Tigana

GUY GAVRIEL KAY

A ROC BOOK

ROC
Published by the Penguin Group
Penguin Books USA Inc., 375 Hudson Street,
New York, New York 10014, U.S.A.
Penguin Books Ltd, 27 Wrights Lane,
London W8 5TZ, England
Penguin Books Australia Ltd, Ringwood,
Victoria, Australia
Penguin Books Canada Ltd, 2801 John Street,
Markham, Ontario, Canada L3R 1B4
Penguin Books (N.Z.) Ltd, 182–190 Wairau Road,
Auckland 10, New Zealand

Penguin Books Ltd, Registered Offices:
Harmondsworth, Middlesex, England

First published by ROC Books, an imprint of New American Library,
a division of Penguin Books USA Inc.

First Printing, September, 1990
10 9 8 7 6 5 4 3 2 1

The author and publisher are grateful to the following for permission
to quote from copyright works: Princeton University Press for
Edmund Keeley and Philip Sherrard (trans. and eds.), *George Seferis:
Collected Poems 1924–1955,* copyright © Princeton University Press,
1967; New American Library for John Ciardi (trans.), Dante's
The Paradiso.

 ROC is a trademark of Penguin Books USA Inc.

LIBRARY OF CONGRESS CATALOGING IN PUBLICATION DATA:
Kay, Guy Gavriel.
    Tigana / Guy Gavriel Kay.
       p.   cm.
    ISBN 0-670-83333-9
    I. Title.
PR9199.3.K39T5   1990
813′.54—dc20   90-34423
                                                               CIP

Printed in the United States of America
Set in Times Roman
Designed by Leonard Telesca

For my brothers, Jeffrey and Rex

CONTENTS

CONTENTS

ACKNOWLEDGMENTS

IN THE SHAPING OF THIS WORK A GREAT MANY PEOPLE lent me their considerable skills and their support. It is a pleasure to be able to acknowledge that aid. Sue Reynolds once again offered me a map that not only reflected but helped to guide the development of my story. Rex Kay and Neil Randall offered both enthusiasm and perceptive commentary from the early stages of the novel through to its last revisions. I am deeply grateful to both of them.

I am indebted to the scholarship of a great many men and women. It is a particular pleasure to record my admiration for Carlo Ginzberg's *Night Battles (I Benandanti).* I have also been stimulated and instructed by the work of, among others, Gene Brucker, Lauro Martines, Jacob Burckhardt, Iris Origo, and Joseph Huizinga. In this regard, I wish also to pay grateful tribute to the memory of two men for whom I have long held the deepest respect, and whose work and sources of inspiration have so profoundly guided my own: Joseph Campbell and Robert Graves.

Finally, while it may often appear to be a matter of ritual or rote when an author mentions the role of a spouse in the creation of a book, I can only affirm that it is with both gratitude and love that I wish to acknowledge the sustaining encouragement and counsel I have received in the writing of *Tigana,* both in Tuscany and at home, from my wife Laura.

A Note on Pronunciation

FOR THE ASSISTANCE OF THOSE TO WHOM SUCH THINGS are of importance, I should perhaps note that most of the proper names in this novel should be pronounced according to the rules of the Italian language. Thus, for example, all final vowels are sounded: Corte has two syllables, Sinave and Forese have three. Chiara has the same hard initial sound as chianti but Certando will begin with the same sound as chair or child.

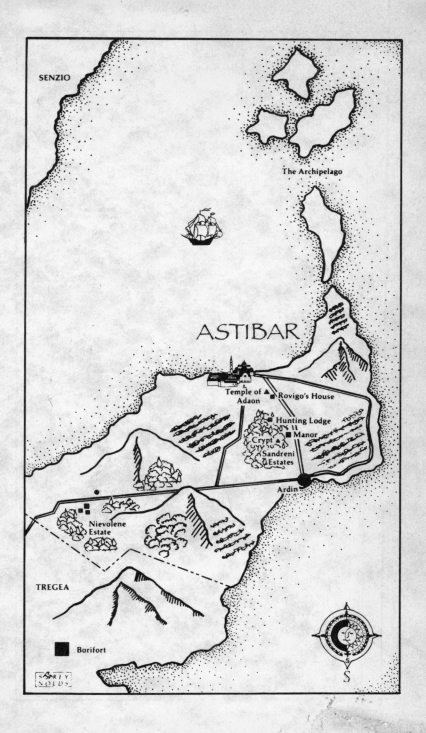

SENZIO

The Archipelago

ASTIBAR

Temple of Adaon

Rovigo's House

Hunting Lodge

Manor

Crypt

Sandreni Estates

Ardin

Nievolene Estate

TREGEA

Borifort

S

CONTENTS

CONTENTS

ACKNOWLEDGMENTS

IN THE SHAPING OF THIS WORK A GREAT MANY PEOPLE lent me their considerable skills and their support. It is a pleasure to be able to acknowledge that aid. Sue Reynolds once again offered me a map that not only reflected but helped to guide the development of my story. Rex Kay and Neil Randall offered both enthusiasm and perceptive commentary from the early stages of the novel through to its last revisions. I am deeply grateful to both of them.

I am indebted to the scholarship of a great many men and women. It is a particular pleasure to record my admiration for Carlo Ginzberg's *Night Battles (I Benandanti)*. I have also been stimulated and instructed by the work of, among others, Gene Brucker, Lauro Martines, Jacob Burckhardt, Iris Origo, and Joseph Huizinga. In this regard, I wish also to pay grateful tribute to the memory of two men for whom I have long held the deepest respect, and whose work and sources of inspiration have so profoundly guided my own: Joseph Campbell and Robert Graves.

Finally, while it may often appear to be a matter of ritual or rote when an author mentions the role of a spouse in the creation of a book, I can only affirm that it is with both gratitude and love that I wish to acknowledge the sustaining encouragement and counsel I have received in the writing of *Tigana*, both in Tuscany and at home, from my wife Laura.

All that you held most dear you will put by
         and leave behind you; and this is the arrow
         the longbow of your exile first lets fly.

You will come to know how bitter as salt and stone
         is the bread of others, how hard the way that goes
         up and down stairs that never are your own.

Dante, The Paradiso

What can a flame remember? If it remembers a little less
than is necessary, it goes out; if it remembers a little
more than is necessary, it goes out. If only it could
teach us, while it burns, to remember correctly.

George Seferis, "Stratis the Sailor Describes a Man"

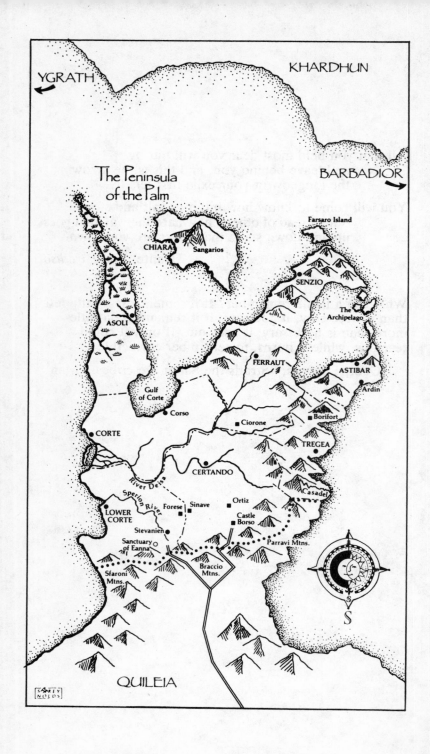

PROLOGUE

BOTH MOONS WERE HIGH, DIMMING THE LIGHT OF ALL but the brightest stars. The campfires burned on either side of the river, stretching away into the night. Quietly flowing, the Deisa caught the moonlight and the orange of the nearer fires and cast them back in wavery, sinuous ripples. And all the lines of light led to his eyes, to where he was sitting on the riverbank, hands about his knees, thinking about dying and the life he'd lived.

There was a glory to the night, Saevar thought, breathing deeply of the mild summer air, smelling water and water flowers and grass, watching the reflection of blue moonlight and silver on the river, hearing the Deisa's murmurous flow and the distant singing from around the fires. There was singing on the other side of the river too, he noted, listening to the enemy soldiers north of them. It was curiously hard to impute any absolute sense of evil to those harmonizing voices, or to hate them quite as blindly as being a soldier seemed to require. He wasn't really a soldier, though, and he had never been good at hating.

He couldn't actually see any figures moving in the grass across the river, but he could see the fires and it wasn't hard to judge how many more of them lay north of the Deisa than there were here behind him, where his people waited for the dawn.

Almost certainly their last. He had no illusions; none of them did. Not since the battle at this same river five days ago. All they had was courage, and a leader whose

1

defiant gallantry was almost matched by the two young
sons who were here with him.

They were beautiful boys, both of them. Saevar regretted that he had never had the chance to sculpt either of
them. The Prince he had done of course, many times.
The Prince called him a friend. It could not be said,
Saevar thought, that he had lived a useless or an empty
life. He'd had his art, the joy of it and the spur, and had
lived to see it praised by the great ones of his province,
indeed of the whole peninsula.

And he'd known love, as well. He thought of his wife
and then of his own two children. The daughter whose
eyes had taught him part of the meaning of life on the
day she'd been born fifteen years ago. And his son, too
young by a year to have been allowed to come north to
war. Saevar remembered the look on the boy's face when
they had parted. He supposed that much the same expression had been in his own eyes. He'd embraced both
children, and then he'd held his wife for a long time, in
silence; all the words had been spoken many times through
all the years. Then he'd turned, quickly, so they would
not see his tears, and mounted his horse, unwontedly
awkward with a sword on his hip, and had ridden away
with his Prince to war against those who had come upon
them from over the sea.

He heard a light tread, behind him and to his left, from
where the campfires were burning and voices were thread-
ing in song to the tune a syrenya played. He turned to
the sound.

"Be careful," he called softly. "Unless you want to trip
over a sculptor."

"Saevar?" an amused voice murmured. A voice he
knew well.

"It is, my lord Prince," he replied. "Can you remember a night so beautiful?"

Valentin walked over—there was more than enough
light by which to see—and sank neatly down on the grass
beside him. "Not readily," he agreed. "Can you see?
Vidomni's waxing matches Ilarion's wane. The two moons
together would make one whole."

"A strange whole that would be," Saevar said.

" 'Tis a strange night."

"Is it? Is the night changed by what we do down here? We mortal men in our folly?"

"The way we see it is," Valentin said softly, his quick mind engaged by the question. "The beauty we find is shaped, at least in part, by what we know the morning will bring."

"What will it bring, my lord?" Saevar asked, before he could stop himself. Half hoping, he realized, as a child hopes, that his dark-haired Prince of grace and pride would have an answer yet to what lay waiting across the river. An answer to all those Ygrathen voices and all the Ygrathen fires burning north of them. An answer, most of all, to the terrible King of Ygrath and his sorcery, and the hatred that *he* at least would have no trouble summoning tomorrow.

Valentin was silent, looking out at the river. Overhead Saevar saw a star fall, angling across the sky west of them to plunge, most likely, into the wideness of the sea. He was regretting the question; this was no time to be putting a burden of false certitude upon the Prince.

Just as he was about to apologize, Valentin spoke, his voice measured and low, so as not to carry beyond their small circle of dark.

"I have been walking among the fires, and Corsin and Loredan have been doing the same, offering comfort and hope and such laughter as we can bring to ease men into sleep. There is not much else we can do."

"They are good boys, both of them," Saevar offered. "I was thinking that I've never sculpted either of them."

"I'm sorry for that," Valentin said. "If anything lasts for any length of time after us it will be art such as yours. Our books and music, Orsaria's green and white tower in Avalle." He paused, and returned to his original thought. "They *are* brave boys. They are also sixteen and nineteen, and if I could have I would have left them behind with their brother . . . and your son."

It was one of the reasons Saevar loved him: that Valentin would remember his own boy, and think of him with the youngest prince, even now, at such a time as this.

To the east and a little behind them, away from the fires, a trialla suddenly began to sing and both men fell silent, listening to the silver of that sound. Saevar's heart was suddenly full, he was afraid that he might shame himself with tears, that they would be mistaken for fear.

Valentin said, "But I haven't answered your question, old friend. Truth seems easier here in the dark, away from the fires and all the need I have been seeing there. Saevar, I am so sorry, but the truth is that almost all of the morning's blood will be ours, and I am afraid it will be all of ours. Forgive me."

"There is nothing to forgive," Saevar said quickly, and as firmly as he could. "This is not a war of your making, nor one you could avoid or undo. And besides, I may not be a soldier but I hope I am not a fool. It was an idle question: I can see the answer for myself, my lord. In the fires across the river."

"And the sorcery," Valentin added quietly. "More that, than the fires. We could beat back greater numbers, even weary and wounded as we are from last week's battle. But Brandin's magic is with them now. The lion has come himself, not the cub, and because the cub is dead there must be blood for the morning sun. Should I have surrendered last week? To the boy?"

Saevar turned to look at the Prince in the blended moonlight, disbelieving. He was speechless for a moment, then found his voice. "I would have gone home from that surrender," he said, with resolution, "and walked into the Palace by the Sea, and smashed every sculpture I ever made of you."

A second later he heard an odd sound. It took him a moment to realize that Valentin was laughing, because it wasn't laughter like any Saevar had ever heard.

"Oh, my friend," the Prince said, at length, "I think I knew you would say that. Oh, our pride. Our terrible pride. Will they remember that most about us, do you think, after we are gone?"

"Perhaps," Saevar said. "But they will remember. The one thing we know with certainty is that they will remember us. Here in the peninsula, and in Ygrath, and Quileia, even west over the sea, in Barbadior and its Empire. We will leave a name."

"And we leave our children," Valentin said. "The younger ones. Sons and daughters who will remember us. Babes in arms our wives and grandfathers will teach when they grow up to know the story of the River Deisa, what happened here, and, even more—what we were in this province before the fall. Brandin of Ygrath can destroy us tomorrow, he can overrun our home, but he cannot take away our name, or the memory of what we have been."

"He cannot," Saevar echoed, feeling an odd, unexpected lift to his heart. "I am sure that you are right. We are not the last free generation. There will be ripples of tomorrow that run down all the years. Our children's children will remember us, and will not lie tamely under the yoke."

"And if any of them seem inclined to," Valentin added in a different tone, "there will be the children or grandchildren of a certain sculptor who will smash their heads for them, of stone or otherwise."

Saevar smiled in the darkness. He wanted to laugh, but it was not in him just then. "I hope so, my lord, if the goddesses and the god allow. Thank you. Thank you for saying that."

"No thanks, Saevar. Not between us and not this night. The Triad guard and shelter you tomorrow, and after, and guard and shelter all that you have loved."

Saevar swallowed. "You know you are a part of that, my lord. A part of what I have loved."

Valentin did not reply. Only, after a moment, he leaned forward and kissed Saevar upon the brow. Then he held up a hand and the sculptor, his eyes blurring, raised his own hand and touched his Prince's palm to palm in farewell. Valentin rose and was gone, a shadow in moonlight, back towards the fires of his army.

The singing seemed to have stopped, on both sides of the river. It was very late. Saevar knew he should be making his own way back and settling down for a few snatched hours of sleep. It was hard to leave though, to rise and surrender the perfect beauty of this last night. The river, the moons, the arch of stars, the fireflies and all the fires.

In the end he decided to stay there by the water. He sat alone in the summer darkness on the banks of the River Deisa, with his strong hands loosely clasped about his knees. He watched the two moons set and all the fires slowly die and he thought of his wife and children and the life's work of his hands that would live after him, and the trialla sang for him all night long.

PART ONE

A BLADE
IN THE SOUL

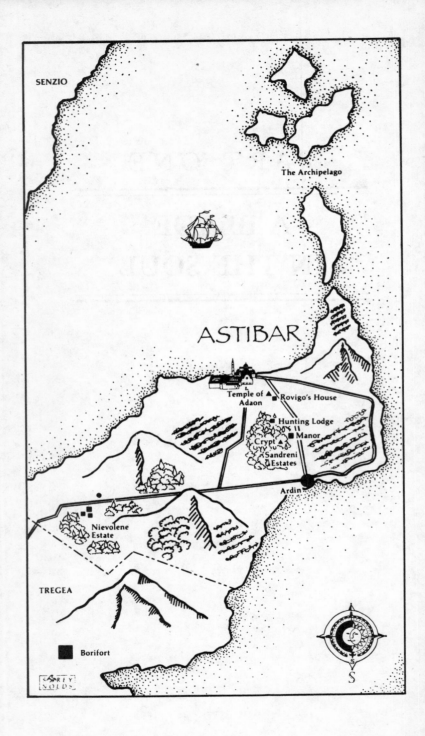

CHAPTER
• 1 •

IN THE AUTUMN SEASON OF THE WINE, WORD WENT FORTH from among the cypresses and olives and the laden vines of his country estate that Sandre, Duke of Astibar, once ruler of that city and its province, had drawn the last bitter breath of his exile and age and died.

No servants of the Triad were by his side to speak their rituals at his end. Not the white-robed priests of Eanna, nor those of dark Morian of Portals, nor the priestesses of Adaon, the god.

There was no particular surprise in Astibar town when these tidings came with the word of the Duke's passing. Exiled Sandre's rage at the Triad and its clergy through the last eighteen years of his life was far from being a secret. And impiety had never been a thing from which Sandre d'Astibar, even in the days of his power, had shied away.

The city was overflowing with people from the outlying distrada and far beyond on the eve of the Festival of Vines. In the crowded taverns and khav rooms truths and lies about the Duke were traded back and forth like wool and spice by folk who had never seen his face and who would have once paled with justifiable terror at a summons to the Ducal court in Astibar.

All his days Duke Sandre had occasioned talk and speculation through the whole of the peninsula men called the Palm—and there was nothing to alter that fact at the time of his dying, for all that Alberico of Barbadior had come with an army from that Empire overseas and exiled Sandre into the distrada eighteen years before. When power is gone the memory of power lingers.

9

Perhaps because of this, and certainly because he tended to be cautious and circumspect in all his ways, Alberico, who held four of the nine provinces in an iron grip and was vying with Brandin of Ygrath for the ninth, acted with a precise regard for protocol.

By noon of the day the Duke died, a messenger from Alberico was seen to have ridden out by the eastern gate of the city. A messenger bearing the blue-silver banner of mourning and carrying, no one doubted, carefully chosen words of condolence to Sandre's children and grandchildren now gathered at their broad estate seven miles beyond the walls.

In The Paelion, the khav room where the wittier sort were gathering that season, it was cynically observed that the Tyrant would have been more likely to send a company of his own Barbadian mercenaries—not just a single message-bearer—were the living Sandreni not such a feckless lot. Before the appreciative, eye-to-who-might-be-listening, ripple of amusement at that had quite died away, one itinerant musician—there were scores of them in Astibar that week—had offered to wager all he might earn in the three days to come, that from the Island of Chiara would arrive condolences in verse before the Festival was over.

"Too rich an opportunity," the rash newcomer explained, cradling a steaming mug of khav laced with one of the dozen or so liqueurs that lined the shelves behind the bar of The Paelion. "Brandin will be incapable of letting slip a chance like this to remind Alberico—and the rest of us—that though the two of them have divided our peninsula the share of art and learning is quite tilted west towards Chiara. Mark my words—and wager who will—we'll have a knottily rhymed verse from stout Doarde or some silly acrostic thing of Camena's to puzzle out, with Sandre spelled six ways and backwards, before the music stops in Astibar three days from now."

There was laughter, though again it was guarded, even on the eve of the Festival, when a long tradition that Alberico of Barbadior had circumspectly indulged allowed more license than elsewhere in the year. A few men with heads for figures did some rapid calculations of sailing-time and the chances of the autumn seas north of

Senzio province and down through the Archipelago, and the musician found his wager quickly covered and recorded on the slate on the wall of The Paelion that existed for just such a purpose in a city prone to gambling.

But shortly after that all wagers and mocking chatter were forgotten. Someone in a steep cap with a curled feather flung open the doors of the khav room, shouted for attention, and when he had it reported that the Tyrant's messenger had just been seen returning through the same eastern gate from which he had so lately sallied forth. That the messenger was riding at an appreciably greater speed than hitherto, and that, not three miles to his rear was the funerary procession of Duke Sandre d'Astibar being brought by his last request to lie a night and a day in state in the city he once had ruled.

In The Paelion the reaction was immediate and predictable: men began shouting fiercely to be heard over the din they themselves were causing. Noise and politics and the anticipated pleasures of the Festival made for a thirsty afternoon. So brisk was his trade that the excitable proprietor of The Paelion began inadvertently serving full measures of liqueur in the laced khavs being ordered in profusion. His wife, of more phlegmatic disposition, continued to short-measure all her patrons with benevolent lack of favoritism.

"They'll be turned back!" young Adreano the poet cried, decisively banging down his mug and sloshing hot khav over the dark oak table of The Paelion's largest booth. "Alberico will never allow it!" There were growls of assent from his friends and the hangers-on who always clustered about this particular table.

Adreano stole a glance at the traveling musician who'd made the brash wager on Brandin of Ygrath and his court poets on Chiara. The fellow, looking highly amused, his eyebrows quizzically arched, leaned back comfortably in the chair he had brazenly pulled up to the booth some time ago. Adreano felt seriously offended by the man, and didn't know whether his umbrage had been more aroused by the musician's so-casual assertion of Chiara's preeminence in culture, or by his flippant dismissal of the great Camena di Chiara whom Adreano had been assiduously imitating for the past half-year: both in the fashion of his verses and the wearing of a three-layered cloak by day and night.

Adreano was intelligent enough to be aware that there might be a contradiction inherent in these twinned sources of ire, but he was also young enough and had drunk a more than sufficient quantity of khav laced with Senzian brandy, for that awareness to remain well below the level of his conscious thoughts.

Which remained focused on this presumptuous rustic. The man had evidently journeyed into the city to saw or pluck for three days at some country instrument or other in exchange for a handful of astins to squander at the Festival. How did such a fellow dare sail into the most fashionable khav room in the Eastern Palm and thump his rural behind down onto a chair at the most coveted table in that room? Adreano still carried painfully vivid memories of the long month it had taken him—even after his first verses had appeared in print—to circle warily closer, flinching inwardly at apprehended rebuffs, before he became a member of the select and well-known circle that had a claim upon this booth.

He found himself actually hoping that the musician would presume to contradict his opinion: he had a choice couplet already prepared, about rabble of the road spewing views on their betters in the company of their betters.

As if on cue to that thought, the fellow slumped even more comfortably back in his chair, stroked a prematurely silvered temple with a long finger and said, directly to Adreano, "This seems to be my afternoon for wagers. I'll risk everything I'm about to win on the other matter that Alberico is too cautious to ruffle the mood of the Festival over this. There are too many people in Astibar right now and spirits are running too high even with the half-measured drinks they serve in here to people who should know better."

He grinned, to take some of the sting from the last words. "Far better for the Tyrant to be gracious," he went on. "To lay his old enemy ceremoniously to rest once and for all, and then offer thanks to whatever gods his Emperor overseas is ordering the Barbadians to worship these days. Thanks and offerings, for he can be certain that the geldings Sandre's left behind will be pleasingly swift to abandon the unfashionable pursuit of freedom that Sandre stood for in ungelded Astibar."

By the end of his speech he was not smiling, nor did the wide-set grey eyes look away from Adreano's own.

And here, for the first time, were truly dangerous words. Softly spoken, but they had been heard by everyone in the booth, and suddenly their corner of The Paelion became an unnaturally quiet space amid the unchecked din everywhere else in the room. Adreano's derisive couplet, so swiftly composed, now seemed trivial and inappropriate in his own ears. He said nothing, his heart beating curiously fast. With some effort he kept his gaze on the musician's.

Who added, the crooked smile returning, "Do we have a wager, friend?"

Parrying for time while he rapidly began calculating how many astins he could lay palms on by cornering certain friends, Adreano said, "Would you care to enlighten us as to why a farmer from the distrada is so free with his money to come *and* with his views on matters such as this?"

The other's smile widened, showing even white teeth. "I'm no farmer," he protested genially, "nor from your distrada either. I'm a shepherd from up in the south Tregea mountains and I'll tell you a thing." The grey eyes swung round, amused, to include the entire booth. "A flock of sheep will teach you more about men than some of us would like to think, and goats . . . well, goats will do better than the priests of Morian to make you a philosopher, especially if you're out on a mountain in rain chasing after them with thunder and night coming on together."

There was genuine laughter around the booth, abetted somewhat by the release of tension. Adreano tried unsuccessfully to keep his own expression sternly repressive.

"Have we a wager?" the shepherd asked one more time, his manner friendly and relaxed.

Adreano was saved the need to reply, and several of his friends were spared an amount of grief and lost astins by the arrival, even more precipitous than that of the feather-hatted tale-bearer, of Nerone the painter.

"Alberico's given permission!" he trumpeted over the

roar in The Paelion. "He's just decreed that Sandre's
exile ended when he died. The Duke's to lie in state
tomorrow morning at the old Sandreni Palace and have a
full-honors funeral with all nine of the rites! Provided"—
he paused dramatically—"provided the clergy of the Triad
are allowed in to do their part of it."

The implications of all this were simply too large for
Adreano to brood much upon his own loss of face—young,
overly impetuous poets had that happen to them every
second hour or so. But these—these were great events!
His gaze, for some reason, returned to the shepherd. The
man's expression was mild and interested, but certainly
not triumphant.

"Ah well," the fellow said with a rueful shake of his
head, "I suppose being right will have to compensate me
for being poor—the story of my life, I fear."

Adreano laughed. He clapped the portly, breathless
Nerone on the back and shifted over to make room for
the painter. "Eanna bless us both," he said to him. "You
just saved yourself more astins than you have. I would
have touched you to make a wager I would have just lost
with your tidings."

By way of reply Nerone picked up Adreano's half-full
khav mug and drained it at a pull. He looked around
optimistically, but the others in the booth were guarding
their drinks, knowing the painter's habits very well. With
a chuckle the dark-haired shepherd from Tregea proffered
his own mug. Self-taught never to query largesse, Nerone
quaffed it down. He did murmur a thank-you when the
khav was drained.

Adreano noted the exchange, but his mind was racing
down unfamiliar channels to an unexpected conclusion.

"You have also," he said abruptly, addressing Nerone
but speaking to the booth at large, "just reaffirmed how
shrewd the Barbadian sorcerer ruling us is. Alberico has
now succeeded, with one decree, in tightening his bonds
with the clergy of the Triad. He's placed a perfect condition upon the granting of the Duke's last wish. Sandre's
heirs will have to agree—not that they'd ever *not* agree to
something—and I can't even begin to guess how many
astins it's going to cost them to assuage the priests and
priestesses enough to get them into the Sandreni Palace

tomorrow morning. Alberico will now be known as the man who brought the renegade Duke of Astibar back to the grace of the Triad at his death."

He looked around the booth, excited by the force of his own reasoning. "By the blood of Adaon, it reminds me of the intrigues of the old days when everything was done with this much subtlety! Wheels within the wheels that guided the fate line of the whole peninsula."

"Well, now," said the Tregean, his expression turning grave, "that may be the cleverest insight we've had this noisy day. But tell me," he went on, as Adreano flushed with pleasure, "if what Alberico's done has just reminded you—and others, I've no doubt, though not likely as swiftly—of the way of things in the days before he sailed here to conquer, and before Brandin took Chiara and the western provinces, then is it not possible"—his voice was low, for Adreano's ears alone in the riot of the room—"that he has been outplayed at this game after all? Outplayed by a dead man?"

Around them men were rising and settling their accounts in loud haste to be outside, where events of magnitude seemed to be unfolding so swiftly. The eastern gate was where everyone was going, to see the Sandreni bring their dead lord home after eighteen years. A quarter of an hour earlier, Adreano would have been on his feet with the others, sweeping on his triple cloak, racing to reach the gate in time for a good viewing post. Not now. His brain leapt to follow the Tregean's voice down this new pathway, and understanding flashed in him like a rushlight in darkness.

"You see it, don't you?" his new acquaintance said flatly. They were alone at the booth. Nerone had lingered to precipitously drain whatever khav had been left unfinished in the rush for the doors and had then followed the others out into the autumn sunshine and the breeze.

"I think I do," Adreano said, working it out. "Sandre wins by losing."

"By losing a battle he never really cared about," the other amended, a keenness in his grey eyes. "I doubt the clergy ever mattered to him at all. They weren't his enemy. However subtle Alberico may be, the fact is that he won this province and Tregea and Ferraut and Certando because of his army and his sorcery, and he holds the Eastern Palm only through those things. Sandre d'Astibar ruled this city and its province for twenty-five years through half a dozen rebellions and assassination attempts that I've heard of. He did it with only a handful of sometimes loyal troops, with his family, and with a guile that was legendary even then. What would you say to the suggestion that he refused to let the priests and priestesses into his death-room last ·night simply to induce Alberico to seize that as a face-saving condition today?"

Adreano didn't know what he would say. What he did know was that he was feeling a zest, an excitement, that left him unsure whether what he wanted just then was a sword in his hand or a quill and ink to write down the words that were starting to tumble about inside him.

"What do you think will happen," he asked, with a deference that would have astonished his friends.

"I'm not sure," the other said frankly. "But I have a growing suspicion that the Festival of Vines this year may see the beginning of something none of us could have expected."

He looked for a moment as if he would say more than that, but did not.

Instead he rose, clinking a jumble of coins onto the table to pay for his khav. "I must go. Rehearsal-time: I'm with a company I've never played with before. Last year's plague caused havoc among the traveling musicians— that's how I got my reprieve from the goats."

He grinned, then glanced up at the wager board on the wall. "Tell your friends I'll be here before sunset three days from now to settle the matter of Chiara's poetic condolences. Farewell for now."

"Farewell," Adreano said automatically, and watched as the other walked from the almost empty room.

The owner and his wife were moving about collecting mugs and glasses and wiping down the tables and benches. Adreano signaled for a last drink. A moment later, sipping his khav—unlaced this time to clear his head—he realized that he'd forgotten to ask the musician his name.

CHAPTER
•2•

DEVIN WAS HAVING A BAD DAY.

At nineteen he had almost completely reconciled himself to his lack of size and to the fair-skinned boyish face the Triad had given him to go with that. It had been a long time since he'd been in the habit of hanging by his feet from trees in the woods near the farm back home in Asoli, striving to stretch a little more height out of his frame.

The keenness of his memory had always been a source of pride and pleasure to him, but a number of the memories that came with it were not. He would have been quite happy to be able to forget the afternoon when the twins, returning home from hunting with a brace of grele, had caught him suspended from a tree upside down. Six years later it still rankled him that his brothers, normally so reliably obtuse, had immediately grasped what he was trying to do.

"We'll help you, little one!" Povar had cried joyfully, and before Devin could right himself and scramble away Nico had his arms, Povar his feet, and his burly twin brothers were stretching him between them, cackling with great good humor all the while. Enjoying, among other things, the ambit of Devin's precociously profane vocabulary.

Well, that had been the last time he actually tried to make himself taller. Very late that same night he'd sneaked into the snoring twins' bedroom and carefully dumped a bucket of pig slop over each of them. Sprinting like Adaon on his mountain he'd been through the yard and over the farm gate almost before their roaring started.

He'd stayed away two nights, then returned to his

17

father's whipping. He'd expected to have to wash the sheets himself, but Povar had done that and both twins, stolidly good-natured, had already forgotten the incident.

Devin, cursed or blessed with a memory like Eanna of the Names, never did forget. The twins might be hard people to hold a grudge against—almost impossible, in fact—but that did nothing to lessen his loneliness on that farm in the lowlands. It was not long after that incident that Devin had left home, apprenticed as a singer to Menico di Ferraut whose company toured northern Asoli every second or third spring.

Devin hadn't been back since, taking a week's leave during the company's northern swing three years ago, and again this past spring. It wasn't that he'd been badly treated on the farm, it was just that he didn't fit in, and all four of them knew it. Farming in Asoli was serious, sometimes grim work, battling to hold land and sanity against the constant encroachments of the sea and the hot, hazy, grey monotony of the days.

If his mother had lived it might have been different, but the farm in Asoli where Garin of Lower Corte had taken his three sons had been a dour, womanless place— acceptable perhaps for the twins, who had each other, and for the kind of man Garin had slowly become amid the almost featureless spaces of the flatlands, but no source of nurture or warm memories for a small, quick, imaginative youngest child, whose own gifts, whatever they might turn out to be, were not those of the land.

After they had learned from Menico di Ferraut that Devin's voice was capable of more than country ballads it had been with a certain collective relief that they had all said their farewells early one spring morning, standing in the predictable greyness and rain. His father and Nico had been turning back to check the height of the river almost before their parting words were fully spoken. Povar lingered though, to awkwardly cuff his little, odd brother on the shoulder.

"If they don't treat you right enough," he'd said, "you can come home, Dev. There's a place."

Devin remembered both things: the gentle blow which had been forced to carry more of a burden of meaning down the years than such a gesture should, and the rough, quick words that had followed. The truth was, he really did remember almost everything, except for his mother and their days in Lower Corte. But he'd been less than two years old when she'd died amongst the fighting down there, and only a month older when Garin had taken his three sons north.

Since then, almost everything was held in his mind.

And if he'd been a wagering man—which he wasn't, having that much of careful Asoli in his soul—he'd have been willing to put a chiaro or an astin down on the fact that he couldn't recall feeling this frustrated in years. Since, if truth were told, the days when it looked as if he would never grow at all.

What, Devin d'Asoli asked himself grimly, did a person have to do to get a drink in Astibar? And on the eve of the Festival, no less!

The problem would have been positively laughable were it not so infuriating. It was the doing, he learned quickly enough—in the first inn that refused to serve him his requested flask of Senzio green wine—of the pinch-buttocked, joy-killing priests of Eanna. The goddess, Devin thought fervently, deserved better of her servants.

It appeared that a year ago, in the midst of their interminable jockeying for ascendancy with the clergy of Morian and Adaon, Eanna's priests had convinced the Tyrant's token council that there was too much licentiousness among the young of Astibar and that, more to the point of course, such license bred unrest. And since it was obvious that the taverns and khav rooms bred license . . .

It had taken less than two weeks for Alberico to promulgate and begin enforcing a law that no youth of less than seventeen years could buy a drink in Astibar.

Eanna's dust-dry priests celebrated—in whatever ascetic fashion such men celebrated—their petty triumph over the priests of Morian and the elegant priestesses of the god: both of which deities were associated with darker passions and, inevitably, wine.

Tavern-keepers were quietly unhappy (it didn't do to be loudly unhappy in Astibar) though not so much for the loss of trade as for the insidious manner in which the law was enforced. The promulgated law had simply placed the burden of establishing a patron's age on the owner of each inn, tavern, or khav room. At the same time, if any of the ubiquitous Barbadian mercenaries should happen to drop by, and should happen—arbitrarily—to decide that a given patron looked too young . . . well, that was one tavern closed for a month and one tavern-keeper locked up for the same length of time.

All of which left the sixteen-year-olds in Astibar truly out of luck. Along with, it gradually became evident through the course of a morning, one small, boyish-looking nineteen-year-old singer from Asoli.

After three summary ejections along the west side of the Street of the Temples, Devin was briefly tempted to go across the road to the Shrine of Morian, fake an ecstasy, and hope they favored Senzian green here as a means of succoring the overly ecstatic. As another, even less rational, option he contemplated breaking a window in Eanna's domed shrine and testing if any of the ball-less imbeciles inside could catch him in a sprint.

He forebore to do so, as much out of genuine devotion to Eanna of the Names as to an oppressive awareness of how many very large and heavily armed Barbadian mercenaries patrolled the streets of Astibar. The Barbadians were everywhere in the Eastern Palm of course, but nowhere was their presence so disturbingly evident as it was in Astibar where Alberico had based himself.

In the end, Devin wished a serious head-cold on himself and headed west towards the harbor and then, following his unfortunately still-functioning sense of smell, towards Tannery Lane. And there, made almost ill by the effluence of the tanner's craft, which quite overwhelmed the salt of the sea, he was given an open bottle of green, no questions asked, in a tavern called The Bird, by a shambling, loose-limbed innkeeper whose eyes were probably inadequate to the dark shadows of his windowless, one-room establishment.

Even this nondescript, evil-smelling hole was completely full. Astibar was crammed to overflowing for tomorrow's start of the Festival of Vines. The harvest had been a good one everywhere but in Certando, Devin knew, and there were plenty of people with astins or chiaros to spend, and in a mood to spend them too.

There were certainly no free tables to be had in The
Bird. Devin wedged himself into a corner where the
dark, pitted wood of the bar met the back wall, took a
judicious sip of his wine—watered but not unusually so,
he decided—and composed his mind and soul towards a
meditation upon the perfidy and unreasonableness of
women.

As embodied, specifically, by Catriana d'Astibar these
past two weeks.

He calculated that he had enough time before the
late-afternoon rehearsal—the last before their opening
engagement at the city home of a small wine-estate owner
tomorrow—to muse his way through most of a bottle and
still show up sober. *He* was the experienced trouper
anyhow, he thought indignantly. He was a *partner*. He
knew the performance routines like a hand knew a glove.
The extra rehearsals had been laid on by Menico for the
benefit of the three new people in the troupe.

Including impossible Catriana. Who happened to be
the reason he had stormed out of the morning rehearsal a
short while before he knew that Menico planned to call
the session to a halt. How, in the name of Adaon, was he
supposed to react when an inexperienced new female
who thought she could sing—and to whom he'd been
genuinely friendly since she'd joined them a fortnight
ago—said what she'd said in front of everyone that
morning?

Cursed with memory, Devin saw the nine of them
rehearsing again in the rented back room on the ground
floor of their inn. Four musicians, the two dancers, Menico,
Catriana, and himself singing up front. They were doing
Rauder's "Song of Love," a piece rather predictably requested by the wine-merchant's wife, a piece Devin had
been singing for nearly six years, a song he could manage
in a stupor, a coma, sound asleep.

And so perhaps, yes, he'd been a little bored, a little
distracted, had been leaning a little closer than absolutely
necessary to their newest, red-headed female singer, putting perhaps the merest shading of a message into his
expression and voice, but still, even so . . .

"Devin, in the name of the Triad," had snapped Catriana
d'Astibar, breaking up the rehearsal entirely, "do you

think you can get your mind away from your groin for long enough to do a decent harmony? This is *not* a difficult song!"

The affliction of a fair complexion had hurtled Devin's face all the way to bright red. Menico, he saw—Menico who should have been sharply reprimanding the girl for her presumption—was laughing helplessly, even more flushed than Devin was. So were the others, all of them.

Unable to think of a reply, unwilling to compromise the tattered shreds of his dignity by yielding to his initial impulse to reach up and whack the girl across the back of her head, Devin had simply spun on his heels and left.

He'd thrown one reproachful glance at Menico as he went but was not assuaged: the troupe-leader's ample paunch was quivering with laughter as he wiped tears from his round, bearded face.

So Devin had gone looking for a bottle of Senzio green and a dark place to drink it in on a brilliant autumn morning in Astibar. Having finally found the wine and the tenuous comfort of shadows he fully expected to figure out, about half a bottle from now, what he *should* have said to that arrogant red-maned creature back in the rehearsal room.

If only she wasn't so depressingly *tall,* he thought. Morosely he filled his glass again. Looking up at the blackened crossbeams of the ceiling he briefly contemplated hanging himself from one of them: by the heels of course. For old time's sake.

"Shall I buy you a drink?" someone said.

With a sigh Devin turned to cope with one of the more predictable aspects of being small and looking very young while drinking alone in a sailor's bar.

What he saw was somewhat reassuring. His questioner was a soberly dressed man of middle years with greying hair and lines of worry or laughter radiating at his temples. Even so:

"Thank you," Devin said, "but I've most of my own bottle left and I prefer having a woman to being one for sailors. I'm also older than I look."

The other man laughed aloud. "In that case," he chuckled, genuinely amused, "you can give *me* a drink if you like while I tell you about my two marriageable daughters and the other two who are on their way to that age sooner than I'm ready for. I'm Rovigo d'Astibar, master of the *Sea Maid* just in from down the coast in Tregea."

Devin grinned and stretched across the bar for another glass: The Bird was far too crowded to bother trying to catch the owner's rheumy eye, and Devin had his own reasons for not wanting to signal the man.

"I'll be happy to share the bottle with you," he said to Rovigo, "though your wife is unlikely to be well pleased if you press your daughters upon a traveling musician."

"My wife," said Rovigo feelingly, "would turn ponderous cartwheels of delight if I brought home a cowherd from the Certandan grasslands for the oldest one."

Devin winced. "That bad?" he murmured. "Ah, well. We can at least drink to your safe return from Tregea, and in time for Festival by a fingernail. I'm Devin d'Asoli bar Garin, at your service."

"And I at yours, friend Devin, not-as-young-as-you-look. Did you have trouble getting a drink?" Rovigo asked shrewdly.

"I was in and out of more doorways than Morian of Portals knows, and as dry when I left as when I'd entered." Devin rashly sniffed the heavy air; even among the odors of the crowd and despite the lack of windows, the tannery stench from outside was still painfully discernible. "This would not have been my first or my tenth choice as a place for drinking a flask of wine."

Rovigo smiled. "A sensible attitude. Will I seem eccentric if I tell you I always come straight here when the *Sea Maid* is home from a voyage? Somehow the smell speaks of *land* to me. Tells me I'm back."

"You don't like the sea?"

"I am quite convinced that any man who says he does is lying, has debts on land, or a shrewish wife to escape from and—" He paused, pretending to have been suddenly struck by a thought. "Come to think of it . . ." he added with exaggerated reflectiveness. Then he winked.

Devin laughed aloud and poured them both more wine. "Why do you sail then?"

"Trade is good," Rovigo said frankly. "The *Maid* is small enough to slip into ports down the coast or around on the western side of Senzio or Ferraut that the bigger traders never bother with. She's also quick enough to make it worth my while running south past the mountains to Quileia. It isn't sanctioned, of course, with the trade embargo down there, but if you have contacts in a remote enough place and you don't dawdle about your business it isn't too risky and there's a profit to be made. I can take Barbadian spices from the market here, or silk from the north, and get them to places in Quileia that would never otherwise see such things. I bring back carpets, or Quileian wood carvings, slippers, jeweled daggers, sometimes casks of buinath to sell to the taverns —whatever's going at a good price. I can't do volume so I have to watch my margins, but there's a living in it as long as insurance stays down and Adaon of the Waves keeps me afloat. I go from here to the god's temple before heading home."

"But here first," Devin smiled.

"Here first." They touched glasses and drained them. Devin refilled both.

"What's news in Quileia?" he asked.

"As a matter of fact, I *was* just there," Rovigo said. "Tregea was a stop on the way back. There are tidings, actually. Marius won his combat in the Grove of Oaks again this summer."

"I did hear about that," Devin said, shaking his head in rueful admiration. "A crippled man, and he must be fifty years old by now. What does that make it—six times in a row?"

"Seven," Rovigo said soberly. He paused, as if expecting a reaction.

"I'm sorry," Devin said. "Is there a meaning to that?"

"Marius decided there was. He's just announced that there will be no more challenges in the Oak Grove. Seven is sacred, he's proclaimed. By allowing him this latest triumph the Mother Goddess has made known her will. Marius has just declared himself King in Quileia, no longer only the consort of the High Priestess."

"*What?*" Devin exclaimed, loudly enough to cause some heads to turn. He lowered his voice. "*He's* declared . . . a man . . . I thought they had a matriarchy there."

"So," said Rovigo, "did the late High Priestess."

Traveling across the Peninsula of the Palm, from moun-

tain village to remote castle or manor, to the cities that
were the centers of affairs, musicians could not help but
hear news and gossip of great events. Always, in Devin's
brief experience, the talk had been only that: a way to
ease the passing of a cold winter's night around an inn
fire in Certando, or to try to impress a traveler in a
tavern in Corte with a murmured confiding that a pro-
Barbadior party was rumored to be forming in that
Ygrathen province.

It was only talk, Devin had long since concluded. The
two ruling sorcerers from east and west across the seas
had sliced the Palm neatly in half between them, with
only hapless, decadent Senzio not formally occupied by
either, looking nervously across the water both ways. Its
Governor remained paralytically unable to decide which
wolf to be devoured by, while the two wolves still warily
circled each other after almost twenty years, each unwilling to expose itself by moving first.

The balance of power in the peninsula seemed to Devin
to have been etched in stone from the time of his first
awareness. Until one of the sorcerers died—and sorcerers were rumored to live a very long time—nothing much
would or could come of khav room or great hall chatter.

Quileia, though, was another matter. One far beyond
Devin's limited experience to sort out or define. He
couldn't even guess what might be the implications of
what Marius had now done in that strange country south
of the mountains. What might flow from Quileia's having
a more than transitory King, one who did not have to go
into the Oak Grove every two years and there, naked,
ritually maimed, and unarmed, meet the sword-wielding
foe who had been chosen to slay him and take his place.
Marius had not been slain, though. Seven times he had
not been slain.

And now the High Priestess was dead. Nor was it
possible to miss the meaning in the way Rovigo had said
that. A little overawed, Devin shook his head.

He glanced up and saw that his new acquaintance was
staring at him with an odd expression.

"You're a thoughtful young man, aren't you?" the
merchant said.

Devin shrugged, suddenly self-conscious. "Not unduly.

I don't know. Certainly not with any insight. I don't hear news like yours every afternoon. What do you think it will mean?"

One answer he was not to receive.

The tavern-keeper, who had quite efficiently succeeded in ignoring Rovigo's intermittent signaling for another bottle of wine now strode to their end of the bar, black anger visible on his features even in the darkened room.

"You!" he hissed. "Your name Devin?"

Taken aback, Devin nodded reflexive agreement. The tavern-keeper's expression grew even more malevolent.

"Get out of here!" he rasped. "Your Triad-cursed sister's outside. Says your father's ordered you home and—Morian blast you both!—that he's minded to turn me in for serving an underage. You gutter-spawned maggot, I'll teach you to put me at risk of being shut down on the eve of the Festival!"

Before Devin could move, a full pitcher of soured black wine was flung into his face, stinging like fire. He scrambled back, wiping at his streaming eyes, swearing furiously.

When he could see again it was to observe an extraordinary sight.

Rovigo—not a big man—had moved along the bar and had grabbed the 'keeper by the collar of his greasy tunic. Without apparent effort he had the man pulled halfway over the bar top, feet kicking ineffectually in mid-air. The collar was twisted to a degree sufficient to cause the helpless tavern-owner's face to begin turning a mottled shade of crimson.

"Goro, I do not like my friends being abused," Rovigo said calmly. "The lad has no father here and I doubt he has a sister.' He cocked an eyebrow at Devin who shook his dripping head vehemently.

"As I say," Rovigo continued, not even breathing hard, "he has no sister here. He is also patently not underage—as should be obvious to any tavern-owner not blinded by swilling buckets of his own slop after hours. Now, Goro, will you placate me a little by apologizing to Devin d'Asoli, my new friend, and offering him two bottles of corked vintage Certando red, by way of showing your sincere contrition? In return I may be persuaded to let you have a cask of the Quileian buinath that's sitting on the *Sea Maid* even now. At an appropriate price or course, given what you can extort for that stuff at Festival-time."

Goro's face had accomplished a truly dangerous hue. Just as Devin felt obliged to caution Rovigo, the tavern-owner gave a jerky, convulsive nod and the merchant untwisted the collar a little. Goro dragged fetid tavern air into his lungs as if it were scented with Chiaran mountain tainflowers and spluttered a three word apology to Devin.

"And the wine?" Rovigo reminded him kindly.

He lowered the other man—still without any evident exertion—enough for Goro to fumble below the bar and resurface with two bottles of what certainly appeared to be Certandan red.

Rovigo let slip another notch of the tightened collar.

"Vintage?" he inquired patiently.

Goro twitched his head up and down.

"Well then," Rovigo declared, releasing Goro completely, "it appears we are quits. I suppose," he said, turning to Devin, "that you should go see who is pretending to be your sister outside."

"I know who it is," Devin said grimly. "Thank you, by the way. I'm used to fighting my own battles, but it's pleasant to have an ally now and again."

"It is *always* pleasant to have an ally," Rovigo amended. "But it seems obvious to me that you aren't keen on dealing with this 'sister,' so I'll leave you to do it in private. Do let me once more commend my own daughters to your kind remembrance. They've been quite well brought up, all things considered."

"I have no doubt of that at all," Devin said. "If I can do you a service in return I will. I'm with the company of Menico di Ferraut and we're here through the Festival. Your wife might enjoy hearing us perform. If you let me know you've come I'll make sure you have good places at either of our public performances, free of charge."

"I thank you. And if your path or your curiosity leads you southeast of town, now or later in the year, our land is about five miles along the road on the right-hand side. There's a small temple of Adaon just before and my gate has a crest with a ship on it. One of the girls designed it. They are all," he grinned, "very talented."

Devin laughed and the two men touched palms formally. Rovigo turned back to reclaim their corner of the bar. Devin, dismally aware that he was soaked with evil-smelling wine from light-brown hair to waist, with stains splotching his hose as well, walked outside clutching his two bottles of Certandan red. He squinted owlishly in the sunshine for a few seconds before spotting Catriana d'Astibar on the other side of the lane, scarlet hair blazing in the light, a handkerchief pressed firmly beneath her nose.

Devin strode briskly into the road and almost collided with a tanner's cart. A brief and satisfying exchange of opinions ensued. The tanner rumbled on and Devin, vowing inwardly not to be put on the defensive this time, crossed the lane to where Catriana had been expressionlessly observing the altercation.

"Well," he said caustically, "I do appreciate your coming all this way to apologize, but you might have chosen a different way of finding me if you were sincere. I rather prefer my clothes unsaturated with spoiled wine. You will offer to wash them for me, of course."

Catriana simply ignored all of this, looking him up and down coldly. "You *are* going to need a wash and a change," she said, from behind the scented handkerchief. "I hadn't counted on that much of a reaction inside. But not having a surplus of astins to spend on bribes I couldn't think of a better way to get tavern-owners to bother looking for you." It was an explanation, Devin noted, but not an apology.

"Forgive me," he said, with exaggerated contrition. "I must talk with Menico—it seems we aren't paying you enough, in addition to all our other transgressions. You must be used to better things."

She hesitated for the first time. "Must we discuss this in the middle of Tannery Lane?" she said.

Without a word Devin sketched a performance bow and gestured for her to lead the way. She started walking away from the harbor and he fell in stride beside her. They were silent for several minutes, until out of the range of the tannery smells. With a faint sigh Catriana put away her handkerchief.

"Where are you taking me?" Devin asked.

Another transgression, it seemed. The blue eyes flashed with anger.

"In the name of the Triad where *would* I be taking you?" Catriana's voice dripped with sarcasm. "We are going to my room at the inn for a session of love-making like Eanna and Adaon at the dawn of days."

"Oh, good," Devin snapped, his own anger rekindling. "Why don't we pool our funds and buy another woman to come play Morian—just so I don't get bored, you understand."

Catriana paled, but before she could open her mouth Devin grabbed her arm with his free hand and swung her around to face him in the street. Looking up into those blue eyes (and cursing the fact that he had to do that) he snapped:

"Catriana, what exactly have I done to you? Why do I deserve that sort of answer? Or what you did this morning? I've been pleasant to you from the day we signed you on—and if you're a professional you know that isn't always the case in troupes on the road. If you must know, Marra, the woman you replaced, was my closest friend in the company. She died of the plague in Certando. I could have made life very hard for you. I didn't and I'm not. I did let you know from the first that I found you attractive. I'm not aware that there is a sin in that if it is done with courtesy."

He released her arm, abruptly conscious that he had been gripping it very hard and that they were in an extremely public place, even with the early-afternoon lull. Instinctively he looked around; thankfully there were no Barbadians passing just then. There was a familiar tight feeling in his chest, as of the apprehended return of pain, that always came with the thought of Marra. The first true friend of his life. Two neglected children, with voices that were gifts of Eanna, telling each other fears and dreams for three years in changing beds across the Palm at night. His first lover. First death.

Catriana, released, remained where she was, and there was a look in her own eyes—perhaps at the naming of death—that made him abruptly revise his estimate of her age downwards. He'd thought she was older than him; now he wasn't sure.

He waited, breathing quickly after his outburst, and at length he heard her say very softly, "You sing too well."

Devin blinked. It was not at all what he'd expected.

"I have to work very hard at performing," she went on, her face flushing for the first time. "Rauder is hard for me—all of his music. And this morning you were doing the 'Song of Love' without even thinking about it, amusing the others, trying to charm me . . . Devin, I have to *concentrate* when I sing! You were making me nervous and I snap at people when I'm nervous."

Devin drew a careful breath and looked around the empty sunlit street for a moment, thinking. He said, "Do you know . . . has anyone ever told you . . . that it is possible and even useful to tell things like this to people—especially the people who have to work with you?"

She shook her head. "Not for me. I've never been able to talk like that, not ever."

"Why do it now, then?" he risked. "Why *did* you come after me?"

A longer pause than before. A cluster of artisans' apprentices swept around the corner, hooting with reflexive ribaldry at the sight of the two of them standing together. There was no malice in it though, and they went by without causing any trouble. A few red and golden leaves skipped over the cobbles in the breeze.

"Something's happened," Catriana d'Astibar said, "and Menico told us all that you are the key to our chances."

"*Menico* sent you after me?" It was almost completely improbable, after nearly six years together.

"No," Catriana said, quickly shaking her head. "No, he said you'd be back in time, that you always were. I was nervous though, with so much at stake. I couldn't just wait around. You'd left a little, um, upset, after all."

"A little," Devin agreed gravely, noting that she finally had the grace to look apologetic. He would have felt even more secure if he hadn't continued to find her so attractive. He couldn't stop himself from wondering—even now—what her breasts would look like, freed from the stiffness of her high-cut bodice. Marra would have told him, he knew, and even helped him with a conquest. They had done that for each other, and shared the tales after, traveling through that last year on the road before Certando where she died.

"You had better tell me what's happened," he said, forcing his thoughts back to the present. There was danger in fantasies and in memories, both.

"The exiled Duke, Sandre, died last night," Catriana said. She looked around but the street was empty again. "For some reason—no one is sure why—Alberico is allowing his body to lie in state at the Sandreni Palace tonight and tomorrow morning, and then . . ."

She paused, the blue eyes bright. Devin, his pulse suddenly leaping, finished it for her:

"A funeral? Full rites? Don't tell me!"

"Full rites! And Devin, Menico's been asked to audition this afternoon! We have a chance to do the most talked-about performance in the whole of the Palm this year!" She looked very young now. And quite unsettlingly beautiful. Her eyes were shining like a child's.

"So you came to get me," he murmured, nodding his head slowly "before I drank myself into a useless stupor of frustrated desire." He had the edge now, for the first time. It was a pleasant turnabout, especially coupled with the real excitement of her news. He began walking, forcing her to fall in stride with him. For a change.

"It isn't like that," she protested. "It's just that this is *so* important. Menico said your voice would be the key to our hopes . . . that you were at your best in the mourning rites."

"I don't know whether to be flattered by that, or insulted that you actually thought I'd be so unprofessional as to miss a rehearsal on the eve of the Festival."

"Don't be either," Catriana d'Astibar said, with a hint of returning asperity. "We don't have time for either. Just be *good* this afternoon. Be the best you've ever been."

He ought to resist it, Devin knew, but his spirits were suddenly much too high.

"In that case, are you *sure* we're not going to your room?" he asked blandly.

More than he could know hung in the balance for the

moment that followed. Then Catriana d'Astibar laughed aloud and freely for the first time.

"Now that," said Devin, grinning, "is much better. I honestly wasn't sure if you had a sense of humor."

She grew quiet. "Sometimes I'm not sure either," she said, almost absently. Then, in a rather different voice: "Devin, I want this contract more than I can tell you."

"Well of course," he replied. "It could make our careers."

"That's right," Catriana said. She touched his shoulder and repeated, "I want this more than I can say."

He might have sought a promise in that touch had he been a little less perceptive, and had it not been for the way she spoke the words. There was, in fact, nothing at all of ambition in that tone, nor of desire in the way that Devin had come to know desire.

What he heard was longing, and it reached towards a space inside him that he hadn't known was there.

"I'll do what I can," he said after a moment, thinking, for no good reason, of Marra and the tears he'd shed.

On the farm in Asoli they had known he was gifted with music quite early but it was an isolated place and none of them had a frame of reference whereby to properly judge or measure such things.

One of Devin's first memories of his father—one that he summoned often because it was a soft image of a hard man—was of Garin humming the tune of some old cradle song to help Devin fall asleep one night when he was feverish.

The boy—four perhaps—had woken in the morning with his fever broken, humming the tune to himself with perfect pitch. Garin's face had taken on the complex expression that Devin would later learn to associate with his father's memories of his wife. That morning though, Garin had kissed his youngest child. The only time Devin could remember that happening.

The tune became a thing they shared. An access to a limited intimacy. They would hum it together in rough, untutored attempts at harmony. Later Garin bought a scaled-down three string syrenya for his youngest child on one of his twice-yearly trips to the market in Asoli town. After that there were actually a few evenings Devin did like to remember, when he and his father and the twins would sing ballads of the sea and hills by the fire at night before bed. Escapes from the drear, wet flatness of Asoli.

When he grew older he began to sing for some of the other farmers. At weddings or naming days, and once with a traveling priest of Morian he sang counterpoint during the autumn Ember Days on the "Hymn to Morian of Portals." The priest wanted to bed him, after, but by then Devin was learning how to avoid such requests without giving offense.

Later yet, he began to be called upon in the taverns. There were no age laws for drinking in northern Asoli, where a boy was a man when he could do a day in the fields, and a girl was a woman when she first bled.

And it had been in a tavern called The River in Asoli town itself on a market day that Devin, just turned fourteen, had been singing "The Ride from Corso to Corte" and had been overheard by a portly, bearded man who turned out to be a troupe-leader named Menico di Ferraut and who had taken him away from the farm that week and changed his life.

"We're next," Menico said, nervously smoothing his best satin doublet over his paunch. Devin, idly picking out his earliest cradle song on one of the spare syrenyae, smiled reassuringly up at his employer. His partner now, actually.

Devin hadn't been an apprentice since he was seventeen. Menico, tired of refusing offers to buy the contract of his young tenor had finally offered Devin journeyman status in the Guild and a regular salary—after first making clear how very much the young man owed him, and how loyalty was the only marginally adequate way to repay such a large debt of gratitude. Devin knew that, in fact, and he liked Menico anyway.

A year later, after another sequence of offers from rival troupe-leaders during the summer wedding season in Corte, Menico had made Devin a ten-percent partner in the company. After making the same speech, almost word for word, as the last time.

The honor, Devin knew, was considerable; only old

Eghano who played drums and the Certandan deep strings, and who had been with Menico since the company was formed, had another partnership share. Everyone else was an apprentice or a journeyman on short-term contract. Especially now, when the aftermath of a plague spring in the south had every troupe in the Palm short of bodies and scrambling to fill with temporary musicians, dancers, or singers.

A haunting thread of sound, barely audible, plucked Devin's attention away from his syrenya. He looked over and smiled. Alessan, one of the three new people, was lightly tracing the melody of the cradle song Devin had been playing. On the shepherd pipes of Tregea it sounded unearthly and strange.

Alessan, black-haired, though greying at the temples, winked at him over the busyness of his fingers on the pipes. They finished the piece together, pipes and syrenya, and humming tenor voice.

"I wish I knew the words," Devin said regretfully as they ended. "My father taught me that tune as a child, but he could never remember how the words went."

Alessan's lean, mobile face was reflective. Devin knew little about the Tregean after two weeks of rehearsal other than that the man was extraordinarily good on the pipes and quite reliable. As Menico's partner, that was all that should matter to him. Alessan was seldom around the inn outside of practice-time, but he was always there and punctual for the rehearsals slated.

"I might be able to dredge them up for you if I thought about it," he said, pushing a hand through his hair in a characteristic gesture. "It's been a long time but I knew the words once." He smiled.

"Don't worry about it," Devin said. "I've survived this long without them. It's just an old song, a memento of my father. If you stay with us we can make it a winter project to try to track them down."

Menico would approve of that last bit, he knew. The troupe-leader had declared Alessan di Tregea to be a find, and cheap at the wages he'd asked.

The other man's expressive mouth crooked sideways, a little wryly. "Old songs and memories of fathers are important," he said. "Is yours dead then?"

Devin made the warding sign with his hand out and two fingers curled down.

"Not last I heard, though I've not seen him in almost six years. Menico spoke to him when he went through the north of Asoli last time, took him some chiaros for me. I don't go back to the farm."

Alessan considered that. "Dour Asolini stock?" he guessed. "No place for a boy with ambition and a voice like yours?" His tone was shrewd.

"Almost exactly," Devin admitted ruefully. "Though I wouldn't have called myself ambitious. Restless, more. And we weren't originally from Asoli in fact. Came there from Lower Corte when I was a small child."

Alessan nodded. "Even so," he said. The man had a bit of a know-it-all manner, Devin decided, but he *could* play the Tregean pipes. The way they might even have sounded on Adaon's own mountain in the south.

In any case, they had no time to pursue the matter.

"We're on!" Menico said, hastily re-entering the room where they were waiting amid the dust and covered furniture of the long-unused Sandreni Palace.

"We do the 'Lament for Adaon' first," he announced, telling them something they'd all known for hours. He wiped his palms on the side of his doublet. "Devin that one's yours—make me proud, lad." His standard exhortation. "Then all of us are together on the 'Circling of Years.' Catriana my love you are sure you can go high enough, or should we pitch down?"

"I'll go high enough," Catriana replied tersely. Devin thought her tone spoke to simple nervousness, but when her gaze met his for a second he recognized that earlier look again: the one that reached somewhere beyond desire towards a shore he didn't know.

"I'd very much like to get this contract," Alessan di Tregea said just then, mildly enough.

"How extremely surprising!" Devin snapped, discovering as he spoke that he too was nervous after all. Alessan laughed though, and so did old Eghano walking through the door with them: Eghano who had seen far too much in too many years of touring to ever be made edgy by a mere audition. Without saying a word, he had, as he always had, an immediately calming effect on Devin.

"I'll do the best I can," Devin said after a moment and for the second time that afternoon, not really certain to whom he was saying it, or why.

In the end, whether because of the Triad or in spite of them—as his father used to say—his best was enough.

The principal auditor was a delicately scented, extravagantly dressed scion of the Sandreni, a man—in his late thirties, Devin guessed—who made it manifest, in his limp posture and the artificially exaggerated shadows that ringed his eyes, why Alberico the Tyrant didn't appear to be much worried about the descendants of Sandre d'Astibar.

Ranged behind this diverting personage were the priests of Eanna and Morian in white and smoke grey. Beside them, vivid by contrast, sat a priestess of Adaon in crimson, with her hair cropped very short.

It was autumn of course, and the Ember Days were coming on: Devin wasn't surprised by her hair. He *was* surprised to see the clergy there for the audition. They made him uncomfortable—another legacy of his father—but this wasn't a situation where he could allow that to affect him, and so he dismissed them from his thoughts.

He focused on the Duke's elegant son, the only one who really mattered now. He waited, reaching as Menico had taught him for a still point inside himself.

Menico cued Nieri and Aldine, the two thin dancers in their grey-blue, almost translucent, chemises of mourning and their black gloves. A moment later, after their first linked pass across the floor, he looked at Devin.

And Devin gave him, gave them all, the lament for Adaon's autumnal dying among the mountain cypresses, as he never had before.

Alessan di Tregea was with him all the way with the high, heart-piercing grief of the shepherd pipes and together the two of them seemed to lift and carry Nieri and Aldine beyond the surface steps of their dance across the recently swept floor and into the laconic, precise articulation of ritual that the "Lament" demanded and was so rarely granted.

When they finished, Devin, traveling slowly back to the Sandreni Palace from the cedar and cypress slopes of

Tregea where the god had died—and where he died again each and every autumn—saw that Sandre d'Astibar's son was weeping. The tracks of his tears had smudged the carefully achieved shadowing around his eyes—which meant, Devin realized abruptly, that he hadn't wept for any of the three companies before them.

Marra, young and intolerantly professional would have been scornful of those tears, he knew: "Why hire a mongrel and bark yourself?" she would say when their mourning rituals were interrupted or marked by displays from their patrons.

Devin had been less stern back then. And was even less so now since she'd died and he had found himself rather desperately fighting back a shameful public grief when Burnet di Corte had led his company through her mourning rites in Certando as a gesture of courtesy to Menico.

Devin also knew, by the smoldering look the Sandreni scion gave him from within the smeared dark rings around his eyes, and the scarcely less transparent glance from Morian's fat-fingered priest—why in the name of the Triad were the Triad so ill-served!—that though they might have just won the Sandreni contract he was going to have to be careful in this palace tomorrow. He made a mental note to bring his knife.

They *had* won the contract. The second number hardly mattered, which is why cunning Menico had begun with the "Lament." Afterwards Menico carefully introduced Devin as his partner when Sandre's son asked to meet him. He turned out to be the middle son of three, named Tomasso. The only one, he explained huskily, holding one of Devin's hands tightly between both his own, with an ear for music and an eye for dance adequate to choosing performers equal to so august an occasion as his father's funeral rites.

Devin, used to this, politely retrieved his fingers, grateful for Menico's experienced tact: presented as a partner he had some slight immunity from overly aggressive wooers, even among the nobility. He was introduced to the clergy next, and promptly knelt before Adaon's priestess in red.

"Your sanction, sister-of-the-god, for what I sang, and for what I am asked to do tomorrow."

Out of the corner of his eye he saw the priest of Morian clench his chubby, ringed fingers at his sides. He accepted the blessing and protection of Adaon—the priestess's index finger tracing the god's symbol on his brow—in the knowledge that he had successfully defused one priest's burgeoning desire. When he rose and turned, it was to catch a wink—dangerous in that room and among that company—from Alessan di Tregea, at the back with the others. He suppressed a grin, but not his surprise: the shepherd was disconcertingly perceptive.

Menico's first price was immediately accepted by Tomasso d'Astibar bar Sandre, confirming in Devin's mind what a sorry creature he was to bear such a magnificent name and lineage.

It would have interested him—and led him a step or two further down the head road towards maturity—to learn that Duke Sandre himself would have accepted the same price, or twice as much, and in exactly the same manner. Devin was not quite twenty though, and even Menico, three times his age, would loudly curse himself back at the inn amid the celebratory wine for not having quoted even more than the extortionate sum he had just received in full.

Only Eghano, aged and placid, softly drumming two wooden spoons on their trestle table, said, "Leave well enough. We need not hold out a greedy palm. There will be more of these from now on. If you are wise you'll leave a tithe at each of the temples tomorrow. We will earn it back with interest when they choose musicians for the Ember Days."

Menico, in high good humor, swore even more magnificently than before, and announced a set intention to offer Eghano's wrinkled body as a tithe to the fleshy priest of Morian instead. Eghano smiled toothlessly and continued his soft drumming.

Menico ordered them all to bed not long after the evening meal. They'd have an early start tomorrow, pointing towards the most important performance of their lives. He beamed benevolently as Aldine led Nieri from the room. The girls would share a bed that night Devin was sure, and for the first time, he suspected. He wished them joy of each other, knowing that they had come together magically as dancers that afternoon and also knowing—for it had happened to him once—how that could spill over into the candles of a late night in bed.

He looked around for Catriana but she had gone upstairs already. She'd kissed him briefly on the cheek though, right after Menico's fierce embrace back in the Sandreni Palace. It was a start; it might be a start.

He bade good night to the others and went up to the single room that was the one luxury he'd demanded of Menico's tour budget after Marra had died.

He expected to dream of her, because of the mourning rites, because of unslaked desire, because he dreamt of her most nights. Instead he had a vision of the god.

He saw Adaon on the mountainside in Tregea, naked and magnificent. He saw him torn apart in frenzy and in flowing blood by his priestesses—suborned by their womanhood for this one autumn morning of every turning year to the deeper service of their sex. Shredding the flesh of the dying god in the service of the two goddesses who loved him and who shared him as mother, daughter, sister, bride, all through the year and through all the years since Eanna named the stars.

Shared him and loved him except on this one morning in the falling season. This morning that was shaped to become the harbinger, the promise of spring to come, of winter's end. This one single morning on the mountain when the god who was a man had to be slain. Torn and slain, to be put into his place which was the earth. To become the soil, which would be nurtured in turn by the rain of Eanna's tears and the moist sorrowings of Morian's endless underground streams twisting in their need. Slain to be reborn and so loved anew, more and more with each passing year, with each and every time of dying on these cypress-clad heights. Slain to be lamented and then to rise as a god rises, as a man does, as the wheat of summer fields. To rise and then lie down with the goddesses, with his mother and his bride, his sister and his daughter, with Eanna and Morian under sun and stars and the circling moons, the blue one and the silver.

Devin dreamt, terribly, that primal scene of women

running on the mountainside, their long hair streaming behind them as they pursued the man-god to that high chasm above the torrent of Casadel.

He saw their clothing torn from them as they cried each other on to the hunt. Saw branches of mountain trees, of spiny, bristling shrubs, claw their garments away, saw them render themselves deliberately naked for greater speed to the chase, seizing blood-red berries of sonrai to intoxicate themselves against what they would do high above the icy waters of Casadel.

He saw the god turn at last, his huge dark eyes wild and knowing, both, as he stood at the chasm brink, a stag at bay at the deemed, decreed, perennial place of his ending. And Devin saw the women come upon him there, with their flying hair and blood flowing along their bodies and he saw Adaon bow his proud, glorious head to the doom of their rending hands and their teeth and their nails.

And there at the end of the chase Devin saw that the women's mouths were open wide as they cried to each other in ecstasy or anguish, in unrestrained desire or madness or bitter grief, but in his dream there was no sound at all to those cries. Instead, piercing through the whole of that wild scene among cedar and cypress on the mountainside, the only thing Devin heard was the sound of Tregean shepherd pipes playing the tune of his own childhood fever, high and far away.

And at the end, at the very last, Devin saw that when the women came upon the god and caught him and closed about him at that high chasm over Casadel, his face when he turned to his rending was that of Alessan.

CHAPTER
•3•

EVEN BEFORE THE COMING OF CAUTIOUS ALBERICO FROM overseas in Barbadior to rule in Astibar, the city that liked to call itself "The Thumb that Rules the Palm" had been known for a certain degree of asceticism. In Astibar the mourning rites were never done in the presence of the dead as was the practice in the other eight provinces: such a procedure was regarded as excessive, too fevered an appeal to emotion.

They were to perform in the central courtyard of the Sandreni Palace, watched from chairs and benches placed around the courtyard, and from the loggias above, leading off the interior rooms on the two upper floors. In one of those rooms, marked by the appropriate hangings—grey-blue and black—lay the body of Sandre d'Astibar, coins over his eyes to pay the nameless doorman at the last portal of Morian, food in his hands and shoes on his feet, for no one living could know how long that final journey to the goddess was.

He would be brought down to the courtyard later, so that all those citizens of his city and its distrada who wished to do so—and who were willing to brave the recording eyes of the Barbadian mercenaries posted outside—could file past his bier and drop blue-silver leaves of the olive tree in the single crystal vase that stood on a plinth in the courtyard even now.

The ordinary citizens—weavers, artisans, shopkeepers, farmers, sailors, servants, lesser merchants—would enter the palace later. They could be heard outside now: gathered to hear the music of the old Duke's mourning rites. The people drifting into the courtyard in the meantime

41

were the most extraordinary collection of petty and high nobility, and of accumulated mercantile wealth that Devin had ever seen in one place.

Because of the Festival of Vines, all the lords of the Astibar distrada had come into town from their country estates. And being in town they could hardly not be present to see Sandre mourned—for all that many or most of them had bitterly hated him while he ruled, and the fathers or grandfathers of some had paid for poison or hired blades thirty years ago and more in the hope that these same rites might have taken place long since.

The two priests and Adaon's priestess were already in their scats, seeming, in the manner of clergy everywhere, to be privy to a mystery that they collectively shielded from lesser mortals with the gravity of their repose.

Menico's company waited in a small room off the court-yard that Tomasso had ordered set aside for their use. All the usual amenities were there, and some that were far from usual: Devin couldn't remember seeing blue wine offered to performers before. An extravagant gesture, that. He wasn't tempted though; it was too early and he was too much on edge. To calm himself he walked over to Eghano who was lazily drumming, as he always seemed to be, on a tabletop.

Eghano glanced up at him and smiled. "It's just a performance," he said in his soft sibilant voice. "We do what we always do. We make music. We move on."

Devin nodded, and forced a smile in return. His throat was dry though. He went to the side-tables, and one of the two hovering servants hastened to pour him water in a gold and crystal goblet worth more than everything Devin owned in the world. A moment later Menico signaled and they went out into the courtyard.

The dancers began it, backed by hidden strings and pipes. No voices. Not yet.

If Aldine and Nieri had burned love candles late last night it didn't show—or if it did, only in the concentration and intensity of their twinned movements that morning.

Sometimes seeming to pull the music forward, sometimes following it, they looked—with their thin, whitened faces, their blue-grey tunics and the jet-black gloves that hid their palms—truly otherworldly. Which was as Menico had trained his dancers to be. Not inviting or alluring as some other troupes approached this dance of the rites, nor a merely graceful prelude to the real performance, as certain other companies conceived it. Menico's dancers were guides, cold and compelling, towards the place of the dead and of mourning for the dead. Gradually, inexorably, the slow grave movements, the expressionless, almost inhuman faces imposed the silence that was proper on that restive, preening audience.

And in that silence the three singers and four musicians came forward and began the "Invocation" to Eanna of the Lights who had made the world, the sun, the two moons and the scattered stars that were the diamonds of her diadem.

Rapt and attentive to what they were doing, using all the contrivances of professional skill to shape an apparent artlessness, the company of Menico di Ferraut carried the lords and ladies and the merchant princes of Astibar with them on a ruthlessly disciplined cresting of sorrow. In mourning Sandre, Duke of Astibar, they mourned—as was proper—the dying of all the Triad's mortal children, brought through Morian's portals to move on Adaon's earth under Eanna's lights for so short a time. So sweet and bitter and short a season of days.

Devin heard Catriana's voice reaching upwards towards the high place where Alessan's pipes seemed to be calling her, cold and precise and austere. He felt, even more than he heard, Menico and Eghano grounding them all with their deep line. He saw the two dancers—now statues in a frieze, now whirling as captives in the trap of time—and at the moment that was proper he let his own voice soar with the two syrenyae into the space that had been left for them to fill, in the middle range where mortals lived and died.

So Menico di Ferraut had shaped his approach to the seldom-performed Full Mourning Rites long ago, bringing forty years of art and a full, much-traveled life to the moment that this morning had become. Even as he began to sing, Devin's heart swelled with pride and a genuine love for the rotund, unassuming leader who had guided them here and into what they were shaping.

They stopped, as planned, after the sixth stage, for their own sake and their listeners'. Tomasso had spoken with Menico beforehand, and the nobles' progression past Sandre's bier would now take place upstairs. After, the company would finish with the last three rites, ending on Devin's "Lament," and then the body would be brought down and the crowd outside admitted with their leaves for the crystal vase.

Menico led them out from the courtyard amid a silence so deep it was their highest possible accolade. They re-entered the room that had been reserved for their use. Caught up in the mood they themselves had created, no one spoke. Devin moved to help the two dancers into the robes they wore between performances and then watched as they paced the perimeter of the room, slender and cat-like in their grace. He accepted a glass of green wine from one of the servants but declined the offered plate of food. He exchanged a glance but not a smile—not now—with Alessan. Drenio and Pieve, the syrenya-players, were bent over their instruments, adjusting the strings. Eghano, pragmatic as ever, was eating while idly drumming the table with his free hand. Menico walked by, restless and distracted. He gave Devin a wordless squeeze on the arm.

Devin looked for Catriana and saw her just then leaving the room through an inner archway. She glanced back. Their glances met for a second, then she went on. Light, strangely filtered, fell from a high unseen window upon the space where she had been.

Devin really didn't know why he did it. Even afterwards when so much had come to pass, flowing outwards in all directions like ripples in water from this moment, he was never able to say exactly why he followed her.

Simple curiosity. Desire. A complex longing born of the look in her eyes before and the strange, floating place of stillness and sorrow where they now seemed to be. None or some or all of these. He felt as if the world wasn't quite as it had been before the dancers had begun.

He drained his wine and rose and he went through the same archway Catriana had. Passing through, he too looked back. Alessan was watching him. There was no judgment in the Tregean's glance, only an intent expression Devin could not understand. For the first time that day he was reminded of his dream.

And because of that, perhaps, he murmured a prayer to Morian as he went on through the archway.

There was a staircase with a high, narrow, stained-glass window on the first-floor landing. In the many-colored fall of light he caught a glimpse of a blue-silver gown swirling to the left at the top of the stairs. He shook his head, struggling to clear it, to slip free of this eerie, dreamlike mood. And as he did, an understanding slid into place and he muttered a curse at himself.

She was from Astibar. She was going upstairs as was entirely fit and proper to pay her own farewell to the Duke. No lord or newly wealthy merchant was about to deny her right to do so. Not after her singing this morning. On the other hand, for a farmer's son from Asoli by way of Lower Corte to enter that upstairs room would be sheerest, ill-bred presumption.

He hesitated, and he would have turned back then, had it not been for the memory that was his blessing and his curse and always had been. He had seen the hanging banners from the courtyard. The room where Sandre d'Astibar lay was to the right, not the left, at the top of these stairs.

Devin went up. He took care now, though still not knowing why, to be quiet. At the landing he bore left as Catriana had done. There was a doorway. He opened it. An empty room, long unused, dusty hangings on the walls. Scenes of a hunt, the colors badly faded. There were two exits, but the dust came to his aid now: he could see the neat print of her sandals going towards the door on the right.

Silently Devin followed that trail through the warren of abandoned rooms on the first floor of the palace. He saw sculptures and objects of glass, exquisite in their delicacy, marred by years of overlaid dust. Much of the furniture was gone, much that remained was covered over. The light was dim; most of the windows were shuttered. A great many darkened, begrimed portraits of stern lords and ladies gazed inimically down upon him as he passed.

He bore right and again right, tracing the path of Catriana's feet, careful to keep from getting too close.

She went straight on after that through the rooms along the outer side of the palace—none that offered onto the crowded balustrades overlooking the courtyard. It was brighter in these rooms. He could hear murmuring voices off to his right and he realized that Catriana was walking around to the far side of the room where Sandre lay in state.

At length he opened a door which proved to be the last. She was alone inside a very large chamber, standing by the side of a huge fireplace. There were three bronze horses on the mantelpiece and three portraits on the walls. The ceiling was gilded in what Devin knew would be gold. Along the outer wall where a line of windows overlooked the street there were two long tables laden with food and drink. This room, unlike the others, had been recently cleaned, but the curtains were still drawn against the morning brightness and the crowd outside.

In the thin, filtered light Devin closed the door behind him, deliberately letting the latch click shut. The sound was a loud report in the stillness.

Catriana wheeled, a hand to her mouth, but even in the half-light Devin could see that what blazed in her eyes was fury and not fear.

"What do you think you are doing?" she whispered harshly.

He took a hesitant step forward. He reached for a witticism, a mild, deflecting remark to shatter the heavy spell that seemed to lie upon him, upon the whole of the morning. He couldn't find one.

He shook his head. "I don't know," he said honestly. "I saw you leave and I followed. It . . . isn't what you think," he finished lamely.

"How would you know what I think?" she snapped. She seemed to calm herself by an act of will. "I wanted to be alone for a few moments," Catriana said, controlling her voice. "The performance affected me and I needed to be by myself. I can see that you were disturbed too, but can I ask you as a courtesy to leave me to my privacy for just a little while?"

It was courteously said. He could have gone then. On any other morning he *would* have gone. But Devin had already passed, half-knowingly, a portal of Morian's.

He gestured at the food on the tables and said, gravely, a quiet observation of fact and not a challenge or accusation, "This is not a room for privacy, Catriana. Won't you tell me why you are here?"

He braced for her rage to flare again, but once more she surprised him. Silent for a long moment, she said at length, "You have not shared enough with me to be owed an answer to that. Truly it will be better if you go. For both of us."

He could still hear muffled voices on the other side of the wall to the right of the fireplace and the bronze horses. This strange room with its laden, sumptuously covered tables and the grim portraits on the dark walls seemed to be a chamber in some waking trance. He remembered Catriana singing that morning, her voice yearning upwards to where the pipes of Tregea called. He remembered her eyes as she paused in the doorway they'd both passed through. Truly he felt as if he were not entirely awake, not in the world he knew.

And in that mood Devin heard himself say, over a sudden constriction in his throat, "Could we not begin then? Is there not a sharing we could start?"

Once more she hesitated. Her eyes were wide but impossible to read in the uncertain light. She shook her head though and remained where she was, standing straight and very still on the far side of the room.

"I think not," she said quietly. "Not on the road I'm on, Devin d'Asoli. But I thank you for asking, and I will not deny that a part of me might wish things otherwise. I have little time now though, and a thing I must do here. Please—will you leave me?"

He had scarcely expected to find or feel so much regret, over and above all the nuances the morning had already carried. He nodded his head—there was nothing else he could think of to do or say, and this time he did turn to go.

But a portal had indeed been crossed in the Sandreni Palace that morning and in exactly the moment that Devin turned they both heard voices again—but this time from *behind* him.

"Oh, Triad!" Catriana hissed, snapping the mood like a fishbone. "I am cursed in all I turn my hands to!" She spun back to the fireplace, her hands frantically feeling around the underside of the mantelpiece. "For the love of the goddesses be silent!" she whispered harshly.

The urgency in her voice made Devin freeze and obey.

"He said he knew who built this palace," he heard her mutter under her breath. "That it should be right over—"

She stopped. Devin heard a latch click. A section of the wall to the right of the fire swung slightly open to reveal a tiny cubbyhole beyond. His eyes widened.

"Don't stand there gawking, fool!" Catriana whispered fiercely. "Quickly!" A new voice had joined the others behind him; there were three now. Devin leaped for the concealed door, slipped inside beside Catriana, and together they pulled it shut.

A moment later they heard the door on the far side of the room click open.

"Oh, Morian," Catriana groaned, from the heart. "Oh, Devin, *why* are you here?"

Addressed thusly, Devin found himself quite incapable of framing an adequate response. For one thing, he still couldn't say why he'd followed her; for another, the closet where they were hiding was only marginally large enough for the two of them, and he became increasingly aware of the fact that Catriana's perfume was filling the tiny space with a heady, unsettling scent.

If he had been half in a dream a moment ago he abruptly found himself wide awake and in dangerous proximity to a woman he had seriously desired for the past two weeks.

Catriana seemed to arrive, belatedly, at the same sort of awareness; he heard her make a small sound in a register somewhat different from before. Devin closed his eyes, even though it was pitch-black in the hidden closet. He could feel her breath tickling his forehead, and he was conscious of the fact that by moving his hands only a very little he could encircle her waist.

He held himself carefully motionless, tilting back from her as best he could, his own breathing deliberately shallow. He felt more than sufficiently a fool for having created this ridiculous situation—he wasn't about to compound his rapidly growing catalogue of sins by making a grope for her in the darkness.

Catriana's robe rustled gently as she shifted position. Her thigh brushed his. Devin drew a ragged breath, which caused him to inhale more of her scent than was entirely good for him, given his virtuous resolutions.

"Sorry," he whispered, though she was the one who'd moved. He felt beads of perspiration on his brow. To distract himself he tried to focus on the sounds from outside. Behind him the shuffling of feet and a steady, diffused murmur made it clear that people were still filing past Sandre's bier.

To his left, in the room they'd just fled, three voices could be distinguished. One was, curiously, almost recognizable.

"I had the servants posted with the body across the way—it gives us a moment before the others come."

"Did you notice the coins on his eyes?" a much younger voice asked, crossing to the outer wall where the laden tables were. "Very amusing."

"Of course I noticed," the first man replied acerbically. Where had Devin heard that tone? And recently. "Who do you think spent an evening scrounging up two astins from twenty years ago? Who do you think arranged for *all* of this?"

The third voice was heard, laughing softly. "And a fine table of food it is," he said lightly.

"That is not what I meant!"

Laughter. "I know it isn't, but it's a fine table all the same."

"Taeri, this is not a time for jests, particularly bad ones. We only have a moment before the family arrives. Listen to me carefully. Only the three of us know what is happening."

"It is only us, then?" the young voice queried. "No one else? Not even my father?"

"Not Gianno, and you know why. I said only us. Hold questions and listen, pup!'

Just then Devin d'Asoli felt his pulse accelerate in a quite unmistakable way. Partly because of what he was hearing, but rather more specifically because Catriana had just shifted her weight again, with a quiet sigh, and Devin became incredulously aware that her body was now pressed directly against his own and that one of her long arms had somehow slipped around his neck.

"Do you know," she whispered, almost soundlessly, mouth close to his ear, "I rather like the thought of this all of a sudden. Could you be *very* quiet?" The very tip of her tongue, for just an instant, touched the lobe of his ear.

Devin's mouth went bone dry even as his sex leaped to full, painful erection within his blue-silver hose. Outside he could hear that voice he almost knew beginning a terse explanation of something involving pall-bearers and a hunting lodge, but the voice and its explanations had abruptly been rendered definitively trivial.

What was not trivial, what was in fact of the vastest importance imaginable was the undeniable fact that Catriana's lips were busy at his neck and ear, and that even as his hands moved—as of their own imperative accord—to touch her eyelids and throat and then drift downward to the dreamt-of swell of her breasts, her own fingers were nimble among the drawstrings at his waist, setting him free.

"Oh, Triad!" he heard himself moan as her cool fingers stroked him, "Why didn't you tell me before that you liked it dangerous?" He twisted his head sharply and their lips met fiercely for the first time. He began gathering the folds of her gown up about her hips.

She settled back on a ledge against the wall behind her to make it easier for him, her own breath now rapid and shallow as well.

"There will be six of us," Devin heard from the room outside. "By second moonrise I want you to be . . ."

Catriana's hands suddenly tightened in his hair, almost painfully, and at that moment the last folds of her robe rode free of her hips and Devin's fingers slipped in among her undergarments and found the portal he'd been longing for.

She made a small unexpected sound and went rigid for just a second, before becoming extremely soft in his arms. His fingers gently stroked the deepest folds of her flesh. She drew an awkward, reaching breath, then shifted again, very slightly and guided Devin into her. She gasped, her teeth sinking hard into his shoulder. For a moment, lost in astonished pleasure and sharp pain, Devin was motionless, holding her close to him, murmuring almost soundlessly, not knowing what he was saying.

"Enough! The others are here," the third voice outside rasped crisply.

"Even so," said the first. "Remember then, you two come your own ways from town—not together!—to join us tonight. Whatever you do be sure you are not followed or we are dead."

There was a brief silence. Then the door on the farthest side of the room opened and Devin, beginning now to thrust slowly, silently into Catriana, finally recognized the voice he'd been hearing.

For the same speaker continued talking, but now he assumed the delicate, remembered, intonations of the day before.

"At last!" fluted Tomasso d'Astibar bar Sandre. "We feared dreadfully that you'd all contrived to lose yourselves in these dusty recesses, never to be found again!"

"No such luck, brother," a voice growled in reply. "Though after eighteen years it wouldn't have been surprising. I need two glasses of wine very badly. Sitting still for that kind of music all morning is cursed thirsty work."

In the closet Devin and Catriana clung to each other, sharing a breathless laughter. Then a newer urgency came over Devin, and it seemed to him it was in her as well, and there was suddenly nothing in the peninsula that mattered half so much as the gradually accelerating rhythm of the movements they made together.

Devin felt her fingernails splay outwards on his back. Feeling his climax gathering he cupped his hands beneath her; she lifted her legs and wrapped them around him. A moment later her teeth sank into his shoulder a second time and in that moment he felt himself explode, silently, into her.

For an unmeasured, enervated space of time they remained like that, their clothing damp where it had been crushed against skin. To Devin the voices from the two rooms outside seemed to come from infinitely far away. From other worlds entirely. He really didn't want to move at all.

At length however, Catriana carefully lowered her legs

to the ground to bear her own weight. He traced her cheekbones with a finger in the blackness.

Behind him the lords and merchants of Astibar were still shuffling past the body of the Duke so many had hated and some few had loved. To Devin's left the younger generation of the Sandreni ate and drank, toasting an end to exile. Devin, wrapped close with Catriana, still sheathed within her warmth, could not have hoped to find words to say what he was feeling.

Suddenly she seized one of his tracing fingers and bit it, hard. He winced, because it hurt. She didn't say anything though.

After the Sandreni left, Catriana found the latch and they slipped out into the room again. Quickly they reorganized their clothes. Pausing only long enough to seize a chicken-wing apiece, they hastily retraced their path back through the rooms leading to the stairway. They met three liveried servants coming the other way and Devin, feeling exceptionally alert and alive now, claimed Catriana's fingers and winked at the servants as they passed.

She withdrew her hand a moment later.

He glanced over. "What's wrong?"

She shrugged. "I'd as soon it wasn't proclaimed throughout the Sandreni Palace and beyond," she murmured, looking straight ahead.

Devin lifted his eyebrows. "What would you rather they thought about us being upstairs? I just gave them the obvious, boring explanation. They won't even bother to talk about it. This sort of thing happens all the time."

"Not to me," said Catriana quietly.

"I didn't mean it that way!" Devin protested, taken aback. But unfortunately they were going down the stairs by then, and so it was with a quite unexpected sense of estrangement that he paused to let her re-enter the room before him.

More than a little confused, he took his place behind Menico as they prepared to go back out into the courtyard.

He had only a minor supporting role in the first two hymns and so he found his thoughts wandering back over the scene just played out upstairs. Back, and then back again, with the memory that seemed to be his birthright focusing like a beam of sunlight upon one detail then another, illuminating and revealing what he had missed the first time around.

And so it was that by the time it was his own turn to step forward to end and crown the mourning rites, seeing the three clergy leaning forward expectantly, noting how Tomasso struck a pose of rapt attentiveness, Devin was able to give the "Lament for Adaon" an undivided soul, for he was confused no longer, but quite decided in what he was going to do.

He began softly in the middle range with the two syrenyae, building and shaping the ancient story of the god. Then, when the pipes of Alessan came in, Devin let his voice leap upward in response to them, as though in flight from mountain glen to crag to chasm brink.

He sang the dying of the god with a voice made pure in the caldron of his own heart and he pitched the notes to rise above that courtyard and beyond it, out among the streets and squares of high-walled Astibar.

High walls he intended to pass beyond that night— beyond, and then following a trail he would find, into a wood where lay a hunting lodge. A lodge where pall-bearers were to carry the body of the Duke, and where a number of men—*six,* the clear voice of his memory reminded him—were to gather in a meeting that Catriana d'Astibar had just done the very best she could short of murder to prevent him learning about. He strove to turn the acrid taste of that knowledge into grief for Adaon, to let it guide and infuse the pain of the "Lament."

Better for both of us, he remembered her saying, and he could recapture in his mind the regret and the unexpected softness in her voice. But a certain kind of pride at Devin's age is perhaps stronger than at any other age of mortal man, and he had already decided, before even he began to sing, here in this crowded courtyard among the great of Astibar, that *he* was going to be the judge of what was better, not she.

So Devin sang the rending of the god at the hands of the women, and he gave that dying on the Tregean mountain slope all he had to give it, making his voice an arrow arching outwards to seek the heart of everyone who heard.

He let Adaon fall from the high cliff, he heard the sound of the pipes recede and fall and he let his grieving voice spiral downward with the god into Casadel as the song came to its end.

And so too, that morning, did a part of Devin's life. For when a portal of Morian's has been crossed there is, as everyone knows, never a turning back.

CHAPTER

•4•

ESCORTING HIS FATHER'S BIER OUT THE EASTERN GATE in the hour before sunset, Tomasso bar Sandre settled his horse to an easy walk and allowed his mind to drift for the first time in forty-eight intensely stressful hours.

The road was quiet. Normally it would have been clogged at this hour with people returning to the distrada before curfew locked the city gates. Normally sundown cleared the streets of Astibar of all save the patrolling Barbadian mercenaries and those reckless enough to defy them in search of women or wine or other diversions of the dark.

This was not a normal time, however. Tonight and for the next two nights there would be no curfew in Astibar. With the grapes gathered and the distrada's harvest a triumphant one, the Festival of Vines would see singing and dancing and things wilder than those in the streets for all three nights. For these three nights in the year Astibar tried to pretend it was sensuous, decadent Senzio. No Duke in the old days—and not even dour Alberico now—had been foolish enough to rouse the people unnecessarily by denying them this ancient release from the sober round of the year.

Tomasso glanced back at his city. The setting sun was red among thin clouds behind the temple-domes and the towers, bathing Astibar in an eerily beautiful glow. A breeze had come up and there was a bite to it. Tomasso thought about putting on his gloves and decided against it: he would have had to remove some of his rings and he quite liked the look of his gems in this elusive, transitory

55

light. Autumn was very definitely upon them, with the Ember Days approaching fast. It would not be long, a matter of days, before the first frost touched those last few precious grapes that had been left on chosen vines to become—if all fell rightly—the icy clear blue wine that was the pride of Astibar.

Behind him the eight servants plodded stolidly along the road, bearing the bier and the simple coffin—bare wood save for the Ducal crest above—of Tomasso's father. On either side of them the two vigil-keepers rode in grim silence. Which was not surprising, given the nature of their errand and the complex, many-generationed hatreds that twisted between those two men.

Those three men, Tomasso corrected himself. It was three, if one chose to count the dead man who had so carefully planned all of this, down to the detail of who should ride on which side of his bier, who before and who behind. Not to mention the rather more surprising detail of exactly which two lords of the province of Astibar should be asked to be his escorts to the hunting lodge for the night-long vigil and from there to the Sandreni Crypt at dawn. Or, to put the matter rather more to the point, the real point: which two lords could and should be entrusted with what they were to learn during the vigil in the forest that night.

At that thought Tomasso felt a nudge of apprehension within his rib cage. He quelled it, as he had taught himself to do over the years—unbelievable how many years—of discussing such matters with his father.

But now Sandre was dead and he was acting alone, and the night they had labored towards was almost upon them with this crimson waning of light. Tomasso, two years past his fortieth naming day knew that were he not careful he could easily feel like a child again.

The twelve-year-old child he had been, for example, when Sandre, Duke of Astibar, had found him naked in the straw of the stables with the sixteen-year-old son of the chief groom.

His lover had been executed of course, though discreetly, to keep the matter quiet. Tomasso had been whipped by his father for three days running, the lash meticulously rediscovering the closing wounds each morning. His mother had been forbidden to come to him. No one had come to him.

One of his father's very few mistakes, Tomasso reflected, thinking back thirty years in autumn twilight. From those three days he knew he could date his own particular taste for the whip in love-making. It was one of what he liked to call his *felicities*.

Though Sandre had never punished him that way again. Nor in any other direct manner. When it became clear— past the point of nursing any hope of discretion that Tomasso's preferences were, to put it mildly, not going to be changed or subdued, the Duke simply ceased to acknowledge the existence of his middle son.

For more than ten years they went on that way, Sandre patiently trying to train Gianno to succeed him, and spending scarcely less time with young Taeri—making it clear to everyone that his youngest son was next in line to his eldest. For over a decade Tomasso simply did not exist within the walls of the Sandreni Palace.

Though he most certainly did elsewhere in Astibar and in a number of the other provinces as well. For reasons that were achingly clear to him now, Tomasso had set out through the course of those years to eclipse the memories of all the dissolute nobility that Astibar still told shocked tales about, even though some of them had been dead four hundred years.

He supposed that he had, to a certain degree, succeeded.

Certainly the "raid" on the temple of Morian that Ember Night in spring so long ago was likely to linger a while yet as the nadir or the paradigm (all came down—or up—to perspective, as he'd been fond of saying then) of sacrilegious debauchery.

The raid hadn't had any impact on his relationship with the Duke. There was no relationship to impact upon ever since that morning in the straw when Sandre had returned from his ride a destined hour too soon. He and his father simply contrived not to speak to or even acknowledge each other, whether at family dinners or formal state functions. If Tomasso learned something he thought Sandre should know—which was often enough, given the circles in which he moved and the chronic danger of their times—he told his mother at one of their weekly breakfasts together and she made sure his father heard. Tomasso also knew she made equally sure Sandre was aware of the source of the tidings. Not that it mattered, really.

She had died, drinking poisoned wine meant for her husband, in the final year of the Duke's reign, still working, to the last morning of her life, towards a reconciliation between Sandre and their middle child.

Greater romantics than were either the father or the son might have allowed themselves to think that, as the Sandreni family pulled tightly together in the bloody, retaliatory aftermath of that poisoning, she had achieved her wistful hope by dying.

Both men knew it was not so.

In fact, it was only the coming of Alberico from the Empire of Barbadior, with his will-sapping sorcery and the brutal efficiency of his conquering mercenaries, that brought Tomasso and Sandre to a certain very late-night talk during the Duke's second year of exile. It was Alberico's invasion and one further thing: the monumental, irredeemable, inescapable stupidity of Gianno d'Astibar bar Sandre, titular heir to the shattered fortunes of their family.

And to these two things there had slowly been added a third bitter truth for the proud, exiled Duke. It had gradually become more and more obvious, past all denial, that whatever of his own character and gifts had been manifested in the next generation, whatever of his subtlety and perception, his ability to cloak his thoughts and discern the minds of others, whatever of such skills he had passed on to his sons, had gone, all of it, to the middle child. To Tomasso.

Who liked boys, and would leave no heir himself, nor ever a name to be spoken, let alone with pride, in Astibar or anywhere else in the Palm.

In the deepest inward place where he performed the complex act of dealing with his feelings for his father, Tomasso had always acknowledged—even back then, and very certainly now on this last evening road Sandre would travel—that one of the truest measures of the Duke's stature as a ruler of men had emerged on that winter night so long ago. The night he broke a decade's stony silence and spoke to his middle son and made him his confidant.

His sole confidant in the painfully cautious eighteen-year quest to drive Alberico and his sorcery and his mercenaries from Astibar and the Eastern Palm. A quest that had become an obsession for both of them, even as Tomasso's public manner became more and more eccentric and decayed, his voice and gait a parody—a self-parody, in fact—of the mincing, lisping lover of boys.

It was planned, all of it, in late-night talks with his father on their estate outside the city walls.

Sandre's parallel role had been to settle visibly and loudly into impotent, brooding, Triad-cursing exile, marked by querulous, blustering hunts and too much drinking of his own wine.

Tomasso had never seen his father actually drunk, and he never used his own fluting voice when they were alone at night.

Eight years ago they had tried an assassination. A chef, traceable only to the Canziano family, had been placed in a country inn in Ferraut near the provincial border with Astibar. For over half a year idle gossip in Astibar had touted that inn as a place of growing distinction. No one remembered, afterwards, where the talk had begun: Tomasso knew very well how useful it was to plant casual rumors of this sort among his friends in the temples. The priests of Morian, in particular, were legendary for their appetites. All their appetites.

A full year from the time they had set things in motion, Alberico of Barbadior had halted on his way back from the Triad Games—exactly as Sandre had said he would—to take his midday meal at a well-reputed inn in Ferraut near the Astibar border.

By the time the sun went down at the end of that bright late-summer day every person in that inn—servants, masters, stable-boys, chefs, children and patrons—had had their backs, legs, arms and wrists broken and their hands cut off, before being bound, living, upon hastily erected Barbadian sky-wheels to die.

The inn was razed to the ground. Taxes in the province of Ferraut were doubled for the next two years, and for a year in Astibar, Tregea and Certando. During the course

of the following six months every living member of the
Canziano family was found, seized, publicly tortured and
burned in the Grand Square of Astibar with their severed
hands stuffed in their mouths so that the screaming might
not trouble Alberico or his advisers in their offices of
state above the square.

In this fashion had Sandre and Tomasso discovered
that sorcerers cannot, in fact, be poisoned.

For the next six years they had done nothing but talk
at night in the manor-house among the vineyards and
gather what knowledge they could of Alberico himself
and events to the east in Barbadior, where the Emperor
was said to be growing older and more infirm with each
passing year.

Tomasso began commissioning and collecting walking
sticks with heads carved in the shape of the male organs
of sex. It was rumored that he'd had some of his young
friends model for the carvers. Sandre hunted. Gianno,
the heir, consolidated a burgeoning reputation as a ge-
nial, uncomplicated seducer of women and breeder of
children, legitimate and illegitimate. The younger Sandreni
were allowed to maintain modest homes in the city as
part of Alberico's overall policy to be as discreet a ruler
as possible—except when danger or civil unrest threatened him.

At which time children might die on sky-wheels. The
Sandreni Palace in Astibar remained very prominently
shuttered, empty and dusty. A useful, potent symbol of
the fall of those who might resist the Tyrant. The superstitious claimed to see ghostly lights flickering there at
night, especially on a blue-moon night, or on the spring
or autumn Ember Nights when the dead were known to
walk abroad.

Then one evening in the country Sandre had told
Tomasso, without warning or preamble, that he proposed
to die on the eve of the Festival of Vines two autumns
hence. He proceeded to name the two lords who were to
be his vigil-keepers, and why. That same night he and
Tomasso decided that it was time to tell Taeri, the youngest son, what was afoot. He was brave, not stupid, and
might be necessary for certain things. They also agreed
that Gianno had somehow sired one likely son, albeit

illegitimate, and that Herado—twenty-one by then and showing encouraging signs of spirit and ambition—was their best hope of having the younger generation share in the unrest Sandre hoped to create just after the time of his dying.

It wasn't, in fact, a question of who in the family could be trusted: family was, after all, family. The issue was who would be *useful* and it was a mark of how diminished the Sandreni had become that only two names came readily to mind.

It had been an entirely dispassionate conversation, Tomasso remembered, leading his father's bier southeast between the darkening trees that flanked the path. Their conversations had always been like that; this one had been no different. Afterwards though, he had been unable to fall asleep, the date of the Festival two years away branded into his brain. The date when his father, so precise in his planning, so judicious, had decided he would die so as to give Tomasso a chance to try again, a different way.

The date that had come now and gone, carrying with it the soul of Sandre d'Astibar to wherever the souls of such men went. Tomasso made a warding gesture to avert evil at that thought. Behind him he heard the steward order the servants to light torches. It grew colder as the darkness fell. Overhead a thin band of high clouds was tinted a somber shade of purple by the last upward-angled rays of light. The sun itself was gone, down behind the trees. Tomasso thought of souls, his father's and his own. He shivered.

The white moon, Vidomni, rose, and then, not long after, came blue Ilarion to chase her hopelessly across the sky. Both moons were nearly full. The procession could have done without torches in fact, so bright was the twinned moonlight, but torchlight suited the task and his mood, and so Tomasso let them burn as the company cut off the road onto the familiar winding path through the Sandreni Woods, to come at length to the simple hunting lodge his father had loved.

The servants laid the bier on the trestles waiting in the center of the large front room. Candles were lit and the two fires built up at opposite ends of the room. Food, they had set up earlier that day. It was quickly uncovered on the long sideboard along with the wine. The windows were opened to air the cabin and admit the breeze.

At a nod from Tomasso the steward led the servants away. They would go on to the manor further east and return at daybreak. At vigil's end.

And so they were left alone, finally. Tomasso and the lords Nievole and Scalvaia, so carefully chosen two years before.

"Wine, my lords?" Tomasso asked. "We will have three others joining us very shortly."

He said it, deliberately, in his natural voice, dropping the artificial, fluting tone that was his trademark in Astibar. He was pleased to see both of them note the fact immediately, their glances sharpening as they turned to him.

"Who else?" growled bearded Nievole who had hated Sandre all his life. He made no comment on Tomasso's voice, nor did Scalvaia. Such questions gave too much away, and these were men long skilled in giving away very little indeed.

"My brother Taeri and nephew Herado—one of Gianno's by-blows, and much the cleverest." He spoke casually, uncorking two bottles of Sandreni red reserve as he spoke. He poured and handed them each a glass, waiting to see who would break the small silence his father had said would follow. Scalvaia would ask, Sandre had said.

"Who is the third?" Lord Scalvaia asked softly.

Inwardly Tomasso saluted his dead father. Then, twirling his own glass gently by the stem to release the wine's bouquet, he said, "I don't know. My father did not name him. He named the two of you to come here, and the three of us and said there would be a sixth at our council tonight."

That word too had been carefully chosen.

"Council?" elegant Scalvaia echoed. "It appears that I have been misinformed. I was naively of the impression that this was a vigil." Nievole's dark eyes glowered above his beard. Both men stared at Tomasso.

"A little more than that," said Taeri as he entered the room, Herado behind him.

Tomasso was pleased to see them both dressed with appropriate sobriety, and to note that, for all the suavely flippant timing of Taeri's entrance, his expression was profoundly serious.

"You will know my brother," Tomasso murmured, moving to pour two more glasses for the new arrivals. "You may not have met Herado, Gianno's son."

The boy bowed and kept silent, as was proper. Tomasso carried the drinks over to his brother and nephew.

The stillness lasted a moment longer, then Scalvaia sank down into a chair, stretching his bad leg out in front of him. He lifted his cane and pointed it at Tomasso. The tip did not waver.

"I asked you a question," he said coldly, in the famous, beautiful voice. "Why do you call this a council, Tomasso bar Sandre? Why have we been brought here under false pretenses?"

Tomasso stopped playing with his wine. They had come to the moment at last. He looked from Scalvaia over to burly Nievole.

"The two of you," he said soberly, "were considered by my father to be the last lords of any real power left in Astibar. Two winters past he decided—and informed me— that he intended to die on the eve of this Festival. At a time when Alberico would not be able to refuse him full rites of burial—which rites include a vigil such as this. At a time when you would both be in Astibar, which would allow me to name you his vigil-keepers."

He paused in the measured, deliberate recitation and let his glance linger on each of them. "My father did this so that we might come together without suspicion, or interruption, or risk of being detected, to set in motion certain plans for the overthrow of Alberico who rules in Astibar."

He was watching closely, but Sandre had chosen well. Neither of the two men to whom he spoke betrayed surprise or dismay by so much as a flicker of a muscle.

Slowly Scalvaia lowered his cane and laid it down on the table by his chair. The stick was of onyx and machial, Tomasso found himself noticing. Strange how the mind worked at moments such as this.

"Do you know," said bluff Nievole from by the larger fire, "do you know that this thought had actually crossed my mind when I tried to hazard why your Triad-cursed father—ah, forgive me, old habits die hard—" His smile was wolfish, rather than apologetic, and it did not reach his narrowed eyes. "—Why Duke Sandre would name me to hold vigil for him. He *must* have known how many times I tried to hasten these mourning rites along in the days when he ruled."

Tomasso smiled in return, just as thinly. "He was certain you would wonder," he said politely to the man he was almost sure had paid for the cup of wine that had killed his mother. "He was also quite certain you would agree to come, being one of the last of a dying breed in Astibar. Indeed, in the whole of the Palm."

Bearded Nievole raised his glass. "You flatter well, bar Sandre. And I must say I do prefer your voice as it is now, without all the dips and flutters and wristy things that normally go with it."

Scalvaia looked amused. Taeri laughed aloud. Herado was carefully watchful. Tomasso liked him very much: though not, as he'd had to assure his father in one diverting conversation, in his own particular fashion.

"I prefer this voice as well," he said to the two lords. "You will both have been deducing in the last few minutes, being who and what you are, why I have conducted certain aspects of my life in certain well-known ways. There are advantages to being seen as aimlessly degenerate."

"There are," Scalvaia agreed blandly, "if you have a purpose that is served by such a misconception. You named a name a moment ago, and intimated we might all be rendered happier in our hearts were the bearer of that name dead or gone. We will leave aside for the moment what possibilities might follow such a dramatic eventuality."

His gaze was quite unreadable; Tomasso had been warned it would be. He said nothing. Taeri shifted uneasily but blessedly kept quiet, as instructed. He walked over and took one of the other chairs on the far side of the bier.

Scalvaia went on "We cannot be unaware that by saying what you have said you have put yourselves completely in our hands, or so it might initially appear. At the same time, I do surmise that were we, in fact, to rise and begin to ride back towards Astibar carrying word of treachery we would join your father among the dead before we left these woods."

It was casually stated—a minor fact to be confirmed before moving on to more important issues.

Tomasso shook his head. "Hardly," he lied. "You do us honor by your presence and are entirely free to leave. Indeed, we will escort you if you wish, for the path is deceptive in darkness. My father did suggest that I might wish to point out that although you could readily have us wristed and death-wheeled after torture, it is exceedingly likely, approaching a certainty, that Alberico would then see compelling cause to do the same to both of you, for having been considered likely accomplices of ours. You will remember what happened to the Canziano after that unfortunate incident in Ferraut some years ago?"

There was a smoothly graceful silence acknowledging all of this.

It was broken by Nievole. "That *was* Sandre's doing, wasn't it?" he growled from by his fire. "Not the Canziano at all!"

"It was our doing," Tomasso agreed calmly. "We learned a great deal, I must say."

"So," Scalvaia murmured drily, "did the Canziano. Your father always hated Fabro bar Canzian."

"They could not have been said to be on the best of terms," Tomasso said blandly. "Though I must say that if you focus on that aspect of things I fear you might miss the point."

"The point you prefer us to take," Nievole amended pointedly.

Unexpectedly, Scalvaia came to Tomasso's aid. "Not fair, my lord," he said to Nievole. "If we can accept anything as true in this room and these times it is that Sandre's hatred and his desire had moved beyond old wars and rivalries. His target was Alberico."

His icy blue eyes held Nievole's for a long moment, and finally the bigger man nodded. Scalvaia shifted in his chair wincing at a pain in his afflicted leg.

"Very well," he said to Tomasso. "You have now told us why we are here and have made clear your father's purpose and your own. For my own part I will make a confession. I will confess, in the spirit of truth that a death vigil should inspire, that being ruled by a coarse, vicious, overbearing minor lord from Barbadior brings little joy to my aged heart. I am with you. If you have a plan I would like to hear it. On my oath and honor I will keep faith with the Sandreni in this."

Tomasso shivered at the invocation of the ancient words. "Your oath and honor are sureties beyond measure," he said, and meant it.

"They are indeed, bar Sandre," said Nievole, taking a heavy step forward from the fire. "And I will dare to say that the word of the Nievolene has never been valued at lesser coin. The dearest wish of my heart is for the Barbadian to lie dead and cut to pieces—Triad willing, by my own blade. I too am with you—by my oath and honor."

"Such terribly splendid words!" said an amused voice from the window opposite the door.

Five faces, four white with shock and the bearded one flushing red, whipped around. The speaker stood outside the open window, elbows resting on the ledge, chin in his hands. He eyed them with a mild scrutiny, his face shadowed by the wood of the window frame.

"I have never yet," he said, "known gallant phrases from however august a lineage to succeed in ousting a tyrant. In the Palm or anywhere else." With an economical motion he hoisted himself upwards, swung his feet into the room and sat comfortably perched on the ledge. "On the other hand," he added, "agreeing on a cause does make a starting point, I will concede that much."

"You are the sixth of whom my father spoke?" Tomasso asked warily.

The man did look familiar now that he was in the light. He was dressed for the forest not the city, in two shades of grey with a black sheepskin vest over his shirt, and breeches tucked into worn black riding boots. There was a knife at his belt, without ornament.

"I heard you mention that," the fellow said. "I actually hope I'm not, because if I am the implications are unsettling, to say the least. The fact is, I never spoke to your father in my life. If he knew of my activities and somehow expected me to find out about this meeting and be here . . . well, I would be somewhat flattered by his confidence but rather more disturbed that he would have known so much about me. On the other hand," he said for a second time, "it is Sandre d'Astibar we're talking about, and I do seem to make six here, don't I?" He bowed, without any visible irony, towards the bier on its trestles.

"You are, then, also in league against Alberico?" Nievole's eyes were watchful.

"I am not," said the man in the window quite bluntly. "Alberico means nothing to me. Except as a tool. A wedge to open a door of my own."

"And what is it lies behind that door?" Scalvaia asked from deep in his armchair.

But in that moment Tomasso remembered.

"I know you!" he said abruptly. "I saw you this morning. You are the Tregean shepherd who played the pipes in the mourning rites!" Taeri snapped his fingers as the recognition came home to him as well.

"I played the pipes, yes," the man on the window-ledge said, quite unruffled. "But I am not a shepherd nor from Tregea. It has suited my purposes to play a role, many different roles, in fact, for a great many years. Tomasso bar Sandre ought to appreciate that." He grinned.

Tomasso did not return the smile. "Perhaps then, under the circumstances, you might favor us by saying who you really are." He said it as politely as the situation seemed to warrant. "My father might have known but we do not."

"Nor, I'm afraid, shall you learn just yet," the other said. He paused. "Though I will say that were I to swear a vow of my own on the honor of my family it would carry a weight that would eclipse both such oaths sworn here tonight."

It was matter-of-factly said, which made the arrogance greater, not less.

To forestall Nievole's predictable burst of anger Tomasso said quickly, "You will not deny us *some* information surely, even if you choose to shield your name. You said Alberico is a tool for you. A tool for what, Alessan not-of-Tregea?" He was pleased to find that he remembered the name Menico di Ferraut had mentioned yesterday. "What *is* your own purpose? What brings you to this lodge?"

The other's face, lean and curiously hollowed with cheekbones in sharp relief, grew still, almost masklike. And into the waiting silence that ensued he said:

"I want Brandin. I want Brandin of Ygrath dead more than I want my soul's immortality beyond the last portal of Morian."

There was a silence again, broken only by the crackle of the autumn fires on the two hearths. It seemed to Tomasso as if the chill of winter had come into the room with that speech.

Then: "Such terribly splendid words!" murmured Scalvaia lazily, shattering the mood. He drew a shout of laughter from Nievole and Taeri, both. Scalvaia himself did not smile.

The man on the window-ledge acknowledged the thrust with the briefest nod of his head. He said, "This is not, my lord, a subject about which I permit frivolity. If we are to work together it will be necessary for you to remember that."

"You, I am forced to say, are an overly proud young man," replied Scalvaia sharply. "It might be appropriate for you to remember to whom you speak."

The other visibly bit back his first retort. "Pride is a family failing," he said finally. "I have not escaped it, I'm afraid. But I am indeed mindful of who you are. And the Sandreni and my lord Nievole. It is why I am here. I have made it my business to be aware of dissidence throughout the Palm for many years. At times I have encouraged it, discreetly. This evening marks the first instance in which I have come myself to a gathering such as this."

"But you have already told us that Alberico is nothing to you." Tomasso inwardly cursed his father for not having better prepared him for this very peculiar sixth figure.

"Nothing in himself," the other corrected. "Will you allow me?" Without waiting for a reply he lifted himself down from the ledge and walked over to the wine.

"Please," said Tomasso, belatedly.

The man poured himself a generous glass of the vintage red. He drained it, and poured another. Only then did he turn back to address the five of them. Herado's eyes, watching him, were enormous.

"Two facts," the man called Alessan said crisply. "Learn them if you are serious about freedom in the Palm. One: if you oust or slay Alberico you will have Brandin upon you within three months. Two: if Brandin is ousted or slain Alberico will rule this peninsula within that same period of time."

He stopped. His eyes—grey, Tomasso noticed now—moved from one to the other of them, challenging. No one spoke. Scalvaia toyed with the handle of his cane.

"These two things must be understood," the stranger went on in the same tone. "Neither I in my own pursuit, nor you in yours, can afford to lose sight of them. They are the core truths of the Palm in our time. The two sorcerers from overseas are their own balance of power and the *only* balance of power in the peninsula right now, however different things might have been eighteen years ago. Today only the power of one keeps the magic of the other from being wielded as it was when they conquered us. If we take them then we must take them both—or make them bring down each other."

"How?" Taeri asked, too eagerly.

The lean face under the prematurely silvering dark hair turned to him and smiled briefly. "Patience, Taeri bar Sandre. I have a number of things yet to tell you about carelessness before deciding if our paths are to join. And I say this with infinite respect for the dead man who seems—remarkably enough—to have drawn us here. I'm afraid you are going to have to agree to submit yourselves to my guidance or we can do nothing together at all."

"The Scalvaiane have submitted themselves willingly to nothing and no one in living memory or recorded history," that vulpine lord said, the texture of velvet in his voice. "I am not readily of a mind to become the first to do so."

"Would you prefer," the other said, "to have your plans and your life and the long glory of your line snuffed out like candles on the Ember Days because of sheer sloppiness in your preparations?"

"You had better explain yourself," Tomasso said icily.

"I intend to. Who was it who chose a double-moon night at double moonrise to meet?" Alessan retorted, his voice suddenly cutting like a blade. "Why are no rear guards posted along the forest path to warn you if some-one approaches—as I just did? Why were no servants left here this afternoon to guard this cabin? Have you even the faintest awareness of how dead the five of you would be—severed hands stuffed into your throats—were I not who I am?"

"My father . . . Sandre . . . said that Alberico would not have us followed," Tomasso stammered furiously. "He was absolutely certain of that."

"And he is likely to have been absolutely right. But you cannot let your focus be so narrow. Your father—I am sorry to have to say it—was alone with his obsession for too long. He was too intent upon Alberico. It shows in everything you have done these past two days. What of the idly curious or the greedy? The petty informer who might decide to follow you just to see what happened here? Just to have a story to tell in the tavern tomorrow? Did you—or your father—give even half a thought to such things? Or to those who might have learned where you planned to come and arranged to be here before you?"

There was a hostile silence. A log on the smaller fire settled with a crack and a shower of sparks. Herado jumped involuntarily at the sound.

"Will it interest you to know," the man called Alessan went on, more gently, "that my people have been guard-ing the approaches to this cabin since you arrived? Or that I've had someone in here since mid-afternoon keep-ing an eye on the servants setting up, and who might follow them?"

"What?" Taeri exclaimed. "In here! In our hunting lodge!"

"For your protection and my own," the other man said, finishing his second glass of wine. He glanced up-wards to the shadows of the half-loft above, where the extra pallets were stored.

"I think that should do it, my friend," he called, pitch-ing his voice to carry. "You've earned a glass of wine after so long dry-throated among the dust. You may as well come down now, Devin."

It had actually been very easy.

Menico, purse jingling with more money than he had ever earned from a single performance in his life, had graciously passed their concert at the wine-merchant's house over to Burnet di Corte. Burnet, who needed the work, was pleased; the wine-merchant, angry at first, was quickly mollified upon learning what Menico's hitherto unfinalized tariff would now have been in the aftermath of the sensation they'd caused that morning.

So, in the event, Devin and the rest of the company had been given the rest of the day and evening off. Menico counted out for everyone an immediate bonus of five astins and benevolently waved them away to the various delights of the Festival. He didn't even offer his usual warning lecture.

Already, just past noon, there were wine-stands on every corner, more than one at the busier squares. Each vineyard in Astibar province, and even some from farther afield in Ferraut or Senzio, had its vintages from previous years available as harbingers of what this year's grapes would offer. Merchants looking to buy in quantity were sampling judiciously, early revelers rather less so.

Fruit vendors were also in abundance, with figs and melons and the enormous grapes of the season displayed beside vast wheels of white cheeses from Tregea or bricks of red ones from northern Certando. Over by the market the din was deafening as the people of the city and its distrada canvassed the offerings of this year's itinerant tradesmen. Overhead the banners of the noble houses and of the larger wine estates flapped brightly in the autumn breeze as Devin strode purposefully towards what he'd just been told was the most fashionable khav room in Astibar.

There were benefits to fame. He was recognized at the doorway, his arrival excitedly announced, and in a matter of moments he found himself at the dark wooden bar of The Paelion nursing a mug of hot khav laced with

flambardion—no awkward questions asked about anyone's age, thank you very much.

It was the work of half an hour to find out what he
needed to know about Sandre d'Astibar. His questions
seemed entirely natural, coming from the tenor who had
just sung the Duke's funeral lament. Devin learned about
Sandre's long rule, his feuds, his bitter exile, and his sad
decline in the last few years into a blustering, drunken
hunter of small game, a wraith compared to what he once
had been.

In that last context, rather more specifically, Devin
asked about where the Duke had liked to hunt. They told
him. They told him where his favorite hunting lodge
had been. He changed the subject to wine.

It was easy. He was a hero of the hour and The Paelion
liked heroes, for an hour. They let him go eventually: he
pleaded an artist's strained sensitivity after the morning's
endeavors. With the benefit of hindsight he now attached
a deal more importance than he had at the time to
glimpsing Alessan di Tregea at a booth full of painters
and poets. They were laughing about some wager concerning certain verses of condolence that had not yet
arrived from Chiara. He and Alessan had saluted each
other in an elaborately showy, performers' fashion that
delighted the packed room.

Back at the inn, Devin had fended off the most ardent
of the group who had walked him home and went upstairs alone. He had waited in his room, chafing, for an
hour to be sure the last of them had gone. Having changed
into a dark-brown tunic and breeches, he put on a cap to
hide his hair and a woolen overshirt against the coming
chill of evening. Then he made his way unnoticed through
the now teeming crowds in the streets over to the eastern
gate of the city.

And out, among several empty wagons, goods all sold,
being ridden back to the distrada by sober, prudent farmers who preferred to reload and return in the morning
instead of celebrating all night in town spending what
they'd just earned.

Devin hitched a ride on a cart part of the way, commis-
erating with the driver on the taxes and the poor rates
being paid that year for lamb's wool. Eventually he jumped

off, feigning youthful exuberance and ran a mile or so along the road to the east.

At one point he saw, with a grin of recognition, a temple of Adaon on the right. Just past it, as promised, was the delicately rendered image of a ship on the roadside gate of a modest country house. Rovigo's home—what Devin could see of it, set well back from the road among cypress and olive trees—looked comfortable and cared for.

A day ago, a different person, he would have stopped. But something had happened to him that morning within the dusty spaces of the Sandreni Palace. He kept going.

A half mile further on he found what he was looking for. He made sure he was alone and then quickly cut to his right, south into the woods, away from the main road that led to the east coast and Ardin town on the sea.

It was quiet in the forest and cooler where the branches and the many-colored leaves dappled the sunlight. There was a path winding through the trees and Devin began to follow it, towards the hunting lodge of the Sandreni. From here on he redoubled his caution. On the road he was simply a walker in the autumn countryside; here he was a trespasser with no excuse at all for being where he was.

Unless pride and the strange, dreamlike events of the morning just past could be called adequate excuses. Devin rather doubted it. At the same time, it remained to be seen whether he or a certain manipulative red-headed personage was going to dictate the shape and flow of this day and those to come. If she were under the impression that he was so easy to dupe—a helpless, youthful slave to his passions, blinded and deafened to anything else by the so-gracious offer of her body—well it was for this afternoon and this evening to show how wrong an arrogant girl could be.

What else the evening might reveal, Devin didn't know; he hadn't allowed himself to slow down long enough to consider the question.

There was no one there when he came to the lodge, though he lay silently among the trees for a long time to be certain. The front door was chained but Marra had been very good with such devices and had taught him a thing or two. He picked the lock with the buckle of his belt, went inside, opened a window, and climbed out to relock the chain. Then he slipped back in through the window, closed it, and took a look around.

There was little option, really. The two bedchambers at the back would be dangerous and not very useful if he wanted to hear. Devin balanced himself on the broad arm of a heavy wooden chair and, jumping, managed to make it up to the half-loft on his second attempt.

Nursing a shin bruised in the process he took a pillow from one of the pallets stored up there and proceeded to wedge himself into the remotest, darkest corner he could find, behind two beds and the stuffed head of an antlered corbin stag. By lying on his left side, eye to a chink in the floorboards, he had an almost complete view of the room below.

He tried to guide himself towards a mood of calm and patience. Unfortunately, he soon became irrationally conscious of the fact that the glassy eye of the corbin was glitteringly fixed upon him. Under the circumstances it made him nervous. Eventually he got up, turned the chestnut head to one side and settled in to his hiding-place again.

And right about then, as the grimly purposeful activities of the day gave way to a time when he could do nothing but wait, Devin began to be afraid.

He was under no real illusions: he was a dead man if they found him here. The secrecy and tension in Tomasso bar Sandre's words and manner that morning made that clear enough. Even without what Catriana had done in her own effort to overhear those words, and then to prevent him from doing so. For the first time Devin began to contemplate where the rash momentum of his wounded pride had carried him.

When the servants came half an hour later to prepare the room they gave him some very bad moments. Bad enough, in fact, to make him briefly wish that he was back home in Asoli guiding a plow behind a pair of stolid water buffaloes. They were fine creatures, water buffaloes, patient, uncomplaining. They plowed fields for you, and their milk made cheese. There was even something to be said for the predictable grey skies of

Asoli in autumn and the equally predictable people. None of their girls, for example, were as irritatingly superior as Catriana d'Astibar who had got him into this. Nor would any Asolini servant, Devin was quite certain, ever have volunteered, as one Triad-blighted fool below was doing even now, to bring down a pallet from the half-loft in case one of the vigil-keeping lords should grow weary.

"Goch, don't be more of a fool than you absolutely must be!" the steward snapped officiously in reply. "They are here to keep a waking watch all night—a pallet in the room is an insult to them both. Be grateful you aren't dependent on your brain to feed your belly, Goch!"

Devin fervently seconded the sentiments of the insult and wished the steward a long and lucrative existence. For the tenth time since the Sandreni servants had entered the lower room he cursed Catriana, and for the twentieth time, himself. The ratio seemed about right.

Finally the servants left; heading back for Astibar to bear the Duke's body here. The steward's instructions were painstakingly explicit. With idiots like Goch around, Devin thought spitefully, they had to be.

From where he lay, Devin could see the daylight gradually waning towards dusk. He found himself softly humming his old cradle song. He made himself stop.

His mind turned back to the morning. To the long walk through empty, dusty rooms of the palace. To the hidden closet at the end. The sudden silken feel of Catriana when her gown had drifted above her hips. He made himself stop that too.

It grew steadily darker. The first owl called, not far away. Devin had grown up in the country; it was a familiar sound. He heard some forest animal rooting in the underbrush at the edge of the clearing. Once in a while a gusting of the wind would set the leaves to rustling.

Then, abruptly, there came a shining of white light through one of the drawn window curtains and Devin knew that Vidomni was high enough to look down upon this clearing amid the tall trees of the wood, which meant that blue Ilarion would be rising even now. Which meant it would not be very much longer.

It wasn't. There was a wavering of torchlight and the

sound of voices. The lock clinked, rattled, and the door
swung open. The steward led in eight men carrying a
bier. Eye glued to his crack in the floor, breathing shal-
lowly, Devin saw them lay it down. Tomasso came in
with the two lords whose names and lineage Devin had
learned in The Paelion.

The servants uncovered and laid out the food and then
they left, Goch stumbling on the threshold and banging
his shoulder pleasingly on the doorpost. The steward, last
to go, shrugged a discreet apology, bowed, and closed
the door behind him.

"Wine, my lords?" said Tomasso d'Astibar in the voice
Devin had heard from the secret closet. "We will have
three others joining us very shortly."

And from then on they had said what they said and
Devin heard what he heard, and so gradually became
aware of the magnitude of what he had stumbled upon,
the peril he was in.

Then Alessan appeared at the window opposite the
door.

Devin couldn't, in fact, see that window but he knew
the voice immediately and it was with disbelief bordering
on stupefaction that he heard Menico's recruit of a fortnight ago deny being from Tregea at all and then name
Brandin, King of Ygrath as the everlasting target of his
soul's hate.

Rash, Devin certainly was, and he would not have
denied that he carried more than his own due share of
impulsive foolishness, but he had not ever been less than
quick, or clever. In Asoli, small boys had to be.

So by the time Alessan named him, and invited him to
come down, Devin's racing mind had put two more pieces
of the puzzle together and he adroitly took the path
offered him.

"*All quiet, since mid-afternoon,*" he called out, extri-
cating himself from his corner and stepping past the
corbin's antlers to the edge of the half-loft. "Only the
servants were here, but they didn't do much of a job
when they chained the door—the lock was easy to pick.
Two thieves and the Emperor of Barbadior could have
been up here without seeing each other or anyone down
there being the wiser."

He said it as coolly as he could. Then he lowered himself, with a deliberately showy flip, to the ground. He registered the looks on the faces of five of the men there—all of whom most certainly recognized him—but his concentration, and his satisfaction, lay in the brief smile of approval he received from Alessan.

For the moment his apprehension was gone, replaced by something entirely different. Alessan had claimed him, given him legitimacy here. He was clearly linked to the man who was controlling events in the room. And the events were on a scale that spanned the Palm. Devin had to fight hard to control his growing excitement.

Tomasso went over to the sideboard and smoothly poured a glass of wine for him. Devin was impressed with the composure of the man. He was also aware, from the exaggerated courtesy and the undeniable sparkle in bar Sandre's accentuated eyes, that although the fluting voice might be faked, Tomasso, in certain matters and propensities, was still very much what he was said to be. Devin accepted the glass, careful not to let their fingers touch.

"I wonder now," drawled Lord Scalvaia in his magnificent voice, "are we to be treated to a recital here while we pass our vigil? There does seem to be a quantity of musicians here tonight."

Devin said nothing, but following Alessan's example did not smile.

"Shall I name you a provincial grower of grapes, my lord?" There was real anger in Alessan's voice. "And call Nievole a grain-farmer from the southwestern distrada? What we do outside these walls has little to do with why we are here, save in two ways only."

He held up a long finger. "One: as musicians we have an excuse to cross back and forth across the Palm, which offers advantages I need not belabor." A second finger shot up beside the first. "Two: music trains the mind, like mathematics, or logic, to precision of detail. The sort of precision, my lords, that would have precluded the carelessness that has marked tonight. If Sandre d'Astibar were alive I would discuss it with him, and I might defer to his experience and his long striving."

He paused, looking from one to another of them, then said, much more softly: "I might, but I might not. It is a vanished tune, that one, never to be sung. As matters stand I can only say again that if we are to work together I must ask you to accept my lead."

He spoke this last directly to Scalvaia who still lounged, elegant and expressionless, in his deep chair. It was Nievole who answered, though, blunt and direct.

"I am not in the habit of delaying my judgment of men. I think you mean what you say and that you are more versed in these things than we are. I accept. I will follow your lead. With a single condition."

"Which is?"

"That you tell us your name."

Devin, watching with rapacious intensity, anxious not to miss a word or a nuance, saw Alessan's eyes close for an instant, as if to hold back something that might otherwise have shown through them. The others waited through the short silence.

Then Alessan shook his head. "It is a fair condition, my lord. Under the circumstances it is entirely fair. I can only pray you will not hold me to it though. It is a grief—I cannot tell you how much of a grief it is—but I am unable to accede."

For the first time he appeared to be reaching for words, choosing them carefully. "Names are power, as you know. As the two tyrant-sorcerers from overseas most certainly know. And as I have been made to know in the bitterest ways there are. My lord, you will learn my name in the moment of our triumph if it comes, and not before. I will say that this is imposed upon me; it is not a choice freely made. You may call me Alessan, which is common enough here in the Palm and happens to be truly the name my mother gave me. Will you be gracious enough to let that suffice you, my lord, or must we now part ways?"

The last question was asked in a tone bereft of the arrogance that had infused the man's bearing and speech from the moment of his arrival.

Just as Devin's earlier fear had given way to excitement, so now did excitement surrender to something else, something he could not yet identify. He stared at Alessan. The man seemed younger than before, somehow—unable to prevent this almost naked showing of his need.

Nievole cleared his throat loudly, as if to dispel an aura, a resonance of something that seemed to have entered the room like the mingled light of the two moons outside. Another owl hooted from the clearing. Nievole opened his mouth to reply to Alessan.

They never knew what he would have said, or Scalvaia.

Afterwards, on nights when sleep eluded him and he watched one or both moons sweep the sky or counted the stars in Eanna's Diadem in a moonless dark, Devin would let his clear memory of that moment carry him back, trying—for reasons he would have found difficult to explain—to imagine what the two lords would have done or said had all their briefly tangled fate lines run differently from that lodge.

He could guess, analyze, play out scenarios in his mind, but he would never *know*. It was a night-time truth that became a queer, private sorrow for him amid all that came after. A symbol, a displacement of regret. A reminder of what it was to be mortal and so doomed to tread one road only and that one only once, until Morian called the soul away and Eanna's lights were lost. We can never truly know the path we have not walked.

The paths that each of the men in that lodge were to walk, through their own private portals to endings near or far were laid down by the owl that cried a second time, very clearly, just as Nievole began to speak.

Alessan flung up his hand. "Trouble!" he said sharply. Then: *"Baerd?"*

The door banged open. Devin saw a large man, his very long, pale-yellow hair held back by a leather band across his brow. There was another leather thong about his throat. He wore a vest and leggings cut in the fashion of the southern highlands. His eyes, even by firelight, gleamed a dazzling blue. He carried a drawn sword.

Which was punishable by death this close to Astibar.

"Let's go!" the man said urgently. "You and the boy. The others belong here—the youngest son and the grandson have easy explanations. Get rid of the extra glasses."

"What is it?" Tomasso d'Astibar asked quickly, his eyes wide.

"Twenty horsemen on the forest path. Continue your

vigil and be as calm as you can—we won't be far away. We'll return after. Alessan, *come on!*"

The tone of his voice pulled Devin halfway to the door. Alessan was lingering though, his eyes for some reason locked on those of Tomasso, and that look, what was exchanged in it, became another one of the things that Devin never forgot, or fully understood.

For a long moment—a very long moment, it seemed to Devin, with twenty horsemen riding through the forest and a drawn sword in the room—no one spoke. Then:

"It seems we will have to continue this extremely interesting discussion at a later hour," Tomasso bar Sandre murmured, with genuinely impressive composure. "Will you take a last glass before you go, in my father's name?"

Alessan smiled then, a full, open smile. He shook his head though. "I hope to have a chance to do so later," he said. "I will drink to your father gladly, but I have a habit I don't think even you can satisfy in the time we have."

Tomasso's mouth quirked wryly. "I've satisfied a number of habits in my day. Do tell me yours."

The reply was quiet, Devin had to strain to hear.

"My third glass of a night is blue," Alessan said. "The third glass I drink is always of blue wine. In memory of something lost. Lest on any single night I forget what it is I am alive to do."

"Not forever lost, I hope," said Tomasso, equally softly.

"Not forever, I have sworn, upon my soul and my father's soul wherever it has gone."

"Then there will be blue wine when next we drink after tonight," said Tomasso, "if it is at all in my power to provide it. And I will drink it with you to our fathers' souls."

"Alessan!" snapped the yellow-haired man named Baerd, "In Adaon's name, I said twenty horsemen! *Will you come?*"

"I will," said Alessan. He hurled his wineglass and Devin's through the nearest window into the darkness. "Triad guard you all," he said to the five in the room. Then he and Devin followed Baerd into the moonlit shadows of the clearing.

With Devin in the middle they ran swiftly around to the side of the cabin farthest from the path that led to the main road. They didn't go far. His pulse pounding furiously, Devin dropped to the ground when the other two men did so. Peering cautiously out from under a cluster of dark-green serrano bushes they could see the lodge. Firelight showed through the open windows.

A moment later Devin's heart lurched like a ship caught by a wave across its bows, as a twig cracked just behind him.

"Twenty-two riders," a voice said. The speaker dropped neatly to the ground on Baerd's other side. "The one in the middle of them is hooded."

Devin looked over. And by the mingled light of the two moons saw Catriana d'Astibar.

"Hooded?" Alessan repeated, on a sharply taken breath. "You are certain?"

"Of course I am," said Catriana. "Why? What does it mean?"

"Eanna be gracious to us all," Alessan murmured, not answering.

"I wouldn't be counting on it now," the man named Baerd said grimly. "I think we should leave this place. They will search."

For a moment Alessan looked as if he would demur, but just then they heard a jingling of many riders from the path on the other side of the lodge.

Without another word spoken the four of them rose and silently moved away.

★　★　★

"This evening," murmured Scalvaia, "grows more eventful by the moment."

Tomasso was grateful for the elegant lord's equanimity. It helped steady his own nerves. He looked over at his brother; Taeri seemed all right. Herado was white-faced, however. Tomasso winked at the boy. "Have another drink, nephew. You look infinitely prettier with color in your cheeks. There is nothing to fear. We are here doing exactly what we have permission to be doing."

They heard the horses. Herado went over to the sideboard, filled a glass and drained it at a gulp. Just as he put the goblet down the door crashed loudly open, banging into the wall beside it, and four enormous, fully-armed Barbadian soldiers strode in, making the lodge seem suddenly small.

"Gentlemen!" Tomasso fluted expertly, wringing his hands. "What is it? What brings you here, to interrupt a vigil?" He was careful to sound petulant, not angry.

The mercenaries didn't even deign to look at him, let alone reply. Two of them quickly went to check the bedrooms and a third seized the ladder and ran up it to examine the half-loft where the young singer had been hiding. Other soldiers, Tomasso registered apprehensively, were taking up positions outside each of the windows. There was a great deal of noise outside among the horses, and a confusion of torches.

Tomasso abruptly stamped his foot in frustration. "What is the meaning of this?" he shrilled as the soldiers continued to ignore him. "Tell me! I shall protest directly to your lord. We have Alberico's express permission to conduct this vigil and the burial tomorrow. I have it in writing under his seal!" He addressed the Barbadian captain standing by the door.

Again it was as if he hadn't even spoken so completely did they disregard him. Four more soldiers came in and spread out to the edges of the room, their expressions blank and dangerous.

"This is intolerable!" Tomasso whined, staying in character, his hands writhing about each other. "I shall ride immediately to Alberico! I shall *demand* that you all be shipped straight back to your wretched hovels in Barbadior!"

"That will not be necessary," said a burly, hooded figure in the doorway.

He stepped forward and threw back the hood. "You may make your childish demand of me right here," said Alberico of Barbadior, Tyrant of Astibar, Tregea, Ferraut and Certando.

Tomasso's hands flew to his throat even as he dropped to his knees. The others, too, knelt immediately, even old Scalvaia with his game leg. A black mind-cloak of numbing fear threatened to descend over Tomasso, trammeling all speech and thought.

"My lord," he stammered, "I did not . . . I could . . . we could not know!"

Alberico was silent, gazing blankly down upon him. Tomasso fought to master his terror and bewilderment. "You are most welcome here," he bleated, rising carefully, "most welcome, most honored lord. You do us too much honor with your presence at my father's rites."

"I do," said Alberico bluntly. Tomasso received the full weight of a heavy scrutiny from the small eyes, close-set and unblinking deep in the folds of the sorcerer's large face. Alberico's bald skull gleamed in the firelight. He drew his hands from the pockets of his robe. "I would have wine," he demanded, gesturing with a meaty palm.

"But of course, of course."

Tomasso stumbled to obey, intimidated as always by the sheer, bulky physicality of Alberico and his Barbadians. They hated him, he knew, and all his kind, over and above everything else these conquerors felt about the people of the Eastern Palm whose world they now ruled. Whenever he faced Alberico Tomasso was overwhelmingly conscious that the Tyrant could crack his bones with bare hands and not think twice about having done so.

It was not a comforting line of thought. Only eighteen years of carefully schooling his body to shield his mind kept his hands steady as they carried a full glass ceremoniously over to Alberico. The soldiers eyed his every movement. Nievole was back by the larger fire, Taeri and Herado together by the small one. Scalvaia stood, braced upon his cane, beside the chair in which he'd been sitting.

It was time, Tomasso judged, to sound more confident, less guilty. "You will forgive me, my lord, for my ill judged words to your soldiers. Not knowing you were here I could only guess they were acting in ignorance of your wishes."

"My wishes change," Alberico said in his heavy, unchanging voice. "They are likely to know of those changes before you, bar Sandre."

"Of course, my lord. But of course. They—"

"I wanted," said Alberico of Barbadior, "to look upon

the coffin of your father. To look, and to laugh." He showed no trace of an inclination toward amusement. Tomasso's blood felt suddenly icy in his veins.

Alberico stepped past him and stood massively over the remains of the Duke. "This," he said flatly, "is the body of a vain, wretched, fatuous old man who decreed the hour of his own death to no purpose. No purpose at all. Is it not amusing?"

He did laugh then—three short, harsh barks of sound that were more truly frightening than anything Tomasso had ever heard in his life. *How had he known?*

"Will you not laugh with me? You three Sandreni? Nievole? My poor, crippled, impotent Lord Scalvaia? Is it not diverting to think how all of you have been brought here and doomed by senile foolishness? By an old man who lived too long to understand how the labyrinthine twistings of his own time could be so easily smashed through with a fist today."

His clenched hand crashed heavily down on the wooden coffin lid, splintering the carved Sandreni arms. With a faint sound of distress Scalvaia sank back into his chair.

"My lord," Tomasso gulped, gesticulating. "What can you possibly mean? What are you—"

He got no further than that. Wheeling savagely Alberico slapped him meatily across the face with an open hand. Tomasso staggered backwards, blood spattering from his ripped mouth.

"You will use your natural voice, son of a fool," the sorcerer said, the words more terrifying because spoken in the same flat tone as before. "Will it at least amuse you to know how easy this was? To learn how long Herado bar Gianno has been reporting to me?"

And with those words the night came down.

The full black cloak of anguish and raw terror Tomasso had been fighting desperately to hold back. *Oh, my father,* he thought, stricken to his soul that it should have been by family that they were now undone. By family. *Family!*

Several things happened then in an extremely short span of time.

"My lord!" Herado cried out in high-pitched dismay. "You promised! You said they would not know! You told me—"

It was all he said. It is difficult to expostulate with a dagger embedded in your throat.

"The Sandreni deal with the scrapings of dirt under their own fingernails," said his uncle Taeri, who had drawn the blade from the back of his boot. Even as he spoke, Taeri pulled his dagger free of Herado and smoothly, part of one continuous motion, sheathed it in his own heart.

"One less Sandreni for your sky-wheels, Barbadian!" he taunted, gasping. "Triad send a plague to eat the flesh from your bones." He dropped to his knees. His hands were on the dagger haft; blood was spilling over them. His eyes sought Tomasso's. "Farewell, brother," he whispered. "Morian grant our shadows know each other in her Halls."

Something was clenched around Tomasso's heart, squeezing and squeezing, as he watched his brother die. Two of the guards, trained to ward a very different sort of blow at their lord, stepped forward and flipped Taeri over on his back with the toes of their boots.

"Fools!" spat Alberico, visibly upset for the first time. "I needed him alive. I wanted both of them alive!" The soldiers blanched at the fury written in his features.

Then the focus of the room went elsewhere entirely.

With an animal roar of mingled rage and pain Nievole d'Astibar, a very big man himself, linked his two hands like a hammer or the head of a mace and swung them full into the face of the soldier nearest to him. The blow smashed bones like splintering wood. Blood spurted as the man screamed and crumpled heavily back against the coffin.

Still roaring, Nievole grappled for his victim's sword.

He actually had it out and was turning to do battle when four arrows took him in the throat and chest. His face went dully slack for an instant, then his eyes widened and his mouth relaxed into a macabre smile of triumph as he slipped to the floor.

And then, just then, with all eyes on fallen Nievole, Lord Scalvaia did the one thing no one had dared to do. Slumped deep in his chair, so motionless they had almost forgotten him, the aged patrician raised his cane with a steady hand, pointed it straight at Alberico's face, and squeezed the spring catch hidden in the handle.

Sorcerers cannot, indeed, be poisoned—a minor protective art, one that most of them master in their youth. On the other hand, they most certainly can be slain, by arrow or blade, or any of the other instruments of violent death—which is why such things were forbidden within a decreed radius of wherever Alberico might be.

There is also a well-known truth about men and their gods—whether of the Triad in the Palm, or the varying pantheon worshiped in Barbadior, whether of mother goddess or dying and reviving god or lord of wheeling stars or single awesome Power above all of these in some rumored prime world far off amid the drifts of space.

It is the simple truth that mortal man cannot understand why the gods shape events as they do. Why some men and women are cut off in fullest flower while others live to dwindle into shadows of themselves. Why virtue must sometimes be trampled and evil flourish amid the beauty of a country garden. Why chance, sheer random chance, plays such an overwhelming role in the running of the life lines and the fate lines of men.

It was chance that saved Alberico of Barbadior then, in a moment that had his name half spelled-out for death. His guards were intent upon the fallen men and on the taut, bleeding form of Tomasso. No one had spared a glance for the crippled lord in his chair.

It was only the fact—mercilessly random—that that evening's Captain of the Guard happened to have moved into the cabin on Scalvaia's side of the room that changed the course of history in the Peninsula of the Palm and beyond. By things so achingly small are lives measured and marred.

Alberico, turning in a white rage to snap an order at his captain, saw the cane come up and Scalvaia's finger jerk upon the handle. Had he been facing straight ahead or turning the other way he would have died of a sharpened projectile bursting into his brain.

It was toward Scalvaia that he turned though, and he was the mightiest wielder of magic, save one, in the Palm in that hour. Even so, what he did—the only single thing he could do—took all the power he had and very nearly more than he could command. There was no time for the spoken spell, the focusing gesture. The bolt that was his ending had already been loosed.

Alberico released his hold upon his body.

Watching in terror and disbelief, Tomasso saw the lethal bolt whip *through* a blurred oozing of matter and air where Alberico's head had been. The bolt smashed harmlessly into the wall above a window.

And in that same scintilla of time, knowing that an instant later would be an instant too late—that his body could be unknit forever, his soul, neither living nor dead, left to howl impotently in the waste that lay in ambush for those who dared essay such magic—Alberico summoned the lineaments of his form back to himself.

It was a near thing.

He had a droop to his right eyelid from that day on, and his physical strength was never again what it had been. When he was tired, ever after, his right foot would have a tendency to splay outward as if retracing the strange release of that momentary magic. He would limp then, much as Scalvaia had done.

Through eyes that fought to focus properly, Alberico of Barbadior saw Scalvaia's silver-maned head fly across the room to bounce, with a sickening sound, on the rush-strewn floor—decapitated by the belated sword of the Captain of the Guard. The deadly cane, crafted of stones and metals Alberico did not recognize, clattered loudly to the ground. The air seemed thick and viscous to the sorcerer, unnaturally dense. He was conscious of a loose, rattling sound to his breathing and a spasmodic trembling at the back of his knees.

It was another moment, etched in the rigid, stunned silence of the other men in the room, before he trusted himself to even try to speak.

"You are dung," he said, thickly, coarsely, to the ashen captain. "You are less than that. You are filth and crawling slime. You will kill yourself. Now!" He spoke as if there were sliding soil clogging and spilling from his mouth. With an effort he swallowed his saliva.

Ferociously straining to make his eyes work properly he watched as the blurry form of his captain bowed jerkily and, reversing his sword, severed his own jugular with a swift, jagged slash. Alberico felt a froth of rage foaming and boiling through his mind. He fought to will an end to a palsied tremor in his left hand. He could not.

There were a great many dead men in the room and he very nearly had been one of them. He didn't even entirely feel as if he lived—his body seemed to have reassembled itself in not quite the same way as before. He rubbed with weak fingers at the drooping eyelid. He felt ill, nauseous. The air was hard to breathe. He needed to be outside, away from this suddenly stifling lodge of his enemies.

Nothing had come to pass as he'd expected. There was only one single element left of his original design for the evening. One thing that might yet offer a kind of pleasure, that might redeem a little of what had gone so desperately awry.

He turned, slowly, to look at Sandre's son. At the lover of boys. He dragged his mouth upwards into a smile, unaware of how hideous he looked.

"Bring him," he said thickly to his soldiers. "Bind him and bring him. There are things we can do with this one before we allow him to die. Things appropriate to what he was."

His vision was still not working properly, but he saw one of his mercenaries smile. Tomasso bar Sandre closed his eyes. There was blood on his face and clothing. There would be more before they were done.

Alberico put up his hood and limped from the room. Behind him the soldiers lifted up the body of the dead captain and supported the man whose face had been broken by Nievole.

They had to help the Tyrant mount his horse, which he found humiliating, but he began to feel better during the torchlit ride back to Astibar. He was utterly devoid of magic though. Even through the dulled sensations of his altered, reassembled body he could feel the void where his power should be. It would be at least two weeks, probably more, before it all came back. If it all came back. What he had done in the flashing of that instant in the lodge had drained more from him than any act of magic ever had in his life.

He was alive though, and he had just shattered the three most dangerous families left in the Eastern Palm. Even more, he had the middle Sandreni son here now as evidence, public proof of the conspiracy for the days to come. The pervert who was said to relish pain. Alberico allowed himself a tiny smile within the recesses of his hood.

It was all going to be done by law, and openly, as had been his practice almost from the day he'd taken power here. No unrest born of arbitrary exercise of might would be permitted to rear its dangerous head. They might hate him, of course they would hate him, but not one citizen of his four provinces would be able to doubt the justice or deny the legitimacy of his response to this Sandreni plot.

Or miss the point of how comprehensive that response was about to be.

With the prudent caution that was the truest wellspring of his character, Alberico of Barbadior began thinking through his actions of the next hours and days. The high gods of the Empire knew this far peninsula was a place of constant danger and needed stern governing, but the gods, who were not blind, could see that he knew how to give it what was needful. And it was growing more and more possible that the Emperor's advisers back home, who were no more sightless than the gods, would see the same things.

And the Emperor was old.

Alberico withdrew his thoughts from these familiar, too seductive channels. He made himself focus on detail again; detail was everything in matters such as this. The neat steps of his planning clicked into place like beads on a djarra string as he rode. Drily, precisely, he assembled the orders he would give. The only commands that caused him an inward flicker of emotion were the ones concerning Tomasso bar Sandre. These, at least, did not have to be made public and they would not be. Only the confession and its revealing details needed to be known outside his palace walls. Whatever took place in certain rooms underground could be extremely private indeed. He surprised himself a little with the anticipation he felt.

At one point he remembered that he'd wanted the hunting lodge torched when they left. Smoothly he adjusted his thinking on that. Let the lesser Sandreni and their servants find the dead when they came at dawn. Let them wonder and fear. The doubt would only last a little while.

Then he would cause everything to be made extremely clear.

CHAPTER
• 5 •

"OH, MORIAN," ALESSAN WHISPERED, WISTFUL RE-
gret infusing his voice. "I could have sent him
to your judgment even now. A child could
have put an arrow in his eye from here."

Not this child, Devin thought ruefully, gauging the
distance and the light from where they were hidden among
the trees north of the ribbon of road the Barbadians had
just ridden along. He looked with even more respect
than before at Alessan and the crossbow he'd picked up
from a cache they'd looped past on the way here.

"She will claim him when she is ready," Baerd said
prosaically. "And you are the one who has spent his life
saying that it will be to no good if either one of them dies
too soon."

Alessan grunted. "Did I shoot?" he asked pointedly.

Baerd's teeth flashed briefly in the moonlight. "I would
have stopped you in any case."

Alessan swore succinctly. Then, a moment later, relaxed into quiet amusement. The two men had a manner
with each other that spoke to long familiarity. Catriana,
Devin saw, had not smiled. Certainly not at him. On the
other hand, he reminded himself, *he* was supposed to be
the one who was angry. The present circumstances made
it a little hard though. He felt anxious and proud and
excited, all at once.

He was also the only one of the four of them who
hadn't noticed Tomasso, bound at wrist and ankle to his
horse.

"We'd better check the lodge," Baerd said as the tran-
sient mood slipped away. "Then I think we will have to

91

travel very fast. Sandre's son will name you and the boy."

"We had better have a talk about the boy first," Catriana said in a tone that made it suddenly very easy for Devin to reclaim his anger.

"The boy?" he repeated, raising his eyebrows. "I think you have evidence to the contrary." He let his gaze rest coldly on hers, and was rewarded to see her flush and turn away.

Briefly rewarded.

"Unworthy, Devin," Alessan said. "I hope not to hear that note from you again. Catriana violated all I know of her nature in doing what she did this morning. If you are intelligent enough to have come here you will be more than intelligent enough to now understand why she did it. You might suspend your own pride long enough to think about how she is feeling."

It was mildly said, but Devin felt as if he had just been punched in the stomach. Swallowing awkwardly, he looked from Alessan back to Catriana, but her gaze was fixed on the stars, away from and above them all. Finally, shamed, he looked down at the darkened forest floor. He felt fourteen years old again.

"I don't particularly appreciate that, Alessan," he heard Catriana saying coldly. "I fight my own wars. You know it."

"Not to mention," Baerd added casually, "the dazzling inappropriateness of your chastising anyone alive for having too much pride."

Alessan chose to ignore that. To Catriana he said, "Bright star of Eanna, do you think I don't know how you can fight? This is different though. What happened this morning cannot be allowed to matter. I can't have this becoming a battle between you if Devin is to be one of us."

"If he *what*?" Catriana wheeled on him. "Are you mad? Is it the music? Because he can sing? Why should someone from Asoli possibly be—"

"Hold peace!" Alessan said sharply. Catriana fell abruptly silent. Not having any good idea where to look or what to feel, Devin continued to simulate an intense interest in the loamy forest soil beneath his feet. His mind and heart were whirling with confusion.

Alessan's voice was gentler when he resumed. "Catriana, what happened this morning was not his fault either. You are not to blame him. You did what you felt you had to do and it did not succeed. He cannot be blamed or cursed for following you as innocently as he did. If you must, curse me for not stopping him as he went through the door. I could have."

"Why didn't you then?" Baerd asked.

Devin remembered Alessan looking at him as he'd paused in the archway of that inner door that had seemed a gateway to a land of dreaming.

"Yes, why?" he asked awkwardly, looking up. "Why did you let me follow?"

The moonlight was purely blue now. Vidomni was over west behind the tops of the trees. Only Ilarion was overhead among the stars, making the night strange with her shining. *Ghostlight,* the country folk called it when the blue moon rode alone.

Alessan had the light behind him so his eyes were hidden. For a moment the only sounds were the night noises of the forest: rustle of leaf in breeze, of grass, the dry crackle of the woodland floor, quick flap of wings to a branch near by. Somewhere north of them a small animal cried out and another answered it.

Alessan said: "Because I knew the tune his father taught him as a child and I know who his father is and he isn't from Asoli. Catriana, my dear, it isn't just the music, whatever you may think of my own weaknesses. He is one of us, my darling. Baerd, will you test him?"

On the most conscious, rational level, Devin understood almost none of this. Nonetheless he felt himself beginning to grow cold even as Alessan spoke. He had a swooping sense, like the descent of a hunting bird, that he had come to where Morian's portal had led him, here in the shadows of this wood under the waxing blue moon.

Nor was he made easier when he turned to Baerd and saw the stricken look on the face of the other man. Even by the distorting moonlight he could see how pale Baerd had become.

"Alessan . . ." Baerd began, his voice roughened.

"You are dearer to me than anyone alive," Alessan said, calm and grave. "You have been more than a brother to me. I would not hurt you for the world, and especially not in this. Never in this. I would not ask unless I was sure. Test him, Baerd."

Still Baerd hesitated, which made Devin's own anxiety grow; he understood less and less of what was happening. Only that it seemed to matter to the others, a great deal.

For a long moment no one moved. Finally Baerd, walking carefully, as if holding tightly to control of himself, took Devin by the arm and led him a dozen steps further into the wood to a small clearing among a circle of trees.

Neatly he lowered himself to sit cross-legged on the ground. After a moment's hesitation Devin did the same. There was nothing he could do but follow the leads he was being given; he had no idea where they were going. *Not on the road I'm on,* he remembered Catriana saying in the palace that morning. He linked his hands together to keep them steady; he felt cold, and it had little to do with the chill of night.

He heard Alessan and Catriana following them but he didn't look back. For the moment what was important was the enormous thing—whatever it was—that he could see building in Baerd's eyes. The blond-haired man had appeared so effortlessly competent until this moment and now, absurdly, he seemed to have become terribly fragile. Someone who could be shattered with unsettling ease. Abruptly, and for the second time in that long day, Devin felt as if he were crossing over into a country of dream, leaving behind the simple, defined boundaries of the daylight world.

And in this mood, under the blue light of Ilarion, he heard Baerd begin the tale, so that it came to him that first time like a spell, something woven in words out of the lost spaces of his childhood. Which is what, in the end, it was.

"In the year Alberico took Astibar," said Baerd, "while the provinces of Tregea and Certando were each preparing to fight him alone, and before Ferraut had fallen, Brandin, King of Ygrath came to this peninsula from the west. He sailed his fleet into the Great Harbor of Chiara and he took the Island. He took it easily, for the Grand Duke killed himself, seeing how many ships had come from Ygrath. This much I suspect that you know."

His voice was low. Devin found himself leaning forward, straining to hear. A trialla was singing sweetly, sadly, from a branch behind him. Alessan and Catriana made no sound at all. Baerd went on.

"In that year the Peninsula of the Palm became a battleground in an enormous balancing game between Ygrath and the Empire of Barbadior. Neither thought it could afford to give the other free rein here, halfway between the two of them. Which is one of the reasons Brandin came. The other reason, as we learned afterward, had to do with his younger, most-beloved son, Stevan. Brandin of Ygrath sought to carve out a second realm for his child to rule. What he found was something else."

The trialla was still singing. Baerd paused to listen, as if finding in its liquescent voice, gentler even than the nightingale's, an echo to something in his own.

"The Chiarans, attempting to rally a resistance in the mountains, were massacred on the slopes of Sangarios. Brandin took Asoli province soon after, and word of his power ran before him. He was very strong in his sorcery, even stronger than Alberico, and though he had fewer soldiers than the Barbadians in the east, his were more completely loyal and better trained. For where Alberico was only a wealthy, ambitious minor lord of the Empire using hired mercenaries, Brandin *ruled* Ygrath and his were the picked soldiers of that realm. They moved south through Corte almost effortlessly, defeating each province's army one by one, for none of us acted together in that year. Or after, naturally." Baerd's voice wasn't quite detached enough for the irony he was trying for.

"From Corte, Brandin himself turned east with the smaller part of his army to meet Alberico in Ferraut and pin him down there. He sent Stevan south to take the last free province in the west and then cross over to join him in Ferraut to meet the Barbadians in the battle that I think they all expected would shape the fate of the Palm.

"It was a mistake, though he could not really have known it then, eighteen years ago. Newly landed here, ignorant of the natures of the different provinces in this peninsula. I suppose he wanted Stevan to have a taste of leadership on his own. He gave him most of the army and his best commanders, relying on his own sorcery to hold Alberico until the others joined him."

Baerd paused for a moment, his blue eyes focused inward. When he resumed, there was a new timbre to his voice; it seemed to Devin to be carrying many different things, all of them old, and all of them sorrowful.

"At the line of the River Deisa," Baerd said, "a little more than halfway between Certando and the sea at Corte, Stevan was met by the bitterest resistance either of the invading armies was to find in the Palm. Led by their Prince—for in their pride they had always named their ruler so—the people of that last province in the west met the Ygrathens and held them, and beat them back from the river with heavy losses on both sides.

"And Prince Valentin of that province . . . the province you know as Lower Corte, slew Stevan of Ygrath, Brandin's beloved son, on the bank of the river at sunset after a bitter day of death."

Devin could almost taste the keenness of old grief in the words. He saw Baerd glance over for the first time to where Alessan was standing. Neither man spoke. Devin never took his own eyes away from Baerd. He concentrated as if his life depended on his doing so, treating each word spoken as if it were a jeweled mosaic piece to be set into the memory that was his own pride.

And right about then it seemed to Devin that a distant bell began to toll in some recess of his mind. Ringing a warning. As might a village bell in a temple of Adaon, summoning farmers urgently back from the fields. A far bell heard, faint but clear, from over morning fields of waving yellow grain.

"Brandin knew what had happened immediately through his sorcery," Baerd said, his voice like the rasp of a file. "He swept back south and west, leaving Alberico a free hand in Ferraut and Certando. He came down with the full weight of his sorcery and his army and with the rage of a father whose son has been slain, and he met the remnant of his last foes where they had waited for him by the Deisa."

Once more Baerd looked over at Alessan. His face was bleak, ghostly in the moonlight. He said:

"Brandin annihilated them. He smashed them to pieces without mercy or respite. Drove them helplessly before him back into their own country south of the Deisa and he burned every field and village through which he passed. He took no prisoners. He had women slain in that first march, and children, which was not a thing he'd done anywhere else. But nowhere else had his own child died. So many souls crossed over to Morian for the sake of the soul of Stevan of Ygrath. His father overran that province in blood and fire. Before the summer was out he had leveled all the glorious towers of the city in the foothills of the mountains—the one now called Stevanien. On the coast he smashed to rubble and sand the walls and the harbor barriers of the royal city by the sea. And in the battle by the river he took the Prince who had slain his son and later that year had him tortured and mutilated and killed in Chiara."

Baerd's voice was a dry whisper now under the starlight and the light of the single moon. And with it there was still that bell warning of sorrows yet to come, tolling in Devin's mind, louder now. Baerd said:

"Brandin of Ygrath did something more than all of this. He gathered his magic, the sorcerous power that he had, and he laid down a spell upon that land such as had never even been conceived before. And with that spell he . . . tore its name away. He stripped that name utterly from the minds of every man and woman who had not been born in that province. It was his deepest curse, his ultimate revenge. He made it as if we had never been. Our deeds, our history, our very name. And then he called us Lower Corte, after the bitterest of our ancient enemies among the provinces."

Behind him now Devin heard a sound and realized that Catriana was weeping. Baerd said, "Brandin made it come to pass that no one living could hear and then remember the name of that land, or of its royal city by the sea or even of that high, golden place of towers on the old road from the mountains. He broke us and he ravaged us. He killed a generation, and then *he stripped away our name.*"

And those last words were not whispered or rasped into the autumn dark of Astibar. They were hurled forth as a denunciation, an indictment, to the trees and the night and stars—the stars that had watched this thing come to pass.

The grief in that accusation clenched itself like a fist within Devin, more tightly than Baerd could ever have known. Than anyone could have known. For no one since Marra had died really knew what memory meant to Devin d'Asoli: the way in which it had come to be the touchstone of his soul.

Memory was talisman and ward for him, gateway and hearth. It was pride and love, shelter from loss: for if something could be remembered it was not wholly lost. Not dead and gone forever. Marra could live; his dour, stern father hum a cradle song to him. And because of this, because this was at the heart of what Devin was, the old vengeance of Brandin of Ygrath smashed into him that night as if it had been newly wrought, pounding through to the vulnerable center of how Devin saw and dealt with the world, and it cut him like a fresh and killing wound.

With an effort he forced himself to steadiness, willing the concentration that would allow him to remember this. All of this. Which seemed to matter more than ever now. Especially now, with the echo of Baerd's last terrible words fading in the night. Devin looked at the blond-haired man with the leather bands across his brow and about his neck, and he waited. He had been quick as a boy; he was a clever man. He understood what was coming; it had fallen into place.

Older by far than he had been only an hour ago, Devin heard Alessan murmur from behind him, "The cradle song I heard you playing was from that last province, Devin. A song of the city of towers. No one not of that place could have learned that tune in the way you told me you did. It is how I knew you as one of us. It is why I did not stop you when you followed Catriana. I left it to Morian to see what might lie beyond that doorway."

Devin nodded, absorbing this. A moment later he said, as carefully as he could, "If this is so, if I have properly understood you, then I should be one of the people who

can still hear and remember the name that has been
. . . otherwise taken away."

Alessan said, "It is so."

Devin discovered that his hands were shaking. He looked
down at them, concentrating, but he could not make
them stop.

He said, "Then this is something that has been stolen
from me all my life. Will you . . . give it back to me?
Will you tell me the name of the land where I was born?"

He was looking at Baerd by starlight, for Ilarion too
was gone now, over west beyond the trees. Alessan had
said it was Baerd's to tell. Devin didn't know why. In the
darkness they heard the trialla one more time, a long,
descending note, and then Baerd spoke, and for the first
time in his days Devin heard someone say:

"Tigana."

Within him the bell he had been hearing, as if in a
dream of unknown summer fields, fell silent. And within
that abrupt, absolute inner stillness a surge of loss broke
over him like an ocean wave. And after that wave came
another, and then a third—the one bearing love and the
other a heart-deep pride. He felt a strange light-headed
dizzying sensation as of a summons rushing along the
corridors of his blood.

Then he saw how Baerd was staring at him. Saw his
face rigid and white, the fear transparent even by starlight, and something else as well: bitterest thirst—an
aching, deprived hunger of the soul. And then Devin
understood, and gave to the other man the release he
needed.

"Thank you," Devin said. He didn't seem to be
trembling anymore. Around a difficult thickness in his
throat he went on, for it was his turn now, his test:

"Tigana. *Tigana.* I was born in the province of Tigana.
My name . . . my true name is Devin di Tigana bar Garin."

Even as he spoke, something akin to glory blazed in
Baerd's face. The fair-haired man squeezed his eyes tightly
shut as if to hold that glory in, to keep it from escaping
into the dispersing dark, to clutch it fiercely to his need.
Devin heard Alessan draw an unsteady breath, and then,
surprised, he felt Catriana touch his shoulder and then
withdraw her hand.

Baerd was lost in a place beyond speech. It was Alessan who said, "That is one of the two names taken away, and the deepest. Tigana was our province and the name of the royal city by the sea. The fairest city under Eanna's lights you would have heard it named. Or perhaps, perhaps only the second most fair."

A thread of something that seemed to genuinely long to become laughter was in his voice. Laughter and love together. For the first time Devin turned to look up at him.

Alessan said, "If you were to have spoken with those from inland and south, in the city where the River Sperion, descending from the mountain, begins its run westward to find the sea, you would have heard it said that second way. For we were always proud, and there was always rivalry between the two cities."

In the end, hard as he tried, his voice could only carry loss.

"You were born in that inland city, Devin, and so was I. We are children of that high valley and of the silver running of that mountain river. We were born in Avalle. In Avalle of the Towers."

There was music in Devin's mind again, with that name, but this time it was different from the bells he'd heard before. This time it was a music that took him back a long way, all the way to his father and his childhood.

He said, "You do know the words then, don't you?"

"Of course I do," said Alessan gently.

"Please?" Devin asked.

But it was Catriana who answered him, in the voice a young mother might have used, rocking her child to sleep on an evening long ago:

Springtime morning in Avalle
And I don't care what the priests say:
I'm going down to the river today
On a springtime morning in Avalle.

When I'm all grown up, come what may,
I'll build a boat to carry me away
And the river will take it to Tigana Bay
And the sea even further from Avalle.

But wherever I wander, by night or by day,
Where water runs swiftly or high trees sway,
My heart will carry me back and away
To a dream of the towers of Avalle.

A dream of my home in Avalle.

The sweet sad words to the tune he'd always known drifted down to Devin, and with them came something else. A sense of loss so deep it almost drowned the light grace of Catriana's song. No breaking waves now, or trumpets along the blood: only the waters of longing. A longing for something taken away from him before he'd even known it was his—taken so completely, so comprehensively he might have lived his whole life through without ever knowing it was gone.

And so Devin wept as Catriana sang. Small boys, young-looking for their age, learned very early in northern Asoli how risky it was to cry where someone might see. But something too large for Devin to deal with had overtaken him in the forest tonight.

If he understood properly what Alessan had just said, this song was one his mother would have sung to him.

His mother whose life had been ripped away by Brandin of Ygrath. He bowed his head, though not to shield the tears, and listened as Catriana finished that bitter-sweet cradle song: a song of a child defying orders and authority, even when young, who was self-reliant enough to want to build a ship alone and brave enough to want to sail it into the wideness of the world, never turning back. Nor ever losing or forgetting the place where it all began.

A child very much as Devin saw himself.

Which was one of the reasons he wept. For he *had* been made to lose and forget those towers, he'd been robbed of any dream he himself might ever have had of Avalle. Or Tigana on its bay.

So his tears followed one another downward in darkness as he mourned his mother and his home. And in the shadows of that wood not far from Astibar those two griefs fused to each other in Devin and became welded in the forge of his heart with what memory meant to him and the loss of memory: and out of that blazing something took shape in Devin that was to change the running of his life line from that night.

He dried his eyes on his sleeve and looked up. No one spoke. He saw that Baerd was looking at him. Very deliberately Devin held up his left hand, the hand of the heart. Very carefully he folded his third and fourth fingers down so that what showed was a simulacrum of the shape of the Peninsula of the Palm.

The position for taking an oath.

Baerd lifted his right hand and made the same gesture. They touched fingertips together, Devin's small palm against the other man's larger, callused one.

Devin said, "If you will have me I am with you. In the name of my mother who died in that war I swear I will not break faith with you."

"Nor I with you," said Baerd. "In the name of Tigana gone."

There was a rustling as Alessan sank to his knees beside them. "Devin, I should be cautioning you," he said soberly. "This is not a thing in which to move too fast. You can be one with our cause without having to break your life apart to come with us."

"He has no choice," Catriana murmured, moving nearer on the other side. "Tomasso bar Sandre will name you both to the torturers tonight or tomorrow. I'm afraid the singing career of Devin d'Asoli may be over just as it truly begins." She looked down on the three men, her eyes unreadable in the darkness.

"It *is* over," Devin said quietly. "It ended when I learned my name." Catriana's expression did not change; he had no idea what she was thinking.

"Very well," said Alessan. He held up his own left hand, two fingers down. Devin met it with his right. Alessan hesitated. "An oath in your mother's name is stronger for me than you could have guessed," he said.

"You knew her?"

"We both did," Baerd said quietly. "She was ten years older than us, but every adolescent boy in Tigana was a little in love with Micaela. And most of the grown men too, I think."

Another new name, and all the hurt that came with it. Devin's father had never spoken it. His sons had never even known their mother's name. There were more avenues to sorrow in this night than Devin could have imagined.

"We all envied and admired your father more than I can tell you," Alessan added. "Though I was pleased that an Avalle man won her in the end. I can remember when you were born, Devin. My father sent a gift to your naming day. I don't remember what it was."

"You *admired* my father?" Devin said, stunned.

Alessan heard that and his voice changed. "Do not judge him by what he became. You only knew him after Brandin smashed a whole generation and their world. Ending their lives or blighting their souls. Your mother was dead, Avalle fallen, Tigana gone. He had fought and survived both battles by the Deisa." Above them Catriana made a small sound.

"I never knew," Devin protested. "He never told us any of that." There was a new ache inside him. *So many avenues.*

"Few of the survivors spoke of those days," Baerd said.

"Neither of my parents did," said Catriana awkwardly. "They took us as far away as they could, to a fishing village here in Astibar down the coast from Ardin, and never spoke a word of any of this."

"To shield you," Alessan said gently. His palm was still touching Devin's. It was smaller than Baerd's. "A great many of the parents who managed to survive fled so that their children might have a chance at a life unmarred by the oppression and the stigma that bore down—that still bear down—upon Tigana. Or Lower Corte as we must name it now.'

"They ran away," said Devin stubbornly. He felt cheated, deprived, betrayed.

Alessan shook his head. "Devin, think. Don't judge yet: think. Do you really imagine you learned that tune by chance? Your father chose not to burden you or your brothers with the danger of your heritage, but he set a stamp upon you—a tune, wordless for safety—and he sent you out into the world with something that would reveal you, unmistakably, to anyone from Tigana, but to no one else. I do not think it was chance. No more than

Catriania's mother giving her daughter a ring that marked her to anyone born where she was born."

Devin glanced back. Catriana held out her hand for him to see. It was dark, but his eyes had adjusted to that, and he could make out a strange, twining shape upon the ring: a man, half human, half creature of the sea. He swallowed.

"Will you tell me of him?" he asked, turning back to Alessan. "Of my father?"

Of stolid, dour Garin, grim farmer in a wet grey land. Who had, it now appeared, come from bright Avalle of the towers in the southern highlands of Tigana and who had, in his youth, wooed and won a woman beloved of all who saw her. Who had fought and lived through two terrible battles by a river and who had—if Alessan was right in his last conjecture—very deliberately sent out into the world his one quick, imaginative child capable of finding what he seemed to have found tonight.

Who had also, Devin abruptly realized, almost certainly lied when he said he'd forgotten the words to the cradle song. It was all suddenly very hard.

"I will tell you what I know of him, and gladly," Alessan said. "But not tonight, for Catriana is right and we must get ourselves away before dawn. Right now I will swear faith with you as Baerd has done. I accept your oath. You have mine. You are as kin to me from now until the ending of my days."

Devin turned to look up at Catriana. "Will you accept me?"

She tossed her hair. "I don't have much choice, do I?" she said carelessly. "You seem to have entangled yourself rather thoroughly here." She lowered her left hand though as she spoke, two fingers curled. Her fingers met his own with a light, cool touch.

"Be welcome," she said. "I swear I will keep faith with you, Devin di Tigana."

"And I with you. I'm sorry about this morning," Devin offered.

Her hand withdrew and her eyes flashed; even by starlight he could see it. "Oh yes," she said sardonically, "I'm sure you are. It was very clear, all along, how regrettable you found the experience!"

Alessan snorted with amusement. "Catriana, my darling," he said, "I just forbade him to mention any details of what happened. How do I enforce that if you bring them up yourself?"

Without the faintest trace of a smile Catriana said, "I am the aggrieved party here, Alessan. You don't enforce anything on me. The rules are not the same."

Baerd chuckled suddenly. "The rules," he said, "have not been the same since you joined us. Why indeed should this be any different?"

Catriana tossed her head again but did not deign to reply.

The three men stood up. Devin flexed his knees to relieve the stiffness of sitting so long in one position.

"Ferraut or Tregea?" Baerd asked. "Which border?"

"Ferraut," Alessan said. "They'll have me placed as Tregean as soon as Tomasso talks—poor man. If I'd been thinking clearly I would have shot him as they rode by."

"Oh, very clear thinking, that," Baerd retorted. "With twenty soldiers surrounding him. You would have had us all in chains in Astibar by now."

"You would have deflected my arrow," Alessan said wryly.

"Is there a chance he won't speak?" Devin interjected awkwardly. "I'm thinking about Menico, you see. If I'm named . . ."

Alessan shook his head. "Everyone talks under torture," he said soberly. "Especially if sorcery is involved. I'm thinking about Menico too, but there isn't anything we can do about it, Devin. It is one of the realities of the life we live. There are people put at risk by almost everything we do. I wish," he added, "that I knew what had happened in that lodge."

"You wanted to check it," Catriana reminded him. "Can we afford the time?"

"I did, and yes, I think we can," said Alessan crisply. "There remains a piece missing in all of this. I *still* don't know how Sandre d'Astibar could have expected me to be the—"

He stopped there. Except for the drone of the cicadas and the rustling leaves it was very quiet in the woods.

The trialla had gone. Alessan abruptly raised one hand
and pushed it roughly through his hair. He shook his
head.

"Do you know," he said to Baerd, in what was almost
a conversational tone, "how much of a fool I can be at
times? It was in the palm of my hand all along!" His
voice changed. "Come on—and pray we are not too
late!"

★　　★　　★

The fires had both died down in the Sandreni lodge.
Only the stars shone above the clearing in the woods.
The cluster of Eanna's Diadem was well over west, following the moons. A nightingale was singing, as if in
answer to the trialla of before, as the four of them
approached. In the doorway Alessan hesitated for a moment then shrugged his shoulders in a gesture Devin
already recognized. Then he pushed open the door and
walked through.

By the red glow of the embers they looked—with eyes
accustomed by now to darkness—on the carnage within.

The coffin still rested on its trestles, although splin-
tered and knocked awry. Around it though, lay dead
men who had been alive when they left this room. The
two younger Sandreni. Nievole, a quiver of arrows in his
throat and chest. The body of Scalvaia d'Astibar.

Then Devin made out Scalvaia's severed head in a
black puddle of blood a terrible distance away and he
fought to control the lurch of sickness in his gorge.

"Oh, Morian," Alessan whispered. "Oh, Lady of the
Dead, be gentle to them in your Halls. They died dreaming of freedom and before their time."

"*Three of them did,*" came a harsh, desiccated voice
from deep in one of the armchairs. "*The fourth should
have been strangled at birth.*"

Devin jumped half a foot, his heart hammering with
shock.

The speaker rose and stood beside the chair, facing
them. He was entirely hidden in shadow. "I thought you
would come back," he said.

The sixth man, Devin realized, struggling to understand, straining to make out the tall, gaunt form by the faint glow of the embers.

Alessan seemed quite unruffled. "I'm sorry I kept you waiting then," he said. "It took me too long to riddle this through. Will you allow me to express my sorrow for what has happened?" He paused. "And my respect for you, my lord Sandre."

Devin's jaw dropped open as if unhinged. He snapped it shut so hard he hurt his teeth; he hoped no one had seen. Events were moving far too fast for him.

"I will accept the first," said the gaunt figure in front of them. "I do not deserve your respect though, nor that of anyone else. Once perhaps; not anymore. You are speaking to an old vain fool—exactly as the Barbadian named me. A man who spent too many years alone, tangled in his own spun webs. You were right in every-thing you said before about carelessness. It has cost me three sons tonight. Within a month, less probably, the Sandreni will be no more."

The voice was dry and dispassionate, objectively damn-ing, devoid of self-pity. The tone of a judge in some dark hall of final adjudication.

"What happened?" Alessan asked quietly.

"The boy was a traitor." Flat, uninflected, final.

"Oh, my lord," Baerd exclaimed. *"Family?"*

"My grandson. Gianno's boy."

"Then his soul is cursed," Baerd said, quiet and fierce. "He is in Morian's custody now, and she will know how to deal with him. May he be trammeled in darkness until the end of time."

The old man seemed not to have even heard. "Taeri killed him," he murmured, wonderingly. "I had not thought he was brave enough, or so quick. Then he stabbed himself, to deny them the pleasure of whatever they might have learned of him. I had not thought he was so brave," he repeated absently.

Through the thick shadows Devin looked at the two bodies by the smaller fire. Uncle and nephew lay so close to each other they seemed almost intertwined on the far side of the coffin. The empty coffin.

"You said you waited for us," Alessan murmured. "Will you tell me why?"

"For the same reason you came back." Sandre moved for the first time, stiffly making his way to the larger fire. He seized a small log and threw it on the guttering flame. A shower of sparks flew up. He nursed it, poking with the iron until a tongue of flame licked free of the ash bed.

The Duke turned and now Devin could see his white hair and beard, and the bony hollows of his cheeks. His eyes were set deep in their sockets, but they gleamed with a cold defiance.

"I am here," Sandre said, "and you are here because it goes on. It goes on whatever happens, whoever dies. While there is breath to be drawn and a heart with which to hate. My quest and your own. Until we die they go on."

"You were listening, then," said Alessan. "From in the coffin. You heard what I said?"

"The drug had worn off by sundown. I was awake before we reached the lodge. I heard everything you said and a great deal of what you chose not to say," the Duke replied, straightening, a chilly hauteur in his voice. "I heard what you named yourself, and what you chose not to tell them. But I know who you are."

He took a step towards Alessan. He raised a gnarled hand and pointed it straight at him.

"I know *exactly* who you are, Alessan bar Valentin, Prince of Tigana!"

It was too much. Devin's brain simply gave up trying to understand. Too many pieces of information were coming at him from too many different directions, contradicting each other ferociously. He felt dizzy, overwhelmed. He was in a room where only a little while ago he had stood among a number of men. Now four of them were dead, with a more brutal violence than he had ever thought to come upon. At the same time, the one man he'd *known* to be dead—the man whose mourning rites he had sung that very morning—was the only man of Astibar left alive in this lodge.

If he *was* of Astibar!

For if he was, how could he have just spoken the name of Tigana, given what Devin had just learned in the wood? How could he have known that Alessan was—

and this, too, Devin fought to assimilate—a Prince? The son of that Valentin who had slain Stevan of Ygrath and so brought Brandin's vengeance down upon them all.

Devin simply stopped trying to put it all together. He set himself to listen and look—to absorb as much as he could into the memory that had never failed him yet—and to let understanding come after, when he had time to think.

So resolved, he heard Alessan say, after a blank silence more than long enough to reveal the degree of his own surprise and wonder: "Now I understand. Finally I understand. My lord, I thought you always a giant among men. From the first time I saw you at my first Triad Games twenty-three years ago. You are even more than I took you for. How did you stay alive? How have you hidden it from the two of them all these years?"

"Hidden what?" It was Catriana, her voice so angry and bewildered it immediately made Devin feel better: he wasn't the only one desperately treading water here.

"He is a wizard," Baerd said flatly.

There was another silence. Then, "The wizards of the Palm are immune to spells not directed specifically at them," Alessan added. "This is true of all magic-users, wherever they come from, however they find access to their power. For this reason, among others, Brandin and Alberico have been hunting down and killing wizards since they came to this peninsula."

"And they have been succeeding because being a wizard has—alas!—nothing to do with wisdom or even simple common sense," Sandre d'Astibar said in a corrosive voice. He turned and jabbed viciously at the fire with the iron poker. The blaze caught fully this time and roared into red light.

"I survived," said the Duke, "simply because no one knew. It involved nothing more complex than that. I used my power perhaps five times in all the years of my reign—and always cloaked under someone else's magic. And I have done *nothing* with magic, not a flicker, since the sorcerers arrived. I didn't even use it to feign my death. Their power is stronger than ours. Far stronger. It was clear from the time each of them came. Magic was never as much a part of the Palm as it was elsewhere. We knew this. All the wizards knew this. You would have thought they would apply their brains to that knowledge, would you not? What good is a finding spell, or a fledgling mental arrow if it leads one straight to a Barbadian death-wheel in the sun?" There was an acid, mocking bitterness in the old Duke's voice.

"Or one of Brandin's," Alessan murmured.

"Or Brandin's," Sandre echoed. "It is the one thing those two carrion birds have agreed upon—other than the dividing line running down the Palm—that theirs shall be the only magic in this land."

"And it is," said Alessan, "or so nearly so as to be the same thing. I have been searching for a wizard for a dozen years or more."

"Alessan!" Baerd said quickly.

"Why?" the Duke asked in the same moment.

"Alessan!" Baerd repeated, more urgently.

The man Devin had just learned to be the Prince of Tigana looked over at his friend and shook his head. "Not this one, Baerd," he said cryptically. "Not Sandre d'Astibar."

He turned back to the Duke and hesitated, choosing his words. Then, with an unmistakable pride, he said, "You will have heard the legend. It happens to be true. The line of the Princes of Tigana, all those in direct descent, can bind a wizard to them unto death."

For the first time a gleam of curiosity, of an actual interest in something appeared in Sandre's hooded eyes. "I do know that story. The only wizard who ever guessed what I was after I came into my own magic warned me once to be wary of the Princes of Tigana. He was an old man, and doddering by then. I remember laughing. You actually claim that what he said was true?"

"It was. I am certain it still is. I have had no chance to test it though. It is our primal story: Tigana is the chosen province of Adaon of the Waves. The first of our Princes, Rahal, being born of the god by that Micaela whom we name as mortal mother of us all. And the line of the Princes has never been broken."

Devin felt a complex stir of emotions working within himself. He didn't even try to enumerate how many things were tangling themselves in his heart. *Micaela.*

He listened and watched, and set himself to remember.
And he heard Sandre d'Astibar laugh.

"I know that story too," the Duke said derisively.
"That hoary, enfeebled excuse for Tiganese arrogance.
Princes of Tigana! Not Dukes, oh no. *Princes!* Descended
of the god!" He thrust the poker toward Alessan. "You
will stand here tonight, now, among the stinking reality
of the Tyrants and of these dead men and the world of
the Palm today and spew that old lie at me? You will do
that?"

"It is truth," said Alessan quietly, not moving. "It is
why we are what we are. It would have been a slight to
the god for his descendants to claim a lesser title. The gift
of Adaon to his mortal son could not be immortality—
that, Eanna and Morian forbade. But the god granted a
binding power over the Palm's own magic to his son, and
to the sons and daughters of his son while a Prince or a
Princess of Tigana lived in that direct line. If you doubt
me and would put it to the test I will do as Baerd would
have had me do and bind you with my hand upon your
brow, my lord Duke. The old tale is not to be lightly
dismissed, Sandre d'Astibar. If we are proud it is because
we have reason to be."

"Not any more," the Duke said mockingly. "Not since
Brandin came!"

Alessan's face twisted. He opened his mouth and closed
it.

"How dare you!" Catriana snapped. Bravely, Devin
thought.

Prince and Duke ignored her, rigidly intent on each
other. Sandre's sardonic amusement gradually receded
into the deep lines etched in his face. The bitterness
remained, in eyes and stance and the pinched line of his
mouth.

Alessan said, "I had not expected that from you. Under all the circumstances."

"You are in no position to have any idea what to
expect from me," the Duke replied, very low. "Under all
the circumstances."

"Shall we part company now then?"

For a long moment something lay balanced in the air
between them, a process of weighing and resolution,

complicated immeasurably by death and grief and rage and the stiff, reflexive pride of both men. Devin, responding with his nerve-endings to the tension, found that he was holding his breath.

"I would prefer not," said Sandre d'Astibar finally. "Not like this," he added, as Devin drew breath again. "Will you accept an apology from one who is sunken as low as he has ever been?"

"I will," said Alessan simply. "And I would seek your counsel before we must, indeed, part ways for a time. Your middle son was taken alive. He will name me and Devin both tomorrow morning if not tonight."

"Not tonight," the Duke said, almost absently. "Alberico apprehends no danger anymore. He will also be quite seriously debilitated by what happened here. He will leave Tomasso until a time when he can enjoy what happens. When he is in a mood to . . . play."

"Tonight, tomorrow," said Baerd, his blunt voice jarring the mood. "It makes little difference. He will talk. We must be away before he does."

"Perhaps, perhaps not," Sandre murmured in the same strangely detached voice. He looked at the four dead men on the floor. "I wish I knew exactly what happened," he said. "Inside the coffin I could see nothing, but I can tell you that Alberico used a magic here tonight so strong it is still pulsating. And he used it to save his own life. Scalvaia did something, I don't know what, but he came very near." He looked at Alessan. "Near to giving Brandin of Ygrath dominion over the whole peninsula."

"You heard that?" Alessan said. "You agree with me?"

"I think I always knew it to be true, and I know I succeeded in denying it within myself. I was so focused on my own enemy here in Astibar. I needed to hear it said, but once will be enough. Yes, I agree with you. They must be taken down together."

Alessan nodded, and some of his own rigidly controlled tension seemed to ease away. He said, "There are those who still think otherwise. I value your agreement."

He glanced over at Baerd, smiling a little wryly, then back to the Duke. "You mentioned Alberico's use of magic as if it should have a meaning now for us.

What meaning then? We are ignorant in these matters."

"No shame. If you aren't a wizard you are meant to be ignorant." Sandre smiled thinly. "The meaning is straightforward though: there is such an overflow of magic spilling out from this room tonight that any paltry power of my own that I invoke will be completely screened. I think I can ensure that your names are not given to the torturers tomorrow."

"I see," said Alessan, nodding slowly. Devin did not see anything; he felt as if he were churning along in the turbulent wake of information. "You can take yourself through space? You can go in there and bring him out?" Alessan's eyes were bright.

Sandre was shaking his head though. He held up his left hand, all five fingers spread wide. "I never chopped two fingers in the wizard's final binding to the Palm. My magic is profoundly limited. I can't say I regret it—I would never have been Duke of Astibar had I done so, given the prejudices and the laws governing wizards here—but it constrains what I am able to do. I can go in there myself, yes, but I am not strong enough to bring someone else out. I can take him something though."

"I see," said Alessan again, but in a different voice. There was a silence. He pushed a hand through his disordered hair. "I am sorry," he said at length, softly.

The Duke's face was expressionless. Above the white beard and the gaunt cheeks his eyes gave nothing away at all. Behind him the fire crackled, sparks snapping outward into the room.

"I have a condition," Sandre said.

"Which is?"

"That you allow me to come with you. I am now a dead man. Given to Morian. Here in Astibar I can speak to no one, achieve nothing. If I am to preserve any purpose now to the botched deception of my dying I must go with you. Prince of Tigana, will you accept a feeble wizard in your entourage? A wizard come freely, not bound by some legend?"

For a long time Alessan was silent, looking at the other man, his hands quiet at his sides. Then, unexpectedly, he grinned. It was like a flash of light, a gleam of warmth cracking the ice in the room.

"How attached are you," he asked, in a quite unexpected tone of voice, "to your beard and your white
hair?"

A second later Devin heard a strange sound. It took
him a moment to recognize that what he was hearing was
the high, wheezing, genuine amusement of the Duke of
Astibar.

"Do with me what you will," Sandre said as his mirth
subsided. "What will you do—tinge my locks red as the
maid's?"

Alessan shook his head. "I hope not. One of those
manes is more than sufficient for a single company. I
leave these matters to Baerd though. I leave a great
many things to Baerd."

"Then I shall place myself in his hands," Sandre said.
He bowed gravely to the yellow-haired man. Baerd, Devin
saw, did not look entirely happy. Sandre saw it too.

"I will not swear an oath," the Duke said to him. "I
swore one vow when Alberico came, and it is the last
vow I shall ever swear. I will say though that it shall be
my endeavor for the rest of my days to ensure that you
do not regret this. Will that content you?"

Slowly Baerd nodded. "It will."

Listening, Devin had an intuitive sense that this, too,
was an exchange that mattered, that neither man had
spoken lightly, or less than the truth of his heart. He
glanced over just then at Catriana and discovered that
she had been watching him. She turned quickly away
though, and did not look back.

Sandre said, "I think I had best set about doing what I
have said I would. Because of the screening of Alberico's
magic I must go and return from this room, but I dare
say you need not spend a night among the dead, however
illustrious they are. Have you a camp in the woods? Shall
I find you there?"

The idea of magic was unsettling to Devin still, but
Sandre's words had just given him an idea, his first really
clear thought since they'd entered the lodge.

"Are you sure you'll be able to stop your son from
talking?" he asked diffidently.

"Quite sure," Sandre replied briefly.

Devin's brow knit. "Well then, it seems to me none of

us is in immediate danger. Except for you, my lord. You must not be seen."

"Until Baerd's done with him," Alessan interposed. "But go on."

Devin turned to him. "I'd like to say farewell to Menico and try to think of a reason to give for leaving. I owe him a great deal. I don't want him to hate me."

Alessan looked thoughtful. "He will hate you a little, Devin, even though he isn't that kind of man. What happened this morning is what a lifelong trouper like Menico dreams about. And no explanation you come up with is going to alter the fact that he needs you to make that dream a real thing now."

Devin swallowed. He hated what he was hearing, but he couldn't deny the truth of it. A season or two of the fees Menico had said he could now charge would have let the old campaigner buy the inn in Ferraut he'd talked about for so many years. The place where he'd always said he'd like to settle when the road grew too stern for his bones. Where he could serve ale and wine and offer a bed and a meal to old friends and new ones passing through on the long trails. Where he could hear and retell the gossip of the day and swap the old stories he loved. And where, on the cold winter nights, he could stake out a place by the fire and lead whoever happened to be there into and out of all the songs he knew.

Devin shoved his hands deep into the pockets of his breeches. He felt awkward and sad. "I just don't like disappearing on him. All three of us at once. We've got concerts tomorrow, too."

Alessan's mouth quirked. "I do seem to recall that," he said. "Two of them."

"Three," said Catriana unexpectedly.

"Three," Alessan agreed cheerfully. "And one the next day at the Woolguild Hall. I also have—it has just occurred to me—a substantial wager in The Paelion that I expect to win."

Which drew an already predictable growl from Baerd. "Do you seriously think the Festival of Vines is going to blithely proceed after what has occurred tonight? You want to go make music in Astibar as if nothing has happened? Music? I've been down this road with you before, Alessan. I don't like it."

"Actually, I'm quite certain the Festival *will* go on." It was Sandre. "Alberico is cautious almost before he is anything else. I think tonight will redouble that in him. He will allow the people their celebrations, let those from the distrada scatter and go home, then slam down hard immediately after. But only on the three families that were here, I suspect. It is, frankly, what I would do myself."

"Taxes?" Alessan asked.

"Perhaps. He raised them after the Canziano poisoning, but that was different. An actual assassination attempt in a public place. He didn't have much choice. I think he'll narrow it this time—there will be enough bodies for his wheels among the three families here."

Devin found it unsettling how casually the Duke spoke of such things. This was his kin they were discussing. His oldest son, grandchildren, nephews, nieces, cousins—all to be fodder for Barbadian killing-wheels. Devin wondered if he would ever grow as cynical as this. If what had begun tonight would harden him to that degree. He tried to think of his brothers on a death-wheel in Asoli and found his mind flinching away from the very image. Unobtrusively he made the warding sign against evil.

The truth was, he was upset just thinking about Menico, and that was merely a matter of costing the man money, nothing more. People moved from troupe to troupe all the time. Or left to start their own companies. Or retired from the road into a business that offered them more security. There would be performers who would be *expecting* him to go on his own after his success this morning. That should have been a helpful thought, but it wasn't. Somehow Devin hated to make it appear as if they were right.

Something else occurred to him. "Won't it look a bit odd, too, if we disappear right after the mourning rites? Right after Alberico's unmasked a plot that was connected with them? We're sort of linked to the Sandreni now in a way. Should we draw attention to ourselves like that? It isn't as if our disappearance won't be noticed."

He said it, for some reason, to Baerd. And was rewarded a moment later with a brief, sober nod of acknowledgment.

"Now that cloth I will buy," Baerd said. "That does make sense, though I'm sorry to say it."

"A good deal of sense," Sandre agreed. Devin fidgeted a little as he came under the scrutiny of those dark, sunken eyes. "The two of you"—the Duke gestured at Devin and Catriana—"may yet redeem your generation for me."

This time Devin refused to look at the girl. Instead his glance went over to the corner where Sandre's grandson lay by the second, dying fire, his throat slashed by a family blade.

Alessan broke the silence with a deliberate cough. "There is also," he said in a curious tone, "another argument entirely. Only those who have spent as many nights outdoors as I have can properly appreciate the depth—as it were—of my preference for a soft bed at night. In short," he concluded with a grin, "your eloquence has quite overcome me, Devin. Lead me back to Menico at the inn. Even a bed shared with two syrenya-players who snore in marginal harmony is a serious improvement over cold ground beside Baerd's relative silence."

Baerd favored him with a forbidding glare. One that Alessan appeared to weather quite easily. "I will refrain," Baerd said darkly, "from a recitation of your own nocturnal habits. I will wait here alone for Duke Sandre to return. We'll have to burn this lodge tonight, for obvious reasons. There's a body that will otherwise be missing when the servants come back in the morning. We'll meet the three of you by the cache three mornings from now, as early as you see fit to rise from your pillows. Assuming," he added with heavy sarcasm, "that soft city living doesn't prevent you from being able to find the cache."

"I'll find it if he gets lost," Catriana said.

Alessan looked from one to the other of them, his expression wounded. "That isn't fair," he protested. "It is just the music. You both know that."

Devin hadn't. Alessan was still gazing at Baerd. "You know it is only the music I'm going back for."

"Of course I know that," Baerd said softly. His expression changed. "I'm only afraid that the music will kill us both one of these days."

Intercepting the look that passed between them then, Devin learned something new and sudden and unexpected—on a night when he'd already learned more things than he could easily handle—about the nature of bonding and about love.

"Go," said Baerd with a scowl, as Alessan still hesitated. Catriana was already by the door. "We will meet you after the Festival. By the cache. Don't," he added, "expect to recognize us."

Alessan grinned suddenly, and a moment later Baerd allowed himself to smile as well. It changed his face a great deal. He didn't, Devin realized, smile very often.

He was still thinking about that as he followed Alessan and Catriana out the door and into the darkness of the wood again.

CHAPTER

• 6 •

A
S IT HAPPENED, THE LONG PATH OF THAT DAY AND
night did not lead back to the inn after all.

The three of them returned through the forest
to the main road from Astibar to Ardin town. They
walked in silence along the road under the arch of the
autumn stars, cicadas loud in the woods on either side.
Devin was glad of his woolen overshirt; it was chilly
now, there might be a frost tonight.

It was strange to be abroad in the darkness so late.
When they were traveling Menico was always careful to
have his company quartered and settled by the dinner
hour. Even with the stern measures both Tyrants had
taken against thieves and brigands, the paths of the Palm
were not often traveled by decent folk at night.

Folk such as he himself had been, only this morning.
He had been secure in his niche and his calling, had even
had—improbably enough—a triumph. He'd been poised
on the edge of a genuine success. And now he was
walking a road in darkness having abandoned any such
prospects or security, and having sworn an oath that
marked him for a death-wheel, in Chiara if not here.
Both places actually, if Tomasso bar Sandre talked.

It was an odd, lonely feeling. He trusted the men he
had joined—he even trusted the girl, if it came to that—
but he didn't *know* them very well. Not like he knew
Menico or Eghano after so many years.

It occurred to him that the same dilemma applied to
the cause he had just sworn to make his own: he didn't
know Tigana either, which was the whole point of what
Brandin of Ygrath had done with his sorcery. Devin was

119

in the process of changing his life for a story told under
the moon, for a childhood song, an evocation of his
mother, something almost purely an abstraction for him.
A name.

He was honest enough to wonder if he was doing this
as much for the adventure of it—for the glamor that
Alessan and Baerd and the old Duke represented—as
for the depth of old pain and grief he'd learned about in
the forest tonight. He didn't know the answer. He didn't
know how much Catriana fitted into his reasons, how
much his father did, or pride, or the sound of Baerd's
voice speaking his loss to the night.

The truth was that if Sandre d'Astibar could stop his
son from talking, as he had promised to do, then there
was nothing to prevent Devin from carrying on exactly as
he had for the past six years. From having the triumph
and the rewards that seemed to lie before him. He shook
his head. It was astonishing in a way, but that course,
with Menico on the road, performing across the Palm—
the life he'd woken to this morning—seemed almost in-
conceivable to him now, as if he'd already crossed to the
other side of some tremendous divide. Devin wondered
how often men did what they did, made the choices
of their lives, for reasons that were clean and uncomplicated and easily understood as they were happening.

He was jolted from his reverie by Alessan abruptly
raising a hand in warning. Without a word spoken the
three of them slipped into the trees again beside the
road. After a moment there was a flicker of torchlight to
the west and Devin heard the sound of a cart approaching. There were voices, male and female both. Revelers
returning home late, he guessed. There *was* a Festival
going on. In some ways it had begun to seem another
irrelevance. They waited for the cart to go by.

It did not. The horse was pulled up, with a soft slap
and jingle of reins just in front of where they were
hiding. Someone jumped down, then they heard him
unlocking a chain on a gate.

"I really am hopelessly overindulgent," they heard
him complain. "Every single time I look at this excuse
for a crest I am reminded that I should have had an

artisan design it. There are limits, or there ought to be, to what a father allows!"

Devin recognized the place and the voice in the same moment. An impulse, a striving back toward the ordinary and familiar after what had happened in the night, made him rise.

"Trust me," he whispered as Alessan threw him a glance. *"This is a friend."*

Then he stepped out into the road.

"I thought it was a handsome design," he said clearly. "Better than most artisans I know. And, to tell the truth, Rovigo, I remember you saying the same thing to me yesterday afternoon in The Bird."

"I know that voice," Rovigo replied instantly. "I know that voice and I am exceedingly glad to hear it—even though you have just unmasked me before a shrewish wife and a daughter who has long been the bane of her father's unfortunate existence. Devin d'Asoli, if I am not mistaken!"

He strode forward from the gate, seizing the cart lantern from its bracket. Devin heard relieved laughter from the two women in the cart. Behind him, Alessan and then Catriana stepped into the road.

"You are not mistaken," Devin said. "May I introduce two of my company members: Catriana d'Astibar and Alessan di Tregea. This is Rovigo, a merchant with whom I was sharing a bottle in elegant surroundings when Catriana arranged to have me assaulted and ejected yesterday."

"Ah!" Rovigo exclaimed, holding the lantern higher. "The sister!"

Catriana, lit by the widened cast of the flame, smiled demurely. "I needed to talk to him," she said by way of explanation. "I didn't much want to go inside that place."

"A wise and a providential woman," Rovigo approved, grinning. "Would that my clutch of daughters were half so intelligent. No one," he added, "should much want to go inside The Bird unless they have a head-cold so virulent that it defeats all sense of smell."

Alessan burst out laughing. "Well-met on a dark road, Master Rovigo—the more so if you are the owner of a vessel called the *Sea Maid.*"

Devin blinked in astonishment.

"I have indeed the great misfortune to own and sail that unseaworthy excuse for a vessel," Rovigo admitted cheerfully. "How do you come to know it, friend?"

Alessan seemed highly amused. "Because I was asked to seek you out if I could. I have tidings for you from Ferraut town. From a somewhat portly, red-faced personage named Taccio."

"My esteemed factor in Ferraut!" Rovigo exclaimed. "Well met, indeed! By the god, where did you encounter him?"

"In another tavern, I am sorry to have to say. A tavern where I had been playing music and he was . . . well, escaping retribution was his own phrase. We two were, as it happened, the last patrons of the night. He wasn't in any great hurry to return home, for what seemed to me prudent reasons, and we fell to talking."

"It is never hard to fall to talking with Taccio," Rovigo assented. Devin heard a giggle from the cart. It didn't sound like the amusement of a ponderous, unmarriageable daughter. He was beginning to take the measure of Rovigo's attitude to his women. In the darkness he found himself grinning.

Alessan said, "The worthy Taccio explained his dilemma to me, and when I came to mention that I had just joined the company of Menico di Ferraut and was bound this way for the Festival he charged me to seek you out and carry verbal confirmation of a letter he says he's had conveyed to you."

"Half a dozen letters," Rovigo groaned. "To it, then: your verbal confirmation, friend Alessan."

"Good Taccio bade me tell you, and to swear it as true by the Triad's grace and the three fingers of the Palm" —Alessan's voice became a flawless parody of a sententious stage messenger—"that did the new bed not arrive from Astibar before the winter frosts, the Dragon that slumbers uneasily by his side would awaken in wrath unimaginable and put a violent end to his life of care in your esteemed service."

There was laughter and applause from the shadows of the cart. The mother, Devin decided, pursuing his earlier thought, didn't sound even remotely shrewish.

"Eanna and Adaon, who bless marriages together, forfend that such a thing should ever come to pass," Rovigo said piously. "The bed is ordered and it is made and it is ready to be shipped immediately the Festival is over."

"Then the Dragon shall slumber at ease and Taccio be saved," Alessan intoned, assuming the sonorous voice used for the "moral" at the end of a children's puppet-show.

"Though why," came a mild, still-amused female voice from the cart, "all of you should be so intimidated by poor Ingonida I honestly don't know. Rovigo, are we bereft entirely of our manners tonight? Will we keep these people standing in the cold and dark?"

"Absolutely not, my beloved," her husband exclaimed hastily. "Alix, it was only the conjured vision of Ingonida in wrath that addled my brain." Devin found that he couldn't stop grinning; even Catriana, he noticed, had relaxed her habitual expression of superior indifference.

"Were you going back to town?" Rovigo asked.

The first tricky moment—and Alessan left it to him. "We were," Devin said. "We'd taken a long walk to clear our heads and escape the noise, but were just about ready to brave the city again."

"I imagine the three of you would have been besieged by admirers all night," Rovigo said.

"We do seem to have achieved a certain notoriety," Alessan admitted.

"Well," said Rovigo earnestly, "all jesting aside, I could well understand if you wanted to rejoin the celebrations—they were nowhere near their peak when we left. It will go on all night, of course, but I confess I don't like leaving the younger ones alone too late, and my unfortunate oldest, Alais, suffers from twitches and fainting spells when over-excited."

"How sad," said Alessan with a straight face.

"Father!" came a softly urgent protest from the cart.

"Rovigo, stop that at once or I shall empty a basin on you in your sleep," her mother declared, though not, Devin judged, with any genuine anger.

"You see the way of things?" the merchant said, gesturing expressively with his free hand. "I am hounded without respite even into my dreams. But, if you are not entirely put off by the grievous stridency of my women and the prospect of three more inside very nearly as unpleasant, you are all most welcome, most humbly welcome to share a late repast and a quieter drink than you are likely to find in Astibar tonight."

"And three beds if you care to honor us," Alix added. "We heard you play and sing this morning at the Duke's rites. Truly, it would be an honor if you joined us."

"You were in the palace?" Devin asked, surprised.

"Hardly," Rovigo murmured in a self-deprecating tone. "We were in the street outside among the crowd." He hesitated. "Sandre d'Astibar was a man I greatly honored and admired. The Sandreni lands are just east of my own small holding—you have been walking by their woods even now. He was an easy-enough neighbor to the very end. I wanted to hear his mourning sung . . . and when I learned that my newest young friend's company had been selected to perform the rites, well . . . *Will* you come in with us?"

This time Devin left it to Alessan.

Who said, still highly amused, his teeth flashing white in the darkness, "We could not dream of refusing an offer so gracious. It will allow us to toast the safe journey of Taccio's new bed and the restful slumbers of his Dragon!"

"Oh, poor Ingonida," said Alix from the cart, trying unsuccessfully not to laugh, "you are all so unfair!"

Inside, there was light and warmth and continuing laughter. There were also three undeniably attractive young women whose names flew past Devin—amid screams and blushes—much too fast to be caught. The oldest of these three though—about seventeen, he guessed—had a musical lilt to her voice and an exceptionally flirtatious glance.

Alais was different.

In the light of the hallway of her home the merchant's oldest daughter turned out to be small and grave and slender. She had long, very straight black hair and eyes of the mildest shade of blue Devin could remember seeing. Beside her, Catriana's own blue gaze looked more challenging than ever and her tumbling red hair resembled nothing so much as the mane of a lioness.

They were ushered by insistent female hands and voices

into immensely comfortable chairs in a sitting-room furnished in shades of green and gold. A huge country fire blazed on the hearth, repudiating the autumn chill. A large carpet in a design that was unmistakably Quileian, even to Devin's untutored eye, covered the floor. The seventeen-year-old—Selvena, it emerged—sank gracefully down upon it at Devin's feet. She looked up at him and smiled. He received, and chose to ignore, a quick, sardonic glance from Catriana as she took a seat nearer to the fire. Alais was elsewhere for the moment, helping her mother.

Just then Rovigo reappeared, flushed and triumphant from some back room, carrying three bottles.

"I hope," he said, beaming down upon them, "that you all have a taste for Astibar's blue wine?"

And for Devin that simple question cast an entirely benevolent aura of fate over his impulsive action in the darkness outside. He glanced over at Alessan, and was rewarded with an odd smile that seemed to him to acknowledge many things.

Rovigo quickly began uncorking and pouring the wine. "If any of my wretched females are bothering you," he said over his shoulder, "feel free to swat them away like cats." A curl of blue smoke could be seen rising from each glass.

Selvena settled her gown more becomingly about her on the carpet, ignoring her father's gibe with an ease that bespoke long familiarity with this sort of thing. Her mother—neat, trim, competent, a laughably far cry from Rovigo's description in The Bird—came in with Alais and an elderly household servant. In a very short while a sideboard was covered with a remarkable variety of food.

Devin accepted a glass from Rovigo, savoring the icy-clean bouquet. He leaned back in his chair and prepared to be extremely content for the next little while. Selvena rose at a glance from her mother, but only to fill a plate of food for Devin. She brought it back to him, smiling, and settled on the carpet again, marginally nearer than before. Alais served Alessan and Catriana while the two youngest daughters sank down on the floor by their father. He aimed a mock-ferocious cuff at each of them.

Devin doubted if he'd ever seen a man so obviously

happy to be where he was. It must have shown in the amused irony of his glance, for Rovigo, catching the look, shrugged.

"Daughters," he lamented, sorrowfully shaking his head.

" 'Ponderous cartwheels,' " Devin reminded him, looking pointedly at the merchant's wife. Rovigo winced. Alix, laughter-lines crinkling at her temples, had overheard the exchange.

"He did it again, did he?" she said, tilting her head to one side. "Let me guess: I was of elephantine proportions and formidably evil disposition, and the four girls had scarcely enough good features among them to make up one passably acceptable woman. Am I right?"

Laughing aloud, Devin turned to see Rovigo—not at all discomfited—beaming with pride at his wife. "Exactly right," Devin said to Alix, "but I must say in his defense that I've never heard anyone give such a description so happily."

He was rewarded with Alix's quick laughter and a wonderfully grave smile over her shoulder from Alais, busy at the sideboard.

Rovigo raised his glass, moving it in small circles to make a pattern in the air with the icy smoke. "Will you join me in drinking to the memory of our Duke and to the glory of music? I don't believe in making idle toasts with blue wine."

"Nor do I," Alessan said quietly. He lifted his own glass. "To memory," he said very deliberately. "To Sandre d'Astibar. To music." Then he added something else, under his breath, before sipping from the wine.

Devin drank, tasting, for only the third or fourth time in his life, the astonishingly rich, cold complexity of Astibar's blue wine. There was nothing like it anywhere else in the Palm. And its price reflected that fact. He looked over and saluted Rovigo with his glass.

"To all of you," Catriana said suddenly. "To kindness on a dark road." She smiled—a smile without any edge or mockery to it. Devin was surprised, then decided it was unfair for him to feel that way.

Not on the road I'm on, she'd said in the Sandreni Palace. And that was something he could understand now. For he too was on that road after all, despite what she'd done to keep him from it. He tried to catch her eye but failed. She was talking to Alix, now seated beside her. Briefly reflective, Devin turned his attention to his food.

A moment later Selvena touched his foot lightly. "Will you sing for us?" she asked with a delicious smile. She didn't move her hand. "Alais heard you, and my parents, but the rest of us have been here all day."

"Selvena!" Mother and older sister snapped the name together. Selvena flinched as if struck but, Devin noticed, it was to her father that she turned, biting her lip. He was looking at her soberly.

"Dear heart," he said, in a voice far removed from the raillery of before, "you have a lesson to learn. Our friends make music for their livelihood. They are our guests here tonight. One does not, light of my life, ask guests to work in one's home." Selvena's eyes brimmed with tears. She lowered her head.

In the same serious tone Rovigo said to Devin, "Will you accept an apology? She meant it in good faith, I can assure you of that."

"I know she did," Devin protested, as Selvena sniffled softly at his feet. "There is no apology needed."

"Truly, none," Alessan added, setting his plate of food aside. "We make music to live, indeed, but we also make music because doing so is most truly to live. It is not work to play among friends, Rovigo."

Selvena wiped her eyes and looked up at him gratefully.

"I shall be happy to sing," Catriana said. She glanced briefly at Selvena. "Unless of course it was only Devin you had in mind?"

Devin winced, even though the slash had not been directed at him. Selvena flinched again, badly flustered for the second time in as many minutes. Out of the corner of his eye Devin saw an intriguing expression cross Alais's face.

Selvena began protesting earnestly that of course she'd meant all three of them. Alessan seemed amused by the entire exchange. Devin had a sudden intuition, looking at him, that this relaxed, sociable man was at least as close to the center of the Prince of Tigana as was the arrogantly precise figure he'd seen in the forest cabin.

He escapes this way, he thought suddenly. And even as the idea entered his mind he knew that it was true. He had heard the man play the "Lament for Adaon."

"Well," said Rovigo, smiling at Catriana, "if you are gracious enough to indulge a shameless child I blush to acknowledge as my own, it happens that I do have a set of Tregean pipes in the house—the Triad alone know why. I seem to remember once having a doting father's fancy that one of these creatures might emerge with a talent of *some* sort."

Alix, from several feet away, mimed a blow with a spoon at her husband. Unabashed, his good spirits restored, Rovigo sent the youngest girl off to fetch the pipes while he set about refilling everyone's glass.

Devin caught Alais looking at him from the seat she'd taken next to the fire. Reflexively he smiled at her. She didn't smile back, but her gaze, mild and serious, did not break away. He felt a small, unsettling skip to the rhythm of his heart.

As it turned out, after the meal was over he and Catriana sang for better than an hour to Alessan's pipes. Part of the way through, as they began one of the rousing old Certandan highland ballads, Rovigo left briefly and returned with a linked pair of Senzian drums. Shyly at first, very softly, he joined in on the refrain, proving as competent at that as at everything else Devin had seen him do. Catriana favored him with a particularly dazzling smile. Rovigo needed no further encouragement to stay with them on the next song, and the next.

No man, Devin found himself thinking, should need more encouragement to do anything in the world than that look from those blue eyes. Not that Catriana had ever favored *him* with anything remotely resembling such a glance. He found himself feeling somewhat confused all of a sudden.

Someone—Alais evidently—had filled his glass a third time. He drank a little more quickly than was good for him, given the legendary potency of blue wine, and then he led the other three into the next number: the last one for the two younger girls, Alix ruled, over protests.

He couldn't sing of Tigana, and he was certainly not about to sing of passion or love, so he began the very old song of Eanna's making the stars and committing the name of every single one of them to her memory, so that nothing might ever be lost or forgotten in the deeps of space or time.

It was the closest he could come to what the night had meant to him, to why, in the end, he had made the choice he had.

As he began it, he received a look from Alessan, thoughtful and knowing, and a quick, enigmatic glance from Catriana as they joined with him. Rovigo's drums fell silent this time as the merchant listened. Devin saw Alais, her black hair backlit by the fire, watching him with grave concentration. He sang one whole verse directly to her, then, in fidelity to the song, he sent his vision inward to where his purest music was always found, and he looked at no one at all as he sang to Eanna herself, a hymn to names and the naming of things.

Somewhere, part of the way through, he had a bright image in his mind of a blue-white star named Micaela aloft in a black night, and he let the keenness of that carry him, high and soaring, up toward Catriana's harmony and then back down softly to an end.

In the quiet of the mood so shaped, Selvena and the two younger girls went to bed with surprising tranquility. A few moments later Alix rose as well, and so, to Devin's disappointment, did Alais.

In the doorway she turned and looked at Catriana. "You must be very tired," Rovigo's daughter said. "If you like I can show you your room now. I hope you don't mind sharing with me. Selvena usually does, but she's in with the girls tonight."

Devin expected Catriana to demur, or worse, at this fairly transparent separation of the women and the men. She surprised him again though, hesitating only a second before rising. "I *am* tired, and I don't mind sharing at all," she said. "It will remind me of home."

Devin, who had been smiling at the irony of the situation suddenly found the expression less appropriate than he'd thought. Catriana had seen him grinning though; he wished, abruptly, that she hadn't. She was sure to misunderstand. It occurred to him, with a genuine sense of unreality, that they had made love together that morning.

For some time after the women had gone the three men sat in silence, each lost in his own thoughts. Rovigo rose at length and refilled their glasses with the last of the wine. He put another log on the fire and watched until it caught. With a sigh he sank back into his chair. Toying with his glass he looked from one to the other of his guests.

It was Alessan who broke the silence though. "Devin's a friend," he said quietly. "We can talk, Rovigo. Though I fear he's about to be extremely angry with both of us."

Devin sat up abruptly and put aside his glass. Rovigo, a wry expression playing about his lips, glanced briefly over at him, and then returned Alessan's gaze tranquilly.

"I wondered," he said. "Though I suspected he might be with us now, given the circumstances." Alessan was smiling too. They both turned to Devin.

Who felt himself going red. His brain raced frantically back over the events of the day before. He glared at Rovigo. "You didn't find me in The Bird by accident. Alessan sent you. You had him follow me, didn't you?" he accused, turning to the Prince.

The two men exchanged another glance before Alessan replied.

"I did," he admitted. "I had a certain suspicion that there would be funeral rites for Sandre d'Astibar coming up and that we might be asked to audition. I couldn't afford to lose track of you, Devin."

"I'm afraid I was behind you most of the way down the Street of the Temples yesterday," Rovigo added. He had the grace to look embarrassed, Devin noted.

He was still furious though, and very confused. "You lied about The Bird then, all that talk about going there whenever you came back from a journey."

"No, that part was true," Rovigo said. "Everything I said was true, Devin. Once you were forced down to the waterfront you happened to end up in a place I know very well."

"And Catriana?" Devin pursued angrily. "What about her? How did she—"

"I paid a boy to run a message back to your inn when I

saw that old Goro was letting you stay inside The Bird. Devin, don't be angry. There was a purpose to all of this."

"There was," Alessan echoed. "You should understand some of it by now. The whole reason Catriana and I were in Astibar with Menico's troupe was because of what I expected to see happen with Sandre's death."

"Wait a minute!" Devin exclaimed. "Expected? How did you know he was going to die?"

"Rovigo told me," Alessan said simply. He let a small silence register. "He has been my contact in Astibar for nine years now. I formed the same impression of him back then that you did yesterday, and about as quickly."

Devin, his mind reeling, looked over at the merchant, the casual friend he'd made the day before. Who turned out to be not so casual at all. Rovigo put down his glass.

"I feel the same way about Tyrants that you do," he said quietly. "Alberico here or Brandin of Ygrath ruling in Chiara and Corte and Asoli, and in that province Alessan comes from whose name I cannot hear or remember, hard as I might try."

Devin swallowed. "And Duke Sandre?" he asked. "How did you know—?"

"I spied on them," Rovigo said calmly. "It wasn't hard. I used to monitor Tomasso's comings and goings. They were wholly focused on Alberico, I was their neighbor here in the distrada, it was easy enough to slip onto their land. I learned of Tomasso's deception years ago, and—though I won't say it is a thing I am proud of—last year I was outside their windows at the estate and at the lodge on many different nights while they shaped the details of Sandre's death."

Devin looked quickly over at Alessan. He opened his mouth to say something, then, without speaking, he closed it.

Alessan nodded. "Thank you," he said. He turned to Rovigo. "There are one or two things here, as there have been before, that you are better off not knowing, for your own safety and your family's. I think you know by now it isn't a matter of trust, or any such thing."

"After nine years I think I do know that," Rovigo

murmured. "What *should* I know about what happened tonight?"

"Alberico arrived just after I joined Tomasso and the vigil-keepers in the lodge. Baerd and Catriana warned us and I had time to hide—with Devin, who had made his way to the cabin on his own."

"On his *own*? How?" Rovigo asked sharply.

Devin lifted his head. "I have my own resources," he said with dignity. Out of the corner of his eye he saw Alessan grin, and he suddenly felt ridiculous. Sheepishly he added, "I overheard the Sandreni talking upstairs between the two sessions of the mourning rites."

Rovigo looked as if he had another question or three, but, with a glance at Alessan, he held them in. Devin was grateful.

Alessan said, "When we went back to the cabin afterwards we found the vigil-keepers dead. Tomasso was taken. Baerd has remained behind to take care of a number of things by the cabin tonight. He will burn it later."

"We passed the Barbadians as we left the city," Rovigo said quietly, absorbing this. "I saw Tomasso bar Sandre with them. I feared for you, Alessan."

"With some cause," Alessan said drily. "There was an informer there. The boy, Herado, Gianno's son was in the service of Alberico."

Rovigo's face registered shock. "Family? Morian damn him to darkness for that!" he rasped harshly. "How could he do such a thing?"

Alessan gave his small characteristic shrug. "A great deal has broken down since the Tyrants came, would you not say?"

There was a silence as Rovigo fought to master his shock and rage. Devin coughed nervously and broke it: "Your own family," he asked. "Do they—"

"They know nothing of this," the merchant said, regaining his calm. "Neither Alix nor any of the girls had ever seen Alessan or Catriana before tonight. I met Alessan and Baerd in Tregea town nine years ago and we discovered in the course of a long night that we had certain dreams and certain enemies in common. They told me something of what their purposes were, and I told them I was willing to assist in those pursuits as best I could without unduly endangering my wife or daughters. I have tried to do that. I will continue to try. It is my hope to live long enough to be able to hear the oath Alessan offers when he drinks blue wine."

He spoke the last words quietly but with obvious passion. Devin looked at the Prince, remembering the inaudible words he had murmured under his breath before he drank.

Alessan gazed steadily at Rovigo. "There is one other thing you should know: Devin is one of us in more than the obvious way. I learned that by accident yesterday afternoon. He too was born in my own province before it fell. Which is why he is here."

Rovigo said nothing.

"What is the oath?" Devin asked. And then, more diffidently, "Is it something that I should know?"

"Not as anything that matters in the scheme of things. I only spoke a prayer of my own." Alessan's voice was careful and very clear. "I always do. I said: *Tigana, let my memory of you be like a blade in my soul.*"

Devin closed his eyes. The words and the voice. No one spoke. Devin opened his eyes and looked at Rovigo.

Whose brow was knotted in fierce, angry consternation.

"My friend, Devin should understand this," Alessan said to him gently. "It is a part of the legacy he has taken on. What did you hear me say?"

Rovigo gestured with helpless frustration. "The same thing I heard the first time this happened. That night nine years ago, when we switched to blue wine. I heard you ask that the memory of something be a blade in you. In your soul. But I didn't hear . . . I've lost the beginning again. The something."

"Tigana," Alessan said again. Tenderly, clear as chiming crystal.

But Devin saw Rovigo's expression grow even more baffled and dismayed. The merchant reached for his glass and drained it. "Will you . . . one more time?"

"Tigana," Devin said before Alessan could speak. To make this legacy, this grief at the heart of things, more truly his own, as properly it was his own. For the land *was* his or it had been, and its name was part of his own, and they were both lost. Taken away.

"Let my memory of you be like a blade in my soul," he said, his voice faltering at the end though he tried hard to keep it as steady as Alessan's had been.

Wondering, disoriented, visibly distressed, Rovigo shook his head.

"And Brandin's magic is behind this?" he asked.

"It is," Alessan said flatly.

After a moment Rovigo sighed and leaned back in his chair. "I am sorry," he said softly. "Forgive me, both of you. I should not have asked. I have opened a wound."

"I was the one who asked," Devin said quickly.

"The wound is always open," said Alessan, a moment later.

There was an extraordinary compassion in Rovigo's face. It was difficult to realize that this was the same man who had been jesting about Senzian rustics as husbands for his daughters. The merchant rose abruptly and became busy tending to the fire again, though the blaze was doing perfectly well. While he did so Devin looked at Alessan. The other man met his gaze. They said nothing though. Alessan's eyebrows lifted a little, and he gave the small shrug Devin had come to know.

"What do we do now, then?" asked Rovigo d'Astibar, returning to stand beside his chair. His color was high, perhaps from the fire. "I am as disturbed by this as I was when we first met. I do not like magic. Especially this kind of magic. It remains a matter of some . . . significance to me to be able to hear one day what I was just debarred from hearing."

Devin felt a rush of excitement run through him again: the other element to his feelings this evening. His pique at having been deceived in The Bird was entirely gone. These two, and Baerd and the Duke, were men to be reckoned with, in every possible way, and they were shaping plans that might change the map of the Palm, of the whole world. And he was here with them, he was one of them, chasing a dream of freedom. He took a long drink of his blue wine.

Alessan's expression was troubled though. He looked, suddenly, as if he were burdened with a new and difficult weight. He leaned slowly back in his chair, his hand going through the tangle of his hair as he looked at Rovigo in silence for a long time.

Turning from one man to the other, Devin felt abruptly lost again, his excitement fading almost as quickly as it had come.

"Rovigo, have we not involved you enough already?" Alessan asked at length. "I must admit this has become harder for me now that I have met your wife and daughters. This coming year may see a change in things, and I cannot even begin to tell you how much more danger. Four men died in that cabin tonight, and I think you know as well as I do how many will be death-wheeled in Astibar in the weeks to come. It has been one thing for you to keep an ear open here and on your travels, to quietly monitor Alberico's doings and Sandre's, for you and Baerd and I to meet every so often and touch palms and talk, friend to friend. But the shape of the tale is changing now, and I greatly fear to put you in danger."

Rovigo nodded. "I thought you might say something like that. I am grateful for your concern. But Alessan, I made up my mind on this a long time ago. I . . . would not expect that freedom could be found or won without a price paid. You said three days ago that the coming spring might mark a turning-point for all of us. If there are ways that I can help in the days to come you must tell me." He hesitated, then: "One of the reasons I love my wife is that Alix would echo this were she with us and did she know."

Alessan's expression was still troubled. "But she isn't with us and she doesn't know," he said. "There have been reasons for that, and there will be more of them after tonight. And your girls? How can I ask you to endanger them?"

"How can you decide for me, or them?" Rovigo replied softly, but without hesitation. "Where is *our* choice, our freedom, if you do that? I would obviously prefer not to do anything that will put them into actual danger, and I cannot afford to suspend my business entirely. But within these confines, is there no aid I can offer that will make a difference?"

Finally understanding the source of Alessan's doubts,

Devin kept grimly silent. This was something to which he had attached no weight at all, while Alessan had been wrestling with it all along. He felt chastened and sobered, and afraid now though not for himself.

There will be people put at risk by everything we do, the Prince had said in the forest, speaking of Menico. And now Devin was beginning to understand, painfully, the reality of that.

He didn't want these people hurt. In any way at all. His excitement quite gone, Devin had driven home for him, for the first time, this one among the many ancillary sorrows that lay on the road he seemed to have found. He was brought face-to-face with the distance that road imposed between them and, it now seemed, almost everyone they might meet. Even friends. Even people who might share a part or all of their dream. He thought of Catriana in the palace again, and he understood her even more now than he had an hour ago.

Watching, letting the growth of wisdom guide him into silence, Devin focused on Alessan's momentarily unguarded face and he saw him come hard to his decision. He watched as the Prince took a deep, slow breath and so shouldered another burden that was the price of his blood.

Alessan smiled, an odd, rueful smile. "Actually, there is," he said to Rovigo. "There *is* something you can do now that will help." He hesitated, then, unexpectedly, the smile deepened and it reached his eyes. "Had you ever given any thought," he said in an elaborately casual voice, "to taking on some business partners?"

For just a moment Rovigo seemed nonplussed, then a quick, answering smile of understanding broadened across his face. I see," he said. "You need access to some places."

Alessan nodded. "That, and there are more of us now, as well. Devin is with us, and there may be others before spring. Things will be different from the years when it was only Baerd and I. I have been giving thought to this since Catriana joined us."

His voice quickened, grew crisper. Devin remembered this tone from the cabin. This was the man he'd first seen there. Alessan said, "In business together you and I will have a more legitimate means of exchanging information and I'm going to need information regularly this winter. As partners we have reason to be writing each other about any affairs that touch on trade. And of course all affairs touch on trade."

"Indeed they do," said Rovigo, his eyes intent on Alessan's face.

"We can communicate directly if you have resources for that, or through Taccio in Ferraut." He glanced over at Devin. "I know Taccio, by the way, that wasn't a coincidence either. I assume you'd figured that out?" Devin hadn't even thought about it actually, but before he could speak Alessan had turned back to Rovigo. "I assume you have a courier service you can trust?" Rovigo nodded.

Alessan said, "You see, the newest problem is that although we could still travel as musicians, after this morning's performance we'd be notorious wherever we went. Had I thought about it in time I'd have botched the music a little, or told Devin to be a little less impressive."

"No you wouldn't have," Devin said quietly. "Whatever other things you would have done, ruining the music isn't one of them."

Alessan's mouth quirked as he acknowledged the hit. Rovigo smiled.

"Perhaps so," the Prince murmured. "It *was* special, wasn't it?"

There was a brief silence. Rovigo got up and put one more log on the fire.

Alessan said, "It all makes sense. There are certain places and certain activities that would be awkward for us as performers. Especially well-known performers. As merchants, we would have a new access to such places."

"Certain islands, perhaps?" Rovigo asked quietly, from by the fire.

"Perhaps," Alessan agreed. "If it comes to that. Though there it may be a matter of five of one hand, five of the other: artists are welcome at Brandin's court on Chiara. This gives us another option, though, and I like having options to work with. It has been necessary once or twice for a character I've assumed to disappear, or die." His voice was quiet, matter-of-fact. He took a sip of his wine.

After a moment he turned back to Rovigo. Who was now stroking his chin in a fine imitation of a shrewdly avaricious businessman.

"Well," the merchant said in a greedy, wheedling voice, "you appear to have made a most . . . *intriguing* proposal, gentlemen. I do have to ask one or two preliminary questions. I've known Alessan for some time, but this particular issue has never come up before, you understand." His eyes narrowed with exaggerated cunning. "What, if anything, do you know about business?"

Alessan gave a sudden burst of laughter, then quickly grew serious again. "Have you any money to hand?" he asked.

"I've my ship just in," Rovigo replied. "Cash from two days' transactions and easy credit based on profits over the next few weeks. Why?"

"I would suggest buying a reasonable but not indiscreet amount of grain in the next forty-eight hours. Twenty-four hours, actually, if you can."

Rovigo looked thoughtful. "I could do that," he said. "And my means are sufficiently limited that no purchase I made would be large enough to be indiscreet. I have a contact, too—the steward at the Nievolene farms by the Ferraut border."

"Not from Nievole," Alessan said quickly.

Another silence. Rovigo nodded his head slowly. "I see," he said, startling Devin again with his quickness. "You think we can expect some confiscations after the Festival?"

"You can," Alessan said. "Among all the other even less pleasant things. Have you another source for buying up grain?"

"I might." Rovigo looked from Alessan to Devin and back again. "Four partners, then," he said crisply. "The three of you and Baerd. Is that right?"

Alessan nodded. "Almost right, but make it five partners. There is one other person who should be brought in to divide our share, if that is all right with you?"

"Why should it not be?" Rovigo shrugged. "That doesn't touch my share at all. Will I meet this person?"

"I hope so, sooner or later," said Alessan. "I expect you will be happy with each other."

"Fine," Rovigo said crisply. "The usual terms for a contraina association are two-thirds to the one investing the funds, and one third to the ones who do the traveling and put in the time. Based on what you have just told me I will accept that you are likely to be able to offer information which will be of real value to our venture. I propose a half interest each way on all affairs we jointly conduct. Is that acceptable?"

He was looking at Devin. With as much composure as he could manage, Devin replied, "It is quite acceptable."

"It is more than fair," Alessan agreed. His expression was troubled again; he looked as if he would go on.

"It is done, then," said Rovigo quickly. "No more to be said, Alessan. We will go into town tomorrow to have the contraina formally drawn up and sealed. Which way do you plan to go after the Festival?"

"Ferraut, I think," said Alessan slowly. "We can discuss what comes after, but I have something to do there, and an idea for some trade with Senzio we might want to consider."

"Ferraut?" said Rovigo, ignoring the latter remarks. A smile slowly widened across his face. "Ferraut! That is splendid. Absolutely splendid! You can save us some money already. I'll give you a cart and all of you can take Ingonida her new bed!"

★　★　★

On the way upstairs Alais couldn't remember when she had last been so happy. Not that she was prone to moodiness like Selvena, but life at home tended to be very quiet, especially when her father was away.

And now so many things seemed to be happening at once.

Rovigo was home after a longer trip than usual down the coast. Alix and Alais were never at ease when he ventured south of the mountains into Quileia, no matter how many times he reassured them of his caution. And on top of that, this trip had come unsettlingly late in the season of autumn winds. But he was home now, and palm to palm with his return had come the Festival of Vines. It was her second one, and Alais had loved every moment of the day and night, absorbing with her wide, alert eyes all she saw. Drinking it in.

In the crowded square in front of the Sandreni Palace that morning she had stood extremely still, listening to a clear voice soar from the inner courtyard out among the unnatural silence of the people gathered. A voice that lamented Adaon's death among the cedars of Tregea so bitterly, so sweetly, that Alais had been afraid she would cry. She had closed her eyes.

It had been a source of astonished pride for her when Rovigo had casually mentioned to her and her mother having had a drink the day before with one of the singers who were doing the Duke's mourning rites. He had even invited the young man, he said, to come meet his four ungainly offspring. The teasing bothered Alais not at all. She would have felt that something was wrong by now had Rovigo spoken about them in any other way. Neither she nor her sisters nursed any anxieties about their father's affection. They had only to look at his eyes.

On the road home late at night, already badly unsettled by the thundering clatter of the Barbadian soldiers they had made way for at the city walls, she had been truly frightened when a voice called out to them from the darkness near their gate.

Then, when her father had replied, and she came gradually to understand who this was, Alais had thought her heart would stop from sheer excitement. She could feel the tell-tale color rising in her cheeks.

When it became clear that the musicians were coming inside, it had taken a supreme act of self-control for her to regain the mien and composure proper to her parents' oldest, most trusted child.

In the house it became easier because the instant the two male guests stepped through the doorway Selvena had gone into her predictable mating frenzy. A course of behavior so embarrassingly transparent to her older sister that it drove Alais straight back into her own habitual, detached watchfulness. Selvena had been crying herself to sleep for much of the year because it looked more and more as if she would still be unmarried when her eighteenth naming day came in the spring.

Devin, the singer, was smaller and younger-looking

than she'd expected. But he was neat and lithe, with an easy smile and quick, intelligent eyes under sandy-brown hair that curled halfway over his ears. She'd expected him to be arrogant or pretentious, despite what her father had said, but she saw nothing of that at all.

The other man, Alessan, looked about fifteen years older, perhaps more. His black, tangled hair was prematurely greying—silvering, actually—at the temples. He had a lean, expressive face with very clear grey eyes and a wide mouth. He intimidated her a little, even though he was joking easily with her father right from the start, in exactly the manner she knew Rovigo most enjoyed.

Perhaps that was it, Alais thought: few people she'd met could keep up with her father, in jesting or in anything else. And this man with the sharp, quizzical features appeared to be doing so effortlessly. She wondered, aware that the thought was more than a little arrogant on her own part, how a Tregean musician could manage that. On the other hand, she reflected, she didn't know very much about musicians at all.

Which made her even more curious about the woman. Alais thought Catriana was terribly beautiful. With her commanding height and the startlingly blue eyes under the blaze of her hair—like a second fire in the room— she made Alais feel small and pale and bland. In a curious way that combined with Selvena's outrageous flirtation to relax rather than unsettle her: this sort of activity, competition, exercise, was simply *not* something with which she was going to get involved. Watching closely, she saw Catriana register Selvena's soft flouncing at Devin's feet and she intercepted the sardonic glance the red-haired singer directed at her fellow musician.

Alais decided to go into the kitchen. Her mother and Menka might need help. Alix gave her a quick, thoughtful glance when she came in, but did not comment.

They quickly put a meal together. Back in the front room Alais helped at the sideboard and then listened and watched from her favorite chair next to the fire. Later she had genuine cause to bless Selvena's shamelessness. None of the rest of them would have dreamt of asking their guests to sing.

This time she could see the singers so she kept her eyes

open. Devin sang directly to her once near the end and Alais, her color furiously rising, forced herself not to look away. For the rest of that last song about Eanna naming the stars she found her mind straying into channels unusual for her—the sort of thing Selvena speculated about at night all the time, in detail. Alais hoped they would all attribute her color to the warmth of the fire.

She did wonder about one thing though, having been an observer of people for most of her life. There was *something* between Devin and Catriana, but it certainly wasn't love, or even tenderness as she understood either of those things. They would look at each other from time to time, usually when the other was unaware, and the glances would be more challenging than anything else. She reminded herself again that the world of these people was farther removed from her own than she could even imagine.

The younger ones said their good nights. Selvena doing so with a highly suspicious lack of protest, and touching, shockingly, fingertip to palm with both men in farewell. Alais caught a glance from her father, and a moment later she rose when her mother did.

It was impulse, nothing more, that led her to invite Catriana to come up with her. Immediately the words were spoken, she realized how they must sound to the other woman—someone so independent and obviously at ease in the company of men. Alais flinched inwardly at her own provincial clumsiness, and braced herself for a rebuff. Catriana's smile, though, was all graciousness as she stood.

"It will remind me of home," she said.

Thinking about that as the two of them went up the stairs past the lamps in their brackets and the wall-hangings her grandfather had brought back south from a voyage to Khardhun years and years ago, Alais tried to fathom what would lead a girl her own age to venture out among the rough and tumble of long roads and uncertain lodging. Of late nights and men who would surely assume that if she was among them she had to be available. Alais tried, but she honestly couldn't grasp it. Despite that, or perhaps because of it, something generous in her spirit opened out toward the other woman.

"Thank you for the music," she said shyly.

"Small return for your kindness," Catriana said lightly.

"Not as small as you think," Alais said. "Our room is over here. I'm glad this reminds you of home . . . I hope it is a good memory." That was probing a little, but not rudely she hoped. She wanted to talk to this woman, to be friends, to learn what she could about a life so remote from her own.

They stepped into the large bedroom. Menka had the fire going already and the two bedspreads turned back. The deep-piled quilts were new this autumn, more contraband brought back by Rovigo from Quileia where winters were so much harsher than here.

Catriana laughed a little under her breath, her eyebrows arching as she surveyed the chamber. "Sharing a room does. This is rather more than I knew in a fisherman's cottage." Alais flushed, fearful of having offended, but before she could speak Catriana turned to her, eyes still very wide, and said casually, "Tell me, will we need to tie your sister down? She seems to be in heat and I'm worried about the two men surviving the night."

Alais went from feeling spoiled and insensitive to red-faced shock in one second. Then she saw the quick smile on the other woman's face and she laughed aloud in a release of anxiety and guilt.

"She's just terrible isn't she? She's vowed to kill herself in some dreadfully dramatic way if she isn't married by the Festival next year."

Catriana shook her head. "I knew some girls like her at home. I've met a few on the road, too. I've never been able to understand it."

"Nor I," said Alais a little too quickly. Catriana glanced at her. Alais ventured a hesitant smile. "I guess that's a thing we have in common?"

"One thing," the other woman said indifferently, turning away. She strolled over to one of the woven pieces on the wall. "This is nice enough," she said, fingering it. "Where did your father find it?"

"I made it," Alais said shortly. She felt patronized suddenly, and it irritated her.

It must have shown in her voice, for Catriana looked quickly back over her shoulder. The two women exchanged a look in silence. Catriana sighed. "I'm hard to make friends with," she said at length. "I doubt it's worth your effort."

"No effort," said Alais quietly. "Besides," she ventured, "I may need your help tying Selvena down later."

Surprised, Catriana chuckled. "She'll be all right," she said, sitting on one of the beds. "Neither of them will touch her while they are guests in your father's house. Even if she slithers into their room wearing nothing but a single red glove."

Shocked for the second time, but finding the sensation oddly enjoyable, Alais giggled and sat down on her own bed, dangling her legs over the side. Catriana's feet, she noticed ruefully, easily reached the carpet.

"She just might do that," she whispered, grinning at the image. "I think she even has a red glove hidden somewhere!"

Catriana shook her head. "Then it's roping her down like a heifer or trusting the men, I guess. But as I say, they won't do anything."

"You know them very well, I suppose," Alais hazarded. She still wasn't sure whether any given remark would earn her a rebuff or elicit a smile. This was not, she was discovering, an easy woman to deal with.

"Alessan, I know better," Catriana said. "But Devin's been on the road a long time and I have no doubt he knows the rules." She glanced away briefly as she said that last, her own color a little high.

Still wary of another rejection Alais said cautiously, "I have no idea about that, actually. *Are* there rules? Do any of them . . . do you have problems when you travel?"

Catriana shrugged. "The kind of problems your sister's longing to find? Not from the musicians. There's an unwritten code, or else the companies would only get a certain kind of woman to tour and that would hurt the music. And the music really does matter to most of the troupes. The ones that last, anyway. Men can be quite badly hurt for bothering a girl too much. Certainly they'll never find work if it happens too often."

"I see," said Alais, trying to imagine it.

"You *are* expected to pair off with someone though," Catriana added. "As if it's the least you can do. Remove yourself as a temptation. So you find a man you like, or some of the girls find a woman, of course. There's a fair bit of that, too."

"Oh," said Alais, clasping her hands in her lap.

Catriana, who was really much too clever by half, flashed a glance of mingled amusement and malice. "Don't worry," she said sweetly, looking pointedly at where Alais's hands had settled like a barrier. "That glove doesn't fit me."

Abruptly Alais put her hands to either side of her, blushing furiously.

"I wasn't particularly worried," she said, trying to sound casual. Then, goaded by the other's mocking expression, she shot back: "What glove *does* fit you, then?"

The other woman's amusement quickly disappeared. There was a small silence. Then: "You do have some spirit in you, after all," Catriana said judiciously. "I wasn't sure."

"That," said Alais, moved to a rare anger, "is patronizing. How would you be sure of anything about me? And why would I let you see it?"

Again there was a silence, and again Catriana surprised her. "I'm sorry," she said. "Truly. I'm really not very good at this. I warned you." She looked away. "As it happens, you hit a nerve and I tend to lash out when that occurs."

Alais's anger, as quick to recede as it was slow to kindle, was gone even as the other woman spoke. This was, she reminded herself sternly, a guest in her house.

She had no immediate chance to reply though, or to try to mend the rift, because just then Menka bustled importantly into the room with a basin of water heated over the kitchen fire, followed by the youngest of Rovigo's apprentices with a second basin and towels draped over both his shoulders. The boy's eyes were desperately cast downwards in a room containing two women as he carried the basin and the towels carefully over to the table by the window.

The garrulous fuss Menka inevitably stirred up wherever she went broke the mood entirely—both the good and the bad parts of it, Alais thought. After the two servants left, the women washed up in silence. Alais, stealing a glance at the other's long-limbed body, felt even more inadequate in her own small, white softness and the sheltered life she'd lived. She climbed into bed, feeling as if she'd like to begin the whole conversation over again.

"Good night," she said.

"Good night," Catriana replied, after a moment. Alais tried to read an invitation to further conversation in her tone, but she wasn't sure. If Catriana wanted to talk, she decided, she had only to say something.

They blew out their bedside candles and lay silently in the semi-darkness. Alais watched the red glow of the fire, curled her toes around the hot brick Menka had put at the foot of her bed, and thought ruefully that the distance to Selvena's side of the room had never seemed so great.

Sometime later, still unsleeping though the fire was down to its embers, she heard a burst of hilarity from the three men downstairs. The warm, carrying sound of her father's laughter somehow worked its way into her and eased her distress. He was home. She felt sheltered and safe. Alais smiled to herself in the darkness. She heard the men come upstairs soon after, and go to their separate rooms.

She remained awake for a while, with an ear perked to catch the sound of her sister in the hallway—though she didn't really believe even Selvena would do that. She heard nothing, and eventually she fell asleep.

She dreamt of lying on a hilltop in a strange place. Of a man there with her. Lowering himself upon her. A mild moonless night glittering with stars. She lay with him upon that windy height amid a scattering of dew-drenched summer flowers, and in the high, unknown place of that dreaming Alais was filled with complex yearnings she could never have named aloud.

It was bitterly cold in the dungeon where they had thrown him at last. The stones were damp and icy, they smelled of urine and feces. He'd only been allowed to put back on his linen underclothing and his hose. There were rats in the cell. He couldn't see them in the blackness but he had been able to hear them from the beginning and he'd been bitten twice already as he dozed.

Earlier, he had been naked. The new Captain of the Guard—the replacement for the one who'd killed himself—had permitted his men to play with their prisoner before locking him up for the night. They all knew Tomasso's reputation. Everyone knew his reputation. He had made sure of that; it had been part of the plan.

So the guards had stripped him in the harsh brightness of the guardroom and they had amused themselves coarsely, pricking him with their swords or with the heated poker from the fire, sliding them around his flaccid sex, prodding him in the buttocks or the belly. Bound and helpless, Tomasso had wanted only to close his eyes and wish it all away.

For some reason it was the memory of Taeri that wouldn't let him do that. He still couldn't believe his younger brother was dead. Or that Taeri had been so brave and so decisive at the end. It made him want to cry, thinking about it, but he was not going to let the Barbadians see that. He was a Sandreni. Which seemed to mean more to him now, naked and near the end, than it ever had before.

So he kept his eyes open and he fixed them bleakly on the new captain. He did his best to ignore the things they were doing to him, and the sniggering, brutal suggestions as to what would happen tomorrow. They weren't very imaginative actually. He knew the morning's reality was going to be worse. Intolerably worse.

They hurt him a little with their blades and drew blood a few times, but nothing very much—Tomasso knew they were under orders to save him for the professionals in the morning. Alberico would be present then, as well. This was just play.

Eventually the captain grew tired of Tomasso's steady gaze, or else he decided that there was enough blood flowing down the prisoner's legs, puddling on the floor. He ordered his men to stop. Tomasso's bonds were cut and they gave him back his undergarments and a filthy pest-infested strip of blanket and they took him down the stairs to the dungeons of Astibar and they threw him into the blackness of one of them.

The entrance was so low that even on his knees he'd scraped his head on the stone when they pushed him in. More blood, he realized, as his hand came away sticky. It didn't actually seem to matter very much.

He hated the rats though. He'd always been afraid of rats. He rolled the useless blanket as tightly as he could and tried to use it as a feeble club. It was hard though in the dark.

Tomasso wished he were a physically braver man. He knew what was coming in the morning, and the thought, now that he was alone, turned his bowels to jelly.

He heard a sound, and realized a moment later that he was whimpering. He fought to keep control of himself. He was alone though, and in freezing darkness in the hands of his enemies, and there were rats. He couldn't entirely keep the sounds from coming. He felt as if his heart was broken, as if it lay in jagged pieces at odd angles in his breast. Among the fragments he tried to assemble a curse for Herado and his betrayal, but nothing seemed equal to what his nephew had done. Nothing seemed large enough to encompass it.

He heard another rat and lashed out blindly with his rolled weapon. He hit something and heard a squeal. Again and again he pounded at the place of that sound. He thought he had killed it. One of them. He was trembling, but the frenzy of activity seemed to help him fight back his weakness. He didn't weep any more. He leaned back against the damp slime of the stone wall, wincing because of his open cuts. He closed his eyes, though he couldn't see in any case, and he thought of sunlight.

It was then that he must have dozed, because he woke suddenly with a shout of pain: one of the rats had bitten viciously at his thigh. He flailed about with the blanket for a few moments, but he was shivering now and beginning to feel genuinely ill. His mouth was swollen and pulpy from Alberico's blow in the cabin. He found it painful to swallow. He felt his forehead and decided he was feverish.

Which is why, when he saw the wan light of a candle, he was sure he was hallucinating. He was able to look around though by its glow. The cell was tiny. There was a dead rat near his right leg and there were two more living ones—big as cats—near the door. He saw, on the wall beside him, a scratched-out image of the sun with notches for days cut into the rim. It had the saddest face Tomasso could ever remember seeing. He looked at it for a long time.

Then he looked back towards the glowing light and realized with certainty that this *was* a hallucination, or a dream.

His father was holding the candle, dressed in the blue-silver robe of his burial, looking down with an expression different from any Tomasso could ever remember seeing on his face.

The fever must be extreme, he decided; his mind was conjuring forth in this abyss an image of something his shattered heart so desperately desired. A look of kindness—and even, if one wanted to reach for the word, even of love—in the eyes of the man who'd whipped him as a child and then designated him as useful for two decades of plotting against a Tyrant.

Which had ended tonight. Which would truly end, most horribly, for Tomasso in the morning, amid pain he didn't even have the capacity to imagine. He *liked* this dream though, this fever-induced fantasy. There was light in it. It kept the rats away. It even seemed to ease the bone-numbing cold of the wet stones beneath him and against his back.

He lifted an unsteady hand towards the flame. Through a dry throat and torn, puffy lips he croaked something. What he wanted to say was, *"I'm sorry,"* to the dream-image of his father, but he couldn't make the words come right.

This was a dream though, his dream, and the image of Sandre seemed to understand.

"You have nothing to be sorry for," Tomasso heard his dream-father say. So gently. "It was my fault and only mine. Through all those years and at the end. I knew Gianno's limitations from the start. I had too many hopes for you as a child. It . . . affected me too much. After."

The candle seemed to waver a little. A part of Tomasso, a corner of his heart, seemed to be knitting itself slowly back together, even though this was only a dream, only his own longing. A last feeble fantasy of being loved before they flayed him.

"Will you let me tell you how sorry I am for the folly that has condemned you to this? Will you hear me if I tell you I have been proud of you, in my fashion?"

Tomasso let himself weep. The words were balm for the deepest ache he knew. Crying made the light blur and swim though, and so he raised his shaking hands and kept trying to wipe the tears away. He wanted to speak but his shattered mouth could not form words. He nodded his head though, over and over. Then he had a thought and he raised his left hand—the heart hand, of oaths and fidelity—toward this dream of his dead father's ghost.

And slowly Sandre's hand came down, as if from a long, long way off, from years and years away, seasons lost and forgotten in the turning of time and pride, and father and son touched fingertips together.

It was a more solid contact than Tomasso had thought it would be. He closed his eyes for a moment, yielding to the intensity of his feelings. When he opened them his father's image seemed to be holding something out towards him. A vial of some liquid. Tomasso did not understand.

"This is the last thing I can do for you," the ghost said in a strange, unexpectedly wistful voice. "If I were stronger I could do more, but at least they will not hurt you in the morning now. They will not hurt you any more, my son. Drink it Tomasso, drink it and this will all be gone. All go away, I promise you. Then wait for me Tomasso, wait if you can in Morian's Halls. I would like to walk with you there."

Tomasso still did not understand, but the tone was so mild, so reassuring. He took the dream-vial. Again it was more substantial than he'd expected it to be.

His father nodded encouragement. With trembling hands Tomasso fumbled and removed the stopper. Then with a last gesture—a final mocking parody of himself—he raised it in a wide, sweeping, elaborate salute to his own powers of fantasy and he drained it to the dregs, which were bitter.

His father's smile was so sad. Smiles are not supposed to be sad, Tomasso wanted to say. He had said that to a boy once, in a temple of Morian at night, in a room where he was not supposed to be. His head felt heavy. He felt as if he were about to fall alseep, even though he already *was* asleep, and dreaming in his fever. He really didn't understand. He especially didn't understand why his father, who was dead, should ask *him* to wait in Morian's Halls.

He looked up again, wanting to ask about that. His vision seemed to be going completely strange on him though.

He knew this was so, because the image of his father, looking down upon him, seemed to be crying. There were tears in his father's eyes.

Which was impossible. Even in a dream.

"Farewell," he heard.

Farewell, he tried to say, in return.

He wasn't sure if he'd actually managed to form the word, or if he'd only thought it, but just then a darkness more encompassing than he had ever known came down over him like a blanket or a mantle, and the difference between the spoken and the unspoken ceased to matter anymore.

PART TWO

DIANORA

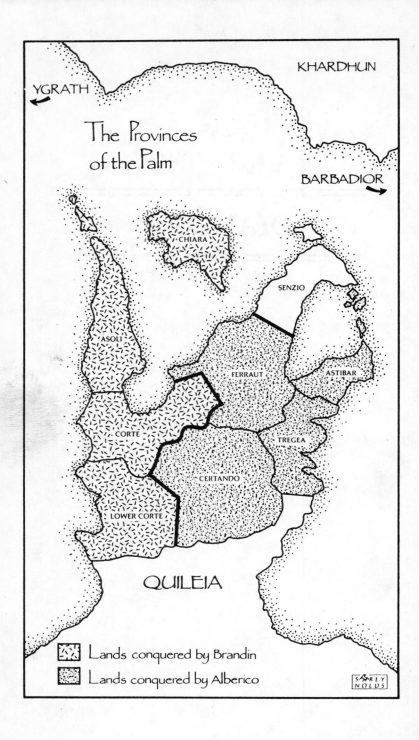

KHARDHUN

YGRATH

The Provinces
of the Palm

BARBADIOR

CHIARA

SENZIO

ASOLI

FERRAUT

ASTIBAR

CORTE

TREGEA

CERTANDO

LOWER CORTE

QUILEIA

⬚ Lands conquered by Brandin

⬚ Lands conquered by Alberico

S. REYNOLDS

CHAPTER
• 7 •

DIANORA COULD REMEMBER THE DAY SHE CAME TO THE Island.

The air that autumn morning had been much like it was today at the beginning of spring—white clouds scudding in a high blue sky as the wind had swept the Tribute Ship through the whitecaps into the harbor of Chiara. Beyond harbor and town the slopes mounting to the hills had been wild with fall colors. The leaves were turning: red and gold and some that clung yet to green, she remembered.

The sails of the Tribute Ship so long ago had been red and gold as well: colors of celebration in Ygrath. She knew that now, she hadn't known it then. She had stood on the forward deck of the ship to gaze for the first time at the splendor of Chiara's harbor, at the long pier where the Grand Dukes used to stand to throw a ring into the sea, and from where Letizia had leaped in the first of the Ring Dives to reclaim the ring from the waters and marry her Duke: turning the Dives into the luck and symbol of Chiara's pride until beautiful Onestra had changed the ending of the story hundreds and hundreds of years ago, and the Ring Dives had ceased. Even so, every child in the Palm knew that legend of the Island. Young girls in each province would play at diving into water for a ring and rising in triumph, with their hair shining wet, to wed a Duke of power and glory.

From near the prow of the Tribute Ship, Dianora had looked up beyond the harbor and palace to gaze at the majesty of snow-crowned Sangarios rising behind them. The Ygrathen sailors had not disturbed her silence. They

155

had allowed her to come forward to watch the Island approach. Once she'd been safely aboard ship and the ship away to sea they'd been kind to her. Women thought to have a real chance at being chosen for the saishan were always treated well on the Tribute Ships. It could make a captain's fortune in Brandin's court if he brought home a hostage who became a favorite of the Tyrant.

Sitting now on the southern balcony of the saishan wing, looking out from behind the ornately crafted screen that hid the women from gawkers in the square below, Dianora watched the banners of Chiara and Ygrath flap in the freshening spring breeze, and she remembered how the wind had blown her hair about her face more than twelve years ago. She remembered looking from the bright sails to the slopes of the tree-clad hills running up to Sangarios, from the blue and white of the sea to the clouds in the blue sky. From the tumult and chaos of life in the harbor to the serene grandeur of the palace just beyond. Birds had been wheeling, crying loudly about the three high masts of the Tribute Ship. The rising sun had been a dazzle of light striking along the sea from the east. So much vibrancy in the world, so rich and fair and shining a morning to be alive.

Twelve years ago, and more. She had been twenty-one years old, and nursing her hatred and her secret like two of Morian's three snakes twining about her heart.

She had been chosen for the saishan.

The circumstances of her taking had made it very likely, and Brandin's celebrated grey eyes had widened appraisingly when she was led before him two days later. She'd been wearing a silken, pale-colored gown, she remembered, chosen to set off her dark hair and the dark brown of her eyes.

She had been certain she would be chosen. She'd felt neither triumph nor fear, even though she'd been pointing her life toward that moment for five full years, even though, in that instant of Brandin's choosing, walls and screens and corridors closed around her that would define the rest of her days. She'd had her hatred and her secret, and guarding the two of them left no room for anything else.

Or so she'd thought at twenty-one.

For all she'd seen and lived through, even by then, Dianora reflected twelve years later on her balcony, she'd known very little—dangerously little—about a great many things that mattered far too much.

Even out of the wind it was cool here on the balcony. The Ember Days were upon them but the flowers were just beginning in the valleys inland and on the hill slopes, and the true onset of spring was some time off even this far north. It had been different at home, Dianora remembered; sometimes there would still be snow in the southern highlands when the springtime Ember Days had come and passed.

Without looking backwards, Dianora raised a hand. In a moment the castrate had brought her a steaming mug of Tregean khav. Trade restrictions and tariffs, Brandin was fond of saying in private, had to be handled selectively or life could be too acutely marred. Khav was one of the selected things. Only in the palace of course. Outside the walls they drank the inferior products of Corte or neutral Senzio. Once a group of Senzian khav merchants had come as part of a trade embassy to try to persuade him of improvements in the crop they grew and the cup it brewed. *Neutral, indeed,* Brandin had said judiciously, tasting. *So neutral, it hardly seems to be there.*

The merchants had withdrawn, consternated and pale, desperately seeking to divine the hidden meaning in the Ygrathen Tyrant's words. Senzians spent much of their time doing that, Dianora had observed drily to Brandin afterward. He'd laughed. She'd always been able to amuse him, even in the days when she was too young and inexperienced to do it deliberately.

Which thought reminded her of the young castrate attending her this morning. Scelto was in town collecting her gown for the reception that afternoon; her attendant was one of the newest castrates, sent out from Ygrath to serve the growing saishan in the colony.

He was well trained already. Vencel's methods might be harsh, but there was no denying that they worked. She decided not to tell the boy that the khav wasn't strong enough; he would very probably fall to pieces, which would be inconvenient. She'd mention it to Scelto and let him handle the matter. There was no need for Vencel to know: it was useful to have some of the castrates grateful to her as well as afraid. The fear came automatically: a function of who she was here in the saishan. Gratitude or affection she had to work at.

Twelve years and more this spring, she thought again, leaning forward to look down through the screen at the bustling preparations in the square for the arrival of Isolla of Ygrath later that day. At twenty-one she'd been at the peak, she supposed, of whatever beauty she'd been granted. She'd had nothing of such grace at fifteen and sixteen she remembered—they hadn't even bothered to hide her from the Ygrathen soldiers at home.

At nineteen she'd begun to be something else entirely, though by then she wasn't at home and Ygrath was no danger to the residents of Barbadian-ruled Certando. Or not normally, she amended, reminding herself—though this was not, by any means, a thing that really needed a reminder—that she was Dianora di Certando here in the saishan. And across in the west wing as well, in Brandin's bed.

She was thirty-three years old, and somehow with the years that had slipped away so absurdly fast she was one of the powers of this palace. Which, of course, meant of the Palm. In the saishan only Solores di Corte could be said to vie with her for access to Brandin, and Solores was six years older than she was—one of the first year's harvest of the Tribute Ships.

Sometimes, even now, it was all a little too much, a little hard to believe. The younger castrates trembled if she even glanced slantwise at them; courtiers—whether from overseas in Ygrath or here in the four western provinces of the Palm—sought her counsel and support in their petitions to Brandin; musicians wrote songs for her; poets declaimed and dedicated verses that spun into hyperbolic raptures about her beauty and her wisdom. The Ygrathens would liken her to the sisters of their god, the Chiarans to the fabled beauty of Onestra before she did the last Ring Dive for Grand Duke Cazal—though the poets always stopped that analogy well before the Dive itself and the tragedies that followed.

After one such adjective-bestrewn effort of Doarde's

she'd suggested to Brandin over a late, private supper that one of the measures of difference between men and women was that power made men attractive, but when a woman had power that merely made it attractive to praise her beauty.

He'd thought about it, leaning back and stroking his neat beard. She'd been aware of having taken a certain risk, but she'd also known him very well by then.

"Two questions," Brandin, Tyrant of the Western Palm, had asked, reaching for the hand she'd left on the table. "Do you think you have power, my Dianora?"

She'd expected that. "Only through you, and for the little time remaining before I grow old and you cease to grant me access to you." A small slash at Solores there, but discreet enough, she judged. "But so long as you command me to come to you I will be seen to have power in your court, and poets will say I am more lovely now than I ever was. More lovely than the diadem of stars that crowns the crescent of the girdled world . . . or whatever the line was."

"*The curving diadem,* I think he wrote." He smiled. She'd expected a compliment then, for he was generous with those. His grey eyes had remained sober though, and direct. He said, "My second question: Would I be attractive to you without the power that I wield?"

And that, she remembered, had almost caught her out. It was too unexpected a question, and far too near to the place where her twin snakes yet lived, however dormant they might be.

She'd lowered her eyelashes to where their hands were twined. *Like the snakes,* she thought. She backed away quickly from that thought. Looking up, with the sly, sidelong glance she knew he loved, Dianora had said, feigning surprise: "Do you wield power here? I hadn't noticed."

A second later his rich, life-giving laughter had burst forth. The guards outside would hear it, she knew. And they would talk. Everyone in Chiara talked; the Island fed itself on gossip and rumor. There would be another tale after tonight. Nothing new, only a reaffirmation in that shouted laughter of how much pleasure Brandin of Ygrath took in his dark Dianora.

He'd carried her to the bed then, still amused, making her smile and then laugh herself at his mood. He'd taken his pleasure, slowly and in the myriad of ways he'd taught her through the years, for in Ygrath they were versed in such things and he was—then and now—the King of Ygrath, over and above everything else he was.

And she? On her balcony now in the springtime morning sunlight Dianora closed her eyes on the memory of how that night, and before that night—for years and years before that night—and after, after even until now, her own rebel body and heart and mind, traitors together to her soul, had slaked so desperate and deep a need in him.

In Brandin of Ygrath. Whom she had come here to kill twelve years ago, twin snakes around the wreckage of her heart, for having done what he had done to Tigana which was her home.

Or had been her home until he had battered and leveled and burned it and killed a generation and taken away the very sound of its name. Of her own true name.

She was Dianora di Tigana bren Saevar and her father had died at Second Deisa, with an awkwardly-handled sword and not a sculptor's chisel in his hand. Her mother's spirit had snapped like a water reed in the brutality of the occupation that followed, and her brother, whose eyes and hair were exactly like her own, whom she had loved more than her life, had been driven into exile in the wideness of the world. He'd been fifteen years old.

She had no idea where he was all these years after. If he was alive, or dead, or far from this peninsula where tyrants ruled over broken provinces that had once been so proud. Where the name of the proudest of them all was gone from the memory of men.

Because of Brandin. In whose arms she had lain so many nights through the years with such an ache of need, such an arching of desire, every time he summoned her to him. Whose voice was knowledge and wit and grace to her, water in the dryness of her days. Whose laughter when he set it free, when she could draw it forth from him, was like the healing sun slicing out of clouds. Whose grey eyes were the troubling, unreadable color of the sea under the first cold slanting light of morning in spring or fall.

In the oldest of all the stories told in Tigana it was from the grey sea at dawn that Adaon the god had risen and come to Micaela and lain with her on the long, dark, destined curving of the sand. Dianora knew that story as well as she knew her name. Her true name.

She also knew two other things at least as well: that her brother or her father would kill her with their hands if either were alive to see what she had become. And that she would accept that ending and know it was deserved.

Her father was dead. Her heart would scald her at the very thought of her brother so, even if death might spare him a grief so final as seeing where she had come, but each and every morning she prayed to the Triad, especially to Adaon of the Waves, that he was overseas and so far away from where tidings might ever reach him of a Dianora with dark eyes like his own in the saishan of the Tyrant.

Unless, said the quiet voice of her heart, unless the morning might yet come when she could find a way to do a thing here on the Island that would still, despite all that had happened—despite the intertwining of limbs at night and the sound of her own voice crying aloud in need assuaged—bring back another sound into the world. Into the voices of men and women and children all over the Palm, and south over the mountains in Quileia, and north and west and east beyond all the seas.

The sound of the name of Tigana, gone. Gone, but not, if the goddesses and the god were kind—if there was any love left in them, or pity—not forever forgotten or forever lost.

And perhaps—and this was Dianora's dream on the nights she slept alone, after Scelto had massaged and oiled her skin and had gone away with his candle to sleep outside her door—perhaps it would come to pass that if she could indeed find a way to do this thing, that her brother, far from home, would miraculously hear the name of Tigana spoken by a stranger in a world of strangers, in some distant royal court or bazaar, and somehow he would know, in a rush of wonder and joy, in the deep core of the heart she knew so well, that it was through her doing that the name was in the world again.

She would be dead by then. She had no doubts as to that. Brandin's hate in this one thing—in the matter of his vengeance for Stevan—was fixed and unalterable. It was the one set star in the firmament of all the lands he ruled.

She would be dead, but it would be all right, for Tigana's name would be restored, and her brother would be alive and would know it had been she, and Brandin . . . Brandin would understand that she had found a way to do this thing while sparing his life on all the nights, the numberless nights, when she could have slain him while he slept by her side after love.

This was Dianora's dream. She used to be driven awake, tears cold on her cheeks, by the intensity of the feelings it engendered. No one ever saw those tears but Scelto though, and Scelto she trusted more than anyone alive.

She heard his quick light footsteps at the doorway and then briskly crossing the floor toward her balcony. No one else in the saishan moved like Scelto. The castrates were notoriously prone to lassitude and to eating too much—the obvious substitutions for pleasure. Not Scelto, though. Slim as he'd been when she met him, he still sought out those errands the other castrates strove to avoid: trips up into the steep streets of the old town, or even farther north into the hills or partway up Sangarios itself in search of healing herbs or leaves or simply meadow flowers for her room.

He seemed ageless, but he hadn't been young when Vencel assigned him to Dianora and she guessed that he must be sixty now. If Vencel ever died—a hard thing to imagine, in fact—Scelto was certainly next in line to succeed him as head of the saishan.

They had never spoken about it, but Dianora knew, as surely as she knew anything, that he would refuse the position if it were offered to him, in order to remain bound to her. She also knew—and this was the thing that touched her—that this would be true even if Brandin stopped sending for her entirely and she became merely another aging ignored item of history in the saishan wing.

And this was the second thing she'd never expected to find when hate had carried her through autumn seas to Chiara on the Tribute Ship: kindness and caring and a friend behind the high walls and ornate screens of the place where women waited among men who had lost their manhood.

Scelto's tread, rapid even after the long climb up the Great Staircase and then another flight up to the saishan, clicked across the mosaics of the balcony floor behind her. She heard him murmur kindly to the boy and dismiss him.

He took another step forward and coughed once, to announce himself.

"Is it terribly hideous?" she asked without turning around.

"It will do," Scelto said, coming to stand beside her. She looked over, smiling to see his close-cropped grey hair, the thin, precise mouth, and the terribly broken hook of his nose. Ages ago, he'd said when she'd asked. A fight over a woman back in Ygrath. He'd killed the other man, who happened to be a noble. Which unfortunate fact had cost Scelto his sex and his liberty and brought him here. Dianora had been more disturbed by the story than he seemed to be. On the other hand, she remembered thinking, it had been new to her, while for him it was only the familiar coinage of his life, from a long time past.

He held up the dark red gown they'd had made in the old town. From his smile which matched her own Dianora knew it had been worth cajoling Vencel for the funds to have this done. The head of the saishan would want a favor later, he always did, but through such exchanges was the saishan run, and Dianora, looking at the gown, had no regrets.

"What is Solores wearing?" she asked.

"Hala wouldn't tell me," Scelto murmured regretfully.

Dianora laughed aloud at the straight face he managed to maintain. "I'm quite sure he wouldn't," she said. "What is she wearing?"

"Green," he said promptly. "High waisted, high neck.

Two shades in pleats below the waist. Gold sandals. A great deal of gold everywhere else. Her hair will be up, of course. She has new earrings."

Dianora laughed again. Scelto allowed himself a tiny smile of satisfaction. "I took the liberty," he added, "of purchasing something else while I was in town."

He reached into a fold of his tunic and handed her a small box. She opened it and wordlessly held up the gem inside. In the bright morning light of the balcony it dazzled and shone like a third red moon to join Vidomni and blue Ilarion.

Scelto said, "I thought it would be better with the gown than anything Vencel would offer you from the saishan jewels."

She shook her head wonderingly. "It is beautiful, Scelto. Can we afford this? Will I have to go without chocolate for all of the spring and summer?"

"Not a bad idea," he said, ignoring her first question. "You ate two pieces this morning while I was gone."

"Scelto!" she exclaimed. "Stop that! Go spy on Solores and see what she's spending her chiaros on. I have my habits and my pleasures, and none of them, so far as I can see, are particularly evil. Do I look fat to you?"

Almost reluctantly he shook his head. "I have no idea why not," he murmured ruefully.

"Well you keep thinking about it till you figure it out," she said with a toss of her head. "In the meantime, that reminds me—the boy this morning was fine, except that the khav was very weak. Will you speak to him about how I like it?"

"I did. I told him to make it a little weak."

"You *what*? Scelto, I absolutely—"

"You always begin drinking more khav at the end of winter, when the weather begins to turn, and every spring you always have trouble sleeping at night. You know this is true, my lady. Either fewer cups or weaker khav. It is my duty to try to keep you rested and tranquil."

Dianora was speechless for a second. "Tranquil!" she finally managed to exclaim. "I might have frightened that poor child to the tips of his fingernails. I would have felt *terrible*!"

"I had told him what to say," Scelto said placidly. "He would have blamed it on me."

"Oh, really. And what if I'd reported it directly to Vencel, instead?" Dianora retorted. "Scelto, he would have had that boy starved and lashed."

Scelto's dignified little sniff conveyed quite clearly what he thought about the likelihood of her having done any such thing.

His expression was so wryly knowing that, against her will, Dianora found herself laughing again. "Very well," she said, surrendering. "Then let it be fewer cups, because I do like it strong, Scelto. It isn't worth the drinking otherwise. Besides, I don't think that's why I can't sleep at night. This season simply makes me restless."

"You were taken as Tribute in the spring," he murmured. "Everyone in the saishan is restless in the season they were taken." He hesitated. "I can't do anything about that, my lady. But I thought perhaps the khav might be making it worse." There was concern and affection in his brown eyes, almost as dark as her own.

"You worry too much about me," she said after a moment.

He smiled. "Who else should I worry about?" There was a little silence; Dianora could hear the noises from far below in the square.

"Speaking of worrying," said Scelto in a transparent effort to change the mood, "we may be concentrating too much on what Solores is doing. We may want to start keeping an eye on the young one with the green eyes."

"Iassica?" Dianora said, surprised. "What ever for? Brandin hasn't even called her to him and she's been here a month already."

"Exactly," said Scelto. He paused, somewhat awkwardly, which piqued her curiosity.

"What are you saying, Scelto?"

"I, um, have been told by Tesios who has been looking after her that he has never seen or heard of a woman in the saishan with such . . . control of her body or such . . . capacity for the climax of love."

He was blushing furiously, which made Dianora abruptly self-conscious too. It was a standard practice—with some quite unstandard variations—for the women of the saishan

to use their castrates to give them physical release if too
much time went by between summonses to the other
wing.

Dianora had never asked Scelto for such a service.
Something about the very idea disturbed her: it seemed
an abuse, in a way she couldn't articulate. He had been a
man, she reminded herself frequently, who had killed
someone for love of a woman. Their relationship, close
as it was, had never entered that dimension. It was strange,
she thought, even amusing, how shy they could both
become at the very mention of the subject—and Triad
knew it came up often enough in the hothouse atmosphere of the saishan.

She turned back to the railing, looking down through
the screen, to give him time to regain his composure.
Thinking about what he'd said though, she found herself
feeling a certain amusement after all. She was already
working out how and when to tell Brandin about this.

"My friend," she said, "you may know me well, but in
exactly the same way and for many of the same reasons I
know Brandin very well."

She glanced back at her castrate. "He is older than
you, Scelto—he is almost sixty-five—and for reasons I
don't entirely understand he has said he must live here in
the Palm another sixty years or so. All the sorcery in the
world would surely not avail him to prolong his life that
long if Iassica is as . . . exceptional as Tesios suggests.
She would wear him out, however pleasantly, in a year or
two."

Scelto blushed again, and glanced quickly back over
his shoulder. They were quite alone though. Dianora
laughed, partly out of genuine amusement, but more
specifically to mask the recurring sorrow she felt whenever this one lie had to be told: the thing she still kept
from Scelto. The one secret that mattered.

Of *course* she knew why Brandin needed to stay here
in the Palm, why he needed to use his sorcery to prolong
his life here in what was surely a place of exile for him in
a land of grief.

He had to wait for everyone born in Tigana to die.

Only then could he leave the peninsula where his son
had been slain. Only then would the full measure of the

vengeance he had decreed be poured out on the bloodied ground. For no one would be left alive in the world who had any true memory of Tigana before the fall, of Avalle of the Towers, the songs and the stories and the legends, all the long, bright history.

It would truly be gone then. Wiped out. Seventy or eighty years wreaking as comprehensive an obliteration as millennia had on the ancient civilizations no one could now recall. Whole cultures that were now only an awkwardly pronounced name of a place, or a deciphered, pompous title—Emperor of All the Earth—on a broken pottery shard.

Brandin could go home after sixty years. He could do whatever he chose. By then she would be long dead and so too would be those from Tigana even younger than she, those born up to the very year of the conquest—the last inheritors.

The last children who could hear and read the name of the land that had been their own. Eighty years, Brandin was giving himself. More than enough, given lifespans in the Palm.

Eighty years to oblivion. To the broken, meaningless pottery shard. The books were gone already, and the paintings, tapestries, sculptures, music: torn or smashed or burned in the terrible year after Valentin's fall when Brandin had come down upon them in the agony of a father's loss, bringing them the reciprocal agony of a conqueror's hate.

The worst year of Dianora's life. Seeing so much of beauty and splendor crumble to rubble and dust or burn down to ashes of loss. She'd been fifteen, then sixteen. Still too young to comprehend the full reality of what was being eradicated. For her father's death and the destruction of his art—the works of his hands and days—she could mourn bitterly. And so too for the deaths of friends and the sudden terrors of an occupied impoverished city. The larger losses, the implications for the future, she couldn't really grasp back then.

Many in the city had gone mad that year.

Others had fled, taking their children away to try to shape a life far from the burning or the memory of burning, of hammers smashing into the statues of the

Princes in the long covered loggia of the Palace by the
Sea. Some had withdrawn so far into themselves—a madness of another kind—that only the merest spark was left
within to make them eat and sleep and somehow walk
through the waste spaces of their days.

Her mother had been one of those.

On the balcony in Chiara so many years later, Dianora
looked up at Scelto and realized, from the blinking concern in his face, that she'd been silent for too long.

She forced a smile. She'd been here for a long time;
she was good at dissembling. At smiling when it was
needful. Even with Scelto whom she hated to deceive.
And especially with Brandin, whom she had to deceive,
or die.

"Iassica is not a concern," she said mildly, resuming
the conversation as if nothing had happened. Indeed,
nothing *had* happened—only old memories come back.
Nothing of weight or import in the world, nothing that
mattered or could matter. Only loss.

She said, skillfully laughing, "She is far too unintelli-
gent to divert him and too young to relax him as Solores
does. I'm glad of your information though—I think we
can use it. Tell me, is Tesios growing weary tending her?
Should I speak to Vencel about assigning someone younger? Or perhaps more than one?"

She made him smile, even as he flushed again. It
always seemed to go this way. If she could make them
smile or laugh it would brush away the clouds like a
wind, a springtime or an autumn wind, leaving behind
the high clear blue of the sky.

Dianora wished, with an aching heart, that she'd known
how to do that eighteen years ago. For her mother and
her brother. For both of them so long ago. No laughter
then. No laughter anywhere, and the blue skies a mockery, looking down upon ruin.

Vencel, more awesomely obese every time she saw him,
approved Solores's gown, Nesaia's, Chylmoene's, and
then her own. Only the four of them—experienced enough
to know how to cope with the exigencies of a formal
reception—were going down to the Audience Chamber.
The envy in the saishan during the past week had been

acute enough to produce a scent, Scelto had said wryly more than once. Dianora hadn't noticed; she was used to it.

Vencel's shrewd eyes widened from deep in the manifold creases of his dark face as he studied her. She had the gem on her brow, set in a band of white gold that held back her hair. Sprawled on his couch of pillows, the head of the saishan played with the billowing folds of his elephantine white robe. The sun shining through the arch of a window behind him glinted distractingly from his bald head.

"I do not recall that stone among our treasures," he murmured in his high, disconcerting voice. It was a voice so utterly inconsequential that it might lead one to underestimate the speaker. Which, as a good many people had discovered over the years, was a serious, sometimes a mortal mistake.

"It isn't," Dianora replied cheerfully. "Though after we return this afternoon may I ask you to guard it in my name among the other treasures?"

Scelto's suggestion, that. Vencel could be corrupt and venal about a great many things, but not when it came to the formal aspects of his office. He was too clever for that. Again, a truth some had paid the ultimate price to discover.

He nodded benignly now. "It seems a very fine stone from this distance." Obediently, Dianora stepped nearer and inclined her head graciously to let him see it more clearly. The scent of tainflowers that he always wore after winter's end enveloped her. It was too sweet, but not unpleasant.

She had feared Vencel once—a fear mixed of physical revulsion at his grossness and rumors of the things he liked to do with the younger castrates and some of the women who were in the saishan for purely political reasons, with no hope of ever seeing the outside world or the west wing of the palace and Brandin's chambers. Long ago though she and the saishan head had reached their understanding. Solores had the same unspoken pact with Vencel, and out of the delicate balance achieved thereby the three of them controlled, as best they could, their enclosed, over-intense, incense-laden world of idle, frustrated women, and half-men.

With a surprisingly delicate finger Vencel touched the gem on her brow. He smiled. "A good stone," he said again, this time in judgment. His breath was fragrant. "I must talk to Scelto about it. I know about such things, you see. Vairstones come from the north, you see. From my own land. They are mined in Khardhun. For years and years I used to play with them as trinkets, a monarch's toys. In the days when I was more than I am now. For as you know, I have been a King in Khardhun."

Dianora nodded gravely. For this too was a part of the unspoken terms of her relationship with Vencel. That however many times he might speak this wild fabrication of a lie—and he said it many times a day, in one variant or another—she was to nod knowingly, reflectively, as if pondering the message hidden in the grandeur of his fall.

Only in her rooms alone with Scelto could she give way to fits of girlish giggling at the very thought of the vasty saishan head being *more* than he was now, or at the subversive, deadly imitation Scelto could give of Vencel's speech and gestures.

"You do that wonderfully," she might say innocently, as Scelto dressed her hair, or polished her curved slippers till they shone.

"It is a thing I know about, you see," he would reply if certain they were alone, his voice pitched high above its normal range. He would gesticulate slowly, expansively. "For as you are aware, I have been a King in Khardhun."

She would laugh like a little girl who knew just how naughty she was being, the more out of control because of that very fact.

She had asked Brandin about it once. His Khardhun campaign had been only a marginal success, she learned. He was frank with her about such things by then. There was real magic in Khardhun, in that hot northern land across the sea, beyond the coastal villages and the desert wastes. A magic far greater than anything in the Peninsula of the Palm and equal to the sorcery of Ygrath.

Brandin had taken one city and established a tenuous control over some lands that lay on the fringes of the great desert stretching north. There had been losses though, serious losses she gathered. The Khardhu had long been celebrated for their skill in battle, nor was this unknown in the Palm: many of them had served as well-paid mercenaries in the warring provinces before the Tyrants had come and made all such feuding irrelevant.

Vencel had been a herald captured late in the campaign, Brandin told her. He'd already been unmanned: a thing they did to messengers in the north, for no reason Brandin had understood. It had been manifestly evident where the castrate belonged when brought back to Ygrath. He had already, Brandin confirmed, been enormous.

Dianora straightened as Vencel withdrew his finger from the red gleam of the vairstone.

"Will you escort us down?" she asked. A ritual.

"I think not," he said judiciously, as if actually giving thought to the matter. "Perhaps Scelto and Hala can manage that office between them. I have some matters that need my attention here this afternoon, you see."

"I understand." Dianora glanced over at Solores and each of them raised a spread palm in respectful salute. In fact, Vencel hadn't left the saishan wing in at least five years. Even when he toured the rooms on this floor it was on a cleverly contrived rolling platform of cushions. Dianora could not remember the last time she'd actually seen him stand upright. Scelto and Solores's Hala attended to virtually all the formal out-of-saishan duties. Vencel believed in delegating.

They went down the stairway that led out from the saishan to the world. One flight below they accepted the scrutiny—respectful but careful—of the two guards posted outside the heavy bronze doors that barred access to and from the level where the women were. Dianora responded to their cautious glances with a smile. One of them returned it shyly. The guards were changed often; she didn't know either of these two, but a smile was a start at bonding and a friend never hurt.

Scelto and Hala, dressed unobtrusively in brown, led the four women out of the saishan wing along the main corridor of the palace to the Grand Staircase in the center. There the two castrates paused to let the women precede them. With some pride but not with hauteur—they were the captives and concubines of a conqueror—

Dianora and Solores led the way down the sweeping stair.

They were noticed of course. The women of the saishan were always noticed when they came out. There were a number of people milling about in the marbled vestibule waiting to enter the Audience Chamber; they made way for the four of them. Some of the newer men smiled in a manner that had taken Dianora some time to accept.

Others knew her better and their expressions were rather different. In the arched doorway to the largest of the formal reception rooms she and Solores paused again side by side, this time entirely for effect—the blood-red gown beside the green—and then walked together into the crowded room of state.

As she did so—every single time she did so—Dianora offered an inward voicing of gratitude for the impulse that had led Brandin to change the rules for his saishan here in the colony he now ruled.

In Ygrath, she knew, this would never have been allowed. For a man other than the King or one of the castrates to see, let alone hold converse with a saishan woman was death for both of them. And, Vencel had told her once, for the head of the saishan wing as well.

Things had been different here in Chiara almost from the start. Over the years Dianora had learned enough to know that some of her gratitude should go to Dorotea, Queen of Ygrath, and her decision to remain there with Girald, her elder son, and not accompany her husband into his self-imposed exile abroad. Dorotea's choice, or, depending on to whom one listened, Brandin's decision not to demand the company of his Queen.

Somewhat instinctively Dianora always preferred the latter version of the story, but she was wise enough to know why that was so, and this was one of the things she never spoke about with Brandin. Not that the matter was taboo; he wasn't that kind of man. It was simply that she wasn't sure if or how she could deal with whatever answer he gave her if the question was ever asked.

In any case, with Dorotea remaining in Ygrath there were few high-born court ladies willing to risk the seas and the Queen's displeasure in journeying to the colony in the Palm. Which meant an extreme scarcity of women at Brandin's new court in Chiara, and this, in turn, led to a change in the role of the saishan. The more so since— especially in the early years—Brandin had deliberately ordered the Tribute Ships to search out daughters of distinguished houses in Corte or Asoli. On Chiara he made the choices himself. From Lower Corte, which had once borne a different name, he took no women at all, as a matter of absolute policy. The hatred there ran both ways and too deep, and the saishan was not a place to let it fester.

He'd sent for only a few of the women from his saishan in Ygrath, leaving it largely intact. The politics were straightforward: control of the saishan was a symbol that would confirm the status and authority of Girald, now ruling as Regent of Ygrath in his father's name.

With such changes here in the colony, the new saishan was a very different place from the old; Vencel and Scelto had both told her that. It had another kind of mood to it, a different character entirely.

It also had, among all those women from Corte and Chiara and Asoli and the handful from Ygrath, one woman named Dianora, from Certando. From Barbadian-ruled Certando.

Or so everyone in the palace thought.

It had almost started a war, Dianora remembered.

In the days after her brother left home, sixteen-year-old Dianora di Tigana, daughter of a sculptor who had died in the war, and of a mother who had scarcely spoken since that day, resolved that she would point her own life towards the killing of the Tyrant on Chiara.

Hardening herself, the way she heard that men in battle were forced to do—the way her father must have tried to do by the Deisa—she had begun preparing to leave her mother in the hollow, echoing house that had once been a place crowded with joy. Where the Prince of Tigana had walked in their courtyard, an arm flung about her father's shoulders, discussing and praising the works in progress there.

Dianora could remember.

Entering the Audience Chamber she checked and approved her reflection in the wall of gold-plated mirrors on the far side of the room, then her eyes sought, instinctively, those of d'Eymon of Ygrath, the Chancellor. The second most powerful man in the court.

He was, predictably, already looking towards Solores and herself, his glance precisely as bleak as it always was. It was a look that had bothered Dianora when first she came. She'd thought d'Eymon had taken a dislike to her, or, worse, that he somehow suspected her. It wasn't long before she realized that he disliked and suspected virtually every person who entered this palace. Everyone received the same glacial, appraising scrutiny. It had been exactly so, she gathered, in Ygrath as well. D'Eymon's loyalty to Brandin was fanatical and unwavering, and so was his zeal in protecting his King.

Over the years Dianora had developed a respect, grudging at first, and then less so, for the grim Ygrathen. She counted it as one of her own triumphs that he seemed to trust her now. For years now—in fact—or she would never have been allowed to spend a night in Brandin's bed while he slept.

A triumph of deception, she thought, with an irony whose teeth were all directed inward against herself.

D'Eymon made an economical circling motion with his head and then repeated the gesture for Solores. It was what they had expected: they were to mingle and converse. Neither of them was to take the chair set beside the Island Throne. They did sometimes—and so had the beautiful, unlamented Chloese before her surprising, untimely death—but Brandin was quite punctilious when guests from Ygrath were among them. At such times the seat beside him stood pointedly empty. For Dorotea, his Queen.

Brandin had not yet entered the room of course, but Dianora saw Rhun, the slack-limbed balding Fool shamble towards one of the servers carrying wine. Rhun, clumsy, grievously retarded, was clad sumptuously in gold and white, and so Dianora knew that Brandin would be as well. It was an integral part of the complex relationship of the Sorcerer Kings of Ygrath and their chosen Fools.

For centuries in Ygrath the Fool had served as shadow and projection for the King. He was dressed like his monarch, ate next to him at public functions, was there when honors were conferred or judgment passed. And every King's chosen Fool was someone visibly, sometimes painfully afflicted or malformed. Rhun's walk was sluggish, his features twisted and deformed, his hands dangled at awkward angles in repose, his speech was badly slurred. He recognized people in the court, but not invariably, and not always in the manner one might expect—which sometimes carried a message. A message from the King.

That part, Dianora didn't entirely comprehend, and doubted she ever would. She knew that Rhun's dim, limited mind was mostly under his own control but she also knew that that was not completely so. There was sorcery at work in this: the subtle magic of Ygrath.

This much she understood: that in addition to serving— very graphically—to remind their King of his mortality and his own limitations, the Fools of Ygrath, dressed exactly like their lord, could sometimes also serve as a voice, an external conduit, for the thoughts and emotions of the King.

Which meant that one could not always be sure whether Rhun's words and actions—slurred or awkward as they might be—were his own, or an important revelation of Brandin's mood. And that could be treacherous ground for the unwary.

Right now Rhun seemed smiling and content, bobbing and bowing jerkily at every second person he encountered, his golden cap slipping off every time. He would laugh though, as he bent to pick it up and set it again on his thinning hair. Every so often an over-anxious courtier, seeking to curry favor in any way he could, would hastily stoop to pick up the fallen cap and present it to the Fool. Rhun would laugh at that too.

Dianora had to admit that he made her uneasy, though she tried to hide that beneath the real pity she felt for his afflictions and his increasingly evident years. But the core truth for her was that Rhun was intimately tied to Brandin's magic, he was an extension of it, a tool, and Brandin's magic was the source of all her loss and fear. And her guilt.

So over the years she had become adroit at avoiding situations where she might find herself alone with the

Fool; his guileless eyes—unnervingly similar to Brandin's—
gave her genuine trouble. They seemed, if she looked
into them for too long, to have no depth, to be only a
surface, reflecting her image back to her in a fashion very
different from that of the gold-plated mirrors, and at
such times she did not like what she was made to see.

From the doorway, with the polished grace of long
experience, Solores drifted to her right as Dianora moved
left, smiling at people she knew. Nesaia and Chylmoene,
chestnut- and amber-tressed, crossed the floor together,
creating a palpable stir where they passed.

Dianora saw the poet Doarde standing with his wife
and daughter. The girl, about seventeen, was obviously
excited. Her first formal reception, Dianora guessed.
Doarde smiled unctuously across the room at her, and
bowed elaborately. Even at a distance, though, she could
read the discomfiture in his eyes: a reception on this scale
for a musician from Ygrath had to be bitter gall for the
most senior poet in the colony. All winter he had preened
with pride over his verses that Brandin had sent east as a
goad for the Barbadian when word had come in the fall
of the death of Sandre d'Astibar. Doarde had been insuf-
ferable for months. Today though, Dianora could sympathize with him a little, even though he was a monumental
fraud in her view.

She'd told Brandin as much once, only to learn that he
found the poet's pompousness amusing. For genuine art,
he'd murmured, he looked elsewhere.

And you destroyed it, she'd wanted to say.

Wanted so much to say. Remembering with an almost
physical pain the broken head and sundered torso of her
father's last *Adaon* on the steps of the Palace by the Sea.
The one for which her brother, finally old enough, had
served as model for the young god. She remembered
looking dry-eyed at the wreckage of that sculpted form,
wanting to weep and not knowing where her tears were
anymore.

She glanced back at Doarde's daughter, at her young,
scarcely contained exhilaration. Seventeen.

Just after her own seventeenth naming day she had
stolen half of the silver from her father's hidden strong-
box, begging pardon of his spirit and her mother's bless-

ing in her heart, and asking the compassion of Eanna who saw all beneath the shining of her lights.

She'd gone without saying good-bye, though she had looked in a last time by carried candlelight, upon the thin, worn figure of her mother, uneasily asleep in the wideness of her bed. Dianora was hardened, as for battle; she did not weep.

Four days later she'd crossed the border into Certando, having forded the river at a lonely place north of Avalle. She'd had to be careful getting there—Ygrathen soldiers were still ranging the countryside and in Avalle itself they were hammering at the towers, bringing them down. Some yet stood, she could see them from her crossing-place, but most were rubble by then, and what she saw of Avalle was through a screen of smoke.

It wasn't even Avalle by then, either. The spell had been laid down. Brandin's magic. The city where the pall of smoke and summer dust hung so heavily was now called Stevanien. Dianora could remember not being able to understand how a man could name the ugly wreckage of a place once so fair after a child he had loved. Later that would become clearer to her: the name had nothing to do with Brandin's memory of Stevan. It was solely for those living there, and elsewhere in what had been Tigana: a constant, inescapable reminder of whose death had meant their ruin. The Tiganese now lived in a province named Lower Corte—and Corte had been their bitterest foe for centuries. The city of Tigana was the city of Lower Corte now.

And Avalle of the Towers was Stevanien. The vengeance of the King of Ygrath went deeper than occupation and burning and rubble and death. It encompassed names and memory, the fabric of identity; it was a subtle thing, and merciless.

There were a number of refugees in the summer Dianora went east, but none had anything remotely resembling her own fixed purpose and so most of them went much further away: to the far side of the Certandan grainlands, to Ferraut, Tregea, Astibar itself. Willing, anxious even, to live under the spreading tyranny of the Barbadian lord in order to put as much distance as they could between

themselves and their images of what Brandin of Ygrath
had done to their home.

But Dianora was clinging to those images, she was
nursing them within her breast, feeding them with hate,
shaping hatred with memory. Twin snakes inside her.

She only went a handful of miles across the border into
Certando. The late-summer fields of corn had been yel-
low and tall, she remembered, but all the men were
gone, away to the north and east where Alberico of
Barbadior, having carefully consolidated his conquests of
Ferraut and Astibar, was now moving south.

He was master of Certando by the end of the fall, and
had taken Borifort in Tregea—the last major stronghold
to stand against him—by the following spring after a
winter siege.

Long before then Dianora had found what she was
looking for, in the western highlands of Certando. A
hamlet—twenty houses and a tavern—south of Sinave
and Forese, the two great forts that watched each other
on either side of the border that divided Certando from
what she learned to call Lower Corte.

The land so near the southern mountains was not nearly
as good as it was farther north. The growing season was
shorter. Cold winds swept down from the Braccio and
Sfaroni Ranges early in fall bringing snow soon after and
a long white winter. Wolves would howl in the wintry
nights and sometimes in the morning strange footmarks
could be found in the deep snow—marks that came down
from the mountains and then returned.

Once, long ago, the village had been near to one of the
roads forking northeast from the main highway down
from the Sfaroni Pass—in the days when there was still
overland trade with Quileia to the south. That was why
the ancient tavern was so large in a village now so small,
why it had four rooms upstairs for the travelers who had
not come for a great many years.

Dianora hid her father's silver south of the village on a
thickly wooded slope away from the goatherd runs, and
she went to work as a serving girl in the tavern. There
was no money to pay her of course. She worked for her
room and the scanty board available that first summer
and fall, and she labored in the fields with the other

women and the young boys to bring home what they could of the harvest.

She told them she was from the north, near Ferraut. That her mother was dead and her father and brother had gone to war. She said her uncle had begun to abuse her and so she had run away. She was good with accents and she had the northern speech right enough for them to believe her. Or at least to ask no questions. There were many transients in the Palm in those days, questions were seldom pushed too far. She ate little and worked as hard as any in the fields. There was actually little enough to do in the inn, with the men away to war. She slept in one of the rooms upstairs, she even had it to herself. They were kind enough to her after their fashion, and given the nature of things in that time.

When the light and the place were right—morning usually, and in certain of the higher fields—she could look away to the west across the border towards the river and see the remaining towers and the smoke above what had been Avalle. One morning, late in the year, she realized that she couldn't see anything anymore. That she hadn't, in fact, seen anything for some time. The last tower was gone.

Around that time the men had begun to come home, beaten and weary. There was work again in the kitchen and waiting on tables or behind the counter of the bar. She was also expected—and had been preparing herself for this as best she could all through the fall—to take a man up to her room if he offered the going rate.

Every village seemed to need one such woman, and she was the obvious candidate here. She tried to make herself not mind, but this was the most difficult thing yet. She had a mission though, a reason for being here, a vengeance to enact, and this, even this, she would tell herself, going up the stairs with someone, was a part of it. She hardened herself, but not always, and not quite enough.

Perhaps that showed through. Several men asked her to marry them. One day she caught herself thinking about one of them as she wiped down the tables after lunch. He was quiet and kind, shy when he took her

upstairs, and his eyes would follow her movements in the
tavern with a fierce concentration whenever he was there.

That day was when she knew it was time for her to
leave.

She was a little surprised to realize that almost three
years had gone by. It was spring.

She slipped away one night, again without a farewell,
remembering her arrival even as she went. Meadow flowers were blooming beside the path into the hills. The air
was clean and mild. By the mingled light of the two
moons she found her buried silver and walked away
without looking back, taking the road north towards the
fort at Sinave. She was nineteen years old.

Nineteen, and sometime in the past two years she had
grown beautiful. Her angular boniness had softened, even
as her face lost its last traces of girlhood. It was oval,
wide at the cheekbones, almost austere. It changed when
she laughed though—and for some reason she still knew
how to laugh—becoming warm and animated, the unexpected dance in her dark eyes seeming to promise things
that went deeper than amusement. Men who had seen
her laughing or who had caused her to smile at them
would encounter that look again in their dreams, or in
the memories that lay on the border of sleep and dream,
years after Dianora had gone away.

At Sinave the Barbadians disturbed her, with their oppressive size and careless, casual brutality. She forced
herself to be calm and to linger there. Two weeks would
be enough she judged. She had to leave an impression
and a memory.

A carefully constructed memory of an ambitious, pretty
country girl from some hamlet near the mountains. A girl
usually silent during the tavern talk at night but who,
when she did speak, told vivid, memorable tales of her
home village to the south. Told them with the distinc-
tively laconic diction and round vowels that would have
marked her anywhere in the Palm as being from the
highlands of Certando.

The tales were usually sad—most stories were in those
years—but once in a while Dianora would offer a wonderfully droll imitation of some highland rustic voicing
his considered opinion on great affairs in the wider world,

and those at the table where she was sitting would laugh for a long time.

She appeared to them to have some money, earned very likely in the way that pretty girls usually came to have some money. But she shared a room with another woman at the better of the two hostelries within the walls of the fort, and neither of them was ever seen to invite a man upstairs. Or to accept an invitation to go elsewhere. The Barbadian soldiers might have been a problem—indeed they had been over the winter—but orders had come from Astibar, and the mercenaries were under a tighter rein that spring.

What she wanted to do, Dianora confided one night to the loosely knit group of young men and women she had joined, was to work in a tavern or dining-place that saw a better class of person coming through its doors. She'd had two hands full and more, thank you, of the other sort of inn, she declared.

Someone mentioned The Queen in Stevanien, across the border in Lower Corte.

With a heartfelt, inward sigh of relief Dianora began asking questions about it.

Questions to which she'd known the answers for three days; during which time she'd sat among these selfsame people every night planting subtle hints in the hope that the name might emerge spontaneously. Subtlety, she'd finally decided, was wasted among young Certandans here on the border, and so she'd practically had to drag the conversation over to the subject she wanted.

Now she listened, seemingly enraptured and wide-eyed, as two of her recent acquaintances animatedly described the newest, most elegant Ygrathen innovation in Lower Corte. A dining-place that boasted a master chef brought all the way from Ygrath itself by the current Governor of Stevanien and its distrada. The Governor, it emerged, was notoriously fond of wine and food, and of good music played in comfortable chambers. He had helped establish the new chef in a set of rooms on the ground floor of a former banking-house, and now he basked in the reflected glory of the most elaborate, most luxurious eating-place in the Palm. He dined there himself several times a week, Dianora learned.

For the second time.

She'd picked up all of this in gossip among the merchants during her days checking out the prices and styles of clothing available in Fort Sinave. She needed some things fit for the city, she knew. It might make a difference.

From the very first time she'd heard the name she'd realized that The Queen would be perfect for the next stage of her plan to change her past.

What she learned from the merchants was that no one from Lower Corte was allowed to dine here. Traders from Corte were cordially greeted, as were those from farther afield, in Asoli or Chiara itself. Any Ygrathen, naturally, soldier, merchant or whoever he might be—come to seek his fortune in the newest colony—was graciously ushered in to salute the portrait of Queen Dorotea that hung on the wall opposite the door. Even those merchants crossing the line that divided the Eastern Palm from the West were more than welcome to leave some of whatever currency they carried in The Queen.

It was only the King's true enemies, the denizens of Lower Corte, of Stevanien itself, who were forbidden to stain or sully the ambience with their pustulent, heir-murdering presence.

They never did, Dianora learned from a Ferraut trader bound back north and east with leather from Stevanien that he expected to sell at a profit, even with that year's tariff levels. What the inhabitants of Stevanien had done in response to the ban was simply refuse to work for the new establishment. Neither as servers or kitchen help or stable hands, nor even as musicians or artisans to help decorate and maintain the splendid rooms.

The Governor, when he learned what was happening, had vowed in red-faced rage to force the contemptible inhabitants to work wherever they were required by their masters of Ygrath. Force them with dungeon and lash and a death-wheel or three if needed.

The master chef, Arduini, had demurred.

One did not, Arduini had said, in a much-quoted display of artistic temperament, build up and maintain an establishment of quality by using enforced, surly labor. His standards were simply too high for that. Even the stable-boys at *his* restaurant, said Arduini of Ygrath, were to be trained and willing, and to have a certain *style* to them.

There had been widespread hilarity when that was reported: stylish stable-hands, indeed. But, Dianora learned, the amusement had turned to respect quite soon, because Arduini, pretentious or not, did know what he was doing. The Queen, the Ferraut trader told her, was like an oasis amid the deserts of Khardhun. In dispirited, broken Stevanien it cast a warm glow of Ygrathen civility and grace. The merchant lamented, though discreetly on this side of the border, the complete absence of any such traits in the Barbadians who had occupied his own province.

But yes, he said, in response to Dianora's apparently casual question, Arduini was still struggling with staff problems. Stevanien was a backwater, and a backwater, moreover, in the most oppressively taxed and militarily subjugated province in the Palm. It was next to impossible to get people to travel there, or stay, and since none of the trickle of adventurers from Ygrath had come so far from home to wash dishes or clear tables or tend to a stable—however stylish a stable it might be—there appeared to be a chronic need for workers from elsewhere in the Palm.

In that moment Dianora had changed every plan she had. She cast the line of her life, with a silent prayer to Adaon, in the direction of this chance information. She had been intending, with some real apprehension, to go northwest to Corte. That had always been the next-to-last destination in her plans. She had seriously wondered, almost every night as she lay awake, whether three years in Certando would be enough to shake off anyone pursuing the true history of her life. She'd had no good ideas about what else she could do, though.

Now she did.

And so it was that a few nights later, in the largest of the taverns in Fort Sinave, a cheerful crowd of young people watched their new friend drink more than was good for her for the first time since she'd arrived. More than one of the men saw cause for cautious optimism in that, with respect to possibilities later in the evening.

"You've settled it then!" Dianora cried in her attractive, south-country voice. She leaned for support against the shoulder of a bemused cartwright. "Hand to the new plow for me tomorrow. I'm over the border as soon as I can to visit The Queen of Ygrath! Triad bless her days!"

Triad shelter and hold my soul, she was thinking as she spoke, absolutely sober, cold to her bones with the sense of the words she was so glibly shouting.

They silenced her, laughing uproariously—in part to cover her words. In Barbadian Certando it was a long way from the path of wisdom to thus salute Ygrath's Queen. Dianora giggled quite endearingly but she subsided. The cartwright and another man tried to see her up to her room afterwards, but found themselves charmingly put off and drinking together amid off-duty mercenaries in the one all-night tavern Fort Sinave possessed.

She was just a little too untutored, too *country,* to succeed in her ambitious hopes, they agreed sagely. They also agreed, a few drinks later, that she had the most extraordinarily appealing smile. Something about her eyes, what happened to them when she was pleased.

In the morning Dianora was dressed and packed and waiting very early at the main gate of the fort. She struck a bargain for passage to Stevanien with a pleasant-enough middle-aged merchant from Senzio carrying Barbadian spices for the luxury trade. His only reason for going to dreary, flattened Stevanien, she learned as they started west, was because of the new restaurant, The Queen. She took that coincidence as a good omen, closing the fingers of her left hand over the thumb three times to make the wish come true.

The roads were better than she remembered; certainly the merchants traveling them seemed to feel safer. Rolling along in the cart, she asked the Senzian about it. He grinned sardonically.

"The Tyrants have cleaned out most of the highway brigands. Just a matter of protecting their own interests. They want to make sure no one else robs us before they do with their border tariffs and taxes." He spat, discreetly, into the dust of the road. "Personally I preferred the brigands. There were ways of dealing with them."

Not long after that she saw evidence of what he was

talking about: they passed two death-wheels beside the roadway, the bodies of would-be thieves spreadeagled upon them, spiraling lazily in the sun, severed hands rotting in their mouths. The smell was very bad.

The Senzian stopped just across the border to do some dealing in the fort at Forese. He also paid his transit duties there scrupulously, waiting patiently in line to have his cart examined and levied. The death-wheels, he pointed out to her after, in the acerbic Senzian manner, were not reserved for highway thieves and captured wizards.

Thus delayed, they spent the night at a coach-house on the well-traveled road, joining a party of Ferraut traders for dinner. Dianora excused herself early and went to bed. She'd paid for a room alone and took the precaution of pushing an oak dresser in front of her door. Nothing disturbed her though, except her dreams. She was back in Tigana and yet she wasn't, because it wasn't there. She whispered the name to herself like a talisman or a prayer before falling into a restless sleep shot through with images of destruction from the burning year.

They spent the second night at another inn beside the river, just outside the walls of Stevanien, having arrived after sundown curfew closed the city gates. They ate alone this time, and she talked to the Senzian until late. He was decent and sober, belying the clichés about his decadent province, and it was clear that he liked her. She enjoyed his company, and she was even attracted to his dry, witty manner. She went to bed alone though. This was not the village in Certando: she had no obligations.

Or not those kinds of obligations. And as for pleasure, or the ordinary needs of human interaction . . . she would have been honestly uncomprehending if anyone had mentioned them to her.

She was nineteen years old and in Tigana that-had-been.

In the morning, just inside the city walls, she bade farewell to the Senzian, touching palm to palm only briefly. He seemed somewhat affected by the night before but she turned and walked away before he could find whatever words his eyes were reaching for.

She found a hostelry not far away, one where her family had never stayed. She wasn't really worried about

being recognized though; she knew how much she had
changed and how many girls named Dianora there were
scattered across the Palm. She paid in advance for three
nights' lodging and left her belongings there.

Then she walked out into the streets of what had been
Avalle of the Towers not very long ago. Avalle, on the
green banks of the Sperion just before the river turned
west to find the sea. There was an ache building in her as
she went, and what hurt most of all, she found, was how
much the same a place could be after everything had
changed.

She went through the leather district and the wool
district. She could remember skipping along beside her
mother when they had all come inland to Avalle to see
one of her father's sculptures ceremoniously placed in
some square or loggia. She even recognized the tiny shop
where she'd purchased her first grey leather gloves, with
coins hoarded from her naming day in the summer for
just such a thing.

Grey was a color for grown young women, not for
little girls, the red-bearded artisan had teased. I *know,*
six-year-old Dianora had said proudly that autumn long
ago. Her mother had laughed. Once upon a time her
mother had been a woman who laughed. Dianora could
remember.

In the wool quarter she saw women and girls working
tirelessly, carding and spinning as they had for centuries
in doorways open to the early-summer early-morning
light. Over by the river she could see and smell the
dyeing sheds and yards.

When Quileia beyond the mountains to the south had
folded inward upon its matriarchy, hundreds upon hundreds of years ago, Avalle had lost a great deal. More
perhaps than any other city in the Palm. Once poised
directly on one of the two main trade routes through the
mountains, it had found itself in danger of sudden incon-
sequentiality. With a collective ingenuity bordering on
genius the city had decisively shifted its orientation and
focus.

Within a generation that city of banking and trade to
north and south had become the principal center in all of

the Palm for works in leather and for sumptuously dyed wool.

Hardly missing a beat, Avalle pursued its new prosperity and its pride. And the towers kept rising.

With a catch to her heart Dianora finally acknowledged that she had been carefully working her way around the edges of Stevanien, the outlying districts, the artisans' quarters, looking outwards only and into doorways. Not into the center, up towards the hill. Where the towers were gone.

And so, realizing that, she did look, standing stock still in the middle of a wide square at the bottom of the street of the Woolguild. There was a small, very beautiful temple of Morian fronting the square, done in marble of a muted rose color. She gazed at it for a moment, then looked up and beyond.

And in that moment Dianora had a truth brought home to her with finality: how something can seem quite unchanged in all the small surface details of existence where things never really change, men and women being what they are, but how the core, the pulse, the kernel of everything can still have become utterly unlike what it had been before.

The wide beautiful streets seemed even wider than before. But that was because they were almost empty. There was a muted swell of noise over to her left where the riverside market still was, but the sound was not a fraction, her memory told her, not a fraction of what it had been in mornings that were lost.

There were too few people. Too many were gone, or dead, and the Ygrathen soldiers were all the more visible because of how empty the streets were. Dianora let her gaze travel past the temple up the line of the broad boulevard beside it towards the heart of the city.

We can and we will build wide and straight, the people of Avalle had said; even in the very beginning, when towns everywhere else were tortuous warrens of twisty alleys and crooked lanes easy to defend. *There will be no city like ours in all the world, and if need comes for defense we will defend ourselves from our towers.*

Which were gone. The squat ugly skyline jarred Dianora with a painful discontinuity. It was as if the eye was tricked, looking ceaselessly for something it *knew* had to be there.

From the earliest days of that broad, elegant city on the banks of the Sperion towers had been associated with Avalle. Assertions of Tiganese pride—sheer arrogance they called it in the provinces of Corte and Chiara and Astibar. They were symbols of internecine rivalry as well—as each noble family or wealthy guild of bankers or traders or artisans thrust its own tower as high as and then higher than they could truly afford. Graceful or warlike, red stone or sandy or grey, the towers of Avalle pushed up towards Eanna's heaven like a forest within the city walls.

The domestic conflicts had actually become dangerous for a time, with murder and sabotage not nearly uncommon enough, and the best masons and architects claiming stupefying fees. It had been the third Prince Alessan in Tigana by the sea who had put an end to the insanity in the simplest possible way more than two hundred years ago.

He commissioned Orsaria, the most celebrated of the architects, to build for him a palace in Avalle. And that palace was to have a tower, said Prince Alessan, that would be—and would remain, by force of law—the highest in the city.

So it had been. The spire of the Prince's Tower, slender and graceful, wrapped in bands of green and white to serve as a memory of the sea this far inland, put an end to the competition for the summit of Avalle. And from then on also, by that Prince Alessan's example which became custom and then tradition, the princes and princesses of Tigana were born in Avalle, in the palace beneath that spire, to mark them as belonging to both of the cities: to Tigana of the Waves and Avalle of the Towers.

There had been over seventy towers once, Dianora knew, crowned in glory by that green and white preeminence. Once? *Four years ago.*

What, Dianora thought, her vision hurting for that absence, is a person who moves through her days as she has always moved, who speaks and walks and labors, eats, makes love, sleeps, sometimes even finds access to laughter, but whose heart has been cut out from her living body? Leaving no scar at all to be seen. No wound by which to remember the sliding blade.

The rubble had all been cleared away. There was no smoke, save from over by the dyeworks, to mar the clear blue of the sky. The day was mild and bright, birds sang a welcome to the coming warmth. There was nothing, nothing at all to show that there had ever been towers in this place. In this low, steadily dwindling town of Stevanien here in its remote corner of the Peninsula of the Palm, in the most oppressed province of them all.

What is such a person? Dianora thought again. That person whose heart was gone? She had no answer, how could she have an answer? Loss coiled to life within her, and hate followed it again, as if both of them were new-born, colder and sharper than before.

She walked up that wide boulevard into the center of Stevanien. She passed the soldiers' barracks and the doors of the Governor's Palace. Not far away she found The Queen. She was hired immediately. To start that same night. Help was badly needed. Help was hard to find. Arduini of Ygrath, who did all his own hiring, decided that this pretty creature from Certando had a certain style to her. She would have to do something though, he admonished her, about that wretchedly vulgar highland accent. She promised to try.

Within six months she was speaking almost like a native of the city, he observed. By then he had her out of the kitchen and into the front room waiting on tables, clad in the cream and dark-brown colors around which he had designed his establishment. Colors that happened to suit her very well.

She was quiet, deft, unassuming, and polite. She remembered names and patrons' preferences. She learned quickly. Four months later, in the spring before she turned twenty-one, Arduini offered her the coveted position at the front of The Queen greeting guests and supervising the staff in the three rooms of dining.

She astonished him by refusing. She astonished a great many people. But Dianora knew that this would be far too prominent a position for her own purposes. Which had not changed. If she was to travel north into Corte soon, and clearly marked by now as being from Certando, she needed to have been associated with The Queen, but not so very prominently. Prominent people had questions asked about them, that much she knew.

So she feigned an attack of country-girl anxiety the night Arduini made his offer. She broke two glasses and dropped a platter. Then she spilled Senzian green wine on the Governor himself.

Tearfully she went to Arduini and begged for more time to grow sure of herself. He agreed. It helped that he was in love with her by then. He invited her, gracefully, to become his mistress. In this, too, she demurred, pleading the inevitable tension that such a liaison would elicit within the staff, badly damaging The Queen. It was the right argument; his establishment was Arduini's true mistress.

In fact, Dianora had resolved to let no man touch her now. She was in Ygrathen territory and she had a purpose. The rules had changed. She had tentatively decided to leave in the fall, north towards Corte. She had been weighing possibilities and excuses for doing so when events had overtaken her so spectacularly.

Slowly circling the Audience Chamber, Dianora paused to greet Doarde's wife whom she liked. The poet seized the opportunity to present his daughter. The girl blushed, but dipped her head, hands pressed together, in a creditable manner. Dianora smiled at her and moved on.

A steward caught up to her, bearing khav in a black chalice set with red gemstones. A gift, years ago, from Brandin. It was her trademark on occasions such as this: she never drank anything stronger than khav at public receptions. With a guilty glance towards the doorway where she knew Scelto would be stationed against the wall, she took a grateful sip of the hot drink. Praise the Triad and the growers of Tregea, it was dark and rich and very strong.

"My dear lady Dianora, you are looking more magnificent than ever."

She turned, smoothly suppressing an expression of distaste. She had recognized the voice: Neso of Ygrath, a minor nobleman from overseas who had recently arrived at Brandin's court on the first ship of the season, solely in the hope of becoming a major nobleman in the colony. He was, so far as Dianora had been able to tell, talentless and venal.

She smiled radiantly at him and allowed him to touch her hand. "My dear Neso, how kind of you to lie so skillfully to an aging woman."

She rather liked saying that sort of thing: for, as Scelto had shrewdly observed once, if she was old, what did that make Solores?

Neso hastened to offer all the emphatic, predictable denials. He praised her gown and the vairstone, noting with a courtier's eye and tongue how exquisitely the stones of her chalice echoed her colors that day. Then, lowering his voice towards an unearned intimacy he asked her for the eighth time at least if she happened to have heard anything further about the planned disposition of that very trivial office of Taxing Master in north Asoli.

It was, in fact, a lucrative position. The incumbent had made his fortune, or enough for his own purposes evidently, and was returning to Ygrath in a few weeks. Dianora hated that sort of graft and she had even been bold enough to say so to Brandin once. A little amused—which had irritated her—he had prosaically pointed out how difficult it was to get men to serve in places as devoid of attraction as the north of Asoli without offering them a chance at modest wealth.

His grey eyes beneath the thick dark eyebrows had rested upon her as she'd wrestled and then finally come to terms with the depressing truth inherent in this. She'd finally looked up and nodded a reluctant agreement. Which made him burst into laughter.

"I am *so* relieved," chuckled Brandin of Ygrath, "that my clumsy reasoning and government meet with your approval." She had gone red to the roots of her hair, but then, catching his mood, had laughed herself at the absurdity of her presumption. That had been several years ago.

Now all she did was try, discreetly, to see that positions such as this one did not go to the most transparently

greedy of the motley crew of petty Ygrathen courtiers
from whom Brandin had to choose. Neso, she had resolved, was *not* getting this posting if she could help it.
The problem was that d'Eymon seemed, for inscrutable
reasons of his own, to be favoring Neso's appointment.
She'd already asked Scelto to see if he could find out
why.

Now she let her smile fade to an earnestly benevolent
look of concern as she gazed at the sleek, plump Ygrathen.
Lowering her voice but without leaning towards him she
murmured, "I am doing what I can. You should know
that there seems to be some opposition."

Neso's eyes narrowed on the far side of the curl of
smoke rising from her khav. With practiced subtlety they
flicked past her right shoulder to where she knew d'Eymon
would still be standing by the King's door. Neso looked
back at her, eyebrows raised very slightly.

Dianora gave a small, apologetic shrug.

"Have you a . . . suggestion?" Neso asked, his brow
furrowed with anxiety.

"I'd start by smiling a little," she said with deliberate
tartness. There was no point in intriguing in such a way
that the whole court knew of it.

Neso forced an immediate laugh and then applauded
stagily as if she'd offered an irresistible witticism.

"Forgive me," he said, smiling as ordered. "This matters a great deal to me."

*It matters a great deal more to the people of Asoli, you
greedy bloodleech,* Dianora thought. She laid a hand
lightly on Neso's puffed sleeve.

"I know it does," she said kindly. "I will do what I
can. If circumstances . . . allow me to."

Neso, whatever he was, was no stranger to this sort of
thing. Once more the false laugh greeted her nonexistent
jest. "I hope to be able to assist the circumstances," he
murmurd.

She smiled again and withdrew her hand. It was enough.
Scelto was going to receive some more money that afternoon. She hoped it would come to a decent part of the
vairstone's cost. As for d'Eymon, she would probably
end up talking directly to him later in the week. Or as
directly as discussions ever got with that man.

Sipping at her khav she moved on. People came up to
her wherever she went. It was bad politics in Brandin's
court not to be on good terms with Dianora di Certando.
Conversing absently and inconsequentially she kept an
ear pitched for the discreet raps of the Herald's staff that
would be Brandin's sole announcement. Rhun, she noted,
was making faces at himself in one of the mirrors and
laughing at the effect. He was in high humor, which was
a good sign. Turning the other way she suddenly noticed
a face she liked. One that was undeniably central to her
own history.

★   ★   ★

In could be said, in many ways, to have been the Governor's own fault. So anxious was he to assuage the evident
frustration of Rhamanus, captain of that year's Tribute
Ship, that he ordered the Certandan serving-girl—who
had apologized so very charmingly after the spilled-wine
incident some time ago—to bring rather more of The
Queen's best vintages than were entirely good for any of
them at the table.

Rhamanus, young enough to still be ambitious, old
enough to feel his chances slipping away, had made some
pointedly acid remarks earlier in the day on board the
river galley about the state of affairs in Stevanien and its
environs. So much of a backwater, so desultory in its
collection of duties and taxes, he murmured a little too
casually, that he wasn't even sure if the galley run upriver
in spring was worthwhile . . . under the present adminis-
trative circumstances.

The Governor, long past the point of ambition but
needing a few more years here skimming his share of
border tariffs and internal levies, along with the criminal
justice fines and confiscations, had winced inwardly and
cursed the conjunctions of his planets. Why, when he
strove so hard to be decent and uncontentious in everything he did, to leave any waters he entered as unruffled
as possible, did he have so little luck?

Short of a massive midsummer military assertion there
was no way to force more money or goods out of this
impoverished region. If Brandin had seriously wanted to

extract real wealth out of Stevanien he would have been better advised not to have so successfully smashed the city and its distrada to its knees.

Not that the Governor would have even dreamt of letting such a furtive thought come anywhere near his lips. But the reality was that he was doing the best he could. If he squeezed the leather or the wool guilds any harder than he was they would simply start to fold. Stevanien, already thinly inhabited—and particularly bereft of men in their prime years—would become a town of ghosts and empty squares. And he had explicit instructions from the King to prevent that.

If the King's various orders and demands rammed so violently up against each other, in such patent contradiction, what, in all fairness, was a middle-echelon administrator to do?

Not that such a plaint could be used with this bristly, unhappy Rhamanus. What care would the captain have for the Governor's dilemmas? The Tribute Ship captains were judged by what came home to Chiara in their holds. Their job was to put as much pressure on the local administrators as they could—even to the point, sometimes, of forcing them to surrender a portion of their own levies to bring the contents of the ship nearer to the mark. The Governor had already resigned himself, dismally, to doing just that by the end of the week if the last hurried sweep of the distrada that he'd ordered didn't produce enough to satisfy Rhamanus. It wouldn't, he knew. This was an ambitious captain he was dealing with, and there had been a tenuous harvest in Corte last fall—Rhamanus's next stop.

His retirement estate in eastern Ygrath, on the promontory he'd already chosen in his mind, seemed farther away this evening than ever before. He signaled for another round of wine for all of them, inwardly grieving for the blue-green sea and the splendid hunting woods by the home he'd probably never be able to build.

On the other hand (as they liked to say here), it appeared that his attempt to soothe the ire of this Rhamanus had been unexpectedly successful. The Governor had asked his wonderful Arduini—the true and only joy there was for him in this benighted place—to prepare an evening meal for them of an unforgettable order.

"*All of my meals are unforgettable,*" Arduini had bridled predictably, but had been mollified by a judicious mixture of flattery, gold ygras, and a quiet reminder (almost certainly not the truth, the Governor reflected unrepentantly) that their guest that evening had ready access to the ear of the King on Chiara.

The meal had been an ascending series of revelations, the service prompt, soothing, and unobtrusive, the wines a sequence of complementary grace notes to Arduini's undeniable artistry. Rhamanus, a man who appeared to keep his trim physique with some difficulty, had progressed from edginess through guarded appreciation, to increasing pleasure, ending up in a volubly expansive good humor.

Somewhere in the next-to-last bottle of dessert wine imported from back home in Ygrath he had also become quite drunk.

Which was the only explanation, the only *possible* explanation, for the fact that, after the dinner was over and The Queen closed for the night, he'd had their evening's dark-haired waitress formally seized as Tribute for Brandin in Chiara and bundled directly onto the galley in the river.

The serving-girl. The serving-girl from *Certando*.

Certando, on the other side of the border, where Alberico of Barbadior held sway, not, alas, Brandin of Ygrath.

The Governor of Stevanien had been awakened at dawn from a fitful, wine-fogged slumber by a terrified, apologetic Clerk of the Council. Unclothed and without so much as a whiff of his morning khav he had heard—through the ominous pounding of a colossal headache—the nature of the news.

"Stop that galley!" he roared, as the horrifying implications fought their way through to register upon his slowly emerging consciousness. He had tried to roar, anyway. What came forth was a pitiful squeal that had been, nonetheless, sufficiently explicit to send the clerk flying, his gown flapping in his haste to obey.

They blocked the River Sperion, stopping Rhamanus just as he was raising anchor.

Unfortunately the Tribute captain then proceeded to reveal a stubbornness that ran stupefyingly counter to the most rudimentary political good sense. He refused to surrender the girl. For one wild, hallucinatory moment of insanity the Governor actually contemplated storming the galley.

The river galley of Brandin, King of Ygrath, Lord of Burrakh in Khardhun, Tyrant of the western provinces of the Peninsula of the Palm. Said galley then flying—rather pointedly—Brandin's own device as well as the royal banner of Ygrath.

Death-wheels, the Governor reflected, were lovingly made for minor functionaries who essayed such maneuvers.

Desperately, his brain curdling in the unfair brightness of the morning sunlight by the river, the Governor tried to find a way of communicating reason to a Tribute captain seized by the manifest throes of a midsummer madness.

"Do you want to start a war?" he shouted from the dock. He had to shout from the dock; they wouldn't let him on the galley. The wretched girl was nowhere to be seen; stowed, doubtless in the captain's cabin. The Governor wished she were dead. He wished that he himself was dead. He wished, in the most grievous inner sacrilege of all, that Arduini the master chef had never set foot in Stevanien.

"And why," Captain Rhamanus called blandly from the middle of the river, "should my doing my precise duty by my King cause any such a thing?"

"Has the sea salt rotted your miserable excuse for a brain?" the Governor screamed, ill-advisedly. The captain's brow darkened. The Governor pushed on, dripping with sweat in the sun.

"She's a *Certandan,* in the name of the seven holy sisters of the god! Do you have any *idea* how easy it will be to goad Alberico into starting a border war over this?" He mopped at his brow with the square of red cloth a servant belatedly produced.

Rhamanus, cursedly composed despite having drunk at least as much as the Governor the night before, seemed unimpressed.

"As far as I'm concerned," he pronounced airily, the

words drifting over the water, "she's living in Stevanien, she's working in Stevanien, and she was taken in Stevanien. By my reckoning that makes her perfectly suitable for the saishan, or whatever our King, in his wisdom, decides to do with her." He leveled a finger suddenly at the Governor. "Now clear the river of these boats or I will ram and sink them in the name of each of the seven sisters and the King of Ygrath. Unless," he added, leaning forward, lowering his hand to the railing, "you would care to farspeak Chiara and have the King settle this himself?"

They had a saying here in the colony: *naked between a fist and a fist.* It was an exact phrase for the place where that insidious, cleverly calculated, viciously unfair proposition put the man to whom it was addressed. A phrase that described in precise and graphic terms where the Governor of Stevanien abruptly felt himself to be. The red cloth swabbed repeatedly, and ineffectually, at his forehead and neck.

One did not farspeak the King without, it had been painstakingly impressed upon all the regional administrators in the Western Palm, *very* compelling reason. The power demanded of Brandin to sustain such a link with his non-sorcerous underlings was considerable.

One most particularly did not willingly undertake such a course of action in the very early morning hours when the King might be asleep. Most relevant of all, perhaps, one did not hasten to bespeak the mental presence of one's monarch with a mind clogged and befuddled with the miasmic aftermath of wine, and over an issue that—in essence—might be seen to involve no more than the Tribute seizure of a common farm girl.

That was one of the fists.

The other was war on the border. With the brain-battering possibility of more than that. For who, in the name of the sisters and the god, knew how the devious pagan mind of Alberico of Barbadior worked? How he might regard—or decide to regard—an incident such as this? Despite Rhamanus's glib analysis, the fact that the girl worked in The Queen made it obvious that she wasn't really a Lower Cortean. In the name of the sisters, they couldn't even *seize* a Lower Cortean for tribute! They weren't allowed to, by order of the King. To take the woman, she had to be Certandan. If Rhamanus wanted to argue she was a resident of Stevanien, well that made her a Lower Cortean which meant that they *couldn't* take her! Which meant that . . . he didn't *know* what that meant. The Governor held out his sopping kerchief and it was exchanged for a fresh one. His brain felt as if it was frying in the sun.

All he had wanted out of his declining years in service was the quiet, mildly lucrative postings his family's long, if fairly minor, support of Brandin's original claim to succession in Ygrath had earned them. That was it. All he wanted. With a decent house on that eastern promontory one day where he could watch the sun come up out of the sea and go hunting in the woods with his dogs. So very much to ask?

Instead, a fist and a fist.

He briefly considered washing his hands of the whole affair—and let the cursed inhabitants of this peninsula chew on *that* for a phrase!—letting the imbecilic Tribute captain row his galley down the river just as he pleased. In fact, he realized, lamentably too late, if he had stayed in bed and pretended he'd not received the message in time he would have been entirely blameless in this affair of a drunken captain's blunder. He closed his eyes, tasting the exquisite, vanished sweetness of such a possibility.

Too late. He was standing by the riverside in the blinding light and the heat of the sun, and half of Stevanien had heard what he and Rhamanus had just shouted back and forth across the water.

With a small, diffident prayer to his own patron gods of food and forest, and a poignantly clear image of that seaside estate, the Governor chose his fist.

"Let me on board then," he said as briskly as he could manage. "I'm not about to farspeak the King while standing on this dock. I want a chair and some quiet and an extremely strong mug of whatever passes for khav on a galley."

Rhamanus was visibly nonplussed. The Governor was able to derive a certain sour pleasure from that.

They gave him everything he asked for. The woman was taken below deck and he was left alone in the captain's cabin. He took a deep breath and then several more. He drank the khav, scalding his tongue which, as much as anything else, woke him up. Then, for the first time in three years of office, he narrowed his mind down to a pinpoint image as Brandin had taught him, and he framed, questioningly, the name of the King in his thoughts.

With profoundly unsettling speed Brandin's crisp, cool, always slightly mocking voice was in his head. It was dizzying. The Governor fought to keep his composure. As carefully but as quickly as he could—speed mattered, they had all been taught—he outlined the situation they faced. He apologized twice, en route, but dared not risk the time required for a third, however much his lifetime's instincts bade him to. What good were a career diplomat's lifetime instincts when enmeshed in sorcery? He felt sick to his stomach with the strain and the discontinuity of the farspeaking.

Then, with a surging of his spirit, with glory, with paeans of praise to twenty different deities chorusing within him, the Governor of Stevanien was given to understand that his King was not angered. More: that he had been exactly correct in this farspeaking. That the political timing could not be better for such a testing of Alberico's resolve. That, accordingly, Rhamanus should indeed be allowed to take the girl as Tribute but, and the King stressed this, very clearly identified as a Certandan. A Certandan who happened to be in Lower Corte. That fact was to be their claim of authority: no evasions about her being a resident of Stevanien or some such thing. They would see what sort of spirit this minor Barbadian sorcerer had after all.

The Governor had done well, the King said.

The image of the house by the sea grew almost incandescently vivid in the back of the Governor's mind even as he heard himself babbling—silently over the link Brandin made—his most abject protestations of love and obedience. The King cut him short.

"We must end now," he said, "Do go easier on the wine down there." Then he was gone. The Governor sat alone in the captain's cabin for a long time, trying to reassure himself that Brandin's last tone had been amused, not reproving. He was fairly certain it was. He was almost sure.

A very tense period had ensued. The galley was allowed to leave that same morning. In the fortnight that followed the King had farspoken him twice. Once to order the border garrison at Forese quietly increased but not by so much as to amount to further provocation in itself. The Governor spent an anguished sleepless night trying to calculate what number of soldiers would suit that command.

Reinforcements from the city of Lower Corte arrived up the river to supplement his own forces in Stevanien. Later he was instructed by the King to watch for a possible Barbadian envoy from Certando, and to greet such a one with utmost cordiality, referring all questions to Chiara for resolution. He was also warned to be on full alert for a retaliatory border raid from Sinave—and to annihilate any and all Barbadian troops that might venture into Lower Corte. The Governor had very little personal experience at annihilation but he swore to obey.

Merchants, he was told, were to be advised to delay their plans to travel east for a little while; no orders, nothing official, merely a piece of advice a prudent businessman might wish to heed. Most did.

In the end nothing happened.

Alberico chose to entirely ignore the affair. Short of a willingness to have things escalate a long way there was nothing else he could do without losing face. For a while there was speculation he might punish some merchant or itinerant musician from the Western Palm who happened to be in his provinces, but there was no sign of this either. The Barbadians simply treated the girl as having been an established resident of Lower Corte—exactly as Rhamanus had so blithely opined the morning he'd seized her.

In the Ygrathen provinces, though, the girl was deliberately described as Certandan from the start—the woman from Barbadian territory that Brandin had seized, mocking Alberico all the while. She was said to be beautiful as well.

Rhamanus made his slow progression home through the rest of that summer and into the early fall. The galley took them downriver and all the collected inland tributes were transferred to the great Tribute Ship itself with its broad, filling sails. Slowly it made its way up the coast, collecting taxes and tariffs at the designated places in Corte and Asoli.

The harvest had indeed been bad in Corte, they had to struggle to meet the quotas there. Twice they rested at anchor for long periods while the captain led a company to an inland post. And all the while Rhamanus searched for women who might be useful as more than hostages or symbols of Ygrath's manifest dominance. Women who might credit the saishan itself and so make the career of a certain Tribute captain who was just about ready for a landside posting after twenty years at sea.

Three possibilities were found. One was of noble birth, her existence revealed by an informer. She was taken only after her father's manor in Corte had been, somewhat regretfully, burned to the ground.

At length, in the autumn turning of the year, beautiful even in flat, unlovely Asoli when the rains chose to relent, the Tribute Ship slipped through the tricky passages of the Strait of Asoli and entered the waters of the Chiaran Sea. A few days later, red and gold sails billowing triumphantly, it had sailed into the Great Harbor of the Island, celebrated in song for more years than could be counted.

The Tribute Ship of Rhamanus had carried gold and gems and silver and coinage of various kinds. It bore leather from Stevanien and wood carvings from Corte and great huge wheels of saull cheese from the west coast of Asoli. They had spices and herbs and knives, stained glass and wool and wine. There were two women from Corte and one from Asoli, and besides these three there was another woman and this one was different. This one was the dark-haired, brown-eyed beauty known throughout the peninsula by the time their voyage ended as the woman who'd come near to starting a war.

Dianora di Certando, her name was.

Dianora, who had intended to come to the Island from the very first, from the earliest glimmerings of her plan when she had sat alone before a dead fire one summer night in her father's silent house. Who had hardened herself—as men in battle were said to have to do—to the thought of being captured and brought here and locked for life inside the saishan of the Tyrant. She had worked it out that far five years ago, a girl with death in her heart, with a father dead and a brother gone and a mother gone even farther away: images of all three of them rising in her dreams from the ashes of the burning in her land.

And death was still there, still with her on that ship. She still had those dreams, but with them now, as fabled Chiara drew nearer under the brightness of the sky was something else: a bemused, an almost numbed incredulity at how the line of her life had run. How things had fallen out so completely wrong, and yet so precisely as she had planned from the first.

She had tried to see that as an omen, closing her left hand three times over her thumb to make her wish come true, as she entered that new world.

CHAPTER
•8•

IT WAS STRANGE, DIANORA THOUGHT, STILL MOVING through the crowded Audience Chamber as spring sunlight filtered down on Brandin's court from the stained-glass windows above, how the so clear portents of youth were alchemized by time into the many-layered ambiguities of adult life.

Sipping from her jeweled cup she considered the alternative. That she had simply *allowed* things to become nuanced and difficult. That the real truths were exactly the same as they had been on the day she arrived. That all she was doing was hiding: from what she had become, and what she had not yet done.

It was the central question of her life and once more she pushed it away to the edges of her awareness. Not today. Not in any daytime. Those thoughts belonged to nights alone in the saishan when only Scelto by her door might know how sleepless she was, or find the tracks of tears along her cheeks when he came to wake her in the morning.

Night thoughts, and this was bright day, in a very public place.

So she walked over towards the the man she'd recognized and let her smile reach her eyes. Balancing her chalice gracefully she sketched a full Ygrathen salute to the portly, soberly dressed personage with three heavy gold chains about his neck.

"Greetings," she murmured, straightening and moving nearer. "This is a surprise. It is rare indeed that the so-busy Warden of the Three Harbors deigns to spare a moment from his so-demanding affairs to visit old friends."

Unfortunately Rhamanus was as hard to ruffle or disconcert as he had ever been. Dianora had been trying to get a rise out of him ever since the night he'd had her bundled like a brown heifer out of the street in front of The Queen and onto the river galley.

Now he simply grinned, heavier with the years gone by and, latterly, his shore-bound duties, but umistakably the man who'd brought her here.

One of the few men from Ygrath she genuinely liked.

"Not so much flavor from you, girl," he mock-growled. "It is not for idle women who do nothing all day but put their hair up and down and up again for exercise to criticize those of us who have stern and arduous tasks that shorten our nights and put grey in our hair."

Dianora laughed. Rhamanus's thick black curls—the envy of half the saishan—showed not a trace of grey. She let her gaze linger expressively on his dark locks.

"I'm a liar," Rhamanus conceded with untroubled equanimity, leaning forward so only she could hear. "It's been a dead-quiet winter. Not much to do at all. I could have come to visit but you know how much I hate these goings-on at court. My buttons pop when I bow."

Dianora laughed again and gave his arm a quick squeeze. Rhamanus had been kind to her on the ship, and courteous and friendly ever since, even when she'd been merely another new body—if a slightly notorious one—in the saishan of the King. She knew he liked her and she also knew, from d'Eymon himself, that the former Tribute Ship captain was an efficient and a fair administrator.

She had helped him get the posting four years ago. It was a high honor for a seaman, supervising harbor rules and regulations at the three main ports of Chiara itself. It was also, to judge from Rhamanus's slightly threadbare clothing, a little too near the seat of power for any real gains to be extracted.

Thinking, she clicked her tongue against her upper teeth, a habit Brandin teased her about. He claimed it always signaled a request or a suggestion. He knew her very well, which frightened her at least as much as it did anything else.

"This is the merest thought," she said now to Rhamanus quietly, "but would you have any interest at all in living

in north Asoli for a few years? Not that I want to get rid
of you. It's a dreadful place, everyone knows that, but
there *are* opportunities and I'd as soon a decent man
reaped them as some of the greedy clutch that are hovering about here."

"The taxing office?" he asked, very softly.

She nodded. His eyes widened slightly but, schooled to
discretion, he gave no other sign of interest or surprise.

What he did do, an instant later, was glance quickly
beyond her shoulder towards the throne. Dianora was
already turning by then, an inexplicable sense, almost an
antenna, having alerted her.

So she was facing the Island Throne and the doorway
behind it by the time the herald's staff rapped the floor
twice, not loudly, and Brandin came into the room. He
was followed by the two priests, and the priestess of
Adaon. Rhun shambled quickly over to stand near by,
dressed identically to the King except for his cap.

The truer measure of power, Brandin had once said to
her, wouldn't be found in having twenty heralds deafen a
room by proclaiming one's arrival. Any fool in funds for
a day could rivet attention that way. The more testing
course, the truer measure, was to enter unobtrusively
and observe what happened.

What happened was what always happened. The Audience Chamber had been collectively poised as if on the
edge of a cliff for the past ten minutes, waiting. Now,
just as collectively, the court plummeted into obeisance.
Not one person in the whole crowded room was still
speaking by the time the herald's muted staff of office
proclaimed the King. In the silence the two discreet raps
on the marbled floor sounded like echoing thunder.

Brandin was in high good humor. Dianora could have
told that from halfway across the room, even if she
hadn't had a hint from Rhun already. Her heart was
beating very fast. It always did whenever Brandin entered a room where she was. Even after twelve years.
Even still, and despite everything. So many lines of her
life led to or from this man or came together, hopelessly
intertwined, in him.

He looked to d'Eymon first, as always, and received
the other's expressionless bow, sketched low in the

Ygrathen fashion. Then, as always, he turned and smiled at Solores.

Then at Dianora. Braced as she was, as she always tried to be, she still could not quite master what happened to her when the grey eyes found and held her own. His glance was like a touch, a gliding presence, fiery and glacial both—as Brandin was.

And all this from a look across a very crowded room.

Once, in bed, years before, she had dared to ask him a question that had long troubled her.

"Is there sorcery involved when you love me here, or when we first meet in a public place?"

She hadn't known what answer she wanted, or what to expect by way of reaction. She'd thought he might be flattered by the implication, or at least amused. You could never be sure with Brandin though, his mind ran through too many different channels and with too much subtlety. Which is why questions, especially revealing ones, were dangerous. This had been important to her though: if he said yes she was going to try to use that to kindle her killing anger again. The anger she seemed to have lost here in the strange world that was the Island.

Her expression must have been very grave; he turned on his pillow, head propped on one hand to regard her from beneath level brows. He shook his head.

"Not in any way you are thinking. Nothing that I control or shape with my magic, other than the matter of children. I will not have any more heirs, you know that." She did know that; all his women did. He said, after a pause, carefully, "Why do you ask? What happens to you?"

For a second she thought she'd heard uncertainty in his voice, but one could never be sure of such things with Brandin.

"Too much," she'd answered. "Too much happens."

And she'd been speaking, for that one time, the unshielded truth of a no longer innocent heart. There was an acute understanding in his clear eyes. Which frightened her. She moved herself—moved by all the layers of her need—to slide over against his body again and then above and upon it that it might begin once more, the whole process. All of it: betrayal and memory mixed with yearning, as in the amber-colored wine the Triad were said to drink—too potent for mortals to taste.

"Are you truly serious about that posting in Asoli?" Rhamanus's voice was soft. Brandin had not gone to the throne but was making a relaxed circuit of the room—more evidence of his benign mood. Rhun, with his lop-sided smile, shambled in his wake.

"I confess I had never even given it a thought," the former Tribute captain added.

With an effort Dianora forced her thoughts back to him. For a second she had forgotten her own query. Brandin did that to her. It was not a good thing, she thought. For many reasons it was not a good thing.

She turned again to Rhamanus. "I'm quite serious," she said. "But I'm not sure if you would want the position—even if it were possible. You have more status where you are, and this is Chiara, after all. Asoli can offer you some chance at wealth, but I think you have an idea what would be involved. What matters to you, Rhamanus?"

It was more bluntly put than courtesy would have deemed appropriate, especially with a friend.

He blinked, and fingered one of his chains of office.

"Is that what it comes down to?" he asked hesitantly. "Is that how you see it? Can a man not perhaps be moved by the prospect of a new challenge, or even—at the risk of sounding foolish—by the desire to serve his King?"

Her turn to blink.

"You shame me," she said simply, after a moment. "Rhamanus, I swear you do." She stilled his quick pro-tests with a hand on his sleeve. "Sometimes I wonder what is happening to me. All the intriguing that goes on here."

She heard footsteps approaching and what she said next was spoken as much to the man behind as to the one in front of her. "Sometimes I wonder what this court is doing to me."

"Should I be wondering as well?" asked Brandin of Ygrath.

Smiling, he joined them. He did not touch her. He very seldom touched the saishan women in public, and

this was an Ygrathen reception. They knew his rules.
Their lives were shaped by his rules.

"My lord," she said, turning and sketching her saluta-
tion. She kept her voice airily provocative. "Do you find
me more cynical than I was when this terrible man brought
me here?"

Brandin's amused glance went from her to Rhamanus.
It was not as if he'd needed the reminder of which
Tribute captain had brought him Dianora. She knew
that, and he knew she did. It was all part of their verbal
dance. His intelligence stretched her to her limits, and
then changed what those limits were. She noticed, perhaps because the subject had come up with Rhamanus,
that there was as much grey in his beard now as black.

He nodded judiciously, simulating a deep concern over
the question. "I would have to say so, yes. You have
grown cynically manipulative in almost exactly the same
proportion as the terrible man has grown fat."

"So much?" Dianora protested. "My lord, he is *very*
fat!"

Both men chuckled. Rhamanus patted his belly affec-
tionately.

"This," he said, "is what happens when you feed a
man cold salt meat for twenty years at sea and then
expose him to the delights of the King's city."

"Well then," said Brandin, "we may have to send you
away somewhere until you are sleek as a seal again."

"My lord," said Rhamanus instantly, "I am yours to
command in all things." His expression was sober and
intense.

Brandin registered that and his tone changed as well.
"I know that," he murmured. "I would that I had more
of you at court. At both of my courts. Portly or sleek,
Rhamanus, I am not unmindful of you, whatever our
Dianora may think."

Very high praise, a promise of sorts, and a dismissal
for the moment. Bright-eyed, Rhamanus bowed formally
and withdrew. Brandin walked a couple of paces away,
Rhun shuffling along beside him. Dianora followed, as
she was expected to. Once out of earshot of anyone but
the Fool, Brandin turned to her. He was, she was sorry
to see, suppressing a smile.

"What did you do? Offer him north Asoli?"

Dianora heaved a heartfelt sigh of frustration. This happened all the time. "Now that," she protested, "is unfair. You *are* using magic."

He let the smile come. She knew that people were watching them. She knew what they would say amongst each other.

"Hardly," Brandin murmured. "I wouldn't waste it or drain myself on something so transparent."

"Transparent!" she bridled.

"Not you, my cynical manipulator. But Rhamanus was too serious too quickly when I jested about posting him away. And the only position of significance currently available is north Asoli and so . . ."

He let the sentence trail off. Laughter lingered in his eyes.

"Would he be such a bad choice?" Dianora asked defiantly. It was genuinely disconcerting how easily Brandin could sound the depths of things. If she allowed herself to dwell on that she could become frightened again.

"What do you think?" he asked by way of reply.

"I? Think?" She lifted her plucked eyebrows in exaggerated arches. "How should a mere object of the King's occasional pleasure venture to have an opinion on such matters?"

"Now that," said Brandin nodding briskly, "is an intelligent observation. I shall have to consult Solores, instead."

"If you get an intelligent observation out of her," Dianora said tartly, "I shall hurl myself from the saishan balcony into the sea."

"All the way across the harbor square? A long leap," said Brandin mildly.

"So," she replied, "is an intelligent observation for Solores."

And at that he laughed aloud. The court was listening. Everyone heard. Everyone would draw their own conclusions, but they would all be the same conclusion in the end. Scelto, she reflected, was likely to receive discreet contributions from sources other than Neso of Ygrath before the day was out.

"I saw something interesting on the mountain this morning," Brandin said, his amusement subsiding. "Something quite unusual."

This, she realized, was why he'd wanted to speak to her alone. He'd been up on Sangarios that morning; she was one of the few who knew about it. Brandin kept this venture quiet, in case he should fail. She'd been prepared to tease him about it.

At the beginning of spring, just as the winds began to change, before the last snows melted in Certando and Tregea and the southern reaches of what had been Tigana, came the three Ember Days that marked the turning of the year.

No fires not already burning were lit anywhere in the Palm. The devout fasted for at least the first of the three days. The bells of the Triad temples were silent. Men stayed within their doors at night, especially after darkfall on the first day which was the Day of the Dead.

There were Ember Days in autumn as well, halfway through the year, when the time of mourning came for Adaon slain on his mountain in Tregea, when the sun began to fade as Eanna mourned and Morian folded in upon herself in her Halls underground. But the spring days inspired a colder dread, especially in the countryside, because so much depended upon what would follow them. Winter's passing, the season of sowing, and the hope of grain, of life, in the summer's fullness to come.

In Chiara there was an added ritual, different from anything elsewhere in the Palm.

On the Island the tale was told that Adaon and Eanna had first come together in love for three full days and nights on the summit of Sangarios. That in the surging climax of her desire on the third night Eanna of the Lights had created the stars of heaven and strewn them like shining lace through the dark. And the tale was told that nine months later—which is three times three—the Triad was completed when Morian was born in the depths of winter in a cave on that same mountain.

And with Morian had come both life and death into the world, and with life and death came mortal man to walk under the newly named stars, the two moons of the night's warding, and the sun of day.

And for this reason had Chiara always asserted its

preeminence among the nine provinces of the Palm, and for this reason as well did the Island name Morian as guardian of its destiny.

Morian of Portals, who had sway over all thresholds. For everyone knew that all islands were worlds unto themselves, that to come to an island was to come to another world. A truth known under the stars and moons, if not always remembered by the light of day.

Every three years then, at the beginning of each Year of Morian, on the first of the springtime Ember Days, the young men of Chiara would vie with each other in a dawn race up to the summit of Sangarios, there to pluck a blood-dark sprig of sonrai, the intoxicating berries of the mountain, under the watchful eye of the priests of Morian who had kept vigil on the peak all night long among the waking spirits of the dead. The first man down the mountain was anointed Lord of Sangarios until the next such run in three years' time.

In the old days, the very old days, the Lord of Sangarios would have been hunted down and slain on his mountain by the women six months later on the first of the Ember Days of fall.

Not anymore. Not for a long time. Now the young champion was likely to find himself in fierce demand as a lover by women seeking the blessing of his seed. A different sort of hunt, Dianora had said to Brandin once.

He hadn't laughed. He didn't find the ritual amusing. In fact, six years ago the King of Ygrath had elected to run the course himself, the morning before the actual race. He had done it again three years past. No small achievement, really, for a man of his years, considering how hard and how long the runners trained for this. Dianora didn't know what to find more whimsical: the fact that Brandin would do this thing, in such secrecy, or the ebullient masculine pride he'd felt both times he'd made it up to the summit of Sangarios and down again.

In the Audience Chamber Dianora asked the question she was clearly expected to ask: "What did you see, then?"

She did not know, for mortals seldom do know when they approach a threshold of the goddess, that the question would mark the turning of her days.

"Something unusual," Brandin repeated. "I had of course outstripped the guards running with me."

"Of course," she murmured, giving him a sidelong glance.

He grinned. "I was alone on the path part of the way up. The trees were still very thick on either side, mountain ash, mostly, some sejoias."

"How interesting," she said.

This time he quelled her with a look. Dianora bit her lip and schooled her expression dutifully.

"I looked over to my right," Brandin said, "and saw a large grey rock, almost like a platform at the edge of the trees. And sitting on the rock there was a creature. A woman, I would swear, and very nearly human."

"Very nearly?"

She wasn't teasing anymore. Within the actual archway of a portal of Morian we sometimes do know that a thing of importance is happening.

"That's what was unusual. She certainly wasn't entirely human. Not with green hair and such pale skin. Skin so white I swear I saw blue veins beneath, Dianora. And her eyes were unlike any I've ever seen. I thought she was a trick of light—the sun filtering through trees. But she didn't move, or change in any way, even when I stopped to look at her."

And now Dianora knew exactly where she was.

The ancient creatures of water and wood and cave went back in time as far as the Triad did almost, and from the description she knew what he had seen. She knew other things as well and was suddenly afraid.

"What did you do?" she asked, as casually as she could.

"I wasn't sure what to do. I spoke; she didn't answer. So I took a step towards her and as soon as I did she leaped down from the rock and backed away. She stopped among the trees. I held out my open palms, but she seemed to be startled by that, or offended, and a moment later she fled."

"Did you follow?"

"I was about to, but by then one of the guards had caught up to me."

"Did he see her?" she asked. Too quickly.

Brandin gave her a curious look. "I asked. He said no, though I think he would have answered that way, regardless. Why do you ask?"

She shrugged. "It would have confirmed she was real," she lied.

Brandin shook his head. "She was real. This was no vision. In fact," he added, as if the thought had just occurred to him, "she reminded me of you."

"With . . . what was it? Green skin and blue hair?" she replied, letting her court instincts guide her now. Something large was happening here though. She labored to hide the turmoil she felt. "I thank you so much my gracious lord. I suppose if I talked to Scelto and Vencel we could achieve the skin color, and blue hair should be easy enough. If it excites you so dramatically . . ."

He smiled but did not laugh. "Green hair, not blue," he said, almost absently. "And she did, Dianora," he repeated, looking at her oddly. "She did remind me of you. I wonder why. Do you know anything about such creatures?"

"I do not," she said. "In Certando we have no tales of green-haired women in the mountains." She was lying. She was lying as well as she could, wide-eyed and direct. She could scarcely believe what she had just heard, what he had seen.

Brandin's good humor was still with him.

"What mountain tales *do* you have in Certando?" he queried, smiling expectantly.

"Stories of hairy things that walk on legs like tree stumps and eat goats and virgins in the night."

His smile broadened. "Are there any?"

"Goats, yes," she said with a straight face. "Fewer virgins. Hairy creatures with such specific appetites are not an incentive to chastity. Are you sending out a party to search for this creature?" A question so important she held her breath awaiting his reply.

"I think not," Brandin said. "I suspect such things are only seen when they want to be."

Which, she knew for a fact, was absolutely true.

"I haven't told anyone but you," he added unexpectedly.

There was no dissembling in the expression she felt come over her face at that. But over and above everything else there was something new inside her with these tidings. She badly needed to be alone to think. A vain hope. She wouldn't get that chance for a long time yet today; best to push his story as far back as she could, with all the other things she was always pushing to the edges of her mind.

"Thank you, my lord," she murmured, aware that they had been talking privately for some time. Aware, as ever, of how that would be construed.

"In the meantime," Brandin suddenly said, in a quite different tone, "you still have not yet asked me how I did on the run. Solores, I have to tell you, made it her first question."

Which carried them back to familiar ground.

"Very well," she said, feigning indifference. "Do tell me. Halfway? Three-quarters?"

A glint of royal indignation flickered in the grey eyes. "You *are* presumptuous sometimes," he said. "I indulge you too much. I went, if you please, all the way to the summit and came down again this morning with a cluster of sonrai berries. I will be extremely interested to see if any of tomorrow's runners are up and down as quickly."

"Well," she said quickly, unwisely, "they won't have sorcery to help them."

"Dianora, have done!"

And that tone she recognized and knew she'd gone too far. As always at such moments she had a dizzying sense of a pit gaping at her feet.

She knew what Brandin needed from her; she knew the reason he granted her license to be outrageous and impertinent. She had long understood why the wit and edge she brought to their exchanges were important to him. She was his counterbalance to Solores's soft, unquestioning, undemanding shelter. The two of them, in turn, balancing d'Eymon's ascetic exercise of politics and government.

And all three of them in orbit around the star that Brandin was. The voluntarily exiled sun, removed from the heavens it knew, from the lands and seas and people, bound to this alien peninsula by loss and grief and revenge decreed.

She knew all this. She knew the King very well. Her

life depended on that. She did not often stray across the line that was always there, invisible but inviolate. When she did it was likely to be over something as apparently trivial as this. It was such a paradox for her how he could shrug off or laugh at or even invite her caustic commentary on court and colony—and yet bridle like a boy with affronted pride if she teased about his ability to run up and down a mountain in a morning.

At such times he had only to say her name in a certain way and endless chasms opened before her in the delicately inlaid floor of the Audience Chamber.

She was a captive here, more slave than courtesan, at the court of a Tyrant. She was also an impostor, living an ongoing lie while her country slowly died away from the memories of men. And she had sworn to kill this man, whose glance across a room was as wildfire on her skin or amber wine in her mortal blood.

Chasms, everywhere she turned.

And now this morning he had seen a riselka. He, and very possibly a second man as well. Fighting back her fear she forced herself to shrug casually, to arch her eyebrows above a face schooled to bland unconcern.

"This amuses me," she said, reaching for self-possession, knowing precisely what his need in her was, even now. Especially now. "You profess to be pleased, even touched, by Solores's doubtlessly agitated query about your mountain run. The first thing she asked, you say. *How* she must have wondered whether or not you succeeded! And yet when I—knowing as surely as I know my own name that you were up on the summit this morning—treat it lightly, as something small, never in doubt . . . why then the King grows angry. He bids me sternly to have done! But tell me, my lord, in all fairness, which of us, truly, has honored you more?"

For a long time he was silent and she knew that the court would be avidly marking the expression on his face. For the moment she cared nothing for them. Or even for her past, or his encounter on the mountainside. There was one specific chasm here that began and ended in the depths of the grey eyes that were now searching her own.

When he spoke it was in a different voice again, but this tone she happened to know exceedingly well and, in spite of everything that had just been said, and in spite of where they were and who was watching them, she felt herself go weak suddenly. Her legs trembled, but not with fear now.

"I could take you," said Brandin, King of Ygrath, thickly, his face flushed, "on the floor of this room right now before all of my gathered court."

Her throat was dry. She felt a nerve flutter beneath the skin of her wrist. Her own color was high, she knew. She swallowed with some difficulty.

"Perhaps tonight would be wiser," she murmured, trying to keep her tone light but not really managing it, unable to hide the swift response in her eyes—spark to spark like the onset of a blaze. The jeweled khav chalice trembled in her hand. He saw that, and she saw that he did and that her response, as always, served as kindling for his own desire. She sipped at her drink, holding it with both hands, clinging to self-control.

"Better tonight, surely," she said again, overwhelmed as always by what was happening to her. She knew what he needed her to say though, now, at this moment, in this room of state thronged with his court and emissaries from home.

She said it, looking him in the eyes, articulating carefully: "After all my lord, at your age you should marshal your strength. You *did* run partway up a hill this morning."

An instant later, for the second time, the Chiaran court of Brandin of Ygrath saw their King throw back his handsome, bearded head and they heard him laugh aloud in delight. Not far away, Rhun the Fool cackled in simultaneous glee.

"Isolla of Ygrath!"

This time there were trumpets and a drum, as well as the herald's staff resounding as it struck the floor by the double doors at the southern end of the Audience Chamber.

Standing most of the way towards the throne, Dianora had time to observe the stately progress of the woman Brandin had called the finest musician in Ygrath. The assembled court of Chiara was lined several rows deep, flanking the approach to the King.

"A handsome woman still," murmured Neso of Ygrath, "and she's fifty years old if she's a day." Somehow he had managed to end up next to her in the front row.

His unctuous tone irritated her, as always, but she tried not to let it show. Isolla was clad in the simplest possible robe of dark blue, belted at the waist with a slender gold chain. Her hair, brown with hints of grey, was cut unfashionably short—although the spring and summer fashion might change after today, Dianora thought. The colony always took its cue in these matters from Ygrath.

Isolla walked confidently, not hurrying, down the aisle formed by the courtiers. Brandin was already smiling a welcome. He was always immensely pleased when one or another of Ygrath's artists made the long, often dangerous, sea voyage to his second court.

Several steps behind Isolla, and carrying her lute in its case as if it were an artifact of immeasurable worth, Dianora saw—with genuine surprise—the poet Camena di Chiara, clad in his ubiquitous triple-layered cloak. There were murmurs from the assembly: she wasn't the only one caught off guard by this.

Instinctively she threw a glance across the aisle to where Doarde stood with his wife and daughter. She was in time to see the spasm of hate and fear that flickered across his face as his younger rival approached. An instant later the revealing expression was gone, replaced by a polished mask of sneering disdain at Camena's vulgar lowering of himself to serve as porter for an Ygrathen.

Still, Dianora considered, this *was* an Ygrathen court. Camena, she guessed in a flash of intuition, had probably had one of his verses set to music. If Isolla was about to sing a song of his it would be a dazzling coup for the Chiaran poet. More than sufficient to explain why he would offer to further exalt Isolla—and Ygrathen artists—by serving as a bearer for her.

The politics of art, Dianora decided, was at least as complex as that of provinces and nations.

Isolla had stopped, as was proper, about fifteen steps

from the dais of the Island Throne, very close to where Dianora and Neso stood.

Neatly she proceeded to perform the triple obeisance. Very graciously—a mark of high honor—Brandin rose to his feet to bid her welcome. He was smiling. So was Rhun, behind him and to his left.

For no reason she would ever afterwards be able to name or explain Dianora turned from monarch and musician back to the poet bearing the lute. Camena had stopped a further half a dozen paces behind Isolla and had knelt on the marble floor.

What detracted from the grace of the tableau was the dilation of his eyes. *Nilth leaves,* Dianora concluded instantly. *He's drugged himself.* She saw beads of perspiration on the poet's brow. It was not warm in the Audience Chamber.

"You are most welcome, Isolla," Brandin was saying with genuine pleasure. "It has been far too long since we have seen you, or heard you play."

Dianora saw Camena make a small adjustment in the way he held the lute. She thought he was preparing to open the case. It did not look like an ordinary lute though. In fact—

Afterwards she was able to know one thing only with certainty: it had been the story of the riselka that made her so sharp to see. The story, and the fact that Brandin wasn't certain if the second man—his guard—had seen her or not.

One man meant a fork in the path. Two men meant a death.

Either way, something was to happen. And now it did.

All eyes but hers were on Brandin and Isolla. Only Dianora saw Camena slip the velvet cover off the lute. Only Dianora saw that it was not, in fact, a lute. And only she had heard Brandin's tale of the riselka.

"*Die, Isolla of Ygath!*" Camena screamed hoarsely; his eyes bulged as he hurled the velvet away and leveled the crossbow he carried.

With the lightning reaction of a man half his years Brandin reflexively threw out his hand to cast a sorcerer's shield around the threatened singer.

Exactly as he was expected to, Dianora realized.

"Brandin, no!" she screamed. *"It's you!"*

And seizing the gape-mouthed Neso of Ygrath by the near shoulder she propelled herself and him both into the aisle.

The crossbow bolt, aimed meticulously to the left of Isolla on a line for Brandin's heart, buried itself instead in the shoulder of a stupefied Neso. He shrieked in pain and shock.

Her momentum drove Dianora stumbling to her knees beside Isolla. She looked up. And for the rest of her days never forgot the look she met in the singer's eyes.

She turned away from it. The emotion, the hatred was too raw. She felt physically ill, trembling with aftershock. She forced herself to stand; she looked at Brandin. He hadn't even lowered his hand. There was still the shimmer of a protective barrier around Isolla.

Who had never been in danger at all.

The guards had Camena by now. He'd been dragged to his feet. Dianora had never seen anyone look so white. Even his eyes were white, from the drug. For a moment she thought he was going to faint, but then Camena threw his head back as far as he could in the iron grip of the Ygrathen soldiers. He opened his mouth, as if in agony.

"Chiara!" he cried once, and then, *"Freedom for Chiara!"* before they silenced him, brutally.

The echoes rang for a long time. The room was large and the stillness was almost absolute. No one dared to move. Dianora had a sense that the court wasn't even breathing. No one wanted the slightest attention drawn to them.

On the mosaic-inlaid floor Neso moaned again in fear and pain, breaking the tableau. Two soldiers knelt to tend to him. Dianora was still afraid she was going to be sick; she couldn't make her hands stop trembling. Isolla of Ygrath had not moved.

She *could* not move, Dianora realized: Brandin was holding her in a mindlock like a flower pressed flat on a sheet. The soldiers lifted Neso and helped him from the room. Dianora stepped back herself, leaving Isolla alone before the King. Fifteen very proper paces away.

"Camena was a tool," Brandin said softly. "Chiara has

virtually nothing to do with this. Do not think that I am
unaware of that. I can offer you nothing now but an
easier death. You must tell me why you did this." His
voice was rigidly measured, careful and uninflected.
Dianora had never heard such a tone from him. She
looked at Rhun: the Fool was weeping, tears streaking
his distorted features.

Brandin lowered his hand, freeing Isolla to move and
speak.

The blazing flash of hatred left her features. In its
place was a defiant pride. Dianora wondered if she had
actually thought the deception would work. If after the
King had been slain she had really expected to walk
freely from this room. And if not—if she had not expected to do so—what did that mean?

Holding herself very straight, Isolla gave part of an
answer. "I am dying," she said to Brandin. "The physi-
cians have given me less than a season before the growth
inside reaches my brain. Already there are songs I can no
longer remember. Songs that have been mine for forty
years."

"I am sorry to hear it," said Brandin formally, his
courtesy so perfect it seemed a violation of human nature. He said, "All of us die, Isolla. Some very young.
Not all of us plot the death of our King. You have more
to tell me before I may grant you release from pain."

For the first time Isolla seemed to waver. She lowered
her gaze from his eerily serene grey eyes. Only after a
long moment did she say, "You had to have known that
there would be a price for what you did."

"Exactly what is it that I did?"

Her head came up. "You exalted a dead child above
the living one, and revenge above your wife. And more
highly than your own land. Have you spared a thought, a
fraction of a thought, for any of them while you pursued
your unnatural vengeance for Stevan?"

Dianora's heart thudded painfully. It was a name not
spoken in Chiara. She saw Brandin's lips tighten in a way
she had seen only a handful of times. But when he spoke
his voice was as rigidly controlled as before.

"I judged that I had considered them fairly. Girald has
governance in Ygrath as he was always going to have. He

even has my saishan, as a symbol of that. Dorotea I invited here several times a year for the first several years."

"Invited here that she might wither and grow old while you kept yourself young. A thing no Sorcerer-King of Ygrath has ever done before, lest the gods punish the land for that impiety. But for Ygrath you never spared a thought, did you? And Girald? He is no King—his father is. That is *your* title, not his. What does the key to a saishan mean against that reality? He is even going to die before you, Brandin, unless you are slain. And what will happen then? It is unnatural! It is all unnatural, and there is a price to be paid."

"There is always a price," he said softly. "A price for everything. Even for living. I had not expected to pay it in my own family." There was a silence. "Isolla, I must extend my years to do what I am here to do."

"Then you pay for it," Isolla repeated, "and Girald pays and Dorotea. And Ygrath."

And Tigana, Dianora thought, no longer trembling, her own ache come back like a wound in her. *Tigana pays too; in broken statues and fallen towers, in children slain and a name gone.*

She watched Brandin's face. And Rhun's.

"I hear you," the King said at length to the singer. "I have heard more than you have chosen to say. I need only one thing further. You must tell me which of them did this." It was said with visible regret. Rhun's ugly face was screwed up tightly, his hands gestured with a random helplessness.

"And why," said Isolla, drawing herself up and speaking with the frigid hauteur of one who had nothing left to lose, "should you imagine their purposes to be at odds in this? Why the one or the other, King of Ygrath?" Her voice rang out, harsh as the message it bore.

Slowly he nodded. The hurt was clear in him now; Dianora could see it in the way he stood and spoke, however much he controlled himself. She didn't even need to look at Rhun.

"Very well," Brandin said. "And you, Isolla? What could they have offered to make you do this thing. Can you really hate me so much?"

The woman hesitated only for an instant. Then, as proudly, as defiantly as before, she said, "I can love the Queen so much."

Brandin closed his eyes. "How so?"

"In all the ways that you forsook when you chose exile here and love of the dead over the heart and the bed of your wife."

In any normal, any halfway normal time there would have been a reaction to this from the court. There would have had to be. Dianora heard nothing though, only the sound of a great many people breathing carefully as Brandin opened his eyes again to look down upon the singer. There was an unveiled triumph in the Ygrathen woman's face.

"She was invited here," he repeated almost wistfully. "I could have compelled her but I chose not to do so. She had made her feelings clear and I left the choice to her. I thought it was the kinder, fairer action. It would appear that my sin lies in not having ordered her to take ship for this peninsula."

So many different griefs and shapes of pain seemed to be warring for preeminence within Dianora. Behind the King she could see d'Eymon; his face was a sickly grey. He met her eyes for only an instant then quickly looked away. Later she might think of ways to use this sudden ascendancy over him but right now she felt only pity for the man. He would offer to resign tonight, she knew. Offer, probably, to kill himself after the old fashion. Brandin would refuse, but after this nothing would be quite the same.

For a great many reasons.

Brandin said, "I think you have told me what I had need to know."

"The Chiaran acted alone," Isolla volunteered unexpectedly. She gestured at Camena, in the bone-cracking grip of the soldiers behind her. "He joined us when he visited Ygrath two years ago. Our purposes appeared to march together this far."

Brandin nodded. "This far," he echoed quietly. "I thought that might be the case. Thank you for confirming it," he added gravely.

There was a silence. "You promised me an easy death," Isolla said, holding herself very straight.

"I did," Brandin said. "I did promise you that." Dianora stopped breathing. The King looked at Isolla without expression for what seemed an unbearably long time.

"You can have no idea," he said at last, in a voice little above a whisper, "how happy I was that you had come to make music for me again."

Then he moved his right hand, in exactly the same casual gesture he would use to dismiss a servant or a petitioner.

Isolla's head exploded like an overripe fruit smashed with a hammer. Dark blood burst from her neck as her body collapsed like a sack. Dianora was standing too near; the blood of the slain woman spattered thickly on her gown and face. She stumbled backwards. A hideous illusion of reptilian creatures was coiling and twisting in the place where Isolla's head had been mashed to a formless, oozing pulp.

There was screaming everywhere and a frenzied pandemonium as the court backed away. One figure suddenly ran forward. Stumbling, almost falling in its haste, the figure jerked out a sword. Then awkwardly, with great clumsy two-handed slashes, Rhun the Fool began hacking at the dead body of the singer.

His face was weirdly distorted with rage and revulsion. Foam and mucus ran from his mouth and nose. With one savage butcher's blow he severed an arm from the woman's torso. Something dark and green and blind appeared to undulate from the stump of Isolla's shoulder, leaving a trail of glistening black slime. Behind Dianora someone gagged with horror.

"*Stevan!*" she heard Rhun cry brokenly. And amid nausea and chaos and terror, an overwhelming pity suddenly laid hard siege to her heart. She looked at the frantically laboring Fool, clad exactly like the King, bearing a King's sword. Spittle flew from his mouth.

"Music! Stevan! Music! Stevan!" Rhun shouted obsessively, and with each slurred, ferocious articulation of the words his slender, jeweled court sword went up and down, glinting brilliantly in the streaming light, hewing the dead body like meat. He lost his footing on the slippery floor and fell to his knees with the force of his own fury. A grey thing with eyes on waving stalks appeared to attach itself like a bloodleech to his knee.

"Music," Rhun said one last time, softly, with unexpected clarity. Then the sword slipped through his fingers and he sat in a puddle of blood beside the mutilated corpse of the singer, his balding head slewed awkwardly down and to one side, his white-and-gold court garments hopelessly soiled, weeping as though his heart was broken.

Dianora turned to Brandin. The King was motionless, standing exactly as he had been throughout, his hands relaxed at his sides. He gazed at the appalling scene in front of him with a frightening detachment.

"There is always a price," he said quietly, almost to himself, through the incessant screaming and tumult that filled the Audience Chamber. Dianora took one hesitant step towards him then, but he had already turned and, with d'Eymon quickly following, Brandin left the room through the door behind the dais.

With his departure the slithering, oleaginous creatures immediately disappeared, but not the mangled body of the singer or the pitiful, crumpled figure of the Fool. Dianora seemed to be alone near them, everyone else had surged back towards the doors. Isolla's blood felt hot where it had landed on her skin.

People were tripping and pushing each other in their frantic haste to quit the room now that the King was gone. She saw the soldiers hustling Camena di Chiara away through a side door. Other soldiers came forward with a sheet to cover Isolla's body. They had to move Rhun away to do it; he didn't seem to understand what was happening. He was still weeping, his face grotesquely screwed up like a hurt child's. Dianora moved a hand to wipe at her cheek and her fingers came away streaked with blood. The soldiers placed the sheet over the singer's body. One of them gingerly picked up the arm Rhun had severed and pushed it under the sheet as well. Dianora saw him do that. There seemed to be blood all over her face. On the very edge of losing all control she looked around for help, any kind of help.

"Come, my lady," said a desperately needed voice that

was somehow by her side. "Come. Let me take you back to the saishan."

"Oh, Scelto," she whispered. "Please. Please do that, Scelto."

The news blazed through the dry tinder of the saishan setting it afire with rumor and fear. An assassination attempt from Ygrath. With Chiaran participation.

And it had very nearly succeeded.

Scelto hustled Dianora down the corridor to her rooms and with a bristling protectiveness slammed the door on the nervous, fluttering crowd that clung and hovered in the hallway like so many silk-clad moths. Murmuring continuously he undressed and washed her, and then wrapped her carefully into her warmest robe. She was shivering uncontrollably, unable to speak. He lit the fire and made her sit before it. In docile submission she drank the mahgoti tea he prepared as a sedative. Two cups of it, one after the other. Eventually the trembling stopped. She still found it difficult to speak. He made her stay in the chair before the fire. She didn't want to leave it anyway.

Her brain felt battered, numb. She seemed to be utterly incapable of marshaling any understanding, of shaping an adequate response to what had just happened.

One thought only kept driving the others away, pounding in her head like the hammer of a herald's staff on the floor. A thought so impossible, so disabling, that she tried, with all she could, through the blinding pulse of an onrushing headache, to block it out. She couldn't. The hammering crashed through, again and again: *she had saved his life.*

Tigana had been a single pulsebeat away from coming back into the world. The pulsebeat of Brandin that the crossbow would have ended.

Home was a dream she'd had yesterday. A place where children used to play. Among towers near the mountains, by a river, on curving sweeps of white or golden sand beside a palace at the edge of the sea. Home was a longing, a desperate dream, a name in her dreams. And this afternoon she had done the one thing she could

possibly have done to bar that name from the world, to
lock it into a dream. Until all the dreams, too, died.

How was she to deal with that? How possibly cope
with what it meant? She had come here to kill Brandin of
Ygrath, to end his life that lost Tigana might live again.
And instead . . .

The shivering started once more. Fussing and murmuring, Scelto built up the fire and brought yet another
blanket for her knees and feet. When he saw the tears on
her face he made a queer helpless sound of distress.
Someone knocked loudly on her door sometime later
and she heard Scelto driving them away with language
she had never known him to use before.

Gradually, very slowly, she began to pull herself together. From the color of the light that gently drifted
down through the high windows she knew that the afternoon would be waning towards dusk. She rubbed her
cheeks and eyes with the backs of her hands. She sat up.
She had to be ready when twilight came; twilight was
when Brandin sent to the saishan.

She rose from her chair, pleased to find that her legs
were steadier. Scelto rushed up, protesting, but when he
saw her face he quickly checked himself. Without another word he led her through the inner doors and down
that hallway to the baths. His ferocious glare silenced the
attendants there. She had a sense that he would have
struck them if they had spoken; she had never heard of
him doing a single violent act. Not since he had killed a
man and lost his own manhood.

She let them bathe her, let the scented oils soften her
skin. There had been blood on it that afternoon. The
waters swirled around her and then away. The attendants
washed her hair. After, Scelto painted the nails of her
fingers and toes. A soft shade, dusty rose. Far from the
color of blood, far from anger or grief. Later she would
paint her lips the same shade. She doubted they would
make love, though. She would hold him and be held. She
went back to her room to wait for the summons.

From the light she knew when evening had fallen.
Everyone in the saishan always knew when evening fell.
The day revolved towards and then away from the hour

of darkness. She sent Scelto outside, to receive the word when it came.

A short time after he came back and told her that Brandin had sent for Solores.

Anger flamed wildly within her. It exploded like . . . like the head of Isolla of Ygrath in the Audience Chamber. Dianora could scarcely draw breath, so fierce was her sudden rage. Never in her life had she felt anything like this—this white hot caldron in her heart. After Tigana fell, after her brother was driven away, her hatred had been a shaped thing, controlled, channeled, driven by purpose, a guarded flame that she'd known would have to burn a long time.

This was an inferno. A caldron boiling over inside her, prodigious, overmastering, sweeping all before it like a lava flow. Had Brandin been in her room at that moment she could have ripped his heart out with her nails and teeth—as the women tore Adaon on the mountainside. She saw Scelto take an involuntary backwards step away from her; she had never known him to fear her or anyone else before. It was not an observation that mattered now.

What mattered, *all* that mattered, the *only* thing, was that she had saved the life of Brandin of Ygrath today, trampling into muck and spattered blood the clear, unsullied memory of her home and the oath she'd sworn in coming here so long ago. She had violated the essence of everything she once had been; violated herself more cruelly than had any man who'd ever lain with her for a coin in that upstairs room in Certando.

And in return? In return, Brandin had just sent for Solores di Corte, leaving her to spend tonight alone.

Not, not a thing he should have done.

It did not matter that even within the fiery heat of her own blazing Dianora could understand why he might have done this thing. Understand how little need he would have tonight for wit or intelligence, for sparkle, for questions or suggestions. Or desire. His need would be for the soft, unthinking, reflexive gentleness that Solores gave. That she herself apparently did not. The cradling worship, tenderness, the soothing voice. He would need shelter tonight. She could understand: it was what she needed too, needed desperately, after what had happened. But she needed it from him.

And so it came to be that, alone in her bed that night, sheltered by no one and by nothing, Dianora found herself naked and unable to hide from what came when the fires of rage finally died.

She lay unsleeping through the first and then through the second chiming of the bells that marked off the triads of the dark hours, but before the third chiming that heralded the coming of grey dawn two things had happened within her.

The first was the inexorable return of the single strand of memory she'd always been careful to block out from among all the myriad griefs of the year Tigana was occupied. But she truly was unsheltered and exposed in the dark of that Ember Night, drifting terribly far from whatever moorings her soul had found.

While Brandin, on the far wing of the palace sought what comfort he could in Solores di Corte, Dianora lay as in an open space and alone, unable to deflect any of the images that now came sweeping back from years ago. Images of love and pain and the loss of love in pain that were far too keen—too icy keen a wind in the heart—to be allowed at any normal time.

But the finger of death had rested on Brandin of Ygrath that day, and she alone had guided it away, steering the King past the darkest portal of Morian, and tonight was an Ember Night, a night of ghosts and shadows. It could not be anything like a normal time, and it was not. What came to Dianora, terribly, one after another in unceasing progression like waves of the dark sea, were her last memories of her brother before he went away.

He had been too young to fight by the Deisa. No one under fifteen, Prince Valentin had proclaimed before riding sternly north to war. Alessan, the Prince's youngest child, had been taken away south in hiding by Danoleon, the High Priest of Eanna, when word came that Brandin was coming down upon them.

That was after Stevan had been slain. After the one victory. They had all known; the weary men who had fought and survived, and the women and the aged and the children left behind—that Brandin's coming would mark the end of the world they had lived in and loved.

They hadn't known then how literally true that was: what the Sorcerer-King of Ygrath could do and what he did. This they were to learn in the days and months that followed as a hard and brutal thing that grew like a tumor and then festered in the souls of those who survived.

The dead of Deisa are the lucky ones. So it was said, more and more often, in whispers and in pain in the year Tigana died, by those who endured the dying.

Dianora and her brother were left with a mother whose mind had snapped like a bowstring with the tidings of Second Deisa. Even as the vanguard of the Ygrathens entered the city itself, occupying the streets and squares of Tigana, the noble houses and the delicately colored Palace by the Sea, she seemed to let slip her last awareness of the world to wander, mute and gentle, through a space neither of her children could travel to with her.

Sometimes she would smile and nod at invisible things as she sat amid the rubble of their courtyard that summer, with smashed marble all around her, and her daughter's heart would ache like an old wound in the rains of winter.

Dianora set herself to run the household as best she could, though three of the servants and apprentices had died with her father. Two others ran away not long after the Ygrathens came and the destruction began. She couldn't even blame them. Only one of the women and the youngest of the apprentices stayed with them.

Her brother and the apprentice waited until the long wave of burnings and demolition had passed, then they sought work clearing away rubble or repairing walls as a limited rebuilding started under Ygrathen orders. Life began to return towards a normality. Or what passed for normality in a city now called Lower Corte in a province of that name.

In a world where the very word *Tigana* could not be heard by anyone other than themselves. Soon they stopped using it in public places. The pain was too great: the twisting feeling inside that came with the blank look of incomprehension on the faces of the Ygrathens or the traders and bankers from Corte who had swarmed quickly down to seek what profit they could among the rubble and the slow rebuilding of a city. It was a hurt for which, truly, there was no name.

Dianora could remember, with jagged, sharp-edged clarity, the first time she'd called her home Lower Corte. They all could, all the survivors: it was, for each of them, a moment embedded like a fish hook in the soul. The dead of Deisa, First or Second, were the lucky ones, so the phrase went that year.

She watched her brother come into a bitter maturity that first summer and fall, grieving for his vanished smile, laughter lost, the childhood too soon gone, not knowing how deeply the same hard lessons and absences were etched in her own hollow, unlovely face. She was sixteen in the late summer, he turned fifteen in the fall. She made a cake on his naming day, for the apprentice, the one old woman, her mother, her brother and herself. They had no guests; assembly of any kind was forbidden throughout that year. Her mother had smiled when Dianora gave her a slice of the dark cake—but Dianora had known the smile had nothing to do with any of them.

Her brother had known it too. Preternaturally grave he had kissed his mother on the forehead and then his sister, and had gone out into the night. It was, of course, illegal to be abroad after nightfall, but something kept driving him out to walk the sreets, past the random fires that still smoldered on almost every corner. It was as if he was daring the Ygrathen patrols to catch him. To punish him for having been fourteen in the season of war.

Two soldiers were knifed in the dark that fall. Twenty death-wheels were hoisted in swift response. Six women and five children were among those bound aloft to die. Dianora knew most of them; there weren't so very many people left in the city, they all knew each other. The screaming of the children, then their diminishing cries were things she needed shelter from in her nights forever after.

No more soldiers were killed.

Her brother continued to go out at night. She would lie awake until she heard him come in. He always made a sound, deliberately, so she would hear him and be able to fall asleep. Somehow, he knew she would be awake, though she had never said a word.

He would have been handsome, with his dark hair and deep brown eyes if he hadn't been so thin and if the eyes were not shadowed and ringed by sleeplessness and grief. There was not a great deal of food that first winter—most of the harvest had been burned, and the rest confiscated—but Dianora did the best she could to feed the five of them. About the look in his eyes there was nothing she could do. Everyone had that look that year. She could see it in her mirror.

The following spring the Ygrathen soldiers discovered a new form of sport. It had probably been inevitable that they would, one of the evil growths that sprang from the deep-sown seeds of Brandin's vengeance.

Dianora remembered being at an upstairs window the day it began. She was watching her brother and the apprentice—no longer an apprentice, of course—walking through a sun-brightened early morning across the square on their way to the site where they were laboring. White clouds had been drifting by overhead, scudding with the wind. A small cluster of soldiers came from the opposite side and accosted the two boys. Her window was open to air the room and catch the freshness of the breeze; she heard it all.

"Help us!" one of the soldiers bleated with a smirk she could see from her window. "We're lost," he moaned, as the others quickly surrounded the boys. He drew sly chuckles from his fellows. One of them elbowed another in the ribs.

"Where are we?" the soldier begged.

Eyes carefully lowered, her brother named the square and the streets leading from it.

"That's no good!" the soldier complained. "What good are street names to me? I don't even know what cursed *town* I'm in!" There was laughter; Dianora winced at what she heard in it.

"Lower Corte," the apprentice muttered quickly, as her brother kept silent. They noticed the silence though.

"What town? *You* tell me," the spokesman said more sharply, prodding her brother in the shoulder.

"I just told you. Lower Corte," the apprentice intervened loudly. One of the soldiers cuffed him on the side of the head. The boy staggered and almost fell; he refused to lift a hand to touch his head.

Her pulse pounding with fright, Dianora saw her brother look up then. His dark hair gleamed in the morning sunlight. She thought he was going to strike the soldier who had dealt that blow. She thought he was going to die. She stood up at her window, her hands clenched on the ledge. There was a terrible silence in the square below. The sun was very bright.

"Lower Corte," her brother said, as though he were choking on the words.

Laughing raucously the soldiers let them go.

For that morning.

The two boys became the favorite victims of that company, which patrolled their district between the Palace by the Sea and the center of town where the three temples stood. None of the temples of the Triad had been smashed, only the statuary that stood outside and within them. Two had been her father's work. A young, seductively graceful Morian, and a huge, primal figure of Eanna stretching forth her hands to make the stars.

The boys began leaving the house earlier and earlier as spring wore on, taking roundabout routes in an attempt to avoid the soldiers. Most mornings, though, they were still found. The Ygrathens were bored by then; the boys' very efforts to elude them offered sport.

Dianora used to go to that same upstairs window at the front of the house when they left by way of the square, as if by watching whatever happened, sharing it, she could somehow spread the pain among three, not two, and so ease it for them. The soldiers almost always accosted them just as they reached the square. She was watching on the day the game changed to something worse.

It was afternoon that time. A half-day of work only, because of a Triad holiday—part of the aftermath to the springtime Ember Days. The Ygrathens, like the Barbadians to the east, had been scrupulous not to tamper with the Triad and their clergy. After their lunch the two boys went out to do an afternoon's work.

The soldiers surrounded them in the middle of the square. They never seemed to tire of their sport. But that afternoon, just as the leader began his familiar litany of being lost a group of four merchants came trudging up the hill from the harbor and one of the soldiers had an inspiration born of sheerest malice.

"Stop!" he rasped. The merchants did, very abruptly. One obeyed Ygrathen commands in Lower Corte, wherever one might be from.

"Come here," the soldier added. His fellows made way for the merchants to stand in front of the boys. A premonition of something evil touched Dianora in that moment like a cold finger on her spine.

The four traders reported that they were from Asoli. It was obvious from their clothing.

"Good," the soldier said. "I know how grasping you lot are. Now listen to me. These brats are going to name their city and their province to you. If you can tell me what they say, on my honor and in the name of Brandin, King of Ygrath, I'll give the first man who says the name back to me twenty gold ygras."

It was a fortune. Even from where she sat, high up and screened behind her window, Dianora could see the Asoli traders react. That was before she closed her eyes. She knew what was coming and how it was going to hurt. She wanted her father alive in that moment with a longing so acute she almost wept. Her brother was down there though, among soldiers who hated them. She forced back her tears and opened her eyes. She watched.

"You," said the soldier to the apprentice—they always started with him—"your province had another name once. Tell them what it was."

She saw the boy—Naddo was his name—go white with fear or anger, or both. The four merchants, oblivious to that irrelevance, leaned forward, straining with anticipation. Dianora saw Naddo look at her brother for guidance, or perhaps for dispensation.

The soldier saw the glance. "None of that!" he snapped. Then he drew his sword. "For your life, say the name."

Naddo, very clearly, said, "Tigana."

And of course not one of the merchants could say back the word he spoke. Not for twenty golden ygras or twenty times so many. Dianora could read the bafflement, the balked greed in their eyes, and the fear that confronting sorcery always brought.

The soldiers laughed and jostled each other. One of them had a shrill cackle like a rooster. They turned to her brother.

"No," he said flatly before they could even command him. "You have had your sport. They cannot hear the name. We all know it—what is left to prove?"

He was fifteen, and much too thin, and his dark-brown hair was too long over his eyes. It had been over a month since she'd cut it for him; she'd been meaning to do so all week. One of her hands was squeezing the window-ledge so tightly that all the blood had rushed away; it was white as ice. She would have cut it off to change what was happening. She noticed other faces at other windows along the street and across the square. Some people had stopped down below as well, seeing the large clustering of men, sensing the sudden tension that had taken shape.

Which was bad, because with an audience the soldiers would now have to clearly establish their authority. What had been a game when done in private was something else now. Dianora wanted to turn away. She wanted her father back from the Deisa, she wanted Prince Valentin back and alive, her mother back from whatever country she wandered through.

She watched. To share it. To bear witness and remember, knowing even then that such things were going to matter, if anything mattered in the days and years to come.

The soldier with the drawn blade placed the tip of it very carefully against her brother's breast. The afternoon sunlight glinted from it. It was a working blade, a soldier's sword. There came a small sound from the people gathered around the edges of the square.

Her brother said, a little desperately, "They cannot hold the name. You know they cannot. You have destroyed us. Is it necessary to go on causing pain? Is it necessary?"

He is only fifteen, Dianora prayed, gripping the ledge

like death, her hand a claw. *He was too young to fight.*
He was not allowed. Forgive him this. Please.

The four Asolini traders, as one man, stepped quickly
out of range. One of the soldiers—the one with the high
laugh—shifted uncomfortably, as if regretting what this
had come to. But there was a crowd gathered. The boy
had had his fair chance. There was really no choice now.

The sword pushed delicately forward a short way and
then withdrew. Through a torn blue tunic a welling of
blood appeared and hung a moment, bright in the springtime light, as if yearning towards the blade, before it
broke and slid downwards, staining the blue.

"The name," said the soldier quietly. There was no
levity in his voice now. He was a professional, and he
was preparing himself to kill, Dianora realized.

A witness, a memory, she saw her younger brother
spread his feet then, as if to anchor himself in the ground
of the square. She saw his hands clench into fists at his
sides. She saw his head go back, lifting towards the sky.

And then she heard his cry.

He gave them what they demanded of him, he obeyed
the command, but not sullenly or diffidently, and not in
shame. Rooted in the land of his fathers, standing before
the home of his family he looked towards the sun and let
a name burst forth from his soul.

"Tigana!" he cried that all should hear. All of them,
everyone in the square. And again, louder yet: *"Tigana!"*
And then a third, a last time, at the very summit of his
voice, with pride, with love, with a lasting, unredeemed
defiance of the heart.

"TIGANA!"

Through the square that cry rang, along the streets, up
to the windows where people watched, over the roofs of
houses running westward to the sea or eastward to the
temples, and far beyond all of these—a sound, a name,
a hurled sorrow in the brightness of the air. And though
the four merchants could not cling to the name, though
the soldiers could not hold it, the women at the windows
and the children with them and the men riveted stone-
still in street and square could hear it clearly, and clutch
it to themselves, and they could gather and remember
the pride at the base of that spiraling cry.

And that much, looking around, the soldiers could see plainly and understand. It was written in the faces gathered around them. He had done only what they themselves had ordered him to do, but the game had been turned inside out, it had turned out wrong in some way they could but dimly comprehend.

They beat him of course.

With their fists and feet and with the flats of their cared-for blades. Naddo too—for being there and so a part of it. The crowd did not disperse though, which would have been the usual thing when a beating took place. They watched in a silence unnatural for so many people. The only sound was that of the blows falling, for neither boy cried out and the soldiers did not speak.

When it was over they scattered the crowd with oaths and imprecations. Crowds were illegal, even though they themselves had caused this one to form. In a few moments everyone was gone. There were only faces behind half-drawn curtains at upstairs windows looking down on a square empty save for two boys lying in the settling dust, blood bright on their clothing in the clear light. There had been birds singing all around and all through what had happened. Dianora could remember.

She forced herself to remain where she was. Not to run down to them. To let them do this alone, as was their right. And at length she saw her brother rise with the slow, meditated movements of a very old man. She saw him speak to Naddo and then carefully help him to his feet. And then, as she had known would happen, she saw him, begrimed and bleeding and hobbling very badly, lead Naddo east without a backwards look, towards the site where they were assigned to work that day.

She watched them go. Her eyes were dry. Only when the two of them turned the corner at the far end of the square and so were gone from sight did she leave her window. Only then did she loosen her white-clawed hold on the wood of the window-ledge. And only then, invisible to everyone with her curtains drawn, did she allow her tears to fall: in love, and for his hurts, and terrible pride.

When they came home that night she and the servant-woman heated water and drew baths for them and afterwards they dealt with the wounds and the black and purpling bruises as best they could.

Later, over dinner, Naddo told them he was leaving. That same night, he said. It was too much, he said, awkwardly twisting in his seat, speaking to Dianora, for her brother had turned his face away at Naddo's first announcement.

There was no life to be made here, Naddo said with passionate urgency through a torn and swollen mouth. Not with the viciousness of the soldiers and the even more vicious taxes. If a young man, a young man such as himself, was to have any hope of doing something with his life, Naddo said, he had to get away. Desperately his eyes besought her understanding. He kept glancing nervously over to where her brother had now fully turned his back on both of them.

Where will you go, Dianora had asked him.

Asoli, he'd told her. It was a hard, wet land, unbearably hot and humid in summer, everyone knew that. But there was room there for new blood. The Asolini made people welcome, he'd heard, more so than in the Barbadian lands to the east. He would never ever go to Corte or Chiara. People from Tigana did not go there, he said. Her brother made a small sound at that but did not turn; Naddo glanced over at him again and swallowed, his Adam's apple bobbing in his throat.

Three other young men had made plans, he said to Dianora. Plans to slip out from the city tonight and make their way north. He'd known about it for some time, he said. He hadn't been sure. He hadn't known what to do. What had happened this morning had made up his mind for him.

Eanna light your path, Dianora had said, meaning it. He had been a good apprentice and then a brave and loyal friend. People were leaving all the time. The province of Lower Corte was a bad place in a very bad time. Naddo's left eye was completely swollen shut. He might easily have been killed that afternoon.

Later, when he'd packed his few belongings and was ready to leave, she gave him some silver from her father's hidden store. She kissed him in farewell. He'd begun weeping then. He commended himself to her mother

and opened the front door. On the threshold he'd turned
back again, still crying.

"Goodbye," he'd said, in anguish, to the figure staring
stonily into the fire on the front-room hearth. Seeing the
look on Naddo's face Dianora silently willed her brother
to turn around. He did not. Deliberately he knelt and
laid another log on the fire.

Naddo stared at him a moment longer, then he turned
to look at Dianora, failed to achieve a tremulous, tearful
smile, and slipped out into the dark and away.

Much later, when the fire had been allowed to die, her
brother went out as well. Dianora sat and watched the
embers slowly fade, then she looked in on her mother
and went to bed. When she lay down it seemed to her
that a weight was pressing upon her body, far heavier than
the quilted comforter.

She was awake when he came in. She always was. She
heard him step loudly on the landing as was his habit, to
let her know he was safely home, but she didn't hear the
next sound, which should have been the opening and
closing of his bedroom door.

It was very late. She lay still for another moment,
surrounded and mastered by all the griefs of the day.
Then, moving heavily, as if drugged or in a waking dream,
she rose and lit a candle. She went to her door and
opened it.

He was standing in the hallway outside. And by the
flickering of the light she bore she saw the river of tears
that was pouring without surcease down his bruised, distorted face. Her hands began to shake. She could not
speak.

"Why didn't I say goodbye to him?" she heard him say
in a strangled voice. "Why didn't you make me say
goodbye to him?" She had never heard so much hurt in
him. Not even when word had come that their father had
died by the river.

Her heart aching, Dianora put the candle down on a
ledge that once had held a portrait bust of her mother by
her father. She crossed the narrow distance and took her
brother in her arms, absorbing the hard racking of his
sobs. He had never cried before. Or never so that she
could see. She guided him into her room and lay down

beside him on her bed, holding him close. They wept together, thus, for a very long time. She could not have said how long.

Her window was open. She could hear the breeze sigh through the young leaves outside. A bird sang, and another answered it from across the lane. The world was a place of dreaming or of sorrow, one or both of those. One or both. In the sanctuary of night she slowly pulled his tunic over his head, careful of his wounds, and then she slipped free of her own robe. Her heart was beating like the heart of a captured forest creature. She could feel the race of his pulse when her fingers touched his throat. Both of the moons had set. The wind was in all the leaves outside. And so.

And so in all that darkness, dark over and about and close-gathered around them, the full dark of moonless night and the darkness of their days, the two of them sought a pitiful illicit shelter in each other from the ruin of their world.

"What are we doing?" her brother whispered once.

And then, a space of time later when pulsebeats had slowed again, leaving them clinging to each other in the aftermath of a headlong, terrifying need, he had said, one hand gentle in her hair, "What have we done?"

And all these long years later, alone in the saishan on the Island as this most hidden memory came back, Dianora could remember her reply.

"Oh, Baerd," she'd said. "What has been done to us?"

It lasted from that first night through the whole of spring and into the summer. The sin of the gods, it was named, what they did. For Adaon and Eanna were said to have been brother and sister at the beginning of time, and Morian was their child.

Dianora didn't feel like a goddess, and her mirror offered no illusions: only a too thin face with enormous, staring eyes. She knew only that her happiness terrified her, and consumed her with guilt, and that her love for Baerd was the whole of her world. And what frightened her almost as much was seeing the same depth of love, the same astonished passion in him. Her heart misgave her constantly, even as they reached for their fugitive joy: too bright this forbidden flame in a land where any kind of brightness was lost or not allowed.

He came to her every night. The woman slept downstairs; their mother slept—and woke—in her own world. In the dark of Dianora's room they escaped into each other, reaching through loss and the knowledge of wrong in search of innocence.

He was still driven to go out some nights to walk the empty streets. Not as often as before, for which she gave thanks and sought a kind of justification for herself. A number of young men had been caught after curfew and killed on the wheels that spring. If what she was doing kept him alive she would face whatever judgment lay in wait for her in Morian's Halls.

She couldn't keep him every night though. Sometimes a need she could not share or truly understand would drive him forth. He tried to explain. How the city was different under the two moons or one of them or the stars. How softer light and shadow let him see it as Tigana again. How he could walk silently down towards the sea and come upon the darkened palace, and how the rubble and ruin of it could somehow be rebuilt in his mind in darkness towards what it had been before.

He had a need for that, he said. He never baited the soldiers and promised her he never would. He didn't even want to see them, he said. They crashed into the illusions he wanted. He just needed to be abroad inside his memory of the city that had gone. Sometimes, Baerd told her, he would slip through gaps he knew in the harbor walls and walk along the beach listening to the sea.

By day he labored, a thin boy at a strong man's job, helping to rebuild what they were permitted to rebuild. Rich merchants from Corte—their ancient enemies—had been allowed to settle in the city, to buy up the smashed buildings and residential palaces very inexpensively, and to set about restoring them for their own purposes.

Baerd would come home at the end of a day sometimes with gashes and fresh bruises, and once the mark of a whip across his shoulders. She knew that if one company of soldiers had ended their sport with him there were others to pick it up. It was only happening here, she'd heard. Everywhere else the soldiers restrained themselves and the King of Ygrath was governing with care, to consolidate his provinces against Barbadior.

In Lower Corte they were special, though. They had killed his son.

She would see those marks on Baerd and she had not the heart to ask him to deny himself his lost city at night when the need rose in him. Even though she lived a hundred terrors and died half a hundred deaths every time the front door closed behind him after dark—until she heard it open again and heard his loved, familiar footstep on the stairs, and then the landing, and then he came into her room to take and hold her in his arms.

It went on into summer and then it ended. It all ended, as her knowing heart had forewarned her from that first time in darkness, listening to the birds singing and the wind in the trees outside.

He came home no later than he usually did from walking abroad one night when blue Ilarion had been riding alone through a high lacework of clouds. It had been a beautiful night. She had sat up late by her window watching the moonlight falling on the rooftops. She'd been in bed when he came home though, and her heart had quickened with the familiar intermingling of relief and guilt and need. He had come into her room.

He didn't come to bed. Instead, he sank into the chair she'd sat in by the window. With a queer, numb feeling of dread she had struck tinder and lit her candle. She sat up and looked at him. His face was very white, she could see that even by candlelight. She said nothing. She waited.

"I was on the beach," Baerd said quietly. "I saw a riselka there."

She had always known it would end. That it had to end.

She asked the instinctive question. "Did anyone else see her?"

He shook his head.

They looked at each other in silence. She was amazed at how calm she was, how steady her hands were upon the comforter. And in that silence a truth came home to her, one she had probably known for a long time. "You have only been staying for me, in any case," she said. A statement. No reproach in it. He had seen a riselka.

He closed his eyes. "You knew?"

"Yes," she lied.

"I'm sorry," he said, looking at her. But she knew that this would be easier for him if she were able to hide how new and deathly cold this actually was for her. A gift; perhaps the last gift she would give him.

"Don't be sorry," she murmured, her hands lying still, where he could see them. "Truly, I understand." Truly, she did, though her heart was a wounded thing, a bird with one wing only, fluttering in small circles to the ground.

"The riselka—" he began. And halted. It was an enormous, frightening thing, she knew.

"She makes it clear," he went on earnestly. "The fork of the prophecy. That I *have* to go away." She saw the love for her in his eyes. She willed herself to be strong enough. Strong enough to help him go away from her. *Oh, my brother,* she was thinking. *And will you leave me now?*

She said, "I know she makes it clear, Baerd. I know you have to leave. It will be marked on the lines of your palm." She swallowed. This was harder than she could ever have imagined. She said, "Where will you go?" *My love,* she added, but not aloud, only inside, in her heart.

"I've thought about that," he said. He sat up straighter now. She could see him taking strength from her calm. She clung to that with everything she had.

"I'm going to look for the Prince," he said.

"What, Alessan? We don't even know if he's alive," she said in spite of herself.

"There's word he is," Baerd said. "That his mother is in hiding with the priests of Eanna, and that the Prince has been sent away. If there is any hope, any dream for us, for Tigana, it will lie with Alessan."

"He's fifteen years old," she said. Could not stop herself from saying. *And so are you,* she thought. *Baerd, where did our childhood go?*

By candlelight his dark eyes were not those of a boy. "I don't think age matters," he said. "This is not going to be a quick or an easy thing, if it can ever be done at all. He will be older than fifteen when the time comes."

"So will you," she said.

"And so will you," Baerd echoed. "Oh, Dia, what will you do?" No one else but her father ever called her that. Stupidly it was the name that nearly broke her control.

She shook her head. "I don't know," she said honestly. "Look after mother. Marry. There is money for a while yet if I'm careful." She saw his stricken look and moved to quell it. "You are not to worry about it, Baerd. Listen to me: *you have just seen a riselka!* Will you fight your fate to clear rubble in this city for the rest of your days? No one has easy choices anymore, and mine will not be as hard as most. I may," she had added, tilting her head defiantly, "try to think of some way to chase the same dream as you."

It astonished her, looking back, that she had actually said this on that very night. As if she herself had seen the riselka and her own path had been made clear, even as Baerd's forked away from her.

Lonely and cold in the saishan she was not half so cold or alone as she had been that night. He had not lingered once she'd given her dispensation. She had risen and dressed and helped him pack a very few things. He had flatly refused any of the silver. She assembled a small satchel of food for his first sunrise on the long road alone. At the doorway, in the darkness of the summer night, they had held each other close, clinging without words. Neither wept, as if both knew the time for tears had passed.

"If the goddesses love us, and the god," Baerd said, "we will surely meet again. I will think of you each and every day of my life. I love you, Dianora."

"And I you," she'd said to him. "I think you know how much. Eanna light your path and bring you home." That was all she'd said. All she could think to say.

After he'd gone she had sat in the front room wrapped in an old shawl of her mother's, gazing sightlessly at the ashes of last night's fire until the sun came up.

By then the hard kernel of her own plan had been formed.

The plan that had brought her here, all these years

after, to this other lonely bed on an Ember Night of
ghosts when she should not have had to be alone. Alone
with all her memories, with the reawakening they carried, and the awareness of what she had allowed to
happen to her here on the Island. Here in Brandin's
court. Here with Brandin.

And so it was that two things came to Dianora that
Ember Night in the saishan.

The memories of her brother had been the first, sweeping over her in waves, image after image until they ended
with the ashes of that dead fire.

The second, following inexorably, born of that same
long-ago year, born of memory, of guilt, of the whirlwind
hurts that came with lying here alone and so terribly
exposed on this night of all nights . . . the second thing,
spun forth from all these interwoven things, was, finally,
the shaping of a resolution. A decision, after so many
years. A course of action she now knew she was going to
take. Had to take, whatever might follow.

She lay there, chilled, hopelessly awake, and she was
aware that the cold she felt came far more from within
than without. Somewhere in the palace, she knew, the
torturers would be attending to Camena di Chiara who
had tried to kill a Tyrant and free his home. Who had
done so knowing he would die and how he would die.

Even now they would be with him, administering their
precise measures of pain. With a professional pride in
their skill they would be breaking his fingers one by one,
his wrists and his arms. His toes and ankles and legs.
They would be doing it carefully, even tenderly, solici-
tously guarding the beat of his heart, so that after they
had broken his back—which was always the last—they
could strap him alive on a wheel and take him out to the
harbor square to die in the sight of his people.

She would never have dreamt Camena had such courage or so much passion in his heart. She had derided him
as a poseur, a wearer of three-layered cloaks, a minor,
trivial artist angling for ascension at court.

Not anymore. Yesterday afternoon had compelled a
new shape to her image of him. Now that he had done
what he had done, now that his body had been given to
the torturers and then the wheel there was a question

that could no more be buried than could her memories of Baerd. Not tonight. Not unsheltered as she was and so awake.

What, the thought came knifing home like a winter wind in the soul, *did Camena's act make her?*

What did it make of that long-ago quest a sixteen-year-old girl had so proudly set herself the night her brother went away? The night he'd seen a riselka under moonlight by the sea and gone in search of his Prince.

She knew the answers. Of course she did. She knew the names that belonged to her. The names she had earned here on the Island. They burned like sour wine in a wound. And burning inside, even as she shivered, Dianora strove one more time to school her heart to begin the deathly hard, never yet successful, journey back to her own dominion from that room on the far wing of the palace where lay the King of Ygrath.

That night was different though. Something had changed that night, because of what had happened, because of the finality, the absoluteness of what she herself had done in the Audience Chamber. Acknowledging that, trying to deal with it, Dianora began to sense, as if from a very great distance, her heart's slow, painful retreat from the fires of love. A returning, and then a turning back, to the memory of other fires at home. Fields burning, a city burning, a palace set aflame.

No comfort there of course. No comfort anywhere at all. Only an absolute reminder of who she was and why she was here.

And lying very still in darkness on an Ember Night when country doors and windows were all closed against the dead and the magic in the fields, Dianora told over softly to herself the whole of the old foretelling verse:

> One man sees a riselka
> his life forks there.
> Two men see a riselka
> one of them shall die.
> Three men see a riselka
> one is blessed, one forks, one shall die.
> One woman sees a riselka
> her path comes clear to her.

Two women see a riselka
   one of them shall bear a child.
Three women see a riselka
   one is blessed, one is clear, one shall bear a child.

In the morning, she said to herself amid cold and fire
and all the myriad confusions of the heart. *In the morning it will begin as it should have begun and ended long ago.*
   The Triad knew how bitter, how impossible all choices
had seemed to her. How faint and elusive had been her
dream within these walls of making it all come right for
all of them. But of one truth she was now, finally, certain: she had needed *something* to be made clear along
the twisting paths to betrayal that seemed to have become her life—and from Brandin's own lips she had
learned how that clear path might be offered her.
   In the morning she would begin.
   Until then she could lie here, achingly awake and
alone, as on another night at home so many years ago,
and she could remember.

PART THREE

EMBER TO EMBER

CHAPTER

· 9 ·

IT WAS COLD IN THE GULLY BY THE SIDE OF THE ROAD. There was a thin, sheltering line of birch trees between them and the gates of the Nievolene estate, but even so the wind was a knife whenever it picked up.

There had been snow last night, a rare thing this far north, even in midwinter. It had made for a white, chilled second night of riding from Ferraut town where they had started, but Alessan had refused to slow their pace. He had said increasingly little as the night wore on, and Baerd said little at the best of times. Devin had swallowed his questions and concentrated on keeping up.

They had crossed the Astibar border in darkness and arrived at the Nievolene lands just after dawn. The horses were tethered in a grove about a half mile to the southwest, and the three men had made their way to this gully on foot. Devin dozed off at intervals through the morning. The snow made the landscape strange and crisp and lovely when the sun was out, but around mid-afternoon the grey clouds had gathered heavily overhead and it was only cold now, not beautiful at all. It had snowed again, briefly, about an hour before.

When Devin heard the jingle of horses approaching through the greyness, he realized that the Triad, for once, were holding open palms toward them. Or that, alternatively, the goddesses and the god had decided to give them a chance to do something fatally rash. He pressed himself as flat as he could to the wet ground of the gully. He thought of Catriana and the Duke, warm and sheltered with Taccio in Ferraut.

A company of about a dozen Barbadian mercenaries

materialized out of the gray landscape. They were laughing and singing in boisterous exuberance. Their horses' breath and their own made white puffs of smoke in the cold. Flat in the gully Devin watched them go by. He heard Baerd's soft breathing beside him. The Barbadians stopped at the gates of what had once been Nievolene lands. They weren't anymore, of course; not since the confiscations of the fall. The company leader dismounted and strode to the locked gates. With a flourish that drew cheers and laughter from his men he unlocked the iron gates with two keys on an ornate chain.

"First Company," Alessan murmured under his breath. His first words in hours. "He chose Karalius. Sandre said he would."

They watched the gates swing open and saw the horses canter through. The last man locked the iron gates behind him.

Baerd and Alessan waited another few moments then rose to their feet. Devin stood up as well, wincing at how stiff he felt.

"We'll need to find the tavern in the village," Baerd said, his voice so unusually grim that Devin glanced sharply at him in the growing gloom. The other man's features were unreadable.

"Not to go inside, though," Alessan said. "What we do here, we do unknown."

Baerd nodded. He pulled a much-creased paper from an inner pocket of his sheepskin vest. "Shall we start with Rovigo's man?"

Rovigo's man turned out to be a retired mariner who lived in the village a mile to the east. He told them where the tavern was. He also, for a fairly significant sum of money, gave them a name: that of a known informer for Grancial and his Second Company of Barbadians. The old sailor counted his money, spat once, meaningfully, then told them where the man lived, and something of his habits.

Baerd killed the informer, strangling him two hours later as he walked along a country lane from his small farm towards the village tavern. It was full-dark by then. Devin helped him carry the body back towards the Nievolene gates and hide it in the gully.

Baerd didn't speak, and Devin could think of nothing to say. The informer was a paunchy, balding man of middle years. He didn't look especially evil. He looked like a man surprised on the way to his favorite tavern. Devin wondered if he'd had a wife and children. They hadn't asked Rovigo's man about that; he was just as happy they hadn't.

They rejoined Alessan at the edge of the village. He was keeping watch on the tavern from there. Without speaking he pointed to a large dun-colored horse among those tethered outside the inn. A soldier's horse. The three of them doubled back west half a mile and lay down to wait again, prone and watchful by the side of the road. Devin realized he wasn't cold anymore, or tired; he hadn't had time to think about such things.

Later that night under the cold white gaze of Vidomni in the clearing winter sky Alessan killed the man they'd been waiting for. By the time Devin heard the soft jingle of the soldier's horse, the Prince was no longer by his side and it had been mostly accomplished.

Devin heard a soft sound, more like a cough than a cry. The horse snorted in alarm, and Devin belatedly rose up to try to deal with the animal. By then, though, he realized that Baerd wasn't beside him either. When he finally clambered out of the ditch to the road, the soldier—wearing the insignia of the Second Company—was dead and Baerd had the horse under control. The man, obviously off duty, from the casual look of his uniform, had evidently been on his way back to the border fort. The Barbadian was a big man, they all were, but this one's face seemed very young under the moonlight.

They threw the body across his horse and made their way back to the Nievolene gates. They could hear the men of the First Company singing loudly from the manorhouse along the curving drive. The sound carried a long way in the stillness of the wintry air. There were stars out now beside the moon; the clouds were breaking up. Baerd pulled the Barbadian off the horse and leaned him against one of the gate pillars. Alessan and Devin claimed the other dead man from where they had left him in the gully; Baerd tethered the Barbadian's horse some distance off the road.

Some distance, but not too far. This one was meant to be found later.

Alessan touched Devin briefly on the shoulder. Using the skills Marra had taught him—it seemed several lifetimes ago—Devin picked the two elaborate locks. He was glad to be able to make a contribution. The locks were showy but not difficult. The arrogant Nievolene had not had much fear of trespassers.

Alessan and Baerd each shouldered a body and carried them through. Devin swung the gates silently shut and they entered the grounds. Not toward the manor though. They let the pale moonlight lead them over the snow to the barns.

There they found trouble. The largest barn was locked from the inside, and Baerd pointed silently, with a grimace, to a spill of torchlight that showed from under the double doors. He mimed the presence of a guard.

The three of them looked up. There was, clearly illuminated by Vidomni's glow, a single small window open, high up on the eastern side.

Devin looked from Alessan to Baerd and then back to the Prince. He looked at the bodies of the two men already dead.

He pointed to the window and then to himself.

After a long moment Alessan nodded his head.

In silence, listening to the ragged singing from over in the manor-house, Devin climbed the outer wall of the Nievolene barn. By moonlight and by feel he deciphered hand and footholds in the cold. When he reached the window he looked over his shoulder and saw Ilarion, just rising in the east.

He slipped through and into the upper loft. Below, a horse whickered softly and Devin caught his breath. His heart thudding, he froze where he was, listening. There was no other response. In the sudden, seductive warmth of the barn he crawled cautiously forward and looked down.

The guard was comprehensively asleep. His uniform was unbuttoned and the lantern on the floor by his side illuminated an empty flask of wine. He must have lost a dice roll, Devin thought, to have been posted so boringly on guard against nothing here among the horses and the straw.

He went down the ladder without a sound. And in the flickering light of that barn, amid the smell of hay and animals and spilled red wine Devin killed his first man, plunging his dagger into the Barbadian's throat as the man slept. It was not the way his dreams of valiant deeds had ever had him doing this.

It took him a moment to fight back the churning nausea that followed. It's the smell of the wine, he tried to tell himself. There was also more blood than he'd thought there would be. He wiped his blade clean before he opened the door for the other two.

"Well done," Baerd said, taking in the scene. He briefly laid a hand on Devin's shoulder.

Alessan said nothing, but by the wavering light Devin read a disquieting compassion in his eyes.

Baerd had already set about doing what they had to do.

They left the guard where he was to be burned. The informer and the soldier from the Second Company they dragged towards one of the outbuildings. Baerd studied the situation carefully for a few moments, refusing to be rushed, then he placed the two bodies in a particular way, and wedged the door in front of them convincingly shut with what Devin assumed would later appear to be a dislodged beam.

The singing from the manor had gradually been fading away. Now it had come down to a single voice drunkenly caroling a melancholy refrain about love lost long ago. Finally that voice, too, fell silent.

Which was Alessan's cue. At his signal they simultaneously set fire to the dry straw and wood in the guarded barn and two of the adjacent outbuildings, including the one where the dead men were trapped. Then they fled. By the time they were off the property the Nievolene barns were an inferno of flame. Horses were screaming.

There was no pursuit. They hadn't expected any. Alessan and Sandre had worked it out very carefully back in Ferraut. The charred bodies of the informer and the Second Company soldier would be found by Karalius's men. The mercenaries of the First Company would draw the obvious conclusion.

They reclaimed their horses and headed west. They spent the night outside again in the cold taking turns on watch. It had gone very well. It seemed to have gone exactly as planned. Devin wished they'd been able to free the horses, though. Their screaming ran through his fitful dreams in the snow.

In the morning Alessan bought a cart from a farmer near the border of Ferraut and Baerd bargained with a woodcutter for a load of fresh-cut logs. They paid the new transit duty and sold the wood at the first fort across the border. They also bought some winter wool to carry to Ferraut town where they were to rejoin the others.

There was no point, Alessan said, in missing a chance at a profit. They did have responsibilities to their partners.

In fact, a disconcerting number of untoward events had ruffled the Eastern Palm in the autumn and winter that followed the unmasking of the Sandreni conspiracy. In themselves, none of them amounted to very much; collectively they unsettled and irritated Alberico of Barbadior to the point where his aides and messengers began finding their employment physically hazardous, in so far as their duties brought them into proximity with the Tyrant.

For a man noted for his composure and equanimity— even back in Barbadior when he'd been only the leader of a middle-ranking family of nobility—Alberico's temper was shockingly close to the surface all winter long.

It had begun, his aides agreed amongst each other, after the Sandreni traitor, Tomasso, had been found dead in the dungeons when they came to bring him to the professionals. Alberico, waiting in the room of the implements, had been terrifyingly enraged. Each of the guards— from Siferval's Third Company—had been summarily executed. Including the new Captain of the Guard; the previous one had killed himself the night before. Siferval himself was summoned back to Astibar from Certando for a private session with his employer that left him limp and shaking for hours afterwards.

Alberico's fury had seemed to border on the irrational. He had clearly, his aides decided, been radically unsettled by whatever had happened in the forest. Certainly he didn't look well; there was something odd about one of his eyes, and his walk was peculiar. Then, in the days and weeks that followed, it became manifest, as the local informers for each of the three companies began to bring in their reports, that Astibar town simply did not believe —or chose not to believe—that *anything* had happened in the forest, that there had been any Sandreni conspiracy at all.

Certainly not with the Lords Scalvaia and Nievole, and most certainly not led by Tomasso bar Sandre. People were commenting cynically all over the city, the word came. Too many of them knew of the bone-deep hatreds that divided those three families. Too many knew the stories about Sandre's middle son, the alleged leader of this alleged plot. He might kidnap a boy from a temple of Morian, Astibar was saying, but plot against a Tyrant? With Nievole and Scalvaia?

No, the city was simply too sophisticated to fall for that. Anyone with the slightest sense of geography or economics could see what was really going on. How, by trumping up this "threat" from three of the five largest landowners in the distrada, Alberico was merely creating a sleek cover for an otherwise naked land grab.

It was only sheerest coincidence, of course, that the Sandreni estates were central, the Nievolene farms lay to the southwest along the Ferraut border, and Scalvaia's vineyards were in the richest belt in the north where the best grapes for the blue wine were grown. An immensely convenient conspiracy, all the taverns and khav rooms agreed.

And every single conspirator was dead overnight, as well. Such swift justice! Such an accumulation of evidence against them! There had been an informer among the Sandreni, it was proclaimed. He was dead. Of course. Tomasso bar Sandre had led the conspiracy, they were told. He too, most unfortunately, was dead.

Led by Astibar itself all four provinces of the Eastern Palm reacted with bitter, sardonic disbelief. They may have been conquered, ground under the heavy Barbadian

heel, but they had not been deprived of their intelligence
or rendered blind. They knew a Tyrant's scheming when
they saw it.

Tomasso bar Sandre as a skilled, deadly plotter? Astibar,
reeling under the economic impact of the confiscations,
and the horror of the executions, still found itself able to
mock. And then there arrived the first of the viciously
funny verses from the west—from Chiara itself—written
by Brandin himself some said, though rather more likely
commissioned from one of the poets who hovered about
that court. Verses lampooning Alberico as seeing plots
hatching in every barnyard and using them as an excuse
to seize fowls and vegetable gardens all over the Eastern
Palm. There were also a few, not very subtle sexual
innuendos thrown in for good measure.

The poems, posted on walls all over the city—and
then in Tregea and Certando and Ferraut—were torn
down by the Barbadians almost as fast as they went up.
Unfortunately they were memorable rhymes, and people
didn't need to read or hear them more than once . . .

Alberico would later acknowledge to himself that he'd
lost control a little. He would also admit inwardly that a
great deal of his rage stemmed from a fierce indignation
and the aftermath of fear.

There *had* been a conspiracy led by that mincing
Sandreni. They had very nearly *killed* him in that cursed
cabin in the woods.

This once, he was telling the absolute truth. There was
no pretense or deception. He had every claim of justice
on his side. What he didn't have was a confession, or a
witness, or any evidence at all. He'd needed his informer
alive. Or Tomasso. He'd *wanted* Tomasso alive. His dreams
that first night had been shot through with vivid images
of Sandre's son, bound and stripped and curved invitingly
backwards on one of the machines.

In the aftermath of the pervert's inexplicable death,
and the unanimous word from all four provinces that no
one believed a word of what had happened, Alberico had
abandoned his original, carefully measured response to
the plot.

The lands were seized of course, but in addition all the
living members of all three families were searched out

and death-wheeled in Astibar. He hadn't expected there
to be quite so many, actually, when he gave that order.
The stench had been deplorable and some of the children
lived an unconscionably long time on the wheels. It made
it difficult to concentrate on business in the state offices
above the Grand Square.

He raised taxes in Astibar and introduced, for the first
time, transit duties for merchants crossing from one of
his provinces to another, along the lines of the existing
tariff levied for crossing from the Eastern to the Western
Palm. Let them pay—literally—if they chose not to believe what had happened to him in that cabin.

He did more. Half the massive Nievolene grain harvest
was promptly shipped home to Barbadior. For an action
conceived in anger he considered that one to be inspired.
It had pushed the price of grain down back home in the
Empire, which hurt his family's two most ancient rivals
while making him exceptionally popular with the people.
In so far as the people mattered in Barbadior.

At the same time, here in the Palm, Astibar was forced
to bring in more grain than ever from Certando and
Ferraut, and with the new duties Alberico was going to
rake a healthy cut of that inflated price as well.

He could almost have slaked his anger, almost have
made himself happy, watching the effects of all this ripple
through, if it wasn't that small things kept happening.

For one, his soldiers began to grow restless. With an
increase in hardship came an increase in tension; more
incidents of confrontation occurred. Especially in Tregea
where there were always more incidents of confrontation.
Under greater stress the mercenaries demanded—predictably—higher pay. Which, if he gave it to them, was
going to soak up virtually everything he might gain from
the confiscations and the new duties.

He sent a letter home to the Emperor. His first request
in over two years. Along with a case of Astibar blue
wine—from what were now his own estates in the
north—he conveyed an urgent reiteration of his plea to
be brought under the Imperial aegis. Which would have
meant a subsidy for his mercenaries from the Treasury in
Barbadior, or even Imperial troops under his command.
As always, he stressed the role he alone played in block-

ing Ygrathen expansion in this dangerous halfway peninsula. He might have begun his career here as an independent
adventurer, he conceded, with what he saw as a nice turn
of phrase, but as an older, wiser man he wished to bind
himself more tightly and more usefully to his Emperor
than ever before.

As for wanting to *be* Emperor, and wanting the cloak
of Imperial sanction thrown over him—however belatedly
—well, such things surely did not have to be put into a
letter?

He received, by way of reply, an elegant wall-hanging
from the Emperor's Palace, commendations on his loyal
sentiments, and polite regret that circumstances at home
precluded the granting of his request for financing. As
usual. He was cordially invited to sail home to all suitable
honors and leave the tiresome problems of that far land
overseas to a colonial expert appointed by the Emperor.

That, too, was as usual. Turn your new territory over
to the Empire. Surrender your army. Come home to a
parade or two, then spend your days hunting and your
money on bribes and hunting gear. Wait for the Emperor
to die without naming a successor. Then knife and be
knifed in the brawl to succeed him.

Alberico sent back sincerest thanks, deep regrets, and
another case of wine.

Shortly thereafter, at the end of the fall, a number
of men in the disgruntled, out-of-favor Third Company
withdrew from service and took late-season ship for home.
The commanders of the First and Second used that same
week to formally present—purely coincidence of course—
their new wage demands and to casually remind him of
past promises of land for the mercenaries. Starting, it was
suggested delicately, with their commanders.

He'd wanted to order the two of them throttled. He'd
wanted to fry their greedy, wine-sodden brains with a
blast of his own magic. But he couldn't afford to do it;
added to which, exercising his powers was still a process
of some real strain so soon after the encounter in the
woods that had nearly killed him.

The encounter that no one in this peninsula even believed had taken place.

What he had done was smile at the two commanders

and confide that he had already marked off in his mind a significant portion of the newly claimed Nievolene lands for one of them. Siferval, he said, more in sorrow than in anger, had been put out of the running by the conduct of his own men, but these two . . . well, it would be a hard choice. He would be watching them closely over the next while and would announce his decision in due course.

How long a while, exactly, had pursued Karalius of the First.

Truly, he could have killed the man even as he stood there, helmet under his arm, eyes hypocritically lowered in a show of deference.

Oh, spring, perhaps, he'd said airily, as if such matters should not be of great moment to men of good will.

Sooner would be better, had said Grancial of the Second, softly.

Alberico had chosen to let his eyes show just a little of what he felt. There were limits.

Sooner would let whichever of us you choose have time to see to the proper handling of the land before spring planting, Grancial explained hastily. A little ruffled, as he should be.

Perhaps it is so, Alberico had said, noncommittally. I will give thought to this.

"By the way," he added, as they reached the door. "Karalius, would you be good enough to send me that very competent young captain of yours? The one with the forked black beard. I have a special, confidential task that needs a man of his evident qualities." Karalius had blinked, and nodded.

It was important, very important, not to let them grow too confident, he reflected after they had gone and he'd managed to calm himself. At the same time, only a genuine fool antagonized his troops. The more so, if he had ultimate plans to lead them home. By invitation of the Emperor, preferably, but not necessarily. Not, to be sure, necessarily.

On further reflection, triggered by that line of thought, he did raise taxes in Tregea, Certando, and Ferraut to match the new levels in Astibar. He also sent a courier to Siferval of the Third in the Certandan highlands, praising his recent work in keeping that province quiet.

You lashed them, then enticed them. You made them fear you, and know that their fortunes could be made if you liked them enough. It was all a matter of balance.

Unfortunately, small things continued to go wrong with the balancing of the Eastern Palm as autumn turned into winter in the unusually cold weeks that followed.

Some cursed poet in Astibar chose that dank and rainy season to begin posting a series of elegies to the dead Duke of Astibar. The Duke had died in exile, the head of a scheming family, most of whom had been executed by then. Verses lauding him were manifestly treasonous.

It was difficult though. Every single writer brought in during the first sweep of the khav rooms denied authorship, and then—with time to prepare—every writer in the second sweep *claimed* to have written the verses.

Some advisers suggested peremptory wheels for the lot of them, but Alberico had been giving thought to a larger issue. To the marked difference between his court and the Ygrathen's. On Chiara, the poets vied for access to Brandin, quivering like puppies at the slightest word of praise from him. They wrote paeans of exaltation to the Tyrant and obscene, scathing attacks on Alberico at request. Here, every writer in the Eastern Palm seemed to be a potential rabble-rouser. An enemy of the state.

Alberico swallowed his anger, lauded the technical skill of the verses, and let both sets of poets go free. Not before suggesting, however, as benignly as he could manage, that he would enjoy reading verses as well-crafted on one of the many possible themes of rich satiric possibility having to do with Brandin of Ygrath. He had managed a smile. He would be *very* pleased to read such verses, he'd said, wondering if one of these cursed writers with their lofty airs could take a hint.

None did. Instead, a new poem appeared on walls all over the city two mornings later. It was about Tomasso bar Sandre. A lament about his death, and claiming—unbelievably—that his perverse sexuality had been a deliberately chosen path, a living metaphor for his conquered, subjugated land, for the perverse situation of Astibar under tyranny.

He'd had no choice after that, once he'd understood what the poet was saying. Not bothering with inquiries again, he'd had a dozen writers pulled at random out of the khav rooms that same afternoon, and then broken, wristed, and sky-wheeled among the still-crowded bodies of the families of the conspirators before sundown. He closed all khav rooms for a month. No more verses appeared.

In Astibar. But the same evening his new taxes were proclaimed in the Market Square in Tregea, a black-haired woman elected to leap to her death from one of the seven bridges in protest against the measures. She made a speech before she jumped, and she left behind— the gods alone knew how she'd come into possession of them—a complete sheaf of the "Sandreni Elegies" from Astibar. No one knew who she was. They dragged the icy river for her body but it was never found. Rivers ran swiftly in Tregea, out of the mountains to the eastern sea.

The verses were all over that province within a fortnight, and had crossed to Certando and southern Ferraut before the first heavy snows of the winter began to fall.

Brandin of Ygrath sent an elegantly fur-clad courier to Astibar with an elegantly phrased note lauding the Elegies as the first decent creative work he'd seen emanating from Barbadian territory. He offered Alberico his sincerest congratulations.

Alberico sent a polite acknowledgment of the sentiments and offered to commission one of his newly competent verse-makers to do a work on the glorious life and deeds in battle of Prince Valentin di Tigana.

Because of the Ygrathen's spell, he knew, only Brandin himself would be able to read that last word, but only Brandin mattered.

He thought he'd won that one, but for some reason the woman's suicide in Tregea left him feeling too edgy to be pleased. It was too *intense* an action, harking back to the violence of the first year after he'd landed here. Things had been quiet for so long, and this level of intensity—of very public intensity—never boded well. Briefly he even considered rolling back the new taxes, but that would look too much like a giving in rather than a gesture of benevolence. Besides, he still needed the money for the army. Back home the word was that the Emperor was sinking more rapidly now, that he was seen in public less and less often. Alberico knew he had to keep his mercenaries happy.

In the dead of winter he made the decision to reward Karalius with fully half of the former Nievolene lands.

The night after the announcement was made public—among the troops first, then cried in the Grand Square of Astibar—the horse barn and several of the outbuildings of the Nievolene family estate were burned to the ground.

He ordered an immediate investigation by Karalius, then wished, a day later, that he hadn't. It seemed that they had found two bodies in the smoldering ruins, trapped by a fallen beam that had barred a door. One was that of an informer linked to Grancial and the Second Company. The other was a Barbadian soldier: from the Second Company.

Karalius promptly challenged Grancial to a duel at any time and place of the latter's choosing. Grancial immediately named a date and place. Alberico quickly made it clear that the survivor of any such combat would be death-wheeled. He succeeded in halting the fight, but the two commanders stopped speaking to each other from that point on. There were a number of small skirmishes among men of the two companies, and one, in Tregea, that was not so small, leaving fifteen soldiers slain and twice as many wounded.

Three local informers were found dead in Ferraut's distrada, stretched on farmers' wagon-wheels in a savage parody of the Tyrant's justice. They couldn't even retaliate—that would involve an admission that the men had been informers.

In Certando, two of Siferval's Third Company went absent from duty, disappearing into the snow-white countryside, the first time that had ever happened. Siferval reported that local women did not appear to be involved. The men had been extremely close friends. The Third Company commander offered the obvious, disagreeable hypothesis.

Late in the winter Brandin of Ygrath sent another suave envoy with another letter. In it he profusely thanked Alberico for his offer of verses, and said he'd be delighted to read them. He also formally requested six Certandan women, as young and comely as the one Alberico had so kindly allowed him to take from the Eastern Palm some years ago, to be added to his saishan. Unforgivably the letter somehow became public information.

Laughter was deadly.

To quell it, Alberico had six old women seized by Siferval in southwestern Certando. He ordered them blinded and hamstrung and set down under a courier's flag on the snow-clad border of Lower Corte between the forts at Sinave and Forese. He had Siferval attach a letter to one of them asking Brandin to acknowledge receipt of his new mistresses.

Let them hate him. So long as they feared.

On the way back east from the border, Siferval said in his report, he had followed an informer's tip and found the two runaway soldiers living together at an abandoned farm. They had been executed on the site, with one of them—the appropriate one, Siferval had reported—castrated first, so that he could die as he'd lived. Alberico sent his commendations.

It was an unsettling winter though. Things seemed to be happening *to* him instead of moving to a measure he dictated. Late at night, and then at other times as well, more and more as the Palm gradually turned towards a distant rumor of spring, Alberico found himself thinking about the ninth province that no one yet controlled, the one just across the bay. Senzio.

★　　★　　★

The grey-eyed merchant was making a great deal of sense. Even as he found himself reluctantly agreeing with the man, Ettocio wished the fellow had chosen someone else's roadside tavern for his midday repast. The talk in the room was veering in dangerous directions and, Triad knew, enough Barbadian mercenaries used the main highway between Astibar and Ferraut towns. If one of them stopped in here now, he would be unlikely in the extreme to indulge the current tenor of the conversation as merely an excess of springtime energy. Ettocio's license would probably be gone for a month. He kept glancing nervously towards the door.

"Double taxation now!" the lean man was saying bitterly as he pushed a hand through his hair. "After the kind of winter we've just had? After what he did to the price of grain? So we pay at the border, and now we pay at the gates of a town, and where in the name of Morian is profit?"

There were truculent murmurs of agreement all around the room. In a tavern full of merchants on the road, agreement was predictable. It was also dangerous. Ettocio, pouring drinks, was not the only man keeping an eye on the door. The young fellow leaning on the bar looked up from his crusty roll and wedge of country cheese to give him an unexpectedly sympathetic look.

"Profit?" a wool-merchant from northern Ferraut said sarcastically. "Why should Barbadior care if we make a profit?"

"Exactly!" The grey eyes flashed in vigorous agreement. "The way I hear it, all he wants to do is soak the Palm for everything he can, in preparation for a grab at the Emperor's Tiara back in Barbadior!"

"Shush!" Ettocio muttered under his breath, unable to stop himself. He took a quick, rare pull at a mug of his own beer and moved along the bar to close the window. It was a shame, because the spring day was glorious outside, but this was getting out of hand.

"Next thing you know," the lean trader was saying now, "he'll just go right ahead and seize the rest of our land like he's already started to do in Astibar. Any wagers we're servants or slaves within five years?"

One man's contemptuous laughter rode over the snarling chorus of response triggered by that. The room fell abruptly silent as everyone turned to confront the person who appeared to find this observation diverting. Expressions were grim. Ettocio nervously wiped down the already clean bartop in front of him.

The warrior from Khardhun continued laughing for a long time, seemingly oblivious to the stares he was receiving. His sculpted, black features registered genuine amusement.

"What," said the grey-eyed one coldly, "is so very funny, old man?"

"You are," said the old Khardhu cheerfully. He grinned like a death's head. "All of you. Never seen so many blind men in one room before."

"You care to explain exactly what that means?" the Ferraut wool-merchant rasped.

"You need it explained?" the Khardhu murmured, his eyes wide in mock surprise. "Well, now. Why in the name of your gods or mine or his should Alberico bother trying to enslave you?" He jabbed a bony finger towards the trader who'd started all this. "If he tried that my guess is there's still enough manhood in the Eastern Palm—barely—that you might take offense. Might even . . . *rise up!*" He said that last in an exaggerated parody of a secretive whisper.

He leaned back, laughing again at his own wit. No one else did. Ettocio looked nervously at the door.

"On the other side of the coin," the Khardhu went on, still chuckling, "if he just slowly squeezes you dry with taxes and duties and confiscations he can get to exactly the same place without making anyone *mad* enough to *do* anything about it. I tell you, gentlemen," he took a long pull at his beer, "Alberico of Barbadior's a smart man."

"And you," said the grey-eyed man leaning across his own table, bristling with anger, "are an arrogant, insolent foreigner!"

The Khardhu's smile faded. His eyes locked on those of the other man and Ettocio was suddenly very glad the warrior's curved sword was checked with all the other weapons behind the bar.

"I've been here some thirty years," the black man said softly. "About as long as you've been alive, I'd wager. I was guarding merchant trains on this road when you were wetting your bed at night. And if I *am* a foreigner, well . . . last time I inquired, Khardhun was a free country. We beat back our invader, which is more than anyone here in the Palm can say!"

"You had magic!" the young fellow at the bar suddenly burst out, over the outraged din that ensued. "We didn't! That's the only reason! The only reason!"

The Khardhu turned to face the boy, his lip curling in

contempt. "You want to rock yourself to sleep at night thinking that's the only reason, you go right ahead, little man. Maybe it'll make you feel better about paying your taxes this spring, or about going hungry because there's no grain here in the fall. But if you want to know the truth I'll give it to you free of charge."

The noise level had abated as he spoke, but a number of men were on their feet, glaring at the Khardhu.

Looking around the room, as if dismissing the boy at the bar as unworthy of his attention, he said very clearly, "We beat back Brandin of Ygrath when he invaded us because Khardhun fought as a country. As a whole. You people got whipped by Alberico and Brandin both because you were too busy worrying about your border spats with each other, or which Duke or Prince would lead your army, or which priest or priestess would bless it, or who would fight on the center and who on the right, and where the battlefield would be, and who the gods loved best. Your nine provinces ended up going at the sorcerers one by one, finger by finger. And they got snapped to pieces like chicken-bones. I always used to think," he drawled into what had become a quiet room, "that a hand fought best when it made a fist."

He lazily signaled Ettocio for another drink.

"Damn your insolent Khardhu hide," the grey-eyed man said in a strangled voice. Ettocio turned from the bar to look at him. "Damn you forever to Morian's darkness for being right!"

Ettocio hadn't expected that, and neither had the others in the room. The mood grew grimly introspective. And, Ettocio realized, more dangerous as well, entirely at odds with the brightness of the spring outside, the cheerful warmth of the returned sun.

"But what can we do?" the young fellow at the bar said plaintively, to no one in particular.

"Curse and drink and pay our taxes," said the wool-merchant bitterly.

"I must say, I do sympathize with the rest of you," said the lone trader from Senzio smugly. It was an ill-advised remark. Even Ettocio, notoriously slow to rouse, was irritated.

The young man at the bar was positively enraged.

"Why you, you . . . I don't believe it! What right do *you* have—" He hammered the bar in incoherent fury. The plump Senzian smiled in the superior manner all of them seemed to have.

"What right indeed!" The grey eyes were icy as they returned to the fray. "Last time I looked, Senzio traders all had their hands jammed so deep in their pockets paying tribute money east *and* west that they couldn't even get their equipment out to please their wives!"

A raucous, bawdy shout of laughter greeted that. Even the old Khardhu smiled thinly.

"Last *I* looked," said the Senzian, red-faced, "the Governor of Senzio was one of our own, not someone shipped in from Ygrath or Barbadior!"

"What happened to the Duke?" the Ferraut merchant snapped. "Senzio was so cowardly your Duke demoted himself to Governor so as not to upset the Tyrants. Are you *proud* of that?"

"Proud?" the lean merchant mocked. "He's got no time to be proud of anything. He's too busy looking both ways to see which emissary from which Tyrant he should offer his wife to!"

Again, coarse, bitter laughter.

"You've a mean tongue for a conquered man," the Senzian said coldly. The laughter stopped. "Where are you from that you're so quick to cut at other men's courage."

"Tregea," said the other quietly.

"*Occupied* Tregea," the Senzian corrected viciously. "Conquered Tregea. With its Barbadian Governor."

"We were the last to fall," the Tregean said a little too defiantly. "Borifort held out longer than anywhere else."

"But it fell," the Senzian said bluntly, sure of his advantage now. "I wouldn't be so quick to talk about other men's wives. Not after the stories we all heard about what the Barbadians did there. And I also heard that most of your women weren't that unwilling to be—"

"*Shut your filthy mouth!*" the Tregean snarled, leaping to his feet. "Shut it, or I'll close it for you permanently, you lying Senzian scum!"

A babble of noise erupted, louder than any before.

Furiously clanging the bell over the bar, Ettocio fought to restore order.

"Enough!" he roared. "Enough of this, or you're all out of here right now!" A dire threat, and it quelled them.

Enough for the Khardhu warrior's sardonic laughter to be audible again. The man was on his feet. He dropped coins on the table to pay his account, and surveyed the room, still chuckling, from his great height.

"See what I mean?" he murmured. "All these stick-like little fingers jabbing and poking away at each other. You've always done that, haven't you? Guess you always will. Until there's nothing left here but Barbadior and Ygrath."

He swaggered to the bar to claim his sword.

"You," said the grey-eyed Tregean suddenly, as Ettocio handed over the curved, sheathed blade. The Khardhu turned slowly.

"You know how to use that thing as well as you use your mouth?" the Tregean asked.

The Khardhu's lips parted in a mirthless smile. "It's been reddened once or twice."

"Are you working for anyone right now?"

Insolently, appraisingly, the Khardhu looked down on the other man. "Where are you going?"

"I've just changed my plans," the other replied. "There's no money to be made up in Ferraut town. Not with double duties to be paid. I reckon I'll have to go farther afield. I'll give you going rates to guard me south to the Certandan highlands."

"Rough country there," the Khardhu murmured reflectively.

The Tregean's face twitched with amusement. "Why do you think I want you?" he asked.

After a moment the smile was returned. "When do we go?' the warrior said.

"We're gone," the Tregean replied, rising and paying his own account. He claimed his own short sword and the two of them walked out together. When the door opened there was a brief, dazzling flash of sunlight.

Ettocio had hoped the talk would settle down after that. It didn't. The youngster at the bar mumbled something about uniting in a common front—a remark that would have been merely insane if it wasn't so dangerous. Unfortunately—from Ettocio's point of view, at any rate—the comment was overheard by the Ferraut wool-trader, and the mood of the room was so aroused by then that the subject wouldn't die.

It went on all afternoon, even after the boy left as well. And that night, with an entirely different crowd, Ettocio shocked himself by speaking up during an argument about ancestral primacy between an Astibarian wine-dealer and another Senzian. He made the same point the tall Khardhu had made—about nine spindly fingers that had been broken one by one because they never formed a fist. The argument made sense to him; it sounded intelligent in his own mouth. He noticed men nodding slowly even as he spoke. It was an unusual, flattering response—men had seldom paid any attention to Ettocio except when he called time in the tavern.

He rather liked the new sensation. In the days that followed he found himself raising the point whenever the opportunity arose. For the first time in his life Ettocio began to get a reputation as a thoughtful man.

Unfortunately, one evening in summer he was overheard by a Barbadian mercenary standing outside the open window. They didn't take away his license. There was a very high level of tension across the whole of the Palm by then. They arrested Ettocio and executed him on a wheel outside his own tavern, with his severed hands stuffed in his mouth.

A great many men had heard the argument by then, though. A great many had nodded, hearing it.

★　★　★

Devin joined the other four about a mile south of the crossroads inn on the dusty road leading to Certando. They were waiting for him. Catriana was alone in the first cart but Devin climbed up beside Baerd in the second.

"Bubbling like a pot of khav," he said cheerfully in response to a quizzical eyebrow. Alessan rode up on one side. He'd buckled on his sword, Devin saw. Baerd's bow was on the cart, just behind the seat and within very quick reach. Devin had had occasion, several times in six months, to see just how quick Baerd's reach could be. Alessan smiled over at him, riding bareheaded in the bright afternoon.

"I take it you stirred the pot a little after we left?"

Devin grinned. "Didn't need much stirring. The two of you have that routine down like professional players by now."

"So do you," said the Duke, cantering up on the other side of the cart. "I particularly admired your spluttering anger this time. I thought you were about to throw something at me."

Devin smiled up at him. Sandre's teeth flashed white through the improbable black of his skin.

Don't expect to recognize us, Baerd had said when they'd parted in the Sandreni woods half a year ago. So Devin had been prepared. Somewhat, but not enough.

Baerd's own transformation had been disconcerting but relatively mild: he'd grown a short beard and removed the padding from the shoulders of his doublet. He wasn't as big a man as Devin had first thought. He'd also somehow changed his hair from bright yellow to what he said was his natural dark brown. His eyes were brown now as well, not the bright blue of before.

What he had done to Sandre d'Astibar was something else entirely. Even Alessan, who'd evidently had years to get used to this sort of thing, gave a low whistle when he first saw the Duke. Sandre had become—amazingly—an aging black fighting man from Khardhun across the northern sea. One of a type that Devin knew had been common on the roads of the Palm twenty or thirty years ago in the days when merchants went nowhere except in company with each other, and Khardhu warriors with their wickedly curved blades were much in demand as insurance against outlaws.

Somehow, and this was the uncanny thing, with his own beard shaven and his white hair tinted a dark grey, Sandre's gaunt, black face and deep-set, fierce eyes were exactly those of a Khardhu mercenary. Which, Baerd had explained, had been almost the first thing he'd noticed about the Duke when he'd seen him in daylight. It was what had suggested the rather comprehensive disguise.

"But *how?*" Devin remembered gasping.

"Lotions and potions," Alessan had laughed.

It turned out, as Baerd explained later, that he and the Prince had spent a number of years in Quileia after Tigana's fall. Disguises of this sort—colorings for skin and hair, even tints for eyes—were a perfected, important art south of the mountains. They assumed a central role in the Mysteries of the Mother Goddess, and in the less secret rites of the formal theater, and they had played pivotal, complex parts in the tumultuous religion-torn history of Quileia.

Baerd did not say what he and Alessan had been doing there, or how he had come to learn this secret craft or possess the implements of it.

Catriana didn't know either, which made Devin feel somewhat better. They'd asked Alessan one afternoon, and had received, for the first time, an answer that was to become routine through the fall and winter.

In the spring, Alessan told them. In the spring a great deal would be made clearer, one way or another. They were moving towards something of importance, but they would have to wait until then. He was not going to discuss it now. Before the Ember Days of spring they would leave their current Astibar—Tregea—Ferraut loop and head south across the wide grainlands of Certando. And at that point, Alessan had said, a great many things might change. One way or another, he'd repeated.

He hadn't smiled, saying any of this, though he was a man with an easy smile.

Devin remembered how Catriana had tossed her hair then, with a knowing, almost an angry look in her blue eyes.

"It's Alienor, isn't it?" she demanded, virtually an accusation. "It's that woman at Castle Borso."

Alessan's mouth had twisted in surprise and then amusement. "Not so, my dear," he'd said. "We'll stop at Borso, but this has nothing to do with her at all. If I didn't know better, if I didn't know your heart belonged only to Devin, I'd say you sounded jealous, my darling."

The gibe had entirely the desired effect. Catriana had stormed off, and Devin, almost as embarrassed himself, had quickly changed the subject. Alessan had a way of doing that to you. Behind the deep, effortless courtesy and the genuine camaraderie, there existed a line they learned not to try to cross. If he was seldom harsh, his jests—always the first measure of control—could sting memorably. Even the Duke had discovered that it was best not to press Alessan on certain subjects. Including this one, it emerged: when asked, Sandre said he knew as little as they did about what would happen come spring.

Thinking about it, as fall gave way to winter and the rains and then the snows came, Devin was deeply aware that Alessan was the Prince of a land that was dying a little more with each passing day. Under the circumstances, he decided, the wonder wasn't that there were places they could not trespass upon but, rather, how far they could actually go before reaching the guarded regions that lay within.

One of the things Devin began to learn during that long winter was patience. He taught himself to hold his questions for the right time, or to restrain them entirely and try to work out the answers for himself. If fuller knowledge had to wait for spring, then he would wait. In the meantime he threw himself, with an unleashed, even an unsuspected passion, into what they were doing.

A blade had been planted in his own soul that starry autumn night in the Sandreni Woods.

He'd had no idea what to expect when they'd set out five days later with Rovigo's horse-drawn cart and three other horses, bound for Ferraut town with a bed and a number of wooden carvings of the Triad. Taccio had written Rovigo that he could sell Astibarian religious carvings at a serious profit to merchants from the Western Palm. Especially because, as Devin learned, duty was not levied on Triad-related artifacts: part of a successful attempt by both sorcerers to keep the clergy placated and neutralized.

Devin learned a great deal about trade that fall and winter, and about certain other things as well. With his new, hard-won patience he would listen in silence as Alessan and the Duke tossed ideas back and forth on the long roads, turning the rough coals of a concept into the diamonds of polished plans. And even though his own dreams at night were of raising a surging army to liberate

Tigana and storm the fabled harbor walls of Chiara, he quickly came to understand—on the cold paths of day— that theirs would have to be a wholly different approach.

Which was, in fact, why they were still in the east, not the west, and doing all they could—with the small glittering diamonds of Alessan and Sandre's plans—to unsettle things in Alberico's realm. Once Catriana confided to him—on one of the days when, for whatever reason, she deemed him worth speaking to—that Alessan was, in fact, moving much more aggressively than he had the year before when she'd first joined them. Devin suggested it might be Sandre's influence. Catriana had shaken her head. She thought that was a part of it, but that there was something else, a new urgency from a source she didn't understand.

We'll find out in the spring, Devin had shrugged. She'd glared at him, as if personally affronted by his equanimity.

It had been Catriana though who'd suggested the most aggressive thing of all as winter began: the faked suicide in Tregea. Along with the idea of leaving behind her a sheaf of the poems that that young poet had written about the Sandreni. Adreano was his name, Alessan had informed them, unwontedly subdued: the name was on the list of the twelve poets Rovigo had reported as being randomly death-wheeled during Alberico's retaliation for the verses. Alessan had been unexpectedly disturbed by that news.

There was other information in the letter from Rovigo, aside from the usual covering business details. It had been held for them in a tavern in north Tregea that served as a mail drop for many of the merchants in the northeast. They had been heading south, spreading what rumors they could about unrest among the soldiers. Rovigo's latest report suggested, for the second time, that an increase in taxes might be imminent, to cover the mercenaries' newest pay demands. Sandre, who seemed to know the Tyrant's mind astonishingly well, agreed.

After dinner, when they were alone around the fire, Catriana had made her proposal. Devin had been incredulous: he'd seen the height of the bridges of Tregea and the speed of the river waters below. And it was winter by then, growing colder every day.

Alessan, still upset by the news from Astibar, and evidently of the same mind as Devin, vetoed the idea bluntly. Catriana pointed out two things. One was that she had been brought up by the sea: she was a better swimmer than any of them, and better than any of them knew.

The second thing was that—as Alessan knew perfectly well, she said—a leap such as this, a suicide, *especially* in Tregea, would fit seamlessly into everything they were trying to achieve in the Eastern Palm.

"That," Devin remembered Sandre saying after a silence, "is true, I'm sorry to say."

Alessan had reluctantly agreed to go to Tregea itself for a closer look at the river and the bridges.

Four evenings later Devin and Baerd had found themselves crouched amid twilight shadows along the riverbank in Tregea town, at a point that seemed to Devin terribly far away from the bridge Catriana had chosen. Especially in the windy cold of winter, in the swiftly gathering dark, beside the even more swiftly racing waters that were rushing past them, deep and black and cold.

While they waited, he had tried, unsuccessfully, to sort out his complex mixture of feelings about Catriana. He was too anxious though, and too cold.

He only knew that his heart had leaped, moved by some odd, tripled conjunction of relief and admiration and envy when she swam up to the bank, exactly where they were. She even had the wig in one hand, so it would not be tangled up somewhere, and found. Devin stuffed it into the satchel he carried while Baerd was vigorously chafing Catriana's shivering body and bundling her into the layers of clothing they'd carried. As Devin looked at her—shaking uncontrollably, almost blue with the cold, her teeth chattering—he had felt his envy slipping away. What replaced it was pride.

She was from Tigana, and so was he. The world might not know it yet, but they were working together—however elliptically—to bring it back.

The following morning their two carts had slowly rattled out of town, going north and west to Ferraut again with a full load of mountain khav. A light snow had been

falling. Behind them the city was in a state of massive
ferment and turmoil because of the unknown dark-haired
girl from the distrada who had killed herself. After that
incident Devin had found it increasingly hard to be sharp
or petty with Catriana. Most of the time. She did continue to indulge herself in the custom of deciding that he
was invisible every once in a while.

It had become difficult for him to convince himself that
they had actually made love together; that he had really
felt her mouth soft on his, or her hands in his hair as she
gathered him into her.

They never spoke of it, of course. He didn't avoid her,
but he didn't seek her out: her moods swung too unpre-
dictably, he never knew what response he'd get. A newly
patient man, he let her come to ride a cart or sit before a
tavern fire with him when she wanted to. She did,
sometimes.

In Ferraut town that winter for the third time, after the
leap in Tregea, they had all been wonderfully fed by
Ingonida—still in raptures over the bed they'd brought
her. Taccio's wife continued to display a particularly so-
licitous affection for the Duke in his dark disguise—a
detail which Alessan took some pleasure in teasing Sandre
about when they were alone. In the meantime, the rotund, red-faced Taccio copiously wined them all.

There had been another mail packet waiting from Rovigo
in Astibar. Which, when opened, proved to contain two
letters this time, one of which gave off—even after its
time in transit—an extraordinary effusion of scent.

Alessan, his eyebrows elaborately arched, presented
this pale-blue emanation to Devin with infinite suggestive-
ness. Ingonida crowed and clasped her hands together in
a gesture doubtless meant to signify romantic rapture.
Taccio, beaming, poured Devin another drink.

The perfume, unmistakably, was Selvena's. Devin's
expression, as he took cautious possession of the envelope, must have been revealing because he heard Catriana
giggle suddenly. He was careful not to look at her.

Selvena's missive was a single headlong sentence—much
like the girl herself. She did, however, make one vivid
suggestion that induced him to decline when the others
asked innocently if they might peruse his communication.

In fact, though, Devin was forced to admit that his
interest was rather more caught by the five neat lines
Alais had attached to her father's letter. In a small,
businesslike hand she simply reported that she'd found
and copied another variant of the "Lament for Adaon"
at one of the god's temples in Astibar and that she
looked forward to sharing it with all of them when they
next came east. She signed it with her initial only.

In the body of the letter Rovigo reported that Astibar
was very quiet since the twelve poets had been executed
among the families of the conspirators in the Grand
Square. That the price of grain was still going up, that he
could usefully receive as much green Senzian wine as
they could obtain at current prices, that Alberico was
widely expected to announce, very soon, a beneficiary
among his commanders for the greater part of the confiscated Nievolene lands, and that his best information was
that Senzian linens were still underpriced in Astibar but
might be due to rise.

It was the news about the Nievolene lands that triggered the next stage of spark-to-spark discussion between
Alessan and the Duke.

And those sparks had led to the blaze.

The five of them did a fast run along the well-maintained
highway north to Senzio with more of the religious artifacts. They bought green wine with their profit on the
statuettes, bargained successfully for a quantity of linens—
Baerd, somewhat surprisingly had emerged as their best
negotiator in such matters—and doubled quickly back to
Taccio, paying the huge new duties at both the provincial
border forts and the city-walls.

There had been another letter waiting. Among the
various masking pieces of business news, Rovigo reported
that an announcement on the Nievolene lands was expected by the end of the week. His source was reliable,
he added. The letter had been written five days before.

That night Alessan, Baerd, and Devin had borrowed a
third horse from Taccio—who was deeply happy to be
told nothing of their intentions—and had set out on the
long ride to the Astibar border and then across to a gully
by the road that led to the Nievolene gates.

They were back seven days later with a new cart and a

load of unspun country wool for Taccio to sell. Word of the fire had preceded them. Word of the fire was everywhere, Sandre reported. There had already been a number of tavern brawls in Ferraut town between men of the First and Second Companies.

They left the new cart with Taccio and departed, heading slowly back towards Tregea. They didn't need three carts. They were partners in a modest commercial venture. They made what slight profit they could, given the taxes and duties that trammeled them. They talked about those taxes and duties a great deal, often in public. Sometimes more frankly than their listeners were accustomed to hearing.

Alessan quarreled with the sardonic Khardhu warrior in a dozen different inns and taverns on the road, and hired him a dozen different times. Sometimes Devin played a role, sometimes Baerd did. They were careful not to repeat the performance anywhere. Catriana kept a precise log of where they had been and what they had said and done there. Devin had assured her they could rely on his memory, but she kept her notes nonetheless.

In public the Duke now called himself "Tomaz." "Sandre" was an uncommon-enough name in the Palm, and for a mercenary from Khardhun it would be sufficiently odd to be a risk. Devin remembered growing thoughtful when the Duke had told them his new name back in the fall. He'd wondered what it was like to have had to kill his son. Even to outlive his sons. To know that the bodies of everyone even distantly related to himself were being spreadeagled alive on the death-wheels of Barbadior. He tried to imagine how all of that would feel.

Life, the processes of living and what it did to you, seemed to Devin to grow more painfully complex all through that fall and winter. Often he thought of Marra, arbitrarily cut off on the way to her maturity, to whatever she had been about to become. He missed her with a dull ache that could grow into something heavy and difficult at times. She would have been someone to talk to about such things. The others had their own concerns and he didn't want to burden them. He wondered about Alais bren Rovigo, if she would have understood these things he was wrestling with. He didn't think so; she had lived too sheltered, too secluded a life for such thoughts to trouble her. He dreamt of her one night though, an unexpectedly intense series of images. The next morning he rode beside Catriana in the lead cart, unwontedly quiet, stirred and unsettled by the nearness of her, the crimson fall of her hair in the pale winter landscape.

Sometimes he thought about the soldier in the Nievolene barn—who had lost a roll of dice and carried a jug of wine to a lonely place away from the singing, and had had his throat slit there while he slept. Had that soldier been born into the world only to become a rite of passage for Devin di Tigana?

That was a terrible thought. Eventually, mulling it over through the long, cold winter rides, Devin worked his way through to deciding it was untrue. The man had interacted with other people through his days. Had caused pleasure and sorrow, doubtless, and had surely known both things. The moment of his ending was not what defined his journey under Eanna's lights, or however that journey was named in the Empire of Barbadior.

It was difficult to sort out though. Had Stevan of Ygrath lived and died so that his father's grief might work the destruction of a small province and its people and their memories? Had Prince Valentin di Tigana been born only to swing the killing blade that caused this to happen? And what about his youngest son then?

And what about the youngest son of the Asolini farmer who had fled from Avalle when it became Stevanien? Truly, it was hard to puzzle through.

In Senzio one morning, with the first elusive hints of spring softening the northern air, Baerd had come back from the celebrated weapons market with a bright, beautifully balanced sword for Devin. There was a black jewel in the hilt. He offered no explanation, but Devin knew it had to do with what had happened in the Nievolene barn. The gift did nothing to answer any of his new questions, but it helped him none the less. Baerd began giving him lessons during their midday breaks on the road.

Devin worried about Baerd, in part because he knew that Alessan did.

His first impression in the cabin had been mostly wrong: a big, blond man, intimidatingly cool and competent. But Baerd was dark-haired and not actually large at all and, though his competence ran to such an astonishing number of things that it could still be intimidating after six months, he wasn't really cool. Only guarded, careful. Closed tightly around the kernel of the hurt he had lived with for a long time.

In some ways, Devin realized, Alessan had it easier than Baerd. The Prince could find a temporary release in talk, in laughter, and most of all, and almost always, in music. Baerd seemed to have no release at all; he walked through a world shaped and reshaped every single moment around the knowledge that Tigana was gone.

It would drive him out at night sometimes, away from sleep, or from a fire they'd built up by a road. He would rise without warning, neatly, quietly, and go out into the darkness alone.

Devin would watch Alessan watching Baerd as he went away.

"I knew a man like him once," Sandre said gravely one night after Baerd had left a warm room in a tavern for a fog-shrouded winter night in the Tregean hills near Borifort. "He used to have to go away by himself to fight off a need to kill."

"That would be a part of it," Alessan had said.

Thoughts of winter, mood of a winter's night.

But it was spring now, and as the sap of the earth rose green-gold to the warming light so did Devin feel his own mood lifting to the stir and quickening of the world through which they rode.

Wait for springtime, Alessan had said amid the browns and reds of autumn trees and the bare, harvested vines. And spring was upon them now, with the Ember Days approaching fast and at last—at long last—they were on the road for Certando and whatever answers lay there. Devin could not quell and did not want to quell the sense rising within him like sap in the green woods that whatever was going to happen was going to begin to happen soon.

In the second cart beside Baerd he felt gloriously,

importantly alive. Ahead of them the glint of afternoon
sunlight in Catriana's hair was doing something strange
and wonderful to his blood. He was aware of Baerd
giving him a curious scrutiny, and caught a half-smile
playing across the other's face. He didn't care. He was
even glad. Baerd was his friend.

Devin began a song. A very old ballad of the road,
"The Song of the Wayfarer":

I'm a long way from the house where I was born
And this is just another winding trail,
But when the sun goes down both of the moons will rise
And Eanna's stars will hear me tell my tale . . .

Alessan, whatever his mood might be, was almost always ready to join in a song and, sure enough, Devin had
the Tregean pipes with him by the second verse. He
looked over and caught a wink from the Prince riding
beside them.

Catriana glanced back at them reprovingly. Devin
grinned at her and shrugged, and Alessan's pipes suddenly spun into a wilder dance of invitation. Catriana
tried and failed to suppress a smile. She joined them on
the third verse and then led them into the next song.

Later, in the summer, Devin would revive that image
of the five of them in the first hour of the long ride south
and the memory would make him feel very old.

He was young that day. In a way they all were, briefly—
even Sandre, joining in on the choruses he knew in a
passable baritone voice, reborn into his new identity,
with a new hope to his long, unfading dream.

Devin took the third song back from Catriana, and
sent his high clear voice along the road before them to
lead the way down the sunlit, winding trail to Certando,
to the Lady of Castle Borso, whoever she might be, and
to whatever it was that Alessan had to find in the highlands.

First though, nearing sundown, they overtook a traveler on the road.

In itself that wasn't unusual. They were still in Ferraut, in
the populated country north of Fort Ciorone where busy
highways from Tregea and Corte met the north-south

road they were on. Solitary travelers, on the other hand, were sufficiently rare for Devin to join Baerd in scanning the sides of the road to see if others were hidden in ambush.

A routine precaution, but they were in country where thieves would not survive long and in any case it was still daylight. Then as they drew nearer Devin saw the small harp slung over the man's back. A troubadour. Devin grinned; they were almost always good company.

The man had turned and was waiting for them to catch up. The deep bow he offered Catriana as she pulled the lead cart to a halt beside him was of such courtly grace it almost looked like a parody on the lonely road.

"I've been enjoying the sound of you for the last mile," he said, straightening. "I must say I'm enjoying the sight of you even more." He was tall, no longer young, with long, greying hair and quick eyes. He gave Catriana the sort of smile for which the troubadours of the Palm were notorious. His teeth were white and even in a leathery face.

"Heading south with the spring?" she asked, smiling politely at his flattery. "The old route?"

"I am indeed," he replied. "The old route at the usual time. And I'd hate to tell someone as young and beautiful as you how many years I've been doing it."

Devin jumped down from beside Baerd and strolled closer to the man to confirm something. "I could probably guess," he said, grinning, "because I think I remember you. We did a wedding season in Certando together. Did you play harp for Burnet di Corte two years ago?"

The sharp eyes looked him up and down. "I did," the troubadour admitted after a moment. "I'm Erlein di Senzio and I was with damned Burnet for a season all right. Then he cheated me of my wages and I decided I was happier on my own again. I *thought* those were professional voices behind me. You are?"

"Devin d'Asoli." The lie came easily. "I was with Menico di Ferraut for a few years."

"And have clearly moved on to other, better things," Erlein said, glancing at their laden carts. "Is Menico still on the road? Is he any fatter than he was?"

"Yes to both," Devin said, concealing the guilt that

still assailed him when he thought of his former troupe-
leader. "So is Burnet last I heard."

"Rot him," Erlein said mildly. "He owes me money."

"Well," Alessan said, looking down from his horse,
"we can't do anything about that but if you like we *can*
run you up to Ciorone and a bed before curfew. You can
ride with Baerd," he added quickly, as Erlein glanced at
the empty seat beside Catriana.

"I would be most profoundly grateful—" Erlein began.

"I don't like Fort Ciorone," Sandre broke in suddenly.
"They cheat you there and too many people learn what
you're carrying and where you're going. Too many of the
wrong kind of people. It's a mild night coming—I think
we're better off out here."

Devin glanced over at the Duke in surprise. This was
the first time he'd offered any such opinion.

"Well, really Tomaz, I don't see why—" Alessan began.

"You hired me, merchant," Sandre growled. "You
wanted me to do a job for you and I'm doing it. You
don't want to listen, pay me now and I'll find someone
who will." His eyes were fierce within the hollows of his
blackened face.

And his tone was one that none of them could mistake.
Whatever it was, Sandre had a reason for what he was
doing.

"A little courtesy if you please," Alessan snapped,
turning his horse to face the Duke's. "Or I will indeed
turn you away and let you carry your old bones back to
find someone else idiot enough to put up with you. I
have managed," he said, swinging back to Erlein, "to
find the most arrogant Khardhu on the roads of the
Palm."

"They are all arrogant," the troubadour replied with a
shake of his head. "Comes with the curved swords."

Alessan laughed. So too, following his lead, did Devin.

"There's a good hour of daylight left," Baerd said in a
complaining voice. "We can make the Fort easy. Why
sleep on the ground?"

Alessan sighed. "I know," he said. "But I'm sorry.
We're new to this run and Tomaz isn't. I suppose we
ought to listen to him or we're wasting his fee, aren't

we?" He looked back at Erlein and shrugged. "There goes your ride to Ciorone."

"Can't lose what you never had," the troubadour smiled. "I'll manage."

"You're welcome to share our fire," Devin interjected, trusting that he'd read the Duke's brief glance correctly. He still wasn't sure what Sandre was doing.

Surprisingly, Erlein flushed; he looked somewhat embarrassed. "As to that, I thank you, but I've nothing with me to bring to table or hearth."

"You *have* been on the road a long time," Sandre said in a quieter voice. "I haven't heard a Palm-born use that phrase in years. It's a lost tradition, that one."

"You have a harp, don't you?" Catriana said, at just the right moment and in her sweetest voice. She glanced directly at Erlein for an instant, then demurely lowered her eyes again.

"I do," said the troubadour after a moment, affirming the obvious. He was devouring Catriana with his gaze.

"Then you are far from empty-handed," Alessan said crisply. "Devin and my sister both sing, as you've heard, and I can manage these pipes a little bit. A harp will go gentle after dinner under the stars."

"Say no more," said Erlein. "You'll be better company by a long go than my mouth talking wisdom with only my own ears to hear."

Alessan laughed again.

"There's trees over west, and a stream beyond them, if I remember rightly," Sandre said. "A good place to camp."

Before anyone else could say a word Erlein di Senzio had jumped up and settled himself at Catriana's side. Devin, his mouth agape, closed it quickly at Sandre's hidden, urgent gesture.

Catriana pulled west off the road to lead them toward the trees the Duke had pointed out. Devin heard her giggle at something the troubadour said.

He was looking at Sandre though. So were Baerd and Alessan.

The Duke glanced at Erlein whose back was to the four of them, then very briefly he held up his left hand with the third and fourth fingers carefully curled down.

He gazed at Alessan deliberately and then back to the man beside Catriana.

Devin didn't understand. *An oath?* he thought, confused.

Sandre lowered his hand but his eyes remained locked on the Prince's. There was an odd, challenging expression in them. Alessan had suddenly gone pale.

And in that moment Devin understood.

"Oh, Adaon," Baerd whispered on a rising note, as Devin leaped up on the cart beside him. "I do not believe this!"

Neither did Devin.

What Sandre was telling them, quite plainly, was that Erlein di Senzio was a wizard. One who had cut two fingers in his linking to the magic of the Palm.

And Alessan bar Valentin was a Prince of the blood of Tigana. Which meant, if the old tale of Adaon and Micaela was true, that he could bind a wizard to his service. Sandre had not believed it back in the cabin in the fall. Devin remembered that.

But now he was giving Alessan his chance. Which explained the challenge in his gaze.

A chance, or at least the beginnings of a chance. Thinking as fast as he ever had in his life, Devin turned to Baerd. "Follow my lead when we get there," he said softly. "I have an idea." Only later would he have time to reflect what a change six months had made. Only six months, one Ember season to another. For him to speak so to Baerd, speak and be listened to . . .

There was indeed a stream, as Sandre had known, or guessed. Not far from its banks they halted the carts. The usual twilight routine began. Catriana seeing to the horses, Devin to wood for the fire. Alessan and the Duke laid out the sleeping-rolls and organized the cooking gear and the food they carried.

Baerd took his bow and disappeared into the trees. He was back in twenty minutes, no more than that, with three rabbits and a plump, wingless grele.

"I'm impressed," Erlein said from beside Catriana and the horses. His eyes were wide. "I'm very impressed."

"I'm buying your music for later," Baerd said with a rare smile. The one he usually reserved for bargaining sessions at town fairs.

Devin had been watching Erlein as unobtrusively as he could. When he could manage to focus on the troubadour's left hand—which never seemed to be still for more than an instant—there *did* seem to be an odd blurring, an occluding of air around it.

He had been waiting for Baerd to come back, now he waited no longer.

"You," he said, grinning at the returning hunter, "look like something that should be hunted yourself. You are going to terrify every civilized merchant we meet. You need a haircut before you are fit for society, my friend."

Baerd was very quick.

"I wouldn't talk, scamp," he shot back, tossing his prey over to Sandre by the wood gathered for the fire. "Not the way you look yourself. Or are you deliberately trying to be scruffy to scare away Alienor at Borso?"

Alessan laughed. So did Erlein.

"Nothing scares away Alienor," the troubadour chuckled. "And that one is exactly the right age for her."

"What 'right age'?" Alessan grinned slyly. "Over twelve and not yet buried suits her fine."

"I don't like that," Catriana said primly as the five men laughed.

"Sorry," Alessan said trying to keep a straight face, as she stepped in front of him, hands firmly on her hips.

"You are not at all sorry, but you should be!" Catriana snapped. "You know very well I don't like that kind of talk. How do you think it makes me look? And you only do it when you're idle. Do something useful. Cut Devin's hair. He does look awful, even worse than usual."

"Me?" Devin squeaked in protest. *"My* hair? What do you mean? It's Baerd, not me! What about him? He's the one who—"

"You *all* need a haircut," Catriana pronounced with a blunt finality that admitted of no rebuttal. Her cold scrutiny rested critically on Erlein's shaggy mane for a second. She opened her mouth, hesitated, then closed it, in a brilliant miming of polite restraint. Erlein flushed. His right hand went uneasily to tug at his shoulder-length strands.

His left hand never stopped playing restlessly with some pebbles he'd gathered by the stream.

"I think," Devin said spitefully, "that you've just insulted our guest. That should make him feel properly welcome here."

"I didn't say a word, Devin," she flared.

"You didn't have to," Erlein said ruefully. "Those magnificent eyes were somewhat less than pleased with what they saw."

"My sister's eyes are almost never pleased with what they see," Alessan grunted. He was crouched beside one of the packs and after a moment's rummaging pulled out a scissors and a comb. "I am fairly obviously being ordered to duty here. There's half an hour of light left. Who's first victim?"

"Me," said Baerd quickly. "You aren't touching me in twilight, I'll tell you that much."

Erlein watched with interest as Alessan led Baerd over to a rock by the stream and proceeded—quite competently, in fact—to trim the other man's hair. Catriana went back to the horses, though not before offering Erlein another quick, enigmatic glance. Sandre stacked the wood for the fire and began skinning the rabbits and the grele, humming tunelessly to himself.

"More wood, lad," he said abruptly to Devin, without looking up. Which was perfect, of course.

Oh, Morian, Devin thought, a heady blend of excitement and pride racing through him. *They are all so good.*

"Later," was all he said, lounging casually on the ground. "We've got enough for now and I'm next with Alessan."

"No you're not," Alessan called from by the river, picking up Sandre's gambit. "Get the wood, Devin. There isn't enough light to do three of you. I'll cut yours tomorrow, and Erlein's now if he wants. Catriana will just have to endure you looking fearsome for one more night."

"As if a haircut's going to change that!" she called from the other side of the clearing. Erlein and Baerd laughed.

Grumbling, Devin stood up and ambled off toward the trees.

Behind him he heard Erlein's voice.

"I'd be grateful to you," the troubadour was saying to Alessan. "I'd hate to have another woman look at me the way your sister just did."

"Ignore her," Devin heard Baerd laugh as he strode back toward the fire.

"She is impossible to ignore," Erlein said in a voice pitched to carry to where the horses were tethered. He stood up and walked over to the riverbank. He sat down on the rock in front of Alessan. The sun was a red disk, westering beyond the stream.

Carrying an armful of wood, Devin looped quietly around in the growing shadows to where Catriana stood among the horses. She heard him come up but continued brushing the brown mare. Her eyes never left the two men by the river.

Neither did Devin's. Squinting into the setting sun it seemed to him as if Alessan and the troubadour had become figures in some timeless landscape. Their voices carried with an unnatural clarity in the quiet of the gathering twilight.

"When was this last done for you?" he heard Alessan ask casually, his scissors busy in the long grey tangles of Erlein's hair.

"I don't even remember," the troubadour confessed.

"Well," Alessan laughed, bending to wet his comb in the stream, "on the road we don't exactly have to keep up with court fashions. Tilt a little this way. Yes, good. Do you brush it across in front or straight back?"

"Back, by preference."

"Fine." Alessan's hands moved up to the crown of Erlein's head, the scissors flashing as they caught the last of the sun. "That's an old-fashioned look, but troubadours are supposed to look old-fashioned, aren't they? Part of the charm. *You are bound by Adaon's name and my own. I am Alessan, Prince of Tigana, and wizard you are mine!*"

Devin took an involuntary step forward. He saw Erlein try, reflexively, to jerk away. But the hand of binding held his head, and the scissors, so busy a moment before, were now sharp against his throat. They froze him for an instant and an instant was enough.

"Rot your flesh!" Erlein screamed as Alessan released him and stepped back. The wizard sprang from the stone as if scalded, and wheeled to face the Prince. His face was contorted with rage.

Fearing for Alessan, Devin began moving toward the river, reaching for his blade. Then he saw that Baerd had an arrow already notched to his bow, and trained on Erlein's heart. Devin slowed his rush and then stopped. Sandre was right beside him, the curved sword drawn. He caught a glimpse of the Duke's dark face and in it—though he couldn't be absolutely sure in the uncertain light—he thought he read fear.

He turned back to the two men by the river. Alessan had laid down the scissors and comb neatly on the rock. He stood still, hands at his sides, but his breath was coming quickly.

Erlein was literally shaking with fury. Devin looked at him and it was as if a curtain had been drawn back. In the wizard's eyes hatred and terror vied for domination. His mouth worked spasmodically. He raised his left hand and pointed it at Alessan in a gesture of violent negation.

And Devin saw, quite clearly now, that his third and fourth fingers had indeed been chopped off. The ancient mark of a wizard's binding to his magic and the Palm.

"Alessan?" Baerd said.

"It is all right. He cannot do anything with his power now against my will." Alessan's voice was quiet, almost detached, as if this was all happening to someone else entirely. Only then did Devin realize that the wizard's gesture had been an attempt to cast a spell. Magic. He had never thought to be so near it in his life. The skin prickled at the back of his neck, and not because of the twilight breeze.

Slowly Erlein lowered his hand and slowly his trembling stopped. "Triad curse you," he said, low and cold. "And curse the bones of your ancestors and blight the lives of your children and your children's children for what you have done to me." It was the voice of someone wronged, brutally, grievously.

Alessan did not flinch or turn away. "I was cursed almost nineteen years ago, and my ancestors were, and whatever children I or any of my people might have. It is a curse I have set my life to undo while time yet allows. For no other reason have I bound you to me."

There was something terrible in Erlein's face. "Every

true Prince of Tigana," the wizard said with bitter intensity, "has known since the beginning how awful a gift the god gave them. How savage a power over a free, a living soul. Do you even know—" He was forced to stop, white-faced, his hands clenched, to regain control of himself. "Do you even know how seldom this gift has been used."

"Twice," Alessan said calmly. "Twice, to my knowledge. The old books recorded it so, though I fear all the books have been burned now."

"Twice!" Erlein echoed, his voice skirling upwards. "Twice in how many generations stretching back to the dawn of records in this peninsula? And you, a puling princeling without even a land to rule have just casually—viciously—set your hands upon my life!"

"Not casually. And only *because* I have no home. Because Tigana is dying and will be lost if I do not do something."

"And what part of that little speech gives you rights over *my* life and death?"

"I have a duty," Alessan replied gravely. "I must use what tools come to hand."

"*I am not a tool!*" Erlein cried from the heart. "I am a free and living soul with my own destiny!"

Watching Alessan's face Devin saw how that cry shafted into him. For a long moment there was silence by the river. Devin saw the Prince draw air into his lungs carefully, as if steadying himself under yet another burden, a new weight joined to those he already carried. Another part added to the price of his blood.

"I will not lie and say that I am sorry," Alessan said finally, choosing his words with care. "I have dreamt of finding a wizard for too many years. I will say—and this is true—that I understand what you have said and why you will hate me, and I can tell you that I grieve for what necessity demands."

"It demands nothing!" Erlein replied, shrill and unrelenting in his righteousness. "We are free men. There is always a choice."

"Some choices are closed to some of us." It was, surprisingly, Sandre.

He moved forward to stand a little in front of Devin.

"And some men must make choices for those who cannot, whether through lack of will or lack of power." He walked nearer to the other two, by the dark, quiet rushing of the stream. "Just as we *may* choose not to slay the man who is trying to kill our child, so Alessan may have chosen not to bind a wizard who might be needed by his people. His children. Neither refusal, Erlein di Senzio, is a true alternative for anyone with honor."

"Honor!" Erlein spat the word. "And how does honor bind a man of Senzio to Tigana's fate? What Prince *compels* a free man to a sure death at his side and then speaks of honor?" He shook his head. "Call it naked power and have done."

"I will not," the Duke replied in his deep voice. It was quite dark now; Devin could no longer see his hooded eyes. From behind them all he heard the sounds of Baerd beginning to light the fire. Overhead the first stars were emerging in the blue-black cloak of the sky. Away west, across the stream, there was a last hint of crimson along the line of the horizon.

"I will not," Sandre said again. "The honor of a ruler, and his duty, lies in his care for his land and his people. That is the only true measure. And the price, part of the price of that, comes when he must go against his own soul's needs and do such things that will grieve him to the very bones of his hands. Such things," he added softly, "as the Prince of Tigana has just done to you."

But Erlein's voice shot back, unpersuaded, contemptuous. "And how," he snarled, "does a bought sword from Khardhun presume to use the word *honor* or to speak about the burdens of a prince?" He wanted the words to hurt, Devin could see, but what came through in the inflections of his voice was the sound of someone lost and afraid.

There was a silence. Behind them the fire caught with a rush, and the orange glow spun outward, illuminating Erlein's taut rage and Sandre's gaunt, dark face, the bones showing in high relief. Beyond them both, Devin saw, Alessan had not moved at all.

Sandre said, "The Khardhu warriors I have known

were deeply versed in honor. But I will claim no credit
for that. Be not deceived: I am no Khardhu. My name is
Sandre d'Astibar, once Duke of that province. I know a
little about power."

Erlein's mouth fell open.

"I am also a wizard," Sandre added matter-of-factly.
"Which is how you were known: by the thin spell you use
to mask your hand."

Erlein closed his mouth. He stared fixedly at the Duke
as if seeking to penetrate his disguise or find confirmation in the deep-hooded eyes. Then he glanced downwards, almost against his will.

Sandre already had the fingers of his left hand spread
wide. All five fingers.

"I never made the final binding," he said. "I was
twelve years old when my magic found me. I was also the
son and heir of Tellani, Duke of Astibar. I made my
choice: I turned my back on magic and embraced the rule
of men. I used my very small power perhaps five times in
my life. Or six," he amended. "Once, very recently."

"Then there *was* a conspiracy against the Barbadian,"
Erlein murmured, his rage temporarily set aside as he
wrestled with this. "And then . . . yes, of course. What
did you do? Kill your son in the dungeon?"

"I did." The voice was level, giving nothing away at
all.

"You could have cut two fingers and brought him
out."

"Perhaps."

Devin looked over sharply at that, startled.

"I don't know. I made my choice long ago, Erlein di
Senzio." And with those quiet words another shape of
pain seemed to enter the clearing, almost visible at the
edges of the firelight.

Erlein forced a corrosive laugh. "And a fine choice it
was!" he mocked. "Now your Dukedom is gone and your
family as well, and you've been bound as a slave wizard
to an arrogant Tiganese. How happy you must be!"

"Not so," said Alessan quickly from by the river.

"I am here by my own choice," Sandre said softly.
"Because Tigana's cause is Astibar's and Senzio's and

Chiara's—it is the same choice for all of us. Do we die
as willing victims or while trying to be free? Do we skulk
as you have done all these years, hiding from the sorcerers? Or can we not join palm to palm—for *once* in this
folly-ridden peninsula of warring provinces locked into
their pride—and drive the two of them away?"

Devin was deeply stirred. The Duke's words rang in
the firelit dark like a challenge to the night. But when he
ended, the sound they heard was Erlein di Senzio clap-
ping sardonically.

"Wonderful," he said contemptuously. "You really must
remember that for when you find an army of simpletons
to rally. You will forgive me if I remain unmoved by
speeches about freedom tonight. Before the sun went
down I was a free man on an open road. I am now a
slave."

"You were not free," Devin burst out.

"And I say I was!" Erlein snapped, rounding fiercely
on him. "There may have been laws that constrained me,
and one government ruling where I might have wished
for another. But the roads are safer now than they ever
were when *this* man ruled in Astibar or *that* one's father
in Tigana—and I carried my life where I wanted to go.
You will all have to forgive my insensitivity if I say that
Brandin of Ygrath's spell on the name of Tigana was not
the first and last thought of my days!"

"We will," Alessan said then in an unnaturally flat
voice. "We *will* all forgive you for that. Nor will we seek
to persuade you to change your views now. I will tell you
this, though: the freedom you speak of will be yours
again when Tigana's name is heard in the world once
more. It is my hope—vain, perhaps—that you will work
with us willingly in time, but until then I can say that the
compulsion of Adaon's gift will suffice me. My father
died, and my brothers died by the Deisa, and the flower
of a generation with them, fighting for freedom. I have
not lived so bitterly or striven so long to hear a coward
belittle the shattering of a people and their heritage."

"Coward!" Erlein exclaimed. "Rot you, you arrogant
princeling! What would you know about it?"

"Only what you have told us yourself," Alessan replied, grimly now. "Safer roads, you said. One government where you *might* have wished for another." He took a step toward Erlein as if he would strike the man, his composure finally beginning to break. "You have been the worst thing I know: a willing subject of two tyrants. Your idea of freedom is exactly what has let them conquer us, and then hold us. You called yourself *free*? You were only free to hide . . . and to soil your breeches if a sorcerer or one of their Trackers came within ten miles of your little screening spell. You were free to walk past death-wheels with your fellow wizards rotting on them, and free to turn your back and continue on your way. Not anymore, Erlein di Senzio. By the Triad, you are in it now! You are in it as deep as any man in the Palm! Hear my first command: you are to use your magic to conceal your fingers exactly as before."

"No," said Erlein flatly.

Alessan said nothing more. He waited. Devin saw the Duke take a half-step towards the two of them and then stop himself. He remembered that Sandre had not believed that this was possible.

Now he saw. They all saw, by the light of the stars and the fire Baerd had made.

Erlein fought. Understanding next to nothing, unnerved by almost all that was happening, Devin gradually became aware that a horrible struggle was taking place within the wizard. It could be read in his rigid, straining stance and his gritted teeth, heard in the rasp and wheeze of his shortening breath, seen in tightly closed eyes and the suddenly clenched fingers at his sides.

"No," Erlein gasped, once and then again and again, with more effort each time. "No, no, no!" He dropped to his knees as if felled like a tree. His head bent slowly downward. His shoulders hunched as if resisting some overmastering assault. They began to shake with erratic spasms. His whole body was trembling.

"No," he said again in a high, cracked whisper. His hands spread open, pressing flat against the ground. In the red firelight his face was a mask of staring agony. Sweat poured down it in the chill of night. His mouth suddenly gaped open.

Devin looked away in pity and terror just before the wizard's scream ripped the night apart. In the same moment Catriana took two quick running steps and buried her head against Devin's shoulder.

That cry of pain, the scream of a tormented animal, hung in the air between fire and stars for what seemed an appallingly long time. Afterwards Devin became aware of the intensity of the silence, broken only by the occasional crackle of the fire, the river's soft murmur, and Erlein di Senzio's choked, ragged breathing.

Without speaking Catriana straightened and released her grip on Devin's arm. He glanced at her but she didn't meet his eye. He turned back to the wizard.

Erlein was still on his knees before Alessan in the new spring grass by the riverbank. His body still shook, but with weeping now. When he lifted his head Devin could see the tracks of tears and sweat and the staining mud from his hands. Slowly Erlein raised his left hand and stared at it as if it was something alien that didn't even belong to him. They all saw what had happened, or the illusion of what had happened.

Five fingers. He had cast the spell.

An owl suddenly called, short and clear from north along the river, nearer to the trees. Devin became aware of a change in the sky. He looked up. Blue Ilarion, waning back to a crescent, had risen in the east. *Ghostlight,* Devin thought, and wished he hadn't.

"Honor!" Erlein di Senzio said, scarcely audible.

Alessan had not moved since giving his command. He looked down on the wizard he had bound and said, quietly, "I did not enjoy that, but I suppose we needed to go through it. Once will be enough, I hope. Shall we eat?"

He walked past Devin and the Duke and Catriana to where Baerd was waiting by the fire. The meat was already cooking. Caught in a vortex of emotion, Devin saw the searching look Baerd gave Alessan. He turned back in time to see Sandre reaching out a hand to help Erlein rise.

For a long moment Erlein ignored him, then, with a sigh, he grasped the Duke's forearm and pulled himself erect.

Devin followed Catriana back toward the fire. He heard the two wizards coming after them.

Dinner passed in near silence. Erlein took his plate and glass and went to sit alone on the rock by the stream at the very farthest extent of the fire's glow. Looking over at his dark outline, Sandre murmured that a younger man would very likely have refused to eat. "He's a survivor that one," the Duke added. "Any wizard who's lasted this long has to be."

"Will he be all right then," Catriana asked softly. "With us?"

"I think so," Sandre answered, sipping his wine. He turned to Alessan. "He'll try to run away tonight though."

"I know," the Prince said.

"Do we stop him?" It was Baerd.

Alessan shook his head. "Not you. I will. He cannot leave me unless I let him. If I call he must return. I have him . . . tethered to my mind. It is a queer feeling."

Queer indeed, Devin thought. He looked from the Prince to the dark figure by the river. He couldn't even imagine what this must feel like. Or rather, he could almost imagine it, and the sensation disturbed him.

He became aware that Catriana was looking at him and he turned to her. This time she didn't look away. Her expression, too, was strange; Devin realized she must be feeling the same edginess and sense of unreality that he was. He suddenly remembered, vividly, the feel of her head against his shoulder an hour ago. At the time he'd hardly registered the fact, so intent had he been on Erlein. He tried to smile reassuringly, but he didn't think he managed it.

"Troubadour, you promised us harp music!" Sandre called out abruptly. The wizard in the darkness didn't respond. Devin had forgotten about that. He didn't feel much like singing and he didn't think Catriana did either.

So, in the event, what happened was that Alessan expressionlessly claimed his Tregean pipes and began to make music alone beside the fire.

He played beautifully, with a pared-down economy of sound—melodies so sweetly offered that Devin, in his current mood, could almost imagine Eanna's stars and the blue crescent of the one moon pausing in their movements overhead so as not to have to wheel inexorably away from the grace of that music.

Then a short while later Devin realized what Alessan was doing and he felt, abruptly, as if he was going to cry. He held himself very still, to keep control, and he looked at the Prince across the red and orange of the flames.

Alessan's eyes were closed as he played, his lean face seemed almost hollowed out, the cheekbones showing clearly. And into the sounds he made he seemed to pour, as from a votive temple bowl, both the yearning that drove him, and the decency and care that Devin knew lay at the root of him. But that wasn't it, that wasn't what was making Devin want to cry:

Every song that Alessan was playing, every single tune, achingly high and sweet, heartbreakingly clear, one after another, was a song from Senzio.

A song for Erlein di Senzio, cloaked in bitterness and the shadows of night by the riverbank alone.

I will not say I am sorry, Alessan had told the wizard as the sun had set. *But I can tell you that I grieve.*

And that night, listening to the music the Prince of Tigana made upon his pipes, Devin learned the difference between the two. He watched Alessan, and then he watched the others as they looked at the Prince, and it was when he was gazing at Baerd that the need to weep did grow too strong. His own griefs rose to the call of the mountain pipes. Grief for Alessan and overmastered Erlein. For Baerd and his haunted night walking. For Sandre and his ten fingers and his dead son. For Catriana and himself, all their generation, rootless and cut off from what they were in a world without a home. For all the myriad accumulations of loss and what men and women had to do in order to seek redress.

Catriana went to the baggage and she opened and poured another bottle of wine. The third glass. And as always, it was blue. She filled Devin's glass in silence. She'd scarcely spoken a word all night, but he felt closer to her than he had in a long time. He drank slowly, watching the cold smoke rise from his glass and drift away in the cool night. The stars overhead were like icy points of fire and the moon was as blue as the wine and as far away as freedom, or a home.

Devin finished his glass and put it down. He reached for his blanket and lay down himself, wrapping it around him. He found himself thinking about his father and of the twins for the first time in a long time.

A few moments later Catriana lay down not far away. Usually she spread her sleeping-roll and blanket on the far side of the fire from where he was, next to the Duke. Devin was wise enough now to know that there was a certain kind of reaching out in what she did, and that tonight might even mark a chance to begin the healing of what lay badly between them, but he was too drained to know what to do or say among all these complicated sorrows.

He said good-night to her, softly, but she did not reply. He wasn't sure if she'd heard him, but he didn't say it again. He closed his eyes. A moment later he opened them again, to look at Sandre across the fire. The Duke was gazing steadily into the flames. Devin wondered what he saw there. He wondered, but he didn't really want to know. Erlein was a shadow, a darker place in the world against the dark by the riverbank. Devin lifted himself on one elbow to look for Baerd, but Baerd had gone away, to walk alone in the night.

Alessan hadn't moved, or opened his eyes. He was still playing, lonely and high and sorrowful, when Devin fell asleep.

He woke to Baerd's firm hand on his shoulder. It was still dark and quite cold now. The fire had been allowed to die to ember and ash. Catriana and the Duke were still asleep, but Alessan was standing behind Baerd. He looked pale but composed. Devin wondered if he'd gone to bed at all.

"I need your help," Baerd murmured. "Come."

Shivering, Devin rolled out of his blankets and began pulling on his boots. The moon was down. He looked east but there was no sign of dawn along the horizon. It was very still. Sleepily he shrugged into the woolen vest Alais had sent him by way of Taccio in Ferraut. He had no idea how long he'd been asleep or what time it was.

He finished dressing and went to relieve himself in the trees by the river. His breath smoked in the frosty air. Spring was coming, but it wasn't quite here yet, not in the middle of the night. The sky was brilliantly clear and full of stars. It would be a beautiful day later when the sun came. Right now he shivered, and did up the drawstrings of his breeches.

Then he realized that he hadn't seen Erlein anywhere.

"What happened?" he whispered to Alessan as he returned to the camp. "You said you could call him back."

"I did," the Prince said shortly. Standing closer Devin could see now how weary he looked. "He fought it so hard that he passed out just now. Somewhere out there." He gestured south and west.

"Come on," Baerd said again. "Bring your sword."

They had to cross the stream. The icy cold water drove all the sleep out of Devin. He gasped with the shock of it.

"I'm sorry," Baerd said. "I'd have done it alone, but I don't know how far away he is or what else is out here in this country. Alessan wants him back in camp before he revives. It made sense to have two men."

"No, no, that's fine," Devin protested. His teeth were chattering.

"I suppose I could have woken the old Duke from his rest. Or Catriana could have helped me."

"What? No, really, Baerd. I'm fine. I'm—"

He stopped, because Baerd was laughing at him. Belatedly Devin caught on to the teasing. It warmed him in a curious way. This was, in fact, the first time he'd ever been out alone in the night with Baerd. He chose to see it as another level of trust, of welcoming. Little by little he was beginning to feel more of a part of what Alessan and Baerd had been trying to achieve for so many years. He straightened his shoulders and, walking as tall as he could, followed Baerd west into the darkness.

They found Erlein di Senzio at the edge of a cluster of olive trees on a slope, about an hour's walk from the camp. Devin swallowed awkwardly when he saw what had happened. Baerd whistled softly between his teeth; it wasn't a pretty sight.

Erlein was unconscious. He had tied himself to one of the tree-trunks and appeared to have knotted the rope at least a dozen times. Bending down, Baerd held up the wizard's waterflask. It was empty: Erlein had soaked the knots to tighten them. His pack and his knife lay together on the ground, a deliberate distance out of reach.

The rope was frayed and tangled. It looked as if a number of knots had been undone, but five or six still held.

"Look at his fingers," Baerd said grimly. He drew his dagger and began cutting the rope.

Erlein's hands were shredded into raw strips. Dried blood covered both of them. It was brutally clear what had happened. He had tried to make it impossible for himself to yield to Alessan's summons. What had he hoped for, Devin wondered. That the Prince would assume he had somehow escaped and would therefore forget about him?

Devin doubted, in fact, if what Erlein had done carried any such weight of rational thought. It was defiance, pure and simple, and one had to acknowledge—not even grudgingly—the ferocity of it. He helped Baerd cut through the last of the bonds. Erlein was breathing, but showed no signs of consciousness. His pain must have been devastating, Devin realized, with a flashing memory of the wizard beaten to his knees and screaming by the river. He wondered what screams the night had heard, here in this wild and lonely place.

He felt an awkward mixture of respect and pity and anger as he gazed down at the grey-haired troubadour. Why was he making this so hard for them? Why forcing Alessan to shoulder so much more pain of his own?

Unfortunately, he knew some of the answers to that, and they were not comforting.

"Will he try to kill himself?" he asked Baerd abruptly.

"I don't think so. As Sandre said, this one is a survivor. I don't think he'll do this again. He had to run once—to test the limits of what would happen to him. I would have done the same thing." He hesitated. "I didn't expect the rope though."

Devin took Erlein's pack and gear and Baerd's bow and quiver and sword. Baerd slung the unconscious wizard over his shoulder with a grunt and they started back east. It was slower going back. On the horizon in front of them when they reached the stream the first grey of false dawn was showing, dimming the glow of the late-rising stars.

The others were up and waiting for them. Beard laid Erlein down by the fire—Sandre had it burning again. Devin dropped the gear and weapons and went back to the river with a basin for water. When he returned Catriana and the Duke began cleaning and wrapping Erlein's mangled hands. They had opened his shirt and turned up the sleeves, revealing angry weals where he had writhed against the ropes in his struggle to be free.

Or is that backwards, Devin thought grimly. Wasn't the *binding* of the rope his real struggle to be free? He looked over and saw Alessan gazing down at Erlein. He could read absolutely nothing in the Prince's expression.

The sun rose, and shortly after that Erlein woke.

They could see him register where he was.

"Khav?" Sandre asked him casually. The five of them were sitting by the fire, eating breakfast, drinking from steaming mugs. The light from the east was a pale, delicate hue, a promise. It glinted and sparkled on the water of the stream and turned the budding leaves green-gold on the trees. The air was filled with birdsong and the leap and splash of trout in the stream.

Erlein sat up slowly and looked at them. Devin saw him become aware of the bandages on his hands. Erlein glanced over at the saddled horses and the two carts, packed and ready for the road.

His gaze swung back and steadied on Alessan's face. The two men, so improbably bound, looked at each other without speaking. Then Alessan smiled. A smile Devin knew. It opened his stern face to warmth and lit the slate-grey of his eyes.

"Had I known," Alessan said, "that you hated Tregean pipes quite that much I honestly wouldn't have played them."

A moment later, horribly, Erlein di Senzio began to laugh. There was no joy in that sound, nothing infectious, nothing to be shared. His eyes were squeezed shut and tears welled out of them, pouring down his face.

No one else spoke or moved. It lasted for a long time. When Erlein had finally composed himself he wiped his face on his sleeve, careful of his bandaged hands and looked at Alessan again. He opened his mouth, about to speak, and then closed it again.

"I know," Alessan said quietly to him. "I do know."

"Khav?" Sandre said again, after a moment.

This time Erlein accepted a mug, cradling it awkwardly in both muffled hands. Not long after they broke camp and started south again.

CHAPTER

• 10 •

FIVE DAYS LATER, ON THE EVE OF THE EMBER DAYS OF spring, they came to Castle Borso.

All that last afternoon as they moved south Devin had been watching the mountains. Any child raised in the watery lowlands of Asoli could not help but be awed by the towering southland ranges: the Braccio here in Certando, the Parravi east towards Tregea and, though he'd never seen them, the rumor of the snow-clad Sfaroni, highest of all, over west where Tigana once had been.

It was late in the day. Far to the north on that same afternoon Isolla of Ygrath lay dead and dismembered under a bloody sheet in the Audience Chamber of the palace on Chiara.

The sun setting behind a thrust spur of the mountains dyed the peaks to burgundy and red and a somber purple hue. On the very highest summits the snow still shone and dazzled in the last of the light. Devin could just make out the line of the Braccio Pass as it came down: one of the three fabled passes that had linked—in some seasons, and never easily—the Peninsula of the Palm with Quileia to the south.

In the old days, before the Matriarchy had taken deep root in Quileia there had been trade across the mountains, and the brooding piety of the springtime Ember Days had also presaged a quickening and stir of commercial life with the promise of the passes opening again. The towns and fortress-castles here in the southern highlands had been vibrant and vital then. Well-defended too, because where a trade caravan could cross, so could an army. But no King of Quileia had ever been secure

302

enough on his throne to lead an army north; not with the High Priestesses standing by at home to see him fail or fall. Here in Certando the private armies had mostly bloodied their blades and arrows against each other, in savage southland feuds that ranged over generations and became the stuff of legend.

And then the Quileian Matriarchy had come to power after all, in the time of Achis and Pasitheia, several hundred years ago. Quileia under the priestesses had folded inward upon itself like a flower at dusk and the caravans ended.

The southland cities dwindled into villages, or, if flexible and energetic enough, they changed their character and turned their faces northward and to other things, as Avalle of the Towers had done in Tigana. Here in the Certandan highlands the mighty lords who had once held glittering court in their huge warlike castles became living anachronisms. Their forays and battles with each other—once integral to the flow of events in the Palm—became more and more inconsequential, though not the less bitter or vicious for that.

To Devin, touring with Menico di Ferraut, it had sometimes seemed that every second ballad they sang was of some lord or younger son pursued by enemies among these crags; or of ill-fated southland lovers divided by the hatred of their fathers; or of the bloody deeds of those fathers, untamed as hawks in their stern high castles among these foothills of the Braccio.

And of those ballads, whether wild with battle and blood and villages set afire, or lamenting parted lovers drowning themselves in silent pools hidden in the misty hills—of all those songs, half again, it seemed to Devin, were of the Borso clan and set in and around the massive, piled, grim splendor of Castle Borso hard under Braccio Pass.

There hadn't been any new ballads for a long time, very few in fact since the Quileian caravans had stopped. But of fresh stories and rumors there had been many in the past two decades. A great many. In her own particular way, and in her own lifetime, Alienor of Castle Borso had already become a legend among the men and women of the road.

And if these newer stories were about love, as so many of the older songs had been, they had little to do with anguished youth bewailing fate on windswept crags, and rather more to tell about certain changes within Castle Borso itself. About deep woven carpets and tapestries, about imported silk and lace and velvet, and profoundly disconcerting works of art in rooms that had once seen hard men plan midnight raids at trestle-tables, while unruly hunting dogs had fought for flung bones among the rushes of the floor.

Riding beside Erlein in the second cart, Devin dragged his gaze away from the last shining of light on the peaks and looked at the castle they were nearing. Tucked into a fold of hills, with a moat around it and a small village just beyond, Borso was already in shadow. Even as he watched, Devin saw lights being lit in the windows. The last lights until the end of the Ember Days.

"Alienor is a friend," was all that Alessan had volunteered. "An old friend."

That much, at least, was evident from the greeting she gave him when her seneschal—tall and stooped, with a magnificent white beard—ushered them gravely into the firelit warmth of the Great Hall.

Alessan's color was unusually high when the lady of the castle unlaced her long fingers from his hair and withdrew her lips from his own. She hadn't hurried the encounter. Neither, even more interestingly, had he. Alienor stepped back, smiling a little, to survey his companions.

She favored Erlein with a nod of recognition. "Welcome back, troubadour. Two years, is it?"

"Even so, my lady. I am honored that you remember." Erlein's bow harkened back to an earlier age, to the manner they'd seen before Alessan had bound him.

"You were alone then, I remember. I am pleased to see you now in such splendid company."

Erlein opened his mouth and then closed it without replying. Alienor glanced at Alessan, a fleeting inquiry in her very dark eyes.

Receiving no response she turned to the Duke and the curiosity in her face sharpened. Thoughtfully she laid a finger against her cheek and tilted her head slightly to one side. The disguised Sandre endured her scrutiny impassively.

"Very well done," said Alienor of Borso, softly so the servants and the seneschal by the doors could not hear. "I imagine that Baerd has the whole Palm taking you for a Khardhu. I wonder who you really are, under all of that." Her smile was quite ravishing.

Devin didn't know whether to be impressed or unsettled. An instant later that particular dilemma was rendered irrelevant.

"You don't know?" said Erlein di Senzio loudly. "A terrible oversight. Allow me the introduction. My lady, may I present to you the—"

He got no further.

Devin was the first to react, which surprised him, thinking about it afterwards. He'd always been quick though, and he was closest to the wizard. What he did—the only thing he could think of to do—was pivot sharply and bury his fist as hard as he could in Erlein's belly.

As it was, he was only a fraction of a second ahead of Catriana on Erlein's other side. She had leaped to clap her hand over the wizard's mouth. The force of Devin's blow doubled Erlein over with a grunt of pain. This in turn had the unintended effect of throwing Catriana off balance and stumbling forward. To be smoothly caught and braced by Alienor.

The whole thing had taken perhaps three seconds.

Erlein sank to his knees on the opulent carpet. Devin knelt beside him. He heard Alienor dismissing her servants from the room.

"You are a fool!" Baerd snarled at the wizard.

"He certainly is," Alienor agreed in a rather different tone, all exaggerated petulance and flounce. "Why would *anyone* think I'd want the burden of knowing the true identity of a disguised Khardhu warrior?" She was still holding Catriana around the waist, quite unnecessarily. Now she let her go, with an amused expression at the girl's rapid retreat.

"You are an impetuous creature, aren't you?" she murmured silkily.

"Not especially," said Catriana hardily, stopping a few feet away.

Alienor's mouth quirked. She looked Catriana up and down with an expert eye. "I am horribly jealous of you," she pronounced at length. "And I would be, even if you had that hair chopped off and those eyes sewn shut. What magnificent men you are traveling with!"

"Are they?" Catriana's voice was indifferent, but her color was suddenly high.

"*Are* they?" Alienor echoed sharply. "You mean you haven't established that for yourself? Dear child, what have you been *doing* with your nights? Of course they are! Don't waste your youth, my dear."

Catriana looked at her levelly. "I don't think I am," she said. "But I doubt we'd have the same thoughts on that subject."

Devin winced, but Alienor's answer was mild. "Perhaps not," she agreed, unruffled. "But, in truth, I think the overlap would actually be greater than you imagine." She paused. "You may also find as you get older that ice is for deaths and endings, not for beginnings. Any kind of beginnings. On the other hand, I will ensure," she added, with a smile that was all kindness, "that you have a sufficiency of blankets to keep you warm tonight."

Erlein groaned, dragging Devin's attention away from the two women. He heard Catriana say, "I thank you for your solicitude," but he missed her expression. From the tone he could hazard a guess at what it would be.

He supported Erlein's head as the wizard labored to get his wind back. Alienor simply ignored them. She was greeting Baerd now with a friendly civility—a tone that was cheerfully matched, Devin noted instinctively, by Baerd's own manner towards her.

"I'm sorry," he whispered to Erlein. "I couldn't think of anything else."

Erlein waved a feeble, still-unhealed hand. He'd insisted on removing the bandages before they'd entered the castle. "*I'm* sorry," he wheezed, surprising Devin considerably. "I forgot about the servants." He wiped his lips with the back of one hand. "I won't achieve much for myself if I get us all killed. Not my idea of freedom, that. Nor, frankly, is this posture my notion of middle-aged dignity.

Since you knocked me down you can kindly help me up."
For the first time Devin heard a faint note of amusement
in the troubadour's voice. *A survivor,* Sandre had said.

As tactfully as he could he helped the other man stand.

"The extremely violent one," Alessan was saying drily,
"is Devin d'Asoli. He also sings. If you are very good he
may sing for you."

Devin turned away from Erlein, but perhaps because
he'd been distracted by what had just happened he was
quite unprepared to deal with the gaze he now encountered.

There is no possible way, he found himself thinking,
that this woman is forty years old. He reflexively sketched
the performer's bow Menico had taught him, to cover his
confusion. She *was* almost forty and he knew it: Alienor
had been widowed two years after she'd been wed, when
Cornaro of Borso had died in the Barbadian invasion of
Certando. The stories and descriptions of the beautiful
widow in her southland castle had begun very shortly
after that.

They didn't come even near to catching what she was—
what he saw standing before him in a long gown of a
blue so deep it was nearly black. Her hair *was* black,
worn high upon her head and held by a diadem of white
gold studded with gems. A few tendrils of hair had been
artlessly allowed to fall free, framing the perfect oval of
her face. Her eyes were indigo, almost violet under the
long lashes, and her mouth was full and red and smiling a
private smile as she looked at Devin.

He forced himself to meet that look. Doing so, he felt
as though all the sluice-gates in his veins had been hurled
open and his blood was a river in flood, racing through a
steep wild course at an ever-increasing speed. Her smile
grew deeper, more private, as if she could actually see
that happening inside him, and the dark eyes grew wider
for an instant.

"I suppose," said Alienor di Certando, before turning
back to Alessan, "that I shall have to try to be very good
then, if that will induce you to sing for me."

Her breasts were full and high, Devin saw, could not
help but see. The gown was cut very low and a diamond
pendant hung against her skin, drawing the eye like a
blue-white fire.

He shook his head, fighting to clear it, a little shocked at his own reaction. This was ridiculous, he told himself sternly. He had been overheated by the stories told, his imagination rendered unruly by the opulent, sensuous furnishings in the room. He looked upwards for distraction and then wished he hadn't.

On the ceiling someone not a stranger to the act of love had painted Adaon's primal coupling with Eanna. The face of the goddess was very clearly that of Alienor and the painting showed—just as clearly—that she was in the very moment of rapture when the stars had streamed into being from her ecstasy.

There were indeed stars streaming all across the background of the ceiling fresco. It was, however, difficult to look at the background of the fresco. Devin forced his eyes down. What helped him reclaim his composure was meeting Catriana's glance just then: a mingled look of caustic irony and a second thing he couldn't quite recognize. For all her own splendor and the wild crimson glory of her hair, Catriana looked exceptionally young just then. Almost a child, Devin thought sagely, not yet fully realized or accomplished in her womanhood.

The Lady of Castle Borso was complete in what she was, from her sandaled feet to the band in her lustrous hair. Her nails, Devin noticed belatedly, were painted the same blue-black dangerous color as her gown.

He swallowed, and looked away again.

"I expected you yesterday," Alienor was saying to Alessan. "I was waiting for you and I'd made myself beautiful for you but you didn't come."

"Just as well, then," Alessan murmured, smiling. "Had I seen you any more beautiful than you are now I might never have found the strength to leave."

Her mouth curled mischievously. She turned to the others. "You see how the man torments me? Not a quarter of an hour in my home and he speaks of leaving. Am I well served in such a friend?"

The question was addressed, as it happened, directly to Devin. His throat was dry; her glance did disruptive things to the orderly flow of messages from brain to tongue. He essayed a smile, suspecting rather that the expression produced fell somewhere between the fatuous and the imbecilic.

Wine, Devin thought desperately. He was in serious need of an effective glass of something.

As if summoned by an art of timing more subtle than wizardry three servants in blue livery reappeared, each bearing seven glasses on a tray. Two of the trays, Devin saw, bore a red wine that was almost certainly Certandan.

The wine in the third set of glasses was blue.

Devin turned to Alessan. The Prince was looking at Alienor with an expression that spoke to something private and shared far in the past. For a moment her own expression and demeanor altered: as if she had laid aside for an instant the reflexive spinning of her webs of enticement. And Devin, a far more perceptive man than he had been six months before, thought he saw the hint of a sadness in her eyes.

Then she spoke and he was certain that he'd seen it. In some subtle way it calmed him, and shed a different, milder light on the mood in the room.

"It is not a thing I am likely to forget," she said softly to Alessan, gesturing towards the blue wine.

"Nor I," he replied. "Since it began here."

She was silent a moment, eyelids lowered. Then the moment passed. Alienor's eyes were sparkling again when they lifted. "I have the usual collection of letters for you. But one is very recent," she said. "Brought two days ago by a very young priest of Eanna who was terrified of me the whole time he was here. He wouldn't even stay the night though he only arrived at sunset. I swear he rode out so fast he must have feared I'd have his robe off if he lingered for a meal."

"And would you have?" Alessan grinned.

She made a face. "Unlikely. Eanna's sort are seldom worth the trouble. Though he *was* pretty. Almost as pretty as Baerd, come to think of it."

Baerd, quite unperturbed, simply smiled. Alienor's glance lingered flirtatiously on him. *There too,* Devin noted. An exchange that spoke to events and things shared a long way back. He felt young suddenly, and out of his depth.

"Where is the new message from?" Alessan asked.

Alienor hesitated. "West," was all she said. She glanced at the rest of them with a veiled question in her eyes.

Alessan noted it. "You may speak freely. I trust every man and woman here." He was careful not to even look at Erlein. Devin did look, but if he'd expected a reaction from the wizard he was disappointed.

With a gesture Alienor dismissed her servants. The old seneschal had already withdrawn to see to the preparation of their rooms. When they were alone Alienor walked over to a writing-table by one of the four blazing fireplaces and claimed a sealed envelope from a drawer. She came back and gave it to Alessan.

"It is from Danoleon himself," she said. "From your own province whose name I cannot yet hear or say."

And that, Devin had not expected at all.

"Forgive me," Alessan murmured. He strode quickly toward the nearest fire, tearing the letter open as he went. Alienor became very busy offering glasses of the red wine. Devin took a long drink from his. Then he noticed that Baerd had not touched his wine and that his gaze was fixed on Alessan across the room. Devin followed the look. The Prince had finished reading. He was standing rigidly, staring into the fire.

"Alessan?" Baerd said.

Alienor turned swiftly at that. Alessan did not move; seemed not to have even heard.

"Alessan?" Baerd said again, more urgently. "What is it?"

Slowly the Prince of Tigana turned from the flames to look at them. Or not really at *them*, Devin amended inwardly. At Baerd. There was something bleak and cold in his face. *Ice is for endings*, Devin thought involuntarily.

"It *is* from Danoleon, I'm afraid. From the Sanctuary." Alessan's voice was flat. "My mother is dying. I will have to start home tomorrow."

Baerd's face had gone as white as Alessan's. "The meeting?" he said. "The meeting tomorrow?"

"That first," Alessan said. "After the meeting, whatever happens, I must ride home."

Given the shock of that news and the impact Alessan's words and manner had on all of them, the knock on

Devin's chamber door late that night came as a disorienting surprise.

He had not been asleep. "Wait," he called softly and
struggled quickly into his breeches. He pulled a loose
shirt on over his head and padded in his stockings across
the floor, wincing at the cold of the stones where the
carpeting ended. His hair disordered, feeling rumpled
and confused, he opened the door.

In the hallway outside, holding a single candle that cast
weird, flickering shadows along the corridor wall was
Alienor herself.

"Come," was all she said. She did not smile and he
could not see her eyes behind the flame. Her robe was a
creamy white, lined with fur. It was fastened at the throat
but Devin could discern the swell of her breasts beneath.
Her hair had been loosened, tumbling over her shoulders
and down her back in a black cascade.

Devin hesitated, his mouth dry again, his mind scattered and lagging. He put up a hand to try to straighten
the hopeless tangle of his hair.

She shook her head. "Leave it like that," she said. Her
free hand with the long dark nails came up and pushed
through his brown curls. "Leave it," she said again, and
turned.

He followed her. Her and the single candle and the
unleashed chaos of his blood down a long corridor then a
shorter one, through an angled sequence of empty public
rooms then up a curving flight of stairs. At the top of the
stairs an orange spill of light came from beyond a pair of
open doors. Devin passed through those doors behind
the Lady of Castle Borso. He had time to register the
blaze of the fire, the rich, intricate hangings on the walls,
the profusion of extravagant carpets on the floor, and the
huge canopied bed strewn with pillows of all colors and
sizes. A lean hunting dog, grey and graceful, regarded
him from by the fire but did not rise.

Alienor laid her candle down. She closed the two doors
and turned to him, leaning back against the polished
wood. Her eyes were enormous, uncannily black. Devin
felt his pulse like a hammer. The rush of his blood
seemed loud in his veins.

"I am burning up," Alienor said.

Somewhere a part of him, where proportion lived and irony took shape, wanted to protest, even to be amused at such a pronouncement. But as he looked at her he saw the quickening draw of her breathing and how shallow it was, saw the deep flush of her coloring . . . one of his hands as if of its own will came up and touched her cheek.

It was burning hot.

With a sound deep in her throat Alienor trapped his hand with one of her own and sank her teeth in the flesh of his palm.

And with that pain desire was loosed in Devin as it never had been in his life. He heard an oddly distorted sound and realized it had come from him. He took a half-step toward her and she was in his arms. Her fingers locked and twisted in his hair and her mouth met his with an avidness, a hunger that raked the rising fires of his own need to a point where awareness fled and drifted far away.

Everything was gone, or going. Tigana. Alessan, Alais, Catriana. His memories. Memory itself, that was his most sure anchor and his pride. Even the memory of the hallways to this room, the roads and years and rooms, all the other rooms that led to this one. And her.

He tore at the fastenings of her robe and buried his face between her breasts as they spilled free. She gasped, and her hands clawed at his shirt until it came away. He felt her nails tear the skin along his back. He twisted his head and bit her then and tasted blood. He heard her laugh.

Never, ever, had he done such a thing before.

Somehow they seemed to be on the bed among the colored splay of the pillows. And then Alienor was naked above him, impaled on his sex, her mouth descending to his own as the two of them surged together through the arc of an act that strove to cast the world away. As far away as it could be hurled.

For an instant Devin thought he understood. In some unthinking flash of visceral illumination he thought he grasped why Alienor did this. The nature of her need, which was not what it seemed to be. Given another moment, a still place in the firmament, he could have

reached out to put a name to it, a frame for the blurred
awareness. He reached . . .

She cried out with her climax. Her hands slid along his
skin, curving down. Desire obliterated thought, any straining towards thought. With a racking twist he virtually
threw her to one side and swung himself above her,
never leaving the warm shelter between her thighs. Cushions scattered around them, fell on the floor. Her eyes
were tightly shut, her mouth forming soundless words.

Devin began to drive himself into her as if to drive
away all the demons and the hurts, all the brutal deaden-
ing truths that were the world of the Palm in their day.
His own climax when it came left him shuddering and
limp, lost to where he was, only dimly clinging to what he
knew to be his name.

He heard her whispering it softly, over and over. She
moved gently out from under him. He rolled over on his
back, eyes closed. He felt her fingers glide along his skin.
He could not move. She was playing with his hands,
caressing and guiding them out from his sides. Her lips
and fingers danced down his chest and belly, over his
satiated sex and further down, exploring along his thighs
and legs, and down.

By the time he was aware of what she'd done he was
bound hand and foot to the four posts of her bed,
spreadeagled beneath her. His eyes flew open, startled
and alarmed. He struggled. Uselessly—he was held in
bonds of silk looped and knotted.

"That," said Alienor in a husky voice, "was a wonderful beginning to a night. Shall I teach you something
now?" She reached, naked and magnificent, flushed and
scored with his marks upon her, and brought something
up from the floor beside the bed. His eyes grew wide
when he saw what it was she held.

"You are binding me against my will," Devin said, a
little desperately. "This is not my idea of how to come
together in love." He twisted hard again, at shoulder and
hip; the silken bonds held firm.

Alienor's answering smile was luminous. She was more
beautiful in that moment than he could ever have imagined a woman being. In the huge dark pools of her eyes
something stirred, primal and dangerous and terrifyingly

arousing. He felt, improbably soon, a quickening in his sex. She saw it. Her smile deepened. One long fingernail stroked lightly, almost meditatively along his gathering tumescence.

"It will be," murmured his dark lady, the Lady of Castle Borso. Her lips parted showing the sharp white teeth behind. He registered the taut firmness of her nipples as she opened her legs to straddle him again. He saw her caress what she had claimed from the carpet by the bed. Beyond her, by the fire, the wolfhound had its handsome head raised, watching them.

"It will be," Alienor said again. "Trust me. Let me teach you now, and show you, this, and then this, and soon it *will* be your idea of how to come together. Oh yes, Devin, it will be very soon."

She moved upon his body and the candlelight was deflected and then hidden as she came down over him. He struggled but only for a moment for his heart was pounding again and desire was overwhelmingly upon him, just as Alienor was, just as her own complex needs could be seen rising in her again, in the darkness of her eyes before they closed, in her movements above him, and in the ragged, reaching, upward straining of her breath.

And before the night was over, before the half of it had passed, with the last candles of winter burning down, she had proven herself right, terribly, over and over again. And at the end even, she was the one who lay bound and open between the four pillars of the world that was her bed and Devin was no longer quite sure of who he was that he should be doing to her the things he was. The things that made her whisper and then cry aloud his name as she did, over and again. But he did know that she had changed him and had found a place within him where his need to seek oblivion was equal to her own.

The candle on his side of the bed burned out some time later. There was a small, scented drifting of smoke. The pattern of light and shade in the room changed; neither of them was asleep, they both noticed it. The fire was down to its embers; the dog still lay before it, its magnificent head stretched out on its paws.

"You had better go," Alienor said, stroking his near shoulder absently. "While there's a candle for you to carry. It is easy to lose your way in the dark."

"You observe the Ember Days?" he asked, a little surprised at such piety. "No fires?"

"No fires," she said ruefully. "Half my household staff would leave me, and I don't even want to guess at what the tenant farmers or the villagers would do. Storm the castle. Call down some ancient curse with ears of corn soaked in blood. These are the southern highlands, Devin—they take their rites seriously up here."

"As seriously as you take yours?"

She smiled at that and stretched like a cat. "I suppose so. The farmers will do things tonight and tomorrow that I prefer not to know about." With a sinuous motion she curled downwards towards the foot of the bed and reached for something on the carpet by the bedposts. Her body was a smooth, candlelit curve of white flesh, with the marks he had made on her still showing red.

She straightened and handed him his breeches. It felt abrupt, a dismissal, and Devin gave her a long stare, not moving. She met the look, but her eyes were neither hard nor dismissive.

"Don't be angry," Alienor said softly. "You were too splendid to be leaving in anger. I'm telling you truths: I do observe the Ember rites and it *is* hard to find your way back without a light." She hesitated a moment, then added, "And I have always slept alone since my husband died."

Devin said nothing. He rose and dressed. His shirt he found halfway between the bed and the doors. It was shredded so badly it should have been amusing. He wasn't amused though. In fact, he *was* angry—or some feeling beyond anger, or beside it, a more complex thing. Lying naked and uncovered among the scattered pillows of her bed, Alienor watched him clothe himself. He looked at her, marveling still at her feline magnificence and even—despite the change of mood—even aware of how easy it would be for her to stir his desire again.

But as he gazed at her a dormant thought surfaced from wherever thought had been driven in the primitive frenzy of the last few hours. He arranged the shirt as best he could and walked over to claim one of the candles in a brass holder.

She had turned on her side to follow his movements, her head now resting on one hand, the black hair tumbling about her, her body offered to his sight as a gift, a glory in the shifting light. Her eyes were wide and direct, her smile generous, even kind.

"Good-night," she said. "I don't know whether you know it, but you are welcome back should you choose to come one day."

He hadn't expected that. He knew, without having to be told, that she was honoring him with this. But his thought, his disquiet from before was strong now and intermingled with other images, so that, although he smiled in return and nodded, it was neither pride nor honor that he felt.

"Good night," he said and turned to go.

At the doors he stopped and, as much because he had remembered Alessan saying that the blue wine had begun with her as for any other single reason that he knew—then or later—Devin turned back to her. She had not moved. He looked, drinking in the opulence of the chamber and the proffered beauty of the woman on the bed. Even as he stood there another candle died on the far side of the room.

"Is this what happens to us?" Devin said then, quietly, reaching for words to frame this new, hard thought. "When we are no longer free. Is this what happens to our love?"

He could see her eyes change, even from this distance and in this wavering of light and dark. For a long time she looked back at him.

"You are clever," she said finally. "Alessan has chosen well in you."

He waited.

"Ah!" said Alienor throatily, simulating astonishment. "He actually wants an answer. A true answer from a lady in her castle at the edge of the world." It may have been a trick of the uncertain light, but she seemed to look away then, beyond where Devin stood, even beyond the tapestried walls of her room.

"It is one of the things that happens to us," she said at

last. "A kind of insurrection in the dark that somehow stands against the laws of day that bind us and cannot be broken now."

Devin thought about it.

"Possibly that," he agreed softly, working it through. "Or else an admission somewhere in the soul that we deserve no more than this, nothing that goes deeper. Since we are not free and have accepted that."

He saw her flinch then, and close her eyes.

"Did I deserve that?" she asked.

A terrible sadness passed over Devin. He swallowed with some difficulty. "No," he said. "No, you didn't."

Her eyes were still closed when he left the room.

He felt heavy and burdened, beyond merely tired; leaden with the weight of his thoughts, slowed by them. He stumbled going down the stairwell and had to fling out his free hand to brace himself against the stone wall. The motion left the candle unguarded and it went out.

It was very dark then. The castle was utterly still. Moving carefully, Devin reached the bottom of the stairs and he put the spent flame down on a ledge there. At intervals, high in the walls, tall thin windows let slanting moonlight fall across the corridor but the angle and the hour did not allow for any real illumination.

Briefly he considered going back for another candle but then, after standing still a moment to let his eyes adjust, Devin set out along what he thought to be the way they had come.

He was lost very soon, though not really alarmed. In his present mood there seemed to be something apposite about padding thus silently down the darkened hallways of this ancient highland castle in the dead of night, the stones cold against his feet.

There are no wrong turnings. Only paths we had not known we were meant to walk.

Who had told him that? The words had come unbidden to his mind from some recess of memory. He turned into an unfamiliar corridor and passed through a long room hung with paintings. Part of the way through, he found a voice for the words: it had been the old priest of Morian at the goddess's temple by his family's farm in Asoli. He had taught the twins and then Devin how to read and do sums, and when it appeared that the youngest boy, the small one, could sing he had given Devin his first lessons in the rudiments of harmony.

No wrong turnings, Devin thought again. And then, with a shiver he could not suppress, he remembered that this was not just the nadir of a night, it was the end of winter, the first of the Ember Days—when the dead were said to walk abroad.

The dead. Who were his dead? Marra. His mother, whom he had never known. Tigana? Could a country, a province, be said to have died? Could it be lost and mourned like a living soul? He thought of the Barbadian he had slain in the Nievolene barn.

He did quicken his pace then, over the dark, sporadically moonlit stones of the vast and silent castle.

It seemed to Devin that he walked for an endless time—or a time outside of time—passing no one, hearing nothing save for his own breathing or the soft tread of his feet, before he finally recognized a statue in an alcove. He had admired it by torchlight earlier in the evening. He knew his room was just ahead and around a corner to the right. Somehow he had come entirely the wrong way along the whole far wing of Castle Borso.

He also knew, from earlier in the evening, that the room directly opposite the small fine statue of the bearded archer drawing a bow, was Catriana's.

He looked up and down the corridor but saw only greater and lesser shadows among the bands of white moonlight falling from above. He listened, and heard no sound. If the dead were abroad they were silent.

No wrong turnings, Ploto the priest had told him long ago.

He thought of Alienor, lying with her eyes closed among her bright cushions and all her candles and he was sorry for what he'd said to her at the end. He was sorry for many things. Alessan's mother was dying. His own was dead.

Ice is for deaths and endings, Alienor had said to Catriana in the hall.

He was cold, and very sad. He moved forward and ended the silence, knocking gently on Catriana's door.

*   *   *

She'd had a restless night, for many reasons. Alienor had disturbed her: both the unbridled sensuousness that emanated from the woman, and the obviously close, unknown past she shared with Alessan and Baerd.

Catriana hated unknown things, information hidden from her. She *still* didn't know what Alessan was going to do tomorrow, what this mysterious meeting in the highlands was all about, and ignorance made her uneasy and even, on a less acknowledged level, afraid.

She wished she could be more like Devin sometimes, matching his seemingly tranquil acceptance of what he could or could not know. She had seen him storing away the pieces of what he did learn and patiently waiting to receive another piece, and then putting them together like the tiles of a children's puzzle game.

Sometimes she admired that, sometimes it made her wild and contemptuous to see him so accepting of Alessan's occasional reticence or Baerd's chronic reserve. Catriana needed to *know*. She had been ignorant for so much of her life, shielded from her own history in that tiny fishing village in Astibar. She felt that there was so much lost time to be regained. Sometimes it made her want to weep.

That was how she'd been feeling this evening before drifting into a shallow, uneasy sleep and a dream of home. She often dreamt of home since she'd left, especially of her mother.

This time she saw herself walking through the village just after sunrise, passing the last house—Tendo's, she even saw his dog—and then rounding the familiar curve of the shore to where her father had bought a derelict cottage and repaired it and raised a family.

In her dream she saw the boat already far out, trawling among the early-morning swell of the sea. It seemed to be springtime. Her mother was in the doorway of the cottage mending nets in the good light of the sunrise. Her eyes had been going bad for years and it was hard for her to work with her needle in the evenings. Catriana had gradually taken over the night-time needlework in her last year at home.

It was a beautiful morning in the dream. The stones of

the beach gleamed and the breeze was fresh and light off the water. All the other boats were out as well, taking advantage of the morning, but it was easy to tell which one was their own. Catriana walked up the path and stood by the newly mended porch, waiting for her mother to look up and see her and leap to her feet with a cry, and fold her daughter in her arms.

Her mother did glance up from her work, but only to gaze seaward, squinting toward the light, to check the position of their boat. An old habit, a nervous one, and one that had probably done much to hurt her eyes. She'd a husband and three sons in that small boat though.

She didn't see her daughter at all. Catriana realized with a queer pain that she was invisible here. Because she had gone, because she had left them and wasn't there any longer. There was more grey, she saw, in her mother's hair, and her heart ached as she stood there in mild sunlight to see how worn and hard her mother's hands were, and how tired the kind face was. She had always thought of her mother as a young woman, until Tiena, the baby, had died in the plague six years ago. Things had changed after that.

It isn't fair, she thought, and in the dream she cried aloud and was not heard.

Her mother sat on a wooden chair on the porch in the early light, working on the nets, occasionally looking up to check the position of one small boat among so many bobbing on this alien eastern sea so far from the one she'd loved.

Catriana woke, her body twisting violently away from all the hurts embedded in that image. She opened her eyes, waiting for her heartbeat to slow, lying under several blankets in a room in Castle Borso. Alienor's castle.

Alienor, who was the same age as Catriana's worn, tired mother. It truly was not fair. Why should she be carrying such guilt, seeing such sad, hurtful images in her sleep, for having gone away? Why, when it was her mother who had given her the ring when she was fourteen, in the year the baby died. The ring that marked her as from Tigana and by the sea for anyone who knew the ancient symbols, and for no one else.

The ring that had so marked her for Alessan bar

Valentin two years ago when he and Baerd had seen her selling eels and fresh-caught telanquy in Ardin town just up the coast from the village.

She had not been a trusting person at eighteen. She could not have said, then or now, why she'd trusted the two of them and joined them for that walk upriver out of town when the market was done. If pushed to an answer she would have said that there was something about Baerd that had reassured her.

It was on that walk that they had told her about her ring and about Tigana, and the axis of her life had tilted another way. A new running of time had begun from that moment, and with it the need to know.

At home that evening after dinner, after the boys had gone to bed, she told her parents that she now knew where they were from, and what her ring meant. And she asked her father what he was going to do to help her bring Tigana back, and what he had been doing all these years. It was the only time in her life she'd ever seen her mild, innocuous father in a rage, and the only time he'd ever struck her.

Her mother wept. Her father stormed about the house in the awkward manner of a man unused to raging, and he swore upon the Triad that he'd not taken his wife and daughter away before the Ygrathen invasion and the fall only to be sucked back into that ancient grief now.

And thus had Catriana learned the second thing that had changed her life.

The youngest of the boys had begun crying. Her father had stomped out then, slamming the door, rattling the windows. Catriana and her mother had looked at each other in silence a long time while a frightened child gradually subsided in the loft above their heads. Catriana held up her hand and showed the ring she'd worn for the past four years. She had looked a question with her eyes, and her mother had nodded once, not weeping now. The embrace they exchanged was one they both expected to be their last.

Catriana had found Alessan and Baerd at the best-known of the inns in Ardin town. It had been a bright night, she remembered, both moons high and nearly full. The night watchman at the inn had leered at her and groped when she sidled by him up the stairs toward the room he'd identified.

She had knocked and Alessan had opened to her name. His grey eyes, even before she spoke, had been curiously dark, as if anticipating a burden or a grief.

"I am coming with you," she had said. "My father was a coward. We fled before the invasion. I intend to make that up. I will not sleep with you though. I've never slept with any man. Can I trust you both?"

Awake in Castle Borso she blushed in the darkness, remembering that. How impossibly young she must have sounded to them. Neither man had laughed though, or even smiled. She would never forget that.

"Can you sing?" was all that Alessan had said.

She fell asleep again, thinking about music, about all the songs she'd sung with him, crossing the Palm for two years. This time when she dreamt it was about water—about swimming in the sea at home, her greatest, sweetest joy. Diving for shells at summer twilight among the startled flashing fish, feeling the water wrap her like a second skin.

Then without warning or transition the dream changed and she was on the bridge in Tregea again in a gathering of winter dark and wind, more terrified than she had imagined a soul could be. Only herself to blame, her own pride, her gnawing, consuming, unslaked need to make redress for the fact that they had fled. She saw herself mount and balance on the railing again, saw the racing, black tumultuous water far below, heard, even over the loud rush of the river, the pounding of her heart . . .

And woke a second time just before the nightmare of her leap. Woke because what she had heard as the beat of her heart was a knocking at her door.

"Who is it?" she called.

"Devin. Will you let me come in?"

Abruptly she sat up in bed and pulled the topmost blanket to her chin.

"What is it?" she called.

"I'm not sure, actually. May I come in?"

"The door isn't locked," she said finally. She made sure the blankets were covering her, but the room was so dark it didn't really matter.

She heard him enter, but saw only the outline of his form.

"Thank you," he said. "You should lock your door, you know."

She wondered if he had any idea how much she hated being told things like that. "The only person likely to be roaming tonight was our hostess, and she was unlikely to be coming for me. There's a chair to your left."

She heard him reach for it and sink back with a sigh into the deep armchair. "I suppose that's true enough," he said in a drained voice. "And I'm sorry, you don't really need me to be telling you how to take care of yourself."

She listened for irony but heard none. "I seem to have managed tolerably well without your guidance," she said mildly.

He was silent. Then: "Catriana, I honestly don't know why I'm here. I'm in such a strange mood tonight. I feel ridiculously sad."

There was something extremely odd in his voice. She hesitated a moment, then, carefully adjusting the blankets, reached over to strike a flint.

"You light fires on the Ember Days?" he asked.

"Evidently."

She lit the candle by her bed. Then, somewhat regretting the waspishness of that reply, added, "My mother used to light one—just one, as a reminder to the Triad, she used to say. Though I only understood what she meant after I met Alessan."

"That's strange. So did my father," Devin said wonderingly. "I've never thought about that. I never knew why he did it. My father was not a man who explained things."

She turned to look at him, but he was deep in the chair and the wings hid his face.

"A reminder of Tigana?" she said.

"It would have to have been. As if . . . as if the Triad didn't deserve full devotion or observance because of what they'd allowed." He paused, then in a meditative tone added, "It's another example of our pride, isn't it? Of that Tiganese arrogance Sandre always talks about. We make bargains with the Triad, we balance scales with them: they take away our name, we take away a part of their rites."

"I suppose so," she said, though it didn't really strike her that way. Devin talked like this sometimes. She didn't see the action as one of pride, or bargaining, just as a reminder to the self of how great a wrong had come to pass. A reminder, like Alessan's blue wine.

"My mother is not a proud woman," she said, surprising herself.

"I don't know what mine was like," he said in that tightened voice. "I don't even know if I could say that my father is proud. I guess I don't know very much about him either." He really did sound peculiar.

"Devin," she said sharply, "lean forward. Let me look at you." She checked her blankets; they covered her to the chin.

Slowly he shifted forward: the candlelight spilled across his wildly disheveled hair, the torn shirt and the visible scratches and marks of teeth. She felt a quick surge of anger, and then a slower, deeper anxiety that had nothing to do with him. Or not directly.

She masked both reactions behind a sardonic laugh. "She *was* roaming, I see. You look like you've been to war."

With an effort he managed a brief smile, but there was something somber in his eyes: she could read it even by candlelight.

It unsettled her. "What is it then?" she pursued with broad sarcasm, "You tired her out and came here wanting more? I can tell you—"

"No," he said quickly. "No, it isn't that. It is . . . hardly that, Catriana. It has been a . . . difficult night."

"You certainly look as if it was," she retorted, her hands gripping the blankets.

He pushed on doggedly. "Not that way. It's so strange. So complicated. I think I learned something there. I think—"

"Devin, I really *don't* want the details!" She was angry with herself for how edgy this sort of thing made her feel.

"No, no. Not like that, though yes, there was that at the beginning. But . . ." He drew a breath. "I think what I learned was something about what the Tyrants have done to us. Not just Brandin, and not just in Tigana. Alberico too. Both of them, and to all of us."

"Such insight," she mocked, reflexively. "She must be even more skillful than you imagined."

Which silenced him. He leaned back in the chair again and she couldn't see his face. In the quiet that followed her breathing grew calmer.

"I'm sorry," she said at length. "I didn't mean that. I'm tired. I've had some bad dreams tonight. What do you want from me, Devin?"

"I'm not sure," he said. "I guess, to be a friend."

Again she felt pushed and uneasy. She resisted an instinctive, nervous urge to suggest he go write a letter to one of Rovigo's daughters. She said, "I've never been good at that, even as a child."

"Nor I," he said, shifting forward again. He had pushed his hair into a semblance of order. He said, "It is more than that between you and I though. You hate me sometimes, don't you."

She felt her heart thump. "We do not have to discuss this, Devin. I don't hate you."

"Sometimes you do," he pursued in that strange, dogged tone. "Because of what happened in the Sandreni Palace." He paused, and drew a shaky breath. "Because I was the first man you ever made love with."

She closed her eyes. Tried, unsuccessfully, to will that last sentence not to have been spoken. "You knew?"

"Not then. I figured it out later."

Pieces of another puzzle. Patiently putting it together. Figuring her out. She opened her eyes and gazed bleakly at him. "And is it your idea that discussing this interesting subject will make us friends?"

He winced. "Probably not. I don't know. I thought I'd tell you I want to be." There was a silence. "I honestly don't know, Catriana. I'm sorry."

Surprisingly, her shock and anger had both passed. She saw him slump back again, exhausted, and she did the same, reclining against the wooden headboard of her bed. She thought for a while, marveling at how calm she felt.

"I don't hate you, Devin," she said finally. "Truly, I don't. Nothing like that. It is an awkward memory, I won't deny that, but I don't think it has ever hindered us in what we have to do. Which is what really matters, isn't it?"

"I suppose so," he said. She couldn't see his face. "If that is all that matters."

"I mean, it's true what I said before: I've always been bad at making friends."

"Why?"

Pieces of the puzzle again. But she said, "As a girl, I'm not sure. Maybe I was shy, perhaps proud. I never felt easy in our village, even though it was the only home I'd ever known. But since Baerd named Tigana for me, since I heard the name, that has been all there is in the world for me. All that counts for anything at all."

She could almost hear him thinking about that.

He said, "Ice is for endings."

Which is exactly what Alienor had said to her. He went on, "You are still a living person, Catriana. With a heart, a life to live, access to friendship, even to love. Why are you sealing yourself down to the one thing only?"

And she heard herself reply: *"Because my father never fought. He fled Tigana like a coward before the battles at the river."*

She could have ripped her tongue bleeding from her mouth, out at the very root, the moment she had spoken.

"Oh," he said.

"Not a word, Devin! Don't say a word!"

He obeyed, sitting very still, almost invisible in the depths of his chair. Abruptly she blew out the candle; she didn't want light now. And then, because it was dark, and because he was so obligingly silent she was gradually able to regain control of herself. To move past the meaning of this moment without weeping. It took a long time in the darkness but eventually she was able to draw a long, steady breath and know she was all right.

"Thank you," she said, not entirely sure what she was thanking him for. Mostly, the silence.

There was no reply. She waited a moment then softly called his name. Again no answer. She listened, and eventually was able to make out the steady rise and fall of his breathing in sleep.

She had enough of a sense of irony to find that amusing. He had evidently had a difficult night though, and not just in the obvious ways.

She thought about waking him and sending him back to his own room. It would most certainly raise eyebrows if they were seen leaving here together in the morning. She discovered, though, that she didn't really care. She also realized that she minded less than she'd expected that he'd figured out the one truth about her and had just learned another. About her father, but really more about herself. She wondered about that, why it didn't bother her more.

She considered putting one of the blankets over him but resisted the impulse. For some reason she didn't really want him waking in the morning and knowing she'd done that. Rovigo's daughters did that sort of thing, not she. Or no: the younger daughter would have had him in this bed and inside her by now, strange moods and exhaustion notwithstanding. The older? Would have woven a new quilt at miraculous speed and tucked it around him with a note attached as to the lineage of the sheep that had given the wool and the history of the pattern she'd chosen.

Catriana smiled to herself in the darkness and settled back to sleep. Her restlessness seemed to have passed and she did not dream again. When she woke, just after dawn, he was gone. She didn't learn until later just how far.

CHAPTER
• 11 •

ELENA STOOD BY THE OPEN DOOR OF MATTIO'S HOUSE looking up the dark road to the moat and the raised drawbridge, watching the candles flicker and go out one by one in the windows of Castle Borso. At intervals people walked past her into the house, offering only a nod or a brief greeting if anything at all. It was a night of battle that lay ahead of them, and everyone arriving was aware of that.

From the village behind her there came no sound at all, and no light. All the candles were long snuffed out, fires banked, windows covered over, even the chinks at the base of doors blocked by cloth or rags. The dead walked on the first of the Ember Nights, everyone knew that.

There was little noise from within the house behind her, though fifteen or twenty people must have arrived by now, crowding into Mattio's home at the edge of the village. Elena didn't know how many more Walkers were yet to join them here, or later, at the meeting-place; she did know that there would be too few. There hadn't been enough last year, or the year before that, and they had lost those battles very badly. The Ember Night wars were killing the Walkers faster than young ones like Elena herself were growing up to replace them. Which is why they were losing each spring, why they would almost certainly lose tonight.

It was a starry night, with only the one moon risen, the white crescent of Vidomni as she waned. It was cold as well, here in the highlands at the very beginning of spring. Elena wrapped her arms about herself, gripping her elbows with her hands. It would be a different sky, a different feel to the night entirely, in only a few hours, when the battle began.

Carenna walked in, giving her quick warm smile, but not stopping to talk. It was not a time for talking. Elena was worried about Carenna tonight; she had just had a child two weeks before. It was too soon for her to be doing this. But she was needed, they were all needed, and the Ember Night wars did not tarry for any man or woman, or for anything that happened in the world of day.

She nodded in response to a couple she didn't know. They followed Carenna past her into the house. There was dust on their clothing; they had probably come from a long way east, timing their arrival here for after the sundown closing of the doors and windows in the town and in all the lonely farmhouses out in the night of the fields. Behind all those doors and windows, Elena knew, the people of the southern highlands would be waiting in darkness and praying.

Praying for rain and then sun, for the earth to be fruitful through spring and summer to the tall harvest of fall. For the seedlings of grain, of corn, to flourish when sown, take root and then rise, yellow and full of ripened promise, from the dark, moist, giving soil. Praying—though they knew nothing within their wrapped dark homes of what would actually happen tonight—for the Night Walkers to save the fields, the season, the grain, save and succor all their lives.

Elena instinctively reached up to finger the small leather ornament she wore about her neck. The ornament that held the shriveled remnant of the caul in which she had been born, as all the Walkers had been—sheathed in the transparent birthing sac as they came crying from the womb.

A symbol of good fortune, birthwomen named the caul elsewhere in the Palm. Children born sheathed in that sac were said to be destined for a life blessed by the Triad.

Here at the remote southern edges of the peninsula, in these wild highlands beneath the mountains, the teachings and the lore were different. Here the ancient rites went deeper, further back, were passed from hand to hand, from mouth to mouth down from their beginnings long ago. In the highlands of Certando a child born with a caul was not said to be guarded from death at sea, or naïvely named for fortune.

It was marked for war.

For this war, fought each year on the first of the Ember Nights that began the spring and so began the year. Fought in the fields and for the fields, for the not yet risen seedlings that were hope and life and the offered promise of earth renewed. Fought for those in the great cities, cut off from the truths of the land, ignorant of such things, and fought for all the living here in Certando, huddled behind their walls, who knew only enough to pray and to be afraid of sounds in the night that might be the dead abroad.

From behind Elena a hand touched her shoulder. She turned to see Mattio looking quizzically at her. She shook her head, pushing her hair back with one hand.

"Nothing yet," she said.

Mattio did not speak, but the pale moonlight showed his eyes bleak above the full black beard. He squeezed her shoulder, out of a habit of reassurance more than anything else, before turning to go back inside.

Elena watched him go, heavy-striding, solid and capable. Through the open doorway she saw him sit down again at the long trestle-table, across from Donar. She gazed at the two of them for a moment, thinking about Verzar, about love and then desire.

She turned away again to look out into the night toward the huge brooding outline of the castle in whose shadow she had spent her whole life. She felt old suddenly, far older than her years. She had two small children sleeping with her mother and father tonight in one of those shut-up cottages where no lights burned. She also had a husband sleeping in the burying field—a casualty, one of so many, of the terrible battle a year ago when the numbers of the Others seemed to have grown so much larger than ever before and so cruelly, malevolently triumphant.

Verzar had died a few days after that defeat, as all the victims of the night battles did.

Those touched by death in the Ember Night wars did

not fall in the fields. They acknowledged that cold, final touch in their souls—like a finger on the heart, Verzar had said to her—and they came home to sleep and wake and walk through a day or a week or a month before yielding to the ending that had claimed them for its own.

In the north, in the cities, they spoke of the last portal of Morian, of longed-for grace in her dark Halls. Of priestly intercessions invoked with candles and tears.

Those born with the caul in the southern highlands, those who fought in the Ember wars and saw the shapes of the Others who came to battle there, did not speak in such a way.

Not that they would ever be so foolish as to deny Morian of Portals or Eanna or Adaon; only that they knew that there were powers older and darker than the Triad, powers that went beyond this peninsula, beyond even, Donar had once told her, this very world with its two moons and its sun. Once a year the Night Walkers of Certando would have—would be forced to have—a glimpse of these truths under a sky that was not their own.

Elena shivered. There would be more claimed for death tonight, she knew, and so fewer to fight the next year, and fewer the next. And where it would end she did not know. She was not educated in such things. She was twenty-two, a mother and a widow and a wheelwright's daughter in the highlands. She was also a child born with the caul of the Night Walkers into a time when all the battles were being lost, year by year.

She was also known to have the best eyesight in the dark of all of them, which is why Mattio had placed her here by the door, watching the road for the one Donar had said might come.

★ ★ ★

It was a dry season; the moat, as he'd expected, was shallow. Once, long ago, the lords of Castle Borso had been pleased to keep their moat stocked with creatures that could kill a man. Baerd didn't expect to find such things; not now, not for a long time now.

He waded across, hip-deep, under the high stars and the thin light of Vidomni in the sky. It was cold, but it had been many years since the elements bothered him much. Nor did it disturb him to be abroad on an Ember Night. Indeed, it had become a ritual of his own over the years: knowing that all across the Palm the holy days were observed and marked by people waiting in silent darkness behind their walls offered him a deepened sense of the solitude his soul seemed to need. He was profoundly drawn to this sense of moving through a scarcely breathing world that lay as if crouched in primitive darkness under the stars with no mortal fires cast back at the sky—only whatever flames the Triad created for themselves with lightning out of the heavens.

If there were ghosts and spirits awake in the night he wanted to see them. If the dead of his past were walking abroad he wanted to beg their forgiveness.

His own pain was spun of images that would not let him go. Images of vanished serenity, of pale marble under moonlight such as this, of graceful porticos shaped of harmonies a man might spend a lifetime studying to understand, of quiet voices heard and almost understood by a drowsy child in another room, of sure, confident laughter following, then morning sunlight in a known courtyard and a steady, strong, sculptor's hand upon his shoulder. A father's hand.

Then fire and blood and ashes on the wind, turning the noon sun red.

Smoke and death, and marble hammered into fragments, the head of the god flying free, to bounce like a boulder on scorched earth and then be ground remorselessly down into powder like fine sand. Like the sand on the beaches walked in the dark later that year, infinite and meaningless by the cold uncaring sea.

These were the bleak visitants, the companions of his nights, these and more, endlessly, through almost nineteen years. He carried, like baggage, like a cart yoked to his shoulders, like a round stone in his heart, images of his people, their world destroyed, their name obliterated. Truly obliterated: a sound that was drifting, year by year, further away from the shores of the world of men, like some tide withdrawing in the grey hour of a winter dawn. Very like such a tide, but different as well, because tides came back.

He had learned to live with the images because he had
no choice, unless it was a choice to surrender. To die. Or
retreat into madness as his mother had. He defined himself by his griefs; he knew them as other men knew the
shape of their own hands.

But the one thing that could drive him awake, barred
utterly from the chambers of sleep or any kind of rest,
what could force him abroad now, as he had been driven
abroad as a boy in a ruined place, was, in the end, none
of these things. Neither a flash of splendor gone, nor an
image of death and loss. It was, instead, over and above
everything else, the remembrance of love among those
ashes of ruin.

Against the memory of a spring and summer with
Dianora, with his sister, his barriers could not hold in the
dark.

And so Baerd would go out into the nights across the
Palm, doubly moonlit, or singly, or dark with only stars.
Among the heathered summer hills of Ferraut, or through
the laden vineyards of autumn in Astibar or Senzio,
along snow-mantled mountain slopes in Tregea, or here,
on an Ember Night at the beginning of spring in the
highlands.

He would go out to walk in the enveloping dark, to
smell the earth, feel the soil, listen to the voice of winter's wind, taste grapes and moonlit water, lie motionless
in a forest tree to watch the night predators at their hunt.
And once in a great while, when waylaid or challenged
by brigand or mercenary, Baerd would kill. A night
predator in his own incarnation, restless and soon gone.
Another kind of ghost, a part of him dead with the dead
of the River Deisa.

In every corner of the mainland Palm except his own,
which was gone, he had done these things for years upon
years, feeling the slow turning of the seasons, learning
the meaning of night in this forest and that field, by this
dark river, or on that mountain ridge, reaching out or
back or inward all the time toward a release that was
ever and again denied.

He had been here in the highlands many times before
on this same Ember Night. He and Alessan went back a
long way and had shared a great deal with Alienor of

Borso, and there was the other, larger reason why they came south to the mountains at the beginning of every second year. He thought of the news from the west. From home. He remembered the look on Alessan's face reading Danoleon's letter and his heart misgave him. But that was for tomorrow, and more Alessan's burden than his own, however much he might want—as he always wanted—to ease or share the weight.

Tonight was his own, and it called to him. Alone in the darkness, but hand in hand with a dream of Dianora, he walked away from the castle. Always before he had gone west and then south from Borso, curving his way into the hills themselves below the Braccio Pass. Tonight, for no reason he knew, his footsteps led him the other way, southeast. They carried him along the road to the edge of the village that lay beneath the castle walls and there, as he passed a house with an unexpectedly open door, Baerd saw a fair-haired woman standing in the moonlight as if she had been waiting for him and he stopped.

★   ★   ★

Sitting at the table, resisting the temptation to count their numbers one more time, trying to appear as if all were as normal as it could be on this night of war, Mattio heard Elena call his name and then Donar's from outside the house. Her voice was soft, as it always was, but his senses were pitched toward her, as they had been for years. Even before poor Verzar had died.

He glanced across the table at Donar, but the older man was already reaching for his crutches and rising to swing on his one leg toward the door. Mattio followed. A number of the others looked over at them, edgy and apprehensive. Mattio forced himself to smile reassuringly. Carenna caught his eye and began speaking soothingly to a few of the more visibly nervous people.

Not at all easy himself, Mattio stepped outside with Donar and saw that someone had come. A dark-haired man, neatly bearded and of middle height, stood motionless before Elena, glancing from her to the two of them, not speaking. He had a sword slung in a scabbard on his back in the Tregean fashion.

Mattio looked over at Donar whose face was quite impassive. For all his experience of Ember Night wars and of Donar's gift he could not repress a shiver.

"Someone may come," their one-legged leader had said yestereve. And now someone was indeed here in the moonlight in the very hour before battle. Mattio looked over at Elena; her eyes had not left the stranger. She was standing very straight, slender and motionless, hands holding her elbows, hiding fear and wonder as best she could. But Mattio had spent years watching her, and he could see that her breathing was shallow and fast. He loved her for her stillness, and for wanting to hide her fear.

He glanced at Donar again, and then stepped forward, extending two open palms to the stranger. Calmly he said, "Be welcome, though it is not a night to be abroad."

The other man nodded. His feet were planted wide and solid on the earth. He looked as though he knew how to use his sword. He said, "Nor, as I understand the highlands, is it a night to have doors and windows open."

"Why would you think you understand the highlands?" Mattio said. Too quickly. Elena still had not looked away from this man. There was an odd expression on her face.

Moving a little nearer to stand beside her, Mattio realized that he had seen this man before. This was one who had come several times to the Lady's castle. A musician, he seemed to remember, or a merchant of some sort. One of those landless men who endlessly crossed and recrossed the roads of the Palm. His heart, which had lifted to see the sword, sank a little.

The stranger had not responded to his sharp retort. He appeared, as much as the moonight revealed, to be giving the matter thought. Then he surprised Mattio.

"I'm sorry," he said. "If I am trespassing upon a custom in ignorance, forgive me. I walk for reasons of my own. I will leave you to your peace."

He actually turned away then, clearly intending to leave.

"No!" Elena said urgently.

And in the same moment Donar spoke for the first time.

"There is no peace tonight," he said in the deep voice they all trusted so much. "And you are not trespassing. I thought someone might come along this road. Elena was watching for you."

And at that the stranger turned. His eyes seemed wider in the dark, and something new, cooler, more appraising, gleamed in them now.

"Come for what?" he asked.

There was a silence. Donar shifted his crutches and swung forward. Elena moved to one side to let him stand in front of the stranger. Mattio looked across at her; her hair was falling over one shoulder, white-gold in the moonlight. She never took her eyes from the dark-haired man.

Who was gazing steadily at Donar. "Come for what?" he repeated, mildly enough.

Still Donar hesitated, and in that moment Mattio realized with a shock that the miller, their Elder, was afraid. A sickening lurch of apprehension rose in Mattio, for he suddenly understood what Donar was about to do.

And then Donar did it. He gave them away to one from the north.

"We are the Night Walkers of Certando," he said, his voice steady and deep. "And this is the first of the Ember Nights of spring. This is our night. I must ask you: wherever you were born, was there a mark . . . did the birthwomen who attended declare a blessing found?" And slowly he reached a hand inside his shirt and drew forth the leather sac he wore there, holding the caul that had marked him at his birth.

Out of the side of his eye Mattio saw Elena biting her lower lip. He looked at the stranger, watched him absorb what Donar had said, and he began gauging his chances of killing the man if it should come to that.

This time the silence stretched. The muted sounds from the house behind them seemed loud. The dark-haired man's eyes had grown wide now, and his head was lifted high. Mattio could see that he was weighing what lay behind what had just been revealed.

Then, still not speaking, the stranger moved one hand to his throat and reaching inside his shirt he brought out, so that the three of them could see, by starlight and moonlight, the small leather sac he too wore.

Mattio heard a small sound, a release of breath, and realized belatedly that he had made it himself.

"Earth be praised!" Elena murmured, unable to stop herself. She had closed her eyes.

"Earth, and all that springs from it and returns," Donar added. His voice, amazingly, trembled.

They left it for Mattio to finish. "Returns, to spring forth again in the cycle that has no end," he said, looking at the stranger, at the sac he bore, almost identical to Mattio's own, to Elena's, to Donar's, to the one they all carried, every one of them.

It was with the words of invocation spoken in sequence by the three of them that Baerd finally understood what he had stumbled upon.

Two hundred years ago, in a time of seemingly unending plagues, a time of harvest failures, of violence and blood, the Carlozzini heresy had taken root here in the south. And from the highlands it had begun to spread throughout the Palm, gaining momentum and adherents with frightening speed. And against Carlozzi's central teaching: that the Triad were younger deities, subject to and agents of an older, darker set of powers, the priesthood of the Palm had grimly and in concert set their hands.

Faced with such rare and absolute unity among the clergy, and caught up in the panic of a decade of plague and starvation, the Dukes and Grand Dukes and even Valcanti, Prince of Tigana, had seen themselves as having no choice. The Carlozzini had been hunted down and tried and executed all across the peninsula, by whatever means executions were conducted in each province in that time.

A time of violence and blood. Two hundred years ago.

And now he was standing here showing the leather that held the caul of his birth, and speaking to three who had just declared themselves to be Carlozzini.

And more. *Night Walkers,* the one-legged old man had said. The vanguard, the secret army of the sect. Chosen in some way that no one knew. But now he did know, they had shown him. It occurred to him that he might be in danger now, having been granted this knowledge, and indeed, the bigger, bearded man seemed to be holding himself carefully, as if prepared for violence.

The woman who had stood watch was weeping though. She was very beautiful, though not in the way of Alienor, whose every movement, every spoken word might hint at a feline undercurrent of danger. This woman was too young, too shy, he could not make himself believe in a threat from her. Not weeping as she was. And all three of them had spoken words of thanks, of praise. His instincts were on guard, but not in a way that warned of immediate danger. Deliberately Baerd forced his muscles to relax. He said, "What have you to tell me, then?"

Elena wiped the tears from her face. She looked at the stranger again, absorbing his square, neat, quiet solidity, his *reality*, the improbable fact that he was here. She swallowed with difficulty, painfully aware of the racing of her heart, trying to move past the moment when she had seen this man emerge from night and shadow to stand before her. And then the long interval when they had faced each other in the moonlight before she had impulsively reached out to touch his hand, to be sure that he was real. And had only then called for Mattio and Donar. Something odd seemed to be happening to her. She made herself concentrate on what Donar was saying.

"What I tell you now gives you power of life and death over a great many people," he said softly. "For the priesthood still want us destroyed and the Tyrant in Astibar will bide by what the clergy say in such things. I think you know this."

"I know this," the dark-haired one echoed, equally quietly. "Will you say why you are confiding in me?"

"Because tonight is a night of battle," Donar said. "Tonight I lead the Night Walkers into war, and yesterday at sunset I fell into a sleep and dreamt of a stranger coming to us. I have learned to trust my dreams, though not to know when they will come."

Elena saw the stranger nod, calm, unruffled, acknowledging this as easily as he had acknowledged her presence in the road. She saw that his arms were ridged with muscle under his shirt, and that he held himself as a man who had known fighting in his days. There seemed to be a sadness in his face, but it was really too dark to tell so much, and she chided herself for letting her imagination run free at such a time.

On the other hand, he was abroad and alone on an Ember Night. Men without griefs of their own would never do such a thing, she was certain. She wondered where he was from. She was afraid to ask.

"You are the leader then, of this company?" he said to Donar.

"He is," Mattio cut in sharply. "And you would do well not to dwell upon his infirmity." From the defiance of his tone it was clear he had misinterpreted the question. Elena knew how protective he was of Donar; it was one of the things she most respected in him. But this was too huge, too important a moment for misunderstandings. She turned to him and shook her head urgently.

"Mattio!" she began, but Donar had already laid a hand on the blacksmith's arm, and in that moment the stranger smiled for the first time.

"You leap at a slight that is not meant," he said. "I have known others, as badly injured or worse, who led armies and governed men. I seek only to find my bearings. It is darker here for me than it is for you."

Mattio opened his mouth and then closed it. He made a small, awkward gesture of apology with his shoulders and hands. It was Donar who replied.

"I am Elder of the Walkers, yes," he said. "And so mine, with Mattio's aid, is leadership in battle. But you must know that the war we are to fight tonight is not like any battle you might know. When we come out again from this house it will be under a different sky entirely than the one above us now. And under that sky, in that changeling world of ghosts and shadows, few of us will appear as we do here."

The dark-haired man shifted uneasily for the first time. He glanced downward, almost reluctantly, to look at Donar's hands.

Donar smiled, and held out his left hand, five fingers spread wide.

"I am not a wizard," he said softly. "There is magic here, yes, but we step into it and are marked for it, we do not shape it. This is not wizardry."

The stranger nodded at length. Then said, with careful courtesy, "I can see that. I do not understand it, but I can only assume you are telling me these things to a purpose. Will it please you now to tell me what that is?"

And so Donar said then, finally, "Because we would ask aid of you in our battle tonight."

In the silence that followed, Mattio spoke, and Elena had an idea how much pride he swallowed in saying: "We have need. Very great need."

"Who do you fight?" the other man said.

"We call them the Others," Elena said herself, as neither Donar nor Mattio spoke. "They come to us year by year. Generation after generation."

"They come to ruin the fields and blight the seedlings and the harvest," Donar said. "For two hundred years the Night Walkers of Certando would battle them on this Ember Night, and for all this time we were able to hold them in check as they come upon us from the west."

Mattio said, "For almost twenty years now, though, it has grown worse and worse for us. And on the last three Ember Nights we have been very badly beaten. Many of us have died. And Certando's droughts have grown worse; you will know about that, and about the plagues here. They have—"

But the stranger had flung up a hand suddenly, a sharp, unexpected gesture.

"Almost twenty years? And from the west?" he said harshly. He came a step nearer and turned to Donar. "The Tyrants came almost twenty years ago. And Brandin of Ygrath landed in the west."

Donar's gaze was steady as he leaned on his crutches looking at the other man. "This is true," he said, "and it is a thought that has occurred to some of us, but I do not think it signifies. Our battles on this night each year go far beyond the daily concerns of who governs in the Palm in a given generation, and how they govern, and from where they come."

"But still—" the stranger began.

"But still," Donar said, nodding his head, "there are mysteries to this that are beyond my power to grasp. If you discern a pattern that I do not . . . who am I to question or deny that it might be true?"

He reached up to his neck and touched the leather sac. "You carry the mark we all bear, and I dreamt your presence here tonight. Notwithstanding that, we have no claim upon you, none at all, and I must tell you that death will be there to meet us in the fields when the Others come. But I can also tell you that our need goes beyond these fields, beyond Certando, and even, I think, beyond this Peninsula of the Palm. Will you fight with us tonight?"

The stranger was silent a long time. He turned away and looked upwards then, at the thin moon and the stars, but Elena had a sense that his truer vision was inwards, that he was not really looking up at the lights.

"Please?" she heard herself say. "Will you please?"

He made no sign that he had even heard her. When he turned back it was to look at Donar once more.

He said, "I understand little of this. I have my own battles to fight, and people to whom I owe a sworn allegiance, but I hear no evil in you, and no untruth, and I would see for myself the shape these Others take. If you dreamt my coming here I will let myself be guided by your dream."

And then, as her eyes began brimming with tears again, Elena saw him turn to her. "Yes, I will," he said levelly, not smiling, his dark eyes grave. "I will fight with you tonight. My name is Baerd."

And so it seemed that he had heard her, after all.

Elena mastered her tears, standing as straight as she could. There was a tumult, a terrible chaos, rising within her though, and in the midst of that chaos it seemed to Elena that she heard a sound, as of a single note plucked on her heart. Beyond Donar, Mattio said something but she didn't hear what it was. She was looking at this stranger, and realizing, as his gaze met her own, that she had been right before, that her instincts had not misled. There was so deep a sadness in him it could not possibly be missed by any man or woman with eyes to see, even in night and shadow.

She looked away, and then closed her eyes tightly for a moment, trying to hold back something of her heart for herself, before it all went seeking in the magic and the strangeness of this night. *Oh, Verzar,* she thought. *Oh, my dead love.*

She opened her eyes again and took a careful breath.

"I am Elena," she said. "Will you come in and meet the others?"

"Yes," said Mattio gruffly, "come in with us, Baerd. Be welcome in my home." This time she heard the hurt that came through in his voice, though he tried to mask it. She winced inwardly at that sound, caring for him, for his strength and his generosity, hating so much to give sorrow. But this was an Ember Night and the tides of the heart could scarcely be ruled even by the light of day.

Besides, she had a very grave doubt, already, as the four of them turned to go into the house, whether there would be any joy for her to find in what had just happened to her. Any joy in this stranger who had come to her out of darkness, in answer to or called by Donar's dream.

★   ★   ★

Baerd looked at the cup that the woman named Carenna had just placed in his hands. It was of earthenware, rough to the touch, chipped at one edge, the unpainted color of red soil.

He looked from Carenna to Donar, the older, maimed man—the Elder, they called him—to the bearded one, to the other girl, Elena. There was a kind of light in her face as she looked back at him, even in the shadows of this house, and he turned away from that as something— perhaps the one thing—he could not deal with. Not now, perhaps not ever in his life. He cast his gaze out over the company assembled there. Seventeen of them. Nine men, eight women, all holding their own cups, waiting for him. There would be more at the meeting-place, Mattio had said. How many more they could not tell.

He was being reckless, he knew. Swept away by the power of an Ember Night, by the undeniable truth of Donar's dream, the fact that they had been waiting for him. By, if he were honest with himself, the look in Elena's eyes when he had first come up to her. A complex tempting of fate, that aspect of it, something he seldom did.

But he was doing it now, or about to do it. He thought of Alessan, and of all the times he'd chided or derided the Prince, his brother of the soul, for letting his passion for music take him down one dangerous path or another. What would Alessan say now, or quick-tongued Catriana? Or Devin? No, Devin would say nothing: he would watch, with that careful, focused attention, and come to his own conclusions in his own time. Sandre would call him a fool.

And perhaps he was. But something had responded deep within him to the words Donar had spoken. He had borne the caul of his birth in leather all his life, a minor, a trivial superstition. A charm against drowning, he had been told as a child. But it was more here, and the cup he held in his hands would mark his acceptance of that.

Almost twenty years, Mattio had said.

The Others from the west, Donar had said.

There might be little in it, or a great deal, or nothing at all, or everything.

He looked at the woman, Elena, and he drained the cup to the lees.

It was bitter, deathly bitter. For one panicked, irrational moment he feared he was undone, poisoned, a blood sacrifice in some unknown Carlozzini rite of spring.

Then he saw the sour face Carenna made as she drank from her own cup, and saw Mattio wince ruefully at the taste of his, and the panic passed.

The long table had been put away, lifted from its trestles. Pallets had been spread about the room for them to lie upon. Elena moved towards him and gestured, and it would have been ungracious to hold back. He walked with her toward one wall and took the pallet she offered him. She sat down, unspeaking, on the one beside it.

Baerd thought of his sister, of that clear image of walking hand in hand with Dianora down a dark and silent road, only the two of them abroad in the wide world.

Donar the miller swung himself towards the pallet on Baerd's other side. He leaned his crutches against the wall and subsided on the mat.

"Leave your sword here," he said. Baerd raised his eyebrows. Donar smiled, a hieratic expression, devoid of mirth. "It will be useless where we are going. We will find our weapons in the fields."

Baerd hesitated a moment longer; then, aware of even greater recklessness, of a mystic folly he could not have explained, he slipped the back-scabbard over his head and laid it against the wall beside Donar's crutches.

"Close your eyes," he heard Elena saying from beside him. "It is easier that way." Her voice sounded oddly distant. Whatever he had drunk was beginning to act upon him. "It will feel like sleep," she said, "but it will not be. Earth grant us grace, and the sky her light." It was the last thing he heard.

It was not sleep. Whatever it was, it was not sleep, for no dream could be this vivid, no dream-wind this keen in his face.

He was in an open field, wide and fallow and dark, with the smell of spring soil, and he had no memory at all of coming here. There were a great many people—two hundred perhaps, or more—in the field with him, and he had no memory of any of them either. They must have come from other villages in the highlands, from gatherings in other homes like Mattio's.

The light was strange. He looked up.

And Baerd saw that the moon in the sky was round and large and full, and it was green like the first green-gold of spring. It shone with that green and golden light among stars in constellations he had never seen. He wheeled around, dizzied, disoriented, his heart pounding, searching for a pattern that he knew in the heavens. He looked south, to where the mountains should be, but as far as his eyes could track in the green light he saw level fields stretching away, some fallow, some fully ripe with summer grain in a season that should only be spring. No mountains at all. No snow-clad peaks, no Braccio Pass with Quileia beyond. He spun again. No Castle Borso to north or east. Or west?

West. With a sudden premonition he turned to look there. Low hills rose and fell in seemingly endless progression. And Baerd saw that the hills were bare of trees, of grass, bare of flower and shrub and bush, bleak and waste and barren.

"Yes, look there," Donar's deep voice said from behind him, "and understand why we are here. If we lose tonight the field in which we stand will be desolate as those hills next year when we come back. The Others are down into these grainlands now. We have lost the battles of those hills over the past years. We are fighting in the plain now, and if this goes on, one Ember Night not far from now our children or their children will stand with their backs to the sea and lose the last battle of our war."

"And?" Baerd's eyes were still on the west, on the grey, stony ruin of the hills.

"And all the crops will fail. Not just here in Certando. And people will die. Of hunger or of plague."

"All over the Palm?" He could not look away from the desolation that he saw. He had a vision of a lifeless world looking like that. He shivered. It was sickening.

"The Palm and beyond, Baerd. Make no mistake, this is no local skirmish, no battle for a small peninsula. All over this world, and perhaps beyond, for it is said that ours is not the only world scattered by the Powers among time and the stars."

"Carlozzi taught this?"

"Carlozzi taught this. If I understand his teaching rightly, our own troubles here are bound up with even graver dangers elsewhere; in worlds we have never seen or will see, except perhaps in dream."

Baerd shook his head, still looking out at the hills in the west. "That is too remote for me. Too difficult. I am a worker in stone and a sometime merchant and I have learned how to fight, against my will and inclination, over many years. I live in a peninsula overrun by enemies from overseas. That is the level of evil I can grasp."

He turned away from the western hills then and looked at Donar. And despite the warning they'd given him, his eyes widened with amazement. The miller stood on two sound legs; his grey, thinning hair had become a thick dark brown like Baerd's own, and he stood with his broad shoulders straight and his head held high, a man in his prime.

A woman came up to them, and Baerd knew Elena, for she was not greatly changed. She seemed older here though, less frail; her hair was shorter, though still white-gold despite the strangeness of the light. Her eyes, he saw, were a very deep blue.

"Were your eyes that same color an hour ago?" he asked.

She smiled, pleased and shy. "It was more than an hour. And I don't know what I look like this year. It changes a little for me every time. What color are they now?"

"Blue. Extremely blue."

"Well then, yes, they have always been blue. Perhaps not *extremely* blue, but blue." Her smile deepened. "Shall I tell you what you look like?" There was an incongruity, a lightness in her voice. Even Donar had an amused expression playing about his lips.

"Tell me."

"You look like a boy," she said with a little laugh. "A fourteen- or fifteen-year-old boy, beardless now and much too thin and with a shock of brown hair I would love to cut if we had but half a chance."

Baerd felt his heart thud like a mallet in his breast. It actually seemed to stop for an instant before beginning again, laboriously, to beat. He turned sharply away from the others, looking down at his hands. They did seem different. Smoother, less lined. And a knife scar he'd got in Tregea five years ago was not there. He closed his eyes, feeling suddenly weak.

"Baerd?" Elena said behind him, concerned. "I'm sorry. I did not mean to—"

He shook his head. He tried to speak but found that he could not. He wanted to reassure her, her and Donar, that it was all right, but he seemed, unbelievably, to be weeping, for the first time in almost twenty years.

For the first time since the year he had been a fourteen-year-old boy forbidden to go to war by his Prince's orders and his father's. Forbidden to fight and die with them by the red banks of the River Deisa when all the shining had come to an end.

"Be easy, Baerd," he heard Donar saying, deep and gentle. "Be easy. There is always a strangeness here."

Then a woman's hands were briefly upon his shoulders and then reaching around him from behind to meet and

clasp at his chest. Her cheek rested against his back and
she held him so, strong and sharing and generous, while
he brought his hands up to cover his face as he cried.

Above them on the Ember Night the full moon was
green-gold and around them the strange fields were fallow, or newly sown, or full with ripened grain before the
planting-time, or utterly bare and desolate and lost, in
the west.

"They are coming," someone said, walking up to them.
"Look. We had best claim our weapons."

He recognized Mattio's voice. Elena released him and
stepped back. Baerd wiped his eyes and looked to the
west again.

And he saw then that the Ember war was giving him
another chance. A chance to make right what had gone
so bitterly wrong in the world the summer he was fourteen.

Over the hills from the west, far off yet but unnaturally
clear in the unnatural light, the Others were coming: *and
they were clad, all of them, in the livery of Ygrath.*

"Oh, Morian!" he whispered on a sharply taken breath.

"What do you see?" Mattio said.

Baerd turned. The man was leaner, and his black beard
was differently trimmed, but he was recognizably the
same. "Ygrathens," he said on a rising note of excitement. "Soliders of the King of Ygrath. You may never
have seen them here, this far east, but that is exactly
what they are, your Others.'

Mattio looked suddenly thoughtful. He shook his head,
but it was Donar who spoke.

"Be not deceived, Baerd. Remember where we are,
what I have told you. You are not in our peninsula, this
is no battle of the day against your invaders from overseas."

"I *see* them, Donar. I know what I see."

"And shall I tell you that what I see out there are
hideous shapes in grey and dun, naked and hairless,
dancing and coupling with each other as they mock us
with their numbers?"

"And the Others for me are different again," Mattio
said bluntly, almost angrily. "They are large, larger than
men, with fur on their spines running down into a tail
like the mountain cats. They walk upon two legs but they

have claws on their hands, and razored teeth in their mouths."

Baerd wheeled again, his heart hammering, looking west in the eerily lucid green light of wherever they were. But still, in the middle distance, pouring down out of the hills, he saw soldiers with weapons: swords and pikes and the undulating knives of Ygrath.

He turned to Elena, a little desperate.

"I do not like to name what I see," she murmured, lowering her eyes. "They frighten me too much. They are creatures of my childhood fears. But it is not what you are seeing, Baerd. Believe me. Believe us. You may see the Others in the shape of your heart's hate, but this is not the battle of your daytime world."

He shook his head in fierce denial. There was a deep surging in his spirit, a rushing of blood in his veins. The Others were nearer now, hundreds of them, streaming out of the hills.

"I am always fighting the same battle," he said to her. To her and the two men. "All my life. Wherever I am. And I know what I see out there. I can tell you that I am fifteen years old now, not fourteen or I could not be here. They would not have allowed me." A thought struck him. "Tell me: is there a stream west of us, a river below where they are descending now?"

"There is," Donar said. "Do you want to join battle there?"

A red, fierce joy was running through Baerd, wild and uncontrollable.

"I do," he said. "Oh, I do. Mattio, where do we claim our weapons?"

"There." Mattio pointed southeast to a small nearby field where tall stalks of corn were growing, in defiance of what should have been the season. "Come. They will be at your stream very soon."

Baerd did not speak. He followed Mattio's lead. Elena and Donar went with them. Other men and women were in that field of corn already and Baerd saw that they were reaching down to pluck a stalk to be their weapon in the night. It was uncanny, incredible, but he was beginning to take a part of the measure of this place, to understand the magic that was at work here, and a corner of his mind, which worked outside and around the stern logic of day, grasped that the tall yellow grain that was so endangered was the only weapon possible tonight. They would fight for the fields with grain in their hands.

He stepped in among the others in that cornfield, careful of where he walked, and he bent down and grasped a stalk for himself. It came free easily, even willingly to his hand in that green night. He walked out on to fallow ground again and hefted it in his hand and swung it cautiously, and he saw that already the stalk had stiffened like metal forged. It sliced through the air with a keen whistling sound. He tested it with a finger and drew blood. The stalk had grown as sharp as any blade he'd ever held, and as true to his hand, and it was many-edged like the fabled blades of Quileia, centuries ago.

He looked away to the west. The Ygrathens were descending the nearest of the hills. He could see the glint of their weapons under the moon. *This is not a dream*, he told himself. Not a dream.

Donar was beside him, grim and unwavering. Mattio stood beyond, a passionate defiance in his face. Men and women were gathering behind them and all around, and all of them held corn swords in their hands, and all of them looked the same: stern and resolute and unafraid.

"Shall we go?" Donar said then, turning to look out upon them all. "Shall we go and fight them for the fields and for our people? Will you come with me now to the Ember war?"

"For the fields!" the Night Walkers cried, and raised their living swords aloft to the sky.

What Baerd di Tigana bar Saevar cried he cried only in his heart and not aloud, but he went forward with all of them, a stalk of corn like a long blade in his hand, to do battle under the pale green moon of that enchanted place.

When the Others fell, scaly and grey, blind and crawling with maggots, there was never any blood. Elena understood why that was so, Donar had told her years ago: blood meant life, and their foes tonight were the enemies, the opposite, of any kind of life. When they fell to the corn swords nothing flowed from them, nothing seeped away into the earth.

There were so many of them. There always were, swirling in a grey mass like slugs, pouring down out of the hills and swarming into the stream where Donar and Mattio and Baerd had come to make their stand.

Elena prepared herself to fight, amid the loud, whirling, green-tinted chaos of the night. She was frightened, but she knew she could deal with that. She remembered how deathly afraid she'd been in her first Ember war, wondering how she—she who could scarcely have even lifted a sword in the daytime world—could possibly battle such hideous creatures as the nightmare ones she saw.

But Donar and Verzar had assuaged her fears: here in this green night of magic it was the soul and the spirit that mattered, here it was courage and desire that shaped and drove the bodies in which they found themselves. Elena felt so much stronger on the Ember Nights, so much more lithe and quick. That had frightened her, too, the first time and even afterward: under this green moon she was someone who could kill. It was a realization she had to deal with, an adjustment to be made. They all did, to one degree or another. None of them were exactly what they were under the sun or the two moons of home. Donar's body on this night of war reached backwards, further every year, toward a lost image of what he once had been.

Just as Baerd's, very clearly, reached back as well, more than one might have guessed or expected. Fifteen, he had said. Not fourteen, or he would not have been allowed. She didn't understand that, but she had no time to puzzle such things out. Not now. The Others were in the stream, and now they were trying to clamber out, clad in the hideous shapes her mind gave them.

She dodged a scything axe-blow from a creature dripping with water as it scrambled up the bank towards her, and as she did she gritted her teeth and slashed downward with an instinctive deadliness she would have never known was hers. She felt her blade, her living sword, crunch hard through scaly armor and bury itself in the maggot-infested body of her foe.

She pulled the weapon free with an effort, hating what

she had done, but hating the Others more, infinitely
more. She turned—barely in time to block another ascending blow and withdraw a step before two new, gape-
jawed assailants on her right. She lifted her blade in a
desperate attempt to ward.

Then suddenly only one of the Others was standing
there. Then neither of them.

She lowered her sword and looked at Baerd. At her
stranger on the road, her promise given by the night. He
smiled grimly at her, tight-lipped, standing over the bodies of the Others he had just killed. He smiled, and he
had saved her life, but he said nothing to her at all. He
turned and went forward to the edge of the river. She
watched him go, saw his boy's body stride into the thickness of battle, and she wasn't sure whether to give way to
a rush of hope because of his deadly skill or to grieve for
the look in his too young eyes.

Again, no time for such thoughts. The river seethed
and boiled now with the churning of the Others as they
waded into it. Screams of pain, cries of rage and fury cut
the green night like blades of sound. She saw Donar
along the bank to the south swinging his sword two-
handed in wheeling circles of denial. Saw Mattio beside
him, slashing and stabbing, neat-footed among the fallen
bodies, absolute in his courage. All about her the Night
Walkers of Certando plunged into the caldron of their
war.

She saw a woman fall, then another, swarmed over and
hacked down by the creatures from the west. She cried
out herself then, in fury and revulsion, and she moved
back up to the edge of the river, running to where Carenna
was, her sword swinging forward, her blood—her blood
which was life, and the promise of life—raging with the
need to drive them back. Back now, tonight, and then
again a year from now, and after that, and again and
again on each of these Ember Nights, that the spring
sowing might be fruitful, that the earth be allowed to
bear its bounty in the fall. This year and the next year,
and the next.

In the midst of that chaos of noise and motion, Elena
glanced up. She checked the height of the still-climbing

moon, and then—she could not stop herself—she looked
to the nearest of the devastated hills beyond the stream,
apprehension clutching at her heart. There was no one
there. Not yet.

There would be, though. She was almost certain there
would be. And then? She pulled herself back from that.
What would happen would happen. Around her there
was war, here and now, and more than enough terror in
the Others massed before her, surging up out of the river
on either side.

She tore her thoughts from the hill and struck downwards, hard, feeling her blade bite into a scabrous shoulder. She heard the Other make a wet, bubbly sound. She
jerked her sword free and spun left barely in time to
block a sideways blow, scrambling to keep her footing.
Carenna's free hand braced her from behind; she didn't
even have time to look but she knew who it was.

It was wild under the unknown stars, under the green
light of that moon, it was frenzy and chaos; there was
screaming and shouting everywhere now, and the riverbank was muddy, slippery and treacherous. Elena's Others were wet and grey, dark with their parasites and open
sores. She clenched her teeth and fought, letting this
Ember Night body's grace be guided by her soul, the
stalk that was her sword dancing with a life that seemed
to come from within itself as much as it did from her. She
was splashed with mud and water, and she was sure there
must be blood, but there was no time to check, no time
now to do anything at all but parry and hammer and
slash, and fight to keep one's footing on the slope of the
riverbank, for to fall would be to die.

She was aware, in scattered, hallucinatory flashes, of
Donar beside her and Carenna for a time. Then she saw
him stride away with a handful of others to quell a
movement to the south. Baerd came up on her left at one
point, guarding her open side, but when she glanced over
again—and now the moon was very high—she saw he
was gone.

Then she saw where. He was in the river, not waiting
for the Others to come to him. He was attacking them in
the water, screaming incoherent words she could not

understand. He was slim and young and very beautiful, and deadly. She saw bodies of the Others piling before his feet like grey sludge blocking the stream. He would be seeing them differently, she knew. He had told them what he saw: he would be seeing soldiers of Ygrath, of Brandin, the Tyrant in the west.

His blade seemed almost to vanish in a blur, it moved so fast. Knee-deep in the stream he stood rooted like a tree and they could not force him back, or survive in front of him. The Others were falling back from him there, scrambling to withdraw, trying to work their way around their own dead to get further down the stream. He was driving them away, battling alone in the water, the moonlight strange on his face and strange on the living stalk that was his sword, and he was a fifteen-year-old boy. Only that. Elena's heart ached for him, even as she fought an overwhelming weariness.

She willed herself to hold her own ground, north of where he was, up on the muddy bank. Carenna was further south along the river now, fighting beside Donar. Two men and a woman from another village came up beside Elena, and together the four of them fought for their stretch of slippery ground, trying to move in concert, to be of one mind.

They were not fighters, not trained for battle. They were farmers and farmers' wives, millers and blacksmiths and weavers, masons and serving-girls, goatherds in the hills of the Braccio Range. But each and every one of them had been born with a caul in the highlands and named in childhood for Carlozzi's teachings and for the Ember war. And under the green moon—which had passed its apex and would be setting now—the passion of their souls taught their hands to speak for life with the blades the tall grain had become.

So the Night Walkers of Certando did battle by that river, fighting for the deepest, oldest dream of the wide-spreading country fields beyond all the high city walls. A dream of Earth, of the life-giving soil, rich and moist and flourishing in its cycle of seasons and years; a dream of the Others driven back, and farther back, and finally away, one bright year none of them would live to see.

And there came a time, amid the tumult and the frenzy,

the loud, blurred, spinning violence by the river, when
Elena and her three companions forged a respite for
themselves. She had a moment to look up and she saw
that the stream was thinning of foes. That the Others
were milling about, disorganized and confused west of
the river. She saw Baerd splash further into the water,
hip-deep now, crying for the enemy to come to him,
cursing them in a voice so tormented it was scarcely
knowable as his own.

Elena could barely stand. She leaned on her sword,
sucking in air with heaving sobs, utterly spent. She looked
over and saw that one of the men who had fought beside
her was down on one knee, clutching his right shoulder.
He bled from an ugly, ragged wound. She knelt beside
him, tearing weakly at her clothing for a strip to bind it
with. He stopped her though.

He stopped her and touched her shoulder and, mutely,
he pointed across the stream. She looked where he pointed,
away to the west, fear rising in her again. And in that
moment of seeming victory Elena saw that the crown of
the nearest hill was not empty anymore. That there was
something standing there.

"*Look!*" a man cried just then, from further down the
river. "He is with them again! We are undone!"

Other voices took up that cry along the riverbank, in
grief and horror and cold fear, for they saw, they all saw
now, that the shadow figure had come. Within the darkest spaces of her heart Elena had known that he would.

Just as he almost always had these last years. Fifteen
years, twenty; though never before that, Donar had said.
When the moon began to set, green and full, just when—so
much of the time—it seemed as if they might have a
chance to force the Others back, that dark figure would
appear, to stand wrapped in fog and mist as in a shroud
at the back of the enemy ranks.

And it was this figure the Walkers would see come
forward in the years of their defeats, when they were
retreating, having been driven back. It was he who would
step onto the bitterly contested places of battle, the lost
fields, and claim them for his own. And blight and dis-
ease and desolation spread where he passed, wherever he
walked upon the earth.

He stood now on the nearest of the wasted hills west of the river, clouds of obscuring mist rising and flowing all around him. Elena could not discern his face—none of them ever had—but from within that smoke and darkness she saw him raise his hands and stretch them out toward them, reaching, reaching for the Walkers on the river-bank. And as he did Elena felt a sudden shaft of coldness come into her heart, a terrible, numbing chill. Her legs began to tremble. She saw that her hands were shaking and it seemed that there was nothing she could do, nothing at all, to hold her courage to her.

Across the stream the Others, his army or his allies or the amorphous projections of his spirit, saw him stretch his arms toward the battlefield. Elena heard a sudden savage exultation in their cries; she saw them massing west of the river to come at them again. And she remembered, weary and spent, with a grim despair reaching into her heart, that this was exactly how it had been last year, and the spring before that, and the spring before as well. Her spirit ached with the knowledge of loss to come, even as she fought to find a way to ready her exhausted body to face another charge.

Mattio was beside her. "No!" she heard him gasp, with a dull, hopeless insistence, blindly fighting the power of that figure on the hill. "Not this time! Not! Let them kill me! Not retreat again!"

He could scarcely speak, and he was bleeding, she saw. There was a gash in his right side, another along his leg. When he straightened to move to the river she saw that he was limping. He was doing it though, he was moving forward, even into the face of what was being leveled at them. Elena felt a sob escape her dry throat.

And now the Others were coming again. The wounded man beside her struggled gamely up from his knees, holding his sword in his left hand, his useless right arm dangling at his side. Further along the bank she saw men and women as badly wounded or worse. They were all standing though, and lifting their blades. With love, with a shafting of pride that was akin to pain, Elena saw that the Night Walkers were not retreating. None of them. They were ready to hold this ground, or to try. And some of them were going to die now she knew, many of them would die.

Then Donar was beside her, and Elena flinched at what she saw in his white face. "No," he said. "This is folly. We must fall back. We have no choice. If we lose too many tonight it will be even worse next spring. I *have* to play for time, to hope for something that will make a change." The words sounded as if they were scraped from his throat.

Elena felt herself beginning to cry, from exhaustion as much as anything else. And even as she was nodding from within the abyss of her weariness, trying to let Donar see her understanding, her support, wanting to ease the rawness of his pain, even as the Others drew near again, triumphant, hideous, unwearied, she abruptly realized that Baerd wasn't with them on the bank. She wheeled toward the river, looking for him, and so she saw the miracle begin.

He was never in any doubt, none at all. From the moment the mist-wrapped figure appeared on the black hill Baerd knew what it was. In an odd way he had known this even *before* the shadow-figure came. It was why he was here, Baerd realized. Donar might not know it, but this was why the Elder had had a dream of someone coming, why Baerd's steps that night had taken him to the place where Elena was watching in the dark. It seemed to have been a long time ago.

He couldn't see the figure clearly but that didn't matter, it really didn't. He *knew* what this was about. It was as if all the sorrows and the lessons and the labors of his life, his and Alessan's together, had brought him to this river under this green moon that someone here might know exactly what the figure on the black hill was, the nature of its power. The power the Night Walkers had not been able to withstand because they could not understand.

He heard a splash behind him and knew instinctively that it would be Mattio. Without turning he handed him his strange sword. The Others—the Ygrathens of his dreams and hate—were massing again on the western bank.

He ignored them. They were tools. Right now they did
not matter at all. They had been beaten by the courage
of Donar and the Walkers; only the shadow-figure signi-
fied now, and Baerd knew what was needed to deal with
that. Not a prowess of blades, not even with these swords
of grain. They were past that now.

He drew a deep breath, and he raised his hands from
his sides and pointed up at that shrouded figure on the
hill, exactly as the figure was pointing down at them.
And with his heart full to overflowing with old grief and
a young certainty, conscious that Alessan would say it
better, but knowing that this had become his task, and
knowing also what had to be done, Baerd cried aloud in
the strangeness of that night:

"Be gone! We do not fear you! I know what you are
and where your power lies! Be gone or I shall name you
now and cut your strength apart—we both know the
power of names tonight!"

Gradually the raucous cries subsided on the other side
of the river, and the murmurs of the Walkers faded. It
grew very still, deathly still. Baerd could hear Mattio's
labored, painful breathing just behind him. He didn't
look back. He waited, straining to penetrate the mist that
wrapped the figure on the hill. And as he stared it seemed
to him, with a surge in his heart, that the upraised arms
were lowered slightly. That the concealing mist dissipated
a very little.

He waited no longer.

"Be gone!" he cried again, more loudly yet, a ringing
sureness in his voice now. "I have said I know you and I
do. You are the spirit of the violators here. The presence
of Ygrath in this peninsula, and of Barbadior. Both of
them! You are tyranny in a land that has been free. *You*
are the blight and the ruin in these fields. You have used
your magic in the west to shape a desecration, to obliterate a name. Yours is a power of darkness and shadow
under this moon, *but I know you and can name you, and
so all your shadows are gone!*"

He looked, and even as he was speaking the words that
came to him he saw that they were true! It was happening. He could see the mist drifting apart, as if taken by a

wind. But even in the midst of joy something checked him: a knowledge that the victory was only here, only in this unreal place. His heart was full and empty at one and the same time. He thought of his father dying by the Deisa, of his mother, of Dianora, and Baerd's hands went flat and rigid at his sides, even as he heard the murmurs of disbelieving hope rising at his back.

Mattio whispered something in a choked voice. Baerd knew it would be a prayer.

The Others were milling about in disarray west of the stream. Even as Baerd watched, motionless, his hands held outwards, his heart in turmoil, more of the shadows cloaking their leader lifted and spread, beginning to blow away over the brow of the hill. For one moment Baerd thought he saw the figure clearly. He thought he saw it bearded and slim, and of medium height, and he knew which of the Tyrants that one would be, which one had come from the west. And something rose within him at that sight, crashing through to the surface like a wave breaking against his soul.

"My sword!" he rasped. "Quickly!"

He reached back. Mattio placed it in his hand. In front of them the Others were starting to fall back, slowly at first, then faster, and suddenly they were running. But that didn't even matter; that didn't matter at all.

Baerd looked up at the figure on the hill. He saw the last of the shadows blowing away and he lifted his voice once more, crying aloud the passion of his soul:

"*Stay for me!* If you are Ygrath, if you are truly the sorcerer of Ygrath I want you now! Stay for me—I am coming! In the name of my home and of my father I am coming for you now! I am Baerd di Tigana bar Saevar!"

Wildly, still screaming his challenge, he splashed forward and clambered out of the stream, scrambling up the other bank. The ruined earth felt cold as ice through his wet boots. He realized that he had entered a terrain that had no real place for life, but tonight, now, with that figure before him on the hill, that didn't matter either. It didn't matter if he died.

The army of the Others was in flight, they were throwing down their weapons as they ran. There was no one to

gainsay him. He glanced up again. The moon seemed to
be setting unnaturally fast. It looked as if it was resting
now, round and huge, on the very crown of the black
hill. Baerd saw the figure standing there silhouetted against
that green moon; the shadows were gone, almost he saw
it clearly again across the dead lands between.

Then he heard a long laugh of mockery, as if in response to his crying of his name. It was the laughter of
his dreams, the laughter of the soldiers in the year of the
fall. Still laughing, not hurrying at all, the shadow-figure
turned and stepped down from the crown of the hill and
away to the west.

Baerd began to run.

"Baerd, wait!" he heard the woman, Carenna, cry
from behind him. "You must not be on the wastelands
when the moon goes down! Come back! We have won!"

They had won. But *he* had not, whatever the Walkers
of the highlands might think, or say. His battle, his and
Alessan's, was no nearer resolution than it had been
before tonight. Whatever he had done for the Night
Walkers of Certando, this night's victory was not his, it
could not be. He knew that in his heart. And his enemy,
the image of his soul's hate, knew that as well as he and
was laughing at him even now just out of sight beyond
the brow of that low hill.

"Stay for me!" Baerd screamed again, his young, lost
voice ripping through the night.

He ran, flashing over the dead earth, his heart bursting
with the need for speed. He overtook stragglers among
the army and he killed them as he ran, not even breaking
stride. It hardly mattered, it was only for the Walkers in
their war, for next year. The Others scattered north and
south, away from him, from the line that led to the hill.
Baerd reached the slope and went straight up, scrabbling
for a foothold on the cold waste ground. Then he breasted
the hill with a surge and a gasp.

And he stood upon the summit, exactly where the
shadow-figure had stood, and he looked away to the west,
toward all the empty valleys and ruined hills beyond,
and saw nothing. There was no one there at all.

He turned quickly north and then south, his chest

heaving, and saw that the army of the Others, too, seemed to have entirely melted away. He spun back to the west and then he understood.

The green moon had set.

He was alone in this wasteland under a clear, high dome of brilliant, alien stars and Tigana was no nearer to coming back than it had ever been. And his father was still dead and would never come back to him, and his mother and sister were dead, or lost somewhere in the world.

Baerd sank to his knees on the ruined hill. The ground was cold as winter. It was colder. His sword slipped from his suddenly nerveless fingers. He looked at his hands by starlight, at the slim hands of the boy he had been, and then he covered his face with those hands for the second time in that Ember Night, and he wept as though his heart were breaking now and not broken long ago.

Elena reached the hill and began to climb. She was breathless from running but the slope was not steep. Mattio had grabbed her arm when she started to enter the river. He had said it might mean death to be among the ruined lands after moonset, but Donar had told her it would be all right now. Donar had been unable to stop smiling since Baerd had made the shadow-figure withdraw. There was a stunned, incredulous glory in his face.

Most of the Walkers had gone back, wounded and weary, intoxicated with triumph, to the field where they had claimed their weapons. From there they would be drawn home before sunrise. So it had always happened.

Carefully avoiding Mattio's eyes, Elena had crossed the river and come after Baerd. Behind her as she went she could hear the singing begin. She knew what would follow in the sheltering hollows and the darkness of that field after an Ember victory. Elena felt her pulse accelerate with the very thought. She could guess what Mattio's face would have revealed as she walked away from him into the river and then across. In her heart she offered him an apology, but her stride as she went did not falter, and then, halfway to the hill, she began to run, suddenly afraid for the man she sought, and for herself, alone in all this wide dark emptiness.

Baerd was sitting on the crown of the hill, where the shadow-figure had stood in front of the setting moon just before he fled. He glanced up as she approached, and a queer, frightened expression flickered for an instant across his face in the starlit dark.

Elena stopped, uncertain.

"It is only me," she said, trying to catch her breath.

He was silent a moment. "I'm sorry," he said. "I wasn't expecting anyone. For a moment . . . for a moment you looked almost exactly like a . . . like something I saw once as a boy. Something that changed my life."

Elena didn't know what to say to that. She had thought no further than getting here. Now that she had found him she was suddenly unsure of herself again. She sat down on the dead earth facing him. He watched her, but said nothing else.

She took a deep breath and said, bravely, "You *should* have expected someone. You should have known that I would come." She swallowed hard, her heart pounding.

For a long moment Baerd was very still, his head tilted a little to one side, as if listening to the echo of her words. Then he smiled. It lit up his young, too thin face and the hollow, wounded eyes.

"Thank you," he said. "Thank you for that, Elena." It was the first time he'd used her name. In the distance they could hear the singing from the cornfield. Overhead the stars were almost impossibly bright in the black arch of the sky.

Elena felt herself flushing. She glanced down and away from his direct gaze. She said, awkwardly, "After all, it is dangerous here in the dead lands, and you wouldn't have known. Not having been here before. With us, I mean. You wouldn't even know how to get back home."

"I have an idea," he said gravely. "I imagine we have until sunrise. And in any case, these aren't the dead lands anymore. We won them back tonight. Elena, look at the ground where you walked."

She turned to look back. And caught her breath in wonder and delight to see that along the path she'd taken to this hill white flowers were blooming in what had been barren earth.

Even as she watched she saw that the flowers were spreading in all directions from where she had passed. Tears sprang to her eyes and spilled over, gliding unheeded down her cheeks, making her vision blur. She had seen enough though, she understood. This was the Earth's response to what they had done tonight. Those delicate white flowers coming to life under the stars were the most beautiful things she had seen in all her days.

Quietly, Baerd said, "You have caused this, Elena. Your being here. You must teach Donar and Carenna and the others this. When you win the Ember war it is not only a matter of holding the line of battle. You must follow the Others and drive them back, Elena. It is possible to regain lands lost in battle years before."

She was nodding. Hearing in his words an echo of something known and forgotten long ago. She spoke the memory: "The land is never truly dead. It can always come back. Or what is the meaning of the cycle of seasons and years?" She wiped her tears away and looked at him.

His expression in the darkness was much too sad for a moment such as this. She wished she knew a way to dispel that sorrow, and not only for tonight. He said, "That is mostly true, I suppose. Or true for the largest things. Smaller things can die. People, dreams, a home."

Impulsively Elena reached forward and took his hand. It was fine and slender and it lay in hers quietly but without response. In the distance, east of the river, the Night Walkers were singing songs to celebrate and welcome the spring, to cry the blessing of the season on the crops that summer would see. Elena wished with all her heart that she were wiser, that she might have an answer to what lay so deeply and hurtfully inside this man.

She said, "If we die that is part of the cycle. We come back in another form." But that was Donar's thought, his way of speaking, not her own.

Baerd was silent. She looked at him, but she could find

nothing within her to say that wouldn't sound wrong, or be someone else's words. So instead, thinking it might somehow help him to speak, she asked, "You said you knew the shadow-figure. How, Baerd? Can you tell me?" It was a strange, almost an illicit pleasure to speak his name.

He smiled at her then, gently. He had a gentle face, especially young as it was now. "Donar had all the clues himself, and Mattio, all of you. You had been losing for twenty years or so they told me. Donar said I was too much tied to the transitory battles of day, do you remember?"

Elena nodded.

"He wasn't wholly wrong," Baerd went on. "I saw Ygrathen soldiers here, and they were not truly so of course. I understand that now. Dearly as I might have wished them to be. But I wasn't wholly wrong either." For the first time his hand put an answering pressure on her own. "Elena, evil feeds on itself. And the evils of day, however transitory, must add to the power of what you face here on the Ember Nights. They *must*, Elena, it cannot but be so. Everything connects. We cannot afford to look only at our own goals. That is the lesson the dearest friend of my life has taught me. The Tyrants in our peninsula have shaped a wrong that goes deeper than who governs in a given year. And that evil has spilled over into this battlefield where you fight Darkness in the name of Light."

"Darkness adding to Darkness," she said. She wasn't certain what had led her to say that.

"Exactly," Baerd said. "Exactly so. I understand your battles here now, how far they go beyond my own war in the daylight world. But going far beyond doesn't mean there is no connection. That was Donar's mistake. It was before him all along, if only he could have seen."

"And the naming," Elena asked. "What did the naming have to do with it?"

"Naming has everything to do with it," Baerd said quietly. He withdrew his hand from hers and rubbed it across his eyes. "Names matter even more here in this place of magic than they do at home where we mortals live and die." He hesitated. And after a silence made deeper by the singing far away, he whispered, "Did you hear me name myself?"

It seemed almost a silly question. He had cried it at the top of his voice. All of them had heard. But his expression was too intense for her to do anything but answer.

"I did," she said. "You named yourself Baerd di Tigana bar Saevar."

And moving very slowly then, very deliberately, Baerd reached for and claimed her hand, and brought it to his lips, as though she were the lady of one of the highland castles, and not only the wheelwright's widowed daughter from the village below Borso.

"Thank you," he said, in a queer voice. "Thank you so much. I thought . . . I thought it might possibly be different tonight. Here."

The back of her hand was tingling where his lips had touched her and her pulse was suddenly erratically fast. Fighting for composure, Elena asked, "I don't understand. What did I do?"

His sorrow was still there, but somehow it seemed gentler now, less naked in his face. He said, quite calmly, "Tigana is the name of a land that was taken away. Its loss is part of the evil that brought the shadow-figure to this hill, and to all your other battlefields for twenty years now. Elena, you won't understand this completely, you can't, but believe me when I tell you that you could not have heard the name of that land back in your village, whether by the light of day or under the two moons. Not even if I spoke it to you from as near as we are now, or cried it louder than I did within the stream."

And now, finally, she did understand. Not the difficult sum of what he was trying to convey, but the thing that mattered more for her: the source of his grief, of that look in the dark of his eyes.

"And Tigana is your home," she said. Not a question. She knew.

He nodded. Very calm. He was still holding her hand, she realized. "Tigana is my home," he echoed. "Men call it Lower Corte now."

She was silent a long moment, thinking hard. Then, "You must speak of this to Donar," she said. "Before morning takes us back. There may be something he knows about such matters, something he can do to help. And he will want to help."

Something flickered in his face. "I'll do that," he said. "I'll speak to him before I go."

They were both silent then. *Before I go.* Elena pushed that away as best she could. She became aware that her mouth was dry and her heart was still pounding, almost as it had in battle. Baerd did not move. He looked so young. Fifteen, he had said. She glanced away, uncertain again, and saw that all around them now the hill itself was covered with a carpet of white flowers.

"Look!" she said, delighted and awed.

He looked around, and smiled then, from the heart.

"You brought them with you," he said.

Below them and east, in the field of corn across the river only a few voices were still singing. Elena knew what that would mean. This was the first of the Ember Nights of spring. The beginning of the year, of the cycle of sowing and harvest. And tonight they had won the Ember war. She knew what would be happening among the men and women in that field. Overhead, the stars seemed to have come nearer, to be almost as close to them as the flowers.

She swallowed, and summoned her courage again. She said: "There are other things that are different about tonight. Here."

"I know," Baerd said softly.

And then he moved, finally, and was on his knees before her among all the young white flowers. He released her palm then, but only to take her face between his two hands, so carefully it seemed as if he feared she might break or bruise to his touch. Over the rapidly growing thunder of her pulse, Elena heard him whisper her name once, as if it were a kind of prayer, and she had time to answer with his—with all of his name, as a gift—before he lowered his mouth to hers.

She could not have spoken after that, for desire and need crashed over her and bore her away as something—a chip of wood, a fragment of bark—carried by a huge and rushing wave. Baerd was with her, though. They were together here in this place, and then they were naked among the newly sprung white flowers of that hill.

And as she drew him down and into her, feeling the keenness of longing and an aching tenderness, Elena looked up for a moment past his shoulder at all the circling, luminous stars of the Ember Night. And it came to her as a wonderful and joyous thought that every single diamond of those stars would have a name.

Then Baerd's rhythm changed above her, and her own awakened desire with it, and all thoughts scattered from her like dust strewn between those stars. She moved her head so her mouth could seek and find his own and she closed her arms around him and gathered him to her and closed her eyes, and they let that high wave carry them into the beginning of spring.

CHAPTER
• 12 •

THE COLD AND A CRAMPED STIFFNESS WOKE DEVIN ABOUT an hour before sunrise. It took him a moment to remember where he was. It was still dark in the room. He massaged his neck and listened to Catriana's quiet breathing from under her blankets in the bed. A rueful expression crossed his face.

It was strange, he reflected, twisting his head from side to side to try to ease the soreness, how only a few hours in a soft armchair could leave one feeling more knotted and uncomfortable than a whole night out on cold ground.

He felt surprisingly awake though, given the night he'd just had and the fact that he couldn't have been asleep for more than three hours or so. He considered going back to his own bed but realized that he wasn't going to be able to sleep any more that night. He decided to go down to the kitchens and see if any of the household staff could be induced to make him a pot of khav.

He left the room, concentrating on closing the door silently behind him. So much so that when he saw Alessan standing in the hallway watching him from in front of his own door he jumped involuntarily.

The Prince walked over, eyebrows arched.

Devin shook his head firmly. "We just talked. I slept in the chair. Got a kink in my neck to show for it."

"I'm sure," Alessan murmured.

"No, really," Devin insisted.

"I'm sure," Alessan repeated. He smiled. "I believe you. If you had essayed more I would have heard screaming—yours with an unpleasant injury, most likely."

367

"Very likely," Devin agreed. They walked away from Catriana's door.

"How was Alienor though?"

Devin felt himself going red. "How . . . ?" he began, then gradually became aware of the condition of his clothing and the amused scrutiny Alessan was giving him.

"Interesting," he offered.

Alessan smiled again. "Come downstairs with me and help solve a problem. I need some khav for the road anyhow."

"I was on the way to the kitchens myself. Give me two minutes to change my clothes."

"Not a bad idea," Alessan murmured, eyeing the torn shirt. "I'll meet you down there."

Devin ducked into his own chamber and quickly changed. For good measure he pulled on the vest Alais had sent him. Thinking of her, of her sheltered, quiet innocence, took him back—by polarity—to what had happened last night. He stood stock-still in the middle of his room for a moment and tried to properly grasp what he had done, and had done to him.

Interesting, he had just called it. Language. The process of sharing with words seemed such a futile exercise sometimes. A remnant of the sadness he'd felt, leaving Alienor, washed back over him and it picked up Catriana's sorrows too. He felt as if he'd been washed up by the sea on some grey beach at a bleak hour.

"Khav," Devin said aloud. "Or I'll never get out of this mood."

On the way downstairs he realized, belatedly, what Alessan had meant by "for the road." His meeting, wherever it was, was today—the encounter they'd been pointing toward for half a year.

And after that he would be riding west. To Tigana. Where his mother lay dying in a Sanctuary of Eanna.

Wide awake, his mind snapping from night reflections into the sharper agitations of the day, Devin followed a glow of light to the huge kitchens of Castle Borso and he paused in the arched doorway, looking within.

Sitting by the roaring fire, Alessan was carefully sipping steaming khav from an oversized mug. In a chair beside him Erlein di Senzio was doing the same. The two

men were both gazing into the flames while all around
them there was already a purposeful stir and bustle in the
kitchen.

Devin stood in the doorway a moment, unnoticed, and
found himself looking closely at the two men. In their
silent gravity they seemed to him to be a part of a frieze,
a tableau, emblematic in some complex way of all such
pre-dawn hours for those on the long roads. Neither man
was a stranger to this hour, Devin knew, to sitting thus
before a castle kitchen fire among the servants in the last
dark hour before dawn, easing into wakefulness and a
fugitive warmth, preparing for the road again and whatever turnings it might offer in the day that had not yet
begun.

It seemed to Devin that Alessan and Erlein, sitting
together as they were, were bonded in some way that
went beyond the harsh thing that had happened by that
twilit stream in Ferraut. It was a linkage that had nothing
to do with Prince and wizard, it was shaped of the things
they each had done. The same things done. Memories
they would each have and could share, if these two men
could truly share anything after what had happened between them.

For years they had each been traveling. There had to
be so many images that overlapped and could evoke the
same mood, emotions, the same sounds and smells. Like
this one: darkness outside, the edge of grey dawn and the
castle stir the sun would bring, chill of the corridors and
knowledge of wind outside the walls, cut by the crackle
and roar of the kitchen fire; the reassuring steam and
smell rising from their cradled mugs; sleep and dream
receding, the mind slowly turning forward to the day that
lay ahead swathed in ground mist. Looking at their stillness amid the bustle of the kitchen Devin felt another
return of the sadness that seemed to be his legacy from
this long strange night in the highlands.

Sadness, and a distinct stir of longing. Devin realized
that he wanted that shared history for himself, wanted to
be a part of that self-contained, accomplished fraternity
of men who knew this scene so well. He was young
enough to savor the romance of it, but old enough—
especially after this past winter and his time with Menico—

to guess at the price demanded for those memories and the contained, solitary, competent look of the two men in front of him.

He stepped through the doorway. A pretty servant noticed him and smiled shyly. Without a word she brought him a scalding mug of khav. Alessan glanced over at him and hooked a third chair with his long leg, pulling it into a position near him by the fire. Devin walked over and sank gratefully down near the warmth. His stiffened neck was still bothering him.

"I didn't even have to be charming," Alessan reported cheerfully. "Erlein was already here and had started in on a fresh pot of khav. There were people in the kitchen all night to keep the fires going. Couldn't have lit new ones on an Ember Day."

Devin nodded, sipping carefully and with intense gratitude from his steaming mug. "And the other question you mentioned?" he asked guardedly, with a glance at Erlein.

"Solved," the Prince said promptly. He seemed unnaturally bright, brittle as kindling. "Erlein's going to have to come with me. We've established that I can't let him get too far away or my summons won't work. And if that's the case, well he simply has to go where I go. All the way west. We really do seem to be tied together, don't we?" He flashed his teeth in a smile at the wizard. Erlein didn't bother to respond; he continued to sip his drink, gazing expressionlessly into the fire.

"Why were you up so early?" Devin asked him, after a moment.

Erlein made a sour face. "Slavery doesn't agree with my rest," he mumbled into his khav.

Devin elected to ignore that. There were times when he really did feel sorry for the wizard, but not when Erlein trotted out his reflexive self-pity.

A thought struck Devin. He turned to Alessan. "Is he going to your meeting this morning, too?"

"I suppose," Alessan said with apparent carelessness. "A small reward for his loyalty and the long ride he'll have afterward. I expect to travel without stopping very much." His tone was genuinely odd; too deliberately casual, as if denying the very possibility of strain.

"I see," Devin said, as neutrally as he could manage. He turned his gaze to the fire and kept it there.

There was a silence. When it stretched, Devin looked back and saw Alessan looking at him.

"Do you want to come?" the Prince asked.

Did he want to come? For half a year, from the moment Devin and Sandre had joined the other three, Alessan had been telling them that everything they wanted to achieve would point toward and wait upon a meeting in these southern highlands on the first of the Ember Days.

Did he want to come?

Devin coughed, spilling some khav on the stone floor. "Well," he said, "not if I'm in the way, naturally. Only if you think I could be useful and if maybe I could . . ."

He trailed off because Alessan was laughing at him.

Even Erlein had been roused from his sulk to a faint, reluctant snort of amusement. The two older men exchanged a glance.

"You are a terrible liar," the wizard said to Devin.

"He's right," Alessan said, still chuckling. "But never mind. I don't actually think you can be useful—it isn't in the nature of what I have to do. But I'm certain you won't do any harm and you and Erlein can keep each other entertained. It'll be a very long ride."

"What? To the meeting?" Devin asked, startled.

Alessan shook his head. "Only two or three hours there, depending on the state of the pass this morning. No, Devin, I'm inviting you west with me." His voice altered. "Home."

"*Pigeon!*" the balding, burly-chested man cried, though they were still some distance away. He sat in a massive oak chair set squarely down in the middle of the Braccio Pass. There had been early spring flowers blooming on the lower slopes but not very many this far up. On either side of the path piled rock and stone yielded to forest. Further up, to the south, there was only rock and snow.

Carrying-poles were attached to the oak chair and six men stood behind it in burgundy livery. Devin thought they were servants, but when he came nearer he saw from their weapons that he was wrong: these were soldiers, and guards.

"Pigeon," the man in the chair repeated loudly. "You have risen in the world! You bring companions this time!"

It was with a genuine sense of disorientation that Devin realized that the childish name and the raucous, carrying words were addressed to Alessan.

Who had the oddest look to his face all of a sudden. He said nothing by way of reply though as they rode up to the seven men in the pass. Alessan dismounted; behind him Devin and Erlein did the same. The man in the chair did not rise to greet them, but his bright, small eyes followed every move that Alessan made. His enormous hands were motionless on the carved arms of the chair. He wore at least six rings; they sparkled in the light of the morning sun. He had a hooked much-broken nose in a leathery, weather-beaten face that showed two livid scars. One was an old wound, slanting down his right cheek in a white line. The other, much more recent, raked redly across his forehead to the greying, receding hairline above his left ear.

"Company for the ride," Alessan said mildly. "I wasn't sure if you'd come. They both sing. Could have consoled me on the way back. The young one is Devin, the other is Erlein. You've grown monstrous fat in a year."

"And why should I not grow fat?" the other roared in delight. "And how *dare* you doubt that I would come! Have I ever not kept faith with you?" The tone was boisterous in the extreme, but Devin saw that the small eyes were alert and very watchful.

"Not ever," Alessan agreed calmly. His own febrile manner had gone, to be replaced by an almost preternatural calm. "But things have changed since two years ago. You don't need me anymore. Not since last summer."

"Not need you!" the big man cried. "Pigeon, *of course* I need you. You are my youth, my memory of what I was. *And* my talisman of fortune in battle."

"No more battles though," said Alessan quietly. "Will you allow me to offer my humblest congratulations?"

"No!" the other growled. "No, I will not allow you. No such mewling courtly claptrap from you. What I want is for you to come here and hug me and stop this imbecilic maundering! Who are we to be chittering like this? The two of us!"

And with the last words he propelled himself upright with a ferocious push of his two muscled arms. The huge oak chair rocked backwards. Three of the liveried guards sprang to balance it.

The big man took two awkward, crippled, hopping steps forward as Alessan strode to meet him. And in that moment Devin abruptly realized—a bucket of ice down the length of his spine—who this scarred, maimed man had to be.

"Bear!" said Alessan, laughter catching in his throat. He threw his arms fiercely about the other man. "Oh, Marius, I truly didn't know if you would come."

Marius.

Stupefied by more than altitude and a sleepless night, Devin saw the self-crowned King of Quileia—the crippled man who'd killed seven armed challengers barehanded in the sacred grove—lift the Prince of Tigana clean off his feet and kiss him loudly on both cheeks. He lowered a red-faced Alessan to the path and held him at arms' length for a close scrutiny.

"It is true," he said at length as Alessan's grin faded. "I can see it. You really did doubt me. I should be outraged, Pigeon. I should be wounded and hurt. What did Pigeon Two say?"

"Baerd was sure you would be here," Alessan admitted ruefully. "I'm afraid I owe him money."

"At least one of you has grown up enough to have some sense," Marius growled. Then something seemed to register with him. "What? You two young scamps were *wagering* on me? How dare you!" He was laughing, but the blow he suddenly clapped on Alessan's shoulder made the other man stagger.

Marius hobbled back to his chair and sat down. Again Devin was struck by the all-embracing nature of the glance he turned on them. Only for an instant did it flit over Devin himself, but he had the uncanny sense that Marius had, in that one second, sized him up quite comprehensively, that he would be recognized and remembered should they meet by chance even a decade hence.

He experienced a weird, fleeting moment of pity for the seven warriors who had had to battle this man, bring-

ing merely swords or spears, and armor and two good
legs to meet him in a night grove.

Those arms like tree-trunks and the message in those
eyes told Devin all he needed to know about which way
the balance would have tilted in those battles despite the
ritual maiming—the severed ankle tendons—of the consort who was supposed to die in the grove, to the greater
glory of the Mother Goddess and her High Priestess.

Marius had not died. For anyone's greater glory. Seven
times he had not died. And now, since that seventh time,
there was a true King in Quileia again and the last High
Priestess was dead. It had been Rovigo, Devin remembered suddenly, who had first given him that news. In a
rancid tavern called The Bird, either half a year or half a
lifetime ago.

"You must have been slipping or lazy or already fat
last summer in the Grove," Alessan was saying. He gestured toward the scar on Marius's forehead. "Tonalius
should never have been able to get that close to you with
a blade."

The smile on the face of the King of Quileia was not,
in truth, a pleasant thing to see. "He didn't," Marius said
grimly. "I used our kick-drop from the twenty-seven tree
and he was dead before we both hit the ground. The scar
is a farewell token from my late wife in our last encounter. May the sacred Mother of us all guard her ever-
blessed spirit. Will you take wine and a midday meal?"

Alessan's grey eyes blinked. "We would be pleased
to," he said.

"Good," said Marius. He gestured to his guards. "In
that case, while my men attend to laying things out for us
you can tell me, Pigeon, and I hope you *will* tell me, why
you hesitated just now before accepting that invitation."

It was Devin's turn to blink; he hadn't even registered
the pause. Alessan was smiling though. "I wish," he said,
with a wry twist of his mouth, "that you would miss
something once in a while."

Marius smiled thinly, but did not speak.

"I have a long ride ahead of me. At least three days,
flat out. Someone I must get to, as soon as I can."

"More important than me, Pigeon? I am desolated."

Alessan shook his head. "Not more important, or I

wouldn't be here now. More compelling perhaps. There was a message from Danoleon waiting for me at Borso last night. My mother is dying."

Marius's expression changed swiftly. "I am deeply sorry," he said. "Alessan, truly I am." He paused. "It could not have been easy for you to come here first, knowing that."

Alessan gave his small characteristic shrug. His eyes moved away from Marius, gazing past him up the pass toward the high peaks beyond. The soldiers had finished spreading a quite extravagant golden cloth over the level ground in front of the chair. Now they began laying out multi-colored cushions upon it and putting down baskets and dishes of food.

"We will break bread together," Marius said crisply, "and discuss what we are here to discuss—then you must go. You trust this message? Is there danger for you in returning?"

Devin hadn't even thought about that.

"I suppose there is," Alessan said indifferently. "But yes, I trust Danoleon. Of course I do. He took me to you in the first place."

"I am aware of that," Marius said mildly. "I remember him. I also know that unless things have greatly changed he is not the only priest in that Sanctuary of Eanna, and your clergy in the Palm have not been noted for their reliability."

Alessan gave his shrug again. "What can I do? My mother is dying. I've not seen her in almost two decades, Bear." His mouth crooked. "I don't think I am likely to be recognized by many people, even without Baerd's disguises. Would you not say I have changed somewhat since I was fourteen?" There was a slight challenge in the words.

"Somewhat," Marius said quietly. "Not so much as one might think. You were a grown man even then, in many ways. So was Baerd when he came to join you."

Again Alessan's eyes seemed to drift away up the line of the pass, as if chasing a memory or a far-off image to the south. Devin had an acute sense that there was much more being said here than he was hearing.

"Come," Marius said, levering his hands on the chair arms. "Will you join me on our carpet in the meadow?"

"Stay in the chair!" Alessan rapped sharply. His expression remained incongruously benign and untroubled. "How many men came here with you, Bear?"

Marius had not moved. "A company to the foothills. These six through the pass. Why?"

Moving easily, smiling carelessly, Alessan sat down on the cloth at the King's feet. "Hardly wise, to bring so few up here."

"There is little enough danger. My enemies are too superstitious to venture into the mountains. You know that, Pigeon. The passes were named as taboo long ago when they shut down trade with the Palm."

"In that case," Alessan said, still smiling, "I am at a loss to explain the bowman I just saw behind a rock up the trail."

"You are certain?" Marius's voice was as casual as Alessan's, but there was suddenly ice in his eyes.

"Twice now."

"I am deeply distressed," said the King of Quileia. "Such a person is unlikely to be here for any reason other than to kill me. And if they are breaking the mountain taboo I am going to be forced to rethink a number of assumptions. Will you take some wine?" He gestured, and one of the men in burgundy poured with a hand that trembled slightly.

"Thank you," Alessan murmured. "Erlein, can you do anything here without it being known?"

The wizard's face went pale, but he too kept his voice level. "Not any sort of attack. It would take too much power, and there is nothing here to screen it from any Tracker in the highlands."

"A shield for the King?"

Erlein hesitated.

"My friend," Alessan said gravely, "I need you and I am going to continue to need you. I know there is danger in using your magic—for all of us. I must have honest answers though, to make intelligent decisions. Pour him some wine," he said to the Quileian soldier.

Erlein accepted a glass and drank. "I can do a low-level screen behind him against arrows." He stopped. "Do you want it? There is some risk."

"I think I do," Alessan said. "Put up the shield as unobtrusively as you can."

Erlein's mouth tightened but he said nothing. His left hand moved very slightly from side to side. Devin could see the two missing fingers now, but nothing else happened, so far as he could tell.

"It is done," Erlein said grimly. "The risk will increase the longer I hold it up." He drank again from his wine.

Alessan nodded, accepting a wedge of bread and a plateful of meat and cheese from one of the Quileians. "Devin?"

Devin had been waiting. "I see the rock," he said quietly. "Up the path. On the right side. Arrow range. Send me home."

"Take my horse. There's a bow in the saddle."

Devin shook his head. "He may notice—and I'm not good enough with the bow anyhow. I'll do what I can. Can you arrange to be noisy in about twenty minutes?"

"We can be very noisy," said Marius of Quileia. "The climb back up and around will be easier to your left as you go down, just past the point where this path bends. I'd very much like this person alive, by the way."

Devin smiled. Marius suddenly roared with laughter and Alessan followed suit. Erlein was silent as Alessan swept an imperious hand out toward Devin.

"If you forgot it then you can fetch it, thimble-brain! We'll be here, enjoying our meal. We *may* leave something for you."

"It wasn't my fault!" Devin protested loudly, letting his smile fade to petulance. He turned back to where the horses were tethered. Shaking his head, visibly disconsolate, he mounted his grey and rode down the path along which they had come.

As far as the bend in the trail.

He dismounted and tethered the horse. After a moment's thought he left his sword where it was, hanging from the saddle. He was aware that it was a decision that might cost him his life. He'd seen the wooded slopes beside the pass though; a sword would be awkward and noisy when he began to climb.

Cutting to the west he soon found himself among the trees. He doubled back south and up, as far off the line of the pass as the terrain allowed. It was hard, sweaty going, and he had to hurry, but Devin was fit and he'd always been quick and agile—compensations for a lack of size. He scrambled up the steep slopes, weaving among mountain trees and dark serrano bushes, grasping roots wedged deep into the slanting soil.

Part of the way up, the trees briefly gave out before a short, steep cliff to the south and west. He could go up or he could go around, angling back toward the pass. Devin tried to guess his bearings but it was difficult—no sounds reached him this far off the trail. He couldn't be sure if he was already above the place where the Quileian cloth was spread for lunch. *Twenty minutes,* he'd told them. He gritted his teeth, offered a quick prayer to Adaon, and began to climb the rock. It occurred to him that there was something profoundly incongruous about an Asolini farmer's son from the northern marshes struggling up a cliff-face in the Braccio Range.

He wasn't an Asolini farmer's son though. He was from Tigana and his father was, and his Prince had asked him to do this thing.

Devin skittered sideways along the rock-face trying not to dislodge any pebbles. He reached an outcrop of stone, changed grip, hung free for a second, and then boosted himself straight up and onto it. He scrambled quickly across some level ground, dropped flat on his stomach and, breathing hard, looked up to the south.

And then straight down. He caught his breath, realizing how lucky he'd been. There was a single figure hiding behind a boulder almost directly below him. Devin had quite certainly been visible on the last part of his climb where the cliff-face broke clear of the trees. His silence had served him well though, for the figure below was oblivious to him, avidly intent on the group feasting on the path. Devin couldn't see them, but their voices carried to him now. The sun moved behind a cloud and Devin instinctively flattened himself, just as the assassin glanced up to gauge the change in the light.

For an archer it would matter, Devin knew. It was a long shot, downhill and partly screened by the guards.

There would also be time, most likely, for only one arrow. He wondered if the tips were poisoned. Probably, he decided.

Very carefully he started crawling uphill, trying to work his way further around behind the assassin. His brain was racing as he slipped into a higher stand of trees. How was he going to get close enough to deal with an archer?

Just then he heard the sound of Alessan's pipes followed, a measure later, by Erlein's harp. A moment after that a number of voices started in on one of the oldest, most rollicking highland ballads of all. About a legendary band of mountain outlaws who had ruled these hills and crags with arrogant impunity until they were surprised and defeated by Quileia and Certando together:

Thirty brave men rode apace from the north
And forty Quileians met them side by side.
There in the mountains each pledged to the other
And Gan Burdash high in his roost defied!

The booming voice of Marius led the others into the refrain. By then Devin had remembered something and he knew what he was going to try to do. He was aware that there was more than an element of lunacy in his planning, but he also knew he didn't have much time, or many options.

His heart was pounding. He wiped his hands dry on his breeches and began moving more quickly through the trees along the line of the ridge he'd climbed. Behind him was the singing; beneath him now, perhaps fifteen feet east of this higher ridge and twenty feet below was an assassin with a bow. The sun came out from behind the clouds.

Devin was above and behind the Quileian now. Had he been carrying a bow and been at all accomplished with one he would have had the other at his mercy.

Instead, what he had was a knife, and a certain pride and trust in his own coordination, and a tall giant of a mountain pine tree rising all the way up to his ridge from just behind the boulder that sheltered the archer. He could see the other clearly now, clad in a masking green

for the mountain trail, with a strung bow and half a
dozen arrows to hand.

Devin knew what he had to do. He also knew—because
there had been woods at home, if not mountain passes—
that he could not climb down that tree with any hope of
silence. Not even with the loud, seriously off-key voices
screening his sounds from below.

Which left, so far as he could judge, only the one
option. Others might have planned it better, but others
weren't on this ridge. Devin wiped his damp palms very
carefully dry again and began concentrating on a large
branch that stretched out and away from the others. The
only one that might do him any good. He tried to calculate angle and distance as best he could, given an almost
total lack of experience at this particular maneuver.
What he was about to try was not a thing one did for
practice, anywhere.

He checked the hang of the dagger in his belt, wiped
his hands one last time, and stood up. Absurdly, the flash
of memory that came to him then was of the day his
brothers had surprised him hanging upside down from a
tree, trying to stretch his height.

Devin smiled tightly and stepped to the edge of the
cliff. The branch looked absurdly far away, and it was
only half of the way down to the level of the pass. He
swore an inward oath that if he survived this Baerd was
going to teach him how to use a bow properly.

From the path below he heard the ragged voices swirling erratically towards the climax of the ballad:

Gan Burdash ruled in the mountain heights
And with his band he ranged from crag to glen,
But seventy brave men tracked him to his lair
And when the moons had set the peaks were free again!

Devin jumped. Air whistled past his face. The branch
flew up to meet him, blurred, very fast. He stretched his
hands, clutched it, swung. Only a little. Only enough to
change his angle of descent, cut his momentum. Bring
him directly down upon the killer behind the rock.

The branch held, but the leaves crackled loudly as
he pivoted. He'd known they would. The Quileian

flung a startled glance skyward and grappled for the bow.

Not nearly fast enough. Screaming at the top of his lungs, Devin plummeted like some hunting bird of these high places. By the time his target began to move Devin was already there.

Our kick-drop from the twenty-seven tree, he thought.

Falling, he tilted his torso so that it angled sideways across the upper body of the Quileian and he kicked out hard with both feet as he did. The impact was sickening. He felt his legs make jarring contact, even as he crashed into the other, driving all the air from his own lungs.

They smashed into the ground together, tumbling and rolling away from the base of the boulder. Devin gasped agonizingly for breath, he felt the world sway and rock wildly in his sight. He gritted his teeth and groped for his dagger.

Then he realized it was not necessary.

Dead before we both hit the ground, Marius had said. With a shuddering heave Devin forced air into his tortured lungs. There was an odd, knifing pain running up his right leg. He forced himself to ignore it. He rolled free of the unconscious Quileian and struggled, gasping and wheezing, for another breath of precious air. And then he looked.

The assassin was a woman. Under all the circumstances, not a great surprise. She was not dead. Her forehead appeared to have glanced off the rock under the impact of his sprawling descent. She was lying on her side, bleeding heavily from a scalp wound. He had probably broken a number of her ribs with his kick. She had a profusion of cuts and scrapes from their tumble down the slope.

So, Devin noted, did he. His shirt was torn and he was badly scratched again, for the second time in half a day. There was a joke, something that ought to be amusing in that, but he couldn't reach to it. Not yet.

He seemed to have survived though. And to have done what he'd been asked to do. He managed to draw one full, steadying breath just as Alessan and one of the Quileian soldiers came sprinting up the path. Erlein was just behind them, Devin saw with surprise.

He started to stand, but the world spun erratically and he had to be braced by Alessan. The Quileian guard flipped the assassin over on her back. He stood staring down upon her and then spat, very deliberately, into her bleeding face.

Devin looked away.

His eyes met Alessan's. "We saw you jump from down there. You're really supposed to have wings before trying that sort of thing," the Prince said. "Didn't anyone ever tell you?"

The expression in the grey eyes belied the lightness of his tone. "I feared for you," he added softly.

"I couldn't think of anything else to do," Devin said apologetically. He was aware of a deep pride beginning to well up within him. He shrugged. "The singing was driving me mad. I had to do something to stop it."

Alessan's smile widened. He reached an arm around and squeezed Devin's shoulder. Baerd had done that too, in the Nievolene barn.

It was Erlein who laughed at the joke. "Come back down," the wizard said. "I'll have to clean out those cuts for you."

They helped him descend the slope. The Quileian carried the woman and her bow. Devin saw that it was made of a very dark wood, almost black, and was carved into a semblance of a crescent moon. From one end of it there hung a gathered and twisted lock of greying hair. He shivered. He had a fair idea of whose it would be.

Marius was on his feet, one hand on the back of his chair, as he watched them come down. His eyes barely flicked over the four men and the carried assassin. They locked, cold and grim, on the black curve of the moon bow. He looked frightening.

And the more so, Devin thought, because not at all afraid.

"I think we are past the need to dance in words around each other," Alessan said. "I would like to tell you what I need and you will tell me if you can do it and that will be all we need say."

Marius held up a hand to stop him.

He had now joined the three of them among the cushions on the golden cloth. The dishes and baskets had been cleared away. Two of the Quileians had taken the woman back up over the pass to where the rest of their company waited. The other four were posted some distance away. The sun was high, as high as it would get at noon this far south, this early in the spring. It had turned into a mild, generous day.

"This Bear is a very bad word-dancer, Pigeon," the King of Quileia said soberly. "You know that. You probably know something else: how much it will grieve me to deny you any request at all. I would like to do this differently. I would like to tell you what I cannot do, so you will not ask it and force me to refuse."

Alessan nodded. He remained silent, watching the King.

"I cannot give you an army," Marius said flatly. "Not yet, and perhaps never. I am too green in power, too far from the stability I need at home to lead or even order troops over these mountains. There are several hundreds of years of tradition I have to set about changing in very little time. I am not a young man anymore, Pigeon."

Devin felt a leap of excitement within himself and struggled to master it. This was too serious an occasion for childlike feelings. He could hardly believe he was here, though, so close to—at the very heart of—something of this magnitude. He stole a sidelong glance at Erlein and then looked more closely: the same quick spark of interest was in the other's face. For all his years and his long travels, Devin seriously doubted if the troubadour-wizard had ever been so near to great events.

Alessan was shaking his head. "Bear," he said, "I would never ask you for that. For our sake as much as for your own. I will not have my name remembered as the man who first invited the newly awakened might of Quileia north into the Palm. If an army ever ventures from Quileia through these passes—and I hope we are both long dead before such a day—the wish of my heart will be for it to be slaughtered and driven back with losses so bloody that no King in the south ever tries again."

"If there is a King in the south and not another four hundred years of the Mother and her priestesses. Very well," Marius said, "then tell me what it is you do need."

Alessan's legs were neatly crossed, his long fingers laced in his lap. He looked for all the world as if he was discussing nothing of greater moment than, perhaps, the sequence of songs for an evening's performance.

Except that his fingers, Devin saw, were so tightly squeezed together they were white.

"A question first," Alessan said, controlling his voice. "Have you received letters offering to open trade?"

Marius nodded. "From both of your Tyrants. Gifts, messages of felicitation, and generous offers to reopen the old trade routes by sea and land."

"And each urged you to scorn the other as being untrustworthy and unstable in his power."

Marius was smiling faintly now. "Are you intercepting my mail, Pigeon? Each did exactly that."

"And what," Alessan asked, direct as an arrow, "have you replied?" For the first time, unmistakably, there was a taut cord of tension in his voice.

Marius heard it too. "Nothing yet," he said, his smile fading. "I want a few more messages from each of them before I move."

Alessan looked down and seemed to notice his clenched fingers for the first time. He unlaced them and ran a hand, predictably, through his hair.

"You will have to move, though," he said with some difficulty. "You will obviously need trade. In your position you have to begin showing Quileia some of the benefits you can offer. Traffic north will be the quickest way, won't it?" There was an awkward kind of challenge in his tone.

"Of course," Marius said simply. "I have to do it. Why else am I King? It is only a question of timing—and with what happened this morning I think my timing has just been moved up."

Alessan nodded, as if he'd known all this already.

"What will you do, then?" he asked.

"Open the passes for both of them. No preferences, no tariffs for either. I will let Alberico and Brandin send me all the gifts and goods and envoys they want. I'll let their trade make me truly a King—a King who brings new prosperity to his people. And I need to start doing it soon. Immediately, I now suspect. I have to put Quileia so firmly on a new path that the old one recedes as fast as I can make it. Otherwise I'll die having done nothing but live somewhat longer than most Year Kings, and the priestesses will be in power again before my bones are picked clean underground."

Alessan closed his eyes. Devin became aware of the rustling of leaves all around them and the sporadic calling of birds. Then Alessan looked up at Marius again, the grey eyes wide and calm, and he said, bluntly:

"My request: that you give me six months before deciding on trade. And something else, in that interval."

"The time alone is a great deal," Marius said very softly. "But tell me the rest, Pigeon. The something else."

"Three letters, Bear. I need three letters sent north. First letter: you say yes to Brandin, conditionally. You ask for time to consolidate your own position before exposing Quileia to outside influences. You make it clear that your inclination toward him is based on his appearing stronger than Alberico, more likely to endure. Second letter: you reject, sorrowfully, all overtures from Astibar. You write Alberico that you are intimidated by Brandin's threats. That you would dearly love to trade with the Empire of Barbadior, need to trade with them, but the Ygrathen seems too strong in the Palm for you to risk offending him. You wish Alberico all good fortune. You ask him to keep in contact with you, discreetly. You say you will be watching events in the north with close interest. You have not yet given Brandin a final decision, and will delay as long as you can. You send your warmest regards to the Emperor."

Devin was lost. He reverted to his trick of the winter: listen, remember, think about it later. Marius's eyes were bright though, and the cold, unsettling smile was back.

"And my third letter?" he asked.

"Is to the Governor of the Province of Senzio. Offering immediate trade, no tariffs, first choice of prime goods, secure anchorage in your harbors for their ships. Expressing deep admiration for Senzio's brave independence and enterprise in the face of adversity." Alessan paused. "And this third letter, naturally—"

"Will be intercepted by Alberico of Barbadior. Pigeon,

do you know what you would be setting in motion? How incredibly dangerous a game this is?"

"Wait a minute!" Erlein di Senzio suddenly interjected, starting to rise.

"*You be silent!*" Alessan literally snarled the command in a voice Devin had never heard him use.

Erlein's mouth snapped shut. He subsided, breathing harshly, his eyes coals of anger and burgeoning understanding. Alessan didn't even look at him. Neither did Marius. The two of them sat on a golden carpet high in the mountains, seemingly oblivious to the existence of anything in the world but each other.

"You *do* know, don't you?" Marius said finally. "You know exactly." There was a certain wonder in his voice.

Alessan nodded. "I've had enough time to think about it, Triad knows. Once the trade routes open I think my province and its name are lost. With what you can offer him, Brandin will be a hero in the west, not a Tyrant. He will be so secure that there will be nothing I can do, Bear. Your Kingship may be my undoing. And my home's."

"Are you sorry you helped me to it?"

Devin watched Alessan wrestle with that. There were currents of emotion running here, far beneath the surface of what he could see and understand. He listened, and remembered.

"I should be sorry," Alessan murmured at length. "In a way it is a kind of treachery that I am not. But no, how can I possibly regret what we worked so hard to achieve?" His smile was wistful.

Marius said, "You know I love you, Pigeon. Both of you."

"I know. We both know."

"You know what I am facing back home."

"I do. I have reason to remember."

In the silence that followed Devin felt a sadness come over him, an echo of his mood at the end of the night. A sense of the terrible spaces that always seemed to lie between people. The gulfs that had to be crossed for even a simple touching.

And how much wider those gulfs must be for men such as these two, with their long dreams and the burdens of being who they were, and what. How hard it seemed, how brutally hard, for hands to reach out across so much history and such a weight of responsibility and loss.

"Oh, Pigeon," said Marius of Quileia, his voice little more than a whisper, "you may have been an arrow shot from the white moon into my heart eighteen years ago. I love you as my son, Alessan bar Valentin. I will give you six months and your three letters. Build a bonfire to my memory if you hear that I have died."

Even with what little he understood, on the uttermost edges of this, Devin felt a lump gather in his throat, making it difficult to swallow. He looked at the two of them and he couldn't have said which man he admired more in that moment. The one who had asked, knowing what he asked, or the one who had given, knowing what he gave. He had an awareness though, humbling, inescapable, of how far yet he had to travel—a distance he might never traverse—before he could name himself a man after the fashion of these two.

"Does either of you have any idea," Erlein di Senzio broke into the stillness, his voice grim as death, "how many innocent men and women may be butchered because of what you are about to do?"

Marius said nothing. Alessan wheeled on the wizard though.

"Have *you* any idea," he said, his eyes like chips of grey ice, "how close I am to killing you for saying that?" Erlein paled but did not draw back. Nor did his own eyes flinch away.

"I did not ask to be born into this time, charged by my birth with trying to set it right," Alessan said, his voice held tightly again as if under a leash. "I was the youngest child. This should have been my brothers' burden, either or both of them. They died by the Deisa. Among the lucky ones." Bitterness cracked through for a moment.

And was beaten back. "I am trying to act for the whole of the Palm. Not just for Tigana and her lost name. I have been reviled as a traitor and a fool for doing so. My mother has cursed me because of this. I will accept that from her. To her I will hold myself accountable for blood and death and the destruction of what Tigana was if I fail. I will *not* hold myself subject to your judgment,

Erlein di Senzio! I do not need you to tell me who or what is at risk in this. I need you to do what I tell you, nothing more! If you are going to die a slave you might as well be mine as anyone else's. You are going to fight with me, Senzian. Whether through your will or against it you are going to fight with me for freedom!"

He fell silent. Devin felt himself trembling, as if a titanic thunderstorm had shaken the sky above the mountains and gone.

"Why do you let him live?" Marius of Quileia asked.

Alessan fought to collect himself. He seemed to consider the matter. "Because he is a brave man in his own way," he answered at length. "Because it is true that his people will be placed in great danger by this. Because I have wronged him by his lights, and by my own. And because I have need of him."

Marius shook his large head. "It is bad to have need of a man."

"I know, Bear."

"He may come back to you, even years later, and ask you for something very large. Something your heart will not let you refuse."

"I know, Bear," said Alessan. The two men looked at each other, sitting motionless on the golden carpet.

Devin turned away, feeling like an intruder on that exchange of glances. In the stillness of that pass below the heights of the Braccio Range birdsong rang out with piercing sweetness and, looking up to the south, Devin saw that the last of the high white clouds had drifted apart, revealing the dazzle of sunlit snow on the peaks. The world seemed to be a place of more beauty and more pain than he could ever have imagined it to be.

When they rode back down from the pass Baerd was waiting for them a few miles south of the castle, alone on his horse among the green of the foothills.

His eyes widened when he saw Devin and Erlein, and a rare amusement was visible even behind his beard, as Alessan pulled to a halt in front of him.

"You," said Baerd, "are even worse at these things than I am, despite everything you say."

"Not worse. As bad, perhaps," Alessan said, ruefully

ducking his head. "After all, your *only* reason for refusing to come was so that he wouldn't feel any extra pressure to—"

"And after lashing me verbally for that, you go and take two complete strangers to reduce the pressure even more. I stand my ground: you are worse than I am."

"Lash me verbally," Alessan said.

Baerd shook his head. "How is he?"

"Well enough. Under strain. Devin stopped an assassination attempt up there."

"What?" Baerd glanced quickly at Devin, noting the torn shirt and hose and the scrapes and cuts.

"You are going to have to teach me how to use a bow," Devin said. "There's less wear and tear."

Baerd smiled. "I will. First chance we have." Then something seemed to occur to him. "An assassination?" he said to Alessan. "In the *mountains*? Surely not!"

Alessan's expression was grim. "I'm afraid so. She carried a moon bow with a lock of his hair. The mountain taboo has obviously been lifted—at least for the purposes of murder."

Baerd's features creased with concern. He sat on his horse quietly a moment, then: "So he had no option really. He needs to act immediately. He said no?"

"He said yes. We have six months and he will send the letters." Alessan hesitated. "He asked us to build a bonfire to his memory if he dies."

Baerd suddenly turned his horse away. He sat staring fixedly off to the west. The late-afternoon sun was shedding an amber glow over the heather and bracken of the hills.

"I love that man," Baerd said, still gazing into the distance.

"I know," said Alessan. Slowly, Baerd turned back to him. They exchanged a look in silence.

"Senzio?" said Baerd.

Alessan nodded. "You will have to explain to Alienor how to set up the interception. These two will come west with me. You and Catriana and the Duke go north and then into Tregea. We start reaping what we've sown, Baerd. You know the timing as well as I do, and you'll know what to do until we meet again, who we'll want from the east. I'm not sure about Rovigo—I'll leave that to you."

"I'm not happy about separate roads," Baerd murmured.

"Neither am I, if you must know. If you have an alternative I'd be grateful to hear it."

Baerd shook his head. "What will you do?"

"Speak to some people on the way. See my mother. After that it depends on what I find. My own reaping in the west before summer comes."

Baerd glanced briefly at Devin and Erlein. "Try not to let yourself be hurt," he said.

Alessan gave his shrug. "She's dying, Baerd. And I've hurt her enough in eighteen years."

"You have not!" the other replied with sudden anger. "You only wound yourself if you think that way."

Alessan sighed. "She is dying unknown and alone in a Sanctuary of Eanna in a province called Lower Corte. She is not in the Palace by the Sea in Tigana. Do not say she has not been hurt."

"But not by you!" Baerd protested. "Why do you do this to yourself?"

Again the shrug. "I have made certain choices in a dozen years since we came back from Quileia. I am willing to accept that others may disagree with those choices." His eyes flicked to Erlein. "Leave it, Baerd. I promise not to let this unbalance me, even without you there. Devin will help if I need help."

Baerd grimaced behind his beard and looked as if he would pursue the matter further, but when he spoke again it was in a different voice. "You think this is it, then? You think it truly might happen now?"

"I think it *has* to happen this summer or it never will. Unless, I suppose, someone does kill Marius in Quileia and we go back to stasis here, with nothing at all to work with. Which would mean that my mother and a great many other people were right. In which case you and I will simply have to sail into Chiara harbor and storm the palace walls alone and kill Brandin of Ygrath and watch the Palm become an outpost of Barbadior's Empire. And what price Tigana then?"

He checked himself. Then continued in a lower voice: "Marius is the one wild card we have ever had, the one thing I've been waiting for and working for all these years. And he's just agreed to let us play him as we need. We have a chance. It may not hurt to do some praying, all of us, in the days to come. This has been long enough in arriving."

Baerd was very still. "Long enough," he echoed finally, and something in his voice sent a chill into Devin. "Eanna light your path through the Ember Days and beyond." He paused, glanced at Erlein. "All three of you."

Alessan's expression spoke a world of things. "And yours, the three of you," was all he said though, before he turned his horse and started away to the west.

Following him, Devin glanced back once and saw that Baerd had not moved. He sat astride his horse watching them, and the sunlight fell on his hair and beard burnishing them back toward the golden color Devin remembered from their first meeting. He was too far away for his expression to be discerned.

Devin raised a hand in farewell, palm spread wide and then, surprised and gladdened, saw Erlein abruptly do the same.

Baerd lifted one arm high in salute to them, then twitched his horse's reins and turned north to ride away.

Alessan, setting a steady pace into the setting sun, did not look back at all.

PART FOUR

THE PRICE OF BLOOD

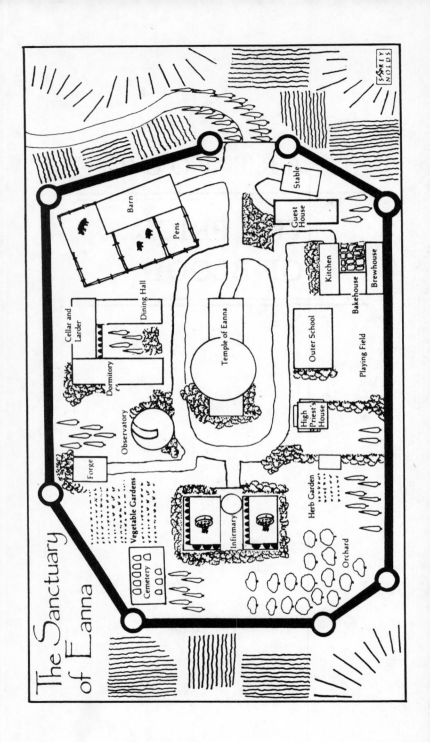

The Sanctuary of Eanna

SORLEY
NOLDS

Barn

Pens

Stable

Guest House

Kitchen

Bakehouse

Brewhouse

Cellar and Larder

Dining Hall

Dormitory

Temple of Eanna

Outer School

Playing Field

Observatory

Forge

High Priest's House

Herb Garden

Vegetable Gardens

Infirmary

Orchard

Cemetery

CHAPTER
· 13 ·

SOME TIME BEFORE DAWN—SHE WASN'T SURE WHAT HOUR it was—Dianora rose from bed and walked to the windows overlooking her balcony. In the end, she had not slept all night. Neither, as it happened, had her brother, a very long way to the south, fighting in the Ember war and then sharing the beginning of spring on a hilltop won from the Darkness.

She herself had shared nothing with anyone that night, lying alone in her bed, visited by ghosts and memories. Now she looked out upon a cold darkness that had little in it of springtime or the promise of growth to come. The late stars still shone though the moon had long since set. A wind blew in from off the sea. She could just make out the banners flapping from the masts of the ships in the harbor beyond the Ring Dive pier.

One of those ships was newly in from Ygrath. It had carried Isolla the singer here. It would not carry her back.

"Khav, my lady?" Scelto said quietly from behind her.

She nodded without turning. "Please. And then come sit with me, we have something to talk about." If she moved quickly enough, she thought, if she set it all in motion without giving herself time for hesitation or fear, she might possibly do this thing. Otherwise she was lost.

She could hear Scelto bustling efficiently in the small kitchen that was a part of her suite of rooms. The fire had been kept going all night. Ygrath might not observe the same spring and autumn rituals as the Palm, but Brandin had seldom interfered with local customs or religion, and Dianora never lit a new flame on any of the

Ember Days. Neither did most of the women in the saishan, if it came to that. The eastern wing of the palace would be a dark place after sunset for two more nights.

She thought about stepping out on the balcony, but it looked much too cold. There were no signs of life yet down below. She thought about Camena di Chiara. At sunrise they would probably bring him out, his bones broken, to die on a wheel in the sight of the people. She turned her mind away from that image too.

"Here is the khav," Scelto said. "I made it very strong," he added awkwardly.

She did turn at that, and her heart ached a little to see the helpless worry in his eyes. She knew how he would have grieved for her last night. The marks of sleeplessness were in his face; she supposed they were in her own as well. She could guess how she must look this morning. She forced a smile and accepted the mug he offered. It was warm to her hand and comforting, even before she drank.

She sat in one of the chairs by the window and motioned him to the other. He hesitated a moment and then sat down. She was silent, weighing her words. She realized, abruptly, that she had no idea how to do this subtly. So much, she thought wryly, for the cynical manipulator of the court.

Taking a deep breath, she said, "Scelto, I need to be out on the mountain this morning alone. I know all of the difficulties, but I have my reasons and they are important. How can we arrange it?"

His smooth brow furrowed. He said nothing though, and she realized that he was thinking about an answer to her question, not trying to judge or understand it. She had feared a different sort of reaction, but realized, belatedly, that she should not have. Never with him.

He said, "It will depend on whether they do the mountain run today."

Her heart swelled with love for him. He hadn't even asked her reasons. "Why would they not run it?" she asked stupidly, and realized the answer even as he replied.

"Camena," he said. "I don't know if the King will allow the spring run on the same day as an execution. If they *are* doing the race then you will be invited to come watch the ending from the King's pavilion in the meadow as you always are."

"I have to be alone," she repeated. "And up the mountain."

"Alone with me," he modified. It was almost a plea.

She sipped her khav. This was the difficult part. "Some of the way, Scelto," she said. "There is a thing I must do there by myself. I will have to leave you partway up."

She watched him wrestle with that. Before he could speak she added, "I would not say this if it were not necessary. There is no one I would rather have by my side."

She did not say what it was necessary *for* and she saw him fighting to hold back the question. He did hold it back though, and she knew what it would have cost him.

He rose. "I'll have to find out what is happening then. I'll be back soon. If they are running we will at least have an excuse to be outside. If they aren't, we'll have to think further on this."

She nodded gratefully and watched him go, neat and trim, infinitely reassuring in his competence. She finished her khav, looking out the window. It was still dark outside. She walked into the other room to wash and dress herself, doing so with some care, knowing it might matter today. She chose a simple brown woolen robe, and belted it at the waist. This was an Ember Day, not a time for splendor of apparel. There was a hood to hide her hair; that too might matter.

By the time she was done Scelto had returned. He had a queer expression on his face.

"They are running," he said. "And Camena is not going to be executed on the wheel."

"What happened to him?" she asked, feeling an instinctive dread.

Scelto hesitated. "The word is being put about that he has been granted a merciful death already. Because the actual conspiracy was from Ygrath and Camena was merely a victim, a tool."

She nodded. "And what has really happened."

Scelto's face was troubled. "This may be a thing you were better not to know, my lady."

It probably was, she thought. But she had come too far

in the night, and had too far yet to go. This was no morning for sheltering, or trying to seek shelter. "Perhaps," was all she said. "But I would prefer you to tell me, Scelto."

He said, after a moment: "I have been told that he is going to be . . . altered. Rhun is growing old and the King must have a Fool. It is necessary to have one in readiness, and it can take a long time, depending on the circumstances."

The circumstances, Dianora thought, sickened. Such as whether the Fool-in-waiting had been a healthy, gifted, normal young man with a love of his home.

Even understanding what the Fools of Ygrath were to their Kings, even grasping that Camena had forfeited his life by what he had done yesterday, she still could not stop her stomach from turning at the implications of Scelto's words. She remembered Rhun hacking at Isolla's body yesterday. She remembered Brandin's face. She forced her mind away from that. She couldn't afford to think about Brandin this morning. In fact, she was better off not thinking about anything at all.

"Have I been summoned yet?" she asked tersely.

"Not yet. You will be." She could hear tension in his voice; the news about Camena had evidently disturbed him as well.

"I know I will," she said. "I don't think we can wait though. If I go out with the others it will be impossible to slip away. What do you think would happen if we two tried to walk down together now?"

Her tone was steady and calm; Scelto's face grew thoughtful. "We can try," he said after a moment.

"Then come."

Her fear was very simple: if she waited too long, or considered this too much she would be paralyzed by doubt. The thing was to move, and to keep on moving, until she reached a certain place.

What would happen then, if anything, she would leave to the Triad's grace.

Her heart beating rapidly, she followed Scelto out of her rooms and into the main saishan corridor. The first thin streaks of light were showing now through the windows at the eastern end. The two of them went the other

way, passing two young castrates who were moving toward
Vencel's rooms. Dianora looked straight at them. She
was pleased—for the first time—to see fear spark in the
eyes of both of the boys. Today fear was a weapon, a
tool, and she would need all the tools she could find.

Scelto led her, not hurrying, down the wide stairway
towards the double doors that led to the outside world.
She caught up to him just as he rapped. When the guard
outside opened she stepped through without waiting for
his challenge or Scelto's announcement. She fixed him
with a cool glance as she went by, and saw his eyes widen
as he recognized her. She began walking down the long
hallway. As she went past the other guard she saw that
he was the young one she'd smiled at yesterday. Today
she did not smile.

Behind her she heard Scelto speak one quick, cryptic
sentence, and then another in answer to a question. Then
she heard his footsteps coming down the corridor. A
moment later the door swung shut behind them. Scelto
caught up to her.

"I think it will take a brave man to stop you today," he
said quietly. "They all know what happened yesterday. It
is a good morning to be trying this."

It was the *only* morning she would ever be trying this,
Dianora thought.

"What did you tell them?" she asked, continuing to
walk.

"The only thing I could think of. You are going to a
meeting with d'Eymon about what happened yesterday."

She slowed a little, considering that, and as she did,
the glimmerings of a proper plan came to her, like the
first faint illumination of the sun rising in the east above
the mountains.

"Good," she said, nodding her head. "Very good,
Scelto. That is exactly what I'm doing." Two other guards
walked past them, taking no notice at all. "Scelto," she
said, when they were alone again, "I need you to find
d'Eymon. Say I want to speak with him alone before we
all go out this afternoon for the end of the race. Tell him
I'll be waiting in the King's Garden two hours from
now."

Two hours might or might not be enough; she didn't

know. But somewhere in the vast expanse of the King's Garden on the north side of the palace she knew there was a gate that led out to the meadows, and then the slopes of Sangarios beyond.

Scelto stopped, forcing her to do the same.

"You are going to go without me, aren't you?" he said.

She would not lie to him. "I am," she said. "I expect to be back in time for that meeting. After you give him the message go back to the saishan. He doesn't know we're out already, so he'll have to send for me. Make sure the message goes directly to you, I don't care how."

"They usually do," he said quietly, clearly unhappy.

"I know that. When he does send we'll have our excuse for being out. Two hours from now come back down yourself. I should be in the garden with him. Look for us there."

"And if you aren't?"

She shrugged. "Stall. Hope. I *have* to do this, Scelto, I told you."

He looked at her a moment longer, and then nodded his head once. They went on. Just before reaching the sweep of the Grand Staircase on their left Scelto turned right and they went down a smaller stairwell to the ground level. It brought them out into another east-west corridor. There was no one there. The palace was only just beginning to stir.

She looked over at Scelto. Their eyes met. For a fleeting moment she was sorely tempted to confide in him, to make an ally of a friend. What could she say, though? How explain in the middle of a dawn corridor the dark night and the train of years that had led her here?

She put a hand on his shoulder and squeezed. "Go now," she said. "I'll be all right."

Without looking back she walked alone a little way down the hallway, pushed open the two glass doors leading to the labyrinth of the King's Garden, and went out into the grey, cold beginning of dawn.

It hadn't always been known as the King's Garden, nor had it always been as wild as it was now. The Grand Dukes of Chiara had shaped this pleasure ground for themselves over successive generations, and it had changed over the years as tastes and styles in the Island court had changed.

When Brandin of Ygrath had first arrived it had been a glittering exercise in topiary: hedges artfully trimmed in the shapes of birds and animals, trees precisely spaced and arranged throughout the enormous walled expanse of the garden, wide walks with sculpted benches at easy intervals, each one under a sejoia planted for fragrance and shade. There had been one tidy box-hedged maze with a lover's seat at the center, and rows and rows of flowers carefully arrayed in complementary colors.

Tame and boring, the King of Ygrath had labeled it the first time he walked through.

Within two years the garden had changed again. A great deal this time. The walkways were less wide now, dappled and overhung with leaves in summer and fall. They twisted seemingly at random through the densely planted groves of trees—brought down with some labor from the mountain slopes and the forests on the north side of the Island. Some of the sculpted benches remained, and the thick and fragrant flower beds, but the bird hedges and the animal bushes had been the first things to go, and the neat, symmetrically pruned shrubs and serrano bushes had been allowed to grow out, higher and darker, like the trees. The maze was gone: the whole of the garden was a maze now.

An underground stream had been tapped and diverted and now the sound of running water was everywhere. There were leafy pools one might stumble upon, with overhanging trees for shade in the summer's heat. The King's Garden was a strange place now, not overgrown and most certainly not neglected, but deliberately shaped to give a sense of stillness and isolation and even, at times, of danger.

Times such as this, with the dawn wind still cold and the scarcely risen sun just beginning to warm the air. Only the earliest buds were on the branches of the trees, and only the first flowers of the season—anemones and wild caiana roses—adding flashes of color to the wan morning. The winter trees stood tall and dark against the grey sky.

Dianora shivered and closed the glass doors behind

her. She took a deep breath of the sharp air and looked
up at the clouds piled high above the mountain, hiding
the peak of Sangarios. Over to the east the clouds were
beginning to break up; it would be a mild day later. Not
yet though. She stood at the edge of the wildness of an
end-of-winter garden and tried to guide herself towards
steadiness and calm.

She knew there was a gate in the northern wall, but
she wasn't sure she remembered where. Brandin had
showed it to her one summer's night years ago when they
had walked for miles aimlessly amid fireflies and the
drone of crickets and the sound of unseen water splashing in the darkness beyond the torchlit paths. He had
brought her to a gate he'd stumbled upon one day, half-
hidden by climbing vines and a rose bush. He had shown
it to her in the darkness, with torches behind them and
blue Ilarion overhead.

He had held her hand that night as they walked, she
remembered, and talked to her about herbs and the
properties of flowers. He had told her an Ygrathen fairy
tale of a forest princess born in some far distant other-
world, on an enchanted bed of snow-white flowers that
bloomed only in the dark.

Dianora shook her head, pushing the memory away,
and set off briskly down one of the smaller, pebbly paths
leading northeast through the trees. After twenty strides
she could no longer see the palace when she looked back.
Overhead the birds were beginning to sing. It was still
cold. She put up her hood, feeling, as she did so, like the
brown-robed priestess of some unknown sylvan god.

And thinking so, she prayed to the god she did know
and to Morian and Eanna, that the Triad might send her
wisdom and the clear heart she had come out this Ember
morning to find. She was intensely aware of what day this
was.

At almost exactly the same moment, Alessan, Prince
of Tigana was riding out from Castle Borso in the
Certandan highland towards a meeting in the Braccio
Pass that he thought might change the world.

Dianora walked past a bed of anemones, much too
small and delicate yet to pick. They were white, which
made them Eanna's. The red ones were Morian's, except

in Tregea where they were said to be stained by the blood of Adaon on his mountain. She stopped and looked down at the flowers, their fragile petals shaken by the breeze; but her thoughts were back with Brandin's fairy tale of the far away princess born under summer stars, cradled on such flowers.

She closed her eyes then, knowing that this would not do.

And slowly, deliberately, searching out pain as a spur, a goad, she built up a mental image of her father riding away, and then of her mother, and then of Baerd among the soldiers in the square. When she opened her eyes to go on there were no fairy tales in her heart.

The paths twisted hopelessly, but the main cloud mass was to the north over the mountain and she kept that in front of her as best she could. It was strange to be wandering like this, almost lost among the trees, and Dianora realized, with a start, that it had been a great many years since she'd last been so alone.

She had only two hours and a long way to go. She quickened her pace. A little later the sun came up on her right and the next time she looked up part of the sky was blue above her and gulls were wheeling against that blue. She pushed back her hood and shook her long hair free, and just then she saw the thick, high grey stone of the northern wall through a screen of olive trees.

Vines and clumps of laren moss were growing along the wall, purple and dark green. The path ended at the olives, forking east and west. She stood a moment, irresolute, trying to orient herself within a memory of summer and torches at night. Then she shrugged and went west, because her heart always did that.

Ten minutes later, winding past a pool and a ruffled reflection of white clouds within it, Dianora came to the gate.

She stopped, suddenly cold again, though the morning was warmer now with the sun. She looked at the arched shape and the rusted iron hinges. The gate was very old; there seemed to have been something carved on it once, but whatever image or symbol had been there was almost entirely worn away. The gate was overgrown with ivy and vines. The rose bush she remembered was bare yet on this first day of spring, but the thorns were long and sharp. She saw the heavy bolt, as rusted as the hinges. There was no lock, but she was suddenly uncertain whether she would even be able to move the corroded bolt. She wondered who had last gone through this gate into the meadows beyond. Who and when and why. She thought about climbing, and looked up. The wall was ten feet high, but she thought there might be hand and toeholds there. She was about to move forward when she heard a sound behind her.

Thinking about it afterwards she tried to understand why she hadn't been more frightened than she was. Somewhere in her mind, she decided, she must have thought that this might happen. The grey rock on the mountainside had been only a starting point. There was no reason in the world to expect that she might find that rock, or find what she needed there.

She turned in the King's Garden, alone among the trees and the earliest flowers, and saw the riselka combing her long green hair beside a pool.

They are only found when they want to be, she remembered. And then she had another thought and she looked quickly around to see if anyone else was there.

They were quite alone in the garden though, or in this part of the garden. The riselka smiled, as if reading Dianora's mind. She was naked, small and very slender, but her hair was so long it almost served her as a robe. Her skin was as translucent as Brandin had said it had been and the eyes were enormous, almost frighteningly so, pale as milk in the pale white face.

She looks like you, Brandin had said. Or, no. *She reminded me of you,* was what he'd said. And in an eerie, chilling fashion Dianora had a sense of what he meant. She had a memory of herself in the year Tigana fell, too thin and pale, her eyes almost as huge as these in the hollows of her face.

But Brandin had never seen or known her then.

Dianora shivered. The riselka's smile deepened. There was nothing of warmth in her, or comfort. Dianora didn't know if she had expected either of those. She didn't really know what she had expected to find. She had come for the clear path of the old foretelling verse, and it seemed that if she was to find it, it would be here among the intricately winding ways of the King's Garden.

The riselka was beautiful, heartbreakingly so, in a fashion that had little to do with mortal beauty. Dianora's mouth was dry. She didn't even try to speak. She stood very still in her plain brown robe, her own dark hair unbound and falling down her back, and she watched the riselka lay a bone-white comb down on the stone bench by the pool and motion to her.

Slowly, her hands beginning to tremble, Dianora walked off the path and under an arch of trees to stand before that pale, elusive creature of legend. She was so near she could see the green hair shine in the soft morning light. The pale eyes had shadings to them, and depth. The riselka lifted one hand, its fingers longer and more slender than any mortal's could be, and she brought it up to Dianora's face and touched her.

The touch was cool, but not so cold as she might have feared. Gently, the riselka stroked her cheek and throat. And then, the hieratic, alien smile deepening again, she slipped her hand further down, undid a button of Dianora's robe, and reached within to touch her breasts. One, and then the other, not hurrying, smiling that entirely secret smile all the while.

Dianora was trembling; she could not make herself stop. Incredulous and afraid, she felt her body respond involuntarily to the exploration of that touch. She could see the riselka's childlike breasts half-hidden beneath the curtain of hair. Her knees were weak suddenly. The riselka's smile showed small, sharp, very white teeth. Dianora swallowed, feeling a hurt inside her she could not even begin to understand. She shook her head mutely, unable to speak. She felt herself beginning to weep.

The riselka's smile faded. She withdrew her hand and, almost apologetically it seemed, did up the robe again. She reached, as gently as before, and touched one of the tears on Dianora's cheek. Then she brought her finger to her lips and tasted it.

She *is* a child, Dianora thought suddenly, a thought cast up on the beach of her mind as if by a tide. And even as it came to her, she knew that this was true, however many years this creature might have lived. She

wondered if this was the same slender, numinous figure
Baerd had met under moonlight by the sea the night he
went away.

The riselka touched and then tasted another tear. Her
eyes were so large Dianora had a sense that she could fall
into them and never come out again. It was a deeply
seductive imagining, a pathway to oblivion. She looked
for another moment and then slowly, with an effort, shook
her head again.

"Please?" she said then, whispered it, needing, and
afraid of her need. Afraid that words or need or longing—
anything—could drive a riselka away.

The green-haired creature turned, and Dianora's hands
clenched at her sides. But the riselka looked back over
her shoulder, grave now, unsmiling, and Dianora understood that she was to follow.

They came to the edge of the pool. The riselka was
looking down into the water and so Dianora did the
same. She saw a reflection of blue sky overhead, of a
single white gull slicing across the space above the pool,
dark green cypresses like sentinels and the branches of
other trees not yet in leaf. And even as she looked, she
realized, with a chill like winter come back too soon,
what was wrong. The wind was blowing above them and
all around, she could hear it among the trees and feel it
on her face and in her hair, but the water of the pool was
like the glass of her mirror, absolutely calm, unruffled by
so much as a tendril of the breeze or any movement in its
own depths.

Dianora drew back from the edge and turned to the
riselka. The creature was looking at her, the green hair
lifted by the breeze and blown back from her small white
face. The eyes were darker now, cloudy, and she no
longer looked like a child. She looked like a power of the
natural world, or an emissary of such a power, and not
one with any warmth for mortal man or woman. No
kindness or shelter there. But Dianora, fighting a rising
fear, reminded herself that she had not come here for
shelter, but for a signing of her road, and she saw then
that the riselka held a small white stone in her hand, and
she saw her throw that stone into the pool.

No ripples. No movement at all. The stone sank without a trace of its passage. But the surface of the water changed soon after, and darkened, and then the reflections were gone. No cypresses. No morning circle of sky overhead. No bare trees framing the slant of gulls. The water had grown too dark, it cast nothing back. But Dianora felt the riselka take her hand and draw her gently but inexorably back to the edge of the pool, and she looked down, having come out from the saishan to find this truth, this signing. And in the dark waters she saw a reflection.

Not herself or the riselka, nor anything at all of the King's Garden on this first of the Ember Days. Instead, an image of another season, late spring or summer, another place, bright with color, a great many people gathered, and, somehow, she could even hear the sound of them in the image, and beneath that sound, constantly, was the surge and sigh of waves.

And in the depths of the pool Dianora saw an image of herself, clad in a robe green as the riselka's hair, moving alone between those gathered people. And then she saw, in the pool, where her steps were leading her.

Fear touched her in that moment with an icy hand for one second and then was gone. She felt her racing heartbeat slow, and then grow slower yet. A deep calm came over her. And a moment later, not without its burden of sorrow, came acceptance. For years her nights had known dreams of such an ending. This morning she had come out of the saishan looking for this certainty. And now, above this pool, her path came clear to her at last and Dianora saw that it led to the sea.

The sounds of gathered people faded away, and then all the images, the bright sun of summer. The pool was dark again giving nothing back at all.

Some time later, it might have been moments or hours, Dianora looked up again. The riselka was still beside her. Dianora looked into the pale eyes, so much lighter than the enchanted waters but seemingly as deep, and she saw herself as a child again, so many years ago. Yet not so many, a blink of an eye or the moment it took an autumn leaf to fall, as this creature would measure time.

"Thank you," she whispered. And: "I understand."

And she stood very still, not flinching at all, as the

riselka rose up on tiptoe and kissed her, soft as the wing
of a butterfly, upon the lips. There was no hint of desire
this time, in the giving or receiving. This was the aftermath, the consummation had come and gone. The riselka's
mouth tasted of salt. The salt, Dianora knew, of her own
tears. She no longer felt any fear at all; only a quiet
sadness like a smooth stone in the heart.

She heard a ripple of sound and turned back to the
pool. The cypresses were reflected again, their images
ruffled and broken now by the movement of the water in
the wind.

When she looked away again, pushing her hair back
from her face, she saw that she was alone.

When she came back out to the open space before the
palace doors d'Eymon was waiting for her, dressed formally in grey, his Seal of Office about his neck. He was
sitting on one of the stone benches, his staff resting
beside him. Scelto hovered by the doors, and Dianora
saw the flash of relief he could not hide when she came
out from among the trees.

She stopped and looked at the Chancellor allowing a
slight smile to show on her face. It was artifice of course,
but an act she could do unconsciously by now. In
d'Eymon's normally inscrutable expression she read edginess and anger, and other signs of what had happened
yesterday. He would probably be spoiling for a fight, she
guessed. It was difficult, amazingly difficult, to switch
back to the manners and affairs of state. It was also
something that had to be done.

"You were late," she said mildly, walking towards
him. He had risen, with perfect courtesy, as she approached. "I went walking in the garden. There are
anemones beginning already."

"I was precisely on time," d'Eymon said.

She might once have been intimidated, but not now.
He would be wearing the Seal as an attempt to reinforce
his authority, but she knew how badly yesterday would
have unsettled him. She was fairly certain he would have
offered to kill himself last night; he was a man for whom
the old traditions mattered. In any case, she was armored
against him: she had seen a riselka this morning.

"Then I must have been early," she said carelessly. "Forgive me. It is good to see you looking so well after yesterday's . . . confusions. Have you been waiting long?"

"Long enough. You wanted to talk about yesterday, I gather. What is it?" Dianora didn't think she had ever heard an inconsequential remark from d'Eymon, let alone a pleasantry.

Refusing to be rushed she sat down on the bench he had just vacated and brushed her brown robe smooth over her knees. She clasped her fingers in her lap and looked up, letting her expression grow suddenly as cold as his own.

"He almost died yesterday," she said flatly, deciding only in that moment what her tack would be. "He would have died. Do you know why, Chancellor?" She didn't wait for his answer. "The King almost died because your people were too complacent or too slovenly to bother searching a party of Ygrathens. What did you think? That danger could only come from the Palm? I expect yesterday's guards to be dealt with, d'Eymon. And soon."

The use of his name and not his title was deliberate. He opened his mouth and closed it, visibly biting back a swift retort. She was pushing things, Triad knew how hard she was pushing with this, but if ever there was going to be a chance for her to do so, this would be it. D'Eymon's face was white with anger and shock. He took a deep breath to control himself.

"They have been dealt with already," he said. "They are dead."

She hadn't expected that. She managed, with an effort, to keep her discomfiture out of her eyes. "There is more," she went on pressing her advantage. "I want to know why Camena di Chiara was not watched when he went to Ygrath last year."

"He *was* watched. What would you have had us do? You know who was behind yesterday's attack. You heard."

"We all heard. Why did you not know about Isolla and the Queen?" This time the bite she put into the words was real, not merely tactical.

For the first time she saw a flicker of hesitation in his eyes. He fingered his Seal, then seemed to become aware that he was doing so and dropped his hand to his side. There was a brief silence.

"I did know," he said finally. His eyes met her own, a question in them like an angry challenge.

"I see," said Dianora a moment later, and looked away. The sun was higher now, slanting across most of the clearing. If she moved a little along the bench its warmth would fall upon her. The harsh, unspoken question in d'Eymon's eyes hung in the air: Would *you* have told the King, knowing these things about his Queen?

Dianora was silent, tracking implications to their endings. With this admission, she realized, d'Eymon was hers, if he hadn't already been so after his failure yesterday and what she had done to save the King. She was also, she thought, in fairly immediate danger as a consequence. The Chancellor was not a man to be treated lightly, ever. Most of the saishan had their suspicions as to how Chloese di Chiara had died ten years ago, and why.

She looked up, and let her rising anger keep the anxiety from showing. "Wonderful," she said acidly. "Such efficient security. And now, of course, because of what I was forced to do your pet courtier Neso simply *has* to receive the posting in Asoli, doesn't he. With a wound of honor earned saving the life of the King. How marvelously clever of you, d'Eymon!"

She had miscalculated. For the first time he smiled, a narrow, mirthless expression. "Is *that* what this is about?" he asked softly.

She bit back a swift denial. It was not inconvenient for him to think so, she realized.

"Among other things," she admitted, as if grudgingly. "I want to know why you have been favoring him for the Asoli posting. I had been meaning to talk to you about this."

"I thought as much," he said, a measure of his usual complacency returning. "I have also been keeping track of some—not all, I have no doubt—of the gifts Scelto has been receiving in your name these past weeks. That was a splendid necklace yesterday, by the way. Did Neso's money pay for it? In an attempt to have you win me over to his side?"

He was immensely well-informed, and he was shrewd. She had always known these things. It was never wise to underestimate the Chancellor.

"It helped pay for it," she said briefly. "You haven't answered my question. Why do you favor him? You must know what sort of man he is."

"Of course I know," d'Eymon replied impatiently. "Why do you think I want him out of here? I want him posted to Asoli because I don't trust him at court. I want him away from the King and in a place where he can be killed without undue inconvenience. I trust that answers your question?"

She swallowed. *Never, ever underestimate him,* she told herself again. "It does," she said. "Killed by whom?"

"That should be obvious. It will be put about that the Asolini did it themselves. I expect it will not take Neso long to give them cause."

"Of course. And then?"

"And then the King will investigate and find that Neso was guilty of gross corruption, which we need not doubt he will be. We execute some man or other for the murder but the King declares his firm renunciation of Neso's methods and greed. He appoints a new Taxing Master and promises fairer measures in the future. I think that should quiet affairs in north Asoli for a time."

"Good," said Dianora, trying to ignore the casual indifference of that *some man or other*. "And very tidy. I have only one thing to add: the new officer will be Rhamanus." She was taking another risk, she knew. When it came down to bedrock, she was a captive and a concubine, and he was the Chancellor of Ygrath and of the Western Palm. On the other hand, there were other ways to measure the balance here, and she fought to focus on those.

D'Eymon looked coolly down at her. She kept her gaze on his, her eyes wide and disingenuous.

"It has long amused me," he said at length, "that you so favored the man who captured you. One would think you hadn't minded, that you *wanted* to come."

Perilously, uncannily near to the mark, but she could see he was baiting her, not serious in his thrust. She forced herself to relax, and smiled. "How could I mind

being here? I'd never have had a chance at pleasant
meetings such as this. And in any case," she let her tone
change, "I *do* favor him, yes. On behalf of the people
of this peninsula I do. And you know that that will
always be my concern, Chancellor. He is a decent man.
There are not many such Ygrathens, I'm afraid."

He was silent a moment. Then: "There are more than
you think." But before she could manage to interpret
either his words or the surprising voice in which they were
spoken, he added, "I seriously thought of having you
poisoned last night. Either that, or suggesting you be
freed and made a citizen of Ygrath."

"What extremes, my dear!" She could feel herself growing cold though. "Didn't you teach us all that balance is
everything?"

"I did," he said soberly, not rising to her bait. He
never did. "Have you *any* idea what you've done to the
equilibrium at this court?"

"What," she said with real asperity, "would you have
preferred me to do yesterday?"

"That is not at all the point. Obviously." There was a
rare spot of color in his cheeks. When he resumed,
though, it was in his usual tones. "I was thinking of
Rhamanus for Asoli myself. It shall be as you suggest. In
the meantime, I very nearly forgot to mention that the
King has sent for you. I intercepted the message before it
reached the saishan. He will be waiting in the library."

She shot to her feet, as agitated as he must have
known she would be. "How long ago?" she asked quickly.

"Not very. Why? You don't seem to mind being late.
There are anemones in the garden, you could tell him
that."

"I could tell him some other things as well, d'Eymon."
Anger almost choked her. She fought for control.

"And so could I. And so, I suppose, could Solores. We
seldom do, do we? The balance, as you have just pointed
out, is everything. That is why I should still be very
careful, Dianora, despite what happened yesterday. The
balance is all. Do not forget it."

She tried to think of a response, a last word, but failed.
Her mind was whirling. He had spoken of killing her, of
freeing her, had agreed with her choice for Asoli, and

then threatened her again. All in a span of minutes! And all the while the King had been waiting for her, and d'Eymon had known.

She turned, abruptly and dismally conscious of her nondescript robe and the fact that she had no time to go back up to the saishan and change. She could feel herself flushing with anger and anxiety.

Scelto had evidently overheard the Chancellor's last remarks. His eyes above the broken nose were vividly concerned and apologetic, though with d'Eymon intercepting the message there was nothing he could have done.

She stopped by the palace doors and looked back. The Chancellor stood alone in the garden leaning upon his stick, a tall, gray, thin figure against the bare trees. The sky above him had turned overcast again. *Of course it has*, Dianora thought spitefully.

Then she remembered the pool and her mood changed. What did these court maneuvers matter, in the end? D'Eymon was only doing what he had to do, and so now, would she. She had seen her path. She found herself able to smile, letting that inner quiet descend upon her again, though with a stone of sorrow at its center still. She sank low in a very formal curtsey. D'Eymon, taken aback, sketched an awkward bow.

Dianora turned and went through the doors that Scelto was holding for her. She went back down the corridor and up the stairs, along a north-south hallway and past two heavy doors. She stopped in front of the third pair of doors. Out of reflex and habit more than anything else she checked her reflection in the bronze shield that hung on the wall. She adjusted her robe and pushed both hands through her hopelessly wind-blown hair.

Then she knocked on the library doors and entered, holding hard to her calm and the vision of the pool, a round stone of knowledge and sorrow in her heart that she hoped would anchor it in her breast and keep it from flying away.

Brandin was standing with his back to the door looking at a very old map of the then known world that hung above the larger of the fires. He did not turn. She looked up at the map. On it, the Peninsula of the Palm and even the larger land mass of Quileia beyond the mountains running all the way south to the Ice, were dwarfed by the size of Barbadior and its Empire to the east and by Ygrath to the west overseas.

The velvet window curtains of the library were drawn against the morning light and a fire was blazing, which bothered her. She found it difficult to deal with flames on an Ember Day. Brandin held a fire-iron in one hand. He was dressed as carelessly as she, in black riding clothes and boots. His boots were muddy; he must have been out riding very early.

She put the encounter with d'Eymon behind her, but not the riselka in the garden. This man was the center of her life; whatever else had changed that had not, but the riselka's vision had offered her a path, and Brandin had let her lie alone and awake all last night.

She said, "Forgive me, my lord. I was with the Chancellor this morning and he chose to only just now tell me you were waiting here."

"Why were you meeting with him?" The nuanced, familiar voice was only mildly interested. He seemed engrossed in the map.

She did not lie to the King. "The Taxing Master question in Asoli. I wanted to know why he favored Neso."

There was a faint hint of amusement in his voice. "I'm sure d'Eymon told you something plausible." He turned finally, and gazed at her for the first time. He looked exactly the same as he always did, and she knew what always happened when their glances first met.

But she had seen a riselka an hour ago and something seemed to have changed. Her calm did not leave her; her heart stayed home. She closed her eyes for an instant, but more to acknowledge the meaning of that change and the passing of a long truth than anything else. She felt that she would weep, for many reasons, if she were not extremely careful now.

Brandin sank into a chair by the fire. He looked tired, as much as anything. It showed only in small ways, but she had known him a long time. "I *will* have to give it to Neso now," he said. "I think you know that. I'm sorry."

Some things, it seemed, had not changed: always that grave, unexpected courtesy when he spoke to her of such things. What need had the King of Ygrath to apologize to her for choosing one of his courtiers over another? She moved into the room, clinging to her resolution, and at his gesture she took the chair opposite his. Brandin's eyes rested on her with an odd, almost a detached scrutiny. She wondered what he would see.

She heard a sound from the far end of the room and, glancing over, saw Rhun sitting by the second fire, aimlessly leafing through a picture-book. His presence reminded her of something, and she felt her anger suddenly come back.

"Of *course* you have to offer it to Neso," she said. "Asoli is his prize for gallantry in the service of his King." He scarcely responded. Briefly his mouth quirked, his expression mildly ironic; he still seemed preoccupied though, only half attending to what she said.

"Gallantry, courage. They'll call it something of that sort," he said absently. "Not getting out of the way in time, it really was. D'Eymon was already arranging last night to have word spread that it was Neso who saved my life."

She would not rise to that. She refused. She didn't even understand why he was saying this to her.

She said, instead, looking across the room at Rhun, not at the King: "That makes sense, and you must surely know that I don't care. What I do *not* understand is why you are putting out lies about Camena's fate." She took a breath, and then plunged ahead. "I know the truth. It is such an ugly, vicious thing to do. If you must prepare a Fool to follow Rhun, why mar a whole man and a healthy one? Why do such a thing?"

He did not answer for a long time and she was afraid to look at him. Rhun, too far away to hear, and nonetheless stopped leafing through his book and was looking over at them.

"As it happens, there are precedents," was what Brandin said at length, his tone still mild. But then, a moment later, he added, "I should probably have taken Scelto away from you a long time ago. You both learn too much, too quickly."

She opened her mouth, but no words came out. What could she say? She had asked for this. For exactly this.

But then, glancing out of the corner of her eye, she saw that Brandin was smiling. An odd smile, and there was something strange about his eyes as he looked at her. He said, "As it also happens, Scelto would have been right this morning, but his tidings are wrong by now."

"What do you mean?" She felt the stirrings of a genuine uneasiness. There was a strangeness to his manner this morning that she could not lay a finger on. It was more than tiredness though, she knew that much.

"I rescinded yesterday's orders after my ride," Brandin said quietly. "Camena is probably dead by now. An easy death. Exactly as word has been put about."

She discovered that her hands were clutching each other in her lap. She said fatuously, without thinking, "Is this true?"

He only raised his eyebrows, but she felt herself flush deep red. "I have no need to deceive you, Dianora. I told them to arrange for witnesses among the Chiarans, so there would be no doubt. What would confirm it for you: shall I have his head sent to your rooms?"

She looked down again, thinking of Isolla's head bursting like a smashed fruit. She swallowed; he had done that with a gesture of his hand. She looked back at the King. Mutely she shook her head. What had happened on that ride? What was happening here?

Then, abruptly, she remembered what else had occurred to him yesterday. On the mountainside, at a place where a grey rock stood beside the runners' track. *One man sees a riselka: his path forks there.*

Brandin turned back towards the fire, one leg crossed over the other. He laid the point of the iron down on the hearthstone, leaning it against his chair.

"You haven't asked me why I changed the orders. That's unlike you, Dianora."

"I'm afraid to," she said, truthfully.

He glanced over at that, his dark brows level now, the gray eyes intimidating with their intelligence. "That's unlike you as well."

"You aren't very . . .like yourself either this morning."

"Fair enough," he said quietly. He looked at her for a moment in silence, then seemed to consider something else. "Tell me, did d'Eymon make things difficult for you just now? Did he . . . warn you, or threaten?"

It *wasn't* sorcery, she told herself fiercely. Not mind-reading. It was only Brandin being what he was, aware of all the nuances that affected those in their orbits around him.

"Not directly," she said awkwardly. Once she might have seen this as an opportunity, but the mood this morning was so strange. "He was . . . upset about yester-day. Afraid, I think, of balances shifting here at the court. Once word is safely out that it was Neso who saved your life I think the Chancellor will be easier. It won't be a difficult story for him to spread; things hap-pened very fast. I doubt anyone saw it clearly."

This time, Brandin's smile as he listened was one she knew and cherished: equal to equal, their minds sharing the track of a complex thought. But when she finished, his expression changed.

"I did," he said. "I saw it clearly."

She looked away and down again, at her hands in her lap. *Your path is clear now,* she told herself as sternly as she could. *Remember that.* She had been offered a vision of herself in green beside the sea. And her heart was her own now after last night. There was a stone holding it there, safe within her breast.

Brandin said, "It would be easy to tell the Neso story, I agree. But I did a great deal of thinking last night and then on my ride this morning. I'll be talking to d'Eymon later today, after we watch the runners come home. The tale that goes around will be the true one, Dianora."

She wasn't sure she had heard him rightly, and then she *was* sure, and something seemed to reach a brim and then spill over a little, like an overflowing wineglass inside her.

"You should go riding more often," she mumbled. He heard. He laughed softly but she didn't look up. She had a very strong sense that she couldn't afford to look up.

"Why?" she asked, intent on her interlocked fingers. "Why to both things, then: Camena's fate, and now this?"

He was silent so long that eventually she did glance up, cautiously. He had turned back to the fire though, and was prodding it with the iron. On the far side of the room Rhun had closed his book and was now standing beside his table looking over at the two of them. He was dressed in black, of course. Exactly like the King.

"Did I ever tell you," said Brandin of Ygrath, very softly, "the legend my nurse used to tell me as a child about Finavir?"

Her mouth was dry again. Something in his tone, the way he was sitting, the discontinuity of his reply.

"No," she said. She tried to think of something witty to add, but failed.

"Finavir, or Finvair," he went on, not really waiting for her response, not looking over at her. "When I grew older and looked in the books of such tales it was written either way, and in one or two other fashions sometimes. That often happens with the stories that come from before the days when we wrote things down."

He leaned the iron against the chair arm again and sat back, still gazing into the flames. Rhun had walked a little nearer to them, as if drawn by the story. He was leaning against one of the heavy window draperies now, kneading a bunched fold of it in both hands.

Brandin said, "In Ygrath the tale is sometimes told and sometimes believed that this world of ours, both here in the southern lands and north beyond the deserts and the rain forests—whatever lies there—is but one of many worlds the gods sent into Time. The others are said to be far off, scattered among the stars, invisible to us."

"There has been such a belief here as well," Dianora said quietly when he paused. "In Certando. In the highlands they once had a teaching that was much the same, though the priests of the Triad burned people for saying as much." It was true; there had been mass burnings for the Carlozzini heresy in the plague years, long ago.

Brandin said, "We never burned or wheeled people for that thought. They were laughed at sometimes, but that is another thing. What my nurse used to tell me was what her mother told her, and her mother's mother before, I have no doubt: that some of us are born over and again into various of these worlds until, at the last, if we have earned it by the manner of our lives, we are born a final time into Finavir or Finvair which is the nearest of all the worlds to where the true gods dwell."

"And after that?" she asked. His quiet words seemed to have become a part of the unfolding spell of this day.

"After, no one knew, or would tell me. Nor did any of the parchments and books I read when I grew older." He shifted in his seat, his beautiful hands resting on the carved arms of the chair. "I never liked my nurse's legend of Finavir. There are other kinds of stories, some of them quite different and many of them I loved, but for some reason that one stayed with me. It bothered me. It seemed to make our lives here merely a prelude, inconsequential in themselves, of importance only for where they would lead us next. I have always needed to feel that what I am doing matters, here and now."

"I think I would agree with you," she said. Her own hands were gentle in her lap now; he had shaped a different mood. "But why are you telling me this, if you have never liked the story?"

The simplest of questions.

And Brandin said, "Because during the nights this past year and more I have had recurring dreams of being reborn far away from all of this, in Finavir." He looked straight at her then for the first time since beginning the tale, and his grey eyes were calm and his voice was steady as he said: "And in all of those dreams you have been at my side and nothing has held us apart, and no one has come between."

She had had no warning. None at all, though perhaps the clues had been there all along and she too blind to see. And suddenly she *was* blind now, helpless tears of shock and wonder overflowing in her eyes and a desperate, urgent hammering that she knew to be her heart.

Brandin said, "Dianora, I needed you so much last night I frightened myself. I did not send for you only because I had to somehow try to come to terms with what happened to me when you blocked Camena's arrow. Solores was a court deception, no more than that: so they might not think me unmanned by danger. I spent the whole night pacing or at my desk, trying to riddle out where my life has now come. What it *means* that my wife and only living son should try to kill me, and fail only because of you. And thinking about that, consumed by it, I only realized near dawn that I had left you alone all night. My dear, will you ever forgive me for that?"

I want time to stop, she was thinking, wiping vainly at her tears, trying to see him clearly. *I want never to leave this room, I want to hear these words spoken over and over, endlessly, until I die.*

"I made a decision on my ride," he said. "I was thinking about what Isolla had said and I was finally able to accept that she was right. Since I will not, since I cannot possibly change what I am committed to doing here, I must be prepared to pay all of the price myself, not through others in Ygrath."

She was shaking, quite unable to stop her tears. He had not touched her, or even moved towards her. Behind him Rhun's face was a twisted mask of pain and need, and something else. The thing she sometimes saw there, and could not face. She closed her eyes.

"What will you do?" she whispered. It was hard to speak.

And then he told her. All of it. Named for her the fork in the road he had chosen. She listened, her tears falling more slowly now, welling up from an over-full heart, and at length she came to understand that the wheel was coming full circle.

Listening to Brandin's grave voice over the crackle of flames on an Ember Day, Dianora saw only images of water in her mind. The dark waters of the pool in the garden, and the vision of the sea she'd been given there. And though she had no gift of foreknowing she could see where his words were taking them, taking them all, and now she understood the showing of the pool.

She searched her heart and knew, with an enormous grief, that it was his, it had not come back to her after all. Yet even so, and most terribly of all, she knew what was about to come, what she was going to do.

She had dreamt on other nights alone through her years in the saishan of finding a path like the one that was opening for her now with the words he spoke. At one point, listening to him, thinking thus, she could bear the physical distance between them no longer. She moved from her chair to the carpet at his feet and laid her head in his lap. He touched her hair and began stroking it, down and down, ceaselessly, as he spoke of what had come to him in the night and on his ride; spoke of being willing, finally, to accept the price of what he was doing here in the Palm; and spoke to her about the one thing she could never have made herself ready for. About love.

She wept quietly, she could not stop weeping as his words continued to flow, as the fire slowly died on the hearth. She wept for love of him, and for her family and her home, for the innocence she had lost to the years and for all that he had lost, and she wept most bitterly of all for the betrayals yet to come. All the betrayals that lay waiting outside this room where time, which would not stop, was going to carry them.

CHAPTER
• 14 •

"RIDE!" ALESSAN CRIED, POINTING TOWARDS A GAP in the hills. "There's a village beyond!"

Devin swore, lowered his head over his horse's neck, and dug his heels into the animal's flanks, following Erlein di Senzio west towards the gap and the low red disk of the sun.

Behind him, thundering out of the brown twilight hills, were at least eight, possibly a dozen brigands of the highlands. Devin hadn't looked back, after their first startled glimpse of the outlaws and the shouted command to halt.

He didn't think they had a chance, however close this village might be. They had been riding at a bone-jarring pace for hours and the horses Alienor had given them were tired. If this was to be a flat-out race against fresh-mounted outlaws they were probably dead. He gritted his teeth and rode, ignoring the ache in his leg and the sting of reopened cuts from his leap in the mountains earlier that day.

The wind whistled past him as they rode. He saw Alessan turn in his saddle, an arrow notched to his fully drawn bow. The Prince fired backwards once and then again into the twilight, his muscles ridged and corded with the effort. An improbable, desperate attempt at such speed in the wind.

Two men screamed. Devin quickly looked back and saw one of them fall. A handful of erratic arrows dropped well short of the three of them.

"They've slowed!" Erlein rasped, glancing back as well. "How far to this village!"

"Through the gap and twenty minutes beyond! Ride!"
Alessan did not shoot again, bending low to urge more
speed from his own grey. They fled into the wind along
the track of the sun, between the shadowy bulk of two
heathery hills and into the gap between.

They didn't get out.

Just where the path bent to follow the curve of the
encroaching ridges eight riders were waiting in a line
across the gap, bows calmly leveled at the three of them.

They pulled their horses to rearing halts. Devin flung a
glance back over his shoulder and saw the pursuing outlaws entering the pass behind them. There was one rider-
less horse, and another man clutched at his shoulder
where an arrow was still embedded.

He looked at Alessan, saw the desperate, defiant look
in the Prince's eye.

"Don't be a fool!" Erlein snapped. "You can't run
through and you can't kill this many men."

"I can try," Alessan said, his eyes darting across the
defile and up the steep hills on either side, wild to find a
way out. He had stopped his horse though, and did not
raise the bow.

"Straight into a trap. What a splendid ending to two
decades of dreaming!" His voice was corrosively bitter,
raw with self-laceration.

It was true though, Devin realized, rather too late.
This pass between the hills was a natural place for an
ambush, and the Triad knew there were enough outlaws
in the wilds of southern Certando, where even the Barbadian mercenaries seldom went, and honest men were
never abroad this close to the fall of night. On the other
hand, they hadn't had much choice, given how far they
had to go, and how fast.

It didn't seem as if they were going to get there. Or
anywhere. There was still enough light to make out the
outlaws, and their appearance did not reassure. Their
clothing might be random and carelessly worn, but the
horses were far from the beaten-down creatures most
brigands rode. The men in front of them looked disciplined, and the weaponry leveled at the three of them
was formidable. This had also been, very clearly, a carefully laid trap.

One man rode a few paces forward from the silent line. "Release your bows," he said with easy authority. "I don't like talking with armed men."

"Neither do I," Alessan replied grimly, staring at the man. But a moment later he let his bow fall to the ground. Beside Devin, Erlein did the same.

"And the boy," the outlaw leader said, still softly. He was a big man of middle years, with a large face and a full beard that showed deep red in the waning light. He wore a dark wide-brimmed hat that hid his eyes.

"I don't carry a bow," Devin said shortly, letting fall his sword.

There was mocking laughter at that from the men in front of them.

"Magian, why were your men in arrow range?" The bearded man said, more loudly now. He himself had not laughed. "You knew my instructions. You know how we do this."

"I didn't think we were," came an angry voice behind them, amid a clattering of hooves. Their pursuers had come up. The trap was closed, before and behind. "He fired a long way in half-light and wind. He was lucky, Ducas."

"He wouldn't have had a chance to be lucky if you had done your job properly. Where's Abhar?"

"Took an arrow in the thigh and fell. Torre's gone back to bring him."

"Waste," the red-bearded man scowled. "I don't like waste." He was a dark, bulky presence, silhouetted against the low sun. Behind him the other seven riders kept their bows leveled.

Alessan said, "If waste offends you, you won't like this evening's work at all. We have nothing to give you beyond our weapons. Or our lives, if you are the sort who kill for pleasure."

"Sometimes," the man named Ducas said, not raising his voice. He sounded unsettlingly calm, Devin thought, and very much in control of his band. "Will my two men die? Do you use poisoned arrows?"

Alessan's expression was contemptuous. "Not even against the Barbadians. Why? Do you?"

"Sometimes," the outlaw leader said again. "Especially against the Barbadians. These *are* the highlands, after all." He smiled for the first time, a cold, wolfish grin. Devin had a sudden sense that he wouldn't want to have this man's memories, or his dreams.

Alessan said nothing. It was growing darker in the pass. Devin saw him glance over at Erlein, a sharp query in his face. The wizard shook his head, a minute, almost invisible gesture. "Too many," he whispered. "And besides—"

"The grey-haired one is a wizard!" came an emphatic voice from the line beyond Ducas.

A chunky, round-faced man moved his horse forward beside the leader's. "Don't even think of it," he continued, looking straight at Erlein. "I could block anything you tried." Startled, Devin glanced at the man's hands, but at this distance it was too dark for him to see if two fingers were missing. They would have to be though.

They had come upon another wizard; much good it would do them.

"And precisely how long do you think it would take a Tracker to find you then?" Erlein was saying, his voice silken. "With the backspill of magic from the both of us leading to this place?"

"There are a sufficiency of arrows trained on your heart and throat," the leader interjected, "to ensure that such an event would not happen. But I confess this grows more interesting every moment. An archer and a wizard riding abroad on an Ember Day. Aren't you afraid of the dead? What does the boy do?"

"I'm a singer," Devin said grimly. "Devin d'Asoli, lately from the company of Menico di Ferraut, if that means anything to you." The thing, obviously, was to keep the talk going somehow. And he had heard stories— wishful thinking on the road, perhaps—of outlaw bands sparing musicians in exchange for a night of song. Something occurred to him: "You thought we *were* Barbadians, didn't you? From a distance. That's why you laid the trap."

"A singer. A clever singer," Ducas murmured. "If not clever enough to stay indoors on an Ember Day. Of course we thought you were Barbadians. Who in the eastern peninsula but Barbadians and outlaws would be abroad today? And all of the outlaws for twenty miles around are part of my band."

"There are outlaws and outlaws," Alessan said softly. "But if you were hunting Barbadian mercenaries you are men with the same hearts as ours. I can tell you—and I do not lie, Ducas—that if you hinder us here, or kill us, you will be giving such comfort to Barbadior—and to Ygrath—as they could not have ever dreamt of asking of you." There was, not surprisingly, a silence. The cold wind knifed into the pass, stirring the young grasses in the growing dark.

"You have a rather large opinion of yourself, it appears," Ducas said at length, thoughtfully. "Perhaps I should know why. I think it is time for you to tell me exactly who you are, and where you are riding at dusk on an Ember Day, and I will draw my own conclusions."

"My name is Alessan. I am riding west. My mother is dying and has summoned me to her side."

"How devoted of you," Ducas said. "But one name tells me nothing, and west is a big place, my friend with the bow. *Who are you and where are you riding?*" The voice was an uncoiled whip this time. Devin jumped. Behind Ducas seven bowstrings were drawn back.

Devin, his heart pounding, saw Alessan hesitate. The sun was almost gone now, a red disk cut in half by the horizon beyond the pass. The wind seemed to be blowing harder, promising a chilly night to come after this first day of spring.

There was a chill in Devin as well. He glanced at Erlein, and discovered that the wizard was staring at him, as if waiting. Alessan had not yet spoken. Ducas shifted meaningfully in his saddle.

Devin swallowed and, knowing that however hard this was for him, it had to be easier than it would be for Alessan, he said: "Tigana. He is from Tigana, and so am I."

He was careful to look straight at the outlaw wizard as he spoke, not at Ducas or the other riders. He saw out of the corner of his eye that Alessan was doing the same thing, so as not to have to see the blank look of incomprehension they both knew would follow. The wizard would be different. Wizards could hear the name.

A murmur rose from the gathered men, before them and behind. And then one man spoke aloud amid the shadows of falling dusk in that lonely place. A voice from the line behind them.

"By the blood of the god!" that voice cried from the heart. Devin wheeled around. A man had dismounted and was striding quickly forward to stand in front of them. Devin saw that the man was small, not much bigger than himself, perhaps thirty years old or a little more, and that he was moving awkwardly and clearly in pain, with Alessan's arrow in his arm.

Ducas was looking at his wizard. "Sertino, what is this?" he said, with an edge in his voice. "I do not—"

"Sorcery," the wizard said bluntly.

"What? His?" Ducas nodded towards Erlein.

"No, not his." It was the wounded man who spoke, his eyes never leaving Alessan's face. "Not this poor wizard's. It is real sorcery, this. It is the power of Brandin of Ygrath that keeps you from hearing the name."

With an angry motion Ducas swept his hat off, revealing a balding dome with a fringe of bright red hair. "And you, Naddo? How do you hear it, then?"

The man on the ground swayed unsteadily on his feet before replying. "Because I was born there too, and so I'm immune to the spell, or another victim of it, whichever you prefer." Devin heard the tautness in his voice, as of someone holding hard to his self-control. He heard the man called Naddo say, looking up at Alessan, "You have been asked for your name, and you only gave him a part. Will you tell us the rest? Will you tell me?" It was hard to see his eyes now, but his voice told an old story.

Alessan was sitting on his horse with an easiness, even after a day in the saddle, that seemed to deny even the possibility of weariness, or the tension of where they were. But then his right hand came up and pushed once, unconsciously, through his already tangled hair, and Devin, seeing the familiar gesture, knew that whatever he himself was feeling now, it was doubled and redoubled in the man he followed.

And then in the stillness of that pass, with the only other sounds the whistle of wind between the hills and the stirring of the horses on the young grass, he heard:

"My name is Alessan di Tigana bar Valentin. If you are as old as you appear to be, Naddo di Tigana, you will know who I am."

With a prickling of hairs on his neck and a shiver he could not control, Devin saw Naddo drop to his knees on the cold ground even before the last words were spoken.

"Oh, my Prince!" the wounded man cried in a raw voice. And covering his face with his one good hand, he wept.

"Prince?" said Ducas, very softly. There was a restive movement among the outlaws. "Sertino, you will explain this to me!"

Sertino the wizard looked from Alessan to Erlein, and then down at the weeping man. A curious, almost a frightened, expression crossed his pale, round face.

He said, "They are from Lower Corte. It had a different name before Brandin of Ygrath came. He has used his sorcery to take that name away. Only people born there, and wizards because of our own magic, can hear the true name. That is what is happening here."

"And 'Prince'? Naddo called him that."

Sertino was silent. He looked over at Erlein, and there was still that odd, uneasy look on his face. He said, "Is it true?"

And Erlein di Senzio, with an ironic half-smile, replied, "Just don't let him cut your hair, brother. Unless you like being bound into slavery."

Sertino's mouth fell open. Ducas slapped his knee with his hat. "Now that," he snapped, "I do not understand at all. There is too much of this I do not understand. I want explanations, from all of you!" His voice was harsh, much louder than before. He did not look at Alessan though.

"I understand it well enough, Ducas," came a voice from behind them. It was Magian, the captain of the group that had driven them into the gap. He moved his horse forward as they turned to look at him. "I understand that we have made our fortunes tonight. If this is the Prince of a province Brandin hates then all we need do is take him west to Fort Forese across the border and turn him over to the Ygrathens there. With a wizard to boot. And who knows, one of them probably likes boys

in his bed, too. Singing boys." His smile was a wide, loose thing in the shadows.

He said, "There will be rewards. Land. Perhaps even . . ."

He said nothing more than that. Ever. In rigid disbelief Devin saw Magian's mouth fall open and his eyes grow briefly wide, then the man slid slowly sideways off his horse to fall with a clatter of sword and bow on the ground beside Erlein.

There was a long-handled dagger in his back.

One of the outlaws from the line behind him, not hurrying at all, dismounted and pulled the dagger free. He wiped it carefully clean on the dead man's surcoat before sheathing it again at his belt.

"Not a good idea, Magian's," he said quietly, straightening to look at Ducas. "Not a good idea at all. We aren't informers here, and we don't serve the Tyrants."

Ducas slapped his hat back on his head, visibly fighting for control. He took a deep breath. "As it happens, I agree. But as it also happens, Arkin, we have a rule here about weapons drawn against each other."

Arkin was very tall, almost gaunt, and his long face was white, Devin saw, even among the shadows of dusk. He said, "I know that, Ducas. It is wasteful. I know. You will have to forgive me."

Ducas said nothing for a long time. Neither did anyone else. Devin, looking past the dead man, saw the two wizards gazing fixedly at each other in the shadows.

Arkin was still looking at Ducas.

Who finally broke the silence. "You are fortunate that I agree with you," he said.

Arkin shook his head. "We would not have stayed together this long otherwise."

Alessan neatly dismounted from his horse. He walked over towards Ducas, ignoring the arrows still trained on him. "If you are hunting Barbadians," he said quietly, "I have some idea as to why. I am doing the same thing, in my own way." He hesitated. "You can do as your dead man suggested: turn me in to Ygrath, and yes, I suspect there would be a reward. Or you can kill us here, and have done with us. You can also let us go our own way

from this place. But there is one other, quite different
thing you can do."

"Which is?" Ducas seemed to have regained his self-
control. His voice was calm again, as it had been at the
beginning.

"Join me. In what I seek to do."

"Which is?"

"To drive both Tyrants from the Palm before this
summer is out."

Naddo looked up suddenly, a brightness in his face.
"Really, my lord? We can do this? Even now?"

"There is a chance," Alessan said. "Especially now.
For the first time there is a chance." He looked back at
Ducas. "Where were you born?"

"In Tregea," the other man said after a pause. "In the
mountains."

Devin had a moment to think about how completely
things had shifted here, that Alessan should be asking the
questions now. He felt a stirring within him, of hope
renewed and of pride.

The Prince was nodding his head. "I thought it might
be so. I have heard the stories of a red-headed Captain
Ducas who was one of the leaders at Borifort in Tregea
during the Barbadian siege there. They never found him
after the fort fell." He hesitated. "I could not help but
notice the color of your hair."

For a moment the two men were motionless as in a
tableau, one on the ground the other on his horse. Then,
quite suddenly, Ducas di Tregea smiled.

"What is left of my hair," he murmured wryly, sweeping off his hat again with a wide gesture.

Releasing his reins he swung down off his horse and,
striding forward, held out an open palm to Alessan. Who
met both—the smile and offered hand—with his own.

Devin found himself gasping with the rush of relief that
swept over him, and then cheering wildly at the top of his
voice with twenty outlaws in that dark Certandan pass.

What he noticed though, even as the cheering reached
a crescendo, was that neither wizard was shouting. Erlein
and Sertino sat very still, almost rigid on their horses, as
if concentrating on something. They gazed at each other,
expressions identically grim.

And because he noticed, because he seemed to be becoming the sort of man who saw things like this, Devin was the first to fall silent, and he had even instinctively raised a hand to quiet the others. Alessan and Ducas lowered their linked palms and gradually, as silence returned to the pass, everyone looked at the wizards.

"What is it?" Ducas said.

Sertino turned to him. "Tracker. Northeast of us, quite close. I just felt the probe. He'll not find me though, I've done no magic for a long time."

"I have," said Erlein di Senzio. "Earlier today, in the Braccio Pass. Only a light spell, a screen for someone. Evidently it was enough. There must have been a Tracker in one of the southern forts."

"There almost always is," Sertino said flatly.

"What," Ducas said, "were you doing in the Braccio Pass?"

"Gathering flowers," Alessan said. "I'll tell you later. Right now we have Barbadians to deal with. How many will be with the Tracker?"

"Not less than twenty. Probably more. We have a camp in the hills south of here. Shall we run for it?"

"They'll follow," Erlein said. "He's got me traced. The spill of my magic will mark me for another day at least."

"I don't much feel like hiding in any case," Alessan said softly.

Devin turned quickly to look at him. So did Ducas. Awkwardly, Naddo rose to his feet.

"How good, exactly, are your men here?" Alessan said, a challenge in his tone and in the grey eyes.

And in the shadows of what was now almost full-dark Devin saw the Tregean outlaw leader's teeth suddenly flash. "They are good enough, and to spare, to deal with a score of Barbadians. This will be more than we've ever tackled, but we've never fought beside a Prince before. I think," he added, in a meditative voice, "that I too am grown tired of hiding, suddenly."

Devin looked over at the wizards. It was hard to make out their features in the dark, but Erlein said, in a hard-edged voice: "Alessan, the Tracker will have to be killed immediately, or he'll send an image of this place back to Alberico."

"He will be," said Alessan quietly. And in his voice, too, there was a new note. The presence of something Devin had never heard. A second later he realized that it was death.

Alessan's cloak flapped in a gust of wind. Very deliberately he drew his hood over his face.

The hard thing for Devin was that Alberico's Tracker turned out to be twelve years old.

They sent Erlein riding west out of the pass, as the lure. He was the one being followed. He had Sertino di Certando, the other wizard, and two other men with them, one of whom was the wounded Naddo, who insisted on being of use even though he could not fight. They had taken the arrow from his arm and bandaged it as best they could. It was clear that he was in difficulty, but even more clear that in the presence of Alessan he was not about to give way to that.

A short while later, under the stars and the low eastward crescent of Vidomni, the Barbadians entered the pass. There were twenty-five of them, and the Tracker. Six carried torches, which made things easier. Though not for them.

Alessan's arrow and Ducas's met in the Tracker's breast, fired from slopes on opposite sides of the defile. Eleven of the mercenaries fell under that first rain of arrows before Devin found himself galloping furiously down with Alessan and half a dozen other men out of their concealment in hollows in the pass. They angled to close the western exit, even as Ducas and nine men sealed off the eastern end the Barbadians had entered from.

And so on that Ember Night, in the company of outlaws in the highlands of Certando far from his lost home, Alessan bar Valentin, Prince of Tigana, fought the first true battle of his long war of return. After the drawn-out years of maneuvering, a subtle gathering of intelligence and the delicate guiding of events, he drew blade against the forces of a Tyrant in that moonlit pass.

No subterfuge, no hidden manipulation anymore from the wings of the stage. This was battle, for the time had come.

Marius of Quileia had made a promise to him that day,

against wisdom and experience and beyond hope. And with Marius's promise everything had changed. The waiting was over. He could loosen the rigid bonds that had held his heart so tightly leashed all these years. Tonight in this pass he could kill: in memory of his father and his brothers and all the dead of the River Deisa and after, in that year when he himself had not been permitted to die.

They had spirited him away and hidden him in Quileia south of the mountains, with Marius, then a captain of the High Priestess's guard. A man with his own reasons for fostering and concealing a young Prince from the northlands. That had been almost nineteen years ago, when the hiding had begun.

He was tired of hiding. The time of running was over now; the season of war had begun. True, it was Barbadior, not Ygrath, whose soldiers drew blade against them now, but in the end it was all the same. Both Tyrants were the same. He had been saying that for all the years since he'd come back north to the peninsula with Baerd. It was a truth hammered into shape like metal on the hard forge of his heart. They had to take them both, or be no nearer freedom than before.

And in the Braccio Pass this morning the taking had begun. The keystone had been set in the arch of his design. And so tonight in this dark defile he could unbind his pent-up passion, his own long memories of loss, and set his sword arm free.

Devin, laboring to keep up with the Prince, rode into his first combat with raw panic and exhilaration vying for mastery in his breast. He did not shout as most of the outlaws did; he was concentrating as much as anything else on ignoring the ache in his wounded leg. He gripped the dark sword Baerd had bought for him, holding it with the blade curving upwards as he had been taught in wintry morning lessons that seemed unimaginably remote from this night's happenings.

He saw Alessan drive straight into the circled ranks of the mercenaries, unswerving as one of his arrows, as if to put behind him in this one act of direct response all the years when such a thing was not allowed.

Frantically, gritting his teeth, Devin followed in Alessan's wake. He was alone though, and half a dozen lengths behind, when a yellow-bearded Barbadian loomed up beside him, enormous on his horse. Devin cried out in shock. Only some blind survival instinct and the reflexes he had been born with saved his life. He pulled his horse hard to the left, veering for a space he saw, and then leaning back to his right, as low to the ground as he could manage, he cut upwards with all his strength. He felt a searing pain in his wounded leg and almost fell. The windrush of the Barbadian's blade sliced empty air where Devin's head had been. A heartbeat later Devin felt his own wickedly curved sword cleave through leathery armor and into flesh.

The Barbadian screamed, a liquid, bubbling sound. He swayed wildly on his mount as his sword fell from his grasp. He brought one hand to his mouth in a curiously childlike gesture. Then, like the slow toppling of a mountain tree, he slid sideways in his saddle and crashed to the ground.

Devin had already pulled his sword free. Wheeling his horse in a tight circle, he looked for adversaries. No one was coming though. Alessan and the others were ahead of him, pounding against the mercenaries, driving to meet Ducas and Arkin's group pressing forward from the east.

It was almost over, Devin realized. There was nothing, really, for him to do. With a complex mixture of emotions that he didn't even try to understand just then, he watched the Prince's blade rise and fall three times and he saw three Barbadians die. One by one the six torches dropped to the ground and were extinguished. And then—only moments after they had ridden into the pass, it seemed to Devin—the last of the Barbadians had been cut down and slain.

It was then that he saw what was left of the Tracker and realized how young he had been. The body had been hideously trampled in the melee. It lay twisted and splayed unnaturally. Somehow the face had been spared, though for Devin, looking down, that was actually the worst thing. The two arrows were still embedded in the child's body, though the upper shaft of one of them had been broken off.

Devin turned away. He stroked the horse Alienor had

given him, and whispered to it. Then he forced himself to ride back towards the man he'd killed. This was not the same as the sleeping soldier in the Nievolene barn. It was not, he told himself. This had been open warfare and the Barbadian had been armed and armored, and he had swung his massive blade seeking Devin's life. Had the Barbadians and the Tracker come upon him and Alessan and Erlein alone in the wilderness Devin had no illusions, none at all, as to what their fate would have been.

It was *not* the same as in the barn. He said it within himself once again, as he gradually became aware of the eerie, disorienting calm that seemed to have descended upon the pass. The wind still blew, as cold as before. He glanced up, and realized belatedly that Alessan had quietly ridden to his side and was also looking down at the man Devin had slain. Both horses stamped and snorted, made restless by the frenzy just past and the smell of blood.

"Devin, believe me, I am sorry," Alessan murmured softly, so that no one else would hear. "It is hardest the first time, and I gave you no chance to prepare."

Devin shook his head. He felt drained, almost numb. "You didn't have much choice. Maybe it was better this way." He cleared his throat awkwardly. "Alessan, you have larger things to worry about. I chose freely in the Sandren Woods last fall. You aren't responsible for me."

"In a way I am."

"Not in a way that matters. I made my own choice."

"Doesn't friendship matter?"

Devin was silent, rendered suddenly diffident. Alessan had a way of doing that to you. After a moment the Prince added, almost as an afterthought, "I was your age when I came back from Quileia."

For a moment he seemed about to add something, but in the end he did not. Devin had an idea of what he meant though, and something kindled quietly within him like a candle.

For a moment longer they looked down at the dead man. Only a crescent, Vidomni's pale light was still bright enough to show the staring pain in his face.

Devin said, "I chose freely, and I understand the need, but I don't think I'm ever going to get used to this."

"I know I never have," said Alessan. He hesitated. "Either one of my brothers would have been so much better at what I was kept alive to do."

Devin turned then, trying to read the expression on the Prince's face in the shadows. After a moment he said, "I never knew them, but will you allow me to say that I doubt it? Truly I doubt it, Alessan."

After a moment the Prince touched his shoulder. "Thank you. There are those who would disagree, I'm afraid. But thank you, nonetheless."

And with those words he seemed to remember something, or be recalled to something. His voice changed. "We had better ride. I must speak with Ducas, and then we'll have to catch up with Erlein and go on. We've a lot of ground to cover yet." He looked at Devin appraisingly. "You must be exhausted. I should have asked before: how is your leg? Can you ride?"

"I'm fine," Devin protested quickly. "Of course I can ride."

Someone behind them laughed sardonically. They both turned. To discover that Erlein and the others had, in fact, returned to the pass.

"Tell me," the wizard said to Alessan, sharp mockery in his voice, "what did you expect him to say? *Of course* he'll tell you he can ride. He'd ride all night, half-dead, for you. So would this one"—he gestured towards Naddo behind him—"on barely an hour's acquaintance. I wonder, Prince Alessan, how does it feel to have such a power over the hearts of men?"

Ducas had ridden over while Erlein was speaking. He said nothing though, and it was too dark now with the torches extinguished, to make out anyone's features clearly. One had to judge by the words, and the inflections given them.

Alessan said quietly, "I think you know my answer to that. In any case, I'm unlikely to think too highly of myself with you around to point these things out to me." He paused, then added, "Triad forfend *you* would ever volunteer to ride all night in any cause but your own."

"I," said Erlein flatly, "have no choice in the matter anymore. Or have you forgotten?"

"I have not. But I've no mind to repeat that quarrel

now, Erlein. Ducas and his men have just put their lives at risk to save your own. If you—"

"To save my own! I would never have been at risk if you hadn't compelled me to—"

"Erlein, enough! We have a great many things to do and I am not of a mind to debate."

In the darkness Devin saw Erlein sketch a mocking bow on horseback. "I most humbly cry your pardon," he said in an exaggerated tone. "You really must let me know when you *are* of a mind to debate. You'll concede it is an issue of some importance to me."

Alessan was silent for what seemed a long time. Then, mildly, he said, "I think I can guess what is behind this now. I understand. It is meeting another wizard, isn't it? With Sertino here you feel what has happened to you the more."

"Don't pretend you understand me, Alessan!" said Erlein furiously.

Still calmly, Alessan said, "Very well then, I won't. In some ways I may never understand you and how you have lived your life—I told you that the evening we met. But for now this issue is a closed one. I will be prepared to discuss it the day the Tyrants are gone from the Palm. Not before."

"You will be dead before that. We will both be dead."

"Don't touch him!" Alessan said sharply. Belatedly Devin saw that Naddo had raised his good hand to strike the wizard. More quietly the Prince added, "If we are both dead, then our spirits can wrangle in Morian's Halls, Erlein. Until then, no more. We will have a great deal to do together in the weeks to come."

Ducas coughed. "As to that," he said, "we two also had better speak. There is a fair bit I'd like to know before I go further than this night's work, much as it has pleased me."

"I know," said Alessan, turning to him in the dark. He hesitated. "Will you ride with us for a little. Only as far as the village. You and Naddo, because of his arm."

"Why there, and why because of the arm? I don't understand," Ducas said. "You should know that we are not much welcome in the village. For obvious reasons."

"I can guess. It won't matter. Not on an Ember Night.

You will understand when we get there. Come. I want my good friend Erlein di Senzio to see something. And I suppose Sertino had better join us too."

"I wouldn't miss this for all the blue wine in Astibar," said the pudgy Certandan wizard. It was interesting, at another time it might even have been amusing, to note what a healthy distance he continued to keep between himself and the Prince. The words he spoke were facetious, but his tone was deadly serious.

"Come on then," said Alessan brusquely. He turned his horse past Erlein's, almost brushing against the other man, and started west out of the pass. The ones he had named began to follow. Ducas spoke a few terse commands to Arkin, too low for Devin to hear. Arkin hesitated for a moment, clearly torn, wanting to come with his leader. But then, without speaking, he turned his horse the other way. When Devin glanced back a moment later, he saw that the outlaws were rifling the Barbadians' bodies for weapons.

He turned to look over his shoulder again a few moments later but they were in open country by then, with the hills in shadow to the south and east and a grassy plain rolling north of them. The entrance to the pass could no longer even be seen. Arkin and the others would be gone from within it soon, Devin knew, leaving only the dead. Only the dead for the scavengers; one of them killed by his own sword, and another one a child.

The old man lay on his bed in the darkness of an Ember Night and the always darkness of his own affliction. Far from sleep, he listened to the wind outside and to the woman in the other room clicking her prayer beads and intoning the same litany over and over.

"Eanna love us, Adaon preserve us, Morian guard our souls. Eanna love us, Adaon preserve us, Morian guard our souls. Eanna love us . . ."

His hearing was very good. It was a compensation most of the time, but sometimes—as tonight, with the woman praying like a demented thing—it was a curse of a particularly insidious kind. She was using her old beads;

he could tell the thin, quick sound even through the wall separating their chambers. He had made her a new ring of beads of rare, polished tanchwood three years ago for her naming day. Most of the time she used that ring, but not on the Ember Days. Then she went back to her old beads and she prayed aloud for most of three days and nights.

In the earliest years here he had slept those three nights in the barn with the two boys who had brought him here, so much did her unceasing litany disturb him. But he was old now, his bones creaked and ached on windy nights such as this, so he kept to his own bed under piled blankets and endured her voice as best he could.

"Eanna love us always, Adaon preserve us from all perils, Morian guard our souls and shelter us. Eanna love us . . ."

The Ember Days were a time of contrition and atonement, but they were also a time when one was to count and give thanks for one's gifts. He was a cynical man, for sufficient and varied reasons, but he would not have called himself unreligious, and he would not, in fact, have said he'd lived a life unblessed, despite the blindness of almost two decades. He had lived much of his life in wealth and near to power. The length of his days was a blessing, and so too was the lifelong grace of his hands with wood. Only a form of play at first, a diversion, it had become something more than that in the years since they had come here.

There was also his other gift of skill, though few people knew of that. Had it been otherwise he would never have been able to shape a quiet life in this highland village, and a quiet life was essential because he was hiding. Still.

The very fact of his survival on the long, sightless journey all those years ago was a blessing of a special kind. He was under no illusions: he would never have survived without the loyalty of his two young servants. The only ones they had allowed to stay with him. The only ones who had wanted to stay.

They weren't young nor were they servants any longer. They were farmers on land they owned with him. No

longer sleeping on the front-room floor in their first small
farmhouse nor out in the barn as they had in the earliest
years, but in their own homes with wives beside them
and children near by. Lying in darkness he offered thanks
for that, as gratefully as for anything he had ever been
given himself.

Either of them would have let him sleep in their home
these three nights, to escape the unending drone of the
woman in the other room, but he would not presume to
ask so much. Not on the Ember Nights, not on any night.
He had his own sense of what was appropriate, and
besides, he liked his own bed more and more with the
passing years.

"Eanna love us as her children, Adaon preserve us as
his children . . ."

He wasn't, clearly, going to be able to fall asleep. He
thought about getting up to polish a staff or a bow, but
he knew Menna would hear him, and he knew she would
make him pay for profaning an Ember Night with labor.
Watery porridge, sour wine, his slippers cruelly moved
from where he laid them down.

"They were in my way," she would say when he complained. Then, when fires were allowed again: burnt meat,
undrinkable khav, bitter bread. For a week, at least.
Menna had her own ways of letting him know what
mattered to her. After all the years they had their tacit
understandings much as any old couple did, though of
course he had never married her.

He knew who he was, and what was appropriate, even
in this fallen state, far from home, from the memory of
wealth or power. Here on this small farm-holding bought
with gold fearfully hidden on his person during that long,
blind journey seventeen years ago, sure that a murderous
pursuit was riding close behind.

He had survived, though, and the boys. Coming to this
village on a day in autumn long ago: strangers arriving in
a dark time. A time when so many people had died and
so many others were brutally uprooted all across the
Palm in the wake of the Tyrants' coming. But the three
of them had somehow endured, had even managed to
make the land put forth a living for them in good years.
In Certando's bad years latterly he had had to deplete his

dwindled reserve of gold, but what else was it for, at this point?

Really, what else would it be for? Menna and the two boys—they were no longer boys, of course—were his heirs. They were all he could claim as family now. They were all he had, if one didn't count the dreams that still came in his nights.

He was a cynical man, having seen a great deal in the days before his darkness came, and after, in a different way of seeing, but he was not so burdened by irony as to defeat wisdom. He knew that exiles always dreamt of home and that the sorely wronged never really forgot. He had no illusions about being unique in this.

"Eanna love us, Adaon preserve us from—*Triad save us!*"

Menna fell silent, very abruptly. And for the same reason the old man sat suddenly upright in bed, wincing at a sharp protest from his spine. They had both heard it: a sound outside in the night. In the Ember Night, when no one should be abroad.

Listening carefully he caught it again: the sound, delicate and faint, of pipes playing in the darkness outside, passing by their walls. Concentrating, the old man could make out footsteps. He counted them. Then, his heart beating dangerously fast, he swung out of bed as quickly as he could and began to dress.

"It is the dead!" Menna wailed in the far room. "Adaon preserve us from vengeful ghosts, from all harm. Eanna love us! The dead have come for us. Morian of Portals guard our souls!"

Despite his agitation the old man paused to note that Menna, even in her fear, still included him in her prayers. For a moment he was genuinely moved. In the next moment he ruefully acknowledged the inescapable fact that the succeeding two weeks of his life—at least—were likely to be sheerest domestic torment.

He was going outside, of course. He knew exactly who this was. He finished dressing and reached for his favorite stick by the door. He moved as quietly as he could, but the walls were thin and Menna's hearing almost as good as his own: there was no point in trying to slip out unheard. She would know what he was doing. And would make him pay the price.

Because this had happened before. On Ember Nights and other nights for almost ten years now. Sure of foot inside the house he went to the front door and used his stick to roll back the chink-blocker on the floor. Then he opened the door and went out. Menna was praying again already:

"Eanna love me, Adaon preserve me, Morian guard my soul."

The old man smiled a wintry smile. Two weeks, at least. Watery porridge in the morning. Burnt, tasteless khav. Bitter mahgoti tea. He stood still for a moment, still smiling faintly, breathing the crisp, cool air. Mercifully, the wind had died down a little, his bones felt fine. Lifting his face to the night breeze he could almost taste the spring to come.

He closed the door carefully behind him and began tapping his way with the stick along the path towards the barn. He had carved this stick when he still had his sight. Many times he had carried it in the palace, an affectation at a dissolute court. He had never expected to need it in this way. Its head was the head of an eagle with the eyes lovingly detailed, wide and fiercely defiant.

Perhaps because he had killed for the second time in his life that night, Devin was remembering that other much larger barn from the winter just past, in Astibar.

This one was far more modest. Only two milk cows and a pair of plow horses stabled. It was well-made though, and warm, with the smell of the animals and clean straw. The walls had no chinks to admit the knife of wind, the straw was freshly piled, the floor swept clean, the tools along the walls neatly laid and stacked.

In fact, if he wasn't careful, the smell and the feel of this barn would take him much further back than last winter: back to their own farm in Asoli, which he tried never to think about. He was tired though, bone tired, after two sleepless nights, and so he supposed he was vulnerable to such memories. His right knee ached fiercely, where he had twisted it on the mountain. It was swollen to twice its normal size and sharply sensitive to touch.

He'd had to walk slowly, making a real effort not to limp.

No one spoke. No one had spoken since they had reached the outskirts of this village of some twenty homes. The only sound for the last few moments after they tethered the horses and began to walk had been Alessan's pipes softly playing. Playing—and Devin wondered if he alone knew this, or if Naddo recognized it too—a certain nursery melody from Avalle.

Here in the barn Alessan was still playing, as gently as before. The tune was one more thing that seemed to be trying to carry Devin back to his family. He resisted: if he went that way in the condition he was in right now he would probably end up crying.

Devin tried to imagine how the haunting, elusive melody would sound to anyone huddled inside the walls of their lightless homes on this Ember Night. A company of ghosts passing by, that was what they would seem to be. The dead abroad, following a small, forgotten tune. He remembered Catriana singing in the Sandreni Woods:

> But wherever I wander, by night or by day,
> Where water runs swiftly or high trees sway,
> My heart will carry me back and away
> To a dream of the towers of Avalle.

He wondered where she was tonight. And Sandre. Baerd. He wondered if he would ever see any of them again. Earlier this evening, pursued into the pass, he had thought he was about to die. And now, two hours later, they had killed twenty-five Barbadians with those same outlaws who had pursued them, and three of the outlaws were here with them in this unknown barn listening to Alessan play a cradle song.

He didn't think he would understand the strangeness of life if he lived to be a hundred years old.

There was a sound outside and the door swung open. Devin stiffened involuntarily. So did Ducas di Tregea, a hand reaching for his sword. Alessan looked at the door, but his fingers never faltered on the pipes and the music continued.

An old man, slightly stooped, but with a leonine combed-back mane of white hair, stood for a moment, backlit by the sudden moonlight, before he stepped inside and pushed the door closed behind him with a stick he carried. After that it was dark again in the barn and hard to see for a few moments.

No one spoke. Alessan did not even look up again. Tenderly, with feeling, he finished the tune. Devin looked at him as he played and wondered if he was the only man here who understood what music meant to the Prince. He thought about what Alessan had been through in this past day alone, about what it was he was riding towards, and something complicated and awkward stirred in his heart as he listened to the wistful ending of the song. He saw the Prince set his pipes aside with a motion of regret. Laying down his release, taking up the burdens again. All the burdens that seemed to be his legacy, the price of his blood.

"Thank you for coming, old friend," he said now, quietly, to the man in the doorway.

"You owe me, Alessan," the old man said in a clear strong voice. "You have condemned me to sour milk and spoiled meat for a month."

"I was afraid of that," Alessan said in the darkness. Devin could hear affection and an unexpected amusement in his voice. "Menna has not changed, then?"

The other man snorted. "Menna and change do not coexist," he said. "You are with new people, and a friend is missing. What has happened? Is he all right?"

"He is fine. A half-day's ride east. There is much to tell. I came with some reason, Rinaldo."

"So much is clear to me. One man with a leg that is torn inside. Another with an arrow wound. The two wizards are not happy but I can do nothing about their missing fingers and neither is ill. The sixth man is now afraid of me, but he need not be."

Devin gasped with astonishment. Beside him Ducas swore aloud.

"Explain this!" he growled furiously. "Explain everything!"

Alessan was laughing. So, more softly, was the man he had called Rinaldo. "You are a spoiled and petty old man," the Prince said, still chuckling, "and you enjoy shocking people simply for the sake of doing it. You should be ashamed of yourself."

"There are so few pleasures left to me in my age," the other retorted. "Would you deny me this one too? There is much to tell, you say? Tell me."

Alessan's voice grew sober. "I had a meeting in the mountains this morning."

"Ah, I was wondering about that! And what follows?"

"Everything, Rinaldo. Everything follows. This summer. He said yes. We will have the letters. One to Alberico, one to Brandin, and one to the Governor of Senzio."

"Ah," said Rinaldo again. "The Governor of Senzio." He said it softly, but could not quite disguise the excitement in his voice. He took a step forward into the room. "I never dreamt I would live to see this day. Alessan, we are going to act?"

"We have already begun. Ducas and his men joined with us tonight in battle. We killed a number of Barbadians and a Tracker pursuing a wizard with us."

"Ducas? That is who this is?" The old man gave a low whistle, a curiously incongruous sound. "Now I know why he is afraid. You have your share of enemies in this village, my friend."

"I am aware of that," said Ducas drily.

"Rinaldo," Alessan said, "do you remember the siege of Borifort when Alberico first came? The stories about a red-bearded captain, one of the leaders of the Tregeans there? The one who was never found?"

"Ducas di Tregea? This is he?" Again the whistle. "Well met then, Captain, though not, as a matter of fact, for the first time. If I remember rightly, you were in the company of the Duke of Tregea when I paid a formal visit there some twenty years ago."

"A visit from where?" Ducas asked, visibly struggling to get his bearings. Devin sympathized: he was doing the same thing, and he knew rather more than the red-bearded man did. "From . . . from Alessan's province?" Ducas hazarded.

"Tigana? But of course," Erlein di Senzio interjected harshly. "Of course he is. This is just another petty injured lordling from the west. Is that why you brought me here, Alessan? To show how brave an old man can be? You will forgive me if I choose to pass on this lesson."

"I didn't hear the beginning of that." It was Rinaldo, speaking softly to the wizard. "What did you say?"

Erlein fell silent, turning from Alessan to the man by the door. Even in darkness Devin could see his sudden confusion.

"He named my province," Alessan said. "They both think you are from my home."

"An outrageous slander," Rinaldo said calmly. He swung his large, handsome head towards Ducas and Erlein. "I am vain enough to have thought you might know me by now. My name is Rinaldo di Senzio."

"What! *Senzio?*" Erlein exclaimed, shocked out of his own composure. "You can't be!"

There was a silence.

"Who, exactly, is this presumptuous man?" Rinaldo asked, of no one in particular.

"My wizard, I'm afraid," Alessan replied. "I have bound him to me with Adaon's gift to the line of our Princes. I spoke to you of that once, I think. His name is Erlein. Erlein di Senzio."

"Ah!" said Rinaldo letting his breath out slowly. "I see. A bound wizard and a Senzian. That explains his anger." He moved another few steps forward, sweeping his stick over the ground in front of him.

It was in that moment that Devin realized that Rinaldo was blind. Ducas registered it in the same moment:

"You have no eyes," he said.

"No," Rinaldo said equably. "I used to, of course, but they were judged inappropriate for me by my nephew, at the suggestion of both Tyrants seventeen years ago this spring. I had the temerity to oppose Casalia's decision to lay down his Ducal status and become a Governor instead."

Alessan was staring fixedly at Erlein as Rinaldo spoke. Devin followed his glance. The wizard looked more confused than Devin had ever seen him.

"I do know who you are, then," he said, almost stammering.

"Of course you do. Just as I know you, and knew your father, Erlein bar Alein. I was brother to the last real

Duke of Senzio and am uncle to the craven disgrace who styles himself Casalia, Governor of Senzio now. And I was as proud to be the one as I am shamed to call myself the other."

Visibly fighting for control, Erlein said, "But then you knew what Alessan was planning. You knew about those letters. He told you. You know what he intends to do with them! You know what it will mean for our province! And you are still with him? You are *helping* him?" His voice rose erratically at the end.

"You stupid, petty little man," Rinaldo said slowly, spacing the words for weight, his own voice hard as stone. "Of course I am helping him. How else are we to deal with the Tyrants? What other battleground is *possible* in the Palm today but our poor Senzio where Barbadior and Ygrath circle each other like wolves and my crapulous nephew drowns himself in drink and spills his seed in the backsides of whores! Do you want freedom to be *easy*, Erlein bar Alein? Do you think it drops like acorns from trees in the fall?"

"He thinks he *is* free," Alessan said bluntly. "Or would be, if it wasn't for me. He thinks he was free until he met me by a river in Ferraut last week."

"Then I have nothing more to say to him," said Rinaldo di Senzio, with contempt.

"How did you . . . how did you find this man?" It was Sertino, speaking to Alessan. The Certandan wizard still kept to the far side of the room from the Prince, Devin noted.

"Finding such men has been my labor for twelve years and more now," Alessan said. "Men and women from my home or yours, from Astibar, Tregea . . . all over the peninsula. People I thought could be trusted and who might have reason to hate the Tyrants as much as I. And a desire to be free that matched my own. Truly free," he said, looking at Erlein again. "Masters of our own peninsula."

With a faint smile he turned to Ducas. "As it happened, you hid yourself well, friend. I thought you might be alive, but had no idea where. We lived in Tregea on and off for more than a year but no one we spoke to knew, or would say anything about your fate. I had to be terribly clever tonight to lure you into finding me instead."

Ducas laughed at that, a deep sound in his chest. Then, sobering, he said, "I wish it had happened earlier."

"So do I. You have no idea how much. I have a friend I think will take to you as much as you will to him."

"Shall I meet him?"

"In Senzio, later this spring, if events fall right. If we can make them fall right."

"If that is so, you had best start by telling us how you need them to fall," Rinaldo said prosaically. "Let me tend to your two wounded while you tell what we should know."

He moved forward, tapping the ground ahead of him as he came up to Devin. "I am a Healer," he explained gravely, the sharpness gone from his voice. "Your leg is bad and needs dealing with. Will you let me try?"

"So *that* is how you knew us," Ducas said, wonder in his voice again. "I have never known a true Healer before."

"There are not many of us and we tend not to announce ourselves," Rinaldo said, the empty sockets of his eyes fixed on nothingness. "That was so even before the Tyrants came: it is a gift with limits and a price. Now we keep ourselves hidden for the same reason the wizards do, or almost the same: the Tyrants are happy to seize us, and force us serve them until they wear us out."

"Can they do that?" Devin asked. His voice was hoarse. He realized that he hadn't spoken for a long time. He cringed at the thought of what he would sound like if he tried to sing tonight. He couldn't remember the last time he had been so exhausted.

"Of course they can," said Rinaldo simply. "Unless we choose to die on their death-wheels instead. Which has been known to happen."

"I will be happy to learn of any difference between that coercion and what this man has done to me," Erlein said coldly.

"And I will be happy to tell you," Rinaldo shot back, "as soon as I finish my work." To Devin he said, "There should be straw behind you. Will you lie down and let me see what I can do?"

In a few moments Devin found himself prone on a bed of straw. With an old man's gingerly caution Rinaldo knelt beside him. The Healer began rubbing his palms slowly against each other.

Over his shoulder Rinaldo said, "Alessan, I'm serious. Talk while I work. Begin with Baerd. I would like to know why he isn't with you."

"*Baerd!*" a voice interrupted. "Is *that* your friend? Baerd bar Saevar?" It was Naddo, the wounded man. He stumbled forward to the edge of the straw.

"Saevar was his father, yes," Alessan said. "You knew him?"

Naddo was so distraught he could scarcely speak. "Knew him? *Of course* I knew him. I was . . . I . . . ." He swallowed hard. "I was his father's last apprentice. I loved Baerd as . . . as an older brother. I . . . we . . . parted badly. I went away in the year after the fall."

"So did he," Alessan said gently, laying a hand on Naddo's trembling shoulder. "Not long after you did. I know who you are now, Naddo. He has often spoken to me of that parting. I can tell you that he grieved for the manner of it. That he still does. I expect he will tell you himself when you meet."

"This is the friend you mentioned?" Ducas asked softly.

"It is."

"He has spoken to you of *me*?" Naddo's voice skirled high with wonder.

"He has."

Alessan was smiling again. Devin, weary as he was, found himself doing the same. The man before them sounded remarkably like a young boy just then.

"Do you . . . does he know what happened to his sister? To Dianora?" Naddo asked.

Alessan's smile faded. "We do not. We have searched for a dozen years, and asked in a great many places, wherever we find survivors of the fall. There are so many women of that name. She went away herself, some time after he left in search of me. No one knows why, or where she went, and the mother died not long after. They are . . . their loss is the deepest hurt I know in Baerd."

Naddo was silent; a moment later they realized that he

was fighting back tears. "I can understand that," he said finally, his voice husky. "She was the bravest girl I ever knew. The bravest woman. And if she wasn't really beautiful she was still so very . . ." He stopped for a moment, struggling for composure, and then said quietly: "I think I loved her. I know I did. I was thirteen years old that year."

"If the goddesses love us, and the god," Alessan said softly, "we will find her yet."

Devin hadn't known any of this. There seemed to be so many things he hadn't known. He had questions to ask, maybe even more than Ducas had. But just then Rinaldo, on his knees beside him, stopped rubbing his palms together and leaned forward.

"You need rest quite badly," he murmured, so softly none of the others could hear. "You need sleep as much as your leg needs care." As he spoke he laid one hand gently on Devin's forehead and Devin, for all his questions and all his perturbation, felt himself suddenly beginning to drift, as on a wide calm sea towards the shores of sleep, far from where men were speaking, from their voices and their grief and their need. And he heard nothing more at all of what was said in the barn that night.

CHAPTER
• 15 •

THREE DAYS LATER AT SUNRISE THEY CROSSED THE BORder south of the two forts and Devin entered Tigana for the first time since his father had carried him away as a child.

Only the most struggling musicians came into Lower Corte, the companies down on their luck and desperate for engagements of any kind, however slight the pay, however grim the ambience. Even so long after the Tyrants had conquered, the itinerant performers of the Palm knew that Lower Corte meant bad luck and worse wages, and a serious risk of falling afoul of the Ygrathens, either inside the province or at the borders going in or out.

It wasn't as if the story wasn't known: the Lower Corteans had killed Brandin's son, and they were paying a price in blood and money and brutally heavy oppression for that. It did not make for a congenial setting, the artists of the roads agreed, talking it over in taverns or hospices in Ferraut or Corte. Only the hungry or the newly begun ventured to take the ill-paying, risk-laden jobs in that sad province in the southwest. By the time Devin had joined him Menico di Ferraut had been traveling for a very long time and had more than enough of a reputation to be able to eschew that particular one of the nine provinces. There was sorcery involved there too; no one really understood it, but the travelers of the road were a superstitious lot and, given an alternative, few would willingly venture into a place where magic was known to be at work. Everyone knew the problems you could find in Lower Corte. Everyone knew the stories.

So this was the first time for Devin. Through the last

451

hours of riding in darkness he had been waiting for the moment of passage, knowing that since they had glimpsed Fort Sinave north of them some time ago, the border had to be near, knowing what lay on the other side.

And now, with the first pale light of dawn rising behind them, they had come to the line of boundary cairns that stretched north and south between the two forts, and he had looked up at the nearest of the old, worn, smooth monoliths, and had ridden past it, had crossed the border into Tigana.

And he found to his dismay that he had no idea what to think, how to respond. He felt scattered and confused. He had shivered uncontrollably a few hours ago when they saw the distant lights of Sinave in darkness, his imagination restlessly at work. *I'll be home soon,* he had told himself. *In the land where I was born.*

Now, riding west past the cairn, Devin looked around compulsively, searching, as the slow spread of light claimed the sky and then the tops of hills and trees and finally bathed the springtime world as far as he could see.

It was a landscape much like what they had been riding through for the past two days. Hilly, with dense forests ranging in the south on the rising slopes, and the mountains visible beyond. He saw a deer lift its head from drinking at a stream. It froze for a minute, watching them, and then remembered to flee.

They had seen deer in Certando, too.

This is home! Devin told himself again, reaching for the response that should be flowing. In this land his father had met and wooed his mother, he and his brothers had been born, and from here Garin di Tigana had fled northward, a widower with infant sons, escaping the killing anger of Ygrath. Devin tried to picture it: his father on a cart, one of the twins on the seat beside him, the other—they must have taken turns—in the back with what goods they had, cradling Devin in his arms as they rode through a red sunset darkened by smoke and fires on the horizon.

It seemed a false picture in some way Devin could not have explained. Or, if not exactly false, it was unreal somehow. Too easy an image. The thing was, it might even be true, it might be *exactly* true, but Devin didn't know. He couldn't know. He had no memories: of that ride, of this place. No roots, no history. This was home, but it wasn't. It wasn't really even Tigana through which they rode. He had never even *heard* that name until half a year ago, let alone any stories, legends, chronicles of its past.

This was the province of Lower Corte; so he had known it all his life.

He shook his head, edgy, profoundly unsettled. Beside him Erlein glanced over, an ironic smile playing about his lips. Which made Devin even more irritable. Ahead of them Alessan was riding alone. He hadn't said a word since the border.

He had memories, Devin knew, and in a way that he was aware was odd or even twisted he envied the Prince those images, however painful they might be. They would be rooted and absolute and shaped of this place which was truly his home.

Whatever Alessan was feeling or remembering now would have nothing of the unreal about it. It would all be raw, brutally actual, the trampled fabric of his own life. Devin tried, riding through the cheerful birdsong of a glorious spring morning, to imagine how the Prince might be feeling. He thought that he could, but only just: a guess more than anything else. Among other things, perhaps first of all things, Alessan was going to a place where his mother was dying. No wonder he had urged his horse ahead; no wonder he wasn't speaking now.

He is entitled, Devin thought, watching the Prince ride, straight-backed and self-contained in front of them. He's entitled to whatever solitude, whatever release he needs. What he carries is the dream of a people, and most of them don't even know it.

And thinking so, he found himself drawn out of his own confusion, his struggling adjustment to where they were. Focusing on Alessan he found his avenue to passion again, to the burning inward response to what had happened here—and was still happening. Every hour of every day in the ransacked, broken-down province named Lower Corte.

And somewhere in his mind and heart—fruits of a long winter of thought, and of listening in silence as older and wiser men spoke—Devin knew that he was not the first and would not be the last person to find in a single man the defining shape and lineaments for the so much harder love of an abstraction or a dream.

It was then, looking all around at the sweep of land under the wide arch of a high blue sky, that Devin felt something pluck at the strings of his heart as if it were a harp. As if *he* were. He felt the drumming of his horse's hooves on the hard earth, following fast behind the Prince, and it seemed to Devin that that drumming was with the harp-strings as they galloped.

Their destiny was waiting for them, brilliant in his mind like the colored pavilions on the plain of the Triad Games that took place every three years. What they were doing now *mattered,* it could make a difference. They were riding at the very center of events in their time. Devin felt something pull him forward, lifting and bearing him into the riptide, the maelstrom of the future. Into what his life would have been about when it was over.

He saw Erlein glance over again, and this time Devin smiled back at him. A grim, fierce smile. He saw the habitual, reflexive irony leave the wizard's lean face, replaced by a flicker of doubt. Devin almost felt sorry for the man again.

Impulsively he guided his horse nearer to Erlein's brown and leaned over to squeeze the other man's shoulder.

"We're going to do it!" he said brightly, almost gaily.

Erlein's face seemed to pinch itself together. "You are a fool,' he said tersely. "A young, ignorant fool." He said it without conviction though, an instinctive response.

Devin laughed aloud.

Later he would remember this moment too. His words, Erlein's, his laughter under the bright, blue cloudless sky. Forests and the mountains on their left and in the distance before them now the first glimpse of the Sperion, a glinting ribbon flowing swiftly north before beginning its curve west to find the sea.

The Sanctuary of Eanna lay in a high valley set within a sheltering and isolating circle of hills south and west of the River Sperion and of what had been Avalle. It was not far from the road that had once borne such a volume of trade back and forth from Tigana and Quileia through the high saddleback of the Sfaroni Pass.

In all nine provinces Eanna's priests and Morian's, and the priestesses of Adaon had such retreats. Founded in out-of-the way parts of the peninsula—sometimes dramatically so—they served as centers of learning and teaching for the newly initiated clergy, repositories of wisdom and of the canons of the Triad, and as places of withdrawal, where priests and priestesses who chose might lay down the pace and burdens of the world outside for a time or for a lifetime.

And not just the clergy. Members of the laity would sometimes do the same, if they could afford "contributions" that were judged as appropriate offerings for the privilege of sheltering for a space of days or years within the ambit of these retreats.

Many were the reasons that led people to the Sanctuaries. It had long been a jest that the priestesses of Adaon were the best birth doctors in the Palm, so numerous were the daughters of distinguished or merely wealthy houses that elected to sojourn at one of the god's retreats at times that might otherwise have been inconvenient for their families. And, of course, it was well known that an indeterminately high percentage of the clergy were culled from the living offerings these same daughters left behind when they returned to their homes. Girl children stayed with Adaon, the boys went to Morian. The white-robed priests of Eanna had always claimed that they would have nothing to do with such goings-on, but there were stories belying that, as well.

Little of this had changed when the Tyrants came. Neither Brandin nor Alberico was so reckless or ill-advised as to stir up the clergy of the Triad against their rule. The priests and the priestesses were allowed to do as they had always done. The people of the Palm were granted their worship, odd and even primitive as it might seem to the new rulers from overseas.

What both Tyrants did do, with greater or lesser success, was play the rival temples against each other, seeing— for it was impossible not to see—the tensions and hostilities that rippled and flared among the three orders of the Triad. There was nothing new in this: every Duke, Grand Duke, or Prince in the peninsula had sought, in each generation, to turn this shifting three-way friction to his own account. Many patterns might have changed with the circling of years, some things might change past all recognition, and some might be lost or forgotten entirely, but not this one. Not this delicate, reciprocal dance of state and clergy.

And so the temples still stood, and the most important ones still flourished their gold and machial, their statuary, and their cloth-of-gold vestments for services. Save in one place only: in Lower Corte, where the statues and the gold were gone and the libraries looted and burned. That was part of something else though, and few spoke of it after the earliest years of the Tyrants. Even in this benighted province, the clergy were otherwise allowed to continue the precisely measured round of their days in city and town, and in their Sanctuaries.

And to these retreats came a great variety of men and women from time to time. It was not only the awkwardly fecund who found reason to ride or be carried away from the turbulence of their lives. In times of strife, whether of the soul or the wider world, the denizens of the Palm always knew that the Sanctuaries were there, perched in snowbound precipitous eyries or half-lost in their misty valleys.

And the people knew as well that—for a price—such a withdrawal into the regimen, the carefully modulated hours of retreats such as this one of Eanna in its valley, could be theirs. For a time. For a lifetime. Whoever they might have been in the cities beyond the hills.

Whoever they might have been.

For a time, for a lifetime, the old woman thought, looking out the window of her room at the valley in sunlight at spring's return. She had never been able to keep her thoughts from going back. There was so much waiting for her in the past and so little here, now, living through the agonizingly slow descent of the years. Season after season falling to the earth like shot birds, arrows in their breasts, through this lifetime that was her own, and her only one.

A lifetime of remembering, by curlew's cry at dawn or
call to prayer, by candlelight at dusk, by sight of chimney
smoke rising straight and dark into winter's wan gray
light, by the driving sound of rain on roof and window at
winter's end, by the creak of her bed at night, by call to
prayer again, by drone of priests at prayer, by a star
falling west in the summer sky, by the stern cold dark of
the Ember Days . . . a memory within each and every
motion of the self or of the world, every sound, each
shade of color, each scent borne by the valley wind. A
remembrance of what had been lost to bring one to this
place among the white-robed priests with their unending
rites and their unending pettiness, and their acceptance
of what had happened to them all.

Which last is what had nearly killed her in the early
years. Which, indeed, she would say—had said last week
to Danoleon—was killing her now, whatever the priest-
physician might say about growths in her breast.

They had found a Healer in the fall. He had come,
anxious, febrile, a lank, sloppy man with nervous mo-
tions and a flushed brow. But he had sat down beside her
bed and looked at her, and she had realized that he did
have the gift, for his agitation had settled and his brow
had cleared. And when he touched her—here, and here—
his hand had been steady and there had been no pain,
only a not unpleasant weariness.

He had shaken his head though in the end, and she
had read an unexpected grief in his pale eyes, though he
could not have known who she was. His sorrow would be
for simple loss, for defeat, not caring who it was who
might be dying.

"It would kill me," he said quietly. "It has come too
far. I would die and I would not save you. There is
nothing I can do."

"How long?" she had asked. Her only words.

He told her half a year, perhaps less, depending on
how strong she was.

How strong? She was very strong. More so than any of
them guessed save perhaps Danoleon, who had known
her longest by far. She sent the Healer from the room,
and asked Danoleon to leave, and then the one slow

servant the priests had allowed to the woman they knew only as a widow from an estate north of Stevanien.

As it happened she had actually known the woman whose identity she had assumed; had had her as one of the ladies of her court for a time. A fair-haired girl, green eyes and an easy manner, quick to laugh. Melina bren Tonaro. A widow for a week; less than that. She had killed herself in the Palace by the Sea when word came of Second Deisa.

The deception was a necessary shielding of identity: Danoleon's suggestion. Almost nineteen years ago. They would be looking for her and for the boy, the High Priest had said. The boy he was taking away, he would soon be safely gone, their dreams carried in his person, a hope living so long as he lived. She had been fair-haired herself, in those days. It had all happened such a long time ago. She had become Melina bren Tonaro and had come to the Sanctuary of Eanna in its high valley above Avalle.

Above Stevanien.

Had come, and had waited. Through the changing seasons and the unchanging years. Waited for that boy to grow into a man such as his father had been, or his brothers, and then do what a descendant in direct line of Micaela and the god should know he had to do.

Had waited. Season after season; shot birds falling from the sky.

Until last autumn, when the Healer had told her the cold large thing she had already guessed for herself. Half a year, he had said. If she was strong.

She had sent them from her room and lain in her iron bed and looked out at the leaves on the valley trees. The change of colors had come. She had loved that once; her favorite season for riding. As a girl, as a woman. It had occurred to her that these would be the last fall leaves she would ever see.

She had turned her mind from such thoughts and had begun to calculate. Days and months, and the numbering of the years. She had done the arithmetic twice, and a third time to be sure of it. She said nothing to Danoleon, not then. It was too soon.

Not until the end of winter, with all the leaves gone and ice just beginning to melt from the eaves, did she summon the High Priest and instruct him as to the letter she wanted sent to the place where she knew—as he knew, alone of all the priests—her son would be on the Ember Days that began this spring. She had done the calculations. Many times.

She had also timed it very well, and not by chance. She could see Danoleon wanting to protest, to dissuade, to speak of dangers and circumspection. But the ground was out from under his feet, she could see it in the way his large hands grew restless and the way his blue eyes moved about the room as if seeking an argument on the bare walls. She waited patiently for him to meet her gaze at last, as she knew he would, and then she saw him slowly bow his head in acceptance.

How did one deny a mother, dying, a message to her only living child? An entreaty to that child to come bid her farewell before she crossed over to Morian. Especially when that child, the boy he himself had guided south over the mountains so many years ago, was her last link to what she had been, to her own broken dreams and the lost dreams of her people?

Danoleon promised to write the letter and have it sent. She thanked him and lay back in her bed after he went out. She was genuinely weary, genuinely in pain. Hanging on. It would be half a year just past the Ember Days of spring. She had done the numbers. She would be alive to see him if he came. And he would come; she knew he would come to her.

The window had been open a little though it was still cold that day. Outside, the snow had lain in gentle drifting folds in the valley and up the slopes of the hills. She had looked out upon it but her thoughts, unexpectedly, had been of the sea. Dry-eyed, for she had not wept since everything fell, not once, not ever, she walked her memory-palaces of long ago and saw the waves come in to break and fall on the white sands of the shore, leaving shells and pearls and other gifts along the curving beach.

So Pasithea di Tigana bren Serazi. Once a princess in a palace by the sea; mother of two dead sons, and of one who yet lived. Waiting, as winter near the mountains turned to spring in that year.

★   ★   ★

"Two things. First, we are musicians," said Alessan. "A newly formed company. Secondly: do not use my name. Not here." His voice had taken on the clipped, hard cadences Devin remembered from the first night in the Sandreni lodge when this had all begun for him.

They were looking down on a valley running west in the clear light of afternoon. The Sperion lay behind them. The uneven, narrow road had wound its way for hours up around the shoulders of an ascending sequence of hills until this highest point. And now the valley unrolled before them, trees and grass touched by the earliest green-gold of spring. A tributary stream, swift-running with the melting snows, slanted northwest out of the foothills, flashing with light. The temple dome in the midst of the Sanctuary gleamed silver in the middle distance.

"What name, then?" Erlein asked quietly. He seemed subdued, whether because of Alessan's tone or the awareness of danger, Devin did not know.

"Adreano," the Prince said, after a moment. "I am Adreano d'Astibar today. I will be a poet for this reunion. For this triumphant, joyous homecoming."

Devin remembered the name: the young poet deathwheeled by Alberico last winter, after the scandal of the "Sandreni Elegies." He looked closely at the Prince for a moment and then away: this was not a day to probe. If he was here for any reason it was to try, somehow, to make things easier for Alessan. He didn't know how he was going to go about doing that though. He felt badly out of his depth again, his earlier rush of excitement fading before the grimness of the Prince's manner.

South of them, towering above the valley, the peaks of the Sfaroni Range loomed, higher even than the mountains above Castle Borso. There was snow on the peaks and even on the middle slopes; winter did not retreat so swiftly this high up, this far south. Below them though, north of the contoured foothills, in the sheltered east–west running of the valley Devin could see green buds swelling on the trees. A grey hawk hung in an updraft for a moment, almost motionless, before wheeling south and down to be lost against the backdrop of the hills. Down on the valley floor the Sanctuary seemed to lie within its walls like a promise of peace and serenity, wrapped away from all the evils of the world.

Devin knew it was not so.

They rode down, not hurrying now, for that would have been unusual in three musicians come here at midday. Devin was keenly, anxiously aware of danger. The man he was riding behind was the last heir to Tigana. He wondered what Brandin of Ygrath would do to Alessan if the Prince was betrayed and taken after so many years. He remembered Marius of Quileia in the mountain pass: *Do you trust this message?*

Devin had never trusted the priests of Eanna in his whole life. They were too shrewd, by far the most subtle of the clergy, by far the most apt to steer events to their own ends, which might lie out of sight, generations away. Servants of a goddess, he supposed, might find it easier to take the longer view of things. But everyone knew that all across the peninsula the clergy of the Triad had their own triple understanding with the Tyrants from abroad: their collective silence, their tacit complicity, bought in exchange for being allowed to preserve the rites that mattered more to them, it seemed, than freedom in the Palm.

Even before meeting Alessan, Devin had had his own thoughts about that. On the subject of the clergy his father had never been shy about speaking his mind. And now Devin remembered again Garin's single candle of defiance twice a year on the Ember Nights of his childhood in Asoli. Now that he had begun to think about it, there seemed to be a great many nuances to the flickering lights of those candles in the dark. And more shadings to his own stolid father than he had ever guessed. Devin shook his head; this was not the time to wander down that path.

When the hill track finally wound its way down to the valley floor, a wider, smoother road began, slanting towards the Sanctuary in the middle of the valley. About half a mile away from the stone outer walls, a double row of trees began on either side of the approach. Elms, coming into early leaf. Beyond them on either side Devin saw men working in the fields, some lay servants and some of them priests, clad not in the white of ceremony, but in nondescript robes of beige, beginning the labors that the soil demanded at winter's end. One man was singing, a sweet, clear tenor voice.

The eastern gates of the Sanctuary complex were open before them, simple and unadorned save for the star-symbol of Eanna. The gates were high though, Devin noted, and of heavy wrought iron. The walls that enclosed the Sanctuary were high as well, and the stone was thick. There were also towers—eight of them—curving forward at intervals around the wide embrace of the walls. This was clearly a place built, however many hundreds of years ago, to withstand adversity. Set within the complex, rising serenely above everything else, the dome of Eanna's temple shone in the sunlight as they rode up to the open gates and passed within.

Just inside Alessan pulled his horse to a halt. From ahead of them and some distance over to the left they heard the unexpected sound of children's laughter. In an open, grassy field set beyond a stable and a large residence hall a dozen young boys in blue tunics were playing maracco with sticks and a ball, supervised by a young priest in the beige work-robes.

Devin watched them with a sudden sharp sadness and nostalgia. He could remember, vividly, going into the woods near their farm with Povar and Nico when he was five years old, to cut and carry home his first maracco stick. And then the hours—minutes more often—snatched from chores when the three of them would seize their sticks and one of the battered succession of balls Nico had patiently wound together out of layers and layers of cloth, to whoop and slash their way about in the mud at the end of the barnyard, pretending they were the Asolini team at the upcoming Triad Games.

"I scored four times one game in my last year of temple schooling," Erlein di Senzio said in a musing voice. "I've never forgotten it. I doubt I ever will."

Surprised and amused, Devin glanced over at the wizard. Alessan turned in his saddle to look back as well. After a moment the three men exchanged a smile. In the distance the children's shouts and laughter gradually subsided. The three of them had been seen. It was unlikely that the appearance of strangers was a common event here, especially so soon after the melting of the snow.

The young priest had left the playing field and was making his way over, as was an older man with a full black leather apron over his robes of beige, coming from where the sheep and goats and cows were kept in pens on the other side of the central avenue. Some distance in front of them lay the arched entrance to the temple and beside it on the right and a little behind, the smaller dome of the observatory—for in all her Sanctuaries the priests of Eanna tracked and observed the stars she had named.

The complex was enormous, even more so than it had seemed from above on the hill slopes. There were a great many priests and servants moving about the grounds, entering and leaving the temple itself, working among the animals, or in the vegetable gardens Devin could see beyond the observatory. From that direction as well came the unmistakable clanging of a blacksmith's forge. Smoke rose up there, to be caught and carried by the mild breeze. Overhead he saw the hawk again, or a different one, circling lazily against the blue.

Alessan dismounted and Devin and Erlein did the same just as the two priests came up to them, at almost exactly the same moment. The younger one, sandy-haired and small like Devin, laughed and gestured at himself and his colleague.

"Not much of a greeting party, I'm afraid. We weren't expecting visitors this early in the year, I must admit. No one even noticed you riding down. Be welcome though, be most welcome to Eanna's Sanctuary, whatever the reason you have come to us. May the goddess know you and name you hers." He had a cheerful manner and an easy smile.

Alessan returned the smile. "May she know and surely name all who dwell within these walls. To be honest, we wouldn't have been certain how to deal with a more official greeting. We haven't actually worked out our entrance routines yet. And as for early in the year—well, everyone knows new-formed companies have to get moving sooner than the established ones or they are likely to starve."

"You are musical performers?" the older priest asked heavily, wiping his hands on the leather apron he wore. He was balding and brown and grizzled, and there was a gap where two of his front teeth ought to have been.

"We are," said Alessan with some attempt at a grand manner. "My name is Adreano d'Astibar. I play the Tregean pipes, and with me is Erlein di Senzio, the finest harp player in all of the peninsula. And I must tell you truly, you haven't heard singing until you've listened to our young companion Devin d'Asoli."

The younger priest laughed again. "Oh, well done! I should bring you along to the outer school to give a lesson to my charges in rhetoric."

"I'd do better to teach the pipes," Alessan smiled. "If music is part of your program here."

The priest's mouth twitched. "Formal music," he said. "This *is* Eanna, not Morian, after all."

"Of course," said Alessan hastily. "Very formal music for the young ones boarding here. But for the servants of the goddess themselves . . . ?" He arched one of his dark eyebrows.

"I will admit," said the sandy-haired young priest, smiling again, "to a preference for Rauder's early music myself."

"And no one plays it better than we," Alessan said smoothly. "I can see we have come to the right place. Should we make our obeisance to the High Priest?"

"You should," said the older man, not smiling. He began untying the apron-strings at his back. "I'll take you to him. Savandi, your charges are about to commit assault upon each other or worse. Have you no control at all over them?"

Savandi spun to look, swore feelingly in a quite unpriestly fashion, and began running towards the games field shouting imprecations. From this distance it did indeed seem to Devin that the maracco sticks were being used by Savandi's young çharges in a fashion distinctly at variance with the accepted rules of the game.

Devin saw Erlein grinning as he watched the boys. The wizard's lean face changed when he smiled. When the smile was a true one, not the ironic, slipping-sideways expression he so often used to indicate a sour, superior disdain.

The older priest, grim-faced, pulled his leather apron over his head, folded it neatly, and draped it over one of the bars of the adjacent sheepfold. He barked a name Devin could not make out and another young man—a servant this time—hastily emerged from the stables on their left.

"Take their horses," the priest ordered bluntly. "See that their goods are brought to the guest house."

"I'll keep my pipes," Alessan said quickly.

"And I my harp," Erlein added. "No lack of trust, you understand, but a musician and his instrument . . ."

This priest was somewhat lacking in Savandi's comfortable manner. "As you will," was all he said. "Come. My name is Torre, I am the porter of this Holy Sanctuary. You must be brought to the High Priest." He turned and set off without waiting for them, on a path going around to the left of the temple.

Devin and Erlein looked at each other and exchanged a shrug. They followed Torre and Alessan, passing a number of other priests and lay servants, most of whom smiled at them, somewhat making up for their dour, self-appointed guide.

They caught up to the other two as they rounded the southern side of the temple. Torre had stopped, Alessan beside him. The balding porter looked around, quite casually, then said, almost as casually: "Trust no one. Speak truth to none but Danoleon or myself. These are his words. You have been expected. We thought it would be another night, perhaps two before you came, but she said it would be today."

"Then I have proved her right. How gratifying," said Alessan in an odd voice.

Devin felt suddenly cold. Off to their left, in the games field, Savandi's boys were laughing again, lithe shapes clad in blue, running after a white ball. From within the dome he could hear, faintly, the sound of chanting. The end of the afternoon invocations. Two priests in formal white came along the path from the opposite direction, arm in arm, disputing animatedly.

"This is the kitchen, and this the bakehouse," Torre

said clearly, pointing as he spoke. "Over there is the brewhouse. You will have heard of the ale we make here, I have no doubt."

"Of course we have," murmured Erlein politely, as Alessan said nothing.

The two priests slowed, registered the presence of the strangers and their musical instruments, and went on. "Just over there is the High Priest's house," Torre continued, "beyond the kitchen and the outer school."

The other two priests, resuming their argument, swept briskly around the curve of the path that led to the front of the temple.

Torre fell silent. Then, very softly, he said: "Eanna be praised for her most gracious love. May all tongues give her praise. *Welcome home my Prince. Oh, in the name of love, be welcome home at last.*"

Devin swallowed awkwardly, looking from Torre to Alessan. An uncontrollable shiver ran along his spine: there were tears, bright-sparkling in the brilliant sunlight, in the porter's eyes.

Alessan made no reply. He lowered his head, and Devin could not see his eyes. They heard children's laughter, the final notes of a sung prayer.

"She is still alive then?" Alessan asked, looking up at last.

"She is," said Torre emotionally. "She is still alive. She is very—" He could not finish the sentence.

"There is no point in the three of us being careful if you are going to spill tears like a child," Alessan said sharply. "Enough of that, unless you want me dead."

Torre gulped. "Forgive me," he whispered. "Forgive me, my lord."

"No! Not 'my lord'. Not even when we are alone. I am Adreano d'Astibar, musician." Alessan's voice was hard. "Now take me to Danoleon."

The porter wiped quickly at his eyes. He straightened his shoulders. "Where do you think we are going?" he snapped, almost managing his earlier tone again. He spun on his heel and strode up the path.

"Good," Alessan murmured to the priest, from behind. "Very good, my friend." Trailing them both, Devin saw Torre's head lift at the words. He glanced at Erlein but this time the wizard, his expression thoughtful, did not return the look.

They passed the kitchens and then the outer school where Savandi's charges—children of noblemen or wealthy merchants, sent here to be educated—would study and sleep. All across the Palm such teaching was a part of the role of the clergy, and a source of a goodly portion of their wealth. The Sanctuaries vied with each other to draw student boarders—and their fathers' money.

It was silent within the large building now. If the dozen or so boys on the games-field with Savandi were all the students in the complex, then Eanna's Sanctuary in Lower Corte was not doing very well.

On the other hand, Devin thought, who of those left in Lower Corte could afford Sanctuary schooling for their children now? And what shrewd businessman from Corte or Chiara, having bought up cheap land here in the south, would not send his son home to be educated? Lower Corte was a place where a clever man from else-where could make money out of the ruin of the inhabi-tants, but it was not a place to put down roots. Who wanted to be rooted in the soil of Brandin's hate?

Torre led them up the steps of a covered portico and then through the open doorway of the High Priest's house. All doors seemed to be open to the spring sunshine, after the shuttered holiness of the Ember Days just past.

They stood in a large, handsome, high-ceilinged sitting-room. A huge fireplace dominated the southwestern end and a number of comfortable chairs and small tables were arranged on a deep-piled carpet. Crystal decanters on a sideboard held a variety of wines. Devin saw two bookcases on the southern wall but no books. The cases had been left to stand, disconcertingly empty. The books of Tigana had been burned. He had been told about that.

Arched doorways in both the eastern and western walls led out to porches where the sunlight could be caught in the morning and at eve. On the far side of the room there was a closed door, almost certainly leading to the bedchamber. There were four cleverly designed, square recesses in the walls and another smaller one above the fire where statues would once have stood. These too were gone. Only the ubiquitous silver stars of Eanna served for painted decoration on the walls.

The door to the bedroom opened and two priests came out.

They seemed surprised, but not unduly so, to see the porter waiting with three visitors. One man was of medium height and middle years, with a sharp face and close-cropped salt-and-pepper hair. He carried a physician's tray of herbs and powders in front of him, supported on a thong about his neck.

It was at the other man that Devin stared, though. It was the other man who carried the High Priest's staff of office. He would have commanded attention even without it, Devin thought, gazing at the figure of what had to be Danoleon.

The High Priest was an enormous man, broad-shouldered with a chest like a barrel, straight-backed despite his years. His long hair and the beard that covered half his chest were both white as new snow, even against the whiteness of his robe. Thick straight eyebrows met in the middle of a serene brow and above eyes as clear and blue as a child's. The hand he wrapped about the massive staff of office held it as if it were no more than a cowherd's hazel switch.

If they were like this, Devin thought, awed, looking up at the man who had been High Priest of Eanna in Tigana when the Ygrathens came, *if the leaders were all like this then there were truly great men here before the fall.*

They couldn't have been so different from today; he knew that rationally. It was only twenty years ago, however much might have changed and fallen away. But even so, it was hard not to feel daunted in the commanding presence of this man. He turned from Danoleon to Alessan: slight, unprepossessing, with his disorderly, prematurely silvered hair and cool, watchful eyes, and the nondescript, dusty, road-stained riding clothes he wore.

But when he turned back to the High Priest he saw that Danoleon was squeezing his own eyes tightly shut as he drew a ragged breath. And in that moment Devin realized, with a thrill that was oddly akin to pain, where, despite all appearances, the truth of power lay between these men. It was Danoleon, he remembered, who had taken the boy Alessan, the last prince of Tigana, south and away in hiding across the mountains all those years ago.

And would not have seen him again since that time. There was gray in the hair of the tired man who stood before the High Priest now. Danoleon would be seeing that, trying to deal with it. Devin found himself hurting for the two of them. He thought about the years, all the lost years that had tumbled and spun and drifted like leaves or snow between these two, then and now.

He wished he were older, a wiser man with a deeper understanding. There seemed to be so many truths or realizations of late, hovering at the edge of his awareness, waiting to be grasped and claimed, just out of reach.

"We have guests," Torre said in his brusque manner. "Three musicians, a newly formed company."

"Hah!" the priest with the medicine-tray grunted with a sour expression. "Newly formed? They'd have to be to venture here and this early in the year. I can't remember the last time someone of any talent showed up in this Sanctuary. Can you three play anything that won't clear a room of people, eh?"

"It depends on the people," said Alessan mildly.

Danoleon smiled, though he seemed to be trying not to. He turned to the other priest. "Idrisi, it is just barely possible that if we offered a warmer welcome we might be graced with visitors happier to display their art." The other man grunted what might or might not have been an apology under the scrutiny of that placid blue gaze.

Danoleon turned back to the three of them. "You will forgive us," he murmured. His voice was deep and soothing. "We have had some disconcerting news recently, and right now we have a patient in some pain. Idrisi di Corte, here, our physician, tends to be distressed when such is the case."

Privately, Devin doubted if distress had much to do with the Cortean priest's rudeness, but he kept his peace. Alessan accepted Danoleon's apology with a short bow.

"I am sorry to hear that," he said to Idrisi. "Is it possible we might be of aid? Music has long been known as a sovereign ease for pain. We should be happy to play for any of your patients.' He was ignoring for the moment, Devin noted, the news Danoleon had mentioned. It was unlikely to be an accident that Danoleon had given them Idrisi's formal name—making clear that he was from Corte.

The physician shrugged. "As you please. She is certainly not sleeping, and it can do no harm. She is almost out of my hands now, in any case. The High Priest has had her brought here against my will. Not that I can do very much anymore. In truth she belongs to Morian now." He turned to Danoleon. "If they tire her out, fine. If she sleeps it is a blessing. I will be in the infirmary or in my garden. I'll check in here tonight, unless I have word from you before."

"Will you not stay to hear us play, then?" Alessan asked. "We might surprise you."

Idrisi grimaced. "I have no leisure for such things. Tonight in the dining hall, perhaps. Surprise me." He flashed a small, unexpected smile, gone as quickly as it appeared, and went past them with brisk, irritated strides out the door.

There was a short silence.

"He is a good man," Danoleon said softly, almost apologetically.

"He is a Cortean," Torre muttered darkly.

The High Priest shook his handsome head. "He is a good man," he repeated. "It angers him when people die in his care." His gaze went back to Alessan. His hand shifted a little on his staff. He opened his mouth to speak.

"My lord, my name is Adreano d'Astibar," Alessan said firmly. "This is Devin . . . d'Asoli, whose father Garin you may perhaps remember from Stevanien." He waited. Danoleon's blue eyes widened, looking at Devin. "And this," Alessan finished, "is our friend Erlein di Senzio, who plays harp among other gifts of his hands."

As he spoke those last words, Alessan held up his left palm with two fingers curled down. Danoleon looked quickly at Erlein, and then back to the Prince. He had grown pale, and Devin was suddenly made aware that the High Priest was a very old man.

"Eanna guard us all," Torre whispered from behind them.

Alessan looked pointedly around at the open archways to the porches. "This particular patient is near death then, I take it?"

Danoleon's gaze, Devin thought, seemed to be devouring Alessan. There was an almost palpable hunger in it, the need of a starving man. "I'm afraid she is," he said keeping his tone steady only with an obvious effort. "I have given her my own chamber that she might be able to hear the prayers in the temple. The infirmary and her own rooms are both too far away."

Alessan nodded his head. He seemed to have himself on a tightly held leash, his movements and his words rigidly controlled. He lifted the Tregean pipes in their brown leather sheath and looked down at them.

"Then perhaps we should go in and make music for her. It sounds as if the afternoon prayers are done."

They were. The chanting had stopped. In the fields behind the house the boys of the outer school were still running and laughing in the sunlight. Devin could hear them through the open doorways. He hesitated, unsure of himself, then coughed awkwardly and said: "Perhaps you might like to play alone for her? The pipes are soothing, they may help her fall asleep."

Danoleon was nodding his head in anxious agreement, but Alessan turned back to look at Devin, and then at Erlein. His expression was veiled, unreadable.

"What?" he said at length. "Would you abandon me so soon after our company is formed?" And then, more softly: "There will be nothing said that you cannot know, and some things, perhaps, that you should hear."

"But she is dying," Devin protested, feeling something wrong here, something out of balance. "She is dying and she is—" He stopped himself.

Alessan's eyes were so strange.

"She is dying and she is my mother," he whispered. "I know. That is why I want you there. There seems to be some news, as well. We had better hear it."

He turned and walked towards the bedroom door. Danoleon was standing just before it. Alessan stopped before the High Priest and they looked at each other. The Prince whispered something Devin could not hear; he leaned forward and kissed the old man on the cheek.

Then he went past him. At the door he paused for a moment and drew a long steadying breath. He lifted a hand as if to run it through his hair but stopped himself. A queer smile crossed his face as if chasing a memory.

"A bad habit, that," he murmured, to no one in particular. Then he opened the door and went in and they followed him.

The High Priest's bedchamber was almost as large as the sitting room in the front, but its furnishings were starkly simple. Two armchairs, a pair of rustic, worn carpets, a wash-stand, a writing desk, a trunk for storage, a small privy set apart in the southeastern corner. There was a fireplace in the northern wall, twin to the one in the front room, sharing the same chimney. This side was lit, despite the mildness of the day, and so the room was warmer though both windows were open, curtains drawn back to admit some slanting light from under the eaves of the porticoes to the west.

The bed on the back wall under the silver star of Eanna was large, for Danoleon was a big man, but it too was simple and unadorned. No canopy, plain pinewood posts in the four corners, and a pine headboard.

It was also empty.

Devin, nervously following Alessan and the High Priest through the door, had expected to see a dying woman there. He looked, more than a little embarrassed, towards the door of the privy. And almost jumped with shock when a voice spoke from the shadows by the fire, where the light from the windows did not fall.

"Who are these strangers?"

Alessan himself had turned unerringly toward the fire the moment he entered the room—guided by what sense, Devin never knew—and so he appeared controlled and unsurprised when that cold voice spoke. Or when a woman moved forward from the shadows to stand by one of the armchairs, and then sit down upon it, her back very straight, her head held high looking at him. At all of them.

Pasithea di Tigana bren Serazi, wife to Valentin the Prince. She must have been a woman of unsurpassed beauty in her youth, for that beauty still showed, even

here, even now, at the threshold of the last portal of
Morian. She was tall and very thin, though part of that,
clearly, was due to the illness wasting her from within. It
showed in her face, which was pale almost to translu-
cence, the cheekbones thrust into too sharp relief. Her
robe had a high, stiff collar which covered her throat; the
robe itself was crimson, accentuating her unnatural, otherworldly pallor—it was as if, Devin thought, she had already crossed to Morian and was looking back at them
from a farther shore.

But there were golden rings, very much of this world,
on her long fingers, and one dazzling blue gem gleamed
from a necklace that hung down over her robe. Her hair
was gathered and bound up in a black net, a style long
out of fashion in the Palm. Devin knew with absolute
certainty that current fashion would mean nothing, less
than nothing, to this woman. Her eyes looked at him just
then with swift, unsettling appraisal, before moving on
to Erlein, and then resting, finally, upon her son.

The son she had not seen since he was fourteen years
old.

Her eyes were grey like Alessan's, but they were harder
than his, glittering and cold, hiding their depths, as if
some semi-precious stone had been caught and set just
below the surface. They glinted, fierce and challenging,
in the light of the room, and just before she spoke
again—not even waiting for an answer to her first
question—Devin realized that what they were seeing in
those eyes was rage.

It was in the arrogant face, in the high carriage and the
fingers that held hard to the arms of her chair. An inner
fire of anger that had passed, long ago, beyond the realm
of words or any other form of expression. She was dying,
and in hiding, while the man who had killed her husband
ruled her land. It was there, it was all there, for anyone
who knew but half the tale.

Devin swallowed and fought an urge to draw back
toward the door, out of range. A moment later he realized that he needn't bother; as far as the woman in the
chair was concerned he was a cipher, a nothing. He
wasn't even there. Her question had not been meant to

be answered; she didn't really care who they were. She had someone else to deal with.

For a long time, a sequence of moments that seemed to hang forever in the silence, she looked Alessan up and down without speaking, her white, imperious features quite unreadable. At last, slowly shaking her head, she said: "Your father was such a handsome man."

Devin flinched at the words and the tone, but Alessan seemed scarcely to react at all. He nodded in calm agreement. "I know he was. I remember. And so were my brothers." He smiled, a small, ironic smile. "The strain must have run out just before it got to me."

His voice was mild, but when he finished he glanced sharply at Danoleon, and the High Priest read a message there. He, in turn, murmured something to Torre who quickly left the room.

To stand guard in front, Devin realized, feeling a chill despite the fire. Words had just been spoken here that could kill them all. He looked over at Erlein and saw that the wizard had slipped his harp out of its case. His expression grim, the Senzian took a position near the eastern window and quietly began tuning his instrument.

Of course, Devin thought: Erlein knew what he was doing. They had come in here ostensibly to play for a dying woman. It would be odd if no music emerged from this room. On the other hand, he didn't much feel like singing just now.

"Musicians," the woman in the chair said with contempt to her son. "How splendid. Have you come to play a jingle for me now? To show me how skillful you are in such an important thing? To ease a mother's soul before I die?" There was something almost unbearable in her tone.

Alessan did not move, though he too had gone pale now. In no other way did he betray his tension though, save perhaps in the almost too casual stance, the exaggerated simulation of ease.

"If it would please you, my lady mother, I will play for you," he said quietly. "There was a time I can remember when the prospect of music would indeed have brought you pleasure."

The eyes of the woman in the chair glittered coldly.

"There was a time for music. When we ruled here. When the men of our family were men in more than name."

"Oh, I know," said Alessan, a little sharply. "True men and wondrous proud, all of them. Men who would have stormed the ramparts of Chiara alone and killed Brandin long ago, if only through his abject terror at their ferocious determination. Mother, can you not let it rest, even now? We are the last of our family and we have not spoken in nineteen years." His voice changed, softened, grew unexpectedly awkward. "Must we wrangle yet, can our speech be no more than the letters were? Did you ask me here simply to say again what you have written so many times?"

The old woman shook her head. Arrogant and grim, implacable as the death that had come for her.

"No, not that," she said. "I have not so much breath in me to waste. I summoned you here to receive a mother's dying curse upon your blood."

"No!" Devin exclaimed before he could stop himself.

In the same second Danoleon took a long stride forward. "My lady, no indeed," he said, anguish in his deep voice. "This is not —"

"I am dying," Pasithea bren Serazi interrupted harshly. There were spots of bright unnatural color in her cheeks. "I do not have to listen to you anymore, Danoleon. To anyone. *Wait,* you told me, all these years. *Be patient,* you said. Well, I have no more time for patience. I will be dead in a day. Morian waits for me. I have no more time to linger while my craven child gambols about the Palm playing ditties at rustic weddings."

There came a discordant jangling of harpstrings.

"That," said Erlein di Senzio from the eastern window, "is ignorant and unfair!" He stopped, as if startled by his own outburst. "Triad knows, I have no cause to love your son. And it is now more than clear to me whence his arrogance comes and his lack of care for other lives, for anything but his own goals. But if you name him a coward simply for not trying to kill Brandin of Ygrath then you are dying a vain, foolish woman. Which, to be perfectly frank, does not surprise me at all in this province!"

He leaned back against the ledge, breathing hard, look-

ing at no one. In the silence that followed Alessan finally
moved. His stillness had seemed inhuman, unnatural,
now he sank to his knees beside his mother's chair.

"You have cursed me before," he said gravely. "Remember? I have lived much of my life in the shadow of
that. In many ways it would have been easier to die years
ago: Baerd and I slain trying to kill the Tyrant in Chiara
. . . perhaps even killing him, through some miracle of
intervention. Do you know, we used to speak of it at
night, every single night, when we were in Quileia, still
boys. Shaping half a hundred different plans for an assassination on the Island. Dreaming of how we would be
loved and honored after death in a province with its
name restored because of us."

His voice was low, almost hypnotic in its cadences.
Devin saw Danoleon, his face working with emotion,
sink back into the other armchair. Pasithea was still as
marble, as expressionless and cold. Devin moved quietly
toward the fire, in a vain attempt to quell the shivering
that had come over him. Erlein was still by the window.
He was playing his harp again, softly, single notes and
random chords, not quite a tune.

"But we grew older," Alessan went on, and an urgency, a terrible need to be understood had come into his
voice. "And one Midsummer's Eve Marius became Year
King in Quileia, with our aid. After that when we three
spoke the talk was different. Baerd and I began to learn
some true things about power and the world. And that
was when it changed for me. Something new came to me
in that time, building and building, a thought, a dream,
larger and deeper than trying to kill a Tyrant. We came
back to the Palm and began to travel. As musicians, yes.
And as artisans, merchants, athletes one time in a Triad
Game year, as masons and builders, guards to a Senzian
banker, sailors on a dozen different merchant-ships. But
even before those journeys had begun, mother, even
before we came back north over the mountains, it had all
changed for me. I was finally clear about what my task in
life was to be. About what had to be done, or tried. You
know it, Danoleon knows; I wrote you years ago what
my new understanding was, and I begged your blessing
for it. It was such a simple truth: we had to take both

Tyrants together, that this whole peninsula might again be free."

His mother's voice overrode his steady passion then, harsh, implacable, unforgiving: "I remember. I remember the day that letter came. And I will tell you again what I wrote you then to that harlot's castle in Certando: you would buy Corte's freedom, and Astibar's and Tregea's at the price of Tigana's name. Of our very existence in the world. At the cost of everything we ever had or were before Brandin came. At the price of vengeance and our pride."

"Our pride," Alessan echoed, so softly now they could barely hear. "Oh, our pride. I grew up knowing all about our pride, mother. You taught me, even more than father did. But I learned something else, later, as a man. In my exile. I learned about Astibar's pride. About Senzio's and Asoli's and Certando's. I learned how pride had ruined the Palm in the year the Tyrants came."

"The Palm?" Pasithea demanded, her voice shrill. "What is the Palm? A spur of land. Rock and earth and water. What is a *peninsula* that we should care for it?"

"What is Tigana?" Erlein di Senzio asked bluntly, his harp silent in his hands.

Pasithea's glance was withering. "I would have thought a bound wizard should know that!" she said corrosively, meaning to wound. Devin blinked at the speed of her perception; no one had told her about Erlein, she had deduced it in minutes from a scattering of clues.

She said: "Tigana is the land where Adaon lay with Micaela when the world was young and gave her his love and a child and a god's gift of power to that child and those who came after. And now the world has spun a long way from that night and the last descendant of that union is in this room with the entire past of his people falling through his hands." She leaned forward, her grey eyes blazing, her voice rising in indictment. "Falling through his hands. He is a fool and a coward, both. There is so much more than freedom in a peninsula in any single generation at stake in this!"

She fell back, coughing, pulling a square of blue silk from a pocket in her robe. Devin saw Alessan begin a movement up from his knees, and then check himself.

His mother coughed, rackingly, and Devin saw, before he could turn his eyes away that the silk came away red when she was done. On the carpet beside her Alessan bowed his head.

Erlein di Senzio, from the far side of the room, perhaps too far to see the blood, said, "And shall I now tell you the legends of Senzio's pre-eminence? Of Astibar's? Will you hear me sing the story of Eanna on the Island shaping the stars from the glory of her love-making with the god? Do you know Certando's claim to be the heart and soul of the Palm? Do you remember the Carlozzini? The Night Walkers in their highlands two hundred years ago?"

The woman in the armchair pushed herself straight again glaring at him. Fearing her, hating her words and manner and the terrible thing she was doing to her son, Devin nonetheless felt humbled in the face of so much courage and such a force of will.

"But that is the point," she said more softly, sparing her strength. "That is the heart of this. Can you not see it? I *do* remember those stories. Anyone with an education or a library, any fool who has ever heard a troubadour's sentimental wailing can remember them. Can hear twenty different songs of Eanna and Adaon on Sangarios. Not us, though. Don't you *see*? Not Tigana anymore. Who will sing of Micaela under the stars by the sea when we are gone? Who will be here to sing, when one more generation has lived and died away in the world?"

"I will," said Devin, his hands at his sides.

He saw Alessan's head come up as Pasithea turned to fix him with her cold eyes. "We all will," he said, as firmly as he could. He looked at the Prince and then, forcing himself, back to the dying old woman raging in her pride. "The whole Palm will hear that song again, my lady. Because your son is *not* a coward. Nor some vain fool seeking a young death and shallow fame. He is trying for the larger thing and he is going to do it. Something has happened this spring and because of it he is going to do what he has said he will do: free this peninsula *and* bring back Tigana's name into the world."

He finished, breathing in hard gasps as if he had been running a race. A moment later, he felt himself go crimson with mortification. Pasithea bren Serazi was laughing. Mocking him, her frail thin body rocking in the chair. Her high laughter turned into another desperate fit of coughing; the blue silk came up, and when it was withdrawn there was a great deal of blood again. She clutched at the arms of her chair to steady herself.

"You are a child," she pronounced finally. "And my son is a child for all the grey in his hair. And I have no doubt that Baerd bar Saevar is exactly the same, with half the grace and the gifts his father had. *'Something has happened this spring,'* " she mimicked with cruel precision. Her voice grew hard and cold as midwinter ice: "Do you infants have any idea what has really just happened in the Palm?"

Slowly her son rose from his knees to stand before her. "We have been riding for a number of days and nights. We have heard no tidings. What is it?"

"I told you there was news," Danoleon said quickly. "But I had no chance to give you the—"

"I am pleased," Pasithea interrupted. "So very pleased. It seems I still have something to tell my son before I leave him forever. Something he hasn't learned or thought out all by himself already." She pushed herself erect again in the chair, her eyes cold and bright like frost under blue moonlight. There was something wild and lost in her voice though, trying to break through. Some terrible fear, and of more than death. She said:

"A messenger came yesterday at sunset, at the end of the Ember Days. An Ygrathen, riding from Stevanien with news from Chiara. News so urgent Brandin had sent it by his sorcerous link to all his Governors with instructions to spread the tidings."

"And the tidings are?" Alessan had braced himself, as if preparing to receive a blow.

"The tidings? The tidings, my feckless child, are that Brandin has just abdicated as King of Ygrath. He is sending his army home. And his Governors. All those who choose to stay with him must become citizens of this peninsula. Of a new dominion: the Kingdom of the Western Palm. Chiara, Corte, Asoli, Lower Corte. Four provinces under Brandin on the Island. He has announced that we are free of Ygrath, no longer a colony. Taxes are to be shared equally among us now, and they have been cut in half. Beginning yesterday. Cut by considerably more than half here in Lower Corte. Our burden will now be equal with the others. The messenger said that the people of this province—the people your father ruled—were singing Brandin's name in the streets of Stevanien."

Alessan, moving very carefully, as if he were carrying something large and heavy, that might shift and fall, turned toward Danoleon. Who was nodding his head.

"It seems that there was an assassination attempt on the Island three days ago," the High Priest said. "Originating in Ygrath: the Queen and Brandin's son, the Regent. It apparently failed only because of one of his Tribute women. The one from Certando who almost started a war. You may remember that, twelve, fourteen years ago? It seems that in the wake of this Brandin has changed his mind about what he has been doing. Not about staying in the Palm, or about Tigana and his revenge, but about what must be done in Ygrath if he continues here."

"And he is going to continue here," Pasithea said. "Tigana will die, still be lost forever to his vengeance, but our people will be singing the Tyrant's name as it dies. The name of the man who killed your father."

Alessan was nodding his head reflexively. He seemed, in fact, scarcely to be listening, as if he had suddenly withdrawn entirely inside himself. Pasithea fell silent in the face of that, looking at her son. It grew deathly still in the room. Outside, far away, the uncontrolled shouts and laughter of the children in the field came to their ears again, the louder for the silence within. Devin listened to that distant mirth and tried to slow the chaos of his heart, to attempt to deal with what they had just heard.

He looked at Erlein, who had laid down his harp on the window-ledge and walked a few steps into the room, his expression troubled and wary. Devin tried desperately to think, to gather his scattered thoughts, but the news had caught him hopelessly unprepared. *Free of Ygrath.* Which was what they wanted, wasn't it? Except that it wasn't. Brandin was staying, they were not free of him, or the weight of his magic. And Tigana? What of Tigana now?

And then, quite unexpectedly, there was something else bothering him. Something different. A distracting, niggling awareness tugging at the corner of his mind. Telling him there was something he should know, should remember.

Then, equally without warning, the something slid forward and into place. In fact . . .

In fact, he knew exactly what was wrong.

Devin closed his eyes for a moment, fighting a sudden paralyzing fear. Then, as quietly as he could, he began working his way along the western wall away from the fireplace where he had been standing all this time.

Alessan was speaking now, almost to himself. He said: "This changes things of course. It changes a great deal. I'm going to need time to think it through, but I believe it may actually help us. This may truly be a gift not a curse."

"How? Are you genuinely simple?" his mother snapped. *"They are singing the Tyrant's name in the streets of Avalle!"*

Devin winced at the old name, the desperate pain at the heart of that cry, but he forced himself to keep moving. A terrifying certainty was rising within him.

"I hear you, I understand. But don't *you* see?" Alessan dropped to his knees on the carpet again, close to his mother's chair. "The Ygrathen army is going home. If he has to fight a war it will have to be with an army of *our* people and what few Ygrathens stay with him. What . . . oh, mother! . . . what do you think the Barbadian in Astibar will do when he hears this?"

"He will do nothing," Pasithea said flatly. "Alberico is a timorous man spun neck-deep in his own webs, all of which lead back to the Emperor's Tiara. At least a quarter of the Ygrathen army will stay with Brandin. And those people singing are the most oppressed people in the peninsula. If *they* are joyous, what do you think is happening elsewhere? Do you not imagine an army can be raised in Chiara and Corte and Asoli to fight against Barbadior for a man who has renounced his own Kingdom for this peninsula?" She began coughing again, her body rocking even more harshly than before.

Devin didn't know the answer. He couldn't even begin to guess. He knew that the balance had completely shifted,

the balance Alessan had spoken about and played with
for so long. He also knew something else.

He reached the window. Its ledge was about the height
of his chest. He was a small man; not for the first time he
regretted it. Then he gave thanks for his compensations,
offered a quick prayer to Eanna and, hands flat on the
ledge for leverage, pushed upward hard and swung himself like a gymnast through to the portico. He heard
Pasithea still coughing behind him, a hard, painful sound.
Danoleon cried out.

He stumbled and fell, crashing into a pillar with his
shoulder and hip. He pushed up and off, scrambling to
his feet in time to see a figure in beige robes leap up from
a crouch beside the window, swearing furiously, and sprint
away. Devin grappled for the knife at his belt, a blind,
thought-obliterating rage rising in him. It *had* been too
uproarious in the games field. The same sound as before,
when the priest had left them alone.

Only this time the priest had left them alone while he
spied on this room.

Alessan was at the window, Erlein just behind him.

"Savandi!" Devin gasped. "He was listening!" He spat
the words over his shoulder because he was already running after the other man. He spared a fleeting moment of
thanks, and wonder, for whatever Rinaldo the Healer
had done to his leg in that Certandan barn. Then anger
swept over him again, and fear, and the absolute need to
catch the other man.

He vaulted the stone balustrade at the back end of the
portico without breaking stride. Savandi, sprinting for all
he was worth, had cut west toward the back of the
Sanctuary grounds. In the distance on their left Devin
could see the children playing in the field. He gritted his
teeth and ran. *These cursed priests!* he was thinking, fury
almost choking him. *Will they undo everything, even now?*

If Alessan's identity became known anywhere in this
Sanctuary Devin had little doubt how swiftly that knowledge would reach Brandin of Ygrath. He had no doubts
at all about what would happen then.

And then he was assailed by another whirling thought,
one that terrified him. He drove himself to even greater
speed, legs pumping, his lungs sucking for air. *The mind-*

link. What if Savandi could link to the King? What if Brandin's spy could directly contact him in Chiara now?

Devin cursed in the depths of his heart but not aloud, sparing his breath for speed. Savandi, lithe and quick himself, raced down the path past a small building on the left and cut sharply right, about twenty strides ahead of Devin, around the back part of the temple itself.

Devin sped around the corner. Savandi was nowhere to be seen. He froze for a moment, seized by panic. There was no door into the temple here. And only a thick barrier of hedges, just coming into green on the left.

Then he saw where the hedges were quivering and he leaped for that spot. There was a gap forced low down. He dropped to his knees and scrambled through, scratching his arms and face.

He was in a cloistered area, large, beautifully serene, gracefully laid out, with a splashing fountain at the center. He had no time to value such things though. At the northwest corner the cloister gave onto another portico and a long building with a small domed roof at the near end. Savandi was just now sprinting up the steps to the portico and then through a doorway into the building. Devin looked up. At one second-story window an old man could be seen, white haired and hollow-cheeked, gazing down without expression on the sunlit cloister.

Running flat out for the doorway, Devin realized where he was. This was the infirmary, and the small dome would be a temple for the sick who sought the comfort of Eanna but could not venture down the path to her larger dome.

He took the three steps to the portico in one flying leap and burst through the doorway, knife in hand. He was aware that following so fast he was an easy target for an ambush if Savandi chose to lie in wait. He didn't think that would happen though—which only increased his deeper fear.

The man seemed to be racing *away* from where his fellow priests might be found, in the temple itself, the kitchens, the dormitory or the dining room. Which meant that he didn't expect help or aid, that he couldn't really be hoping to escape.

Which meant, in turn, that there was probably only one thing he was going to try to do, if Devin gave him enough time.

The doorway gave onto a long corridor and a stairway leading upward. Savandi was out of sight but Devin, glancing down, gave a quick prayer of thanks to Eanna: running across the damp ground of the cloister the priest had picked up mud on his shoes. The trail was unmistakable on the stone floor and it went down the corridor and not up the stairs.

Devin sped in pursuit, flying down the hallway, skidding into a left turn around a corner at the far end. There were rooms at intervals all along and an arched entrance to the infirmary's small temple at the opposite end. Most of the doors were open; most of the rooms were empty.

But then, in that short corridor he came to one closed door; Savandi's trail led there and stopped. Devin clutched the handle and threw his shoulder hard against the heavy wood. Locked. Immovable.

Sobbing for breath he dropped to his knees, grappling in his pocket for the twist of wire he was never without: not since Marra had been alive. Since she had taught him all he knew about locks. He untwisted and tried to shape the wire, but his hands were trembling. Sweat streamed into his eyes. He wiped it furiously away and fought for calm. He *had* to get this door open before the man inside sent the message that would destroy them all.

An exterior door opened behind him. Steps thudded quickly down the hallway.

Without looking up, Devin said: "The man who touches or hinders me dies. Savandi is a spy for the King of Ygrath. Find me a key for this door!"

"It is done!" came a voice he knew. "It is open. Go!"

Devin flung a glance over his shoulder and saw Erlein di Senzio standing there with a sword in his hand.

Springing to his feet Devin twisted the handle again. The door swung open. He charged into the room. There were jars and vials lining shelves around the walls, and instruments on tables. Savandi was there, on a bench in the middle of the room, hands at his temples, visibly straining to concentrate.

"Plague rot your soul!" Devin screamed at the top of

his voice. Savandi seemed to snap awake. He rose with a feral snarl, grabbing for a surgical blade on the table beside him.

He never reached it.

Still screaming, Devin was upon him, his left hand gouging at the priest's eyes. He slashed forward and up with his right in a hard and deadly arc, plunging his blade in between Savandi's ribs. Once, he stabbed, and then again, raking savagely upward, feeling the blade twist, grinding against bone with a sickening sensation. The young priest's mouth gaped open, his eyes widened in astonishment. He screamed, high and short, his hands flying outward from his sides. And then he died.

Devin released him and collapsed on the bench, fighting for breath. Blood pounded in his head; he could feel a vein pulsing at his temple. His vision blurred for a moment and he closed his eyes. When he opened them he saw that his hands were still shaking.

Erlein had sheathed his sword. He moved to stand beside Devin.

"Did . . . did he send . . . ?" Devin found that he couldn't even speak properly.

"No." The wizard shook his head. "You came in time. He didn't link. No message went."

Devin stared down at the blank, staring eyes and the body of the young priest who had sought to betray them. *How long?* he wondered. *How long was he doing this?*

"How did you get here?" he asked Erlein, his voice hoarse. His hands were still shaking. He dropped the bloodied knife with a clatter on the tabletop.

"I followed from the bedchamber. Saw which way you went until I lost you around the back of the temple. Then I needed magic. I traced Savandi's aura here."

"We came through the hedges and across the cloister. He was trying to shake me."

"I can see that. You're bleeding again."

"Doesn't matter." Devin took a deep breath. There were footsteps in the corridor outside. "Why did you come? Why do this for us?"

Erlein looked defensive for an instant, but quickly regained his sardonic expression. "For you? Don't be a fool, Devin. I die if Alessan does. I'm bound, remember? This was self-preservation. Nothing else."

Devin looked up at him, wanting to say something more, something important, but just then the footsteps reached the doorway and Danoleon entered quickly with Torre close behind. Neither of them said a word, taking in the scene.

"He was trying to mind-link with Brandin," Devin said. "Erlein and I got to him in time."

Erlein made a dismissive sound. "Devin did. But I had to use a spell to follow them and another on the door. I don't think they were strong enough to draw attention, but in case there is a Tracker anywhere around here we had better get moving before morning."

Danoleon seemed not to have even heard. He was looking down at Savandi's body. There were tears on his face.

"Don't waste your grief on a carrion bird," Torre said harshly.

"I must," the High Priest said softly, leaning upon his staff. "I must. Don't you understand? He was born in Avalle. He was one of us."

Devin abruptly turned his head away. He felt sick to his stomach, hit by a resurgence of the raging white fury that had sped him here, and had driven him to kill so violently. *One of us.* He remembered Sandre d'Astibar in the cabin in the woods, betrayed by his grandchild. He was seriously afraid he was going to be ill. *One of us.*

Erlein di Senzio laughed. Devin wheeled furiously around on him, his hands clenched into fists. And there must have been something murderous in his eyes, for the wizard quickly sobered, mockery leaving his face as if wiped away with a cloth.

There was a short silence.

Danoleon drew himself up and straightened his massive shoulders. He said, "This will have to be dealt with carefully or the story will spread. We can't have Savandi's death traced to our guests. Torre, when we leave lock this room with the body in it. After dark, when the others are asleep we will deal with him."

"He'll be missed at dinner," Torre said.

"No he won't. You are the porter. You will see him

ride through the gate late this afternoon. He will be going to see his family. It fits, just after the Ember Days, and in the wake of the news from Chiara. He has ridden out often enough, and not always with my permission. I think I have an idea why now. I wonder if he ever really rode to his father's house. Unfortunately for Savandi, this time he is going to be killed by someone on the road just outside our valley."

There was a hardness to the High Priest's voice that Devin had not heard before. *One of us.* He looked down at the dead man again. His third killing. But this one was different. The guard in the Nievolene barn, the soldier in the hill pass, they had been doing what they had come to the Palm to do. Loyal to the power they served, hiding nothing of their nature, true to their manifest cause. He had grieved for their dying, for the lines of life that had brought him together with them.

Savandi was otherwise. This death was different. Devin searched his soul and found that he could not grieve for what he had done. It was all he could do, he realized with a sense of real uneasiness, to refrain from plunging his dagger again in the corpse. It was as if the young priest's corrosive treachery to his people, his smiling deceit, had tapped some violence of passion Devin hadn't known lay within him. Almost exactly, he thought suddenly, the way that Alienor of Castle Borso had done, in a very different sphere of life.

Or, perhaps, at the heart of things, not so very different after all. But that was too hard, too dangerous a knot to try to untie just now, in the staring presence of death. Which reminded him of something, made him suddenly aware of an absence. He looked quickly up at Danoleon.

"Where's Alessan?" he said sharply. "Why didn't he follow?"

But even before he was answered, he knew. There could only be one reason in the world why the Prince hadn't come.

The High Priest looked down at him. "He is still in my chamber. With his mother. Though I am afraid it may be over by now."

"No," Devin said. "Oh, no." And rose, and went to the door, and into the corridor, and then out through the eastern doorway of the infirmary into the slanting light of late afternoon, and began, again, to run.

Along the back curve of the temple dome, past the same small building as before and a little garden he hadn't noticed coming here, then back, flying, down the path to the High Priest's house, and up onto the portico between the pillars, as if rewinding events like a ball of wool, to the window through which he had leaped such a little while ago. As if he could race back not only past Savandi, past their coming here, but all the way back, with a sudden, incoherent longing, to where the seeds of this grief had been planted when the Tyrants came.

But time was not rewound, neither in the heart nor in the world as they knew it. It moved on, and things changed, for better or for worse; seasons changed, the hours of sunlit day went by, darkness fell and lingered and gave way to light at dawn, years spun after each other one by one, people were born, and lived by the Triad's grace, and they died.

And they died.

Alessan was still in the room, still on his knees on the simple carpet, but beside the bed now, not by the heavy, dark oak chair as before. He had moved, time had moved, the sun was further west along the curving sky.

Devin had wanted to somehow run his way back through the moments that had passed. That Alessan might not have been left alone, not with this. On his first day in Tigana since he was a boy. He was no longer a boy; there was grey in his hair. Time had run. Twenty years worth of time had run and he was home again.

And his mother lay on the High Priest's bed. Alessan's two hands were laced around one of her own, cradling it gently as one might hold a small bird that would die of fright if clutched too fast but would fly away forever if released.

Devin must have made some kind of sound at the window for the Prince looked up. Their eyes met. Devin ached inside, wordless with sorrow. His heart felt bruised, besieged. He felt hopelessly inadequate to the needs of such a time as this now was. He wished that Baerd were here, or Sandre. Even Catriana would know what to do better than he.

He said, "He is dead. Savandi. We caught him in time." Alessan nodded, acknowledging this. Then his gaze went down again to his mother's face, serene now as it had not been before. As it very likely had not been for the last long years of her life. Time, moving inexorably forward for her, taking memory, taking pride. Taking love.

"I'm sorry," Devin said. "Alessan, I'm so sorry."

The Prince looked up again, the grey eyes clear but terribly far away. Chasing images backward along a skein of years. He looked as if he would speak but did not. Instead, after another moment, he gave his small shrug, the calm, reassuring motion of acceptance, of shouldering another burden, that they all knew so well.

Devin suddenly felt as if he could not bear it anymore. Alessan's quiet acquiescence was as a final blow in his own heart. He felt torn open, wounded by the hard truths of the world, by the passing of things. He lowered his head to the windowsill and wept like a child in the presence of something too large for his capacity.

In the room Alessan knelt in silence by the bed, holding his mother's hand between his own. And the westering sun of afternoon sent light in a golden slant through the window and across the chamber floor, to fall upon him, upon the bed, upon the woman lying there, upon the golden coins that covered her grey eyes.

CHAPTER

• 16 •

SPRING CAME EARLY IN ASTIBAR TOWN. IT ALMOST ALways did along that sheltered northwestern side of the province, overlooking the bay and the strungout islands of the Archipelago. East and south the unblocked winds from the sea pushed the start of the growing season back a few weeks and kept the smaller fishing boats close to shore this early in the year.

Senzio was already flowering, the traders in Astibar harbor reported, the white blossoms of the sejoia trees making the air fragrant with the promise of summer to come. Chiara was still cold it was said, but that happened sometimes in early spring on the Island. It wouldn't be long before the breezes from Khardhun gentled the air and the seas around her.

Senzio and Chiara.

Alberico of Barbadior lay down at night thinking about them, and rose up in the morning doing the same, after intense, agitated nights of little rest, shot through with lurid, disturbing dreams.

If the winter had been unsettling, rife with small incidents and rumors, the events of early spring were something else entirely. And there was nothing small, nothing only marginally provocative about them.

Everything seemed to be happening at once. Coming down from his bedchamber to his offices of state, Alberico would find his mood darkening with every step in the apprehensive anticipation of what might next be reported to him.

The windows of the palace were open now to let the mild breezes sweep through. It had been some time since

490

it had been warm enough to do that and for much of the autumn and winter there had been bodies rotting on death-wheels in the square. Sandreni bodies, Nievolene, Scalvaiane. A dozen poets wheeled at random. Not conducive to opening windows, that. Necessary though, and lucrative, after his confiscation of the conspirators' lands. He liked when necessity and gain came together; it didn't happen often but when it did the marriage seemed to Alberico of Barbadior to represent almost the purest pleasure to be found in power.

This spring however his pleasures had been few and trivial in scope, and the burgeoning of new troubles made those of the winter seem like minor, ephemeral afflictions—brief flurries of snow in a night. What he was dealing with now were rivers in flood, everywhere he looked.

At the very beginning of spring a wizard was detected using his magic in the southern highlands, but the Tracker and the twenty-five men Siferval had immediately sent after him had been slaughtered in a pass by outlaws, to the last man. An act of arrogance and revolt almost impossible to believe.

And he couldn't even properly exact retribution: the villages and farms scattered through the highlands hated the outlaws as much or more than the Barbadians did. And it had been an Ember Night, with no decent man abroad to see who might have done this unprecedented deed. Siferval sent a hundred men from Fort Ortiz to hunt the brigands down. They found no trace. Only long dead campfires in the hills. It was as if the twenty-five men had been slain by ghosts: which, predictably, is what the people of the highlands were already saying. It *had* been an Ember Night after all, and everyone knew the dead were abroad on such nights. The dead, hungry for retribution.

"How clever of the dead to use new-fletched arrows," Siferval's written report had offered sardonically, when he sent two captains to carry the tidings north. His men had retreated quickly in whey-faced terror at the expression on Alberico's face. It was, after all, the Third Company which had allowed twenty-five of its men to be killed, and had then sent out another hundred incompe-

tents to do no more than elicit laughter, wandering about
in the hills.

It was maddening. Alberico had been forced to fight
back an urge to torch the Certandan hamlet nearest to
those hills, but he knew how destructive that would be in
the longer run. It would undermine all the benefits of the
focused restraint he'd used in the affair of the Sandreni
plot. That night his eyelid began to droop again, the way
it had in the early autumn.

Then, very shortly after, came the news from Quileia.

He had nourished such hopes there after the shocking
fall of the Matriarchy. It was such an enormous, ripe new
market for trade, an absolute harvest for the Empire.
And one, most importantly, that would be brought into
Barbadior's aegis by that ever vigilant guardian of the
western borders of the Empire, Alberico of the Eastern
Palm.

So much rich hope and promise there, and so little
actual prospect of difficulty. Even if this Marius, this
crippled priestess-killer on his precarious throne, chose to
trade west with Ygrath as well as east that was all right.
Quileia was more than large enough to offer bounty both
ways. For a time. Soon enough it should be possible to
make the uncouth fellow see the many-faceted advantages
of focusing his dealings towards Barbadior.

In the evolution of the Barbadian Empire there had
emerged a number of ways, a great many time-honored
ways, some subtle, some rather less so, of causing men to
see things in a particular light. Alberico had a few thoughts
of his own about even newer means of persuading petty
monarchs to view matters usefully. He fully intended to
explore them, once he was home.

Home, as Emperor. For that, after all, was the point,
the point of absolutely everything. Except that the events
of the spring utterly refused to cooperate.

Marius of Quileia sent a gratifyingly swift reply to
Alberico's latest benevolent offer to trade. An emissary
delivered it directly into the hands of Siferval in Fort
Ortiz.

Unfortunately, that brief gratification had been smashed
and annihilated when the letter reached Astibar, carried
north this time, in recognition of its importance, by Siferval

himself. Couched in unexpectedly sophisticated language it contained a message that, however politely and circuitously phrased, was flat and clear: the Quileian regretfully judged that Brandin of Ygrath was the greater, firmer power in the Palm, and as such, and being but green in his own power, he could not risk incurring the anger of the King of Ygrath by trading with Alberico, a minor lord of the Empire, much as he might want to.

It was a letter that could easily drive a man into a killing rage.

Fighting for self-control, Alberico had seen cringing apprehension in his clerks and advisors, and even a quickly veiled fear in the eyes of the captain of the Third Company. Then, when Siferval handed over the second letter, the one, he explained, that he had so cleverly arranged to extract and copy from the saddle pouch of the overly garrulous Quileian emissary, Alberico felt all control deserting him.

He had been forced to turn away, to stride alone to the windows at the back of the offices of state and draw gasping breaths of air to calm his boiling mind. He could feel the tell-tale tremor beginning again in his right eyelid; the fluttering he'd never been able to get rid of since that night he'd almost died in the Sandreni Woods. His huge hands grasping the window-ledge with a grip of iron, he struggled for the equanimity that would let him carefully weigh the implications of this intercepted message, but calm was a swiftly receding illusion and his thoughts in the morning sunlight were black and foaming like the sea in storm.

Senzio! The Quileian fool sought to link himself with those dissolute puppets in the ninth province! It was almost impossible to credit that a man, however new to the world stage, could be such an imbecile.

His back to his advisors and his captains, staring blindly out the window down upon the too bright Grand Square, Alberico abruptly began to consider how this was going to look to the wider world. To the part of the world that mattered: the Emperor, and those who had his ear, and who saw themselves as rivals to Alberico. How would the tidings be read, if Brandin of Ygrath was busily trading south, if Senzian merchants were blithely sailing past the

Archipelago and down the coast beyond Tregea and the mountains to Quileian ports and all the fabled goods of that land, so long kept to themselves under the priestesses? If the Empire alone was denied access to this new market. Denied access because Alberico of Barbadior was judged too infirm in his power here as compared to the Ygrathen in the west . . . Albeico felt himself beginning to sweat; a cold trickle of moisture slid down his side. There was a spasm of pain in his chest as a muscle clenched near his heart. He forced himself to breathe slowly until it passed.

From the source of so much promise it suddenly seemed as if a dagger had materialized, more sharp and deadly than any enemy of his back in Barbadior might have fashioned.

Senzio. He had been thinking and dreaming about the ninth province all through the months of ice and snow, seeking a way in his restless nights to break out, to regain control of a situation that increasingly seemed to be operating upon him, instead of he upon it, as master of his destiny.

And that had been in the winter, even before this news from beyond the mountains.

Then, shortly after, even as the first flowers began blooming in the gardens of Astibar, there was more. In the very same week word came from the west that someone had tried to kill Brandin of Ygrath.

Had tried, and failed. For one blissful night Alberico played out glorious scenarios of triumph in his sleep. Dreaming, over and over again, so keen was the pleasure, that the assassin—using a crossbow, they had learned—had succeeded in his purpose. Oh, it would have been so perfect, it would have been timed so flawlessly for him, dovetailing so neatly with his needs. It would have had to be seen as a gift, a shining upon his face, from the high gods of the Empire. The entire Peninsula of the Palm would have been his in a year, in *half* a year. Quileia's crippled monarch, needing the outer world so desperately, would have had to embrace whatever terms of trade Alberico then chose to offer him.

And the Empire? His, a year after all of that, at the very worst.

With such an unchallenged power base here, he would not have even needed to wait for the ailing Emperor to finally die. He could have sailed home with his armies as the champion and the hero of the people. Having first showered them with grain, with gold, with freely flowing wine from the Palm, and all the newly rediscovered wealth of Quileia.

It would have been glorious. For that one night Alberico let himself dream, smiling in his sleep. Then he woke, and came down the stairs again to the offices of state and found all three of his captains waiting, grim-faced. A new messenger was there with them. From the west again, a single day after the first, with news that smashed twenty years of balancing into tiny, sharp-edged fragments that would never again be reassembled as they had been.

Brandin had abdicated in Ygrath and named himself King of the Western Palm.

On Chiara, the messenger reported, trembling at his lord's visage, they had begun celebrating within hours of the announcement.

"And the Ygrathens?" Karalius of the First asked sharply, though he had no real right to speak.

"Most will go home," the messenger said. "If they stay they must become citizens, only equal citizens, of the new kingdom."

"You say they will go home," Alberico said, his gaze flat and heavy, masking the feverish churning of his emotions. "Do you know this, have you been told this, or do you only guess it to be so?"

The messenger turned grey, stammering some reply about logic and obvious consequences and what anyone could predict . . .

"Have this man's tongue cut out then have him killed," Alberico said. "I don't care how. Feed him to the animals. My messengers bring me the news they learn. *I* draw what conclusions are to be drawn."

The messenger fainted dead away, toppling sideways to the floor. It could be seen that he had soiled himself. Grancial of the Second Company signaled quickly for two men to carry him out.

Alberico didn't bother to watch. In a way he was glad

the man had spoken as fatuously as he had. He had needed an excuse to kill just then.

He gestured with two fingers, and his steward hastily ushered everyone out of the room but the three captains. Not that any of the lesser officials seemed inclined to linger at that particular moment. Which was as it should be. He didn't trust any of them very much.

He didn't entirely trust his captains either, but he needed them, and they needed him, and he had been careful to keep them at odds and on edge with each other. It was a workable arrangement. Or it had been, until now.

But *now* was what mattered, and Brandin had just thrown the peninsula into chaos. Not that the Palm actually mattered, not in itself. It was a gateway, a stepping-stone. He had moved out of Barbadior as a young man, in order to rise in the world and return as a leader in his prime, and there was no point, no point at all to twenty years of exile if he could not sail home in triumph. In more than triumph. In mastery.

He turned his back on the captains and went to the window, surreptitiously massaging his eye. He waited, to see who would speak first, and what he would say. There was a fear growing within him that he was at pains to hide. Nothing was falling right, none of his caution and discretion seemed to have borne the fruit it should.

Karalius said, very softly from behind him, "My lord, there is opportunity here. There is great opportunity."

Which is exactly what he was afraid the man would say. Afraid, because he knew it was true and because it meant moving again, and quickly, committing himself to dangerous, decisive action. But action here and not in the Empire, not back home, where he had been readying himself to return. War far away in this savage, obdurate peninsula where he could lose all, a lifetime's sowing, in striving for a conquest he hardly cared about.

"We had best go carefully," Grancial said quickly. More to oppose Karalius than anything else, Alberico knew. But he noted that *we.*

He turned and fixed the Second Company captain with a wintry glance. "I will indeed do nothing without thought," he said, placing clear emphasis on the first word. Grancial flicked his eyes away. Siferval smiled beneath his curling blond moustaches.

Karalius did not. His expression remained sober and thoughtful. He was the best of the three, Alberico knew. Also the most dangerous, for the two things went hand in hand in such a man. Alberico moved around behind his huge oak desk and sat down again. He looked up at the First Company leader and waited.

Karalius said again, "There is opportunity now. There will be turmoil in the west, disruption, Ygrathens sailing home. Shall I tell you what I think?" His pale skin was flushed with a growing excitement. Alberico understood that: the man saw chances of his own, land and wealth for himself.

It would be a mistake to let Karalius unfold too much. He would end up thinking the planning was his. Alberico said, "I know exactly what you think, to the very words you would speak. Be silent. I know everything that will be happening in the west except one thing: we don't yet know how many of the Ygrathen army will stay. My guess is that most will leave, rather than be lowered to the level of people they have had mastery over all these years. They did not come here to become inconsequential figures in the Palm."

"Neither," said Siferval pointedly, "did we."

Alberico suppressed his anger yet again. It seemed he had been forced to do that so much of late with these three. But they had their own purposes, their own long drawn-out plans, and wealth and fame were at the heart of them. As they had to be for all ambitious men in the Empire: toward what else should an ambitious man aspire?

"I am aware of that," he said, as calmly as he could.

"Then what do we do?" Grancial asked. A real question, not a challenge. Grancial was the weakest and the most loyal—because of that weakness—of the three.

Alberico looked up. At Karalius, not at Grancial.

"You gather my armies," he said deliberately, though his pulse was racing very fast. This was dangerous and might be final, every instinct within him told him that. But he also knew that time and the gods had thrown a glittering gem down toward him from the heavens, and if he did not move it would fall away.

"You gather my armies in all four provinces and take them north. I want them massed together as soon as possible."

"Where?" Karalius's eyes were almost shining with anticipation.

"Ferraut, of course. On the northern border with Senzio." *Senzio,* he was thinking. *The ninth. The jewel. The battleground.*

"How long will it take you?" he asked the three of them.

"Five weeks, no more," Grancial said quickly.

"Four," said Siferval, smiling.

"The First Company," said Karalius, "will be on the border three weeks from now. Count on it."

"I will," said Alberico. And dismissed them.

He sat alone at his desk for a long time after, toying with a paperweight, thinking upon all sides of this, over and around and about. But however he looked upon it all the pieces seemed to slide into place. There was power to be grasped here, and triumph, he could almost see that shimmering jewel falling through the air, over water, over land, into his reaching hand.

He was acting. Shaping events himself, not being impacted upon. His enemy would be vulnerable, enormously so, until this new chaos settled in the west. Quileia's choice could be forced and be no choice at all. The Empire could be made to see, on the eve of his final journey home, just what his sorcery and his armies could do. The time was offering a jewel, truly, falling from the heavens, waiting to be clasped. To be set upon his brow.

He was still uneasy though, almost uncannily so, sitting alone as the morning brightened, trying to convince himself of the truth of all this shining promise. He was more than uneasy; his mouth was dry and the spring sunlight seemed strange to him, almost painful. He wondered if he was ill. There was something gnawing away like a rat in darkness at the unlit corners of his thoughts. He forced himself to turn towards it, trying to make a torch of his careful rationality, to look within himself and root out this anxiety.

And then indeed he did see it, and understood, in that

same moment, that it could not be rooted out, nor ever be acknowledged to a living soul.

For the truth, the poisonous gall of truth, was that he was afraid. Deathly afraid, in the deepest inward places of his being, of this other man. Of Brandin of Ygrath, now Brandin of the Western Palm. The name had been changed, the balance changed utterly.

The truth of fear was exactly as it had been for almost twenty years.

A short while later he left the room and went down the stairs and underground to see how they killed the messenger.

★　　★　　★

Alais knew exactly why she was being granted this unprecedented gift of a journey in the *Sea Maid* with her father: Selvena was getting married at the end of summer.

Catini bar Edinio, whose father owned a good-sized estate of olive trees and vineyards north of Astibar, and a modest but successful banking house in the city, had asked Rovigo for his second daughter's hand early in the spring. Rovigo, urgently forewarned by his second daughter, had given his consent, a decision calculated, among other things, to forestall Selvena's oft-proclaimed intention to do away with herself should she still be living at home and unwed by the autumn. Catini was earnest and pleasant if a little dull, and Rovigo had done business with Edinio in the past and liked the man.

Selvena was tempestuously ecstatic, about plans for the wedding, about the prospect of running her own home— Edinio had offered to set the young couple up in a small house on a hill above his vineyards—and, as Rovigo overheard her telling the younger girls one evening, about the anticipated pleasures of the marriage bed.

He was pleased for her happiness and rather looking forward to the celebration of the marriage. If he had moments of sadness that he strove to mask, he attributed it to the natural feelings of a man who saw that his girl-child had become a woman rather sooner than he had been prepared for. The sight of Selvena making a red glove for her bridal night affected Rovigo more than he had thought it would. He would turn from her bright, feverish chatter to Alais, neat and quiet and watchful, and something akin to sadness would touch his spirit amid the anticipatory bustle of the house.

Alix seemed to understand, perhaps even better than he did himself. His wife had taken to patting his shoulder at sporadic, unexpected moments, as if gentling a restive creature.

He *was* restive. This spring the news from the wider world was unpredictable and of seemingly enormous consequence. Barbadian troops were beginning to clog the roads as they moved up to northern Ferraut, on the border of Senzio. From the newly declared Kingdom of the Western Palm had come no clear response as yet to this provocation. Or none that had reached Astibar. Rovigo hadn't heard a word from Alessan since well before the Ember Days, but he had been told a long time ago that this spring might mark the beginning of something new.

And something *was* in the air, a sense of quickening and of change that fit itself to the mood of burgeoning spring and then went beyond it, into danger and the potential for violence. He seemed to hear it and see it everywhere, in the tramp of armies on the march, in the lowered voices of men in taverns, looking up too quickly whenever anyone came through the door.

One morning when he woke, Rovigo had an image that lingered in his mind, of the great floes of solidly packed river ice he had glimpsed many years ago far to the south on a long voyage down the coast of Quileia. And in his mind-picture, as he lay in bed, suspended between asleep and fully awake, he had seemed to see that ice breaking up and the river waters beginning to run again, carrying the floes crashing and grinding down to the sea.

Over khav that same morning, standing in the kitchen, he had announced that he was going into town to see about equipping the *Maid* for her first run of the season down to Tregea, with goods, perhaps wine—perhaps Edinio's wine—to trade for a ship's hold's worth of early spring wool and Tregean goat's cheese.

It was an impulsive decision, but not an inappropriate one. He usually made a run south in the spring, if a little later in the season, mostly for trade, partly to learn what he could for Alessan. He had been doing it for years, for both reasons, ever since he'd met Alessan and Baerd, spending a long night in a southern tavern with them, and coming away with the knowledge of a shared passion of the soul and a cause that might be a lifetime in the unfolding.

So this spring voyage was a part of his yearly routine. What was not, what was truly impulsive, was his offer, between one sip of early morning khav and the next, to take Alais with him.

His eldest, his pride, his clever one. He thought her beautiful beyond words. No one had asked for her hand. And though he knew she was truly pleased for Selvena and not grieving at all for herself, this knowledge didn't stop him from feeling a difficult sorrow whenever he looked at her amid the already building excitement of Selvena's wedding preparations.

So he asked her, a little too casually, if she wanted to come with him, and Alix glanced up quickly from her labors in the kitchen with a sharp, worried look in her dark eyes, and Alais said, even more quickly, with a fervor rare for her: "Oh, Triad, *yes!* I would love to come!"

It happened to be her dream.

One of her oldest dreams, never requested, never even spoken aloud. Alais could feel how high her tell-tale color had suddenly become. She watched her father and mother exchange a glance. There were times when she envied them that communion of their eyes. No words were spoken, they didn't seem to need words much of the time. Then Alais saw her mother nod, and she turned in time to catch her father's slow smile in response to that, and she knew she was going to sea in the *Maid* for the first time in her life.

She had wanted to do so for so long she couldn't even think back to a time when the desire hadn't been there. She remembered being a small girl, light enough to be lifted up by her father while her mother carried Selvena, going down to the harbor in Astibar to see the new ship that was the key to their small fortune in the world.

And she had loved it so much. The three masts—they

had seemed so tall to her then—aspiring toward the sky, the dark-haired figurehead of a maiden at the prow, the bright-blue coat of fresh paint along the railings, the creak of the ropes and the timber. And the harbor itself: the smell of pitch and pine and fish and ale and cheese, wool and spice and leather. The rumble of carts laden with goods going away to some far part of the known world, or coming in from distant places with names that were a kind of magic to her.

A sailor in red and green walked by with a monkey on his shoulder and her father called a familiar greeting to him. Her father seemed to be at home here, he knew these men, the wild, exotic places from which they came and went. She heard shouts and sudden raucous laughter and voices raised in profane dispute over the weight of this or the cost of that. Then someone cried out that there were dolphins in the bay; that was when her father had lifted her up on his shoulders so she might see them.

Selvena had begun to cry at all the fierce commotion, Alais remembered, and they had gone back to their cart shortly after and ridden away, past the watchful, looming presence of the Barbadians, big, fair-haired men on their big horses, guarding the harbor of Astibar. She had been too young to understand what they were about, but her father's abrupt silence and expressionless face, riding by them, had told her something. Later, she learned a great deal more, growing up into the occupied reality of her world.

Her love of the ships and the harbor had never gone away. Whenever she could she would go with Rovigo down to the water. It was easier in winter, when they all moved to the town house in Astibar, but even in spring and summer and early fall she would find excuses, reasons and ways to accompany him into town and down to where the *Maid* was berthed. She gloried in the scene, and at night she dreamt her dreams of oceans opening before her and salt spray off the waves.

Dreams. She was a woman. Women did not go to sea. And dutiful, intelligent daughters never troubled their fathers by even asking to be allowed such a thing. But it seemed that, sometimes, on some mornings completely unforeseen, Eanna could look down from among her

lights in the sky, and smile, and something miraculous
might be freely offered that would never have been sought.

It seemed she was a good sailor, adjusting easily to the
swing and roll of the ship on the waves as the coastline of
Astibar scrolled by on their right. They sailed north
along the bay and then threaded their way through the
islands of the Archipelago and into the wideness of the
open sea, Rovigo and his five seamen handling the ship
with an ease that seemed to her both relaxed and precise.
Alais was exhilarated, watching everything in this unknown world with an intensity that made them laugh and
tease her for it. There was no malice in the jests though;
she had known all five of these men for most of her life.

They swung around the northern tip of the province; a
cape of storms, one of the men told her. But that spring
day it was an easy, mild place, and she stood at the
railing as they turned back south, and watched the green
hills of her province pass by, sloping down to the white
sand of the shores and the fishing villages dotted along
the coast.

A few nights later there *was* a storm, off the cliffs of
northern Tregea. Rovigo had seen it coming at sunset, or
smelled it in the air, but the coastline was rocky and
forbidding here, with no place to put in for shelter. They
braced for the squall, a respectful distance off shore to
keep clear of the rocks. When it hit, Alais was down
below in her cabin, to keep out of the way.

Even this weather, she was grateful to discover, didn't
bother her very much. There was nothing *pleasant* about
it, feeling the *Sea Maid* groan and shake, buffeted in
darkness by wind and rain, but she told herself that her
father had endured infinitely worse in thirty years at sea,
and she was not going to let herself be frightened or
discomfited by a minor spring squall from the east.

She made a point of going back up on deck as soon as
she felt the waves and the wind die down. It was still
raining, and she covered her head with the hood of her
cape. Careful to stay clear of where the men were
laboring, she stood at one rail and looked up. East of
them the swiftly scudding clouds revealed rifts of clear
sky and briefly Vidomni's light shone through. Later the

wind died down even more, the rain stopped and the clouds broke up, and she saw Eanna's bright, far stars come out above the sea, like a promise, like a gift. She pushed back her hood and shook out her dark hair. She took a deep breath of the fresh clean air, and knew a moment of perfect happiness.

She looked over and saw that her father was watching her. She smiled at him. He did not return the smile, but as he walked over she could see that his eyes were tender and grave. He leaned on the rail beside her, looking west at the coastline. Water glistened in his hair and in the short beard he was growing. Not far away—a series of dark, massive forms touched by the moonlight—the cliffs of Tregea moved slowly by.

"It is in you," her father said quietly, over the slap and sigh of the waves. "In your heart and in your blood. You have it more than I do, from my father and from his." He was silent a moment, then slowly shook his head, "But Alais, my darling, a woman cannot live a life at sea. Not in the world as it is."

Her dream. Clear and bright as the glitter of white Vidomni's light upon the waves. Laid out and then undone in such simple words.

She swallowed. Said, a speech long rehearsed, never spoken: "You have no sons. I am eldest. Will you surrender the *Maid* and all you have worked to achieve when you . . . when you no longer wish to pursue this life?"

"When I die?" He said it gently, but something heavy and hurtful took shape, pressing upon her heart. She looped her hand through the crook of his arm, holding tight, and moved nearer to him, to lean her head on his shoulder.

They were silent, watching the cliffs go by and the play of moonlight on the sea. The ship was never quiet, but she liked the noises it made. She had fallen asleep the past few nights hearing the *Sea Maid's* endless litany of sounds as a night song.

She said, her head still on his shoulder, "Could I be taught? To help you in your business, I mean. Even if not to actually sail on the journeys."

Her father said nothing for a time. Leaning against

him, she could feel his steady breathing. His hands were loosely clasped together over the rail.

He said, "That can be done, Alais. If you want it, it can be done. Women run businesses all over the Palm. Widows, most often, but not only them." He hesitated. "Your mother could keep this going, I think, if she wanted to, if she had good advisors." He turned his head to look down at her, but she did not lift hers from his shoulder. "It is a sharp, cold life though, my darling. For a woman, for a man, without a hearth at the end of day for warmth. Without love to carry you outward and home."

She closed her eyes at that. There was something here that went to the heart of things. They had never pressed her, never harried or urged, though she was almost twenty years old and it was time, it was well past time. And she had had that one strange dream many nights through the dark of the winter just past: herself and a shadowy figure against the moon, a man in a high, unknown place, among flowers, under the arch of stars, his body lowered to her own, her hands reaching to gather him.

She lifted her head, withdrew her arm. Said carefully, looking down at the waves: "I *like* Catini. I'm happy for Selvena. She's ready, she's wanted this for so long and I think he'll be good to her. But father, I need more than what she will have. I don't know what it is, but I need more."

Her father stirred then. She watched him draw a deep breath and then slowly let it out. "I know," she heard him say. "I know you do, my darling. If I knew what, or how, and could give it, it would be yours. The world and the stars of Eanna would all be yours."

She cried then, which she seldom did. But she loved him and had caused him grief, and he had spoken just now, twice, of dying one day, and the white moon on the cliffs and sea after the storm was like nothing she had ever known or was likely to know again.

Catriana couldn't see the road as she climbed the slope from the dell, but from the distant sounds and the way Baerd and Sandre were both standing, rigidly watchful

on the grass at the edge of the trees, she could tell that
something was wrong. Men, she had long since concluded, were significantly worse than women at hiding
their feelings in situations such as this.

Her hair still wet after bathing in the pond—a favorite place of hers, one they had passed every time they
went back and forth between Ferraut and Certando—she
hurried up the slope to see what was happening.

The two men said nothing as she appeared beside
them. The cart had been pulled into the shade off the
north–south road and the two horses let free to graze.
Baerd's bow and quiver were lying in the grass beside the
trees, close to hand if he needed them. She looked at the
road and saw the Barbadian troops passing by, marching
and riding, raising a heavy cloud of dust all around them.

"More of the Third Company," Sandre said, a cold
anger in his voice.

"It looks like they're all going, doesn't it?" Baerd
murmured grimly.

Which was *good*, it was more than good, it was exactly
what they wanted. The anger, the grimness were almost
wholly uncalled for; they seemed to be some instinctive
male response to the nearness of the enemy. Catriana felt
like shaking them both.

It was so clear, really. Baerd himself had explained it
to her and Sandre, and to Alienor of Borso on the day
Alessan met Marius of Quileia in the mountains and rode
west with Devin and Erlein.

And listening that day, forcing herself to be composed
in Alienor's presence, Catriana had finally understood
what Alessan had meant, all this time, when he'd said
they would have to wait until spring. They had been
waiting for Marius to say yes or no. To say if he would
risk his own unstable crown and his life for them. And
that day in the Braccio Pass he'd said he would. Baerd
told them a little, a very little, about why.

Ten days later she and Baerd and Sandre had been on
watch in the hills outside Fort Ortiz when the emissaries
came riding along the road carrying the Quileian flag and
were met with ceremonious honor outside the walls and
escorted within by the Barbadians.

Next morning the Quileians had ridden on, not hurrying, down the road to the north. Two hours after their departure the gates of the fort had opened again and six men had ridden out in extreme haste. One of them—it was Sandre who noted it—was Siferval himself, captain of the Third Company.

"It is done," Baerd had said, a kind of awe in his voice. "I cannot believe it, but I think we have done it!"

A little more than a week later the first troops had begun to move, and they knew he was right. It wasn't until some days after that, in an artisans' village in northern Certando, trading for carvings and finished cloth, that they learned, belatedly, what Brandin of Ygrath had done in Chiara. The Kingdom of the Western Palm.

"Are you a gambling man?" Sandre had said to Baerd. "The dice are rolling now, and no one will hold or control them until they stop." Baerd had said nothing in reply, but something stunned, near to shock in his expression, made Catriana go over and take his hand in hers. Which was not really like her at all.

But everything had changed, or was changing. Baerd was not the same since the Ember Days and their stay at Castle Borso. Something had happened to him there, too, but this part he didn't explain. Alessan was gone, and Devin—and though she hated to admit it, she missed him almost as much as the Prince. Even their role here in the east had completely altered now.

They had waited in the highlands for the emissaries, in case something should go wrong. But now Baerd kept them moving at speed from town to town and he was stopping to speak to men and to some women Catriana had never even heard about, telling them to be ready, that there might be a summer rising.

And with some of them, not many, only a select few, his message was very specific: Senzio. Head north to Senzio before Midsummer. *Have a weapon with you if you can.*

And it was these last words that brought home to Catriana most sharply, most potently, the fact that the time for action had truly come. It was upon them. No more oblique disruptions or hovering on the edge of events. Events had a center now, which was or would soon be in Senzio, and they were going there. What was to happen she didn't yet know. If Baerd did, he wasn't telling.

What he did tell her, and Sandre too, were the names of people.

Scores of them. Names he had held in memory, some for a dozen years. People who were with them in this, who could be trusted. Who needed to be told, here in the provinces ruled by Barbadior, that the movement of Alberico's troops was their own signal to be ready at last. To watch the unfolding of events and be prepared to respond.

They would sit together at night, the three of them, around a campfire under stars or in a secluded corner of an inn in some hamlet or village, and Baerd would recite for them the names they needed to know.

It was only on the third night, falling asleep afterward, that Catriana belatedly realized that the reason they needed to be told this was if Baerd were to die, with Alessan away in the west.

"Ricaso bar Dellano," Baerd would say. "A cooper in Marsilian, the first village south of Fort Ciorone. He was born in Avalle. Could not go to war because of a lame foot. Speak to him. He will not be able to come north, but knows the others near by and will spread the word and lead our people in that district if the need for a rising comes."

"Ricaso bar Dellano," she would repeat. "In Marsilian."

"Porrena bren Cullion. In Delonghi, just inside the Tregean border on the main road from Ferraut. She's a little older than you, Catriana. Her father died at the Deisa. She knows who to speak to."

"Porrena," Sandre would murmur, concentrating, his bony, gnarled hands clasped together. "In Delonghi."

And Catriana marveled at how many names there seemed to be, how many lives Baerd and Alessan had touched in their travels through a dozen years since returning from Quileia, readying themselves and these unknown others for a time, a season, a moment in the future—which was now. Which they had lived to see. And her heart was filled with hope as she whispered the names over and over to herself like talismans of power.

They rode through the next weeks, through the flowering of spring, at an almost reckless pace, barely simulating their role as merchants. Making bad, hasty transactions where they stopped, unwilling to linger to bargain for better ones. Pausing only long enough to find the man or woman who was the key in that village or this cluster of farms, the one who knew the others and would carry the word.

They were losing money, but they had astins to spare from Alienor. Catriana, being honest with herself, realized that she was still reluctant to acknowledge the role that woman had played in Alessan's doings for so many years. Years in which she herself had been growing up in ignorance, a child in a fishing village in Astibar.

Once, Baerd let her make the contact in a town. The woman was a weaver, widely known for her skill. Catriana had found her house at the edge of the village. Two dogs had barked at her approach and had been stilled by a mild voice from within. Inside, Catriana had found a woman only a little younger than her mother. She had made certain they were alone, and then, as Baerd had instructed, had shown her dolphin ring and given Alessan's name and had spoken the message. The same message of readiness as everywhere else. Then she carefully named two men and spoke Baerd's second message: *Senzio. Midsummer. Tell them to be armed if they can.*

The woman had gone pale, standing up abruptly as Catriana began to speak. She was very tall, even more so than Catriana herself. When the second message was done she had remained motionless a moment and then stepped forward to kiss Catriana on the mouth.

"Triad bless you and keep you and the both of them," she had said. "I did not think I would live to see this day." She was crying; Catriana tasted salt on her lips.

She had walked out into the sunshine and back to Baerd and Sandre. They had just finished a purchase of a dozen barrels of Certandan ale. A wretched transaction.

"We're going *north*, you fools," she had exclaimed, exasperated, her trade instincts taking over. "They don't *like* ale in Ferraut! You *know* that."

"Then we'll have to drink it ourselves," Sandre said, swinging up on his horse and laughing. Baerd, who so rarely used to laugh, but who had changed since the

Ember Days, began to chuckle suddenly. And then, sitting beside him on the cart as they rode out of town, so did she, listening to the two of them, feeling the clean freshness of the breeze blowing through her hair, and, as it seemed, through her heart.

It was that same day, early in the afternoon, that they came to the dell she loved and Baerd, remembering, pulled the cart off the road to let her go down to the pool and bathe. When she climbed back up neither man was laughing or amused anymore, watching the Barbadians go by.

It was the way the two of them were standing that caused the trouble, she was sure of it. But by the time she came up beside them it was already too late. It would have been mostly Baerd whose look drew their attention. Sandre in his Khardhu guise was a matter of almost complete indifference to the Barbadians.

But a merchant, a minor trader with a single cart and a second scrawny horse, who stood gazing at an army passing in the way that this one did, coldly, his head arrogantly high, not even remotely submissive or chastened let alone showing any of the fear proper to such a situation . . .

The language of the body, Catriana thought, could be heard far too clearly sometimes. She looked at Baerd beside her, his dark eyes fixed in stony appraisal of the company passing by. It wasn't arrogance, she decided, not just a male pride. It was something else, something older. A primitive response to this display of the Tyrant's power that he could no more hide than he could the dozen barrels of ale they carried on thc cart.

"Stop it!" she whispered fiercely. But even as she did she heard one of the Barbadians bark a terse command and half a dozen of them detached from the moving column of men and horses and galloped over toward them. Catriana's mouth went dry. She saw Baerd glance over to where his bow lay in the grass. He shifted his stance slightly, to balance himself better. Sandre did the same.

"What are you doing?" she hissed. "Remember where we are!"

She had time for no more. The Barbadians came up to

them, huge men on their horses, looking down on a man and a woman of the Palm and this gaunt, grey-haired relic from Khardhun.

"I don't like the look of your face," the leader said, staring at Baerd. The man's hair was darker than most of the others, but his eyes were pale and hard.

Catriana swallowed. This was the first time in a year they'd had a confrontation so direct with the Barbadians. She lowered her eyes, willing Baerd to be calm, to say the right things.

What she did not know, for no one who had not been there could know, was what Baerd was seeing in that moment.

Not six Barbadians on horses by a road in Certando, but as many Ygrathen soldiers in the square before his father's house long ago. So many years, and the memory still sharp as a wound from only yesterday. All the normal measures of time seemed to fall apart and blow away in moments such as this.

Baerd forced himself to avert his gaze before the Barbadian's glare. He knew he had made a mistake, knew this was a mistake he would always make if he wasn't careful. He had been too euphoric though, rushing too fast on a floodtide of emotion, seeing this marching column as dancing to the tune he and Alessan had called. But it was early yet, far too early, so much lay unknown and uncontrollable in the future. And they had to live to see that future or everything would have been wasted. Years and lives, the patient conjuring of dream into reality.

He said, eyes cast down, voice low, "I am sorry if I have offended. I was only marveling at you. We have not seen so many soldiers on the road in years."

"We moved aside to make way," Sandre added in his deep voice.

"You be silent," the Barbadian leader rasped. "If I wish to converse with servants I will inform you." One of the others sidled his horse toward Sandre, forcing him to step backward. Catriana, behind him, felt her legs grow weak. She reached out and gripped the railing of the cart; her palms were damp with fear. She saw two of the Barbadians staring at her with frank, smirking appraisal, and she was suddenly aware of how her clothing would be clinging to her body after her swim in the pond.

"Forgive us," Baerd repeated, in a muffled tone. "We meant no harm, no harm at all."

"Really? Why were you counting our numbers?"

"Counting? Your numbers? Why would I do such a thing?"

"You tell me, merchant."

"It is not so," Baerd protested, inwardly cursing himself as an amateur and a fool. After twelve years, something so clumsy as this! The situation was careening out of control, and the simple fact was that he had indeed been counting the Barbadian numbers. "We are only traders," he added. "Only minor traders."

"With a Khardhu warrior for guard? Not so minor, I would say."

Baerd blinked, and clutched his hands together deferentially. He had made a terrible mistake. This man was dangerously sharp.

"I was afraid for my wife," he said. "There have been rumors of outlaws in the south, of great unrest." Which was true. There were, in fact, more than rumors. Twenty-five Barbadians had been slaughtered in a pass. He was fairly certain Alessan had been there.

"Your wife or your goods?" one of the other Barbadians sneered. "We know which you people value more." He looked past Baerd to where Catriana stood, and there was a loose, heavy-lidded look in his face. The other soldiers laughed. Baerd quickly lowered his head again; he didn't want them to see the death that was in his eyes. He remembered that kind of laughter, the resonance of it. Where it could lead. Had led, in a square in Tigana eighteen years ago. He was silent, eyes downcast, murder in his heart, bound close with memory.

"What are you carrying?" the first Barbadian rapped out, his voice blunt as a trowel.

"Ale," Baerd said, squeezing his hands together. "Only barrels of ale for the north."

"Ale for *Ferraut*? You *are* a liar. Or a fool."

"No, no," Baerd said hastily. "Not Ferraut. We got a very good price. Eleven astins the barrel. Good enough to be worth taking all the way north. We are bound for Astibar with this. We can sell it for three times that."

Which would have been true, had he not paid twenty-three astins for each of these.

At a gesture from the leader two of the Barbadians dismounted. They cracked open one of the barrels, using their swords as levers. The pungent, earthy smell of Certandan beer surrounded them all.

The leader looked over, saw his men nod, and turned back to Baerd. There was a malicious smile on his face.

"Eleven astins a barrel? Truly a good price. So good, that even a grasping merchant will not hesitate to donate them to the army of Barbadior that defends you and your kind."

Baerd had been half expecting this. Careful to stay in character, he said, "If . . . if it is your desire, then yes. Would you . . . would you care to buy it, at only the price I paid?"

There was a silence. Behind the six Barbadians the army was still marching down the road. It had almost passed them by. He had a decent estimate of how many there were. Then the man on the horse in front of him drew his sword. Baerd heard Catriana make a small sound behind him. The Barbadian leaned forward over the neck of his horse, weapon extended, and delicately touched Baerd on his bearded cheek with the flat of his blade.

"We do not bargain," he said softly. "Nor do we steal. We accept gifts. Offer us a gift, merchant." He moved the blade a little. Baerd could feel it nicking and fretting against his face.

"Please accept . . . please accept this ale from us as a gift to the men of the Third Company," he said. With an effort he kept his eyes averted from the man's face.

"Why thank you, merchant," the man said with lazy sarcasm. Slowly, sliding it along Baerd's cheek like an evil caress, he drew back his sword. "And since you have given us these barrels, you will surely not begrudge us the horse and cart that carry them?"

"Take the cart as well," Baerd heard himself saying. He felt suddenly as if he had left his body. As if he were floating above this scene, looking down.

And it was as from that high, detached vantage point that he seemed to see the Barbadians move to claim their wagon. They attached the cart-horse to the traces again. One of them, younger than the others, slung their packs and food out onto the ground. He looked shyly back at Catriana, a little abashed, then he mounted quickly up on the seat and clucked at the horse, and the cart rolled slowly away to where the tail of the Barbadian column was moving along the road.

The five other men, leading his horse, followed after him. They were laughing, the easy, spilling laughter of men among each other, sure of their place and of the shape of their lives. Baerd glanced over at his bow again. He was fairly certain he could kill all six of them, starting with the leader, before anyone could intervene.

He didn't move. None of them moved until the last of the column was out of sight, their cart rumbling after it. Baerd turned then and looked at Catriana. She was trembling, but he knew her well enough to know it was as much with anger as with fear.

"I'm sorry," he said, reaching up a hand to touch her arm.

"I could kill you Baerd for giving me such a fright."

"I know," he said. "And I would deserve to be dead. I underestimated them."

"Could have been worse," Sandre said prosaically.

"Oh, somewhat," Catriana said tartly. "We could all be lying dead here now."

"That would indeed have been worse," Sandre agreed gravely. It took her a moment to realize he was teasing her. She surprised herself by laughing, a little wildly.

Sandre, his darkened face sober, said something quite unexpected then. "You have no idea," he murmured, "how dearly I wish you were of my blood. My daughter, granddaughter. Will you allow me to take pride in what you are?"

She was so surprised she could think of nothing to say. A moment later, deeply moved, she went forward and kissed him on the cheek. He put his long, bony arms around her and held her to his chest for a moment, carefully, as if she was fragile, or very precious, or both.

She couldn't remember the last time someone had held her that way.

He stepped back, clearing his throat awkwardly. She saw that Baerd's expression was unwontedly soft, looking at the two of them.

"This is all extremely lovely," she said, deliberately dry. "Shall we spend the day here telling each other what splendid people we think we are?"

Baerd grinned. "Not a bad idea, but not the very best. I think we'll have to double back to where we bought the ale. We need another cart and horse."

"Good. I could use a flask of ale," Sandre said. Catriana glanced quickly back at him, caught the wry look in his eye, and laughed. She knew what he was doing, but she would never have expected to be able to laugh so soon after seeing a sword against Baerd's face.

Baerd collected his bow and quiver from the grass. They shouldered their packs and made her ride the horse— nothing else, Sandre said, would look right. She wanted to argue but couldn't. And she was secretly grateful for the chance to ride; her knees were still weak.

It was very dusty along the road for a mile or two because of the army, and they kept to the grass beside it. Her horse startled a rabbit and before she could even register the fact, Baerd had notched an arrow and shot, and the animal was dead. They traded it a short while later at a farmhouse for a pitcher of ale and some bread and cheese and then went on.

Late in the day, by the time they had made their slow way back to the village, Catriana had convinced herself that the incident had been unfortunate, but not really important after all.

Eight days later they were in Tregea town. They had seen no other soldiers in the intervening week, their path having taken them far off the major roads. They left the new cart and goods at their usual inn and walked down to the central market. It was late in the afternoon, a warm day for spring. Looking north between the buildings toward the docks, Catriana could see the masts of the first ships to come up the river after the winter. Sandre had stopped at a leather stall to have repairs done to the belt that held his sword. As she and Baerd moved through the crowded square, a Barbadian mercenary, older than most, moving with a limp, and probably drunk on spring wine, stumbled out of a tavern, saw her, and lurched over to grope clumsily at her breasts and between her legs.

She shrieked, more startled than anything else.

And a moment later wished with all her heart that she had not done so. Baerd, just ahead of her, wheeled, saw the man, and with the same deadly, reflexive speed that had killed the rabbit, flattened the Barbadian with a colossal blow to the side of his head.

And Catriana knew—knew in that moment with utter and absolute certainty—that he was striking out not just against a drunken reserve guard, but against the officer who had touched him with a sword by that grove in Certando a week before.

There was a sudden, frightened silence around them. And then an immediate babble of sound. They looked at each other for a blurred, flashing second.

"Run!" Baerd ordered harshly. "Meet tonight by the place where you came up from the river last winter. If I am not there go on by yourselves. You know the names. There are only a handful left. Eanna guard you all!"

Then he was gone, sprinting through the square the way they had come, as a cluster of mercenaries began fanning out quickly through the crowd toward them. The man on the ground had not moved. Catriana didn't wait to see if he would. She cut off the other way as fast as she could run. Out of the corner of her eye she saw Sandre at the leather stall watching them, his face loose with shock. She was careful, desperately careful, not to look at him, not to run that way. That one of them, oh, Triad please be willing, *one* of them might make it from this place alive and free, with the names known and the dream still carried toward Midsummer's fires.

She darted down a crowded street and then sharply left at the first crossing into the warren of twisting lanes that made up the oldest quarter of Tregea near the river. Over her head the second stories of houses leaned crazily out towards each other, and what filtered through of the sunlight was completely blocked in places by the enclosed bridges that connected the ramshackle buildings on either side of the street.

She looked back and saw four of the mercenaries following her, pounding loudly down the lane. One of them shouted a command to halt. If any of them had a bow, Catriana thought, she was quite likely to die in the next few seconds. Dodging from side to side she cut to her right down an alleyway and then quickly right again at the first crossing, doubling back the way she had come.

There were three names on Baerd's list here in Tregea, and she knew where two of them might be found, but there was no way she could go to them for succor, not with the Barbadians so close behind. She would have to lose the pursuit herself, if she could, and leave it to Sandre to make the contact. Or Baerd, if he survived.

She ducked under the flapping ends of someone's wash hanging above the street, and knifed over to her left toward the water. There were people milling about in the lanes, glancing up with mild curiosity as she went by. Their glances would change in a moment, she knew, when the Barbadians rumbled through after her.

The streets were a hopelessly jumbled maze. She wasn't certain where she was, only that the river was north of her; at fleeting intervals she could glimpse the topmost masts of the ships. The waterfront would be dangerous though, much too open and exposed. She doubled back south again, her lungs sucking for air. Behind her, she heard a crashing sound and then a cacophony of irate shouts and curses.

She stumbled going around another corner to her right. Every moment, every turning, she expected this chaos of lanes to lead her straight back into her pursuers. If they fanned out she was probably finished. A wheelwright's cart blocked the lane. She flattened herself against the wall and sidled sideways past. Came to another crossing of roads. Sprinted straight through this time, past half a dozen children playing a skipping game with ropes. Turned at the second crossing.

And was grabbed hard just above her right elbow. She started to scream, but a hand was quickly slapped over her mouth. She bared her teeth to bite, violently twisting to escape. Then suddenly she froze in disbelief.

"Quietly, my heart. And come this way," said Rovigo d'Astibar removing his palm from her mouth. "No running. They are two streets over. Look as if you're walking with me." Hand on her arm he guided her quickly into a tiny, almost deserted lane, looked back once over his shoulder, and then propelled her through the doorway of a fabric shop. "Now down behind the counter, quickly."

"How did you . . . ?" she gasped.

"Saw you in the square. Followed you here. Move, girl!"

She moved. An old woman took her hand and squeezed it, then lifted a hinged counter and Catriana ducked through and dropped to the floor behind it. A moment later the hinge swung up again and her heart stopped as a shadow appeared above her holding something long and sharp.

"Forgive me," whispered Alais bren Rovigo, kneeling beside her. "My father says your hair might give you away when we leave." She held up the scissors she carried.

Catriana went rigid for a moment, then, closing her eyes without a word, she slowly turned her back on the other woman. A moment later she felt her long red tresses gathered and pulled. And then the long sharp cloth-cutter's scissors rasped cleanly through in a line above her shoulders, severing a decade's growth in a moment in the shadows.

There was a burst of noise outside, a clatter and hoarse shouting. It approached, reached them, went loudly past. Catriana realized that she was shaking; Alais touched her shoulder and then diffidently withdrew her hand. On the other side of the counter the old woman moved placidly about in the shadows of her shop. Rovigo was nowhere to be seen. Catriana's breath came in ragged scourings of air and her right side ached; she must have crashed into something in her wild careen. She had no memory of doing so.

There was something lying on the ground beside her feet. She reached down and gathered the thick red curtain of her severed hair. It had happened so fast she'd hardly had time to realize what was being done.

"Catriana, I'm so sorry," Alais whispered again. There was real grief in her voice.

Catriana shook her head. "Nothing . . . this is less than nothing," she said. It was difficult to speak. "Only vanity. What does it matter?" She seemed to be weeping. Her ribs hurt terribly. She put a hand up and touched the shorn remains of her hair. Then she turned sideways a little, on the floor of the shop, down behind the counter, and leaned her head wearily against the other woman's shoulder. Alais's arms came up and around her then, holding her close while she cried.

On the other side of the counter the old woman hummed tunelessly to herself as she folded and sorted cloth of many colors and as many different textures, working by the wan light of afternoon as it filtered down to the street in a quarter where the leaning houses mostly blocked the sun.

★   ★   ★

Baerd lay in the mild darkness by the river, remembering how cold it had been the last time he was here, waiting with Devin at winter twilight to see if Catriana would come floating down to them.

He had lost the pursuit hours ago. He knew Tregea very well. He and Alessan had lived here for more than a year off and on after their return from Quileia, rightly judging this wild, mountainous province as a good place to seek out and nurture any slow flames of revolution.

They had been principally looking for one man they had never found, a captain from the siege of Borifort, but they had discovered others, and spoken to them, and bound them to their cause. And they had been back here many times over the years, in the city itself and in the mountains of its distrada, finding in the harsh simple life of this province a strength and a clean directness that helped carry them both through the terribly slow, twistingly indirect paths of their lives.

He had known the city's maze of streets infinitely better than the Barbadians who were barracked here. Known which houses could be quickly climbed, which roofs led to others, and which to avoid as dangerous dead-ends. It had been important, in the life they'd led, to know such things.

He'd cut south and then east from the market, and then scrambled up to the roof of The Shepherd's Crook, their old tavern here, using the slanting cover of the adjacent woodpile as a springboard. He remembered doing the same thing years ago, dodging the night watch after curfew. Running low and quickly he crossed two roofs and then spanned a street by crawling along the top of one of the ramshackle covered bridges that linked houses on either side.

Behind him, far behind him very soon, he heard the sounds of pursuit being balked by seemingly inadvertent things. He could guess what those things might be: a milk-cart with a loose wheel, a quickly gathered crowd watching two men brawl in the street, a keg of wine spilled as it was wheeled into a tavern. He knew Tregea, which meant knowing the spirit of its people too.

In a short time he was a long way from the market square, having covered the distance entirely from roof to roof, flitting light-footed and unseen. He could have almost enjoyed the chase had he not been so worried about Catriana. At the higher, southern fringes of Tregea the houses grew taller and the streets wider. His memory did not fail him though; he knew which ways to angle in order to continue working upward till he came to the house he sought and leaped to land on its roof.

He remained there for several moments, listening carefully for sounds of alarm in the street below. He heard only the ordinary traffic of late afternoon though, and so Baerd slipped the key out from its old hiding-place under the one burnt shingle, unlocked the flat trapdoor, and slipped down, noiselessly, into Tremazzo's attic.

He lowered the door behind him and waited for his eyes to adjust to the darkness. Down below, in the apothecary's shop itself he could hear voices quite clearly, and he quickly made out the unmistakable rumble of Tremazzo's bass tones. It had been a long time, but some things seemed never to change. Around him he could smell soaps and perfumes, and the odors, astringent or sweet, of various medications. When he could see a little in the gloom he found the tattered armchair that Tremazzo used to leave up here for them and sank down into it. The very action brought back memories from years ago. Some things did not change.

Eventually the voices below fell silent. Listening carefully he could make out only the one distinctive, heavy tread in the shop. Leaning over, Baerd deliberately scratched the floor, the sound a rat might make in an attic room. But only a rat that could scratch three times quickly, and then once again. Three for the Triad as a whole, and one more for the god alone. Tregea and Tigana shared an ancient link to Adaon, and they had chosen to mark it when they devised their signal.

He heard the footsteps below stop, and then, a moment later, resume their measured tread, as if nothing had happened. Baerd leaned back in the chair to wait.

It didn't take long. It was late in the day by now, nearly time to close up shop in any case. He heard Tremazzo sweeping the counter and floor and then the bang of the front door being shut and the click of the bolt driven home. A moment later the ladder was moved into place, footsteps ascended, the lower door swung back, and Tremazzo came into the attic, carrying a candle. He was puffing from exertion, bulkier than ever.

He set the candle on a crate and stood, hands on wide hips, looking down at Baerd. His clothes were very fine, and his black beard was neatly trimmed to a point. And scented, Baerd realized a second later.

Grinning, he rose to his feet and gestured at Tremazzo's finery, pretending to sniff the air. The apothecary grimaced. "Customers," he grunted. "It is the fashion of the day. What they expect now in a shop like this. Soon we'll be as bad as Senzio. Was it you that caused all the hue and cry this afternoon?" No more than that; no greeting, no effusions. Tremazzo had always been thus, cool and direct as a wind out of the mountains.

"I'm afraid so," Baerd replied. "Did the soldier die?"

"Hardly," Tremazzo said in his familiar, dismissive tones. "You aren't strong enough for that."

"Was there word of a woman caught?"

"Not that I heard. Who is she?"

"One of us, Tremazzo. Now listen, there is real news,

and I need you to find a Khardu warrior and give him a message from me." Tremazzo's eyes widened briefly as Baerd began, then narrowed with concentration as the story unfolded. It didn't take long to explain. Tremazzo was nothing if not quick. The bulky apothecary was not a man to venture north to Senzio himself, but he could contact others who were and let them know. And he should be able to find Sandre at their inn. He went down the ladder once more and returned, puffing, with a wheel of bread and some cold meat, and a flask of good wine to go with them.

They touched palms briefly, then he left in search of Sandre. Sitting among the sundry items stored above an apothecary's shop, Baerd ate and drank, waiting for darkness to fall. When he was sure the sun had set he slipped out onto the roof again and started back north through the town. After a while he worked his way down to the ground and, careful of the torches of the watch, threaded eastward through the winding streets to the place at the edge of the city where Catriana had come ashore from her winter leap. There, he sat down in the grass by the river in the almost windless night and settled himself to wait.

He had never really feared he would be caught. He'd had too many years of living this way, body honed and hardened, senses sharpened, mind quick to remember things, to seize and act upon opportunity.

None of which explained or excused what he'd done to get them into this in the first place. His impulsive blow at the drunken Barbadian had been an act of unthinking stupidity, regardless of the fact that it was also something that most of the people in that square had longed to do themselves at one time or another. In the Palm of the Tyrants today one suppressed such longings or died. Or watched people one cared for die.

Which led him back to Catriana. In the starry spring darkness he remembered her emerging like a ghost from winter water. He lay silent in the grass thinking of her, and then, after a time, perhaps predictably, of Elena. And then, always and forever, certain as dawn or dusk or the turning of the seasons, of Dianora who was dead or lost to him somewhere in the world.

There was a rustle, too small to be alarming, in the leaves of a tree behind him. A moment later a trialla began to sing. He listened to it, and to the river flowing, alone and at home in the dark, a man shaped and defined by his need for solitude and the silent play of memory.

His father, as it happened, had done the same thing by the Deisa, the night before he died.

A short time later an owl called from along the river-bank just west of him. He hooted softly in reply, silencing the trialla's song. Sandre came up silently, scarcely disturbing the grass. He crouched down and then sat, grunting slightly. They looked at each other.

"Catriana?" Baerd murmured.

"I don't know. Not caught though, I think. I would have heard. I lingered in the square and around it. Saw the guards come back. The man you hit is all right. They were laughing at him, after. I think this will pass."

Baerd deliberately relaxed his tensed muscles. He said, conversationally, "I am a very great fool sometimes, had you noticed?"

"Not really. You'll have to tell me about it some time. Who was the extremely large man who accosted me?"

"Tremazzo. He's been with us for a long while. We used his upper storage room for meetings when we lived here, and after."

Sandre grunted. "He came up to me outside the inn and offered to sell me a potion to ensure the lust of any woman or boy I desired."

Baerd found himself grinning. "Rumors of Khardu habits precede you."

"Evidently." Sandre's teeth flashed white in the darkness. "Mind you, it was a good price. I bought two vials of the stuff."

Laughing quietly, Baerd felt a curious sensation, as if his heart were expanding outward toward the man here with him. He remembered Sandre the night they had met, when all the plans of his old age had been undone, when a final, savage end had come for the whole Sandreni family. A night that had not come to an end until the Duke had used his magic to go into Alberico's dungeons and kill his own son. Tomasso. *Any woman or boy I desired.*

Baerd felt humbled by the strength of the old man with him. Not once in half a year and more of hard traveling, through the bitter cold and rutted tracks of winter, had Sandre breathed so much as a request for a halt or an easier pace. Not once had he balked at a task, shown weariness, been slow to rise in the predawn dampness of the road. Not once given any sign of the rage or the grief that must have choked him whenever word reached them of more bodies death-wheeled in Astibar. He had given them a gift of all he had, his knowledge of the Palm, the world, and especially of Alberico; a lifetime's worth of subtlety and leadership, offered without arrogance and without reserve, nothing held back.

It was men such as this, Baerd thought, who had been the glory and the grief of the Palm in the days before it fell. Glory in the grandeur of their power, and grief in their hatreds and their wars that had let the Tyrants come and take the provinces one by one in their solitary pride.

And sitting there by the river in darkness Baerd felt again, with certainty, in the deep core of his heart, that what Alessan was doing—what he and Alessan were doing—was right. That theirs was a goal worth the striving for, this reaching out for wholeness in the Palm, with the Tyrants driven away and the provinces bound together in a sharing of the years that would come. A goal worth all the days and nights of a man's life, whether or not it was ever reached, could ever be made real. A goal that lay beside and was bound together with the other vast and bitter thing, which was Tigana and her name.

Certain things were hard for Baerd bar Saevar, almost impossible in fact, and had been since his youth had been torn away from him in the year Tigana fell. But he had lain with a woman on an Ember Night just past, in a place of deepest magic, and had felt in that green darkness as if the stern bindings that wrapped and held his heart were loosening. And this was a dark place too, a quiet one with the river flowing, and things had begun to take shape in the Palm that he had feared would never happen while he lived.

"My lord," he said softly to the old man sitting there with him, "do you know that I have come to love you in the time we have been together?"

"By the Triad!" Sandre said, a little too quickly. "And I haven't even given you the potion!"

Baerd smiled, said nothing, able to guess at the bindings the old Duke must have within himself. A moment later though, he heard Sandre murmur, in a very different voice:

"And I you, my friend. All of you. You have given me a second life and a reason for living it. Even a hope that a future worth knowing might lie ahead of us. For that you have my love until I die."

Gravely, he held out a palm and the two of them touched fingers in the darkness. They were sitting thus, motionless, when they heard the sound of an oar splash gently in the water. Both men rose silently, reaching for their swords. Then they heard an owl hoot from the river.

Baerd called softly back, and a moment later a small boat bumped gently against the sloping bank and Catriana, stepping lightly, came ashore.

At the sight of her Baerd drew a breath of pure relief; he had been more afraid for her than he could ever have said. There was a man behind her in the boat holding the oars but the moons had not yet risen and Baerd couldn't see who it was.

Catriana said, "That was quite a blow. Should I be flattered?"

Sandre, behind him, chuckled. Baerd felt as though his heart would overflow with pride in this woman, in the calm, matter-of-factness of her courage. Matching her tone with an effort he said only, "You shouldn't have shrieked. Half of Tregea thought you were being ravished."

"Yes, well," she said drily. "Do forgive me. I wasn't sure myself."

"What happened to your hair?" Sandre asked suddenly from behind, and Baerd, moving sideways, saw that it had indeed been cropped away, in a ragged line above her shoulders.

She shrugged, with exaggerated indifference. "It was in the way. We decided to cut it off."

"Who is *we*?" Baerd asked. Something within him was grieving for her, for the assumed casualness of her manner. "Who is in the boat? I assume a friend, given where we are."

"A fair assumption," the man in the boat answered for himself. "Though I must say I could have picked a better place for our contraina to have a business meeting."

"*Rovigo!*" Baerd murmured, with astonishment and a swift surge of delight. "Well met! It has been too long."

"Rovigo d'Astibar?" Sandre said suddenly, coming forward. "Is that who this is?"

"I *thought* I knew that voice," Rovigo said, shipping his oars and standing up abruptly. Baerd moved quickly down to the bank to steady the boat. Rovigo took two precise strides and leaped past him to the shore. "I do know it, but I cannot believe I am hearing it. In the name of Morian of Portals, have you come back from the dead, my lord?"

Even as he spoke he knelt in the tall grass before Sandre, Duke of Astibar. East of them, beyond where the river found the sea, Ilarion rose, sending her blue light along the water and over the waving grasses of the bank.

"In a manner of speaking I have," Sandre said. "With my skin somewhat altered by Baerd's craft." He reached down and pulled Rovigo to his feet. The two men looked at each other.

"Alessan wouldn't tell me last fall, but he said I would be pleased when I learned who my other partner was," Rovigo whispered, visibly moved. "He spoke more truly than he could have known. How is this possible, my lord?"

"I never died," Sandre said simply. "It was a deception. Part of a poor, foolish old man's scheme. If Alessan and Baerd had not returned to the lodge that night I would have killed myself after the Barbadians came and went." He paused. "Which means, I suppose, that I have you to thank for my present state, neighbor Rovigo. For various nights through the years outside my windows. Listening to the spinning of our feeble plots."

Under the slanting blue moonlight, there was a certain glint in his eye. Rovigo stepped back a little, but his head was high and he did not avert his gaze. "It was in a cause that you now know, my lord." he said. "A cause you have joined. I would have cut out my tongue before betraying you to Barbadior. I think you must know that."

"I do know that," Sandre said after a moment. "Which is a great deal more than I can say for my own kin."

"Only one of them," Rovigo said quickly, "and he is dead."

"He is dead," Sandre repeated. "They are all dead. I am the last of the Sandreni. And what shall we do about it, Rovigo? What shall we do with Alberico of Barbadior?"

Rovigo said nothing. It was Baerd who answered, from the water's edge.

"Destroy him," he said. "Destroy them both."

PART FIVE

THE MEMORY OF A FLAME

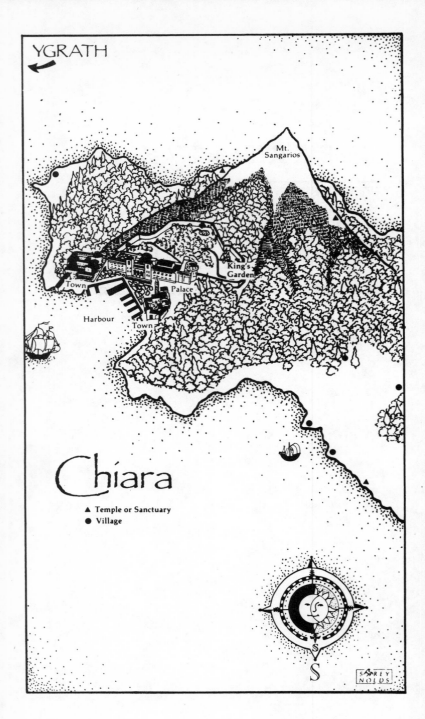

YGRATH

Mt.
Sangarios

King's
Garden

Town

Palace

Harbour

Town

Chiara

▲ Temple or Sanctuary
● Village

S

S

CHAPTER

• 17 •

SCELTO WOKE HER VERY EARLY ON THE MORNING OF the ritual. She had spent the night alone, as was proper, and had made offerings the evening before at the temples of Adaon and Morian both. Brandin was careful now to be seen observing all rites and proprieties of the Palm. In the temples the priests and the priestesses had been almost fawning in their solicitude. In what she was doing there was power for them and they knew it.

She'd had a short and restless sleep and when Scelto touched her awake, gently, and with a mug of khav already to hand, she felt her last dream of the night slipping away from her. Closing her eyes, only half conscious, she tried to chase it, sensing the dream receding as if down corridors of her mind. She pursued, trying to reclaim an image that would hold it, and then, just as it seemed about to fade and be lost, she remembered.

She sat up slowly in bed and reached for the khav, cradling it in both hands, seeking warmth. Not that the room was cold, but she had now remembered what day it was, and there was a chill in her heart that went beyond foreboding and touched certainty.

When Dianora had been a very small girl—perhaps five years old, a little less than that—she had had a dream of drowning one night. Sea waters closing over her head, and a vision of something dark, a shape, final and terrible, approaching to draw her down into lightless depths.

She had come awake gasping and screaming, thrashing about in bed, uncertain of where she even was.

And then her mother had been there, holding Dianora

to her heart, murmuring, rocking her back and forth until the frantic sobbing ceased. When Dianora had finally lifted her head from her mother's breast, she had seen by candlelight that her father was there as well, holding Baerd in his arms in the doorway. Her little brother had been crying too, she saw, shocked awake in his own room across the hall by her screams.

Her father had smiled and carried Baerd over to her, and the four of them had sat there in the middle of the night on Dianora's bed while the candles cast light in circles around them, shaping an island in the dark.

"Tell me about it," she remembered her father saying. Afterward he had made shadow figures for them with his hands on the wall and Baerd, soothed and drowsy, had fallen asleep again in his lap. "Tell me the dream, love."

Tell me the dream, love. On Chiara, almost thirty years after, Dianora felt an ache of loss, as if it had all been but a little while ago. Days, weeks, no time at all. When had those candles in her room lost their power to hold back the dark?

She had told her mother and father, softly so as not to wake Baerd, some of the fear coming back in the stumbling words. The waters closing over her, a shape in the depths drawing her down. She remembered her mother making the sign against evil, to unbind the truth of the dream and deflect it away.

The next morning, before opening his studio and beginning his day's work, Saevar had taken both his children past the harbor and the palace gates and south along the beach, and he had begun to teach them to swim in a shallow cove sheltered from the waves and the west wind. Dianora had expected to be afraid when she realized where they were going, but she was never really afraid of anything when her father was with her, and she and Baerd had both discovered, with whoops of delight, that they loved the water.

She remembered—so strange, the things one remembered—that Baerd, bending over in the shallows that first morning, had caught a small darting fish between his hands, and had looked up, eyes and mouth comically round with surprise at his own achievement, and their father had shouted with laughter and pride.

Every fine morning that summer the three of them had gone to their cove to swim and by the time autumn came with its chill and then the rains Dianora felt as easy in the water as if it were a second skin to her.

Once, she remembered—and there was no surprise to this memory lingering—the Prince himself had joined them as they walked past the palace. Dismissing his retinue, Valentin strolled with the three of them to the cove and disrobed to plunge into the sea beside their father. Straight out into the waves he had gone, long after Saevar stopped, past the sheltering headland of the cove and into the choppy whitecaps of the sea. Then he had turned around and come back to them, his smile bright as a god's, his body hard and lean, droplets of water sparkling in his golden beard.

He was a better swimmer than her father was, Dianora could see that right away, even as a child. She also knew, somehow, that it really didn't matter. He was the Prince, he was *supposed* to be better at everything.

Her father remained the most wonderful man in the world, and nothing she could imagine learning was ever going to change that.

Nothing ever had, she thought, shaking her head slowly in the saishan, as if to draw free of the clinging, spidery webs of memory. Nothing ever had. Though Brandin, in another, better world, in his imaginary Finavir, perhaps . . .

She rubbed her eyes and then shook her head again, still struggling to come awake. She wondered suddenly if the two of them, her father and the King of Ygrath, had seen each other, had actually looked each other in the eye that terrible day by the Deisa.

Which was such a hurtful thought that she was afraid that she might begin to cry. Which would not do. Not today. No one, not even Scelto—especially not Scelto, who knew her too well—must be allowed to see anything in her for the next few hours but quiet pride, and a certainty of success.

The next few hours. The last few hours.

The hours that would lead her to the margin of the sea and then down into the dark green waters which were the vision of the riselka's pool. Lead her to where her path came clear at last and then came, not before time, and not without a certain relief beneath the fear and all the loss, to an end.

It had unfolded with such direct simplicity, from the moment she had stood by the pool in the King's Garden and seen an image of herself amid throngs of people in the harbor, and then alone underwater, drawn toward a shape in darkness that was no longer a source of childhood terror but, finally, of release.

That same day, in the library, Brandin had told her he was abdicating in Ygrath in favor of Girald, but that Dorotea his wife was going to have to die for what she had done. He lived his life in the eyes of the world, he said. Even had he wished to spare her, he would have no real choice.

He didn't wish to spare her, Brandin said.

Then he spoke of what else had come to him on his ride that morning through the pre-dawn mists of the Island: a vision of the Kingdom of the Western Palm. He was going to make that vision real, he said. For the sake of Ygrath itself, and for the people here in his provinces. And for his own soul. And for her.

Only those Ygrathens willing to become people of his four joined provinces would be allowed to stay, he said; all others were free to sail home to Girald.

He would remain. Not just for Stevan and the response shaped in his heart to his son's death, though that would hold, that was constant; but to build a united realm here, a better world than he had known.

That would hold, that was constant.

Dianora had listened to him, had felt her tears beginning to fall, and had moved to lay her head in his lap beside the fire. Brandin held her, moving his hands through her dark hair.

He would need a Queen, he had said.

In a voice she had never heard before; one she had dreamt of for so long. He wanted to have sons and daughters here in the Palm now, Brandin said. To start again and build upon the pain of Stevan's loss, that something bright and fair might emerge from all the years of sorrow.

And then he spoke of love. Drawing his hands gently through her hair he spoke of loving her. Of how that truth had finally come home into his heart. Once, she would have thought it far more likely that she might grasp and hold the moons than ever hear him speak such words to her.

She wept, unable to stop, for in his words it was all gathering now, she could see how it was coming together, and such clarity and prescience was too much for a mortal soul. For her mortal soul. This was the Triad's wine, and there was too much bitter sorrow at the bottom of the cup. She had seen the riselka, though, she *knew* what was coming, where the path would lead them now. For one moment, a handful of heartbeats, she wondered what would have happened had he whispered these same words to her the night before instead of leaving her alone with the fires of memory. And that thought hurt as much as anything ever had in all her life.

Let it go! she wanted to say, wanted so much to say that she bit her lip holding back the words. *Oh, my love, let the spell go. Let Tigana come back and all the world's brightness will return.*

She said nothing. Knowing that he could not do so, and knowing, for she was no longer a child, that grace could not be come by so easily. Not after all these years, not with Tigana and Stevan twined together and embedded so deep down in Brandin's own pain. Not with what he had already done to her home. Not in the world in which they lived.

Besides which, and above everything else, there was the riselka, and her clear path unfolding with every word whispered by the fire. Dianora felt as if she knew everything that was going to be said, everything that would follow. And each passing moment was leading them— she could see it as a kind of shimmer in the room— towards the sea.

Almost a third of the Ygrathens stayed. It was more than he'd expected, Brandin told her, standing on the balcony above the harbor two weeks later, watching most of his flotilla sail away, back to their home, to what had been his home. He was exiled now, by his own will, more truly than he had ever been before.

He also told her later that same day that Dorotea was dead. She didn't ask how, or how he knew. His sorcery was still the thing she did not ever want to face.

Shortly after that came bad tidings though. The Barbadians were beginning to move north toward and through Ferraut, all three armies apparently heading for the border of Senzio. He had not expected that, she saw. Not nearly so soon. It was too unlike careful Alberico to move with such decisiveness.

"Something has happened there. Something is pushing him," Brandin said. "And I wish I knew what it was."

He was weak and vulnerable now, that was the problem. He needed time and they all knew it. With the Ygrathen army mostly gone Brandin needed a chance to shape a new structure of order in the western provinces. To turn the first giddy euphoria of his announcement into the bonds and allegiances that would truly forge a kingdom. That would let him summon an army to fight in his name, among a conquered people lately so hard-oppressed.

He needed time, desperately, and Alberico wasn't giving it to him.

"You could send us," d'Eymon the Chancellor said one morning, as the dimensions of the crisis began to take shape. "Send the Ygrathens we have left and position the ships off the coast of Senzio. See if that will hold Alberico for a time."

The Chancellor had stayed with them. There was never any real doubt that he would. For all his trauma——he had looked ill and old for days after Brandin's announcement——Dianora knew that d'Eymon's deepest loyalty, his love, though he would have shied awkwardly away from that word, was given to the man he served and not to the nation. Moving through those days almost numbed by the divisions in her own heart she envied d'Eymon that simplicity.

But Brandin flatly refused to follow his suggestion. She remembered his face as he explained, looking up from a map and strewn sheets of paper covered with numbers. The three of them together around a table in the sitting-

room off the King's bedchamber; Rhun a nervous, preoc-
cupied fourth on a couch at the far end of the room. The
King of the Western Palm still had his Fool, though the
King of Ygrath was named Girald now.

"I cannot make them fight alone," Brandin said
quietly. "Not to carry the full burden of defending people I
have just made them equal to. This cannot be an Ygrathen
war. For one thing, they are not enough, we will lose.
But it is more than that. If we send an army or a fleet it
must be made up of all of us here, or this Kingdom will
be finished before I start."

D'Eymon had risen from the table, agitated, visibly
disturbed. "Then I must say again what I have said
before: this is folly. The thing to do is to go home and
deal with what has happened in Ygrath. They *need* you
there."

"Not really, d'Eymon. I will not flatter myself. Girald
has been ruling Ygrath for twenty years."

"Girald is a traitor and should have been executed as
such with his mother!"

Brandin looked up at him, the grey eyes suddenly
chilly.

"Must we repeat this discussion? D'Eymon, I am here
for a reason and you know that reason. I cannot go back
on that: it would cut against the very core of what I am."
His expression changed. "No man need stay with me, but
I am bound myself to this peninsula by love and grief,
and by my own nature, and those three things will hold
me here."

"The Lady Dianora could come with us! With Dorotea
dead you would need a Queen in Ygrath and she would
be—"

"D'Eymon! Have done." The tone was final, ending
the discussion.

But the Chancellor was a brave man. "My lord," he
pushed on, grim-faced, his voice low and intense, "if I
cannot speak of this and you will not send our fleet to
face Barbadior I know not how to advise you. The provinces will *not* go to war for you yet, we know that. It is
too soon. They need time to see and to believe that you
are one of them."

"And I *have* no time," Brandin replied with what had

seemed an unnatural calm after the sharp tension of the exchange. "So I have to do it immediately. Advise me on that, Chancellor. How do I show them? Right now. How do I make them believe I am truly bound to the Palm?"

So there it was, and Dianora knew that the moment had come to her at last.

I cannot go back on that; it would cut against the very core of what I am. She had never really nursed any fantasies of his ever freely releasing and unbinding his spell. She knew Brandin too well. He was not a man who went back or reversed himself. In anything. The core of what he was. In love and hate and in the defining shape of his pride.

She stood up. There was an odd rushing sound in her ears, and if she closed her eyes she was certain she would see a path stretching away, straight and clear as a line of moonlight on the sea, very bright before her. Everything was leading her there, leading all of them. He was vulnerable, and exposed, and he would never turn back.

There was an image of Tigana flowering in her heart as she rose. Even here, even now, an image of her home. In the depths of the riselka's pool there had been a great many people gathered under banners of all the provinces as she walked down to the sea.

She placed her hands carefully on the back of her chair and looked down at him where he sat. There was grey in his beard, more, it seemed, each time she noticed it, but his eyes were as they had always been, and there was no fear, no doubt in them as they looked back at her. She drew a deep breath and spoke words that seemed to have been given to her long ago, words that seemed to have simply waited for this moment to arrive.

"I will do it for you," she said. "I will make them believe in you. I will do the Ring Dive of the Grand Dukes of Chiara as it used to be done on the eve of war. You will marry the seas of the peninsula, and I will bind you to the Palm and to good fortune in the eyes of all the people when I bring you back the sea-ring from the sea."

She kept her gaze steady on his own, dark and clear and calm, as she spoke at last, after so many years, the words that set her on the final path. That set him, set them all, the living and the dead, the named and the lost, on that path. As, loving him with a sundered heart, she lied.

She finished her khav and rose from bed. Scelto had drawn the curtains back and she could see sunrise just beginning to lighten the dark sea. The sky was clear overhead and the banners in the harbor could just be seen, moving lazily in the dawn breeze. There was already a huge crowd gathered, hours before the ceremony was to start. A great many people had spent the night in the harbor square, to be sure of a place near the pier to see her dive. She thought she saw someone, a tiny figure at such a distance, lift a hand to point to her window and she stepped quickly back.

Scelto had already laid out the clothes she would wear, the garments of ritual. Dark green for the going down: her outer robe and sandals, the net that would hold her hair and the silken undertunic in which she would dive. For afterwards, after she came back fom the sea, there was another robe, white, richly embroidered with gold. For when she was to represent, to *be* the bride come from the sea with a gold ring in her hand for the King.

After she came back. *If* she came back.

She was almost astonished at her own calm. It was easier actually because she hadn't seen Brandin since early the day before, as was proper for the rite. Easier too, because of how brilliantly clear all the images seemed to be, how smoothly they had led her here, as if she was choosing or deciding nothing, only following a course set down somewhere else and long ago.

Easier, finally, because she had come to understand and accept, deeply, and with certitude, that she had been born into a world, a life, that would not let her be whole.

Not ever. This was not Finavir, or any such dreamplace. This was the only life, the only world, she was to be allowed. And in that life Brandin of Ygrath had come to this peninsula to shape a realm for his son, and Valentin di Tigana had killed Stevan, Prince of Ygrath. This had happened, could not be unmade.

And because of that death, Brandin had come down upon Tigana and her people and torn them out of the known past and the still unfolding pages of the world.

And was staying here to seal that truth forever—blank and absolute—in vengeance for his son. This had happened and was happening, and had to be unmade. So she had come here to kill him. In her father's name and her mother's, in Baerd's name and her own, and for all the lost and ruined people of her home. But on Chiara she had discovered, in grief and pain and glory, that islands were truly a world of their own, that things changed there. She had learned, long ago, that she loved him. And now, in glory and pain and wonder, had been made to understand that he loved her. This had all happened, and she had tried to unmake it, and had failed.

Hers was not a life meant to be made whole. She could see it now so clearly, and in that clarity, that final understanding, Dianora found the wellspring of her calm.

Some lives were unlucky. Some people had a chance to shape their world. It seemed—who could have foretold? —that both these things were true of her.

Of Dianora di Tigana bren Saevar, a sculptor's daughter; a dark-haired dark-eyed child, gawky and unlovely in her youth, serious and grave, though with flashes of wit and tenderness, beauty coming to her late, and wisdom coming later, too much later. Coming only now.

She took no food, though she'd allowed herself the khav—a last concession to years of habit. She didn't think that doing so would violate any rituals. She also knew it didn't really matter. Scelto helped her dress, and then, in silence, he carefully gathered and pinned her hair, binding it in the dark green net that would hold it back from her eyes when she dived.

When he was done she rose and submitted herself, as always before going out into the world, to his scrutiny. The sun was up now; its light flooding the room through the drawn-back curtains. In the distance the growing noise from the harbor could be heard. The crowd must be very large by now, she thought; she didn't go back to the window to look. She would see them soon enough. There was a quality of anticipation to the steady murmur of sound that gave evidence, more clearly than anything else, of the stakes being played for this morning.

A peninsula. Two different dominions here, if it came to that. Perhaps even the very Empire in Barbadior, with the Emperor ill and dying as everyone knew. And one last thing more, though only she knew this, and only she would ever know: Tigana. The final, secret coin lying on the gaming table, hidden under the card laid down in the name of love.

"Will I do?" she asked Scelto, her voice determinedly casual.

He didn't follow that lead. "You frighten me," he said quietly. "You look as though you are no longer entirely of this world. As if you have already left us all behind."

It was uncanny how he could read her. It hurt to have to deceive him, not to have him with her on this last thing, but there was nothing he could have done, no reason to give him grief, and there were risks in the doing so.

"I'm not at all sure that's flattering," she said, still lightly, "but I will attempt to think of it that way."

He refused to smile. "I think you know how little I like this," he said.

"Scelto, Alberico's entire army will be on the border of Senzio two weeks from now. Brandin has no choice. If they walk into Senzio they will not stop there. This is his very best chance, probably his *only* chance, to link himself to the Palm in time. You know all this." She forced herself to sound a little angry.

It was true, it was all true. But none of it was the *truth*. The riselka was the truth this morning, that and the dreams she'd dreamt alone here in the saishan through all the years.

"I know," Scelto said, clearly unhappy. "Of course I know. And nothing I think matters at all. It is just . . ."

"Please!" she said, to stop him before he made her cry. "I don't think I can debate this with you now, Scelto. Shall we go?" *Oh, my dear,* she was thinking. *Oh, Scelto, you will undo me yet.*

He had stopped, flinching at her rebuke. She saw him swallow hard, his eyes lowered. After a moment he looked up again.

"Forgive me, my lady," he whispered. He stepped forward and, unexpectedly, took her hands, pressing them to his lips. "It is only for you that I speak. I am afraid. Please forgive."

"Of course," she said. "Of course. There is really nothing to forgive, Scelto." She squeezed his hands tightly. But in her heart she was bidding him farewell, knowing she must not cry. She looked into his honest, caring face, the truest friend she'd had for so many years, the only real friend actually, since her childhood, and she hoped against hope that in the days to come, he would remember the way she had gripped his hands and not the casual, careless sound of her words.

"Let's go," she said again, and turned her face away from him, to begin the long walk through the palace and out into the morning and then down to the sea.

The Ring Dive of the Grand Dukes of Chiara had been the most dramatic single ritual of temporal power in the Peninsula of the Palm. From the very beginning of their dominion on the Island, the leaders of Chiara had known that theirs was a power granted by and subject to the waters that surrounded them. The sea guarded them and fed them. It gave their ships—always the largest armada in the peninsula—access to trade and plunder, and it wrapped them about and enclosed them in a world within the world. No wonder, as the tale-tellers said, no wonder it was on the Island that Eanna and Adaon had come together to engender Morian and make the Triad complete.

A world within the world, girdled by the sea.

It was said to have been the very first of the Grand Dukes who had begun the ceremony that became the Ring Dive. It had been different in those early days. Not actually a dive, for one thing, only a ring thrown as a gift into the sea in propitiation and token of acknowledgment, in the days when the world turned its face toward the sun and the sailing season began in earnest.

Then one spring, a long time after that, a woman dived into the sea after the ring when the Grand Duke of that time cast it in. Some said later she had been crazed with love or religious possession, others that she was only cunning and ambitious.

In either case, she surfaced from the waters of the harbor with the ring bright in her hand.

And as the crowd that had gathered to watch the Grand Duke wed the sea shouted and babbled in wild confusion and wonder the High Priest of Morian in Chiara suddenly cried aloud, in words that would run down through all the years, never to be lost: "Look and see! See how the oceans accept the Grand Duke as husband to them! How they offer back the sea-ring as a bride piece to a lover!"

And the High Priest moved to the very end of the pier beside the Duke and knelt to help the woman rise from the sea and so he set in motion everything that followed. Saronte the Grand Duke was but new to his power and as yet unwed. Letizia, who had come into the city from a farm in the distrada and had done this unprecedented thing, was yellow-haired and comely and very young. And their palms were joined together then and there over the water by Mellidar, that High Priest of Morian, and Saronte placed the sea-ring on Letizia's finger.

They were wed at Midsummer. There was war that autumn against Asoli and Astibar, and young Saronte di Chiara triumphed magnificently in a naval battle in the Gulf of Corte, south of the Island. A victory whose anniversary Chiara still remembered. And from that time onward, the newly shaped ritual of the Ring Dive was enshrined for use in time of Chiara's need.

Thirty years later, near the end of Saronte's long reign, in one of the recurring squabbles for precedence among the Triad's clergy, a newly anointed High Priest of Eanna revealed that Letizia had been near kin to Mellidar, the priest of Morian who had drawn her from the water and bound her to the Duke. Eanna's priest invited the people of the Island to draw their own conclusions about the schemes of Morian's clergy and their endless striving for preeminence and power.

A number of events, none of them pleasant, had unfolded among the Triad's servants in the months following that revelation, but none of these disturbances had come near to touching the bright new sanctity of the ritual itself. The ceremony had taken hold on the imagination of the people. It seemed to speak to something deep within them, whether of sacrifice or homage, of love or danger, or, in the end, of some dark, true binding to the waters of the sea.

So the Ring Dive of the Grand Dukes remained, long

after all those feuding clergy of the Triad had been lowered to their rest, their names only half-remembered, and only because of their part in the story of the Dive. What had finally brought an end to the ceremony, in much more recent times, was the death of Onestra, wife to Grand Duke Cazal, two hundred and fifty years ago.

It was not, by any means, the first such death: the women who volunteered to dive for the Grand Dukes always had it made absolutely clear to them that their lives were worth infinitely less than the ring they sought to reclaim from the sea. To come back without the ring left one an exile from the Island for life, known and mocked throughout the whole peninsula. The ceremony was repeated with another woman, another ring, until one of the thrown rings was found and claimed.

By contrast, the woman who carried a sea-ring back to the pier was acclaimed as the luck of Chiara and her fortune was made for life. Wealth and honor, an arranged marriage into nobility. More than one had borne a child to her Grand Duke. Two had followed Letizia to the consort's throne. Girls from families of little prospect were not chary about risking their lives for such a glittering, hallucinatory future.

Onestra di Chiara had been different, and because of her and after her everything had changed.

Beautiful as a legend and as proud, Grand Duke Cazal's young bride had insisted on doing the Ring Dive herself, scorning to allocate such a glittering ceremony to some ill-bred creature from the distrada on the eve of a dangerous war. She had been, all the chroniclers of the day agreed, the most beautiful vision any of them had ever seen as she walked down to the sea in the dark-green of ritual.

When she floated, lifeless, to the surface of the water some distance from the shore, in full sight of the watching throng, Duke Cazal had screamed like a girl and fainted dead away.

After which there had been rioting and a terrified pandemonium unmatched before or since on the Island. In one isolated temple of Adaon on the north shore, all the priestesses had killed themselves when one of their number brought back the news. It was the wrath of the god that was coming, so the portents were read, and Chiara almost strangled on its fear.

Duke Cazal, foolhardy and broken, was slain in battle that summer against the joined armies of Corte and Ferraut, after which Chiara endured two generations of eclipse, rising to power again only after the bitter, destructive war fought between the erstwhile allies who had beaten it. Such a process, of course, was hardly noteworthy. It had been the way of things in the Palm as far back as the records went.

But no woman had done the Ring Dive since Onestra died.

All the symbols had changed with her, the stakes had risen too high. If another woman were to die in the Dive, with that legacy of chaos and defeat . . .

It was far too dangerous, successive Grand Dukes declared, the one after the other, and they found ways to keep the Island safe in its sea-girt power without the sanction of that most potent ceremony.

When the Ygrathen fleet had been sighted nineteen years ago the last Grand Duke of Chiara had killed himself on the steps of Eanna's temple, and so there had been no one to cast a ring into the sea that year, even had there been a woman willing to dive for it, in search of Morian's intercession and the god's.

It was eerily silent in the saishan when she and Scelto left her rooms. Normally at this hour the corridors would be loud with the stir and bustle of the castrates, fragrant and colorful with the scented presence of women moving languorously to the baths or to their morning meal. Today was different. The hallways were empty and still save for their own footsteps. Dianora suppressed a shiver, so strange did the deserted, echoing saishan seem.

They passed the doorway to the baths and then the entrance to the dining rooms. Both were empty and silent. They turned a corner toward the stairway that led down and out of the women's wing, and there Dianora saw that one person at least had remained, and was waiting for them.

"Let me look at you," Vencel said, the usual words. "I must approve you before you go down."

The saishan head was sprawled as always among the
many-colored pillows of his rolling platform. Dianora
almost smiled to see his vast bulk, and to hear the familiar words spoken.

"Of course," she said, and slowly turned full circle
before his scrutiny.

"Acceptable," he said at length. The customary judgment, though his high distinctive voice sounded more
subdued than she had ever heard it. "But perhaps . . . perhaps you would like to wear that vairstone from Khardhun
about your throat? For luck? I brought it with me for
you, from the saishan treasures."

Almost diffidently Vencel extended a large soft hand
and she saw that he was holding the red jewel she had
worn the day Isolla of Ygrath had tried to kill the King.

She was about to demur when she remembered that
Scelto had brought this back for her as something special
for that day, just before she had dressed to go down.
Remembering that, and moved by Vencel's gesture, she
said, "Thank you. I would be pleased to wear it." She
hesitated. "Would you put it on for me?"

He smiled, almost shyly. She knelt before him and
with his deft and delicate fingers the enormous saishan
head clasped the jewel on its chain about her neck.
Kneeling so near she was overwhelmed by the scent of
tainflowers that he always wore.

Vencel withdrew his hands and leaned back to look at
her. In his dark face his eyes were unwontedly soft. "In
Khardhun we used to say to someone going on a journey,
Fortune find you there and guide you home. Such is my
wish today." He hid his hands in the billowing folds of
his white robe and looked away, down the empty corridor.

"Thank you," she said again, afraid to say more. She
rose and glanced over at Scelto; there were tears in his
eyes. He wiped them hastily away and moved to lead her
down the stairs. Halfway down she looked back at Vencel,
an almost inhumanly vast figure, draped in billowing
white. He was gazing expressionlessly down after them,
from among the brilliantly colored panoply of his pillows, an exotic creature from another world entirely,
somehow carried ashore and stranded here in the saishan
of Chiara.

At the bottom of the stairs she saw that the two doors had been left unbarred. Scelto would not have to knock. Not today. He pushed the doors open and drew back to let her pass.

In the long hallway outside the priests of Morian and the priestesses of Adaon were waiting for her. She saw the scarcely veiled triumph in their eyes, a collective glittering of expectation.

There was a sound, a drawing of breath, as she came through the doors in the green robes of a rite that had not been performed in two and a half hundred years, her hair drawn back and bound in a net green as the sea.

Trained to control, being what they were, the clergy quickly fell silent. And in silence they made way for her, to follow behind in orderly rows of crimson and smoke-grey.

She knew they would make Scelto trail behind them. He could not be part of this procession of the rites. She knew she had not properly said farewell to him. Hers was not a life meant to be made whole.

They went west down the corridor to the Grand Staircase. At the top of the wide marble stairs Dianora paused and looked down, and she finally understood why the saishan had been so silent. All the women and the castrates were gathered below. They had been allowed out, permitted to come this far to see her pass by. Holding her head very high and looking neither left nor right she set her foot on the first stair and started down. She was no longer herself, she thought. No longer Dianora, or not only Dianora. She was merging further into legend with every step she took.

And then, at the bottom of the staircase, as she stepped onto the mosaic-inlaid tiles of the floor, she realized who was waiting by the palace doors to escort her out and her heart almost stopped.

There was a cluster of men there. D'Eymon, for one, and Rhamanus as well, who had stayed in the Palm as she'd been sure he would, and had been named as Brandin's First Lord of the Fleet. Beside them was Doarde the poet, representing the people of Chiara. She had expected him: it had been d'Eymon's clever idea that the participation of one Island poet could help counterbalance the crime and death of another. Next to Doarde was

a burly, sharp-faced man in brown velvet hung about
with a ransom's worth of gold. A merchant from Corte,
and a successful one clearly enough; very possibly one of
the ghouls who had made their fortune preying on the
ruins of Tigana two decades ago. Behind him was a lean
grey-clad priest of Morian who was obviously from Asoli.
She could tell from his coloring, the native Asolini all
had that look about them.

She also knew he was from Asoli because the last of
the men waiting for her there was from Lower Corte and
she knew him. A figure from her own internal legends,
from the myths and hopes that had sustained her life this
far. And this was the one whose presence here almost
froze the blood in her veins.

In white of course, majestic as she remembered him
from when she was a girl, gripping the massive staff that
had always been his signature, and towering over every
man there, stood Danoleon the High Priest of Eanna in
Tigana.

The man who had taken Prince Alessan away to the
south. So Baerd had told her the night he saw his own
riselka and went away to follow them.

She knew him, everyone had known Danoleon, his
long-striding, broad-shouldered preeminence, the deep,
glorious instrument that was his voice in temple services.
Approaching the doors Dianora fought back a moment
of wild panic before sternly controlling herself. There
was no way he could recognize her. He had never known
her as a child. Why should he have—the adolescent daughter of an artist loosely attached to the court? And she
had changed, she was infinitely changed since then.

She couldn't take her eyes off him though. She had
known d'Eymon was arranging for someone to be there
from Lower Corte, but had never expected Danoleon
himself. In the days when she had worked in The Queen
in Stevanien it was well-known that Eanna's High Priest
had withdrawn from the wider world into the goddess's
Sanctuary in the southern hills.

Now he had come out, and was here, and looking at
him, drinking in his reality, Dianora felt an absurd, an
almost overwhelming swell of pride to see how he seemed

to dominate, merely by his presence, all the people assembled there.

It was for him, and for the men and women like him,
the ones who were gone and the ones who yet lived in a
broken land, that she was going to do what she would do
today. His eyes rested on her searchingly; they were all
doing that, but it was under Danoleon's clear blue gaze
that Dianora drew herself up even taller than before.
Behind them all, beyond the doors which had not yet
been opened, she seemed to see the riselka's path growing brighter all the time.

She stopped and they bowed to her, all six men putting
a straight leg forward and bending low in a fashion of
salute not used for centuries. But this was legend, ceremony, an invocation of many kinds of power, and Dianora
sensed that she must now seem to them like some hieratic figure out of the tapestry scrolls of the distant past.

"My lady," said d'Eymon gravely, "if it pleases you
and you are minded to allow us, we would attend upon
you now and lead you to the King of the Western Palm."

Carefully said, and clearly, for all their words were to
be remembered and repeated. Everything was to be remembered. One reason the priests were here, and a
poet.

"It pleases me," she said simply. "Let us go." She did
not say more; her own words would matter less. It was
not what she would *say* today that was to be remembered.

She still could not take her eyes from Danoleon. He
was the first man from Tigana, she realized, that she had
seen since coming to the Island. In a very direct way it
eased her heart that Eanna, whose children they all were,
had allowed her to see this man before she went into the
sea.

D'Eymon nodded a command. Slowly the massive
bronze doors swung open upon the vast crowd assembled
between the palace and the pier. She saw people spilling
across the square to the farthest ends of the harbor,
even thronging the decks of the ships at anchor there.
The steady murmur of sound that had been present all
morning swelled to a crescendo as the doors swung open,
and then it abruptly stopped and fell away as the crowd
caught sight of her. A rigid, straining silence seemed to

claim Chiara under the blue arch of the sky; and out into that stillness Dianora went.

And it was then, as they moved into the brilliant sunshine along the aisle, the shining path that had been made for her passage, that she saw Brandin waiting by the sea for her, dressed like a soldier-king, without extravagance, bareheaded in the light of spring.

Something twisted within her at the sight of him, like a blade in a wound. *It will end soon,* she told herself steadily. *Only a little longer now. It will all be over soon enough.*

She went toward him then, walking like a queen, slender and tall and proud, clad in the colors of the dark-green sea with a crimson gem about her throat. And she knew that she loved him, and knew her land was lost if he was not driven away or slain, and she grieved with all her being for the simple truth that her mother and her father had had a daughter born to them all those years ago.

For someone as small as he was it was hopeless to try to see anything from the harbor square itself and even the deck of the ship that had brought them here from Corte was thronged with people who had paid the captain for a chance to view the Dive from this vantage point. Devin had made his way over to the mainmast and scrambled up to join another dozen men clinging to the rigging high above the sea. There were compensations inherent in agility.

Erlein was somewhere below amid the crowd on deck. He was still terrified, after three days here, by this enforced proximity to the sorcerer from Ygrath. It was one thing, he had said angrily, to elude Trackers in the south, another for a wizard to walk up to a sorcerer.

Alessan was somewhere among the crowd in the harbor. Devin had spotted him at one point working his way towards the pier, but couldn't see him now. Danoleon was inside the palace itself, representing Lower Corte in the ceremony. The irony of that was almost overwhelming, whenever Devin allowed himself to think about it.

He tried not to because it made him afraid, for all of them.

But Alessan had been decisive when the courteously phrased request had come for the High Priest to travel north and join men of the other three provinces as formal witnesses to the Ring Dive.

"You will go, of course," the Prince had said, as if it were the most natural thing in the world. "And we shall be there as well. I need to take the measure of things on Chiara since this change."

"Are you absolutely mad?" Erlein had gasped, not bothering to hide his disbelief.

Alessan had only laughed, though not, Devin thought, with any real amusement. He had become virtually impossible to read since his mother had died. Devin felt quite inadequate to the task of bridging that space or breaking through. Several times in the days following Pasithea's death he had found himself desperately wishing that Baerd were with them.

"What about Savandi?" Erlein had demanded. "Couldn't this be a trap for Danoleon. Or for you, even?"

Alessan shook his head. "Hardly. You said yourself, no message was sent. And it is entirely plausible that he was killed by brigands in the countryside as Torre made it seem. The King of the Western Palm has larger things to worry about right now than one of his petty spies. I'm not concerned about that, Erlein, but I do thank you for your solicitude." He smiled, a wintry smile. Erlein had scowled and stalked away.

"What *are* you concerned about?" Devin had asked the Prince.

But Alessan hadn't answered that.

High in the rigging of the *Aema Falcon* Devin waited with the others for the palace doors to open, and tried to control the pounding of his heart. It was difficult though; the sense of excitement and anticipation that had been building on the Island for three days had started to become overwhelming this morning, and had taken an almost palpable shape when Brandin himself had appeared and walked calmly down to the pier with a small retinue, including one stooped, balding old man dressed exactly like the King.

"Brandin's Fool," the Cortean in the rigging next to
him said, when Devin asked, pointing. "Something to do
with sorcery, the way they do things in Ygrath." He
grunted. "We're better off not knowing."

Devin had gazed for the first time at the man who had
destroyed Tigana and tried to imagine what it would be
like to have a bow in his hands right now and Baerd or
Alessan's skill at archery. It was a long, but not an
impossible shot, down, and across a span of water to
strike a single soberly clad, bearded man standing by the
sea.

Imagining the flight of that arrow in the morning sun,
he remembered another conversation with Alessan, at
the rail of the *Falcon* the night they reached Chiara.

"What do we *want* to happen?" Devin had asked.

Word had reached the Gulf of Corte just before they
sailed that most of the Second Company of Alberico's
Barbadian mercenaries had now been pulled back from
the border forts and cities in Ferraut and were marching
with the other armies towards Senzio. Hearing that,
Alessan's face had gone pale, and there was a sudden
hard glitter in his gray eyes.

Much like his mother's, Devin had thought, but would
not dream of saying.

On the ship Alessan had turned to him briefly at the
question and then looked back out to sea. It was very
late, nearer dawn than midnight. Neither of them had
been able to sleep. Both moons were overhead and the
water gleamed and sparkled with their mingled light.

"What do we want to happen?" Alessan repeated.
"I'm not completely sure. I think I know, but I can't be
certain yet. That's why we're going to watch this Dive."

They listened to the sounds of the ship in the night sea.
Devin cleared his throat.

"If she fails?" he asked.

Alessan was silent for so long Devin didn't think he
was going to answer. Then, very softly, he said, "If the
Certandan woman fails Brandin is lost I think. I am
almost sure."

Devin looked quickly over at him. "Well then, that
means . . ."

"That means a number of things, yes. One is our name

come back. Another is Alberico ruling the Palm. Before
the year is out, almost certainly."

Devin tried to absorb that. *If we take them then we
must take them both,* he remembered the Prince saying in
the Sandreni lodge, with Devin hiding in the loft above.

"And if she succeeds?" he asked.

Alessan shrugged. In the blue and silver moonlight his
profile seemed more marble than flesh. "You tell me.
How many people of the provinces will fight against the
Empire of Barbadior for a king who has been wedded to
the seas of the Palm by a sea-bride from this peninsula?"

Devin thought about it.

"A lot," he said at length. "I think a lot of people
would fight."

"So do I," said Alessan. "Then the next question
becomes, who would win? And the one after that is: Is
there something we can do about it?"

"Is there?"

Alessan looked over at him then and his mouth crooked
wryly. "I have lived my life believing so. We may find it
put to the test very soon."

Devin stopped his questions then. It was very bright
with the two moons shining. A short while later Alessan
touched his shoulder and pointed with his other hand.
Devin looked and saw a high, dark mass of land rising
from the sea in the distance.

"Chiara," said Alessan.

And so Devin saw the Island for the first time.

"Have you ever been here before?" he asked softly.

Alessan shook his head, never taking his eyes from
that dark, mountainous shape on the horizon.

"Only in my dreams," he said.

"She's coming!" someone shouted from the topmost rigging of the Asolini ship anchored next to them; the cry
was immediately picked up and strung from ship to ship
and along the harbor, peaking in a roar of anticipation.

And then falling away to an eerie, chilling silence as
the massive bronze doors of Chiara Palace swung fully
back to reveal the woman framed within.

Even when she began to walk the silence held. Moving
slowly, she passed among the throngs assembled in the

square, seeming almost oblivious of them. Devin was too far away to see her face clearly yet, but he was suddenly conscious of a terrible beauty and grace. *It is the ceremony,* he told himself; it is only because of where she is. He saw Danoleon behind her, moving among the other escorts, towering above them.

And then, moved by some instinct, he turned from them to Brandin of Ygrath on the pier. The King was nearer to him and he had the right angle. He could see how the man watched the woman approach. His face was utterly expressionless. Icy cold.

He's calculating the situation, Devin thought. The numbers, the chances. He's *using* all of this—the woman, the ritual, everyone gathered here with so much passion in them—for a purely political end. He realized that he despised the man for that, over and above everything else: hated him for the blank, emotionless gaze with which he watched a woman approach to risk her life for him. By the Triad, he was supposed to be in love with her!

Even the bent old man beside him, Devin saw, the King's Fool, dressed exactly like Brandin, was wringing his hands over and about each other in obvious apprehension, anxiety and concern vivid in his face.

By contrast, the face of the King of the Western Palm was a frigid, uncaring mask. Devin didn't even want to look at him anymore. He turned back to the woman, who had come much nearer now.

And because she had, because she was almost at the water's edge, he could see that his first sense had been right and his glib explanation wrong: Dianora di Certando clad in the sea-green robes of the Ring Dive was the most beautiful woman he had ever seen in all his life.

What do we want to happen? he had asked Alessan three nights ago, sailing to this Island.

He still didn't know the answer. But looking down at the woman as she reached the sea a sudden fear rose in him, and an entirely unexpected pity. He grasped the rigging tightly and set himself to watch from high, high above.

She knew Brandin better than anyone alive; it had been

necessary, in order to survive, especially in the beginning, in order to say and do the right things in a mortally dangerous place. Then as the years slipped by necessity had somehow been alchemized into something else. Into love, actually, bitterly hard as that had been to acknowledge. She had come here to kill, with the twin snakes of memory and hatred in her heart. Instead, she had ended up understanding him better than anyone in the world because there was no one else who mattered half so much.

And so what came very near to breaking her, as she passed through that multitude of people to the pier, was seeing how ferociously he was struggling not to show what he was feeling. As if his soul were straining to escape through the doorways of his eyes, and he, being born to power, being what he was, felt it necessary to hold it in, here among so many people.

But he couldn't hide it from her. She didn't even have to look at Rhun to read Brandin now. He had cut himself off from his home, from all that had anchored him in life, he was here among an alien people he had conquered, asking for their aid, needing their belief in him. She was his lifeline now, his only bridge to the Palm, his only link, really, to any kind of future here, or anywhere.

But Tigana's ruin lay between the two of them like a chasm in the world. The lesson of her days, Dianora thought, was simply this: that love was not enough. Whatever the songs of the troubadours might say. Whatever hope it might seem to offer, love was simply not enough to bridge the chasm in *her* world. Which was why she was here, what the riselka's vision in the garden had offered her: an end to the terrible, bottomless divisions in her heart. At a price, however, that was not negotiable. One did not bargain with the gods.

She came up to Brandin at the end of the pier and stopped and the others stopped behind her. A sigh, rising and falling away like a dying of wind, moved through the square. With an odd trick of the mind her vision seemed to detach itself from her eyes for a moment, to look down on the pier from above. She could see how she must appear to the people gathered there: inhuman, otherworldly.

As Onestra must have seemed before the last Dive. Onestra had not come back, and devastation had followed upon that. Which was why this was her chance: the dark doorway history offered to release, and to the incarnation of her long dream in the saishan.

The sunlight was very bright, gleaming and dancing on the blue-green sea. There was so much color and richness in the world. Beyond Rhun, she saw a woman in a brilliant yellow robe, an old man in blue and yellow, a younger, dark-haired man in brown with a child upon his shoulders. All come to see her dive. She closed her eyes for a moment, before she turned to look at Brandin. It would have been easier not to, infinitely easier, but she knew that there were dangers in not meeting his gaze. And, in the end, here at the end, this was the man she loved.

Last night, lying awake, watching the slow transit of the moons across her window, she had tried to think of what she could say to him when she reached the end of the pier. Words beyond those of the ritual, to carry layers of meaning down through the years.

But there, too, lay danger, a risk of undoing everything this moment was to become. And words, the ones she would want to say, were just another reaching out towards making something whole, weren't they? Towards bridging the chasms. And in the end that was the point, wasn't it? There was no bridge across for her.

Not in this life.

"My lord," she said formally, carefully, "I know I am surely unworthy, and I fear to presume, but if it is pleasing to you and to those assembled here I will try to bring you the sea-ring back from the sea."

Brandin's eyes were the color of skies before rain. His gaze never wavered from her face. He said, "There is no presumption, love, and infinite worthiness. You ennoble this ceremony with your presence here."

Which confused her, for these were not the words they had prepared. But then he looked away from her, slowly, as if turning away from light.

"People of the Western Palm!" he cried, and his voice was clear and strong, a King's, a leader of men, carrying resonantly across the square and out among the tall ships and the fishing boats. "We are asked by the Lady Dianora if we find her worthy to dive for us. If we will place our hopes of fortune in her, to seek the Triad's blessing in the war Barbadior brings down upon us. What is your reply? She waits to hear!"

And amid the thunderous roar of assent that followed, a roar as loud and sure as they had known it would be after so much pent-up anticipation, Dianora felt the brutal irony of it, the bitter jest, seize hold of her.

Our hopes of fortune. In her? *The Triad's blessing.* Through her?

In that moment, for the first time, here at the very margin of the sea, she felt fear come in to lay a finger on her heart. For this truly was a ritual of the gods, a ceremony of great age and numinous power and she was using it for her own hidden purposes, for something shaped in her mortal heart. Could such a thing be allowed, however pure the cause?

She looked back then at the palace and the mountains that had defined her life for so long. The snows were gone from the peak of Sangarios. It was on that summit that Eanna was said to have made the stars. And named them all. Dianora looked away and down, and she saw Danoleon gazing at her from his great height. She looked into the calm, mild blue of his eyes and felt herself reach out and back through time to take strength and sureness from his quietude.

Her fear fell away like a discarded garment. It was for Danoleon, and for those like him who had died, for the books and the statues and the songs and the names that were lost that she was here. Surely the Triad would understand that when she was brought to her final accounting for this heresy? Surely Adaon would remember Micaela by the sea? Surely Eanna of the Names would be merciful?

Slowly then, Dianora nodded her head as the roar of sound finally receded; seeing that, the High Priestess of the god came forward in her crimson gown and helped her free of the dark-green robe.

Then she was standing by the water, clad only in the thin green undertunic that barely reached her knees, and Brandin was holding a ring in his hand.

"In the name of Adaon and of Morian," he said, words of ritual, rehearsed and carefully prepared, "and always and forever in the name of Eanna, Queen of Lights, we seek nurture here and shelter. Will the sea welcome us and bear us upon her breast as a mother bears a child? Will the oceans of this peninsula accept a ring of offering in my name and in the name of all those gathered here, and send it back to us in token of our fates bound together? I am Brandin di Chiara, King of the Western Palm, and I seek your blessing now."

Then he turned to her, as a second murmur of astonishment began at his last words, at what he'd named himself, and beneath that sound, as if cloaked and sheltered under it, he whispered something else, words only she could hear.

Then he turned towards the sea and drew back his arm, and he threw the golden ring in a high and shining arc up towards the brightness of the sky and the dazzling sun.

She saw it reach its apex and begin to fall. She saw it strike the sea and she dived.

The water was shockingly cold, so early in the year. Using the momentum of the dive she drove herself downwards, kicking hard. The green net held her hair so she could see. Brandin had thrown the ring with some care but he had known he could not simply toss it near to the pier—too many people would be looking for that. She propelled herself forward and down with half a dozen hard, driving strokes, her eyes straining ahead in the blue-green filtered light.

She might as well reach it. She might as well see if she could claim the ring before she died. She could carry it as an offering, down to Morian.

Her fear, amazingly, was entirely gone. Or perhaps it was not so amazing after all. What was the riselka, what did its vision offer if not this certainty, a sureness to carry her past the old terror of dark waters, to the last portal of Morian? It was ending now. It should have ended long ago.

She saw nothing, kicked again, forcing herself deeper and further out, towards where the ring had fallen.

There *was* a sureness in her, a brilliant clarity, an

awareness of how events had shaped themselves towards
this moment. A moment when, simply by her dying,
Tigana might be redeemed at last. She knew the story of
Onestra and Cazal; every person in this harbor did. They
all knew what disasters had followed upon Onestra's
death.

Brandin had gambled all on this one ceremony, having
no other choice in the face of battle brought to him too
soon. But Alberico would take him now; there could be
no other result. She knew exactly what would follow
upon her death. Chaos and shrill denunciation, the per-
ceived judgment of the Triad upon this arrogantly self-
styled King of the Western Palm. There would be no
army in the west to oppose the Barbadian. The Peninsula
of the Palm would be Alberico's to harvest like a vineyard, or grind like grain beneath the millstones of his
ambition.

Which was a pity, she supposed, but redressing that
particular sorrow would have to be someone else's task.
The soul's quest of another generation. Her own dream,
the task she'd set herself with an adolescent's pride,
sitting by a dead fire in her father's house long years ago,
had been to bring Tigana's name back into the world.

Her only wish, if she were allowed a wish before the
dark closed over her and became everything, was that
Brandin would leave, would find a place to go far from
this peninsula, before the end came. And that he might
somehow come to know that his life, wherever he went,
was a last gift of her love.

Her own death didn't matter. They killed women who
slept with conquerors. They named them traitors and
they killed them in many different ways. Drowning would
do.

She wondered if she would see the riselka here, sea-
green creature of the sea, agent of destiny, guardian of
thresholds. She wondered if she would have some last
vision before the end. If Adaon would come for her, the
stern and glorious god, appearing as he had to Micaela
on the beach so long ago. She was not Micaela though,
not bright and fair and innocent in her youth. She didn't
think that she would see the god.

Instead, she saw the ring.

It was to her right and just above, drifting like a
promise or an answered prayer down through the slow,
cold waters so far below the sunlight. She reached out, in
the dreamlike slowness of all motion in the sea, and she
claimed it and put it on her finger that she might die as a
sea-bride with sea-gold upon her hand.

She was very far under now. The filtered light had
almost disappeared this far down. She knew her last
gathered air would soon be gone as well, the need for the
surface becoming imperative, reflexive. She looked at the
ring, Brandin's ring, his last and only hope. She brought
it to her lips, and kissed it, and then she turned her eyes,
her life, her long quest, away from the surface and the
sunlight, and love.

Downward she went, forcing herself as deep as she
could. And it was then, just then, that the visions began
to come.

She saw her father in her mind, clearly, holding his
chisel and mallet, his shoulders and chest covered with a
fine powder of marble, walking with the Prince in their
courtyard, Valentin's arm familiarly thrown about his
shoulders, and then she saw him as he had been before
he rode away, awkward and grim, to war. Then Baerd
was in her mind: as a boy, sweet-natured, seemingly
always laughing. Then weeping outside her door the night
Naddo left them, then wrapped close in her arms in a
ruined moonlit world, and lastly in the doorway of the
house the night he went away. Her mother next—and
Dianora felt as if she were somehow swimming back
through all the years to her family. For all these images
of her mother were from before the fall, before the
madness had come, from a time when her mother's voice
had seemed able to gentle the evening air, her touch still
soothe all fevers away, all fear of the dark.

It was dark now, and very cold in the sea. She felt the
first agitation of what would soon be a desperate need for
air. There came to her then, as on a scroll unrolling
through her mind, vignettes of her life after she'd left
home. The village in Certando. Smoke over Avalle seen
from the high and distant fields. The man—she couldn't
even remember his name—who had wanted to marry
her. Others who had bedded her in that small room

upstairs. The Queen in Stevanien. Arduini. Rhamanus
on the river galley taking her away. The opening sea
before them. Chiara. Scelto.

Brandin.

And so, at the very end, it was he who was in her mind
after all. And over and above the hard, quick images of a
dozen years and more Dianora suddenly heard again his
last words on the pier. The words she had been fighting
to hold back from her awareness, had tried not to even
hear or understand, for fear of what they might do to her
resolve. What he might do.

My love, he'd whispered, *come back to me. Stevan is
gone. I cannot lose you both or I will die.*

She had not wanted to hear that; anything like that.
Words were power, words tried to change you, to shape
bridges of longing that no one could ever really cross.

Or I will die, he had said.

And she knew, could not even try to deny within
herself that it was true. That he *would* die. That her
false, beneficent vision of Brandin living somewhere else,
remembering her tenderly, was simply another lie in the
soul. He would do no such thing. *My love,* he had called
her. She knew, gods how she and her home had cause to
know, what love meant to this man. How deep it went in
him.

How deep. There was a roaring sound in her ears now,
a pressure of water so far below the surface of the sea.
Her lungs felt as if they were going to burst. She moved
her head to one side, with difficulty.

There seemed to be something there, beside her in the
darkness. A darting figure further out to sea. A glimmer,
glimpse of a form, of a man or a god she could not say.
But it could not be a man down here. Not so far below
the light and the waves, and not glowing as this form
was.

Another inward vision, she told herself. A last one,
then. The figure seemed to be swimming slowly away
from her, light shining around it like an aureole. She was
spent now. There was an aching in her, of longing, a
yearning for peace. She wanted to follow that gentle,
impossible light. She was ready to rest, to be whole and
untormented, without desire.

And then she understood, or thought she did. That figure had to be Adaon. It had to be the god coming for her. But he had turned his back. He was moving away, the calm glow receding away towards blackness here in the depths of the sea.

She did not belong to him. Not yet.

She looked at her hand. The ring upon it was almost invisible, so faint was the light. But she could feel it there, and she knew whose ring it was. She knew.

Far down in the dark of the sea, terribly far below the world where mortal men and women lived and breathed the air, Dianora turned. She pushed her hands above her, touched palms together and parted them, cleaving the water upwards, hurling her body like a spear up through all the layers of the sea, of dark-green death, towards life again and all the unbridged chasms of air and light and love.

When he saw her break the surface of the sea, Devin wept. Even before he saw the flash of gold sparkling on the hand she lifted in weariness, that they all might see the ring.

Wiping at his streaming eyes, his voice raw from screaming with all the others on the ship, on all the ships, all through the harbor of Chiara, he then saw something else.

Brandin of Ygrath, who had named himself Brandin di Chiara, had dropped to his knees on the pier and had buried his face in his hands. His shoulders were shaking helplessly. And Devin understood then how wrong he had been before: that this was not, after all, a man who was only pleased and happy that a stratagem had worked.

With agonizing slowness the woman swam to the pier. An eager priest and priestess helped her from the sea and supported her and wrapped her shivering form in a robe of white and gold. She could scarcely stand. But Devin, still weeping, saw her lift her head high as she turned to Brandin and offered him the sea-ring in a trembling hand.

Then he saw the King, the Tyrant, the sorcerer who

had ruined them with his bitter, annihilating power, gather
the woman into his arms, gently, with tenderness, but
with the unmistakable urgency of a man deprived and
hungry for too long.

Alessan reached up and removed the child from his shoulders, setting it carefully down beside its mother. She
smiled at him. Her hair was yellow as her gown. He
smiled back, reflexively, but found himself turning away.
From her, from the man and woman embracing feverishly next to them. He felt physically ill. There was a
quite substantial level of jubilant chaos erupting all around
in the harbor. His stomach was churning. He closed his
eyes, fighting nausea and dizziness, the tumultuous
overflow.

When he opened his eyes it was to gaze at the Fool—
Rhun, they had said his name was. It was deeply unsettling to see how, with the King releasing his own feelings,
clutching the woman in that grip of transparent need, the
Fool, the surrogate, seemed suddenly empty and hollow.
There was a blank, weighted sadness to him, jarring in its
discontinuity amid the exultation all around. Rhun seemed
a still, silent point of numbness amid a world of tumult
and weeping and laughter.

Alessan looked at the bent, balding figure with his weirdly
deformed face, and felt a blurred, disorienting kinship to
the man. As if the two of them were linked here, if only
in their inability to know how to react to all of this.

He had to have been shielding himself, Alessan repeated in his mind for the tenth time, the twentieth. *He
had to.* He looked at Brandin again, and then away,
hurting with confusion and grief.

For how many years in Quileia had he and Baerd spun
adolescent plots of making their way here? Of coming
upon the Tyrant and killing him, their cries of Tigana's
name ringing in the air, hurtling back into the world.

And this morning, now, he'd been scarcely fifteen feet
away, unsuspected, unknown, with a dagger at his belt
and only one row of people between him and the man
who'd tortured and killed his father.

He had to have been shielding himself against a blade.
But the thing was, the simple fact was, that Alessan
couldn't *know* that. He hadn't tested it; hadn't tried. He
had stood and watched. Observed. Played out his own
cool plan of shaping events, steering them towards some
larger abstraction.

His eyes hurt; there was a dull pulsing behind them, as
if the sun were too bright for him. The woman in yellow
had not moved away; she was still looking up at him with
a slantwise glance hard not to understand. He didn't
know where the child's father was, but it was clear that
the woman didn't greatly care just now. It would be
interesting, he thought, with that perverse, detached quirk
of his mind that was always there, to see how many
children were born in Chiara nine months from now.

He smiled at her again, meaninglessly, and made some
form of mumbled excuse. Then he started back alone
through the celebrating, uproarious crowd towards the
inn where the three of them had been paying for their
room by making music these past three days. Music might
help right now, he thought. Very often music was the only
thing that helped. His heart was still racing weirdly, as it
had started to do when the woman broke the surface of the
water with the ring on her hand after so long undersea.

So long a time he had actually begun to calculate if
there was anything he could do to make use of the shock
and fear that was going to follow upon her death.

And then she had come up, had been there before
them in the water and, in the second before the roaring
of the crowd began, Brandin of Ygrath, who had been
rigidly motionless from the moment she dived, had collapsed to his knees as if struck from behind by a blow
that had robbed him of all his strength.

And Alessan had found himself feeling ill and hopelessly confused even as the screams of triumph and ecstasy began to sweep across the harbor and the ships.

This is *fine,* he told himself now, forcing his way past a
wildly dancing ring of people. This will fit, it can be made
to fit. It is coming together. As I planned. There will be
war. They will face each other. In Senzio. As I planned.

His mother was dead. He had been fifteen feet away
from Brandin of Ygrath with a blade in his belt.

It was too bright in the square, and much too loud. Someone grabbed his arm as he went by and tried to draw him into a whirling circle. He pulled away. A woman careened into his arms and kissed him full upon the lips before she disengaged. He didn't know her. He didn't know anyone here. He stumbled through the crowd, pushed and pulled this way and that, trying numbly to steer himself, a cork in a flood, towards The Trialla, where his room was, and a drink, and music.

Devin was already at the crowded bar when he finally made it back. Erlein was nowhere to be seen yet. Probably still on the ship; staying afloat, as far from Brandin as he could. As if the sorcerer had the faintest scintilla of interest in pursuing wizards right now.

Devin, mercifully, said nothing at all. Only pushed over a full glass and a flagon of wine. Alessan drained the glass and then another very quickly. He had poured and tasted a third when Devin quickly touched his arm and he realized, with a sense of almost physical shock, that he'd forgotten his oath. The blue wine. Third glass.

He pushed the flagon away and buried his head in his hands.

Someone was speaking beside him. Two men arguing.

"You're actually going to do it? You're a goat-begotten fool!" the first one snarled.

"I'm joining up," the second replied, in the flat accents of Asoli. "After what that woman did for him I figure Brandin's blessed with luck. And someone who styles himself Brandin di Chiara is a long sight better than that butcher from Barbadior. What are you, friend, afraid of fighting?"

The other man gave a harsh bark of laughter. "You simple-minded dolt," he said. He flattened his voice in broad mimicry. "*After what that woman did for him.* We all know what she did for him, night after night. That woman is the Tyrant's whore. She spent a dozen years coupling with the man who conquered us all. Spreading her legs for him for her own gain. And here you are, here *all* of you are, making a whore into a Queen over you."

Alessan pushed his head up from his hands. He shifted his feet, pivoting for leverage. Then, without a word spoken, he hammered a fist with all the strength of his body and all the tormented confusion of his heart into the speaker's face. He felt bones crack under his blow; the man flew backwards into the bar and halfway over it, scattering glasses and bottles with a splintering crash.

Alessan looked down at his fist. It was covered with blood across the knuckles, and already beginning to swell. He wondered if he'd broken his hand. He wondered if he was going to be thrown out of the bar, or end up in a free-wheeling brawl for this stupidity.

It didn't happen. The Asolini who had proclaimed his readiness for war clapped him on the back with a hard, cheerful blow and the owner of The Trialla—their employer, in fact—grinned broadly, completely ignoring the shards of broken glass along the bar.

"I was hoping someone would shut him up!" he roared over the raucous tumult in the room. Someone else came over and wrung Alessan's hand, which hurt amazingly. Three men were shouting insistent demands to buy him a drink. Four others picked up the unconscious man and began carting him unceremoniously away in search of medical aid. Someone spat on the man's shattered face as he was carried by.

Alessan turned away from that, back to the bar. There was a single glass of Astibar blue wine in front of him. He looked quickly at Devin who said nothing at all.

Tigana, he murmured under his breath, as a Cortean sailor behind him bellowed his praise and ruffled his hair and someone else pushed over to pound his back, *Oh, Tigana, let my memory of you be like a blade in my soul.*

He drained the glass. Someone—not Devin—immediately reached to pick it up and smash it on the floor. Which started a predictable sequence of other men doing the same with their own drinks. As soon as he decently could he made his way out of the room and went upstairs. He remembered to touch Devin's arm in thanks as he went. In their room he found Erlein lying on his bed, hands behind his head, gazing fixedly at the ceiling. The wizard glanced over as Alessan came in, and his eyes quickly narrowed and grew frankly curious.

Alessan said nothing. He fell onto his pallet and closed his eyes which were still hurting. The wine, naturally, hadn't helped. He couldn't stop thinking about the woman, what she had done, how she had looked rising like some supernatural creature from the sea. He couldn't force out of his mind the image of Brandin the Tyrant falling to his knees and burying his face in his hands.

Hiding his eyes, but not before Alessan, fifteen feet away, only that, had seen the shattering relief and the blaze of love that had shone through like the white light of a falling star.

His hand hurt terribly, but he flexed it gingerly and didn't think he'd broken anything. He honestly couldn't have said why he'd felled that man. Everything he'd said about the woman from Certando was true. All of it was true, yet none of it was the real truth. Everything about today was brutally confusing.

Erlein, unexpectedly tactful, cleared his throat in a way that offered a question.

"Yes?" Alessan said wearily, not opening his eyes.

"This is what you wanted to happen, isn't it?" the wizard asked, unwontedly hesitant.

With an effort Alessan opened his eyes and looked over. Erlein was propped on one elbow gazing at him, his expression thoughtful and subdued. "Yes," he said at length, "this is what I wanted."

Erlein nodded slowly. "It means war, then. In my province."

His head was still throbbing, but less than before. It was quieter up here, though the noise from below still penetrated, a dull, steady background of celebration.

"In Senzio, yes," he said.

He felt a terrible sadness. So many years of planning, and now that they were here, where were they? His mother was dead. She had cursed him before she died, but had let him take her hand as the ending came. What did that mean? Could it be made to mean what he needed it to?

He was on the Island. Had seen Brandin of Ygrath. What would he tell Baerd? The slender dagger at his side felt heavy as a sword. The woman had been so much more beautiful than he'd expected her to be. Devin had had to give him the blue wine; he couldn't believe that. He'd hurt a hapless, innocent man so brutally just now, had shattered the bones of his face. I must look truly terrible, he thought, for even Erlein to be so gentle with me now. They were going to war in Senzio. *This is what I wanted,* he repeated to himself.

"Erlein, I'm sorry," he said, risking it, trying to struggle upwards from this sorrow.

He braced for a stinging reply, he almost wanted one, but Erlein said nothing at all at first. And when he spoke it was mildly. "I think it is time," was what he said. "Shall we go down and play? Would that help?"

Would that help? Since when did his people—Erlein, even—need to minister to him so much?

They went back down the stairs. Devin was waiting for them on the makeshift stage at the back of the Trialla. Alessan took up his Tregean pipes. His right hand was hurting and swollen, but it was not going to keep him from making music. He needed music now, very badly. He closed his eyes and began to play. They fell silent for him in the densely crowded room. Erlein waited, his hands motionless on the harp, and Devin did, leaving him a space in which to reach upwards alone, yearning towards that high note where confusion and pain and love and death and longing could all be left behind him for a very little while.

CHAPTER
• 18 •

NORMALLY WHEN SHE WENT UP ON THE RAMPARTS OF her castle at sunset it was to look south, watching the play of light and the changing colors of the sky above the mountains. Of late though, as springtime turned towards the summer they had all been waiting for, Alienor found herself climbing to the northern ramparts instead, to pace the guard's walk behind the crenellations or lean upon the cool rough stone, gazing into the distance, wrapped in her shawl against the chill that still came when the sun went down.

As if she could actually see as far as Senzio.

The shawl was a new one, brought by the messengers from Quileia that Baerd had told them would come. The ones who carried the messages that could, if all went right, turn the whole world upside down. Not just the Palm: Barbadior too, where the Emperor was said to be dying, and Ygrath, and Quileia itself where, precisely because of what he was doing for them, Marius might not survive.

The Quileian messengers had stopped on their way to Fort Ortiz, as was appropriate, to pay their respects to the Lady of Castle Borso and to bring her a gift from the new King of Quileia: an indigo-colored shawl, a color almost impossible to find here in the Palm, and one which was, she knew, a mark of nobility in Quileia. It was evident that Alessan had told this Marius a fair bit about her involvement with him over the years. Which was fine. Marius of Quileia, it seemed, was one of them; in fact, as Baerd had explained it the afternoon after

Alessan had ridden into the Braccio Pass and then away west, Marius was the key to everything.

Two days after the Quileians passed through, Alienor began a habit of springtime rides that took her, casually, far enough afield to necessitate one or two overnight stays at neighboring castles. At which time she relayed a quite specific message to a half dozen equally specific people.

Senzio. Before Midsummer

Not long afterwards, a silk-merchant and then a singer she rather liked came down to Castle Borso with word of tremendous troop movements among the Barbadians. The roads were absolutely clogged with mercenaries marching north, they said. She had raised her eyebrows in quizzical mystification, but had allowed herself more wine than was customary each of those two nights, and had rewarded both men later, after her own fashion.

Up on the ramparts at sunset now, she heard a footstep on the stair behind her. She had been waiting for it. Without turning, she said, "You are almost too late. The sun is nearly gone." Which was true; the color of the sky and the thin, underlit clouds in the west had darkened from pink through crimson and purple most of the way down to the indigo she wore about her shoulders.

Elena stepped out on the parapet.

"I'm sorry," she said, inappropriately. She was always apologizing, still uneasy in the castle. She moved to the guard's walk beside Alienor and looked out over the gathering darkness of the late-spring fields. Her long yellow hair fanned over her shoulders, the ends lifting in the breeze.

Ostensibly she was here to serve as a new lady-in-waiting to Alienor. She had brought her two young children and her few belongings into Borso two mornings after the Ember Days had ended. It was considered a good idea that she be established here well before the time that might matter. It appeared, incredibly enough, that there could actually come a time when her being here might matter.

Tomaz, the gaunt, aged Khardhu warrior had said that it would be necessary for one of them to stay here. Tomaz, who was very clearly *not* from Khardhun, and just as clearly unwilling to say who he really was. Alienor didn't care about that. What mattered was that Baerd and Alessan trusted him, and in this matter Baerd was deferring to the dark, hollow-cheeked man absolutely.

"One of *whom,* exactly?" Alienor had asked. The four of them had been alone: herself, Baerd and Tomaz, and the red-headed young girl who didn't like her, Catriana.

Baerd hesitated a long time. "One of the Night Walkers," he said finally.

She had raised her eyebrows at that, the small outward gesture serving to show all she was prepared to reveal of her inward astonishment.

"Really? Here? They are still about?"

Baerd nodded.

"And that is where you were last night when you went out?"

After a second Baerd nodded again.

The girl Catriana blinked in manifest surprise. She was clever and quite beautiful, Alienor thought, but she still had rather a great deal to learn.

"Doing what?" Alienor asked Baerd.

But this time he shook his head. She had expected that. There were limits with Baerd; she enjoyed trying to push towards them. One night, ten years ago, she had found exactly where his boundaries of privacy lay, in one dimension at least. Surprisingly perhaps, their friendship had deepened from that time on.

Now, unexpectedly, he grinned. "You could have them all stay here, of course, not just one."

She had grimaced with a distaste only partly feigned. "One will be sufficient, thank you. Assuming it is enough for your purposes, whatever those are?" She said that last to the old man disguised as a Khardhu warrior. His skin coloring was really very good but she knew all about Baerd's techniques of disguise. Over the years he and Alessan had shown up here in an effective diversity of appearances.

"I'm not absolutely sure *what* our purposes are," Tomaz had replied frankly. "But insofar as we need an anchor for what Baerd wants us to at least be able to try, one of them in this castle should be enough."

"Enough for what?" she'd probed again, not really expecting anything.

"Enough for my magic to reach out and find this place," Tomaz had said bluntly.

This time it was she who blinked and Catriana who looked unruffled and superior. Which was unfair, Alienor decided afterwards; the girl must have *known* the old man was a wizard. That was why she hadn't reacted. Alienor had enough of a sense of humor to find their by-play amusing, and even to feel a little regretful when Catriana had gone.

Two days afterwards Elena had come. Baerd had said it would be a woman. He had asked Alienor to take care of her. She had raised her eyebrows at that as well.

On the northern ramparts she glanced over in the twilight. Elena had come up without a cloak; her hands were cupping her elbows tightly against her body. Feeling unreasonably irritated, Alienor abruptly removed her shawl and draped it over the other's shoulders.

"You should know better by now," she said sharply. "It gets cold up here when the sun goes down."

"I'm sorry," Elena said again, quickly motioning to remove the shawl. "But you'll be chilled now. I'll go down and get something for myself."

"Stay where you are!" Alienor snapped. Elena froze, apprehension in her eyes. Alienor looked out past her, past the darkening fields and the emerging flickers of light where night candles and fires were being lit in houses and farms below. She looked beyond all these under the first stars of the evening, her eyes straining north, her imagination winging far beyond her sight to where the others would all be gathering now, or soon.

"Stay here," she said, more gently. "Stay with me."

Elena's blue eyes widened in the darkness as she looked over. Her expression was grave, thoughtful. Unexpectedly, she smiled. And then, even more astonishingly, she moved nearer and drew her arm through Alienor's, pulling her close. Alienor stiffened for a second, then allowed herself to relax against the other woman. She had asked for companionship. For the first time in more years than she could remember, she had asked for this. A completely different kind of intimacy. It felt, of late, as if something rigid and hard was falling away inside her. She had waited for this summer, for what it might mean, for so many years.

What had the young one said, Devin? About being allowed more than the transience of desire, if only one believed it was deserved. No one had ever said such a thing to her in all the years since Cornaro of Borso had died fighting Barbadior. In which dark time his young widow, his bride, alone in a highland castle with her grief and rage, had been set upon the road towards what she had become.

He had gone with Alessan, Devin. By now, they would probably be in the north as well. Alienor looked out, letting her thoughts stream like birds arrowing away through darkness, across the miles between, to where all of their fates would be decided when Midsummer came.

Dark hair and light blown back and mingled by the wind, the two women stood together in that high place for a long time, sharing warmth, sharing the night and the waiting time.

★   ★   ★

It had long been said, sometimes in mockery, sometimes with a bemusement that bordered on awe, that as the days heated up in summer, so did the night-time passions of Senzio. The hedonistic self-indulgence of that northern province, blessed with fertile soil and gentle weather, was a byword in the Palm and even over the seas. You could get whatever you wanted in Senzio, it was said, provided you were willing to pay for it. And fight someone to keep it, the initiated often added.

Towards the end of spring that year it might have been thought that burgeoning tensions and the palpable threat of war would have dampened the nocturnal ardor of the Senzians—and their endless flow of visitors—for wine, for lovemaking in diverse combinations, and for brawling in the taverns and streets.

Someone might indeed have thought such a thing, but not anyone who knew Senzio. In fact, it actually seemed as if the looming portents of disaster—the Barbadians massed ominously on the Ferraut border, the ever-

increasing numbers of ships of the Ygrathen flotilla anchored at Farsaro Island off the northwestern tip of the
province—were simply spurs to the wildness of night in
Senzio town. There were no curfews here; there hadn't
been for hundreds of years. And though emissaries of
both invading powers were prominently housed in opposite wings of what was now called the Governor's Castle,
Senzians still boasted that they were the only free province in the Palm.

A boast that began to ring more hollow with each
passing day and sybaritic night as the entire peninsula
braced itself for a conflagration.

In the face of which onrushing intrusion of reality
Senzio town merely intensified the already manic pace of
its dark hours. Legendary watering-holes like The Red
Glove or Thetaph were packed with sweating, shouting
patrons every night, to whom they dispensed their harsh,
overpriced liquors and a seemingly endless stream of
available flesh, male or female, in the warrens of airless
rooms upstairs.

Those innkeepers who had elected, for whatever reasons, not to trade in purchased love had to offer substan-
tially different inducements to their patrons. For the
eponymous owner of Solinghi's, a tavern not far from the
castle, good food, decent vintages and ales, and clean
rooms in which to sleep were assurances of a respectable
if not an extravagant living, derived primarily from merchants and traders disinclined to traffic in the carnality of
night, or at least to sleep and eat amid that overripe
corruption. Solinghi's also prided itself on offering, by
day or night, the best music to be found in the city at any
given time.

At this particular moment, shortly before the dinner-
hour one day late in the spring, the bar and table patrons
of the almost full tavern were enjoying the music of an
unlikely trio: a Senzian harper, a piper from Astibar, and
a young Asolini tenor who—according to a rumor started
a couple of days before—was the singer who had disappeared after performing Sandre d'Astibar's funeral rites
last fall.

Rumors of every kind were rife in Senzio that spring,
but few believed this one: such a prodigy was unlikely in

the extreme to be singing in a put-together group like
this. But in fact the young tenor had an exceptional voice
and he was matched by the playing of the other two.
Solinghi di Senzio was immensely pleased with their effect on business over the past week.

The truth was, he would have given them employment
and a room upstairs if they had made music like boarhounds
in lust. Solinghi had been a friend of the dark-haired man
who was now calling himself Adreano d'Astibar for almost ten years. A friend, and more than that; as it
happened, almost half the patrons of the inn this spring
were men who had come to Senzio expressly to meet the
three musicians here. Solinghi kept his mouth shut, poured
wine and beer, supervised his cooks and serving-girls,
and prayed to Eanna of the Lights every night before he
went to sleep that Alessan knew what he was doing.

This particular afternoon the patrons enjoying the young
tenor's rousing rendition of a Certandan ballad were
rudely snapped out of their bar-pounding rhythm when
the doors to the street were pushed open, revealing a
largish cluster of new customers. Nothing of note in that,
of course. Or not until the singer cut himself off in the
middle of a chorus with a shouted greeting, the piper
quickly laid down his pipes and leaped off the stage, and
the harper lowered his own instrument and followed, if
more slowly.

The enthusiasms of the reunion that ensued would
have led to predictably cynical conclusions about the
nature of the men involved, given the way of such things
in Senzio, had the new party not included a pair of
exceptionally attractive young women, one with short red
hair, one with raven-dark. Even the harper, a dour,
unsmiling fellow if ever there was one, was drawn almost
against his will into the circle, to be crushed against the
bony breast of a cadaverous looking Khardhu mercenary
who towered over the rest of the party.

A moment later another kind of reunion occurred.
One with a different resonance that even stilled the excitement of the newly mingled group. Another man rose
and walked diffidently over to the five people who had just
arrived. Those who looked closely could see that his
hands were trembling.

"Baerd?" they heard him say.

There followed a moment of silence. Then the man whom he'd addressed said *"Naddo?"* in a tone even the most innocent Senzian could interpret. Any lingering doubts about that were laid to rest a second later by the way the two men embraced each other.

They even wept.

More than one man, eyeing the two women with frank admiration, decided that his chances of a conversation, and who knew what else, might be better than they'd first appeared if the men were all like that.

★   ★   ★

Alais had been moving through the days since Tregea in a state of excitement that brought an almost continuous flush to her pale skin and made her more delicately beautiful than she knew. What she *did* know is why she had been allowed to come.

From the moment the *Sea Maid*'s landing-boat had silently returned to the ship in the moonlit harbor of Tregea, bearing her father and Catriana and the two men they'd gone to meet, Alais had been aware that something more than friendship was involved here.

Then the dark-skinned man from Khardhu had looked at her appraisingly, and at Rovigo with an amused expression on his lined face, and her father, hesitating for only a moment, had told her who this really was. And then, quietly, but with an exhilarating confidence in her, he'd explained what these people, his new partners, were really doing here, and what he appeared to have been doing in secret with them for a great many years.

It appeared that it had not been entirely a coincidence after all that they'd met three musicians on the road outside their home during the Festival of Vines last fall.

Listening intently, trying not to miss a syllable or an implication, Alais measured her own inward response to all of this and was pleased beyond words to discover that she was not afraid. Her father's voice and manner had much to do with that. And the simple fact that he was trusting her with this.

It was the other man—Baerd, they named him—who said to Rovigo, "If you are truly set on coming with us to Senzio, then we will have to find a place on the coast to put your daughter ashore."

"Why, exactly?" Alais had said quickly before Rovigo could answer. She could feel her color rising as all eyes turned to her. They were down below deck, crowded in her father's cabin.

Baerd's eyes were very dark by candlelight. He was a hard-looking, even a dangerous-seeming man, but his voice when he answered her was not unkind.

"Because I don't believe in subjecting people to unnecessary risks. There is danger in what we are about to do. There are also reasons for us to face those dangers, and your father's assistance and that of his men if he trusts them, is important to us. For you to come would be a danger without necessity. Does that make sense?"

She forced herself to be calm. "Only if you judge me a child, incapable of any contribution." She swallowed. "I am the same age as Catriana and I think I now understand what is happening here. What you have been trying to do. I have . . . I can say that I have the same desire as any of you to be free."

"There are truths in that. I think she should come." It was, remarkably, Catriana. "Baerd," she went on, "if this is truly the time that will decide, we have no business refusing people who feel the way we do. No right to decide that they must huddle in their homes waiting to see if they are still slaves or not when the summer ends."

Baerd looked at Catriana for a long time but said nothing. He turned to Rovigo, deferring to him with a gesture. In her father's face Alais could see worry and love warring with his pride in her. And then, by the light of the candles, she saw that inner battle end.

"If we get through this alive," Rovigo d'Astibar said to his daughter, his life, his joy in life, "your mother will kill me. You know that, don't you?"

"I'll try to protect you," Alais said gravely, though her heart was racing like a wild thing.

It had been their talk at the railing of the ship, she knew. She knew it absolutely. The two of them looking at the cliffs under moonlight after the storm.

I don't know what it is, she had said, *but I need more.
I know,* her father had replied. *I know you do. If I
could give it, it would be yours. The world and the stars of
Eanna would all be yours.*

It was because of that, because he loved her and meant
what he had said, that he was allowing her to come with
them to where the world they knew would be put into the
balance.

Of that journey to Senzio she remembered two things
particularly. Standing at the rail early one morning with
Catriana as they moved north up the coast of Astibar.
One tiny village, and then another and another, the roofs
of houses bright in the sun, small fishing boats bobbing
between the *Sea Maid* and the shore.

"That one is my home," Catriana said suddenly, breaking a silence, speaking so softly only Alais could hear.
"And that boat with the blue sail is actually my father's." Her voice was odd, eerily detached from the
meaning of the words.

"We have to stop, then!" Alais had murmured urgently. "I'll tell my father! He'll—"

Catriana laid a hand on her arm.

"Not yet," she'd said. "I can't see him yet. After.
After Senzio. Perhaps."

That was one memory. The other, very different, was of
rounding the northern tip of Farsaro Island early in the
morning and seeing the ships of Ygrath and the Western
Palm anchored in the harbor there. Waiting for war.
She *had* been afraid then, as the reality of what they
were sailing towards was brought home to her in that
vision, at once brightly colorful and forbidding as grey
death. But she had looked over at Catriana, and her
father, and then at the old Duke, Sandre, who named
himself Tomaz now, and she had seen shadings of doubt
and anxiety in each of them as well. Only Baerd, carefully counting the flotilla, had a different kind of expression on his face.

If she'd been forced to put a name to that look she
would have said, hesitantly, that it was desire.

*   *   *

The next afternoon they had come to Senzio, and had
moored the *Maid* in the crowded harbor and gone ashore,
and so had come, at the end of the day, to an inn all the
others seemed to know about. And the five of them had
walked through the doors of that tavern into a flashing of
joy bright and sudden as the sun come up from the rim of
the sea.

Devin embraced her tightly and then kissed her on the
lips, and then Alessan, after a moment's visible anxiety
at her presence and a searching glance at her father, did
exactly the same. There was a lean-faced grey-haired
man named Erlein with them, and then a number of
other men in the tavern came up—Naddo was one name,
Ducas another, and there was an older blind man with
those two whose name she never caught. He walked with
the aid of a magnificent stick. It had the most extraordinary carved eagle's head, with eyes so piercing they seemed
almost to be a compensation for the loss of his own.

There were others as well, from all over, it seemed.
She missed most of their names. There was a great deal
of noise. The innkeeper brought them wine: two bottles
of Senzio green and a third one of Astibar's blue wine.
She had a small, careful glass of each, watching everyone, trying to sort through the chaotic babble of all that
was said. Alessan and Baerd drew briefly apart for a
moment, she noticed; when they returned to the table
both men looked thoughtful and somewhat grim.

Then Devin and Alessan and Erlein had to go back
and make their music for an hour while the others ate,
and Alais, flushed and terribly excited, inwardly relived
the feel of the two men's lips upon hers. She found
herself smiling shyly at everyone, afraid that her face was
giving away exactly what she was feeling.

Afterwards they made their way upstairs behind the
broad back of the innkeeper's wife to their rooms. And
later, when it was quiet on that upper level Catriana led
her from the room they were put in, down the hall to the
bedroom Devin and Alessan and Erlein shared.

They were there, and a number of other men—some
of the ones she'd just met, and a few who were strangers.
Her father entered a moment later with Sandre and Baerd.

She and Catriana were the only women there. She had a moment to feel a little strange about that, and to think about how far she was from home, before everyone fell silent as Alessan pushed a hand through his hair and began to speak.

And as he did, Alais, concentrating, gradually came to understand with the others the dimensions, the truly frightening shape, of what he proposed to do.

At a certain point he stopped and looked at three men one by one. At Duke Sandre first, then at a round-faced Certandan named Sertino sitting with Ducas, and finally, almost challengingly, at Erlein di Senzio.

The three of them were wizards, she understood. It was a hard thing to come to terms with. Especially Sandre. The exiled Duke of Astibar. Their neighbor in the distrada all her life.

The man called Erlein was sitting on his bed, his back against the wall, hands crossed over his breast. He was breathing hard.

"It is clear to me now that you *have* lost your mind," he said. His voice shook. "You have lived in your dreams so long you've lost sight of the world. And now you are going to kill people in your madness."

Alais saw Devin open his mouth and then snap it shut without speaking.

"All of this is possible," Alessan said, with an unexpected mildness. "It is possible I am pursuing a path of madness, though I think not. But yes, there are likely to be a great many people killed. We always knew that; the real madness would have been in pretending otherwise. For the moment though, compose your spirit and ease your soul. You know as well as I do, nothing is happening."

"Nothing? What do you mean?" It was her father.

Alessan's expression was wry, almost bitter. "Haven't you noticed? You were in the harbor, you walked through the town. Have you seen any Barbadian troops? Any Ygrathens, soldiers from the west? *Nothing is happening.* Alberico of Barbadior has his entire army massed on the border, and the man refuses to order them north!"

"He is afraid," said Sandre flatly in the silence that followed. "He's afraid of Brandin."

"Perhaps," her father said thoughtfully. "Or else he is just cautious. Too cautious."

"What do we do then?" asked the red-bearded Tregean named Ducas.

Alessan shook his head. "I don't know. I honestly don't know. This is one thing I never expected. You tell me," he said. "How do we make him cross the border? How do we bring him to war?" He looked at Ducas and then at each of the others in the room.

No one answered him.

★   ★   ★

They would think he was a coward. They were fools. They were all fools. Only a fool went lightly into war. Especially a war such as this, that risked everything for a gain he hardly cared about. *Senzio? The Palm?* What did they matter? Should he throw twenty years away for them?

Every time a messenger arrived from back in Astibar something in him leaped with hope. If the Emperor had died . . .

If the Emperor had died he and his men were gone. Away from this blighted peninsula, home to claim an Emperor's Tiara in Barbadior. *That* was his war, the one he wanted to fight. The one that mattered, the only thing that had really mattered all these years. He would sail home with three armies and wrest the Tiara from the court favorites hovering there like so many ineffectual, fluttering moths.

And after *that* he could make war back here, with all the gathered might of Barbadior. Then let Brandin of Ygrath, of the Western Palm, whatever he chose to name himself, *then* let him try to stand before Alberico, Emperor of Barbadior.

Gods, the sweetness of it . . .

But no such message came from the east, no such glittering reprieve. And so the bald reality was that he found himself camped with his mercenaries here on the border between Ferraut and Senzio, preparing to face the armies of Ygrath and the Western Palm, knowing that the eyes of the entire world would be upon them now. If he lost, he lost everything. If he won . . . well that depended on the cost. If too many of his men died here, what kind of an army would he have to lead home? And too many men dying was a vivid prospect now. Ever since what had happened in the harbor of Chiara. Most of the Ygrathen army had indeed sailed home, exactly as anticipated, leaving Brandin crippled and exposed. Which is why Alberico had moved, why the three companies were here and he with them. The flow and shape of events had seemed to be on their side, in the clearest possible way.

Then the Certandan woman had fished a ring from the water for Brandin.

She haunted his dreams, that never-seen woman. Three times now she'd surfaced like a nightmare in his life. Back when Brandin had first claimed her for his saishan she had nearly drawn him into an insane war. Siferval had wanted to fight, Alberico remembered. The Third Company captain had proposed storming across the border into Lower Corte and sacking Stevanien itself.

Gods. Alberico shuddered even now, long years after, at the thought of such a war far to the west against the Ygrathens in all their power. He had swallowed his bile and absorbed all the mocking gibes Brandin sent east. Even then, long ago, he had preserved his discipline, kept his eyes on the real prize back home.

But he might have had the Peninsula of the Palm without effort this spring, a pure gift fallen from the sky, if that same Dianora di Certando had not saved the Ygrathen's life two months ago. It had been there for him, gently floating down: with Brandin assassinated the Ygrathens would have all sailed home and the western provinces would have lain open before him like so much ripe fruit.

Quileia's crippled King would have hobbled across the mountains to abase himself before Alberico, *begging* for the trade he needed. No elaborate letters then about fearing the mighty power of Ygrath. It would have all been so easy, so . . . elegant.

But it was not so, because of the woman. The woman from one of his own provinces. The irony was coruscat-

ing, it was like acid in his soul. Certando was *his* and
Dianora di Certando was the only reason Brandin was
alive.

And now—her third time in his life—she was the only
reason there was an army from the west, a flotilla anchored in the Bay of Farsaro, waiting for Alberico to
make the slightest move.

"They are fewer than us," his spies reported daily.
"And not as well armed."

Fewer, the three captains echoed each other in mind-
less litany. *Not as well armed*, they gibbered. *We must
move*, they chorused, their imbecilic faces looming in his
dreams, set close together, hanging like lurid moons too
near the earth.

Anghiar, his emissary in the Governor's Castle at Senzio,
sent word that Casalia still favored them; that the Governor realized that Brandin was not as strong as they.
That he had been persuaded to see the virtue of tilting
even further towards Barbadior. The emissary from the
Western Palm, one of the few Ygrathens who had decided to stay with Brandin, was having a more difficult
time each passing day gaining audience with the Governor, but Anghiar dined with plump, sybaritic Casalia
almost every night.

So now even Anghiar, who had grown lazy and self-
indulgent, morally corrupt as any Senzian during his years
there, was saying the same thing as all the others: *Senzio
is a vineyard ripe for harvesting. Come!*

Ripe for harvesting? Didn't they understand? Didn't
any of them realize that there was *sorcery* to reckon
with?

He *knew* how strong Brandin was; he had probed and
backed quickly away from the Ygrathen's power in the
year they had both come here, and that had been when
he himself was in his prime. Not hollow and weakened,
with a bad foot and a drooping eye after almost being
killed in that cursed Sandreni lodge last year. He was not
the *same* anymore; he knew it, if none of the others did.
If he went to war it had to be a decision made in the light
of that. His military edge had to be enough to offset the
Ygrathen's sorcery. He needed to be *certain*. Surely any
man not a fool could see that that had nothing to do with

cowardice! Only with a careful measuring of gains and losses, risks and opportunities.

In his dreams in his tent on the border he thrust the vacuous moon faces of his captains back up into the sky, and under five moons, not two, he slowly dismembered and defiled the staked-out body of the woman from Certando.

Then the mornings would come. Digesting messages like rancid food, he would begin to wrestle again, endlessly, with the other thing that was nagging him this season like an infected wound.

Something felt wrong. Entirely wrong. There was an aspect about this whole chain of events—from the autumn onwards—that jarred within him like a jangling, dissonant chord.

Here on the border with his army all around him he was supposed to feel as if *he* were calling the measure of the dance. Forcing Brandin and the entire Palm to respond to his tune. Seizing control again after a winter of being impacted upon in all those trivial, disconcerting, cumulative ways. Shaping events so that Quileia would have no choice but to seek him out, so that back home in the Empire they could not mistake his power, the vigor of his will, the glory of his conquests.

That was how he was *supposed* to feel. How he had indeed briefly felt the morning he'd heard that Brandin had abdicated in Ygrath. When he'd ordered his three armies north to the border of Senzio.

But something had changed since that day and it was more than just the presence of opposition now waiting in the Bay of Farsaro. There was something else, something so vague and undefined he couldn't even talk about it— even if he'd had anyone to talk to—couldn't even pin it down, but it was there, nagging at him like an old wound in rain.

Alberico of Barbadior had not got to where he was, achieved this power base from which a thrust for the Tiara was imminent, without subtlety and thoughtfulness, without learning to trust his instincts.

And his instincts told him, here on the border, with his captains and his spies and his emissary in Senzio literally begging him to march, that something was wrong.

That he was *not* calling the tune. Someone else was. Somehow, someone else was guiding the dangerous steps of this dance. He had truly no idea who it could be, but the feeling was there each morning when he woke and it would not be shaken off. Neither would it come clear for him under the spring sun, in that border meadow bright with the banners of Barbadior, with irises and asphodels, and fragrant with the scent of the surrounding pines.

So he waited, praying to his gods for word of a death back home, agonizingly aware that the world might soon be laughing at him if he drew back, knowing, as spies kept hastening south in relays, that Brandin was getting stronger in Farsaro every day, but held there on the border by his craftiness, his instinct for survival, by that ache of doubt. Waiting for something to come clear.

Refusing, as the days slipped past, to dance to what might be someone else's tune, however seductively the hidden pipes might play.

She was numbingly afraid. This was worse, infinitely worse than the bridge in Tregea. There she had embraced and accepted danger because there was more than a hope of surviving the leap. It had been only water down below, however frigid it might be, and there had been friends waiting in the darkness around the bend to claim her from the river and chafe her back to life.

Tonight was different. Catriana realized with dismay that her hands were shaking. She stopped in the shadows of a lane to try to steady herself.

She reached up nervously to adjust her hair under the dark hood, fingering the jeweled black comb she'd set in it. On the ship coming here Alais, who had said she was used to doing so for her sisters, had evened and shaped her original swift cropping on the floor of the shop in Tregea. Catriana knew her appearance was perfectly acceptable now—more than that, actually, if the reactions of men in Senzio these past days meant anything.

And they had to mean something. For that was what had brought her out here in the darkness alone, pressed against a rough stone wall in a lane, waiting now for a noisy swarm of revelers to pass by in the street before her. This was a better part of town, so near the castle, but there was no truly safe quarter of Senzio for a woman alone in the streets at night.

She wasn't out here for safety though, which is why none of the others knew where she was. They would never have let her come. Nor would she, being honest with herself, have knowingly let any of them undertake anything like this.

This was death. She was under no illusions.

All afternoon, walking through the market with Devin and Rovigo and Alais, she had been shaping this plan and remembering her mother. That single candle always lit at sunset on the first of the Ember Days. Devin's father had done the same thing, she remembered him saying. Pride, he'd thought it was: withholding something from the Triad because of what they had allowed to happen. Her mother wasn't a proud woman, but neither had she permitted herself to forget.

Tonight Catriana saw herself as being like one of her mother's forbidden candles on those Ember Nights while all the rest of the world lay shrouded in darkness. She was a small flame, exactly like those candles; one that would not last the night, but one that, if the Triad had any love at all for her, might shape a conflagration before she went out.

The drunken revelers finally staggered by, heading in the direction of the harbor taverns. She waited another moment and then, muffled in her hood, went quickly into the street, keeping to the side of it and started the other way. Toward the castle.

It would be much better, she thought, if she could somehow make her hands be still and slow her racing heart. She should have had a glass of wine back at Solinghi's before slipping away, using the outside back stairs so that none of the others would see her. She'd sent Alais down to dinner alone, pleading a woman's illness, promising to follow soon if she could.

She had lied so easily, had even managed a reassuring smile. Then Alais was gone and she was alone, realizing in that precise instant, as the room door gently closed, that she would never see any of the others again.

In the street she shut her eyes, feeling suddenly unsteady; she put her hand on a shop-front for support, drawing deep breaths of the night air. There were tainflowers not far away, and the unmistakable fragrance of sejoia trees. She was near to the castle gardens then. She bit her lips, to force color into them. Overhead the stars were bright and close. Vidomni was already risen in the east, with blue Ilarion to follow soon. She heard a sudden peal of laughter from the next street over. A woman's laughter followed by shouting. The voice of a man. More laughter.

They were going the other way. As she looked up a star fell in the sky. Following its track to her left she saw the garden wall of the castle. The entrance would be further around that way. Entrances and endings, faced alone. But she had been a solitary child, and then solitary as a woman, drawn into an orbit of her own that took her away from others, even those who would be her friends. Devin and Alais only the latest of those who had tried. There had been others back home in the village before she left. She knew her mother had grieved for her proud solitude.

Pride. Again.

Her father had fled Tigana before the battles at the river.

There it was. There it was.

Carefully she drew back her hood. With real gratitude she discovered that her hands were steady now. She checked her earrings, the silver band about her throat, the jeweled ornament in her hair. Then she drew onto her hand the red glove she'd bought in the market that afternoon and she walked across the street and around the corner of the garden wall into the blaze of light at the entrance to the Governor's Castle of Senzio.

There were four guards, two outside the locked gates, two just within. She allowed her hooded cloak fall open, to let them see the black gown she wore beneath.

The two guards outside the gates glanced at each other and visibly relaxed, removing their hands from their

swords. The other two moved nearer, the better to see by
torchlight.

She stopped in front of the first pair. She smiled.
"Would you be kind enough," she said, "to let Anghiar
of Barbadior know that his red vixen has come?" And
she held up her left hand, sheathed in the bright red
glove.

She had actually been amused at first by Devin's reaction
and Rovigo's in the marketplace. Casalia, the plump,
unhealthy looking Governor had ridden through, side by
side with the emissary from Barbadior. They had been
laughing together. Brandin's emissary from the Western
Palm had been several paces behind, among a cluster of
lesser Senzians. The image and the message were as clear
as they could be made.

Alais and Catriana had been standing at a silk-merchant's
stall. They had turned to see the Governor go by.

He had not gone by. Instead, Anghiar of Barbadior
laid a quick restraining hand on Casalia's braceleted wrist
and they stopped their prancing horses directly in front of
the two women. Thinking back on it, Catriana realized
that she and Alais must have made a striking pair. Anghiar,
blond and beefy, with an upturned moustache and hair as
long as her own was now, evidently thought so.

"A mink and a red vixen!" he said, in a voice pitched
for Casalia's ear. The plump Governor laughed, too
quickly, a little too loudly. Anghiar's blue eyes stripped
the women to their flesh under the bright sun. Alais
looked away, but not down. Catriana met the Barbadian's gaze as steadily as she could. She would not turn
away from these men. His smile only deepened. "A red
vixen, truly," he repeated, but this time to her, and not to
Casalia.

The Governor laughed anyhow. They moved on, their
party following, including Brandin's emissary, looking
grimly unhappy for all the beauty of the morning.

Catriana had become aware of Devin at her shoulder
and Rovigo beside his daughter. She looked at them and
registered the clenched fury in their eyes. It was then that
she'd felt amusement, however briefly.

"That," she said lightly, "is exactly how Baerd looked

before he almost had us both killed in Tregea. I don't think I'm prepared to repeat the experience. I have no hair left to cut."

It was Alais, cleverer by far than Catriana had realized at first, who laughed, carrying them past the moment. The four of them walked on.

"I would have killed him," Devin said quietly to her as they paused by a leather goods booth.

"Of course you would have," she said easily. Then realizing how that probably sounded, and that he was quite serious in what he'd said, she squeezed his arm. Not something she would have done six months before. She was changing, they all were.

But just about then, amusement and anger both fading, Catriana began to think about something. It seemed to her that the brightness of the day slid abruptly into shadow for a moment though there were no clouds in the sky at all.

She realized afterwards that she had decided to do it almost as soon as the idea took shape in her mind.

Before the morning market had closed she had managed to be alone long enough to purchase what she needed. Earrings, gown, black comb. Red glove.

And it was while doing these things that she'd begun to think about her mother and to remember the bridge in Tregea. Not surprisingly: the mind worked in patterns like that. Such patterns were why she was doing this, why she'd even been able to think of it. When night fell she would have to come away by herself, telling none of them. A lie of some sort for Alais. No farewells; they would stop her, just as she would have stopped any of them.

But something had to be done, they all knew it. A move *had* to be made, and that morning in the market Catriana had thought she'd discovered what that move might be.

She'd spent the first part of this solitary walk through darkness wishing she were braver though, that her hands would not tremble as they were. But they'd stopped shaking after all when she reached the garden wall and saw a star fall in the blue-black velvet sky.

*   *   *

"We'll have to search you, you understand," said one of
the two guards outside the gates, a crooked smile on his
face.

"Of course," she murmured, stepping nearer. "There
are so few benefits to standing watch here, aren't there?"
The other one laughed, and drew her forward, not
ungently, into the light of the torches and then a little
past them, to the more private shadows at the side of the
square. She heard a brief, low-pitched altercation between the two men on the other side of the gate, ending
in a concise six-word order. One of them, manifestly
outranked, reluctantly began heading inward through the
courtyard to find Anghiar of Barbadior and tell him his
dreams had just come true, or some such thing. The
other hastily unlocked the gates with a key on a ring at
his belt and came out to join the others.

They took some time with her, but were not unkind,
nor did they presume too much in the end. If she was
going to the Barbadian and found favor there, they could
be at risk in offending her. She had counted on something like that. She managed to laugh softly once or
twice, but not so much as to encourage them. She was
thinking of patterns still, remembering the very first evening she'd come to Alessan and Baerd. The night porter
at the inn groping for her as she went by, leering, sure of
why she was there.

I will not sleep with you, she'd said when they opened
to her knock. *I have never slept with any man.* So much
irony in her life, looking back from these tangled shadows, the guards' hands moving over her. What mortal
knew the way their fate line would run? Inevitably perhaps, she thought about Devin in the hidden closet of the
Sandreni Palace. Which had worked out rather differently in almost every way than she had expected it to.
Not that she'd been thinking of futures or fates that day.
Not then.

And now? What should she be thinking now, as the
patterns began to unfold again? The images, she told
herself, cloaked in shadow with three guards: hold hard
to the images. Entrances and endings, a candle starting a
blaze.

By the time they were done with her the fourth guard was back with two Barbadians. They were smiling too. But they treated her with some courtesy as they led her through the open gates and across the central courtyard. Light spilled erratically downward from interior windows above. Before they passed inside she looked up at the stars. Eanna's lights. Every one of them with a name.

They went into the castle through a pair of massive doors guarded by four more men, then up two long flights of marble stairs and along a bright corridor on the highest level. At the end of this last hallway a door was partly open. Beyond it, as they approached, Catriana caught a glimpse of a room elaborately furnished in dark, rich colors.

In the doorway itself stood Anghiar of Barbadior, in a blue robe to match his eyes, holding a glass of green wine and devouring her with his gaze for the second time that day.

She smiled, and let him take her red-gloved fingers in his own manicured hand. He led her into the room. He closed and locked the door. They were alone. There were candles burning everywhere.

"Red vixen," he said, "how do you like to play?"

Devin had been edgy all week, uneasy in his own skin; he knew they all felt the same way. The combination of building tension and enforced idleness, coupled with the awareness—one had only to look at Alessan's face sometimes—of how close they were to a culmination, created a pervasive, dangerous irritability among them all.

In the face of such a mood Alais had been extraordinary, a blessing of grace these past few days. Rovigo's daughter had seemed to grow wiser and gentler and yet more at ease among them with each passing day, as if sensing a need, a reason for her to be here, and so moving to fill that need. Observant, unceasingly cheerful, effortlessly conversational, with questions and bright responses and a declared passion for long anecdotes from all of them, she had, almost single-handedly, prevented three or four mealtimes from degenerating into sullen grimness or fractious rancor. Blind Rinaldo the Healer seemed almost in love with her, so much did he seem to flourish when she was by his side. He wasn't the only one of them, either, Devin thought, almost grateful that the tensions of the time were preventing him from addressing his own inward feelings.

In the hothouse atmosphere of Senzio Alais's delicate, pale beauty and diffident grace singled her out like some flower transplanted here from a garden in a cooler, milder world. Which was, of course, exactly true. An observer himself, Devin would catch Rovigo gazing at his daughter as she drew one or another of their new companions into conversation, and the look in the man's eyes spoke volumes.

Now, at the end of dinner, having spent the last half-hour turning their market expedition of the morning and afternoon into a veritable sea-voyage of discovery, Alais excused herself briefly and went back upstairs. Her departure was followed by an abrupt return of grimness to the table, an inexorable reversion to the single dominating preoccupation of their lives. Even Rovigo was not immune: he leaned towards Alessan and asked a sharp, low-voiced question about the latest foray outside the city walls.

Alessan and Baerd, with Ducas and Arkin and Naddo, had been scouting the distrada, searching out likely battlefields, and so the best place for them to position themselves when the time came for their own last roll of dice. Devin didn't much like thinking about that. It had to do with magic, and magic always bothered him. Besides which, there had to be a battle for anything to happen, and Alberico of Barbadior was hunkered down in his meadow on the border and showing no signs of moving at all. It was enough to drive men mad.

They had begun spending more time apart from each other in the days and evenings, partly for reasons of caution, but undeniably because too much proximity in this mood was good for none of them. Baerd and Ducas were in one of the harbor taverns tonight, braving the blandishments of the flesh-merchants to keep in touch with the Tregean's men and Rovigo's sailors, and a number of the others who had made their way north in response to a long-awaited summons.

They also had a rumor to spread: about Rinaldo di Senzio, the Governor's exiled uncle, said to be somewhere in the city stirring up revolution against Casalia and the Tyrants. Devin had briefly wondered about the wisdom of that, but Alessan had explained, even before Devin could ask: Rinaldo was greatly changed in eighteen years; few people even knew he had been blinded. He had been a much-loved man: for Casalia to have released such a word would have been dangerous back then. They had gouged Rinaldo's eyes to neutralize him, and then kept it very quiet.

The old man, huddled quietly now in a corner of Solinghi's, was unlikely in the extreme to be recognized, and the only thing they could really do these days was contribute as much as they could to raising tensions in the city. If the Governor could be made more anxious, the emissaries a little more uneasy . . .

Rinaldo himself said little, though it was he himself who had first suggested starting the rumor. He seemed to be coiling or gathering himself; with a war to come the demands on a Healer would be severe, and Rinaldo was not young anymore. When he did speak it was mostly with Sandre. The two old men, enemies from rival provinces in the time before the Tyrants, now eased and distracted each other with whispered recollections from bygone years, stories of men and women who had almost all crossed to Morian long ago.

Erlein di Senzio was seldom with them the past few days. He played his music with Devin and Alessan but tended to eat and drink alone, sometimes in Solinghi's, more often elsewhere. A few of his fellow Senzians had recognized the troubadour over the course of their time here, though Erlein seemed no more effusive with them than he was with any of their own party. Devin had seen him walking one morning with a woman who looked so much like him he was sure she was his sister. He had thought of walking over to be introduced, but hadn't felt up to enduring Erlein's abrasiveness. One might have naively thought that as events hung fire here, poised on the edge of a climax, the wizard would lay down his own grudges finally. It was not so.

He wasn't worried about Erlein's absences because Alessan wasn't. For the man to betray them in any way was certain death for himself. Erlein might be enraged and bitter and sullen, but he wasn't, by any stretch, a fool.

He had gone elsewhere to dine this evening as well, though he would have to be back in Solinghi's soon; they were due to play in a few minutes and for their music Erlein was never late. The music was their only sanctuary of harmony these last few days, but Devin knew that only really applied to the three of them. What some of the others scattered about the city were doing for release he couldn't imagine. Or, yes he could. This *was* Senzio.

"Something's wrong!" Blind Rinaldo said abruptly beside him, tilting his head as if sniffing the air. Alessan stopped sketching the distrada terrain on the tablecloth and looked up quickly. So did Rovigo. Sandre had already half-risen from his chair.

Alais hurried up to the table. Even before she spoke Devin felt a finger of dread touch him.

"Catriana's gone!" she said, fighting to keep her voice low. Her eyes flicked from her father to Devin, then rested on Alessan.

"What? How?" Rovigo said sharply. "We would have had to see her when she came down, surely?"

"The back stairs outside," Alessan said. His hands, Devin, noticed, had suddenly flattened on the tabletop. The Prince stared at Alais. "What else?"

The girl's face was white. "She changed her clothes. I don't understand why. She bought a black silk gown and some jewelry in the market this afternoon. I was going to ask her about it but I . . . I didn't want to presume. She's so hard to ask questions of. But they're gone. All the things she bought."

"A *silk gown?*" Alessan said incredulously, his voice rising. "What in Morian's name . . . ?"

But Devin already knew. He knew absolutely.

Alessan hadn't been with them that morning, neither had Sandre. They had no way of understanding. A bone-deep fear dried his mouth and began hammering at his heart. He stood up, tipping over his chair, spilling his wine.

"Oh, Catriana," he said. "Catriana, *no!*" Stupidly, fatuously, as if she were in the room, and could still be stopped, still be kept among them, dissuaded from going out into the dark alone with her silk and jewels, with her unfathomable courage and her pride.

"What? Devin, tell me, what is it?" Sandre, voice like a knife. Alessan said nothing. Only turned, the gray eyes bracing for pain.

"She's gone to the castle," Devin said flatly. "She's gone to kill Anghiar of Barbadior. She thinks that will start the war."

Even as he spoke he was moving, rational thought quite gone, something deeper than that, infinitely deeper, driving him, though if she had reached the castle already there was no hope, no hope at all.

He was flying when he reached the door. Even so, Alessan was right beside him, with Rovigo only a step behind. Devin knocked someone down as they burst into the darkness. He didn't look back.

Eanna, show grace, he prayed silently, over and over as they raced toward the risen moons. *Goddess of Light, let it not be like this. Not like this.*

He said nothing though. He sped toward the castle in the dark, fear in his heart like a living thing, bringing the terrible knowledge of death.

Devin knew how fast he could run, had prided himself on his speed all his life. But moving as if possessed, scarcely touching the ground, Alessan was with him when they reached the Governor's Castle. They careened around a corner side by side and came to the garden wall and there they stopped, looking upward past the branches of a huge, spreading sejoia tree. They could hear Rovigo come up behind them, and someone else further back. They did not turn to see. They were both looking at the same thing.

There was a figure silhouetted against torchlight in one

of the highest windows. A figure they knew. Wearing a long dark gown.

Devin dropped to his knees in the moonlit lane. He thought about climbing the wall, about screaming her name aloud. The sweet scent of tainflowers surrounded him. He looked at Alessan's face, and then quickly away from what he saw there.

How did she like to play?

Mostly, she didn't, and especially not like this. She had not been the playing kind. She had liked swimming, and walks along the beach in the mornings, mostly alone. Other walks inland into the woods, picking mushrooms or mahgoti leaves for tea. She had liked music always, and the more since meeting Alessan. And yes, some six or seven years ago she had begun to have her own intermittent dreams of finding love and passion somewhere in the world. Not often though, and the man seldom had a face in those dreams.

There was a man's face with her now though, and this was not a dream. Nor was it play. It was death. Entrances and endings. A candle shaping fire before it went out.

She was lying on his bed, naked to his sight and touch save for the jewelry shining at wrist and throat and ears and in her hair. Light blazed from all corners of the room. It seemed that Anghiar liked to watch his women respond to what he did. *Come on top of me*, he'd murmured in her ear. *Later*, she had replied. He had laughed, a husky sound deep in his throat, and had moved to be above her, naked as well, save for his ruffled white shirt which hung open showing the delicate blond hairs on his chest.

He was a skillful lover, a deeply experienced one. It was what let her kill him, in the end.

He lowered his head to her breasts before entering her. He took one nipple in his mouth, surprisingly gently, and began to run his tongue in circles over it.

Catriana closed her eyes for a moment. She made a

sound, one she thought was right. She stretched her hands catlike above her head, moving her body sinuously under the pressure of his mouth and hands. She touched the black comb in her hair. *Red vixen.* She moaned again. His hands were on her thighs, moving upward and between, his mouth was still at her breast. She slid the comb free, pressed the catch so the blade sprang open. And then, moving without haste, as if she had all the time in the world, as if this single moment were the gathered sum of all the moments of her life, she brought her weapon down and plunged it into his throat.

Which meant that his life was over.

You could buy anything you wanted in Senzio's weapon market. Anything at all. Including a woman's ornament with a hidden blade. And poison on the blade. An ornament for the hair, in black, with shining jewels, one of which released the spring that freed the blade. An exquisite, deadly thing.

Crafted in Ygrath, of course. For that was central to her plan tonight.

Anghiar's head snapped back in shock. His mouth twisted in an involuntary snarl as his eyes bulged wide in staring agony. There was blood pumping from his throat, soaking into the sheets and the pillows, covering her.

He screamed, a terrible sound. He rolled off her, off the bed, onto the carpeted floor, clutching desperately at his throat. He screamed again. There was so much blood pulsing from him. He tried to stop it, pressing his hands to the wound. It didn't matter. It wasn't the wound that would kill him. She watched him, heard the screaming stop, followed by a wet, bubbling sound. Anghiar of Barbadior toppled slowly over on one side, mouth still open, blood leaking from his throat onto the carpet. And then his blue eyes clouded and closed.

Catriana looked down at her hands. They were steady as stone. And so was the beat of her heart. In a moment that was all the moments in her life. Entrances and endings.

There was a furious pounding on the locked door. Frantic shouting, a panic-stricken volley of curses.

She was not yet done. They could not be allowed to

take her. She knew what sorcery could do to the mind. If they had her alive they had all of her friends. They would know everything. She was under no illusions, had known there was a final step from the time she formed this plan. They were battering against the door now. It was large and heavy, would hold a moment or two. She rose up and put on the gown again. She did not want to be naked now, she couldn't have really said why. Bending over the bed she took the Ygrathen weapon, that glittering agency of death, and, careful of the treated blade, laid it beside Anghiar to be quickly found. It was necessary that it be found.

There was a sharp splintering sound from the door, more shouting, a tumult of noise in the corridor. She thought about setting fire to the room—candle to blaze, it appealed to her—but no, they had to find Anghiar's body and exactly what had killed him. She opened the casement window and stepped up on the ledge. The window was elegantly designed, easily tall enough for her to stand upright before it. She looked outward and down for a moment. The room was over the garden, far above it. More than high enough. The scent of the sejoia trees came drifting up, and the heavy sweetness of tainflowers, and there were other night flowers whose names she did not know. Both moons had risen now, Vidomni and Ilarion watching her. She looked at them for a moment but it was to Morian she prayed, for it was toward Morian she was crossing, through the last portal of all.

She thought of her mother. Of Alessan. Of his dream that had become hers, and for which she was now to die in a land not her own. Briefly she thought of her father, knowing how much this all had to do with making redress, with the way each generation seemed to put its mark upon the next, one way or another. *Let it be enough,* she prayed then, aiming the thought like an arrow of the mind toward Morian in her Halls.

The door burst inward with a grinding crash. Half a dozen men stumbled into the room. It was time. Catriana turned back from the stars and the two moons and the garden. She looked down at the men from the window-ledge. There was a singing in her heart, a crescendo of hope and pride.

"Death to Barbadior's servants!" she screamed at the top of her voice. *"Freedom for Senzio!"* she cried, and then: *"Long live King Brandin of the Palm!"*

One man, quicker than the others, reacted, springing across the room. He was not quite quick enough, not as fast as she. She had already turned, the acid of those last, necessary words eating in her brain. She saw the moons again, Eanna's stars, the wide, waiting darkness between them and beyond.

She leaped. Felt the night wind in her face and in her hair, saw the dark ground of the garden begin to hurtle up toward her, heard voices for an instant, and then none at all, only the loud, rushing wind. She was alone, falling. She had always been alone it seemed. Endings. A candle. Memories. A dream, a prayer of flames, that they might come. Then a last doorway, an unexpectedly gentle darkness seemed to open wide before her in the air. She closed her eyes just before she went through.

CHAPTER
• 19 •

A WARM NIGHT, THE FRAGRANCE OF FLOWERS. MOON-light on the trees, on the pale stones of the garden wall, on the woman standing in the high window.

Devin hears a sound to his left and quickly turns. Rovigo running up, to stop, rigid with shock as his gaze follows Alessan's upward. Behind him now comes Sandre with Alais.

"Help me!" the Duke orders harshly, dropping to the cobblestones beside Devin. His expression is wild, distraught, he has a knife in his hand.

"What? Devin gasps, uncomprehending. "What do you . . . ?"

"My fingers! Now! Cut them! I need the power!" And Sandre d'Astibar slaps the hilt of the knife hard into Devin's palm and curls his own left hand around a loose slab of stone in the street. Only his third and fourth fingers are extended. The wizard's fingers, of binding to the Palm.

"Sandre . . ." Devin begins, stammering.

"No words! *Cut me, Devin!"*

Devin does as he is told. Wincing, gritting his teeth against pain against grief, he poises the sharp slim blade and brings it down on Sandre's exposed fingers, cleaving through. He hears someone cry out. Alais, not the Duke.

But in the moment the knife cuts clean through flesh to grind against stone there is a swift and dazzling flash. Sandre's darkened face is illuminated by a corona of white light that flares like a star about his head and dies away, leaving them blinded for a moment in the after-image of its glow.

Alais is on the Duke's other side, kneeling to quickly wrap a square of cloth about his bleeding hand. Sandre lifts that hand, with an effort, silent in the face of pain. Without a word spoken, Alais helps him, her fingers supporting his arm.

From high above they hear a sharp, distant crash, the sound of men shouting. Silhouetted in the tall window, Catriana becomes suddenly taut. She screams something. They are too far away to make out the words. Too terribly far. They see her turn though, to the darkness, to the night.

"Oh, my dear, no. Not this!" Alessan's voice is a ragged whisper scoured up from his heart.

Too late. Far, far too late.

On his knees in the dusty road, Devin sees her fall.

Not wheeling or tumbling to death, but graceful as she has always been, a diver cleaving the night downward. Sandre thrusts forward his maimed wizard's hand, straining upward. He speaks rapid words Devin cannot understand. There is a sudden weirdly distorting blur in the night, a shimmer as of unnatural heat in the air. Sandre's hand is aimed straight at the falling woman. Devin's heart stops for a moment, seizing at this wild, impossible hope.

Then it starts beating again, heavy as age, as death. Whatever Sandre has tried, it is not enough. He is too far, it is too hard a spell, he is too new to this power. Any of these, all, none. Catriana falls. Unstayed, unchecked, beautiful as a moonlit fantasy of a woman who can fly. Down to a broken, crumpled ending behind the garden wall.

Alais bursts into desperate sobs. Sandre covers his eyes with his good hand, his body rocking back and forth. Devin can hardly see for the tears in his eyes. High above them, in the window where she had stood, the blurred forms of men appear, looking downward into the darkness of the garden.

"We have to move away!" Rovigo croaks, the words scarcely intelligible. "They will be searching."

It is true. Devin knows it is. And if there is any gift, anything at all they can offer back to Catriana now, to where she might be watching with Morian, it is that her dying should not have been meaningless or in vain.

Devin forces himself up from his knees, he helps Sandre to rise. Then he turns to Alessan. Who has not moved, nor taken his eyes from the high window where there are still men standing and gesturing. Devin remembers the Prince the afternoon his mother died. This is the same. This is worse. He wipes at his eyes with the backs of his hands. Turns to Rovigo: "We are too many to stay together. You and Sandre take Alais. Be very careful. They may recognize her—she was with Catriana when the Governor saw them. We'll go another way and meet you in our rooms."

Then he takes Alessan by the arm, and turns him— the Prince does not resist, follows his lead. The two of them start south, stumbling down a lane that will take them away from the castle, from the garden where she lies. He realizes he is still holding Sandre's bloodied dagger. He jams it into his belt.

He thinks about the Duke, about what Sandre has just done to himself. He remembers—his mind playing its familiar tricks with time and memory—a night in the Sandreni lodge last fall. His own first night that has led him here. When Sandre told them he could not take Tomasso out of the dungeon alive because he lacked the power. Because he'd never sacrificed his fingers in the wizard's binding.

And now he has. For Catriana, not his son, and to no good at all. There is something that hurts so much in all of this. Tomasso is nine months dead, and now she lies in a garden in Senzio, dead as any of the men of Tigana who fell in war by the Deisa years ago.

Which was the whole point for her, Devin knows. She had told him as much in Alienor's castle. He begins to cry again, unable to stop himself. A moment later he feels Alessan's hand upon his shoulder.

"Hold hard, for a little longer yet," the Prince says. His first words since her fall. "You lead me and I'll lead you, and afterwards we will mourn together, you and I." He leaves the hand on Devin's shoulder. They make their way through the dark lanes and the torchlit ones.

There is already an uproar in the streets of Senzio as

they go, a careening, breathless thread of rumor about some happening at the castle. The Governor is dead, someone shouts feverishly, sprinting wildly past them. The Barbadians have crossed the border, a woman screams, leaning out from a window above a tavern. She has red hair, Devin sees, and he looks away. There are no guards in the streets yet; they walk quickly and are not stopped by anyone.

Thinking back upon that walk, later, Devin realizes that never, not for a single moment, did he doubt that Catriana had killed the Barbadian before she jumped.

Back at Solinghi's Devin wanted nothing more than to go upstairs to his room and close his eyes and be away from people, from all the invading tumult of the world. But as they came through the door, he and the Prince, a loud, impatient cheer suddenly rose in the packed front room, running swiftly toward the back as well. They were well overdue for the first of the evening's performances, and Solinghi's was jammed with people who'd come to hear them play, regardless of the increasing noises from outside.

Devin and Alessan exchanged a glance. Music.

There was no sign of Erlein, but the two of them slowly made their way through the crowd to the raised platform in the middle space between the two rooms. Alessan took up his pipes and Devin stood beside him, waiting. The Prince blew a handful of testing, tuning notes and then, without a word spoken, began the song Devin had known he would begin.

As the first high, mournful notes of the "Lament For Adaon" spun out into the densely crowded rooms there was a brief, disconcerted murmur, and then silence fell. Into which stillness Devin followed Alessan's pipes, lifting his voice in lament. But not for the god this time, though the words were not changed. Not for Adaon falling from his high place, but for Catriana di Tigana fallen from hers.

Men said after that there had never been such a stillness, such rapt attention among the tables in Solinghi's. Even the servants waiting on patrons and the cooks in the kitchens behind the bar stopped what they had been doing and stood listening. No one moved, no one made a sound. There were pipes playing, and a solitary voice singing the oldest song of mourning in the Palm.

In a room upstairs Alais lifted her head from her tear-soaked pillow and slowly sat up. Rinaldo, tending to Sandre's maimed hand, turned his blind face toward the door and both men were still. And Baerd, who had come back here with Ducas to tidings that smashed his heart in a way he had not thought could ever happen to him again, listened to Alessan and Devin below and he felt as if his soul were leaving him, as it had on the Ember Night, to fly through darkness searching for peace and a home, for a dreamt-of world in which young women did not die in this way.

Out in the street where the sound of the pipes and that pure lamenting voice carried, people stopped in their loud pursuit of rumor or the restless chasing of night's pleasures and they stood outside the doors of Solinghi's, listening to the notes of grief, the sound of love—held fast in the spell of a music shaped by loss.

For a long time after it was remembered in Senzio, that haunting, heartbreaking, utterly unexpected offering of the "Lament" on the mild, moonlit night that marked the beginning of war.

They played only the one song and then ended. There was nothing left in either of them. Devin claimed two open bottles of wine from Solinghi behind the bar and followed Alessan upstairs. One bedroom door was partly open: Alais's, that had been Catriana's too. Baerd was waiting in the doorway; he made a small choking sound and stepped forward into the hallway and Alessan embraced him.

For a long time they stood locked together, swaying a little. When they drew back both of their faces looked blurred, unfocused. Devin followed them into the room. Alais was there and Rovigo. Sandre. Rinaldo, Ducas and Naddo. Sertino the wizard. All of them crowded into this one room; as if being in the room from which she'd gone would somehow hold her spirit nearer to them.

"Did anyone think to bring wine?" Rinaldo asked in a faint voice.

"I did," Devin said, going over to the Healer. Rinaldo looked pale and exhausted. Devin glanced at Sandre's left hand and saw that the bleeding had been stopped. He guided Rinaldo's hand to one of the wine bottles and the Healer drank, not bothering to ask for a glass. Devin gave the other bottle to Ducas, who did the same.

Sertino was gazing at Sandre's hand. "You're going to have to get in the habit of masking those fingers," he said. He held up his own left hand, and Devin saw the now-familiar illusion of completeness.

"I know," Sandre said. "I feel very weak right now though."

"Doesn't matter," Sertino replied. "Two missing fingers seen will mean death for you. However weary we are, the masking must be constant. Do it. Now."

Sandre looked up at him angrily, but the Certandan wizard's round pink face showed nothing but concern. The Duke closed his eyes briefly, grimaced, and then slowly held up his own left hand. Devin saw five fingers there, or the illusion of such. He couldn't seem to stop thinking about Tomasso, dead in a dungeon in Astibar.

Ducas was offering him the bottle. He took it and drank. Passed it over to Naddo, and went to sit beside Alais on the bed. She took his hand, which had never happened before. Her eyes were red with weeping, her skin looked bruised. Alessan had slumped on the floor by the door, leaning against the wall. His eyes were closed. In the light of the candles his face looked hollowed out, the cheekbones showing in angular relief.

Ducas cleared his throat. "We had best do some planning," he said awkwardly. "If she killed this Barbadian there will be a search through the city tonight, and Triad knows what tomorrow."

"Sandre used magic, as well," Alessan said, not opening his eyes. "If there's a Tracker in Senzio he's in danger."

"That we can deal with," Naddo said fiercely, looking from Ducas to Sertino. "We did it once already, remember. And there were more than twenty men with that Tracker."

"You aren't in the highlands of Certando now," Rovigo said mildly.

"Doesn't matter," Ducas said. "Naddo's right. If enough of us are down in the street and Sertino's with us to point out the Tracker then I'd be ashamed of my men if we couldn't contrive a brawl that killed him."

"There's a risk," Baerd said.

Ducas suddenly smiled like a wolf, cold and hard, without a trace of mirth. "I'd be grateful for a risk to take tonight," he said. Devin understood exactly what he meant.

Alessan opened his eyes and looked up from his place against the wall. "Do it, then," he said. "Devin can run any messages back here to us. We'll move Sandre out, back to the ship if we have to. If you send word that—"

He stopped, and then uncoiled in one lithe movement to his feet. Baerd had already seized his sword from where it was leaning against the wall. Devin stood up, releasing Alais's hand.

There came another rattle of sound from the stairway outside the window. Then the window opened as a hand pulled the glass outward and Erlein di Senzio stepped carefully over the ledge and into the room with Catriana in his arms.

In the stony silence he looked at them all for a moment, taking in the scene. Then he turned to Alessan. "If you are worried about magic," he said in a paper-thin voice, "then you had best be very worried. I used a great deal of power just now. If there's a Tracker in Senzio then anyone near me is extremely likely to be captured and killed." He stopped, then smiled very faintly. "But I caught her in time. She is alive."

The world spun and rocked for Devin. He heard himself cry out with an inarticulate joy. Sandre literally leaped to his feet and rushed to claim Catriana's unconscious body from Erlein's arms. He hastened to the bed and laid her down. He was crying again, Devin saw. So, unexpectedly, was Rovigo.

Devin wheeled back to where Erlein stood. In time to see Alessan cross the room in two swift strides and wrap

the exhausted wizard in a bear hug that lifted Erlein,
feebly protesting, clean off the ground. Alessan released
him and stepped back, the grey eyes shining, his face lit
by a grin he couldn't seem to control. Erlein tried, without success, to preserve his own customary cynical expression. Then Baerd came up and, without warning,
seized the wizard by the shoulders and kissed him on
both cheeks.

Again the troubadour struggled to look fierce and dis-
pleased. Again he failed. With an entirely unconvincing
attempt at his usual scowl, he said, "Careful, you. Devin
flattened me to the ground when you all ran out the
door. I'm still bruised." He threw a glare at Devin, who
smiled happily back at him.

Sertino handed Erlein a bottle. He drank, a long,
thirsty pull. He wiped at his mouth. "It wasn't hard to
guess from the way you were running that something was
seriously wrong. I started to follow, but I don't run very
fast anymore so I decided to use magic. I got to the far
end of the garden wall just as Alessan and Devin reached
the near side."

"Why?" Alessan asked sharply, wonder in his voice.
"You *never* use your magic. Why now?"

Erlein shrugged elaborately. "I'd never seen all of you
run anywhere like that before." He grimaced. "I suppose
I was carried away."

Alessan was smiling again; he couldn't seem to hold it
in for very long. Every few seconds he glanced quickly
over at the bed, as if to reassure himself of who was lying
there. "Then what?" he asked.

"Then I saw her in the window, and figured out what
was happening. So I . . . I used my magic to get over the
wall and I was waiting in the garden beneath the window." He turned to Sandre. "You sent an astonishing
spell from so far, but you didn't have a chance. You
couldn't know, never having tried, but you can't stop
someone falling that way. You have to be beneath them.
And they usually have to be unconscious. That kind of
magic works on our own bodies almost exclusively; if we
want to apply it to someone else their will has be suspended or everything gets muddled when they see what is
happening and their mind begins to fight it."

Sandre was shaking his head. "I thought it was my weakness. That I just wasn't strong enough, even with the binding."

Erlein's expression was odd. For a second he seemed about to respond to that, but instead he resumed his tale. "I used a spell to make her lose consciousness partway down, and a stronger one to catch her before she hit. Then a last to get us over the wall again. By then I was completely spent, and terrified they would trace us immediately if there was a Tracker anywhere in the castle. But they didn't, there was too much chaos. I think something else is happening back there. We hid behind the main temple of Eanna for a time, and then I carried her here."

"Carried her through the streets?" Alais asked. "No one noticed that?"

Erlein grinned at her, not unkindly. "It isn't that unusual in Senzio, my dear." Alais flushed crimson, but Devin could see that she didn't really mind. It was all right. Everything was suddenly all right.

"We had better get down into the street then," Baerd said to Ducas. "We'll have to get Arkin and some of the others. Regardless of whether there are Trackers, this changes things. When they don't find her body in the garden there's going to be an unbelievable search of the town tonight. I think there will have to be some fighting."

Ducas smiled again, more like a wolf than ever. "I hope so," was all he said.

"One moment," said Alessan quietly. "I want you all to witness something." He turned back to Erlein and hesitated, choosing his words. "We both know that you did this tonight without any coercion from me, and against your own best interests, in every way."

Erlein glanced over at the bed, two sudden spots of red forming on each of his sallow cheeks. "Don't make too much of it," he warned gruffly. "Every man has his moments of folly. I like red-headed women, that's all. That's how you trapped me in the first place, remember?"

Alessan shook his head. "That may be true, but it is not all, Erlein di Senzio. I bound you to this cause against your will, but I think you have just joined it freely."

Erlein swore feelingly. "Don't be a fool, Alessan! I just told you, I . . ."

"I know what you just told me. I make my own judgments though, I always have. And the truth is, I have been made to realize tonight—by you and Catriana, both— that there are limits to what I wish to do or see done for any cause. Even my own."

As Alessan finished speaking, he stepped forward quickly and laid a hand on Erlein's brow. The wizard flinched, but Alessan steadied him. "I am Alessan, Prince of Tigana," he said clearly, "direct in descent from Micaela. In the name of Adaon and his gift to her children, I release you to your freedom, wizard!"

Both men suddenly staggered apart, as if a taut cord had been cut. Erlein's face was bone-white. "I tell you again," he rasped, "you are a fool!"

Alessan shook his head. "You have called me worse than that, with some cause. But now I will name you something you will probably hate: I will unmask you as a decent man, with the same longing to be free as any of us here. Erlein, you cannot hide anymore behind your moods and rancor. You cannot channel into me your own hatred of the Tyrants. If you choose to leave us, you can. I do not expect you will. Be welcome, freely, to our company."

Erlein looked cornered, assailed. His expression was so confused Devin laughed aloud; the whole situation was clear to him now, and comical, in a bizarre, twisted way. He stepped forward and gripped the wizard. "I'm glad," he said. "I'm glad you're with us."

"I'm not! I haven't *said* that!" Erlein snapped. "I haven't said or done any such thing!"

"Of course you have." It was Sandre, the evidence of exhaustion and pain still vivid in his lined, dark face. "You did it tonight. Alessan is right. He knows you better than any of us. Better, in some ways, than you know yourself, troubadour. How long have you tried to make yourself believe that nothing mattered to you but your own skin? How many people have you convinced that that was true? I'm one. Baerd and Devin. Perhaps Catriana. Not Alessan, Erlein. He just set you free to prove us all wrong."

There was a silence. They could hear shouting from the streets below now, and the sound of running footsteps. Erlein turned to Alessan and the two men gazed at each other. Devin was suddenly claimed by an image, another of his intrusions of memory: that campfire in Ferraut, Alessan playing songs of Senzio for Erlein, an enraged shadow by the river. There were so many layers here, so many charges of meaning.

He saw Erlein di Senzio raise his hand, his left hand, with a simulation of five fingers there, and offer it to Alessan. Who met it with his right so their palms touched.

"I suppose I am with you," Erlein said. "After all."

"I know," said Alessan.

"Come!" said Baerd, a second later. "We have work to do." Devin followed him, with Ducas and Sertino and Naddo, toward the back stairs beyond the window.

Just before stepping through Devin turned to look back at the bed. Erlein noticed, and followed his gaze.

"She's fine," the wizard said softly. "She'll be just fine. Do what you have to do, and come back to us."

Devin glanced up at him. They exchanged an almost shy smile. "Thank you," Devin said, meaning a number of things. Then he followed Baerd down into the tumult of the streets.

★   ★   ★

She was actually awake for a few moments before she opened her eyes. She was lying somewhere soft and unexpectedly familiar, and there were voices drifting towards and away from her, as if on a swelling of the sea, or like slow-moving fireflies in the summer nights at home. At first she couldn't quite make the voices out. She was afraid to open her eyes.

"I think she is awake now," someone was saying. "Will you all do me a great courtesy and leave me alone with her for a few moments?"

She knew *that* voice though. She heard the sound of a number of people rising and leaving the room. A door closed. That voice was Alessan's.

Which meant she could not be dead. These were not

Morian's Halls, after all, with the voices of the dead surrounding her. She opened her eyes.

He was sitting on a chair drawn close to where she lay. She was in her own room in Solinghi's inn, lying under a blanket in bed. Someone had removed the black silk gown and washed the blood from her skin. Anghiar's blood, that had fountained from his throat.

The rush of memory was dizzying.

Quietly, Alessan said, "You are alive. Erlein was waiting in the garden below you. He rendered you unconscious and then caught you with his magic as you fell and brought you back."

She let her eyes fall shut again as she struggled to deal with all of this. With the fact of life, the rise and fall of her chest as she breathed, the beat of her heart, this curiously light-headed sensation, as if she might drift away on the slightest of breezes.

But she wouldn't. She was in Solinghi's and Alessan was beside her. He had asked all the others to leave. She turned her head and looked at him again. He was extremely pale.

"We thought you had died," he said. "We saw you fall from outside the garden wall. What Erlein did, he did on his own. None of us knew. We thought you had died," he repeated after a moment.

She thought about that. Then she said: "Did I achieve anything? Is anything happening?"

He pushed a hand through his hair. "It is too soon to tell for certain. I think you did, though. There is a great deal of commotion in the streets. If you listen you can hear it."

Concentrating, she could indeed make out the sounds of shouting and running feet passing beneath the window.

Alessan seemed unnaturally subdued, struggling with something. It was very peaceful in the room though. The bed was softer than she had remembered it being. She waited, looking at him, noting the perennial unruliness of his hair where his hands were always pushing through it.

He said, carefully, "Catriana, I cannot tell you how frightened I was tonight. You must listen to me now, and try to think this through because it is something that matters very much." His expression was odd, and there was something in his voice she couldn't quite pin down.

He reached out and laid his hand over hers where it lay upon the blanket. "Catriana, I do not measure your worth by your father's. None of us ever has. You must stop doing this to yourself. There was never anything for you to redeem. You are what you are, in and of yourself."

This was difficult ground for her, the most difficult of all, and she found that her heartbeat had quickened. She watched him, blue eyes on his grey ones. His long, slender fingers were covering her own. She said:

"We arrive with a past, a history. Families matter. He was a coward and he fled."

Alessan shook his head; there was still something strained in his expression. "We have to be so careful," he murmured. "So very careful when we judge them, and what they did in those days. There are reasons why a man with a wife and an infant daughter might choose— other than fear for himself—to stay with the two of them and try to keep them alive. Oh, my dear, in all these years I have seen so many men and women who went away for their children."

She could feel her tears starting now and she fought to blink them back. She hated talking about this. It was the hard kernel of pain at the core of all she did.

"But it was *before* the Deisa," she whispered. "He left before the battles. Even the one we won."

Again he shook his head, wincing at the sight of her distress. He lifted her hand suddenly and carried it to his lips. She could not remember his ever having done that before. There was something completely strange about all of this.

"Parents and children," he said, so softly she almost missed the words. "It is so hard; we are so quick to judge." He hesitated. "I don't know if Devin told you, but my mother cursed me in the hour before she died. She called me a traitor and a coward."

She blinked, moved to sit up. Too suddenly. She was dizzy and terribly weak. Devin hadn't told her any such thing; he had said next to nothing about that day.

"How could she?" she said, anger rising in her, against

this woman she had never seen. "You? A coward? Doesn't
. . . didn't she know anything about . . ."

"She knew almost all of it," he said quietly. "She
simply disagreed as to where my duty lay. That is what I
am trying to say, Catriana: it is possible to differ on such
matters, and to reach a place as terrible as that one was
for both of us. I am learning so many things so late. In
this world, where we find ourselves, we need compassion
more than anything, I think, or we are all alone."

She managed this time to push herself up higher in the
bed. She looked at him, imagining that day, those words
of his mother. She remembered what she herself had said
to her father on her own last night at home, words that
had driven him violently out of the house into the dark.
He had still been out there somewhere, alone, when she
had gone away.

She swallowed. "Did it . . . did it end like that with
your mother? Was that how she died?"

"She never unsaid the words, but she let me take her
hand before the end. I don't think I'll ever know if that
meant . . ."

"Of course it did!" she said quickly. "Of course it did,
Alessan. We all do that. We do with our hands, our eyes,
what we are afraid to say." She surprised herself; she
hadn't known she knew any such thing.

He smiled then, and looked down to where his fingers
still covered hers. She felt herself coloring. He said,
"There is a truth there. I am doing that now, Catriana.
Perhaps I am a coward, after all."

He had sent the others from the room. Her heart was
still beating very fast. She looked at his eyes and then
quickly away, afraid that after what she had just said it
would look like she was probing. She felt like a child
again, confused, certain that she was missing something
here. She had always, always hated not understanding
what was happening. But at the same time there seemed
to be this very odd, extraordinary warmth growing inside
her, and a queer sensation of light, brighter than the
candles in the room should have allowed.

Fighting to control her breathing, needing an answer,
but absurdly afraid of what it might be, she stammered,
"I . . . would you . . . explain that to me? Please?"

She watched him closely this time, watched him smile, saw what kindled in his eyes, she even read his lips as they moved.

"When I saw you fall," he murmured, his hand still holding hers, "I realized that I was falling with you, my dear. I finally understood, too late, what I had denied to myself for so long, how absolutely I had debarred myself from something important, even the acknowledging of its possibility, while Tigana was still gone. The heart . . . has its own laws though, Catriana, and the truth is . . . the truth is that you are the law of mine. I knew it when I saw you in that window. In the moment before you leaped I knew that I loved you. Bright star of Eanna, forgive me the manner of this, but you are the harbor of my soul's journeying."

Bright star of Eanna. He had always called her that, from the very beginning. Lightly, easily, a name among others, a teasing for when she bridled, a term of praise when she did something well. *The harbor of his soul.*

She seemed to be crying, silently, tears welling up to slide slowly down her cheeks.

"Oh, my dear, no," he said, with an awkward catch to his voice. "I am so sorry. I am a fool. This is far too sudden, tonight, after what you have done. Not tonight. I should never have spoken. I don't even know if you—"

He stopped just there. But only because she had covered his mouth with her fingers to make him stop. She was still crying, but there seemed to be the most amazing brightness growing inside the room, far more than candles now, more than the moons: a light like the sun beginning to rise beyond the rim of darkness.

She slipped her fingers down from his mouth and claimed the hand he had held her with. *We do with our hands what we cannot say.* She still said nothing; she couldn't speak. She was trembling. She remembered how her hands had been shaking when she walked out earlier tonight. So little time ago she had stood in a castle window and known she was about to die. Her tears fell on his hand. She lowered her head but others kept falling. She felt as though her heart were a bird, a trialla, only newly born, spreading wings, preparing to give voice to the song of its days.

He was on his knees beside the bed. She moved her free hand across and ran it through his hair, in a hopeless attempt at smoothing it. It seemed to be something she had wanted to do for a long time. How long? How long could such needs be present and yet never known, never acknowledged or allowed?

"When I was young," she said finally, her voice breaking, but needing to speak, "I used to dream of this. Alessan, have I died and come back? Am I dreaming now?"

He smiled slowly, the deeply reassuring smile that she knew, that they all knew, as if her words had granted him release from his own fear, freed him to be himself again. To offer the look that had always meant that he was with them and so everything would be made all right.

But then, unexpectedly, he moved forward and lowered his head to rest it against the thin blanket covering her, as if seeking his own shelter, one that was hers to give to him. She understood; it seemed—oh, what goddess could have foretold this?—that she *did* have something to offer him. Something more than her death after all. She lifted her hands and closed them around his head, holding him to her, and it seemed to Catriana in that moment as if that new-born trialla in her soul began to sing. Of trials endured and trials to come, of doubt and dark and all the deep uncertainties that defined the outer boundaries of mortal life, but with love now present at the base of it all, like light, like the first stone of a rising tower.

There *had* been a Barbadian Tracker in Senzio, Devin learned later that night, and he *was* killed, but not by them. Nor did they have to deal with the kind of search party they'd feared. It was nearly dawn by the time they pieced the story together.

It seemed that the Barbadians had gone wild.

Finding the poisoned Ygrathen knife on the floor by Anghiar's body, hearing what the woman cried before she leaped, they had leaped themselves—to all the murderously obvious conclusions.

There were twenty of them in Senzio, an honor guard for Anghiar. They armed themselves, assembled, and made their way across to the western wing of the Governor's Castle. They killed the six Ygrathens on guard there, broke down a door, and burst in upon Cullion of Ygrath, Brandin's representative, as he struggled into his clothing. Then they took their time about killing him. The sound of his screams echoed through the castle.

Then they went back downstairs and through the courtyard to the front gates and hacked to death the four Senzian guards who had let the woman in without a proper search. It was during this that the captain of the Castle Guard came into the courtyard with a company of Senzians. He ordered them to lay down their arms.

The Barbadians were, according to most reports later, about to do so, having achieved their immediate purposes, when two of the Senzians, enraged at the butchery of their friends, fired arrows at them. Two men fell, one instantly dead, one mortally wounded. The dead one was Alberico's Tracker. There ensued a bloody, to-the-death melee in the torchlit courtyard of the castle, soon slippery with blood. The Barbadians were slaughtered to the last man, taking some thirty or forty Senzians with them.

No one knew which man fired the arrow that killed Casalia the Governor as he came hastily down the stairs screaming hoarsely at them all to stop.

In the chaos that followed that death no one gave a thought to going down to the garden for the body of the woman who had started it all. There was an increasingly wild panic in the city as the news spread through the night. A huge, terrified crowd gathered outside the castle. Shortly after midnight two horses were seen racing away from the city walls, heading south for the Ferraut border. Not long after that the five remaining members of Brandin's party in Senzio rode away as well, in a tight cluster under the risen moons. They went north of course, toward Farsaro where the fleet was anchored.

Catriana was asleep in the other bed, her face smooth and untroubled, almost childlike in its peace. Alais could not find rest though. There was too much noise and tumult in the streets and she knew her father was down there, among whatever was happening.

Even after Rovigo came back in and stopped at their door to look in on the two of them and report that there seemed to be no immediate danger, Alais was still unable to sleep. Too much had happened tonight, but none of it to her, and so she was not weary as Catriana was, only excited and unsettled in oddly discontinuous ways. She couldn't even have said all the things that were working upon her. Eventually she put on the robe she'd bought two days before in the market and went to sit on the ledge of the open window.

It was very late by then, both moons were west, down over the sea. She couldn't see the harbor—Solinghi's was too far inland—but she knew it was there, with the *Sea Maid* bobbing at anchor in the night breeze. There were people in the streets even now, she could see shadowy forms pass in the lane below, and she heard occasional shouts from the direction of the tavern quarter, but nothing more now than the ordinary noises of a city without a curfew, prone to be awake and loud at night.

She wondered how near to dawn it was, how long she would have to stay awake if she wanted to see the sunrise. She thought she might wait for it. This was not a night for sleep; or not for her, Alais amended, glancing back at Catriana. She remembered the other time the two of them had shared a room. Her own room at home.

She was a long way from home. She wondered what her mother had thought, receiving Rovigo's letter of carefully phrased almost-explanation sent by courier across Astibar from the port of Ardin town as they sailed north to Senzio. She wondered, but in another way she knew: the trust shared between her parents was one of the sustaining, defining elements of her own world.

She looked up at the sky. The night was still dark, the stars overhead even more bright now that the moons were setting; it probably lacked several hours yet till dawn. She heard a woman's laughter below and realized with an odd sensation that that was the one sound she'd not heard earlier that night amid the tumult in the streets. In a curious, quite unexpected way, the woman's breathless sound, and then a man's murmur following close upon it served to reassure her: in the midst of all else, whatever might come, certain things would still continue as they always had.

There was a footstep on the wood of the stairway outside. Alais leaned backward on the window-ledge, belatedly realizing she could probably be seen from below.

"Who is it?" she called, though softly, so as not to disturb Catriana.

"Only me," Devin said, coming up to stand on the landing outside the room. She looked at him. His clothing was muddy, as if he'd tumbled or rolled somewhere, but his voice was calm. It was too dark to properly see his eyes. "Why are you awake?" he asked.

She gestured, not sure what to say. "Too many things at once, I suppose. I'm not used to this."

She saw his teeth as he smiled. "None of us are," he said. "Believe me. But I don't think anything else will happen tonight. We are all going to bed."

"My father came in a while ago. He said it seemed to have quieted down."

Devin nodded. "For now. The Governor was slain in the castle. Catriana did kill the Barbadian. There was chaos up there, and somebody seems to have shot the Tracker. I think that was what saved us."

Alais swallowed. "My father didn't tell me about that."

"He probably didn't want to disturb your night. I'll be sorry now if I have." He glanced past her toward the other bed. "How is she?"

"She's all right, really. Asleep." She registered the quick concern in his voice. But Catriana had earned that concern, that caring, tonight and before tonight, in ways Alais could scarcely even encompass within her mind.

"And how are you?" Devin asked, in a different tone, turning back to her. And there was something in that altered, deeper voice that made it difficult for her to breathe.

"I'm fine too, honestly."

"I know you are," he said. "Actually, you are a great deal more than that, Alais." He hesitated for a moment, seeming suddenly awkward. She didn't understand that, until he leaned slowly forward to kiss her full upon the lips. For the second time, if you counted the one in the crowded room downstairs, but this was really quite amazingly unlike the first. For one thing, he didn't hurry, and for another, they were alone and it was very dark. She felt one of his hands come up, brushing along the front of her robe before coming to rest in her hair.

He drew back unsteadily. Alais opened her eyes. He looked blurred and softened, where he stood on the landing. Footsteps went past in the lane below, slowly now, not running as before. The two of them were silent, looking at each other. Devin cleared his throat. He said, "It is . . . there are still two or three hours to morning. You should try to sleep, Alais. There will be a . . . a great deal happening in the days to come."

She smiled. He hesitated another moment, then turned to walk along the outer landing toward the room he shared with Alessan and Erlein.

She remained sitting where she was for some time longer, looking up at the brightness of the stars, letting her racing heart gradually slow. She replayed in her mind the ragged, very young uncertainty and wonder in his voice in those last words. Alais smiled again to herself in the darkness. To someone schooled by a life of observation, that voice had revealed a great deal. And it had been simply touching her that had done this to him. Which was, if one lingered to think about it and relive the moment of that kiss, a most astonishing thing.

She was still smiling when she left the window-ledge and returned to her bed and she did fall asleep then, after all, for the last few greatly altered hours of that long night.

All through the next day everyone waited. A pall of doom like smoke hung over Senzio. The city treasurer attempted to assert control in the castle, but the leader of the Guard was disinclined to take orders from him. Their shouted confrontations went on all day. By the time someone thought to go down for the girl her body had already been taken away; no one knew where or by whose orders.

The work of the city ground to a halt. Men and women roamed the streets, feeding on rumor, choking on fear. On almost every corner a different story was heard. It was said that Rinaldo, the last Duke's brother, had come back to the city to take command in the castle; by the middle of the day everyone had heard some version of the tale, but no one had seen the man.

A restless, nervous darkness fell. The streets remained crowded all night long. It seemed that no one in Senzio could sleep. The night was bright and very beautiful, both moons riding through a clear sky. Outside Solinghi's inn a crowd gathered—there was no room at all inside—to hear the three musicians play and sing of freedom, and of the glory of Senzio's past. Songs not sung since Casalia had relinquished his claim to his father's Ducal Throne and allowed himself to be called Governor instead with emissaries from the Tyrants to advise him. Casalia was dead. Both emissaries were dead. Music drifted out from Solinghi's into the scented summer night, spilling along the lanes, rising toward the stars.

Just after dawn, word came. Alberico of Barbadior had crossed the border the afternoon before and was advancing north with his three armies, burning villages and fields as he went. Before noon they heard from the north as well: Brandin's fleet had lifted anchor in Farsaro Bay and was sailing south with a favorable wind.

War had come.

All through Senzio town people left their homes, left the taverns and the streets and began thronging, belatedly, to the temples of the Triad.

In the almost deserted front room of Solinghi's that afternoon one man continued to play the Tregean pipes, faster and faster and higher and higher, in a wild, almost forgotten tune.

CHAPTER
• 20 •

T HE SEA WAS AT THEIR BACK, AT THE END OF A LONG
goatherds' track that wound down the slope to the
sands just south of where they'd beached the ships
and come ashore. About two miles north of them the walls
of Senzio rose up, and from this height Dianora could see
the gleaming of the temple domes and the ramparts of
the castle. The sun, rising over the pine forests to the
east, was bronze in a close, deep blue sky. It was warm
already this early in the day; it would be very hot by
mid-morning.

By which time the fighting would have begun.

Brandin was conferring with d'Eymon and Rhamanus
and his captains, three of them newly appointed from the
provinces. From Corte and Asoli and Chiara itself. Not
from Lower Corte, of course, though there were a number of men from her province in the army below them in
the valley. She had wondered briefly, lying awake one
night in the flagship off Farsaro, if Baerd was one of
them. She knew he wouldn't be though. Just as Brandin
could not change in this, neither could her brother. It
went on. However much might alter, this single thing
would go on until the last generation that knew Tigana
died.

And she? Since the Dive, since rising from the sea, she
had been trying hard not to think at all. Simply to move
with the events she had set in motion. To accept the
shining fact of Brandin's love for her and the terrible
uncertainties of this war. She no longer saw the riselka's
path in her mind's eye. She had some sense of what that
meant, but she made an effort not to dwell upon it during

the day. Nights were different; dreams were always different. She was owner and captive, both, of a bitterly divided heart.

With her two guards just behind her she moved forward on the crown of the hill and looked out over the wide east–west running valley. The dense green pine woods were beyond, with olive trees growing on steeper ridges to the south and a plateau north leading to Senzio town.

Down below the two armies were just stirring, men emerging from their tents and sleeping-rolls, horses being saddled and harnessed, swords cleaned, bowstrings fitted and readied. Metal glinted in the young sun all along the valley. The sound of voices carried easily up to her in the clear bright air. There was just enough breeze to take the banners and lift them to be seen. Their own device was new: a golden image of the Palm itself, picked out against a background of deep blue for the sea. The meaning of Brandin's chosen image was as clear as he could make it—they were fighting in the name of the Western Palm, but the truer claim was to everything. To a united peninsula with Barbadior driven away. It was a good symbol, Dianora knew. It was also the proper, the necessary step for this peninsula. But it was being taken by the man who had been King of Ygrath.

There were even Senzians in Brandin's army, besides the men of the four western provinces. Several hundred had joined them from the city in the two days since they'd landed in the southern part of the bay. With the Governor dead and a squabble for meaningless power going on in the castle, the official policy of Senzian neutrality was in tatters. Helped, no one doubted, by Alberico's decision to torch the lands through which he had come, in retaliation for Barbadian deaths in the city. Had the Barbadians moved faster Rhamanus might have had trouble landing the fleet in the face of opposition, but the winds had been with them, and they reached the city a full day before Alberico. Which let Brandin choose the obvious hill from which to overlook the valley, and to align his men where he wanted them. It was an advantage, they all knew it.

It had seemed less of one the next morning when the

three armies of Barbadior arrived emerging out of the smoke of burning to the south. They had two banners, not one: the Empire's red mountain and golden tiara against their white background, and Alberico's own crimson boar on a yellow field. The red in both banners seemed to dot the plain like stains of blood, while horsemen and foot-soldiers arrayed themselves in crisp, precisely drilled ranks along the eastern side of the valley. The soldiers of the Barbadian Empire had conquered most of the known world to the east.

Dianora had stood on the hill watching them come. It seemed to take forever. She went away into their tent and then came back, several times. The sun began to set. It was over behind her in the west above the sea before Alberico's mercenaries had all marched or ridden into the valley.

"Three to one, perhaps a little better than that," Brandin had said, coming up beside her. His short greying hair was uncovered, ruffled by the late afternoon breeze.

"Are they too many?" she had asked, quietly so no one else would hear.

He looked at her quickly, then took her hand. He often did that now, as if unable to bear not having touched her for any length of time. Their love-making since the Dive had taken on an urgency that would leave them both shattered and drained afterwards, scarcely able to form thoughts of any kind. Which was at the center of things for her, Dianora knew: she *wanted* to numb her mind, to still the voices and the memories. Obliterate the image of that clear, straight path disappearing in the darkness of the sea.

On the hill the day the Barbadians came Brandin laced his fingers through her own and said, "They may be too many. It is hard to judge. I am stronger in my power than Alberico in his. I think that on this hill I am worth the difference in the armies."

Quietly spoken, a careful statement of relevant facts. No arrogance, only the steady, always enduring pride. And why should she doubt his sorcery? She knew exactly what it had done in war some twenty years ago.

That conversation had been yesterday. Afterwards she had turned to watch the sun go down into the sea. The night had been bright and glorious, with Vidomni waxing and Ilarion at her full, blue and mysterious, a moon of fantasy, of magic. She had wondered if they would have time to be alone that night, but in fact Brandin had been down on the plain among the tents of his army through most of the dark hours, and speaking with his captains after that. D'Eymon, she knew was going to remain up here with him tomorrow, and Rhamanus—more a sailor than a military commander—would be on the hill as well to lead the men of the King's Guard in defense, if matters came to that. If matters came to that they were probably dead, she knew.

Both moons had set by the time Brandin came back to their tent on that hill above the sea. Awake in bed, waiting, she could see his weariness. He had maps with him, sketches of terrain to study one last time, but she made him put them down.

He came over to the bed still fully clothed and lay down. After a moment he rested his head in her lap. Neither of them spoke for a long time. Then Brandin shifted a little and looked up at her.

"I hate that man down there," he said quietly. "I hate everything he stands for. There is no passion in him, no love, no pride. Only ambition. Nothing matters but that. Nothing in the world can move him to pity or grief but his own fate. Everything is a tool, an instrument. He wants the Emperor's Tiara, everyone knows it, but he doesn't want it *for* anything. He only wants. I doubt anything in his life has ever moved him to *feel* anything for anyone else . . . love, loss, anything."

He subsided. He was repeating himself in his exhaustion. She pressed her fingers against his temples, looking down at his face as he turned again and his eyes closed and his brow gradually grew smooth under her touch. Eventually his breathing steadied and she knew he was asleep. She stayed awake, her hands moving like a blind woman's over him, knowing from the light outside that the moons were down, knowing the morning was war and that she loved this man more than the world.

She must have slept, because the sky was grey with the

coming of dawn when she opened her eyes again, and Brandin was gone. There was a red anemone on the pillow beside her. She looked at it without moving for a moment, then picked it up and crushed it to her face inhaling the fragile scent. She wondered if he knew the legend of that flower here. Almost certainly not, she thought.

She rose, and a few moments later Scelto came in with a mug of khav in his hand. He was wearing the stiff leather vest of a messenger; lightweight inadequate armor against arrows. He had volunteered to be one of the score of such men running orders and messages up and down the hill. He had come to her first though, as he had every morning in the saishan for a dozen years. Dianora was afraid that thinking about that would make her cry: a brutal omen on such a day. She managed a smile and told him to go back to the King, who needed him more this morning.

After he left, she slowly drank her khav, listening to the growing noises outside. Then she washed and dressed herself and went out of the tent into the rising sun.

Two men of the King's Guard were waiting for her. They went wherever she did, a discreet step or two behind, but not more than that. She would be guarded today, she knew. She looked for Brandin and saw Rhun first. They were both near the front of the flattened ridge, both bare-headed, without armor, though with identical swords belted at their sides. Brandin had chosen to dress today in the simple brown of an ordinary soldier.

She was not fooled. None of them were, or could be.

Not long after that they saw him step alone toward the edge of his hill and raise one hand above his head for all the men in both armies to see. Without a word spoken, any warning at all, a dazzling blood-crimson flare of light sprang from that upthrust hand like a flame into the deep blue of the sky. From below they heard a roar of sound, as, crying their King's name aloud, Brandin's outnumbered army moved forward across the valley to meet the soldiers of Alberico in a battle that had been coming for almost twenty years.

★　★　★

"Not yet," Alessan said steadily, for the fifth time, at least. "We have waited years, we must not be too soon now."

Devin had a sense that the Prince was cautioning himself more than anyone else. The truth was that until Alessan gave the word there was nothing for them to do but watch as men from Barbadior and Ygrath and the provinces of the Palm killed each other under the blazing Senzian sun.

It was noon or a little past it, by the sun. It was brutally hot. Devin tried to grasp how the men below must feel, hacking and battering each other, slipping on blood, treading the fallen in the broiling caldron of battle. They were too high and far away to recognize anyone, but not so distant that they couldn't see men die or hear their screams.

Their vantage point had been chosen by Alessan a week before with a sure prediction of where the two sorcerers would base themselves. And both had done exactly as he judged they would. From this sloping ridge less than half a mile south of the higher, broader rise of land where Brandin was, Devin gazed down over the valley and saw two armies knotted together in a pitiless sending of souls to Morian.

"The Ygrathen chose his field well," Sandre had said with an almost detached admiration earlier that morning as the cries of horses and men began. "The plain is wide enough to allow him room to maneuver, but not so broad as to let the Barbadians flank around him without serious trouble in the hills. They would have to climb out of the valley, and then along the exposed slopes and back down again."

"And if you look, you will see," Ducas di Tregea had added, "that Brandin has most of his archers on his own right flank, toward the south, in case they do try that. They could pick the Barbadians off like deer among the olives on the slopes if they attempt to go around."

One contingent of Barbadians had, in fact, tried just that an hour ago. They had been slaughtered and driven back by a rain of arrows from the archers of the Western

Palm. Devin had felt a quick surge of excitement, but then that congealed within him into turmoil and confusion. The Barbadians were tyranny, yes, and all that it meant, yet how could he possibly exult in any kind of triumph for Brandin of Ygrath?

But should he then desire the death of men of the Palm at the hands of Alberico's mercenaries? He didn't know *what* to think or feel. He felt as though his soul was being stripped raw and exposed here, laid out for burning under the Senzian sky.

Catriana was standing just ahead of him, next to the Prince. Devin didn't think he'd seen them apart from each other since Erlein had brought her back from the garden. He'd spent a disoriented, difficult hour the morning after that, struggling to adjust to the shining thing that had so clearly overtaken them. Alessan had looked as he did when he made music, as if he'd found a hearthstone in the world. When Devin had glanced over at Alais it was to find her watching him with a curious, very private smile on her face; it left him even more confused than before. He had a sense that he wasn't even keeping up with himself, let alone with the changes around him. He also knew that there wasn't going to be any time to deal with such things, not with what was coming to Senzio.

In the next two days, the armies had arrived from north and south bringing with them a bone-deep awareness of destiny hanging before them all as if suspended on some balance scale of gods in the summer air.

On their ridge above the battle Devin looked back and saw Alais offering water to Rinaldo in the partial shade of a twisted olive tree that clung to the slope of their ridge. The Healer had insisted on coming with them instead of remaining hidden with Solinghi in town. *If lives are at risk then my place is there as well,* was all he'd said, and he'd carried his eagle-headed staff up here with all of them before sunrise.

Devin glanced beyond them to where Rovigo stood with Baerd. He should probably be with those two, he knew. His own responsibility here was the same as theirs: to guard this hill if either sorcerer or both should send troops after them. They had sixty men: Ducas's band, Rovigo's brave handful of mariners, and those carefully

chosen men who had made their solitary way north to
Senzio in response to the messages scattered across the
provinces. Sixty men. It would have to be enough.

"Sandre! Ducas!" Alessan said sharply, snapping Devin
out of reverie. "Look now, and tell me."

"I was about to," Sandre said with an emerging note of
excitement in his voice. "It is as we guessed: with his own
presence on the hill Brandin is not outnumbered after all.
His power is too much stronger than Alberico's. More so
than I guessed, even. If you are asking my reading right
now, I would say that the Ygrathen is on the edge of
breaking through in the center before the hour is out."

"Sooner than that," Ducas said in his deep voice.
"When such things begin they happen very fast."

Devin moved forward to see more clearly. The seeth-
ing center of the valley was as choked with men and
horses as before, many of them dead and fallen. But if he
used the banners as his frame of reference, it seemed,
even to his untutored eye, that Brandin's men were pushing their front lines forward now, though the Barbadians
were still more numerous by far.

"How?" he muttered, almost to himself.

"He weakens them with his sorcery," a voice to his
right said. He looked over at Erlein. "The same way they
conquered us years ago. I can feel Alberico trying to
defend them, but I think Sandre has it right: the Barbadian is weakening as we speak."

Baerd and Rovigo came quickly up from where they
too had been looking down.

"Alessan?" Baerd said. Only the name, no more.

The Prince turned and looked at him. "I know," he
said. "We were just thinking the same thing. I think it is
time. I think it has come." He held Baerd's gaze for
another moment; neither of them spoke. Then Alessan
looked away, past the friend of his life, to the three
wizards.

"Erlein," he said softly. "You know what must be
done."

"I do," said the Senzian. He hesitated. "Pray for the
Triad's blessing upon the three of us. Upon all of us."

"Whatever you're going to do, you had better hurry,"

Ducas said bluntly. "The Barbadian center is starting to give."

"We are in your hands," Alessan said to Erlein. He seemed about to say something more, but did not. Erlein turned to Sandre and Sertino who had moved nearer to him. All of the others stepped back a little, to leave the three of them alone.

"*Link!*" said Erlein di Senzio.

★   ★   ★

On the plain at the back of his army, but near to them and in their midst—because distance mattered in magic— Alberico of Barbadior had spent the morning wondering if the gods of the Empire had abandoned him at last. Even the dark-horned god of sorcerers and the night-riding Queen on her Mare. His thoughts, such thoughts as he could manage to coherently form under the ceaseless, mind-pounding onslaught of the Ygrathen, were black with awareness of ruin; it seemed to him as if there were ashes in his heart choking his throat.

It had seemed so simple once. All that would be needed were planning and patience and discipline, and if he had any qualities, any virtues at all, they were those. Twenty years worth of each of them here in the service of his long ambition.

But now as the merciless bronze sun reached its zenith and slipped past and began its descent toward the sea, Alberico knew with finality that he had been right at the first and wrong at the last. Winning the whole of the Palm had *never* mattered, but losing it meant losing everything. Including his life. For there was nowhere to run, or hide.

The Ygrathen was brutally, stupefyingly strong. He had *known* it, he had always known it. Had feared the man not as a coward does, but as one who has taken the measure of something and knows exactly what it is.

At dawn, after that crimson beacon had flamed from Brandin's hand on his hill in the west, Alberico had allowed himself to hope, even briefly to exult. He had only to defend his men. His armies were almost three times as strong and they were facing only a small number of the trained soldiers of Ygrath. The rest of the army of the Western Palm was a flung-together mélange of artisans and traders, fishermen and farmers and scarcely bearded boys from the provinces.

He had only to blunt the thrust of Brandin's sorcery from the hill and let his soldiers do their work. He had no need to push his own powers outward against his foe. Only to resist. Only defend.

If only he could. For as the morning wore on and gathered heat to itself like a smothering cloak, Alberico felt his mind-wall begin, by grudging, agonizing degrees, to flatten and bend under the passionate, steady, numbing insistence of Brandin's attack. Endlessly the Ygrathen's waves of fatigue and weakness flowed down from his hill upon the Barbadian army. Wave after wave after wave, tireless as the surf.

And Alberico had to block them, to absorb and screen those waves, so his soldiers could fight on, unafraid, unsapped in their courage and strength save by the sweltering heat of the sun—which was blazing down upon the enemy too.

Well before noon some of the Ygrathen's spell began to leak through. Alberico couldn't *hold* it all. It just kept coming and coming, monotonous as rain or surf, without alteration in rhythm or degree. Simple power, hugely pouring forth.

Soon—far too soon, too early in the day—the Barbadians began to feel as if they were fighting uphill, even on a level plain, as if the sun actually was fiercer above their heads than on the men they fought, as if their confidence and courage were seeping away with the sweat that poured from them, soaking through their clothing and armor.

Only the sheer weight of numbers kept them level, kept that Senzian plain in balance all morning long. His eyes closed, sitting in the great, canopied chair they had brought for him, Alberico mopped at his face and hair continuously with water-soaked cloths and he fought Brandin of Ygrath through that morning with all his power and all the courage to which he could lay claim.

But shortly after noon, cursing himself, cursing the maggot-eaten soul of Scalvaia d'Astibar who had so nearly killed him nine months ago—and who had weakened him

enough, after all, to be killing him now—cursing his
Emperor for living too long as a useless, senescent, ema-
ciated shell, Alberico of Barbadior confronted the bleak,
pitiless reality that all his gods were indeed leaving him
here under the burning sun of this far-off land. As the
messages began streaming back from the crumbling front
ranks of his army, he began preparing himself, in the way
of his people, for death.

Then the miracle happened.

At first, his mind too punishingly battered, he couldn't
even grasp what was taking place. Only that the colossal
weight of magic pouring down from the hill was suddenly, inexplicably, lightening. It was a fraction, a *half* of
what it had been only a moment before. Alberico could
sustain it. Easily! That level of magic was less than his
own, even weakened as he was now. He could even push
forward against that, instead of only defending. He could
attack! If that was all that Brandin had left, if the Ygrathen
had suddenly reached the end of his reserves . . .

Wildly mind-scanning the valley and the hills around
for a clue, Alberico suddenly came upon the third matrix
of magic, and abruptly realized—with a glory flowering
out of the morning's ashes in his heart—that the horned
god was with him yet after all, and the Night Queen in
her riding.

There were wizards of the Palm here, and they were
helping him! They hated the Ygrathen as much as he!
Somehow, for whatever incomprehensible reason, they
were on *his* side against the man who was King of Ygrath,
whatever he might pretend to call himself now.

"I am winning!" he shouted to his messengers. "Tell
the captains at the front, revive their spirits. Tell them I
am beating the Ygrathen back!"

He heard sudden glad cries around him. Opened his
eyes to see messengers sprinting forward across the valley. He reached out toward those wizards—four or five,
he judged, by their strength, perhaps six of them—seeking
to merge with their minds and their power.

But in that he was balked. He knew exactly where they
were. He could even *see* where they were—a ridge of
land just south of the Ygrathen's hill—but they would
not let him join with them or know who they were. They

must still be afraid of what he did to wizards when he found them.

What he did to wizards? He would *glory* in them! He would give them land and wealth and power, honor here and in Barbadior. Riches beyond their starved, pinched dreams. They would see!

No matter that they did not open to him! It truly mattered not. So long as they stayed, and lent their powers to his defense there was no need to merge. Together they were a match for Brandin. And all they had to do was be a match: Alberico knew he still had more than twice the army in the field that the other had.

But even as hope was pouring back into his soul with these thoughts, he felt the weight beginning to return. Unbelievably, the Ygrathen's power growing again. Frantically he checked: the wizards on their ridge were still with him. Yet Brandin was still pushing forward. He was so strong! So accursedly, unimaginably *strong*. Even against all of them he was exerting his might, tapping deeper into his wellspring of sorcery. How deep could he go? How much more did he have?

Alberico realized, the knowledge like ice amid the inferno of war, the savage heat of the day, that he had no idea. None at all. Which left him only the one course. The only one he'd ever had from the moment the battle had begun.

He closed his eyes again, the better to focus and concentrate, and he set himself, with all the power in him, to resist again. To resist, to hold, to keep the wall intact.

★   ★   ★

"By the seven sisters of the god!" Rhamanus swore passionately. "They are regaining the ground they lost!"

"Something has happened," Brandin rasped in the same moment. They had erected a canopy above him for shade and had brought a chair for him to sit upon. He was standing though—one hand on the back of the chair for support at times—the better to look down on the course of battle below.

Dianora was standing close to him, in case he needed her, for water or comfort, for anything at all that she

could give, but she was trying not to look down. She
didn't want to see any more men die. About the screaming in the valley she could do nothing though, and every
cry below seemed to fly upward and sheath itself in her
like a knife made of sound and human agony.

Had it been like this by the Deisa when her father
died? Had he screamed so with his own mortal wound,
seeing his life's blood leave him, not to be held back,
staining the river red? Had he died in this kind of pain
under the vengeful blades of Brandin's men?

It was her own fault, this sickness rising. She should
not be here. She should have known what images war
would unleash in her. She felt physically ill: from the
heat, the sounds, she could actually smell the carnage
below.

"Something has happened," Brandin said again, and
with his voice a clarity came back into the maelstrom of
the world. She was here and he was the reason why, and
if the others could not, Dianora who knew him so well,
could hear a new note in his voice, a marginal clue to the
strain he was enduring. She walked quickly away and
then back, a beaker of water in her hand and a cloth to
wet his brow.

He took the water, seeming almost oblivious to her
presence, to the touch of the cloth. He closed his eyes,
and then slowly turned his head from side to side, as if
blindly seeking something.

Then he opened his eyes again and pointed. "Over
there, Rhamanus." Dianora followed his gaze. On a ridge
of land south of them, across the uneven, tummocky
ground, a number of figures could be discerned.

"There are wizards there," Brandin said flatly. "Rhamanus, you'll have to take the Guard after them. They
are working with Alberico against me. I don't know why.
One of them looks like a Khardhu, but he isn't; I would
recognize Khardhun magic. There is something extremely
odd about this."

His eyes were a dark, clouded grey.

"Can you match them, my lord?" It was d'Eymon, his
tone deliberately neutral, masking any hint of concern.

"I am about to try," Brandin said. "But I am getting
near to the limit of the power I can safely tap. And I

can't turn my magic on them alone, they are working
with Alberico. Rhamanus, you'll have to get those wizards for me yourself. Take everyone here."

Rhamanus's ruddy face was grim. "I will stop them or
die, my lord. I swear it."

Dianora watched him step out from under the canopy
and summon the men of the King's Guard. In pairs they
fell into step behind him and started quickly down the
goat-track leading west and south. Rhun took a couple of
steps after them, and then stopped, looking confused and
uncertain.

She felt a touch and turned from the Fool as Brandin
took her hand. "Trust me, love," he murmured. "And
trust Rhamanus." After a second he added, with what
was almost a smile: "He brought you to me."

Then he let her go and turned his attention back to the
plain below. And now he did sit down in the chair.
Watching, she could literally see him gather himself to
renew his assault.

She looked over at d'Eymon, then followed the Chancellor's narrowed, speculative gaze south again, across to
the cluster of people on that slope half a mile away. They
were near enough that she could see the dark-skinned
figure Brandin said wasn't really a Khardhu. She thought
she could make out a red-haired woman as well.

She had no idea who they were. But suddenly, for the
first time, looking around at their own thinned-out numbers on the hill, she felt afraid.

"Here they come," Baerd said, looking north, a hand up
to screen his eyes.

They had been waiting for this, and watching for it
from the moment the wizards linked, but anticipation
was not reality and, at the sight of the picked men of
Brandin's Guard moving swiftly down their hill and beginning to cross the ground between, Devin's heart began
thumping hard. There had been war all morning in the
valley below; now it was coming to them.

"How many?" Rovigo asked, and Devin was grateful

to hear the tension in the merchant's voice: it meant he was not alone in what he was feeling now.

"Forty-nine, if he sent them all, and Alessan thought he would," Baerd replied, not turning around. "That is always the number of the King's Guard in Ygrath. It is sacred for them."

Rovigo said nothing. Devin glanced to his right and saw the three wizards standing closely together. Erlein and Sertino had their eyes closed, but Sandre was staring fixedly downwards to where Alberico of Barbadior was at the back of his army. Alessan had been with the wizards but now he came quickly over to join the thirty or so men spread out behind Baerd on the ridge.

"Ducas?" he asked quietly.

"I can't see any of them," Baerd said, with a quick glance at the Prince. The last of the Ygrathen Guard had now descended their hill. The vanguard were already moving rapidly over the uneven ground between. "I still don't believe it."

"Let me take my men to meet them below," Ducas had urged Alessan, the moment the wizards had linked. *"We know he will be coming after us."*

"Of course we do," Alessan had said, "but we are poorly armed and trained. We need the advantage of height up here."

"Speak for yourself," Ducas di Tregea had growled. "There isn't any cover down there. Where could you hide?"

"You are telling *me* whether there is cover?" Ducas replied, feigning anger. His mouth widened in his wolfish grin. "Alessan, go teach your fingers to know your fingernails! I was fighting running battles and ambushes in this kind of terrain while you were still numbering oak trees or some such thing in Quileia. Leave this to me."

Alessan had not laughed. After a moment though, he nodded his head. Not waiting for more, red-bearded Ducas and his twenty-five men had immediately melted away down the slopes of their ridge. By the time the Ygrathens sent the Guard, the outlaws were down below, hidden among the gorse and heather, the high grass and the scattered olive and fig trees in the ground between the hills.

Squinting, Devin thought he could see one of them, but he wasn't sure.

"*In Morian's name!*" Erlein di Senzio suddenly cried from the east end of the ridge. "He is pushing us back again!"

"Then *hold!*" Sandre snarled. "Fight him! Go deeper!"

"I haven't got any deeper to go!" Sertino gasped.

Baerd leaped from his crouch staring at the three of them. He hesitated, visibly wracked by doubt for a moment, then he strode swiftly over to the wizards.

"Sandre, Erlein? Can you hear me?"

"Yes, of course." Sandre's darkened face was streaming with perspiration. He was still staring east, but his gaze was unfocused now, inward.

"Then do it! Do what we talked about. If he's pushing all of you back we have to try or there is no point to any of this!"

"Baerd, they could be . . ." Erlein's words came out one by one as if forced from his lips.

"No, he's right!" Sertino gasped, cutting in. "Have to try. The man's . . . too strong. I'll follow you two . . . know where to reach. Do it!"

"Stay with me then," Erlein said, in a voice leeched of all strength. "Stay with me, both of you."

There were sudden shouts and then screaming below them. Not from the battlefield. From the ground to the north. All of them but the wizards wheeled around to see.

Ducas had sprung his trap. Firing from ambush his outlaws unleashed a score of arrows at the Ygrathens, and then swiftly let fly as many more. Half a dozen, eight, ten of their attackers fell, but the King's Guard of Ygrath were armored against arrows even in the blazing heat, and most of them pushed on, reacting with frightening agility despite the weight they carried, moving toward Ducas's spread-out men.

Devin saw three of the downed men get up again. One pulled an arrow from his own arm and stumbled resolutely on, pressing toward their ridge.

"Some of them will have bows. We have to cover the wizards,' Alessan snapped. "Any man with any kind of shield, over here!"

Half a dozen of the men remaining on the hill rushed over. Five had makeshift shields of wood or leather; the sixth, a man of some fifty years, limped behind them on a twisted foot, carrying nothing but an ancient, battered sword.

"My lord Prince," he said, "my body is shield enough for them. Your father would not let me go north to the Deisa. Do not deny me now. Not again. I can stand between them and any arrows, in Tigana's name."

Devin saw the suddenly blank, frightened look on many of the faces near them: a name had been spoken that they could not hear.

"Ricaso," Alessan began, looking around. "Ricaso, you need not . . . You shouldn't have even come here. There were other ways to . . ." The Prince stopped. For a moment it looked as if he would refuse the man as his father had, but he said nothing more, only nodded his head once and strode away. The lame man and the other five immediately placed themselves in a protective circle around the wizards.

"Spread out!" Alessan ordered the others. "Cover the north and the west sides of the ridge. Catriana, Alais— keep your eyes on the south in case some of them make it around behind us. Shout if you see anything move!"

Sword in hand, Devin raced for the northwest edge of their hill. There were men fanning out all around him. He looked over as he ran, and caught his breath in dismay. Ducas's men were in pitched battle on the un- even ground with the Ygrathens, and though they were holding their own, taking a man, it seemed, for every one of them that fell, that meant that they were falling. The Ygrathens were quick and superbly trained and fero- ciously determined. Devin saw their leader, a big man no longer young, hurl himself against one of the outlaws and hammer the man flat to the ground with a blow of his shield.

"Naddo! Look out!"

A scream, not a shout. Baerd's voice. Wheeling, Devin saw why. Halfway to the other hill, Naddo had just beaten back an Ygrathen, and was continuing a fighting withdrawal toward a clump of bushes where Arkin and two others were. What he didn't see was the man who had flanked wide to the east and was now rushing toward him from behind.

What the running Ygrathen didn't see was the arrow that hit him, fired from the summit of the ridge by Baerd di Tigana with all the strength of his arm and the skill of a lifelong discipline. Far away, unbelievably far, the Ygrathen grunted and fell, an arrow in his thigh. Naddo whirled at the sound, saw the man, and dispatched him with a quick sword.

He looked up at the ridge, saw Baerd, and quickly waved his thanks. He was still waving, hand aloft in salute to the friend he had left as a boy, when an Ygrathen arrow took him in the chest.

"No!" Devin cried out, a fist of grief clenching about his throat. He looked toward Baerd, whose eyes had gone wide with shock. Just as Devin took a step towards him he heard a quick scrabbling sound and a grunt, and behind him Alais screamed, "*Look out!*"

He turned back just in time to see the first of half a dozen Ygrathens surging up the slope. He had no idea how they'd got here so fast. He howled a second warning for the others and rushed forward to engage the first man before he gained the summit of the ridge.

He didn't make it. The Ygrathen was up and balanced, with a shield in his left hand. Charging at him, trying to drive the man backward down the slope, Devin swung his sword as hard as he could. It clanged on the metal shield sending shock waves all along his arm. The Ygrathen thrust straight ahead with his own blade. Devin saw it coming and twisted desperately to one side. He felt a sudden tearing pain as the sword ripped him above the waist.

He let himself drop, ignoring the wound, and as he fell forward he chopped viciously for the unprotected back of the Ygrathen's knee. He felt his sword bite deep into flesh. The man cried out and pitched helplessly forward, trying, even as he tumbled, to bring his own blade down on Devin again. Devin rolled frantically away, dizzy with pain. He clawed to his feet, clutching his ripped side.

In time to see the prone Ygrathen killed by Alais bren Rovigo with a clean swordthrust in the back of his neck.

It seemed to Devin that he knew a moment of almost

hallucinatory stillness then in the midst of carnage. He looked at Alais, at her clear, mild, blue eyes. He tried to speak. His throat was dry. Their gazes locked for a second. It was hard for Devin to absorb, to *understand* this image of her with a reddened sword in her hand.

He looked past her, and instantly the stillness was gone, shattered. Fifteen, perhaps twenty of the Ygrathens were up on the summit. More were coming. And some of them did have bows. He saw an arrow fly, to be embedded in one of the shields around the wizards. There was a sound of quick footsteps ascending the slope to his left. No time to speak, even if he could have. They were here to die if they had to, it had always been possible. There was a reason why they had come. There was a dream, a prayer, a tune his father had taught him as a child. He held his left hand tightly to his wound and turned from Alais, stumbling forward, gripping his sword, to meet the next man scrambling up the ridge.

★   ★   ★

A mild day, the sun in and out of the clouds pushed swiftly along by the breeze. In the morning they had walked in the meadows north of the castle gathering flowers, armfuls of them. Irises, anemones, bluebells. The sejoia trees were just coming into flower now this far south; they left the white blossoms for later in the season.

They were back in Castle Borso drinking mahgoti tea just past midday when Elena abruptly made a small, frightened sound. She stood up rigidly straight, her hands clutching at her head. Her tea spilled unregarded, staining the Quileian carpet.

Alienor quickly laid her own cup down. "It has come?" she said. "The summons? Elena, what can I do?"

Elena shook her head. She could scarcely hear the other woman's words. There was a clearer, harder, more compelling voice in her head. Something that had never happened before, not even on the Ember Nights. But Baerd had been right, her stranger who had come to them out of darkness and changed the shape of the Ember wars.

He had returned to the village late in the day that

followed, after his friends had come down from the pass and ridden west. He had spoken to Donar and Mattio and to Carenna and Elena and said that what the Night Walkers shared had to be a kind of magic, if not the same as wizardry. Their bodies changed in the Ember Nights, they walked under a green moon through lands that were not there by the light of day, they wielded swords of growing corn that altered under their hands. They were wedded in their own fashion, he had said, to the magic of the Palm.

And Donar had agreed that this was so. So Baerd had told them, carefully, what his purpose was, and that of his friends, and he'd asked Elena to come to Castle Borso until summer's end. In case, he'd said, in case it was possible for their power to be tapped in this cause.

Would they do this? There would be danger. He had asked it diffidently, but there had been no hesitation in Elena as she looked into his eyes and answered that she would. Nor in the others when they agreed. He had come to them in their own need. They owed him at least this much, and more. And they too were living through tyranny in their own land. His cause in the daylight was their own.

Elena di Certando? Are you there? Are you in the castle?

She didn't know this mind-voice, but within its clarity she could sense a desperation; there seemed to be chaos all around him.

Yes. Yes, I am. I'm here. What . . . what must I do?

I don't believe it! A second voice joined them, deeper, as imperative. *Erlein, you have reached her!*

Is Baerd there? she asked, a little desperately herself. The sudden link was dizzying, and the sense of tumult all around; she swayed, almost fell. She reached out and put both her hands on the high back of a chair. The room in Castle Borso was beginning to fade for her. Had Alienor spoken now she would not have even heard.

He is, the first man said quickly. *He is here with us and we have terrible need of help. We are at war! Can you link to your friends? To the others? We will help you. Please! Reach for them!*

She had never tried such a thing, not by daylight nor

even under the green moon of the Ember Nights. She
had never known anything like this wizards' link, but she
felt their power resting in her, and she knew where
Mattio would be, and Donar; and Carenna would be at
home with her newest child. She closed her eyes and
reached out for the three of them, straining to focus her
mind on the forge, the mill, Carenna's house in the
village. To focus, and then to call. To summon.

Elena, what . . . ? Mattio. She had him.

Join me! she sent quickly. *The wizards are here. There
is war.*

He asked no more questions. She could feel his steadying presence in her mind as the wizards helped her open
to him. She registered his own sudden, disoriented shock
at the link to the other men. Two of them, no three,
there was a third one there as well.

Elena, has it come? Have they sent? Donar in her
mind, seizing at truth like a weapon to his hand.

I am here, love! Carenna's mind-voice, quick and bright,
exactly the same as her speech. *Elena, what must we do?*

Hold to each other and open to us! the deep presence
of the second wizard was there to answer. *We may now
have a chance. There is danger, I will not lie, but if we
hold together—for once in this peninsula—we may yet
break through! Come, join us, we must forge our minds
into a shield. I am Sandre d'Astibar and I never died.
Come to us now!*

Elena opened her mind to him, and reached out. And
in that moment she felt as though her own body was
entirely gone, as if she were no more than a conduit, like
and yet very unlike what happened on the Ember Nights.
A clammy fear of this unknown thing rose in her. Defiantly she fought it back. Her friends were with her,
and—unbelievably—the Duke of Astibar was there, and
alive, and Baerd was with him in far-off Senzio, battling
against the Tyrants.

He had come to them, to her, in their own war. She
had heard him weep and had lain with him in love on a
hill in the Ember dark after the green moon had set. She
would not fail him now. She would lead the Carlozzini to
him along the pathway of her mind and her soul.

Without warning they broke through. The link was forged. She was in a high place under a fiercely blazing sun, seeing with the eyes of the Duke of Astibar on a hill in Senzio. The vision rocked with stomach-churning dislocation. Then it steadied and Elena saw men killing each other in a valley below, armies grappling together in the heat like beasts in a convulsive embrace. She heard screaming so loud she felt the sound as pain. Then she became aware of something else.

Sorcery. North of them, that hill. Brandin of Ygrath. And in that moment Elena and the three other Night Walkers understood why they had been summoned, feeling in their own minds the punishing weight of the assault they had to resist.

Back in Castle Borso, Alienor stood by, helpless and blind in her uncertainty, understanding nothing of this at all, only knowing that it was happening, that it was upon them at last. She wanted to pray, to reach back toward words not thought or spoken in almost twenty years. She saw Elena bring her hands up to cover her face.

"Oh no," she heard the girl whisper in a voice thin as old parchment. "So strong! How can one man be so strong?"

Alienor's hands gripped each other so tightly the knuckles were white. She waited, desperately seeking a clue to what was happening to all of them, so far to the north where she could not go.

She did not, could not hear Sandre d'Astibar's reply to Elena:

He is strong yes, but with you we will be stronger! Oh, children, we can do it now! In the name of the Palm, together we can be strong enough!

What Alienor did see was how Elena's hands came down, how her white face grew calm, the wild, primitive terror leaving her staring eyes.

"Yes," she heard the other woman whisper. "Yes."

Then there was silence in that room in Castle Borso under the Braccio Pass. Outside, the cool wind of the highlands blew the high white clouds across the sun and away, and across it and away, and a single hunting hawk hovered on motionless wings in that passing of light and shadow over the face of the mountains.

★   ★   ★

In fact, the next man scrabbling up the slope of the cliff
was Ducas di Tregea. Devin had actually begun to swing
his sword before he recognized who it was.

Ducas reached the summit in two hard, churning strides
and stood beside him. He was a fearful sight. His face
was covered in blood, dripping down into his beard.
There was blood all over him, and wet on his sword. He
was smiling though, a terrible red look of battle-lust and
rage.

"You are hurt!" he said sharply to Devin.

"I wouldn't talk," Devin grunted, pressing his left hand
to his torn side. "Come on!"

Quickly they turned back east. More than fifteen of
the Ygrathens were still on their summit, pressing forward against the untrained band of men Alessan had
kept back to defend the wizards. The numbers were
almost even, but the Ygrathens were the picked and
deadly warriors of that realm.

Even so, even with this, they were not getting through.
And they would not, Devin realized with a surge of
exultation in his heart, rising high over pain and grief.

They would not, because facing them, side by side,
swinging blades together in their longed-for battle after
all the long waiting years that had run by, were Alessan,
Prince of Tigana, and Baerd bar Saevar, the only brother
of his soul, and the two of them were absolute and
deadly, and even beautiful, if killing could be so.

Devin and Ducas rushed over. But by the time they
got there five Ygrathens only were left, then three. Then
only two. One of them made as if to lay down his sword.
Before he could do so, a figure moved forward with an
awkward, deceptive swiftness from the ring guarding the
wizards. Dragging his lame foot, Ricaso came up to the
Ygrathen. Before anyone could stay him he swung his
old, half-rusted blade in a passionate, scything arc, cleaving through the links in armor to bury itself in the man's
breast.

Then he fell to his knees on the ground beside the
soldier he'd killed, weeping as though his soul was pouring out of him.

Which left one of them only. And the last was the
leader, the large, broad-chested man Devin had seen
down below. The man's hair was plastered flat to his
head, he was red-faced with heat and exhaustion, sucking
hard for breath, but his eyes glared at Alessan.

"Are you fools?" he gasped. "Fighting for the Barbadian? Instead of with a man who has joined the Palm? Do
you *want* to be slaves?"

Slowly Alessan shook his head. "It is twenty years too
late for Brandin of Ygrath to join the Palm. It was too
late the day he landed here with an invading force. You
are a brave man. I would prefer not to kill you. Will you
give us an oath in your own name and lay down your
sword in surrender?"

Beside Devin, Ducas snarled angrily. But before the
Tregean could speak, the Ygrathen said: "My name is
Rhamanus. I offer it to you in pride, for no dishonor
has ever attached to that name. You will have no oath
from me though. I swore one to the King I love before I
led his Guard here. I told him I would stop you or die. It
is an oath I will keep."

He raised his sword toward Alessan, and gestured—
though not seriously, Devin realized afterwards—to strike
at the Prince. Alessan did not even move to ward the
blow. It was Baerd whose blade came up and then swept
downward to bite with finality into the neck of the
Ygrathen, driving him to the ground.

"Oh, my King," they heard the man say then, thickly,
through the blood rising in his mouth. "Oh, Brandin, I
am so sorry."

Then he rolled over on his back and lay still, his
sightless eyes staring straight at the burning sun.

The sun had been burning hot as well, the morning he
had defied the Governor and taken a young serving-girl
for tribute down the river from Stevanien, so many years
ago.

Dianora saw a man raise his sword on that hill. She
turned her head away so she would not see Rhamanus
die. There was an ache in her, a growing void; she felt as

if all the chasms of her life were opening in the ground before her feet. He had been an enemy, the man who had seized her to be a slave. Sent to claim tribute for Brandin, he had burned villages and homes in Corte and Asoli. He had been an Ygrathen. Had sailed to the Palm in the invading fleet, had fought in the last battle by the Deisa.

He had been her friend.

One of her only friends. Brave and decent and loyal all his life to his King. Kind and direct, ill-at-ease in a subtle court . . . Dianora realized that she was weeping for him, for the good life cloven like a tree by that stranger's descending sword.

"They have failed, my lord." It was d'Eymon, his voice actually showing—or was she imagining it?—the faintest hint of emotion. Of sorrow. "All of the Guards are down, and Rhamanus. The wizards are still there."

From his chair under the canopy Brandin opened his eyes. His gaze was fixed on the valley below and he did not turn. Dianora saw that his face was chalk-white now with strain, even in the red heat of the day. She wiped quickly at her tears: he must not see her thus if he should chance to look. He might need her; whatever strength or love she had to give. He must not be distracted with concern for her. He was one man alone, fighting so many.

And more, in fact, than she even knew. For the wizards had reached the Night Walkers in Certando by now. They were linked, and they were all bending the power of their minds to Alberico's defense.

From the plain below there came a roar, even above the steady noise of battle. Cheering and wild shouts from the Barbadians. Dianora could see their white-clad messengers sprinting forward from the rear where Alberico was. She saw that the men of the Western Palm had been stopped in their advance. They were still outnumbered; terribly so. If Brandin could not help them now then all was done, all over. She looked south toward that hill where the wizards were, where Rhamanus had been cut down. She wanted to curse them all, but she could not.

They were men of the Palm. They were her own people. But her own people were dying in the valley as well, under the heavy blades of the Empire. The sun was a brand overhead. The sky a blank, pitiless dome.

She looked at d'Eymon. Neither of them spoke. They heard quick footsteps on the slope. Scelto stumbled up, fighting for breath.

"My lord," he gasped, dropping to his knees beside Brandin's chair, "we are hard-pressed . . . in the center and on the right. The left is holding . . . but barely. I am ordered . . . to ask if you want us to fall back."

And so it had come.

I hate that man, he had said to her last night, before falling asleep in utter weariness. *I hate everything he stands for.*

There was a silence on the hill. It seemed to Dianora as if she could hear her own heartbeat with some curious faculty of the ear, discerning it even above the sounds from below. The noises in the valley seemed, oddly, to have receded now. To be growing fainter every second.

Brandin stood up.

"No," he said quietly. "We do not fall back. There is nowhere to retreat, and not before the Barbadian. Not ever." He was gazing bleakly out over Scelto's kneeling form, as if he would penetrate the distance with his eyes to strike at Alberico's heart.

But there was something else in him now: something new, beyond rage, beyond the grimness of resolution and the everlasting pride. Dianora sensed it, but she could not understand. Then he turned to her and she saw in the depths of that grey gaze a bottomless well of pain opening up such as she had never seen in him. Never seen in anyone, in all her days. *Pity and grief and love,* he had said last night. Something was happening; her heart was racing wildly. She felt her hands beginning to shake.

"My love," Brandin said. Mumbled, slurred it. She saw death in his eyes, an abscess of loss that seemed to be leaving him almost blind, stripping his soul. "Oh, my love," he said again. "What have they done? See what they will make me do. Oh, see what they make me do!"

"Brandin!" she cried, terrified, not understanding at all. Beginning again to weep, frantically. Grasping only the open sore of hurt he had become. She reached out toward him, but he was blind, and already turning

away, east, toward the rim of the hill and the valley below.

★   ★   ★

"All right," said Rinaldo the Healer, and lifted his hands away. Devin opened his eyes and looked down. His wound had closed; the bleeding had stopped. The sight of it made him feel queasy; the unnatural speed of the healing, as if his senses still expected to find a fresh wound there. "You are going to have an easy scar for women to know you by in the dark," Rinaldo added drily. Ducas gave a bark of laughter.

Devin winced and carefully avoided meeting Alais's eye. She was right beside him, wrapping a roll of linen around his torso to bind the wound. He looked at Ducas instead, whose own cut above his eye had been closed by Rinaldo in the same way. Arkin, who had also survived the skirmish down below, was bandaging it. Ducas, his red beard matted and sticky with blood, looked like some fearful creature out of childhood night terrors.

"Is that too tight?" Alais asked softly.

Devin drew a testing breath and shook his head. The wound hurt, but he seemed to be all right.

"You saved my life," he murmured to her. She was behind him now, tying up the ends of his bandage. Her hands stopped for a moment and then resumed.

"No I didn't," she said in a muffled voice. "He was down. He couldn't have hurt you. All I did was kill a man." Catriana, standing near them, glanced over. "I . . . I wish I hadn't," Alais said. And began to cry.

Devin swallowed and tried to turn, to offer comfort, but Catriana was quicker than he, and had already gathered Alais in her arms. He looked at them, wondering bitterly what real comfort there could be to offer on this bare ridge in the midst of war.

"Erlein! Now! Brandin is standing!" Alessan's cry knifed through all other sounds. His heart suddenly thumping again, Devin went quickly toward the Prince and the wizards.

"It is upon us then," said Erlein, in a hard, flat voice

to the other two. "I will have to pull out now, to track
him. Wait for my signal, but *move* when I give it!"

"We will," Sertino gasped. "Triad save us all." Sweat
was pouring down the pudgy wizard's face. His hands
were shaking with strain.

"Erlein," Alessan began urgently, "He must use it all.
You know what you—"

"Hush! I know exactly what I must do. Alessan, you
have set this in motion, you brought us all here to Senzio,
every single person, the living and the dead. Now it is up
to us. Be still, unless you want to pray."

Devin looked north to Brandin's hill. He saw the King
step forward from under his canopy.

"Oh, Triad," he heard Alessan whisper then in a queerly
high voice. "Adaon, remember us. Remember your children now!" The Prince sank to his knees. "Please," he
whispered again. "Please, let me have been right!"

On his hill to the north of them Brandin of Ygrath
stretched forth one hand and then the other under the
burning sun.

★ ★ ★

Dianora saw him move forward to the very edge of the
hill, out from the canopy into the white blaze of the light.
Scelto scrambled away. Beneath them the armies of the
Western Palm were being hammered back now, center
and left and right. The cries of the Barbadians had taken
on a quality of triumphant malice that fell like blows
upon the heart.

Brandin lifted his right hand and leveled it ahead.
Then he brought up his left beside it so that the palms
were touching each other, the ten fingers pointing together. Pointing straight to where Alberico of Barbadior
was, at the rear of his army.

And Brandin of the Western Palm, who had been the
King of Ygrath when he first came to this peninsula,
cried aloud then, in a voice that seemed to flay and shred
the very air:

"Oh, my son! Stevan, forgive me what I do!"

Dianora stopped breathing. She thought she was going

to fall. She reached out a hand for support and didn't even realize it was d'Eymon who braced her.

Then Brandin spoke again, in a voice colder than she had ever heard him use, words none of them could understand. Only the sorcerer down in the valley would know, only he could grasp the enormity of what was happening.

She saw Brandin spread his legs, as if to brace himself. Then she saw what followed.

"*Now!*" Erlein di Senzio screamed. "Both of you! Get the others out! Cut free *now!*"

"They're loose!" Sertino cried. "I'm out!" He collapsed in a heap to the ground as if he might never rise again.

Something was happening on the other hill. In the middle of day, under the brilliant sun, the sky seemed to be changing, to be darkening where Brandin stood. Something—not smoke, not light, some kind of change in the very nature of the air—seemed to be pouring from his hands, boiling east and down, disorienting to the eye, blurred, unnatural, like a rushing doom.

Erlein suddenly turned his head, his eyes widening with horror.

"*Sandre, what are you doing?*" he shrieked, grabbing wildly at the Duke. "Get out, you fool! In Eanna's name, *get out!*"

"Not . . . yet," said Sandre d'Astibar, in a voice that carried its own full measure of doom.

There had been *more* of them. Four more coming to his aid. Not wizards now, a different kind of magic of the Palm, one he hadn't even known about, didn't understand. But it didn't matter. They were here and on his side, if screened from his mind, and with them, with all of them bending their power to his defense, he had even been able to reach out, and forward, to assert his own strength *against* the enemy.

Who were falling back! There was glory after all under
the sun, and hope, more than hope, a glittering vista of
triumph spreading in the valley before him, a pathway
made smooth with the blood of his foes, leading straight
from here back across the sea and home to the Tiara.

He would bless these wizards, honor them! Make them
lords of unimagined power, here in this colony or in
Barbadior. Wherever they wanted, whatever they chose.
And thinking so, Alberico had felt his own magic flow
like intoxicating wine in his veins and had sent it pouring
forth against the Ygrathens and the men of the Western
Palm, and his armies had laughed aloud in triumph and
felt their swords to be suddenly as light as summer grass.

He heard them beginning to sing, the old battle-song
of the Empire's legions, conquering in far lands centuries
ago. And they were! It was happening again. They weren't
just mercenaries; they *were* the Empire's legions, for he
was, or would be, the Empire. He could see it. It was
here, it was shining before him in the blazing day.

Then Brandin of Ygrath rose and stepped to the rim of
his hill. A distant figure alone under the sun in that high
place. And a moment later, Alberico, who was a sorcerer
himself, felt, for he could not have actually heard, the
dark, absolute words of invocation that Brandin spoke,
and his blood froze in his veins like ice in the dead of a
winter night.

"He cannot," he gasped aloud. "Not after so long! He
cannot do this!"

But the Ygrathen was. He was reaching for all, summoning everything, every last scintilla of his magic, holding nothing back. Nothing, not even the power that had
sustained the vengeance that had kept him here all these
years. He was emptying himself to shape a sorcery such
as had never been wielded before.

Desperately, still half disbelieving, Alberico reached
out for the wizards. To tell them to brace, to be ready.
Crying that there were eight of them, nine, that they
could hold against this. That all they had to do was
survive this moment and Brandin would be nothing, a
shell. Waste, for weeks, months, years! A hollow man with
no magic in him anymore.

Their minds were closed, barred against him. They

were still *there* though, and defending, braced. Oh, if the horned god and the Night Queen were with him! If they were with him yet, he might still . . .

They were not. They were not with him.

For in that instant Alberico felt the wizards of the Palm cut loose, melting away without warning, with terrifying suddenness, to leave him naked and alone. On the hill Brandin had now leveled his hands and from them came blue-grey death, an occluding, obliterating presence in the air, foaming and boiling down across the valley toward him.

And the wizards were gone! He was alone.

Or almost gone, almost alone. One man was still linked, one of them had held with him! And then that one mind opened up to Alberico like the locked door of a dungeon springing back, letting light flood in.

The light of truth. And in that moment Alberico of Barbadior screamed aloud in terror and helpless rage, for illumination came at last and he understood, too late, how he had been undone, and by whom destroyed.

In the name of my sons I curse you forever, said Sandre, Duke of Astibar, his remorseless image rising in Alberico's mind like an apparition of horror from the afterworld. But he was alive. Impossibly alive, and here in Senzio on that ridge, with eyes implacable and utterly merciless. He bared his teeth in a smile that summoned the night. *In the name of my children and of Astibar, die now, forever cursed.*

Then he cut free, he too was gone, as that blue-grey death came boiling down the valley from Brandin's hill, from his outstretched hands, with blurred, annihilating speed, and Alberico, still reeling with shock, clawing frantically upward from his chair, was struck and enveloped and consumed by that death, as a tidal wave of the raging, engorged sea will take a sapling in low-lying fields.

It swept him away with it and sundered his body, still screaming, from his soul, and he died. Died in that far Peninsula of the Palm two days before his Emperor passed to the gods in Barbadior, failing at last one morning to wake from a dreamless sleep.

Alberico's army heard his last scream, and their own cries of exultation turned to panic-stricken horror; in the

face of that magic from the hill the Barbadians felt a fear
such as men should never have had to endure sweep over
them. They could scarcely grip their swords, or flee, or
even stand upright before their foes who advanced un-
touched, unharmed, exalted, under that dread, sun-
blighting sorcery, and began to carve and hew them with
hard and deadly wrath.

Everything, thought Brandin of Ygrath, of the Western
Palm, weeping helplessly on his hill as he looked down
over the valley. He had been driven to this and had
answered, had summoned all he had ever had to this final
purpose, and it was enough. It was sufficient and nothing
less would have been. There had been too much magic
opposed to him, and death had been waiting for his
people here.

He knew what he had been made to do, knew the price
of holding nothing back. He had paid that price and was
paying it now, would go on doing so with every breath he
drew until he died. He had screamed Stevan's name,
aloud and in the echoing chambers of his soul, before the
summoning of that power. Had known that twenty years
of vengeance for that too-soon shattered life were now
undone under this bronze sun. *Nothing held back*. It was
over.

There had been men dying below him though, fighting
under his banner, in his name, and there had been no
retreat for them from that plain. Nor for him. He could
not retreat. He had been driven to this moment, like a
bear to a rocky cliff by a pack of wolves, and the price
was being paid now. Everywhere the price was being
paid. There was butchery in the valley; a slaughter of
Barbadians. His heart was crying. He was a grieving,
torn thing, all the memories of love, of a father's loss,
flooding over him, another kind of tidal wave. *Stevan*.

He wept, adrift in an ocean of loss, far from any shore.
He was aware, dimly, of Dianora beside him, clutching
his hands between her own, but he was lost inside his
pain, power gone now, the core of his being shattered
into fragments, shards, a man no longer young, trying,

without any hope at all, to conceive of how to shape a life that could possibly go forward from this hill.

Then the next thing happened. For he had, in fact, forgotten something. Something he alone could possibly have known.

And so time, which truly would not stop, for grief or pity or love, carried them all forward to the moment no sorcerer or wizard or piper on his ridge had foreseen.

The weight had been the weight of mountains crushing his mind. Carefully, exquisitely judged to leave him that faintest spark of self-awareness, which was where the purest torture lay. That he might always know exactly who he was and had been, and what he was being made to do, utterly unable to control himself. Pressed flat under the burden of mountains.

Which now were gone. He straightened his back, of his own will. He turned east. Of his own will. He tried to lift his head higher but could not. He understood: too many years in the same skewed, sunken position. They had broken the bones of his shoulder several times, carefully. He knew what he looked like, what they had turned him into in that darkness long ago. He had seen himself in mirrors through the years, and in the mirrors of others' eyes. He knew exactly what had been done to his body before they started on his mind.

That didn't matter now. The mountains were gone. He looked out with his own sight, reached back with his own memories, could speak, if he wished to speak, with his own thoughts, his own voice, however much it had changed.

What Rhun did was draw his sword.

Of course he had a sword. He carried whatever weapon Brandin did, was given each day the clothing the King had chosen; he was the vent, the conduit, the double, the Fool.

He was more than that. He knew exactly how much more. Brandin had left him that delicately measured scrap of awareness at the very bottom of his mind, under the burying, piled-up mountains. That had been the whole point, the essence of everything; that and the secrecy, the fact that only they two knew and only they would ever know.

The men who had maimed and disfigured him had been blind, working on him in their darkness, knowing him only by the insistent probing of their hands upon his flesh, reaching through to bone. They had never learned who he was. Only Brandin knew, only Brandin and he himself, with that dim flickering of his identity so carefully left behind after everything else was gone. It had been so elegantly contrived, this answer to what he had done, this response to grief and rage. This vengeance.

No one living other than Brandin of Ygrath knew his true name and under the weight of mountains he had had no tongue to speak it himself, only a heart to cry for what was being done to him. The exquisite perfection of it, of that revenge.

But the mountains that had buried him were gone.

And on that thought, Valentin, Prince of Tigana, lifted his sword on a hill in Senzio.

His mind was his own, his memories: of a room without light, black as pitch, the voice of the Ygrathen King, weeping, telling what was being done to Tigana even as they spoke, and what would be done to him in the months and the years to come.

A mutilated body, his own features sorcerously imposed upon it, was death-wheeled in Chiara later that week then burned to ash and scattered to the winds.

In the black room the blind men began their work. He remembered trying not to scream at first. He remembered screaming. Much later Brandin came and began and ended his own part of that careful patient work. A torture of a different kind; much worse. The weight of mountains in his mind.

Late in that same year the King's Fool from Ygrath died of a misadventure in the newly occupied Palace of Chiara. And shortly afterwards, Rhun, with his weak, blinking eyes, his deformed shoulder and slack mouth, his nearly crippled walk, was brought shambling up from his darkness into twenty years of night.

It was very bright here now, almost blindingly so in the

sunlight. Brandin was just ahead of him. The girl was holding his hand.

The girl. The girl was Saevar's daughter.

He had known her the moment she was first brought to be presented to the King. She had changed in five years, greatly changed, and she would change much more as the years spun past, but her eyes were her father's, exactly, and Valentin had watched Dianora grow up. When he had heard her named, that first day, as a woman from Certando, the dim, allowed spark of his mind had flickered and burned, for he knew, he *knew* what she had come to do.

Then, as the months passed and the years, he watched helplessly with his rheumy eyes from under the crush of his mountains, as the terrible interwovenness of things added love to everything else. He was bound to Brandin unimaginably and he saw what happened. More, he was made to be a part of it, by the very nature of the relationship between the Kings and the Fools of Ygrath.

It was he who first gave expression—beyond his control, he *had* no control—to what was growing in the heart of the King. Back in a time when Brandin still refused to admit even the idea of love into a soul and a life shaped by vengeance and loss it was Rhun—Valentin—who would find himself staring at Dianora, at Saevar's dark-haired daughter, with another man's soul in his eyes.

No more, not ever again. The long night had been rolled back. The sorcery that had bound him was gone. It was over; he stood in sunlight and could speak his true name if he chose. He took an awkward step forward and then, more carefully, another. No one noticed him though. They never noticed him. He was the Fool. Rhun. Even that name, chosen by the King. Only the two of them ever to know. Not for the world, this. The privacy of pride. He had even understood. Perhaps the most terrible thing of all: he had understood.

He stepped under the canopy. Brandin was ahead of him near the edge of the hill. He had never struck a man from behind in all his days. He moved to one side, stumbling a little, and came up on the King's right hand. No one looked at him. He was Rhun.

He was not.

"You should have killed me by the river," he said, very clearly. Slowly, Brandin turned his head, as if just now remembering something. Valentin waited until their eyes meBd held before he drove his sword into the Ygrathen's heart, the way a Prince killed his enemies, however many years it might take, however much might have to be endured before such an ending was allowed.

★　★　★

Dianora could not even scream she was so stunned, so unprepared. She saw Brandin stagger backward, a blade in his chest. Then Rhun—*Rhun!*—jerked it clumsily free and so much blood followed. Brandin's eyes were wide with astonishment and pain, but they were clear, so luminously clear. And so was his voice as she heard him say:

"Both of us?" He swayed, still on his feet. "Father and son, both? *What a harvest, Prince of Tigana.*"

Dianora heard the name as a white burst of sound in her brain. Time seemed to change, to slow unbearably. She saw Brandin sinking to his knees; it seemed to take forever for him to fall. She tried to move toward him; her body would not respond. She heard an elongated, weirdly distorted sound of anguish, and saw stark agony in d'Eymon's face as the Chancellor's blade ripped into and through Rhun's side.

Not Rhun. *Not Rhun.* Valentin the Prince.

Brandin's Fool. All those years. The thing that had been done to him! And she beside him, beside that suffering. *All those years.* She wanted to scream. She could not make a sound, could scarcely breathe.

She saw him falling too, the maimed, broken form crumpling to the ground beside Brandin. Who was still on his knees, a red wound in his chest. And who was looking at her now, only at her. A sound finally escaped her lips as she sank down beside him. He reached out, so slowly, with such a colossal effort of will, with all the control he had, and he took her hand.

"Oh, love," she heard him say. "It is as I told you. We should have met in Finavir."

She tried again to speak, to answer him, but tears were streaming down her face and closing her throat. She gripped his hand as tightly as she could, trying to will life from herself over into him. He slumped sideways against her shoulder, and so she lowered him to her lap and wrapped her arms around him, the way she had last night, only last night when he slept. She saw the brilliantly clear grey eyes slowly grow cloudy, and then dark. She was holding him like that when he died.

She lifted her head. The Prince of Tigana, on the ground beside them, was looking at her with so much compassion in his newly clear eyes. Which was a thing she could not possibly endure. Not from him: not with what he had suffered and what she was, what she herself had done. If he only *knew*, what words would he have for her, what look would there be in those eyes? She could not bear it. She saw him open his mouth as if to speak, then his eyes flicked quickly to one side.

A shadow crossed the sun. She looked up and saw d'Eymon's sword lifted high. Valentin raised a hand, pleading, to ward it.

"*Wait!*" she gasped, forcing the one word out.

And d'Eymon, almost mad with his own grief yet stayed for her voice. Held back his sword. Valentin lowered his hand. She saw him draw breath against the massive final reality of his own wound, and then, closing his eyes to the pain and the fierce light, she heard him speak. Not a cry, only the one word spoken in a clear voice. The one word which was—oh, what else could it have ever been? —the name of his home, offered as a shining thing for the world again to know.

And Dianora saw then that d'Eymon of Ygrath *did* know it. That he did hear the name. Which meant that all men now could, that the spell was broken. Valentin opened his eyes and looked up at the Chancellor, reading the truth of that knowledge in d'Eymon's face, and Dianora saw that the Prince of Tigana was smiling as the Chancellor's sword came down from its great height and drove into his heart.

Even in death the smile remained on the terribly afflicted face. And the echo of his last word, the single name, seemed to Dianora to be hanging yet and spreading outward in ripples through the air around the hill, above the valley where the Barbadians were all dying now.

She looked down at the dead man in her arms, cradling his head and the greying hair, and she could not stop her tears. *In Finavir*, he had said. Last words. Another named place, farther away than dream. And had been right, as so many many times he had been right. They ought to have met, if the gods had any kindness, any pity at all for them, in another world than this. Not here. For love was what it was, but it was not enough. Not here.

She heard a sound from under the canopy and turned in time to see d'Eymon slump forward against Brandin's chair. The hilt of his sword was against the seat-back of the chair. The blade was buried in his breast. She saw it and she pitied him his pain but she could not properly grieve. There was nothing left within her for such a sorrow. D'Eymon of Ygrath could not matter now. Not with the two men lying here with her, beside each other. She could pity, oh, she could pity any man or woman born, but she could not grieve for any but these two. Not now.

Not ever, she realized.

She looked over then and saw Scelto, still on his knees, the only other living person on this hill. He too was weeping. But for her, she realized, even more than for the dead. His first tears had always been for her. He seemed to be far away though. Everything seemed oddly remote. Except Brandin. Except Valentin.

For the last time she looked down at the man for whose love she had betrayed her home and all her dead and her own vengeance sworn before a fire in her father's house so long ago. She looked down upon what remained of Brandin of Ygrath with his soul gone, and slowly, tenderly, Dianora lowered her head and kissed him upon the lips in farewell. "In Finavir," she said. "My love." Then she laid him on the ground beside Valentin and she stood.

Looking south she saw that three men and the woman with red hair had descended the slope of the wizards' ridge and were beginning to swiftly cross the uneven ground between. She turned to Scelto whose eyes had now a terrible foreknowledge in them. He knew her, she remembered, he loved her and he knew her much too well. He knew all save the one thing, and that one secret she would take away with her. That was her own.

"In a way," she said to him, gesturing at the Prince, "it would almost be better if no one ever knew who he was. But I don't think we can do that. Tell them, Scelto. Stay, and tell them when they get here. Whoever they are, they ought to know."

"Oh, my lady," he whispered, weeping. "Must it end like this?"

She knew what he meant. Of course she knew. She would not dissemble with him now. She looked at the people—whoever they were—coming quickly across the ground from the south. The woman. A brown-haired man with a sword, another darker one, a third man, smaller than the other two.

"Yes," she said to Scelto, watching them approach. "Yes, I think it must."

And so she turned and left him with the dead on that hill, to wait for those who were coming even now. She left the valley behind, the hill, left all the noises of battle and pain, walking down the northernmost of the goatherds' tracks as it wound west along the slope of the hill out of sight of everyone. There were flowers growing along the path: sonrai berries, wild lilies, irises, anemones, yellow and white, and then there was a scarlet one. In Tregea they said that flower had been made red by the blood of Adaon where he fell.

There were no men or women on that slope to see her or to stay her as she went, nor was the distance very far to level ground and then to the beginnings of the sand and finally to the margin of the sea where there were gulls wheeling and crying overhead.

There was blood on her garments. She discarded them in a small pile on the wide sweep of that white sand. She stepped into the water—it was cool, but not nearly so cold as the sea of Chiara had been on the morning of the Dive. She walked out slowly until it came to her hips and then she began to swim. Straight out, heading west, toward where the sun would set when it finally went down to end this day. She was a good swimmer; her father had taught her and her brother long ago after a dream she had had. Valentin the Prince had even come with them once to their cove. Long ago.

When she began, at length, to tire she was very far from the shore, out where the blue-green of the ocean near land changes to the darker blue of the deep. And there she dived, pushing herself downward, away from the blue of the sky and the bronze sun and it seemed to her as she went down that there was an odd illumination appearing in the water, a kind of path here in the depths of the sea.

She had not expected that. She had not thought any such thing would be here for her. Not after all that had happened, all that she had done. But there was indeed a path, a glow of light defining it. She was tired now, and deep, and her vision was beginning to grow dim. She thought she saw a shape flicker at the edge of the shimmering light. She could not see very clearly though, there seemed to be a kind of mist coming down over her. She thought for a moment the shape might be the riselka, though she had not earned that, or even Adaon, though she had no claim at all upon the god. But then it seemed to Dianora that there was a last gathering of brightness in her mind at the very end, and the mist fell back a little, and she saw that for her it was neither of these, after all, not the riselka, nor the god.

It was Morian, come in kindness, come in grace, to bring her home.

★ ★ ★

Alone of the living on a hill with the dead, Scelto stood and composed himself as best he could, waiting for those he could see beginning to climb the slope.

When the three men and the tall woman reached the summit he knelt in submission as they surveyed in silence what had happened here. What death had claimed upon this hill. He was aware that they might kill him, even as he knelt. He wasn't sure that he cared.

The King was lying only an arm's length away from Rhun who had slain him. Rhun, who had been a Prince here in the Palm. Prince of Tigana. Lower Corte. If he had a space of time later, Scelto sensed that the pieces of this story might begin to come together for him. Even numbed as he was now, he could feel a lancing hurt in his mind if he dwelt upon that history. So much done in the name of the dead.

She would be near the water by now. She would not be coming back this time. He had not expected her to return on the morning of the Dive; she had tried to hide it, but he had seen something in her when she woke that day. He hadn't understood why, but he had known that she was readying herself to die.

She *had* been ready, he was certain of it; something had changed for her by the water's edge that day. It would not change again.

"You are?"

He looked up. A lean, black-haired man, silvering at the temples, was looking down at him with a clear grey gaze. Eyes curiously like Brandin's had been.

"I am Scelto. I was a servant in the saishan, a messenger today."

"You were here when they died?"

Scelto nodded. The man's voice was calm, though there was a discernible sense of effort in that, as if he were trying with his tone to superimpose some pattern of order upon the chaos of the day.

"Will you tell me who killed the King of Ygrath?"

"His Fool," Scelto said quietly, trying to match the manner of the other man. In the distance below them the noises of battle were subsiding at last.

"How? At Brandin's request?" It was one of the other men, a hard-looking, bearded figure with dark eyes and a sword in his hand.

Scelto shook his head. He felt overwhelmingly weary all of a sudden. She would be swimming. She would be a long way out by now. "No. It was an attack. I think . . ." He lowered his head, fearful of presuming.

"Go on," said the first man gently. "You are in no danger from us. I have had enough of blood today. More than enough."

Scelto looked up at that, wondering. Then he said, "I think that when the King used his last magic he was too intent on the valley and he forgot about Rhun. He used so much in that spell that he released the Fool from his binding."

"He released more than that," the grey-eyed man said softly. The tall woman had come to stand beside him. She had red hair and deep blue eyes; she was young and very beautiful.

She would be far out among the waves. It would all be over soon. He had not said farewell. After so many years. Despite himself, Scelto choked back a sob. "May I know," he asked them, not even sure why he needed this, "may I know who you are?"

And quietly, without arrogance or even any real assertion, the dark-haired man said, "My name is Alessan bar Valentin, the last of my line. My father and brothers were killed by Brandin almost twenty years ago. I am the Prince of Tigana."

Scelto closed his eyes.

In his mind he was hearing Brandin's voice again, clear and cold, laden with irony, even with his mortal wound: *What a harvest, Prince of Tigana.* And Rhun, just before he died, speaking that same name under the dome of the sky.

His own revenge was here then.

"Where is the woman?" the third man asked suddenly, the younger, smaller one. "Where is Dianora di Certando who did the Ring Dive? Was she not here?"

It would be over by now. It would be calm and deep and dark for her. Green tendrils of the sea would grace her hair and twine about her limbs. She would finally be at rest, at peace.

Scelto looked up. He was weeping, he didn't even try to stop, or hide his tears now. "She was here," he said. "She has gone to the sea again, to an ending in the sea."

He didn't think they would care. That they could possibly care about that, any of them, but he saw then that he was wrong. All four of them, even the grim, warlike one with the brown hair, grew abruptly still and then turned, almost as one, to look west past the slopes and the sand to where the sun was setting over the water.

"I am deeply sorry to hear that," said the man named Alessan. "I saw her do the Ring Dive in Chiara. She was beautiful and astonishingly brave."

The brown-haired man stepped forward, an unexpected hesitation in his eyes. He wasn't as stern as he had first seemed, Scelto realized, and he was younger as well.

"Tell me," the man began. "Was she . . . did she ever . . ." He stopped, in confusion. The other man, the Prince, looked at him with compassion in his eyes.

"She was from Certando, Baerd. Everyone knows the story."

Slowly, the other man nodded his head. But when he turned away it was to look out toward the sea again. They don't seem like conquerors, Scelto thought. They didn't seem like men in the midst of a triumph. They just looked tired, as at the end of a very long journey.

"So it wasn't me, after all," the grey-eyed man was saying, almost to himself. "After all my years of dreaming. It was his own Fool who killed him. It had nothing to do with us." He looked at the two dead men lying together, then back at Scelto. "Who was the Fool? Do we know?"

She was gone, claimed by the dark sea far down. She was at rest. And Scelto was so tired. Tired of grief and blood and pain, of these bitter cycles of revenge. He knew what was going to happen to this man the moment he spoke.

They ought to know, she had said, before she walked away to the sea, and it was true, of course it was true. Scelto looked up at the grey-eyed man.

"Rhun?" he said. "An Ygrathen bound to the King many years ago. No one very important, my lord."

The Prince of Tigana nodded his head, his expressive mouth quirking with an inward-directed irony. "Of course," he said. "Of course. No one very important. Why should I have thought it would be otherwise?"

"Alessan," said the younger man from the front of the hill, "I think it is over. Down below, I mean. I think . . . I think the Barbadians are all dead."

The Prince lifted his head and so did Scelto. Men of the Palm and of Ygrath would be standing beside each other down in that valley.

"Are you going to kill us all now?" Scelto asked him.

The Prince of Tigana shook his head. "I told you, I have had enough of blood. There is a great deal to be done, but I am going to try to do it without any more killing now."

He went to the southern rim of the hill and lifted his hand in some signal to the men on his own ridge. The woman went over and stood beside him, and he put an arm around her shoulders. A moment later they heard the notes of a horn ring out over the valley and the hills, clear and high and beautiful, sounding an end to battle.

Scelto, still on his knees, wiped at his eyes with a grimy hand. He looked over and saw that the third man, the one who had tried to ask him something, was still gazing out to sea. There was a pain there he could not understand. There had been pain everywhere today though. He had had it in his grasp, even now, to speak truth and unleash so much more.

His eyes swung slowly down again, away from the hard blue sky and the blue-green sea, past the man at the western edge of the hill, past d'Eymon of Ygrath slumped across the King's chair with his own blade in his breast, and his gaze came to rest on the two dead men beside each other on the ground, so near that they could have touched had they been alive.

He could keep their secret. He could live with it.

EPILOGUE

THREE MEN ON HORSES IN THE SOUTHERN HIGHLANDS looking over a valley to the east. There are pine and cedar woods beyond, hills on either side. The Sperion River sparkles in the distance, flowing down out of the mountains, not far from where it will begin its long curve west to find the sea. The air is bright and cool, with a feel of autumn in the breeze. The colors of the leaves will be changing soon and the year-round snow on the highest peaks of the mountains will begin moving down, closing the pass.

In the tranquil green of the valley below them, Devin sees the dome of Eanna's temple flash in the morning sunlight. Beyond the Sanctuary he can just make out the winding trail they had ridden down in the spring, coming here from the east across the border. It seems a lifetime ago. He turns in the saddle and looks north over the rolling, gradually subsiding hills.

"Will we be able to see it from here, later?"

Baerd glances over and then follows his gaze. "What, Avalle and the Towers? Easily, on any clear day. Meet me here in a year's time and you'll see my green-and-white Prince's Tower, I promise you."

"Where are you getting the marble?" Sandre asks.

"Same place as Orsaria did for the original tower. The quarry is still available, believe it or not, about two days' ride west of us near the coast."

"And you'll have it carried here?"

"By sea to Tigana, then on river barges up the Sperion. The same way they did it back then." Baerd has shaved his beard again. He looks years younger, Devin finds himself thinking.

"How do you know so much about it?" Sandre asks with lazy mockery. "I thought all you knew was archery and how not to fall on your face when you were out alone in the dark."

Baerd smiles. "I was always going to be a builder. I have my father's love of stone if not his gift. I'm a craftsman though, and I knew how to look at things, even back then. I think I know as much as any man alive about how Orsaria built his towers and his palaces. Including one in Astibar, Sandre. Would you like me to tell you where your secret passages are?"

Sandre laughs aloud. "Don't boast, you presumptuous mason. On the other hand, it has been almost twenty years since I was in that palace, you may *have* to remind me of where they are."

Grinning, Devin looks over at the Duke. It has taken him a long time to adjust to seeing Sandre without his dark Khardhu guise. "You will be going back after the wedding, then?" he asks, feeling a sadness at the thought of another parting ahead.

"I think I must, though I will say that I'm torn. I feel too old for governing anyone now. And it isn't as if I have any heirs to groom."

After a moment's stillness, Sandre takes them smoothly past the darkness of those memories: "To be honest, the thing that interests me most right now is what I've been doing here in Tigana. The mind-linking with Erlein and Sertino and the wizards we've managed to find."

"And the Night Walkers?" Devin asks.

"Indeed, Baerd's Carlozzini as well. I must say I'm pleased that the four of them are coming with Alienor to the wedding."

"Not as pleased as Baerd is, I'm sure," Devin adds slyly. Baerd gives him a look, and pretends to be absorbed in scanning the distant line of the road south of them.

"Well, hardly as pleased," Sandre agrees. "Though I do hope he'll spare his Elena for a small part of the time she's here. If we are going to change the attitude of this peninsula to magic there's no better time to start than now, wouldn't you say?"

"Oh, certainly," Devin says, grinning broadly.

"She's not my Elena," Baerd murmurs, keeping his eyes firmly fixed on the road.

"She isn't?" Sandre asks in mock surprise. "Then who's this Baerd person she keeps using me to relay messages to? Would you know the fellow?"

"Never heard of him," Baerd says laconically. He keeps a straight face for a moment longer, then gives way to laughter. "I'm beginning to remember why I preferred keeping to myself. And what about Devin, if you're on that subject? You don't think Alais would be sending him messages if she could?"

"Devin," says the Duke airily, "is a mere child, far too young and innocent to be getting involved with women, especially the likes of that guileful, experienced creature from Astibar." He attempts to look stern and fails; both of the others know his real opinion of Rovigo's daughter.

"There are no inexperienced women in Astibar," Baerd retorts. "And besides, he's old enough. He even has a battle scar on his ribs to show her."

"She's seen it already," Devin says, enjoying this enormously. "She taped it up after Rinaldo healed me," he adds hastily as both of the others raise their eyebrows. "No thrill there." He tries and fails to conceive of Alais as guileful and deceptive. The memory of her on the window-ledge in Senzio keeps coming back to him of late though; the particular smile on her face as he stumbled along the outside landing to his own room.

"They are coming, aren't they?" the Duke asks. "It occurs to me that I could sail home with Rovigo."

"They'll be here," Devin confirms. "They had a wedding of their own last week, or they'd have arrived by now."

"I see you are intimately versed in their timing," Baerd says with a straight face. "Just what do you plan to do after the wedding?"

"Actually," Devin says, "I wish I knew. There must be ten different things I've thought about." He evidently sounds more serious than he'd meant to, for both of his friends turn their attention fully to him.

"Such as?" Sandre asks.

Devin takes a breath and lets it out. He holds up both hands and starts counting on his fingers. "Find my father and help him settle here again. Find Menico di Ferraut and put together the company we should have had before you people side-tracked me. Stay with Alessan and Catriana in Tigana and help them with whatever they have to do. Learn how to handle a ship at sea; don't ask me why. Stay in Avalle and build a tower with Baerd." He hesitates; the others are smiling. He plunges onward: "Spend another night with Alienor at Borso. Spend my life with Alais bren Rovigo. Start chasing down the words and music of all the songs we've lost. Go over the mountains to Quileia and find the twenty-seven tree in the sacred grove. Start training for the sprint race in next summer's Triad Games. Learn how to shoot a bow—which reminds me, you did promise me that, Baerd!"

He stops, because they are laughing now, and so is he, a little breathlessly. "You must have gone past ten somewhere in that list," Baerd chuckles.

"There are more," Devin says. "Do you want them?"

"I don't think I could stand it," Sandre says. "You remind me too painfully of how old I am and how young you are."

Devin sobers at those words. He shakes his head. "Never think that. I don't think there was a moment last year when I didn't have to work to keep up with you wherever we went." He smiles at a thought. "You aren't old, Sandre, you're the youngest wizard in the Palm."

Sandre's expression is wry. He holds up his left hand; they can clearly see the two missing fingers. "There's truth to that. And I may be the first to break the habit of screening what we are, because I never got *into* the habit."

"You're serious about dropping the screening?" Baerd asks.

"Utterly serious. If we are to survive in this peninsula as a whole nation in the world we are going to need magic to match Barbadior and Ygrath. And Khardhun, come to think of it. And I don't even *know* what powers they have in Quileia now; it has been too many years since we dealt with them. We can no longer hide our wizards, or the Carlozzini, we can't afford to be as ignorant as we've always been about how magic is shaped here. Even the Healers, we don't understand *anything* about them. We have to learn our magic, value it, search wizards out and train them, find ways to control them too. The Palm has to discover magic, or magic will undo us again one day the way it did twenty years ago."

"You think we can do that first thing though?" Devin asks. "Make a nation here, out of the nine we are?"

"I know we can. And I think we will. I will wager you both right now that Alessan di Tigana is named King of the Palm at the Triad Games next year."

Devin turns quickly to Baerd, whose color has suddenly risen. "Would he take it?" he asks. "Would he do that, Baerd?"

Baerd looks at Sandre and then slowly back to Devin. "Who else could?" he answers finally. "I don't even think he has a choice. The knitting together of this peninsula has been his life's cause since he was fifteen years old. He was already on that path when I found him in Quileia. I think . . . I think what he'd *really* like to do is find Menico with you, Devin, and spend a few years making music with you two, and Erlein, and Catriana, and some dancers, and someone who can play the syrenya."

"But?" Sandre asks.

"But he's the man who saved us all, everyone knows it, everyone knows who he is now. After a dozen years of being on the roads he knows more people who matter in each province than anyone else. He's the one who gave the rest of us the vision. And he's the Prince of Tigana, too, and in his prime. I'm afraid"—he grimaces at the word—"I don't see how he can avoid this, even if he wanted to. I think for Alessan it is just beginning now."

They are silent a moment.

"What about you?" Devin asks. "Will you go with him? What do you want?"

Baerd smiles. "What do I want? Nothing nearly so high. I'd badly like to find my sister, but I'm beginning to accept that she's . . . gone, and I think that I may never know where, or how. I'll be there for Alessan whenever he needs me, but what I most want to do is build things. Houses, temples, bridges, a palace, half a dozen towers here in Avalle. I need to see things rising, and I . . . I suppose it's part of the same thing, but I want to start a family. We need children here again. Too many people died." He looks away for a moment toward the mountains and then back again. "You and I may be the lucky ones, Devin. We aren't Princes or Dukes or wizards. We're only ordinary men, with a life to start."

"I told you he was waiting for Elena," Sandre says gently. Not a gibe, the voice of a friend, speaking with deep affection. Baerd smiles, looking into the distance again. And in that moment his expression changes, it grows charged with a fierce, bright pleasure:

"Look!" he cries, pointing. "Here he comes!"

From the south, winding out of the mountains and the hills of the highlands along a road that has not been used in hundreds of years there comes a caravan, many-colored, stretching back a long way. There is music playing beside it and ahead, with men and women riding and on foot, donkeys and horses laden with goods, at least fifty banners flapping in the wind. And now the tunes drift up to the three of them, bright and gay, and all the colors are flashing in the morning light as Marius, King of Quileia comes riding down from the mountain pass to the wedding of his friend.

He is to spend the night in the Sanctuary where he will be formally welcomed by the High Priest of Eanna—whom he will remember as the man who brought a fourteen-year-old boy to him over the mountains long ago. There are barges waiting in Avalle to take them down the river to Tigana in the morning.

But the right of first greeting is Baerd's, in Alessan's name, and he has asked the two of them to ride here with him.

"Come on!" he cries now, joy in his face. He urges his horse forward down the sloping path. Devin and Sandre glance at each other and hasten to follow.

"I will never understand," Devin shouts, as they catch

up to Baerd, "how you can possibly be so pleased to see a man who calls you Pigeon Two!"

Sandre gives a cackle of glee. Baerd laughs aloud, and mimes a blow at Devin. The three of them are still laughing as they slow their horses to swing around a cluster of sonrai bushes at a wide curve in the downward trail.

And it is there that they see the riselka, three men see a riselka, sitting on a rock beside the sunlit path, her long sea-green hair blowing back in the freshening breeze.